MW00834279

Copyright © 2018 by Luke Chmilenko

To my ever patient wife, friends and family who had to endure me talking about this book for months on end.

Thank you.

Chapter 1

Friday, March 8th, 2047 - 5:23 a.m.
Far Southeast of Aldford

A pair of moons hung high in the western sky, locked in an eternal chase with one another as they sped through the void. The first moon was large and ponderous as it crossed the firmament, casting a bright crimson light everywhere it glanced, making it appear as if the night itself were on fire.

Far ahead of its crimson mate, a much smaller and nimble orb sped through the starry night, its pale azure hue much too weak to challenge the glow of its larger sibling. Perched on the far edge of the northwestern horizon, the azure moon began its descent, as the dawn of a new day broke to the east.

"Charge!" my hoarse voice barked out as I sprinted through the morning twilight, kicking up a spray of dew behind me.

The sound of thundering feet echoed in my ears, drowning out the crash of the battle before me. A surge of magic sliced through the air, brutally ravaging the bandits' rear ranks, causing them to turn at the unexpected assault. I saw a wave of terror ripple through their line as they spotted us charging out of the night, desperately scrambling to meet our attack.

They were far too slow.

Our vanguard slammed into the panicking horde, overrunning and trampling all in their path as they forced their way towards the front of the battle. In their wake, they left chaos and confusion as shell-shocked bandits picked themselves off the ground, wondering what force of nature had just run them over.

Then our second line arrived.

I slammed into a grey-armored bandit, knocking the rising half-elf back to the ground, plunging Razor deep into the fallen Adventurer's back. Barely breaking my stride, I leaped over the body with a single thought dominating my mind as I forced myself deeper into the chaos.

I hope we're not too late.

A heartbeat later, my sprint carried me through the bandits' shattered battle line, the few survivors of our surprise attack, fighting fiercely in rapidly shrinking pockets. I carefully picked my way through the bodies littering the ground under my feet as I ran deeper into the chaos. I saw the bodies of uniformed guards lying beside others that could have only been Settlers, both caught in the wrong place at the wrong time, but neither hesitating to give up their lives as they stood up to the bandits' sudden raid.

Running hard, I worked to regain my lost speed, tearing my attention from the fallen and instead fixating on an overturned wagon ahead of me. With a quick gesture of my hand, I triggered a spell, immediately feeling lighter on my feet. A gentle hop easily took me to the top of the capsized wagon, and then a powerful leap sent me high into the sky.

Acrid smoke and a wash of heat greeted me as I surveyed the battlefield from above, my augmented vision cutting through the twilight, allowing my eyes to drink in every detail as I momentarily hung free from gravity's grasp. Chaos reigned everywhere I looked, with more than half of the bandits still unaware of our arrival. I saw dozens of wagons, carts, and carriages spread out below me, some having circled next to one another for protection against the bandits' attack. Draft animals wailed with terror as flashes of magic illuminated the morning's dawn, the constant thunderclaps of concussive spells doing little to drown out their sounds.

Damn! I spotted a pair of bloody defenders collapse as a group of six bandits overwhelmed them, opening a clear path to a cowering mass of travelers huddled next to a heavily laden cart. As the other bandits bent down to loot the fallen defenders, I saw one marauder dart forward, moving directly towards the now panicking travelers. My cloak billowed out around me as gravity finally began to pull me back down.

Here we go! I tightened my grip on Razor, focusing on the overeager bandit, and triggered *Blink Step*.

The world blurred for the briefest of instants before I landed on the bandit's back, chopping Razor deep into his shoulder as I rode him to the ground. Chancing a quick glance upward, I saw the eyes of the cringing travelers widen in surprise at my arrival.

Gritting my teeth, I tore my blade out of the stunned marauder and thrust it viciously into the back of his neck, feeling his body go limp under me. Standing up slowly, I turned to face the other bandits that lagged behind their late friend.

Two Humans, possibly Scouts or Rogues, plus an Elf that looks like a Mage. I dispassionately analyzed the attackers as they gaped at my sudden appearance. *The half-orc might be a Shaman, and that dwarf is almost definitely a Warrior.*

"Ah! What the hell?" one of the human bandits shouted, his eyes flicking to his comrade's fallen form, "Where the fuck did he just come from?"

"Well look at that, boys! Someone else wants to play 'Hero'!" The dwarven warrior laughed derisively as he motioned his companions forward. "Let's show him what the *Grey Devils* do to Heroes."

"Careful, Phil, he doesn't look right," the second human bandit called out cautiously. "There's something going o—"

That's all anyone sees now, I thought as I offered the bandits a bitter smile, having seen the same reaction countless times over the last few weeks. *A gaunt, scarred man with skin far too tight for his bones.*

With a burst of cold anger, I leaped forward, covering the short distance between me and the dwarven bandit in the blink of an eye. Caught completely flat-footed, the overconfident dwarf had let his shield arm droop and was still bringing up his axe when I stabbed a crackling Razor into the meat of his arm, discharging a *Shocking Touch* into his body.

"Aaah!" The dwarf yelped in pain, his axe falling from his spasming hand.

Twisting my blade, blood sprayed all over the dwarf's powder-grey leather armor as I pirouetted to the side, evading a reflexive swipe from his shield. Completing my spin, I shifted ever so slightly to let a gleaming short sword pass by my hip harmlessly, finding myself staring into the eyes of one of the human bandits. His eyes flared with horror when my free hand grabbed his outstretched wrist and yanked him forward.

Right into Razor's path.

The battle-worn sword viciously chopped into the base of the bandit's unarmored neck. Fueled by adrenaline and the need for speed, I ruthlessly sawed the blade into the bandit's flesh before tearing it free, causing a gout of blood to erupt from the massive wound. Pulling even harder on the now screaming bandit's arm for a second time, I hauled him completely off balance and sent him staggering into the dwarven bandit behind me.

"Damn it, Welton! Get it together!" I heard the dwarf yell in anger, before realizing the extent of his friend's injury. "Oh, shit! Orsond! Welton needs heals before he bleeds out!"

As if I'm going to let that happen, I thought with a shake of my head, my anger feeling slightly stated. *What do they take me for, an amateur?*

Not waiting to lose the initiative, I dug in my heels and sprinted towards the Elf, managing to cover three long strides before the still standing human bandit moved to intercept me. I could see a hesitant expression on his face as he braced himself to receive my charge, having already seen me brutally wound one of his companions. As I ran, the Elf confirmed my suspicions, identifying himself as a Mage, and beginning to conjure a ball of fire in his hands.

"Rylan, box him in!" I heard the dwarf call out from behind me. "Let Penn wear him down at range!"

Quickly glancing over my shoulder, I saw that the dwarf had begun charging after me, intent on bowling me over from behind, leaving the half-orc all by himself as he urgently tended to the fallen bandit.

I mentally sighed, almost feeling sorry for what I was about to do; it wasn't my fault that this group didn't know the single and most important rule for player-versus-player combat.

Never abandon your healer.

A stride before I crashed into Rylan, I planted my foot, bringing myself to a stop. Caught off guard by my unexpected move, Rylan watched me with a stunned expression on his face as I whirled away, focusing my attention on the distant healer, and triggered *Blink Step.*

Once again, my world blurred as I teleported a short distance, appearing directly behind the half-orc Shaman, who had knelt down to heal his fallen comrade. With no regard to the fairness of the act, I lunged forward and drove Razor straight through the half-orc's back, piercing through the worn leather armor with ease.

I felt the Shaman gasp as he looked down to see my blade protruding from his chest, his magic chant dying on his lips. Pulling myself close to him, I didn't wait to see if my opening blow would be enough to put him down for good. I spoke a word of power, causing a dagger made of fire to appear in my hand.

Leaving Razor buried inside the Shaman, I let go of the hilt and grabbed a fistful of the Shaman's hair, pulling his head backwards sharply. I allowed myself a moment of showmanship, spinning the dagger in my hand before I caught it by the hilt and brutally thrust it into the Shaman's exposed throat, feeling it vanish the moment my attack was complete. The half-orc went limp in my grip.

And that's why you don't leave your healer alone.

I shoved the dead man forward, the body falling heavily on top of the still bleeding Welton. Reaching forward, I grabbed the hilt of Razor and pulled it free, the smell of burning flesh wafting into my lungs as I stood over the body. Flicking the blood off the blade, I turned to face the remaining three bandits.

"Damn it!" I heard the Elf swear as he began conjuring another ball of fire in his hands.

"You're making the biggest fucking mistake, you hear me, you little *freak*?" the dwarf spat venomously. "Even if you manage to beat us, you're still trapped in the middle of our raid, all by yourself! Your best bet is to surrender now and *pray* we kill you quickly!"

I cocked my head, letting the dwarf's words wash over me. "What makes you think I'm alone?"

The words hung in the air, taking a few seconds for the bandits to fully absorb. I could see their faces shift as they realized the echoes of combat raging around us had changed. Screaming voices and shouting had been replaced by the sound of running feet. Sharp thunderclaps of magical explosions could be heard in the distance.

"Phillion!" A loud shout echoed from behind the bandits as a second band of grey armored marauders ran towards the dwarf, a bloodied half-elf in the lead. "We're under attack by another group!"

"What's happening?" the dwarf shouted, not daring to take his eyes off me.

"I don't know! They just hit us out of nowhere!" The half-elf motioned for the group to follow him. "We need to regroup and counterattack! I don't know what happened to our camp, but everyone who dies is respawning in Eberia or Coldscar!"

"That would have been us," I called out, savoring the look of surprise on the bandits' faces. "We were hoping to come by, maybe borrow a cup of sugar while introducing ourselves as friendly neighbors. Imagine how upset we were when we found the remains of half a dozen caravans in your tiny little grotto."

"You...*destroyed* our camp?" the dwarf replied in disbelief, shock visibly running through his body as he took a step backwards.

"*And* spent nearly half the night running and trying to catch up to you all." I let my gaze slide off the dwarf, looking at the half-elf and the other bandits expectantly. "In case you were wondering, this is the part where you all surrender."

"*Surrender?*" the half-elf said with disbelief. "You're outnumbered ten to one, and you expect *us* to surrender?"

"Yeah, and quickly, please, if you don't mind." I motioned to the battle raging distantly around us. "I have places to be, people to save. My schedule is pretty packed this morning."

"Phil, who the fuck is this clown?" the half-elf grunted. "And what the hell is going on with his face and eyes?"

"I don't know, Roc," the dwarf replied, regaining some of his courage now that more of his allies had arrived. "He just appeared out of nowhere and killed Rodgen, Welton, and Orsond without breaking a sweat!"

"Are you fucking serious?" the half-elf exclaimed with surprise, his eyes narrowing as he looked at me. "You let this anorexic little shit kill half your party?"

"Can we get on with the surrendering portion of this conversation?" I called out in the best bored tone I could muster, despite inwardly seething as they spoke about my appearance. "I really do have places to be today."

"I don't think you understand the situation you're in." The half-elf started moving towards me, waving a metal rod in his hand. "You attacked the *Grey Devils*; you're about as fucked as a person can get. By the time lunch rolls around, we'll be setting up our new camp in whatever place *you* call home."

"Somehow, I doubt that," I replied, watching the half-elf continue stalking forward, his retinue not far behind. I held up a hand, motioning for the group to stop. "Last chance before things get violent..."

I paused, looking down at the bodies belonging to the half-orc Shaman and human Rogue, who had since expired from blood loss. "Well, *more* violent."

Unfazed by my threats, the half-elf didn't break his stride as he moved menacingly towards me. "Enough, let's get this over with."

"I was hoping you'd say that."

Before I had even finished speaking, a massive azure blur sailed over the top of my head and slammed into the advancing half-elf, sending him to the ground.

<You talk far too much when there is killing to be done!> a mental voice rang in my head.

"What the hell is that?" one of the bandits yelled in surprise, watching the Ætherwarped puma begin to savage the fallen half-elf. "Oh shit, Roc—"

A thunderclap of magic cut the bandit off as a burst of magefire exploded through the gathered group of marauders, sending them all sprawling off balance. A second later, a large fireball flew through the air and detonated itself against the side of the elven mage. The blast sent the poor bandit flying, landing with a sickening crunch as his armor caught fire, but before the stunned mage could even register what had happened, a black arrow thudded into the side of his chest, followed by two more seconds later.

"Lyr!" I heard a familiar voice boom over the twin magic bursts, spotting Drace's massive form as he sprinted towards the Raiders. "Hit them from both sides!"

Leaping forward at Drace's order, I circled around my familiar as his teeth finally closed on the half-elf's head, ending all resistance with a vicious twist of the neck. Focusing on the now terrified dwarf warrior, I threw a Flare at his face as I closed the distance.

Reacting instinctively, the dwarf brought up his shield to protect his face, the tiny fireball splashing harmlessly against the wood. Capitalizing on the dwarf's momentary blindness, I triggered *Blink Step* once more, this time appearing directly on his unprotected flank. With all my strength and simmering anger behind the attack, I stabbed Razor deep into the dwarf's side, feeling the blade slip past his ribs and bite deep into his flesh.

Roaring in pain, the dwarf tore himself free of my sword, his axe swinging wildly as he tried to buy himself space, forcing me to backpedal to evade his crazed, rage-filled attacks. Howling like a wild animal, the dwarf launched himself at me, seeking to overwhelm my defenses with wild and punishing attacks.

No longer able to baffle the warrior with creative maneuvers, I was forced to stand toe to toe and found myself almost hard-pressed to keep up. For whatever he lacked in tactical sense, the berserk dwarf made up for in sheer ferocity and endurance as I worked to dodge and evade his attacks, unwilling to risk directly parrying an attack.

Shit! I winced, feeling my arm go numb reflexively deflecting a particularly inspired attack, and I felt my balance stagger under the powerful blow as my feet slid across the ground. *That Rage ability is powerful!*

"Need help, Lyr?" Constantine's voice reached my ears the same moment his short sword buried itself deep into the dwarf's kidney. The warrior let out a high-pitched gasp of pain, before falling lifelessly to the ground as Constantine followed up his first attack with an even more devastating stab to the back of the head.

"I had him!" I called to the Rogue, both of us turning to move towards the remaining bandits.

"You mean before the sun comes up?" Constantine grunted dismissively as he fell in beside me. "You were taking too long!"

"I already killed three of them before you got here!" I challenged, catching a bandit's blade on my sword and forcing it high, allowing Constantine the opportunity to disembowel the man.

"Congrats. Do you want a shiny sticker?" he shot back at me while stepping forward and shouldering the now bleeding bandit to the ground.

"Oh, I know where I'll put a sticker alright!" I replied while stabbing the fallen bandit in the chest.

"Is it my butt?" Constantine queried, darting forward to stab a bandit fighting Drace from behind.

"Are you two at it already?" Drace shouted, interrupting our banter as his sword bit deep into the collar of the bandit. "How do you even have the energy? We've literally been running all night!"

"I logged off and took a nap. Couldn't you tell?" Constantine replied, stabbing the bandit a second time. "I feel great!"

"Are you serious?" I thrust a *Shocking Touch*-charged Razor into the shoulder of the last standing bandit, the others having long since been felled by a volley of magic and arrows.

"That depends," Constantine shot back, trapping the stunned bandit's weapon, allowing Drace the time to wind up and cleave into his skull. "How angry will you be if I say yes?"

"Ugh," I grunted at the Rogue in mock frustration, watching the last bandit fall to the ground as Drace pulled his weapon free.

"We've got them on the run," Sierra called out, trotting over to me while carefully scanning our surroundings. "I'm taking a few of the scouts to see if we can cut them off before they make it into the woods. Constantine, Amaranth, let's go."

"On it," Constantine replied, throwing me a mock salute as he started to move. "Catch you guys later."

"Rah," Amaranth cooed in acknowledgment, the familiar's tongue flicking out as it licked the bloody mess covering its maw.

"You got this, Lyr?" Drace asked me, motioning to the people still cowering under the nearby carts. "We're going to see if anyone else needs help."

"Yeah, I should be fine." I waved at the warrior, watching him spin on his heels and run off with a nod, taking Caius and Halcyon with him.

I turned towards the cart where I had seen the cowering travelers, expecting them to recoil from my appearance. To my surprise, however, none looked away from my face, all watching me intently as hope bloomed in their eyes.

"Don't worry," I spoke softly, "you're safe now.

"Virtus is here."

Chapter 2

Aldford

I felt the wagon lurch as it rolled over a rough patch of ground, waking me from a light, if fitful sleep. Opening my eyes, I saw that we had finally begun the final approach towards Aldford; the morning sun had risen into the sky and banished the twin moons of the night.

Blinking myself awake, my mind drifted back to the aftermath of the battle, vaguely recalling Sierra's report that every single *Grey Devil* bandit they could find had been either captured or killed, followed by Caius's excited discovery that the caravan that we had just rescued was in fact the second wave of settlers that we had been expecting for the last two weeks.

My memories of the morning blurred into a jumble of new faces as we re-organized the caravan, tending to the wounded and sorting out the dead. The last thing I remembered after the caravan started moving was hopping into the lead wagon of the rescued caravan, and promptly falling asleep, exhausted.

Loosening the fur cloak I had pulled around myself, I brought up a gloved hand to rub my face, grimacing when my fingers touched hard cheekbones, an instant reminder of my now not-so-new condition.

Damn Ætherwarping, I thought, turning my grimace into a scowl as I attempted to shift myself into a more comfortable position. Although a month had passed since my body had been warped under the twin influences of the *Annulment Sphere* and the raw Æther that *Slave-King Abdiel* had used to manifest his physical presence in the world, I was still having a hard time adjusting to the physical changes that had altered my body.

Resembling nothing like the body I had first designed in character creation all those weeks ago, it was now withered and gaunt, bereft of any excess fat or muscle. My now beardless face had a slightly feral look to it, the scars that Amaranth had inflicted on me while he was my Nemesis having stretched wide across the side of my head and jaw. The result giving me a rather ghoulish appearance that couldn't help but make me feel self-conscious every time someone flinched when meeting my eyes.

Despite the changes to my form, I considered myself lucky the transformation hadn't affected my raw strength, and I had to only make minor adjustments to my fighting style to compensate for my leaner and lighter stature. For what I lost in mass and being able to 'throw my weight around', I gained in being almost impossible to keep hold of, and being able to, quite literally, punch above my weight class.

I sighed, looking up at Aldford in the distance. *At least we're back at the village no-*

"Is that a tree?" the driver sitting beside me exclaimed, his voice full of awe, having long since gotten used to my presence. "Wait... is it really *glowing* or have my eyes gone and cracked?"

"Hmm?" The driver's excitement snapped me out of my thoughts and I looked up to see the now massive Ætherwarped oak tree hanging high over Aldford. "Your eyes aren't lying to you. We really do have a magic tree growing in the heart of the village."

"A magic tree?" the driver echoed in disbelief while turning to glance at me. "How?"

"A gigantic magic-infused spider attacked the village one night not too long ago, and on its death, it erupted into a large puddle of glowing ichor," I explained, my expression completely deadpan as I watched the teamster's eyes grow wider and wider with every word I spoke. "We had no easy way of cleaning up the mess, so we buried it and tossed an acorn down. By the time the morning rolled around... the tree had sprouted nearly a dozen feet."

The driver's mouth hung open for a moment before he shook his head and laughed nervously, "You're having a laugh at me, aren't you?"

"Not at all," I replied. "Ask any of the villagers, and they'll tell you the same."

"Ah..." The man looked at me, trying to gauge how serious I was. After a moment, he let out a strangled cough, and turned his attention forward, shaking his head, "...first bandits, now giant spiders and a magic tree... shoulda stayed on the farm."

I couldn't help but smile slightly at the teamster's reaction as I turned my attention towards Aldford, spotting a large crowd waiting for us just outside of the village. We had sent word ahead with a pair of eager scouts to explain the night's and morning's events to the Bann as well as give Aldford enough time to prepare to receive a little over two hundred more souls.

The wagon slowly ground to a halt as a pair of Adventurers and a handful of villagers began organizing the incoming vehicles into neat lines where they would not impede progress, while still allowing for the quick unloading of the countless goods the settlers had brought with them.

While the wagons and carts were being secured, the new arrivals travelling on foot were greeted enthusiastically by dozens of waiting villagers and Adventurers, quickly finding themselves overwhelmed by the rushing wave of hospitality as their long journey finally came to an end.

I bid a quick farewell to the driver as he moved to check on the horse pulling the cart, leaping down from the vehicle, happy for the opportunity to stretch and readjust my armor.

"We're finally back." Sierra's tired voice filtered into my ears as she walked between the wagons towards me, Amaranth following close on her heels. "It's barely noon and it already feels like it's been a long day. I really need to go take a nap."

"I caught a few hours of sleep while we were travelling," I replied empathetically, taking my gloves off so I could run my hands through Amaranth's fur, the giant cat immediately moving to rub his face on my hip. "Hopefully that'll be enough to get me through the day."

"Are you sure, Lyr?" Sierra asked, pulling off her helmet and running a hand through her bright crimson hair. "You and Constantine have that meeting with the Stream Producers to go to in the afternoon today."

"Yeah... I'll be okay." I shrugged at Sierra before looking back down at Amaranth, who had closed his eyes in bliss once I began scratching his ears. "I managed to get a couple hours before everything... *started* this morning, and I'll likely crash into bed early tonight."

After looking into my eyes for a moment, Sierra eventually nodded her approval, satisfied with what she saw. "Alright, just don't burn yourself out."

<If you rested more often throughout the day, such as I do, perhaps you would not be so weary when rival predators reveal themselves.> Amaranth's cool mental voice filtered through my head as he opened a single azure colored eye to look at me.

I couldn't help but snort at the cat's logic. "Is that what you call sleeping around all day?"

<Bold words for someone so tasty!> Amaranth chided me as he quickly moved his head, gently nipping at my hand.

"Hey!" I yelped as I instinctively pulled my hand free from my familiar's mouth.

"Sassy cat?" Sierra asked, eyebrow raised.

"Sassy cat," I confirmed scowling at my wet hand. "He needs to spend less time with Constantine; he's picking up bad habits."

Sierra couldn't help but laugh. "Remember that time he brought you that giant snake?"

"You mean that one that he didn't actually kill," I looked at Amaranth sternly, "and let wrap itself around my leg while I was still asleep and in bed?"

<I hadn't seen you eat in days!> The Puma let out a frustrated croak. *<You were wasting away before my eyes; I had thought you forgot how to hunt!>*

"Lyrian!" A stern voice cut short any reply I could give my familiar, causing me to turn in its direction. Searching through the milling group of settlers, I saw Aldwin beckoning me towards him.

"Better go report, Lyr," Sierra said with a smile. "I'm going to go help the new Adventurers settle in and figure out what they need. See you in a bit."

"Alright." I waved goodbye to the scout as I turned to walk towards a bewildered Aldwin looking out at the arriving wave of settlers. Amaranth led the way, with me following close behind, the giant cat's presence and my intimidating appearance allowing the two of us to easily cut through the crowd.

"Lyrian…" The knight looked at me incredulously, completely at a loss for words. "I know you sent word ahead, but…I'd rather hear it again straight from your mouth…"

"Well, as you can see… we haven't been abandoned," I told the Bann, watching a wave of relief wash through the older man, "but I haven't had a chance to talk with the settlers yet, so I have no idea what has happened in Eberia over the last month."

Aldwin gave me a grim nod. "Do you think this was just simple banditry?"

"Adventurers rarely make anything simple," I replied shaking my head as my mind went back to the events of the previous night, "but from what we could tell, their motivation was purely greed."

"Tell me what happened after you left," Aldwin said, struggling to keep his voice even. "All I remember was a flurry of shouting when Bax returned… then you all practically sprinted out of the village as if hell itself was chasing after you."

"I didn't feel like Bax's report could wait," I began to explain, referring to the surviving scoutmaster of the ill-fated Eberian Mage's Guild Expedition we had rescued a month ago. "We had him and a handful of others scouting out the southeastern approach towards Aldford, to see if there was any reason why we hadn't seen anyone out this way over the last few weeks."

"From the little we've learned so far, a fairly large group of Adventurers split off from Coldscar and were preying on anyone making their way towards Aldford or further north into the Fens." I paused to take a breath. "They found themselves a grotto that was practically impossible to spot from a distance, unless you happened to know that it was there, and set up a camp."

"From there it seems they raided more than a dozen caravans coming our way, cutting us off from the rest of the world."

"*Gods*," Aldwin cursed, clenching his fists in rage. "Please tell me you put an end to them. *All of them*."

"We did," I replied softly. "But not at their camp."

"Oh?"

"We missed the bandits by an hour."

"Missed them?" The Bann looked at me with a confused expression. "What do you mean?"

"They went out raiding," I replied with a sigh, "only leaving a handful behind to watch over their hideout."

"Then they must have known the settlers were coming," Aldwin stated, turning to gaze at all of the new arrivals. I could see his eyes searching through the crowd, pausing when they landed on bloodstained clothes and damaged vehicles.

"We took their camp and captured those left behind easily enough. Its strength was better suited to not being found, rather than being a defensible location." I nodded as I continued my explanation. "We think they've been there at least three weeks. We found a rather substantial stash of goods that they've looted."

Aldwin closed his eyes momentarily as he absorbed the information. "Were there any survivors?"

"From their earlier raids?" I queried, before shaking my head sadly. "No. At least, none that we could find."

"Damn." Aldwin let out a deep sigh before motioning for me to continue.

"We didn't linger for too long at the bandit camp once we realized that their main force had moved out. The little information we were able to get out of the captured bandits was that they had left to intercept a huge caravan on the way here." I motioned to the settlers behind me. "The bandits had quite a bit of a head start on us, but left a trail that even a blind man could follow."

"We were lucky that the moons were out today too," I added. "It gave us enough light to move at a fast pace and make up for lost time; we managed to find them only a few minutes after the attack had started..."

Aldwin fell silent, looking over the nervous settlers as they slowly began to unwind from their journey. There was a hesitant motion to their actions as they tried to come to grips with their brutal introduction to frontier life. They were quickly realizing that the only safety they would find here would be in the strength of their arms and from the friends standing beside them.

"How many casualties were there?" Aldwin asked hesitantly.

"Ten amongst all the caravan guards, and eight settlers," I replied, remembering the dead. "Plus at least nine Adventurers, but we can't be completely sure in their case."

"And the bandits?" Aldwin's voice took on a hard tone.

"At least ninety," I couldn't help but reply cheerfully.

"We also managed to take a few prisoners as well." I nodded towards the wagons. "I have the guild watching them for the time being."

"Which I will have to request that you remand into my custody," an unfamiliar voice spoke over my shoulder, startling me with how close it was behind me.

<Where did he come from?> Amaranth let out a startled hiss as he twisted to look at something behind me.

Turning around, I found myself staring into a featureless grey helmet that completely obscured the upper half of the speaker's face. Flinching involuntarily, I took a step backward, creating space between me and a tall armor-clad man.

"Ah..." Any reply I had, died in my throat as I realized the man's armor was full plate.

And that he had just snuck up on both Amaranth and I while wearing it.

<I don't know!> I sent back to the cat, swallowing hard as I noticed dry bloodstains streaked along the man's hands and chest, marring the otherwise immaculate grey-tinted armor. The man stood formally, hands clasped in front of him, presumably staring directly at me, though with no visor or eye sockets in the helmet, it was impossible to tell.

How does he even see? My mind had frozen itself at the man's mysterious stare, leaving my mouth hanging open.

Fortunately for me, Aldwin's tongue didn't suffer the same sort of paralysis that had gripped mine. He saluted the man standing before us. "*Justicar!* You honor us with your presence!"

"It is you who honor me, Sir Aldwin," the man spoke, shifting to bow slightly before the knight, then turning to do the same towards Amaranth and me. "I am Justicar Joseph Dyre and I have been *Called* to enforce the Rule of Law in Aldford. My apologies for startling you two with my arrival."

"We are to receive a Justicar?" Aldwin's eyes immediately widened on hearing the man's words. "So soon? I had thought it would be years before the gods graced us with one of your order, if ever!"

"I do not presume to know the gods plans," the Justicar spoke with a neutral tone. "I only live to serve."

<He does not smell,> Amaranth voice filtered through my mind, as he coiled his body around my legs, watching the Justicar carefully. *<I smell blood, leather and metal on him, but no skin or sweat.>*

"Erm," I cleared my throat, my brain finally having had a chance to catch up with the conversation. "What, exactly, is a *Justicar*?"

Aldwin looked at me incredulously. "You have never heard of a Justicar?"

"I really haven't," I replied while looking over Dyre's armor. "I'm pretty sure I would have remembered seeing such... unique armor."

"The Justicars are a sect of warrior-monks and paladins that hold a special place within Eberian society," Aldwin spoke with a tone boarding on reverence. "Without them we would have surely torn ourselves apart shortly after arriving on this continent."

"We are but servants of *Mithus, the God of Law*." I felt Dyre's featureless gaze shift onto me. "We enforce the *Laws of the Land* where we are posted and maintain acceptable order as decreed in the local Writ or Charter."

"Completely neutral in all regard, the Justicars have served as an incorruptible force within Eberia and have been experts in all matters of law for decades," Aldwin continued. "Their numbers have never been great, but their tenacity and ability has long outweighed that. To have one sent to Aldford so soon... it is an honor beyond measure."

"I had no idea..." I turned to look at Dyre, who seemed to be unaffected by Aldwin's praise. "What exactly would your role be within Aldford?"

"Since I am the only Justicar here, I would likely fill a variety of roles wherever my services are needed. I am able to adjudicate legal disputes and form contracts, in addition to every day peacekeeping duties. If our journey was any indication of what to expect from frontier life, I also expect to devote a large portion of my time to keeping Adventurers in check."

"Something we find ourselves in dire need of," Aldwin commented bitterly, casting a glance at me. "While Lyrian and his friends have been a great boon to our settlement, others have not."

"So I saw this morning." Dyre inclined his head ever so slightly in agreement while indicating the blood on his armor. "If you would present the Town's Charter before me, so that I could place my seal upon it, I can begin my duties immediately."

"Certainly!" Aldwin replied, reaching into a pouch tied to his belt. "I have it right here."

"Hang on," I said with a frown. "What do you mean, 'keep Adventurers in check'?"

"Since the appearance of so many Adventurers over the last month, Mithus has decreed that all Justicars are to ensure that Adventurers do not take advantage of their immortality and harm those who are not blessed with the same gift," the Justicar replied patiently, "and to punish those who do so."

"Punish them how exactly?"

"Depending on the scope of their crimes, a monetary fine may suffice in some cases, while others may warrant execution and their subsequent imprisonment for a set time."

"You can change where an Adventurer returns to life?" I asked, a hint of concern creeping into my voice as I pieced together the hidden meaning to the Justicar's words.

"I *personally* cannot. But should Mithus deem it necessary to punish an Adventurer with imprisonment, he can direct the Adventurer's soul wherever he deems necessary," Dyre stated crisply. "Be assured that if you follow the laws set forth in the Town Charter, then there is nothing to be concerned about. My duty is to ensure that all remains safe within the town limits."

"I see," I said slowly mulling over the Justicar's response in my head.

It seems to me that Justicars are Ascend Online's version of police and rule enforcement, I thought, watching Dyre touch a corner of Aldford's Charter, causing a small symbol to appear on the paper. *Much like how high-leveled town guards used to be in other multiplayer games – to keep players from griefing other players, or simply killing everyone in a city.*

"It is done," Dyre said to Aldwin. "Aldford is now under Mithus's watchful eye."

"Thank you, Justicar," the knight replied earnestly, placing the Town Charter back into his pouch. "Your arrival could have not come at a better time."

Dyre silently nodded this thanks to the Bann before turning to look at me. "I would take custody of those prisoners now, it is past time that they answer for their crimes."

I looked towards Aldwin, seeing him give me a gentle nod. "Lyrian, you and Virtus have done more than I could have ever asked to keep the peace in Aldford. These bandits fall under the Justicar's responsibility now. You may release them to any fate he deems fit."

"Well... I'm definitely happy to have *less* work on my plate for a change," I replied, a little taken aback at how fast the Justicar had inserted himself into the town, but if Aldwin trusted him, I was willing to do the same. I motioned for the Justicar to follow me. "I'll take you to the prisoners right away."

The Justicar nodded silently, turning to follow me as we walked back towards the crowd of settlers. To better keep the prisoners contained and protected from the settlers' wrath, we had decided to keep them together in a spare wagon under strict guard.

"What are you going to do with the prisoners?" I asked, curious to hear of Dyre's plans. So far, he hadn't asked if

Aldford had a prison or given any sort of hint to what his intentions were.

"I am going to sentence them," Dyre's voice was completely flat as he spoke.

"To what exactly?"

"They have been caught in the act of Banditry," Dyre replied. "There is only one sentence available to them."

The Justicar paused for a split second.

"Death."

Chapter 3

"Welcome to Aldford. Please grab a rope and pull," Halcyon muttered while all of us, minus Amaranth, looked at the six hanging bandits that Dyre had just unceremoniously hung from a tree just outside of the town. On seeing the hanging bodies, the cat had commented that he was getting particularly hungry, and excused himself to hunt for his meal. None of us dared to argue.

"What else could he have done?" Caius asked with a slow shake of his head. "Each one of them were beyond guilty, they deserved to hang."

"No disagreement here," Halcyon replied with a sigh. "I just expected something *different.*"

"Like what? Cheerleaders?" Caius snorted. "Or maybe snacks and a parade?"

"Well... I don't know," Halcyon's eyes were unfocused while he looked at the hanging bandits. "A trial? Dyre just grabbed a handful of the caravan guards, gave them each a rope and strung up the bandits with barely a second thought."

"I don't think a trial would have done anything other than waste time," I said, casting a glance to the Justicar, who was standing beside Aldwin a short distance away. "You saw the blood on Dyre's armor. He was *there* when the bandits attacked the settlers. There was no doubt of guilt."

"I guess..." Halcyon admitted. "It just caught me a bit off guard how fast it all happened."

"I think it was a warning to all of the Adventurers," Sierra quietly added, speaking up for the first time since the bandits were executed. "Until now, it's been up to us to enforce the rules, and thankfully we haven't had to really do that, barring the whole thing with Graves last month. By hanging the bandits right in front of everyone, Dyre's shown that there'll be *Game* enforced penalties if they take advantage of people."

"Yeah," Constantine agreed. "We've been pretty lucky so far with the Adventurers that joined us after Graves dragged them here. All we've had are growing pains or minor disagreements."

"How many Adventurers do we have in the new arrivals?" Drace asked, looking towards Constantine and Sierra.

"Seventy-eight," Constantine answered. "Though, a handful have already told me that they're only looking to pass through Aldford and head further north to start their own settlement."

"Hrm, I wish them luck with that. They'll definitely have enough work cut out for themselves," Drace grunted in amusement, then nodded towards the massive group of settlers. "What about the settlers? Are they all here to join Aldford, or moving on too?"

"I haven't heard any talking about leaving," Sierra replied. "Which means we're going to have to find places to put a hundred and eleven people, not counting the thirty guards that survived the attack.

There was a quiet pause as we digested those numbers.

"So... counting the Adventurers, we're looking at nearly tripling the number of people we have in the village, *again*..." I said, realizing that Aldford would be boasting nearly three hundred inhabitants, depending on how many Adventurers chose to stay with us.

"Aldford's come a long way from being a little frontier village," Constantine commented wistfully. "I guess it's definitely a town now."

I nodded in agreement with Constantine, turning to look at all the Settlers and Adventurers who had paused to watch the execution of the bandits, feeling a little overwhelmed at just how many people were here now. In not even a day we had gone from being completely cut off and alone on the frontier, without a single new arrival to Aldford since Graves showed up on our doorstep, to scrambling and trying to somehow accommodate two hundred more souls.

"Damn bandits...if we'd known so many were coming, we could have done more to prepare for all of them..." Drace said, reading my mind as he gave one last look at the hanging Adventurers. "Let's get back to Aldford. We should give Léandre a heads up before everyone starts trying to cram themselves into the town and realizes that we have no place to put them."

"We have to go soon too, Lyr," Constantine reminded me as we began to walk towards the town. "Our meeting is at three, and it's probably a good idea to be there early."

"Yeah, you're right," I replied with a nod. "I just need to set up my offline tasks after we talk with Léandre."

"*Right*," Constantine agreed, "I have a ton of leather I've been meaning to clean and have ready for crafting. I've ignored crafting for far too long."

"I'll probably take my rest day tonight too," I added after doing the mental math and realizing I had already been logged in for nine straight days. "Something tells me we might need the extra days once we get everyone settled in."

"That's probably not a bad idea..." Sierra said slowly, rubbing her eyes. "I for one, want to sleep at least a solid twelve hours."

The party chorused their agreement, exhaustion visible on everyone's expression. It had been a long and busy night, with little sleep to go around.

As we walked towards the town, I found my mind focusing on the new settlers. I couldn't believe how much had changed in Aldford since Launch Day, well over a month ago, where I'd found myself separated from the group and dropped completely naked into a veritable horde of goblins.

Aldford's come a long way since then, I thought as I looked up at a new building flanking the town's southeastern entrance. Situated just behind the earthworks, stood the first of Aldford's two watchtowers, which in its current, semi-finished state, measured twenty-five feet tall from ground to roof.

At the moment, the watchtower was essentially a four-posted scaffold with a set of stairs twisting upwards to a semi-covered platform, where the militia or other Adventurers could easily watch the horizon for threats while also enjoying some level of protection from the worst of the elements.

One of our long-term plans was to build a sister tower to match the watch tower on the southern entrance in order to maximize our visibility across the horizon and to better control access into the heart of Aldford. Should the need ever arise, the two watchtowers would be perfectly positioned to rain death and destruction on any who chose to assault the town from the southeastern bridge.

The same applied for the northern entrance to Aldford, where a matching watchtower also stood, giving us a clear view of the land to the north of the town, and any who would approach from the direction of the northeastern forest.

In time, we hoped to finish both sets of watchtowers guarding the two entrances to Aldford, which would then serve as a starting point to begin building the palisade I had originally envisioned circling around the town.

That is if I can ever get Jenkins, Léandre and Drace to agree on a proper design for the finished defenses. I shook my head remembering the rather heated disagreements the trio had found themselves in over the last few weeks. Channeling his expertise from his Real Life career of being a Civil Planner, Drace had quickly become integral to the development of Aldford, happy to have a way to put his education to practical use, something that he'd been unable to do in Reality with the massive downturn in employment.

Walking over the bridge and into the town proper, three large buildings came into view. Set in a row, side by side to one another, were three Viking style longhouses, all bearing noticeable architectural differences, despite each serving the same function.

We had learned early that Léandre viewed using the same design for more than one building something akin to a mortal sin and so we eventually found it easier to give in to his eccentricities, so long as it didn't impact the building's production time or the town's defense.

We'll probably need to build a few more of these, I thought, silently admiring the Tul'Shar's handiwork and the way that he had managed to have the three different designs blend seamlessly together. *On second thought... we need to build more of everything. I haven't the faintest idea where we're going to find enough space to put everyone. I hope they're okay sleeping outside for a few more days.*

Leaving the long houses behind, we cut through what was shaping up to be the residential section of Aldford and approached what once used to be the Workshop, now creatively renamed 'The Crafting Hall' after our countless renovations had drastically changed the single room building into a sprawling, multi-purpose crafting hub.

It had taken a fair bit of arm-twisting and cajoling to convince Jenkins to allow us to modify his treasured Workshop, but as more Adventurers expressed interest in pursuing tradeskills and the demand for construction materials rose, he was forced to admit that the tiny little Workshop wasn't enough to fulfill all of Aldford's needs anymore.

Well, that and we told Shelia that he was being an obstinate fool about the whole thing.

So, with a hesitant Jenkins' ever vigilant supervision and Léandre's expertise, the Workshop had been drastically expanded into a massive, two-story building, with dedicated crafting areas set aside for Leatherworking, Tailoring and Carpentry. Due to its unique requirements, we had decided to move the original forge into its own adjacent and still-in-progress building that we had come to call The Foundry.

Progress on the new crafting hub for the town had advanced far enough that Adventurers were no longer tripping over one another as they worked, but as with practically everything in Aldford, we still had a long way to go until the Crafting Hall was considered complete.

"Ah, our intrepid defenders return." A silky-smooth voice pulled me out of my thoughts as a tan colored Tul'Shar, wearing a simple leather tunic with dark pants, walked out of the Crafting Hall. "You wake a tired old man with such a large ruckus in the night, and now I sense you are all here to bring him even more work, yes?"

"Léandre." I smiled while looking up to see the familiar lion-like form of Aldford's Lead Architect striding towards us. "You know what they say about the reward for doing a good job…"

"But, of course… *more work!*" the cat-man exclaimed with a laugh, causing the numerous tools he had looped along his waist to jingle. "This is how the world works for people such as us. We are destined to be forever busy!"

Revealing a mouth full of sharp teeth, the architect grinned at us in anticipation as he clasped his hands together. "Now, tell poor Léandre what tasks you wish to pile on him, and he will tell you what he can do."

Drace took a deep breath, before starting to explain the events of the night, culminating with our battle against the bandits. "Now we need to find a way to house at least two-hundred and twenty people. At least for the short term until we can build a few more buildings."

"A daunting task…" Léandre replied, crossing his arms in thought for a few seconds before snapping his fingers with a nod, "…for anyone other than myself."

"Y-You came up with a plan already?" I couldn't help but stammer in surprise. Despite having spent nearly a month working with the older architect-turned-gamer, I was often caught off guard by how the man thought and his creative approach to problems.

"Of course!" Léandre waved dismissively. "For most of my life, I have traveled all over the world, volunteering with disaster relief organizations during crises. On several occasions, I have had to do much more… with much less than we find ourselves with today."

The architect paused, his expression falling for a second as his ears drooped, before springing up as he shook his head, "But that is all in the past, and we must worry about what we can do today."

Before any of us could comment on the ghost that we had seen cross Léandre's face, he launched into explaining his plan, already having moved past whatever memory had haunted him. "We will take the entirety of that godawful burlap cloth piling up in the storage room and fashion it into a tarp, from there we will use a few of the timbers we have set aside to dry as supports and we will make ourselves a massive tent."

"A...tent?" Drace repeated slowly before a spark caught in his eye. "*A tent!* You mean like a circus tent! That's a great idea! It'll be perfect for the short term!"

"Thank you, my friends," the Tul'Shar purred with another toothy smile as we all echoed Drace's enthusiasm. "There will be some work involved to create the needed bracing, fastenings and rope, but I am confident that with some help, I can complete the task by nightfall. If need be, we will conscript others for any additional labor we may need. Where do you wish this tent to be placed?"

"Just outside the town to the north," I replied, mentally trying to envision the size of the tent. "I don't want it blocking our view towards the south, and the rivers will provide enough of a defense to keep any creatures away."

"You want to put them outside the northern defenses?" Halcyon asked. "Won't they see that as a snub that we don't trust them?"

"I don't see that we have any other choice," I said, shrugging at the mage. "If we put the tent up within Aldford, they'll be right on top where we're going to be building their new homes anyway."

"Lyr's right," Drace agreed. "The fewer people we have underfoot, the better. If anyone has hurt feelings, tell them to grab a hammer or an axe and help out; we won't turn them away."

"That is for cert—" A pair of loud nervous whinnies interrupted Léandre as a cart, pulled by two large draft horses, rumbled into view, a familiar looking shape pulling on the reins to stop the moment he saw us.

Keeping pace beside the cart on foot, were the two largest Thunder Lizards, Helix and Abaddon, their eyes eagerly scanning the nearby area for threats. Perched on top of the cart, I saw a terrified, white-haired man being practically crushed into his seat as both Myr, and Zethus covered him from either side. A coal-black dwarf held the reins, grinning maniacally while waving towards us with a free hand.

"Thorne!" Sierra called out in concern, all of us instantly on high alert with the sudden arrival of the cart. "What's going on? What are you doing to that man? Where are Freya and Theia?"

"We're protecting him!" Thorne called back to us. "Freya and Theia are sorting out all the new Adventurers. When we found out what was in this cart, we had to get him to safety."

"Is the cart full of bullion?" Constantine snorted while shaking his head. "What the hell does he have in there?"

Before Thorne could reply, the middle-aged man pushed himself free from both Zethus and Myr towards us. "Please, I'm just an Alchemist! I don't even know what's happening! They took one look at my cart, then practically commandeered it! I have done nothing wrong!"

"Thorne, you kidnapped an Alchemist?" Halcyon asked, his voice suddenly filling with worry. "Hang on... that cart isn't packed with naphtha or some other crazy shit that could explode at the drop of a hat, is it?"

"No!" The Alchemist called out. "Nothing like that! I just have a pair of alembics an—"

The older man's words suddenly cut off as Myr covered his mouth with a hand, growling at him loud enough for us to hear, "Sssh, don't sshout that to the world! Are you insssane?!"

"I couldn't let word get out," Thorne replied. "If everyone knew what he had, we'd probably have a riot on our hands within an hour."

"You still haven't told us what he has, Thorne!" Halcyon started to back away from the cart nervously.

"Nothing that can explode," the dwarf answered quickly, holding up his hands placatingly while carefully looking around for other people. Seeing no one else nearby, he then waved us in close to the cart and began speaking very softly. "There's enough equipment, alembics, boiling pots and anything else you could possibly need in here to set up a fully functioning Alchemy Laboratory."

"That's what I told him!" The man exclaimed, having been freed from Myr's grasp. "Then he abducted me!"

"That's... *it?*" Caius asked, his voice filled with disbelief. "It's not illegal to run an Alchemy Lab."

"I don't care about the Alchemy Lab," Thorne replied. "What I care about, is that all that equipment can be used to set up a brewery and a distillery."

There was a pause as we all absorbed that, each of us looking at Thorne blankly before the implications set in.

"Gods... if the other Adventurers find out..." Drace shook his head.

"It would be *chaos*," Léandre agreed.

"Find out what?" The older man demanded. "I don't understand, why would that matter?"

"With your equipment, you are the first person in this town capable of producing spirits or any other kind of alcohol," Caius whispered.

"*What?*" The man's eyes went wide. "You mean this town is *dry?*"

"Dry as a three-dollar wh- *hey!*" Halcyon yelped as Caius swatted him on the arm. "What was that for?"

"Ugh, you know exactly what it was for!" Caius rolled his eyes sarcastically at the mage before looking back at the Alchemist. "Aldford hasn't seen a drop of alcohol since it was founded."

"Then you truly *have* saved me." The man ran a hand through his hair while sighing loudly. "My name is Marlin Carey, I journeyed here with the intention of setting up my own laboratory, though it seems I may find my talents better suited to opening a *distillery* instead…"

"Do you really think that this will be a problem?" Constantine asked, a confused expression still on his face after we had formally introduced ourselves to the Alchemist. "I mean, sure, I could appreciate a stiff drink after a day like today, but I don't get why this is such big deal."

"You *really* need to start paying more attention to Tradeskills, Constantine," Caius scolded gently. "Aside from the fact people would want to *drink it*, alcohol, in general, is a key ingredient for all higher quality recipes for both *Cooking* and *Alchemy*."

"*Leathercrafting* too," I added, remembering one of the newer recipes that I had learned. "I need strong alcohols to tan thicker types of hide, and that's only what I've discovered so far…"

"Almost all potions have an alcohol base too," Marlin added, having visibly relaxed now that he understood Thorne's motivations for getting him clear of the other Adventurers.

"Shit, I didn't realize that." Constantine accepted the rebuke with a nod, pausing for a moment to think, "…the demand is going to be incredible… are you looking for investors?"

"I-Investors? M-me?" Marlin stammered, completely caught by surprise by the offer. "I j-just got here and..."

"Oh, that's a good idea!" Sierra agreed enthusiastically.

"I'm happy to offer up my time to help," Caius said to Marlin. "I have some experience as an Alchemist already."

"Me too!" Zethus spoke up from the Alchemist's side. "I would love to be a part of thiss!"

"Count me in as well," Thorne added with a wave of his hand.

Marlin gaped at all of us, as we stared at him waiting for a reply, his mouth working soundlessly while trying to find any words at all. "I-I, oh, didn't expect to have such *enthusiasm* for my arrival. I-I would certainly be interested in, oh...we would h-have to discuss terms..."

"Perhaps this conversation would be better suited to a more relaxed environment at a later time, yes?" Léandre came to the Alchemist's rescue, seeing that the older man was clearly overwhelmed with everyone standing around him. "I must get to work if we are to see the shelter constructed by nightfall. In the meantime, we can store the Alchemy equipment within the Crafting Hall and keep it out of sight."

"T-That would be wonderful," Marlin nodded eagerly, seizing the lifeline Léandre had cast. "This is just so much to absorb at the moment, a-and after the attack this morning..."

"We completely understand, Marlin," I told the Alchemist. "There is quite a lot to consider; just keep us in mind, and we can talk more about it later."

"Thank you; yes, of course." The man continued to nod as Thorne gathered the reins, ready to move the cart closer to the Crafting Hall.

"Okay, Lyr," Constantine said to me as the cart slowly began to move away, "we really need to get our shit moving for the meeting."

"Yeah, you're right." I sighed in acknowledgment, turning to look at Léandre while opening a menu in my vision. "I'm queuing a bunch of bronze and leather refinement in my offline task list, but I'm also permitting you to assign crafting tasks to me while I'm gone. We're all going to be gone tonight for a full rest cycle to reset our timers."

"Good, I was going to ask that you did so," the architect replied inclining his head as he accepted the prompt I had sent him. "Go to your meeting and do not waste time worrying, we should have everything well in hand until you return."

"Awesome. Thanks, Léandre." I bid the cat-man farewell before I turned towards the rest of the group and gave them a quick wave. "See you all tonight. Send Constantine or me a message if anything comes up that you really need us for."

"No worries, Lyr," Sierra replied with a smile. "We'll be fine! Just make sure you have good news waiting for us tonight!"

"Heh, fingers crossed!" I gave one final wave to the group as I called up a menu I had only seen a handful of times in the last month.

Are you sure you want to log off?

YES / NO

I mentally selected 'YES' and felt my perception begin to change as the world slowly faded to black.

Loading, please wait…

Chapter 4

Toronto, Ontario, Canada
CTI Player Housing Complex – Ninth Floor – Apartment Suite

"Grrr, stupid thing..." I cursed under my breath as I fought to properly adjust my now too-large dress shirt. "If it wasn't enough that my in-game body is all different... so is my fucking *real* one."

"Hey, Marc," I heard Peter's voice call from the hallway, a second before he poked his head into the bathroom. "You ready to go yet?"

"Yeah, one sec." I glanced quickly at Peter then back towards the mirror, my mind forcing me to do a double take as my friend's appearance registered in my head.

Turning to look back, it took a moment for my mind to accept that I was looking at someone I had regularly seen nearly every day for the last month, his physical appearance not matching up to what I normally had pictured in my head.

Standing at nearly six feet tall, with a wild mop of dark-brown hair, I was expecting to see Peter's slightly pudgy face looking back at me, but instead, I saw a lean, unfamiliar face staring back at me. Glancing down, I saw that his shirt hung even looser than mine did and that his pants were struggling to stay hanging around his hips, even with his belt cinched to the tightest notch.

"The Virtual Reality Diet is damned effective, isn't it?" Peter said softly, noticing my prolonged stare.

"Yeah... that it is," I replied slowly. "How much have you lost?"

"So far?" Peter shrugged, something I could barely see through his loose shirt, "about twenty pounds. You?"

"Almost ten."

The 'Virtual Reality Diet' was a term that the media had coined to describe the rather considerable weight loss that all Long-Term Play Players underwent after playing Ascend Online for a prolonged period.

Rather than being an intended outcome by CTI, the weight loss was actually a side effect of the constant anti-atrophy treatments that were performed on the comatose players to stave off muscular and cardiovascular degeneration, a nanite-based treatment program originally designed for coma patients, astronauts, and others confined to immobility for long periods of time.

In order to prevent atrophy, the patient's cardiovascular system was intermittently stimulated to that of a moderate workout, while muscles were forced through tiny, but constant, contractions to ensure that they didn't deteriorate. This whole process also managed the patient's metabolism, preventing the body from consuming valuable muscle mass for energy, instead focusing on stored fat cells and the intravenous solutions fed to the body.

The positive side effect of this process, aside from no muscular deterioration, was that prolonged treatment actually tended to improve the patient's overall physical conditioning and health, though many players were finding it extremely jarring to get used to the changes that their body underwent when they logged themselves out of the game.

It won't be long until you can tell that someone is a Long-Term Player just by looking at them, I thought.

Giving up on adjusting my shirt with a sigh, I moved to leave the bathroom, Peter leading the way as we grabbed our winter jackets and left the suite. A few minutes later we had descended in the elevator and checked out of the secure section of the building.

The lobby was nothing like Launch Day - the two of us only spotting a handful of people loitering in the hall, the eager expressions on their faces hinting that they had finally made it to the end of the incredibly long wait list and were set to join the world of Ascend Online.

I wish them luck wherever they end up. I nodded at a middle-aged woman that made eye contact as Peter and I walked by and stepped outside, feeling the freezing winter wind slice straight through us.

"Couple weeks until spring is here and there's nothing but cold and snow in the forecast," Peter grumbled at the unnaturally cold winter, even by Canadian standards, as he signaled a passing taxi.

A yellow sedan pulled itself out of the steady flow of traffic before us into an unused pickup lane, set directly outside of the CTI building. Moving to get out of the freezing cold, Peter and I practically leaped into the small car, breathing in relief when we found the inside to be pleasantly warm.

"Hello, thank you for choosing CityTaxi," the driverless car greeted us in a smooth male's voice the moment the doors closed. *"Where am I taking you today?"*

I quickly rattled off the address to our Stream Producer's office, having taken the time to memorize it.

"Understood. Your estimated time of arrival is: seven minutes," the car replied as it seamlessly rejoined traffic, the other cars automatically compensating to provide a gap. *"Would you like to engage Quiet Mode, or shall I turn the radio on?"*

"Quiet Mode," I told the car as I belted myself in.

"It always amazes me that our parents had to... were *allowed* to physically drive their cars through the downtown core here," Peter commented wistfully, watching the hundreds of driverless vehicles seamlessly moving through the streets, often with less than a foot of clearance between one another. "I can't imagine how much time they must have wasted in traffic or spent dealing with accidents."

"No kidding," I agreed, shaking my head at the thought.

With all the technological advances over the last twenty years, it was hard to believe that Driverless Vehicles had been relegated to an almost footnote status in history, overshadowed by the advent of Nanotechnology. Commercially released in 2020, the technologies supporting Driverless Vehicles rapidly expanded over the intervening decade as the auto industry competed savagely amongst one another in order to bring the technology fully to market. By the time the early 30's rolled around, practically every car on the road in a first world nation had some sort of automated driving technology.

The natural progression after that was to create the Automated Traffic Control System and fully remove the pesky and unreliable factor that was Human Input. This was then adopted by nearly every major metropolis when it was proved that the ATCS drastically cut down on traffic and fatal accidents. It was now a rarity to even hear of an accident in an ATCS controlled area, as opposed to the almost daily fatalities and accidents in the years that preceded it.

"Nothing but Ascend Online advertisements everywhere you look," Peter commented, waving a hand towards a small truck beside us carrying a digital billboard, currently displaying the game's logo on it.

Turning to look, the moment I made eye contact with the billboard, the display shifted, causing me to flinch as I found myself staring right into my own eyes, or at least those of my avatar's scarred and withered face.

Shit! I winced at my own reaction. It was the first time I had ever had a good look at myself from outside the game. *I think I understand why people look at me the way they do now…*

Plastered right across the digital billboard was me in my Ætherwarped state, along with the rest of the party including Amaranth, each of us poised in a heroic pose as we all gazed into the distance. A caption scrolled across the billboard.

The Birth of Virtue
Episode 1 Starting Tonight @ 9pm – GameTV

"Ha!" Peter gasped, just as the billboard truck pulled away and turned down another street. "What are the odds of that!"

"We're on *GameTV*?" I couldn't help but smile in excitement, pushing away the embarrassment of being startled by my own appearance. "Maybe that's what they wanted to talk to us about."

"Maybe!" Peter nodded excitedly. "We've been out of the loop for over a week… and well until today, we really haven't done anything really interesting. I don't think that we're going to get many more people watching us grind wolverines until we hit level thirteen."

"Well… we have a hell of a lot more people in the town now. I'm sure something interesting will crop up," I replied, hoping that I hadn't just jinxed myself.

"Hopefully nothing as exciting as that whole bit with Graves," Peter commented wistfully.

"Hopefully," I echoed, completely agreeing with Peter's sentiment. "I'm hoping we can get the Foundry up and functional soon. That iron we found back at the Tower is proving damn hard to smelt."

"Man, I really need to play catch up with tradeskills..." Peter let out a deep sigh. "There's just too much work to go around with all the construction we have on the go."

"I hear you there," I said sympathetically, remembering all the work we'd done over the last few weeks. "At least we've found more hands to help out today."

"Yeah, all things considered, we were damn lucky."

The rest of the ride went smoothly, Peter and I chatting to pass the time as we wound our way through the city, until the taxi once again pulled itself out of traffic. Its voice spoke softly, *"We have arrived at your destination. Please ensure you have collected all your belongings before leaving the vehicle. Your account will be automatically charged: six dollars. Thank you for choosing CityTaxi and have a good day!"*

*"*You ready for this?" I asked Peter, looking out into the cold and the big building looming before us.

"Of course." Peter grinned at me while he pulled his jacket tight. "Let's go see how much money we've made."

—～～—

Pushing through the frosted glass door the first thing I noticed was that the entire office was in chaos, construction workers were walking everywhere, along with the sound of countless power tools filling the air. Large areas of the office were sectioned into contained areas by thick walls of plastic to prevent dust from taking over the office.

A single dark-haired secretary sat at a large wooden desk centering the room, perking up the moment that she saw us walk in.

"Hi, there! Welcome to Ætherworld Productions! How can I help you today?"

"Uh, Ætherworld Productions?" I asked, the company name not matching up to the one that I had originally been expecting. "I'm not sure if we're in the right place..."

"You wouldn't happen to be Marcus and Peter by chance?" the woman asked.

"That's us," Peter replied. "I thought this was—"

"Oh good, you're here! Sorry for the confusion!" The woman came around the desk, rushing to greet us with a large smile plastered across her face. "We've actually just changed our company name to help with branding, and it has been hectic getting everything changed over to the new name. My name is Jen by the way."

"Nice to meet you, Jen," I replied graciously, happy that we were in the right place.

"Paul asked me to send you two back to him as soon as you got here, so please follow me." Jen began leading us through the office, almost all of which seemed to be under some sort of renovation. "Sorry about all the construction, we've been long overdue for a facelift here and decided to get it all done in one shot."

"No worries," Peter said. "We understand."

Smoothly gliding around all the construction, Jen led us towards an already finished meeting room at the back of the office, where two men were waiting for us. The moment we stepped into the room, both men leaped to their feet and came around the massive table to shake our hands.

"Marcus! Peter! I'm happy you could both make it today!" Paul greeted us enthusiastically, before motioning towards the other man in the room. "This is our attorney, Andrew. I've asked him to sit in on our meeting today. I think he'll have some interesting advice for you both after we get our update out of the way."

"Pleasure to meet you both," Andrew said softly as he shook our hands.

"Can I interest you two in some coffee or tea?" Jen asked, indicating a pair of carafes on a nearby table.

"Yes, coffee please!" I nodded excitedly, Peter echoing my response.

Moving efficiently, the dark-haired secretary poured a pair of cups for both Peter and me before excusing herself from the meeting room. "Let me know if you need anything else."

"Thanks, Jen!" I called to the secretary's retreating form as the door closed, and I breathed the sweet and tantalizing aroma of the coffee before me, my first cup in well over a week.

"So, we're really excited to hear what's happened over the last couple of weeks," Peter began excitedly. "Just on our way here we saw an ad for our stream on GameTV. I had no idea we were that popular!"

"Yes!" Paul exclaimed cheerfully as he sat back down at the table across from us. "Ascend Online has just been dominating the entertainment market. You wouldn't believe what the demand for quality and entertaining streams are like, which I'm happy to say that your guild ranks among the highest for."

"That's great!" I replied with a smile. "I mean, we've been having a ton of fun *playing* the game, but I'm happy it's working out in the Real World too!"

"Of course," Paul agreed wholeheartedly as he began pulling a handful of papers out of a folder on the table and handing them over to us. "I'm sure you're both eager to know just how much you've made with your streams so far, so here's a general breakdown."

Setting my coffee cup aside, I grabbed the sheet with nervous hands, scanning through the document. My eyes widened as I looked at the final figure, causing me to look back up at the two men with a stupefied expression on my face. "We've made a little over four hundred thousand dollars in not even three weeks of airtime?"

"Well, you've actually made a great deal more than that," Paul added. "Unfortunately, taxes and CTI's five percent cut take a rather substantial portion of your earnings…"

"You're not kidding!" Peter snorted as he pointed out the line where Ætherworld's production fee, taxes and CTI's portion of the revenue were calculated on my sheet of paper. "I'd completely forgotten that CTI had their hands in the revenue stream, but still…*four hundred thousand dollars* is not that shabby…"

"That's incredible!" I exclaimed waving my hand in the air, narrowly missing knocking my coffee mug over. "I was worried that there would be far too much competition from literally every other player that wanted to stream their play time."

"That definitely has an impact on the market," Paul acknowledged. "However, there are very few players that have combined multiple feeds into a single episodic show like you all have."

"Because we've been able to consolidate so many feeds from multiple perspectives and expand the narrative into an actual storyline, such as Freya and her party's journey with Graves, we've managed to maintain steady pacing episode to episode and have retained a high viewership throughout the entire series."

"Given that we now have a timeslot on GameTV, I'm tentatively expecting that your earnings should *at least* double over the course of the next two or three months with just what you have released so far," Paul said optimistically. Then he held up a hand in warning, "*But,* making any more than that largely depends on what sort of content you have coming down the pipe for us. Entertainment isn't what it used to be, like back in the 2010 era, where you could afford to be off the air for six months of the year, viewers are demanding new shows and content on an almost daily basis, and if you can't keep up…"

"You get left behind," Peter finished with an understanding nod, then looked over to me. "We've been fairly busy the last few weeks, but nothing on the same level of excitement when compared to that run-in with Graves."

"Yeah, it's been mostly quiet since people stopped arriving from Eberia. We've managed to get the core group of Virtus up to level thirteen and have spent most of our time building and developing Aldford." I said slowly, watching Paul nod as he followed along with me. "Well, at least until this morning…"

"*Ooh,*" Paul made an excited noise, pulling a pen out of a shirt pocket. "What happened this morning?"

"Well, we found out that the reason why we haven't had anyone new coming to Aldford was that we had a group of Bandits camped out intercepting all the traffic," Peter answered before going on to give a high-level summary of everything that had happened earlier in the day. "I know it'll be quite some time before that part of the feed becomes available…"

"No, this is *great*!" Paul replied eagerly as he made a handful of notes. "This is exactly what we need, a huge battle with the bandits to kick things off… more people coming to the area… we can definitely make this work!"

Paul paused for a moment while looking down at his notes. "You said there were quite a few new Adventurers that arrived too, right? Any chance of them maybe applying to Virtus, and us getting their feed?"

"That was still being sorted out when we left." I looked towards Peter, who simply shrugged at me. "We'll probably get applicants over the next few days. If any make the cut, we'll definitely send over their feeds; it's part of our guild membership requirements anyway."

"Perfect!" Paul exclaimed. "We'll sort through those feeds once we get them, and maybe do a feature on some of the new members since some of those feeds may already be available for use, or will be sooner than today's bandit battle."

"We have a couple other places that we're looking into exploring near Aldford when things settle down," I told the producer. "Though the majority of our focus for the next couple days is going to be getting all the new people settled."

"That's more than understandable, and I have no place to tell you how to run your town. Definitely do what you think is best," Paul replied as he put his pen down and looked intently at Peter and me. "I know I asked this before, but are you sure I can't convince you all to go public with your names and avatars? It would really help with creating a tangible presence for viewers to identify with. Especially if we can line up a few interviews or appearances at events."

"Right now, we'd rather keep our Real World identities private," I said after seeing Peter look towards me again for an answer to the producer's question. "Maybe one day when we can generate the biggest impact with it we can go public, but right now… we'd rather not."

"That's definitely understandable." Paul looked a little disappointed at my reply, but clearly understood our reasoning behind it. "I won't lie, it might slow things down with how quickly you climb the rankings, and your viewership, but then again… *if* you can make it high enough up the rankings without anyone knowing who you are, then that mystery will only make your group even more interesting."

"Hang on." Peter cocked his head in confusion. "There are rankings?"

"Huh?" Paul gave us a blank look, before slapping himself on the forehead. "Geez, I'm sorry about that! I completely forgot that you two have *literally* spent the last few weeks in another world and wouldn't have had a chance to see them yet."

"Rankings, or more specifically *Player Rankings* is something that CTI introduced shortly after the first feeds were released," Paul excitedly began to explain. "The ranking doesn't actually have anything to do with your in-game characters, but instead is a reflection of your Real World popularity for that current month. The more popular you are, the higher your ranking increases the following month. It also aggregates ranking in cases where multiple players submit their feeds into a single feed, giving them all the same ranking based on the overall popularity."

"So, how are we doing right now then?" I asked hesitantly, looking back down at the sheet to see if it was on there.

"Right now, Virtus is currently ranked eight hundred and ninety-ninth out of, well… *several million* players for the month of February," Paul answered with a smile. "So, I'd say you are doing *very well* overall!"

"We're in the *top thousand*?" Peter exclaimed slapping a hand on the table, then shifting to high five me. "Damn, that's awesome!"

"No kidding!" I replied, feeling a little overwhelmed at how high we had climbed already. "That's insane!"

"Has there been any feedback from the viewers?" Peter asked curiously. "I'd be interested to know what they're saying about us."

"It's largely positive actually, especially from the greater gaming community," the producer replied. "To be honest, all feedback has been *overwhelmingly* positive. Practically everyone wants to see more of you all. We've only had a handful of negative complaints, and that's just been due to bad language, and we've pretty much ignored those."

"People still get worked up over salty language?" Peter asked with surprise. "That's pretty fucking ridiculous."

"Yeah..." I shook my head slowly in disbelief. "They're okay with watching us fight and kill things, but their ears are suddenly too sensitive?"

"You'll hear all sorts of it in this business," Paul replied with a shrug. "What's important to focus on though, is that you guys are trending upwards. This new bandit stuff that happened today should keep you guys in the top thousand for the month of March, but if you're looking to climb... we're going to need more exciting things to sell to the viewers until you can build a dedicated following."

"We'll do our best," I told Paul, trying to project some optimism into my voice.

"No doubt!" Paul said enthusiastically before indicating Andrew, who had been patiently listening to the conversation all this time. "Now, the last bit of our update has a few legal components, so I'm going to turn this over to Andrew because he can explain it much better than I can. Then he has a few options to explain to you all."

Still riding high on our excitement, Peter and I shifted our glance towards Andrew, who smiled and leaned forward. "So, to follow up on Paul's excellent segue, have you two ever considered the benefits of turning Virtus into a company?"

Chapter 5

"Peter?" My voice was completely flat as I leaned my head against the side of the elevator wall.

"Yeah, Marc?" I heard his defeated voice reply to me.

"My head hurts."

"Mine too, Marc."

"What happened back there?" I asked, still struggling to understand what had happened in the second half of the meeting.

"We laid the groundwork to form our guild as a corporate entity to make sure all of our guild members get a fair cut of our earnings while employing a more efficient tax structure," Peter explained tonelessly. "It will also allow us to have our members expense their subscription costs of playing Ascend Online to the company, which we can then claim for tax credit. In addition, we can also hire employees to help manage Real World or even Game World duties while working directly for us."

I blinked twice before turning to look at my friend. "Why didn't he just explain it that way? That makes perfect sense."

"He did explain it that way, just with a bunch of more words in between it all," Peter replied with a sigh. "I just happen to have much more experience dealing with lawyers at work."

"I might sound like a terrible friend for asking this, but...you dealt with lawyers at work? I thought you traded digital currency?"

"Yeah, I did," Peter confirmed with a dismissive wave of his hand. "Usually the lawyers came to me representing clients that need money moved in some way, or were looking at exchanging their crypto-currencies for real currency or vice versa. It was all *stupidly boring shit,* and you know just how much I hated talking about my job…or doing it."

"Wait, *hated*?" I finally caught on to Peter's choice of words. "You quit?"

"Hah, yeah!" Peter barked a tired laugh. "Same day that I called you about Ascend Online actually. I just had enough and walked out."

"That's crazy! What were you going to do if the game didn't pan out?" I shook my head, not believing that Peter hadn't told any of us that he had quit his job for well over a month.

"Hell, if I know." Peter shrugged. "Go back to school for something design or art related? That's pretty much the only field there's any real demand for."

"That's a far leap from the economics degree you have now," I replied slowly, still getting over my surprise.

"What else is there to do, Marc? Between you, and the others, you're all in design one way or the other," Peter exclaimed waving his hands in the air. "Food and retail stores are all run by robots, vehicles are almost all automated now, and thanks to the 'Nano-Industrial Revolution' we don't even need *skilled* workers for our manufacturing industry anymore, let alone unskilled ones. If it wasn't for the Basic Living Income giving people money to spend… the world economy would have collapsed ages ago.

"I don't disagree with you there," I replied with a sigh, having heard a similar version of Peter's rant before.

The Basic Living Income was a measure enacted by almost all of the world governments in response to nanotechnology and robotics rendering the majority of the global workforce obsolete over the last decade. Almost all labor or service based industries had been fully automated, only needing a handful of individuals to manage and direct their robotic workforce, leaving billions out of work as their professions simply ceased to exist. Mines were now run by fully automated robots, vehicles drove themselves, and once sprawling farms had been converted with massive, completely automated, multi-story complexes.

To keep society from falling into chaos when bank accounts dried up and the threat of hunger drove people to riot, the government was forced to essentially give people free money, with the goal of providing a basic level of income to keep them from destabilizing the world economy. The money ensured that goods were still purchased, services were still used, houses were built, and the fabric of society kept itself together.

Once the threat of global destabilization was averted, the government turned their efforts to reeducating their obsolete workforce by subsidizing almost all levels of education and encouraging their citizens to study science, engineering or entertainment.

However, that ran into its own problems, with only a fraction of the displaced workforce choosing to re-educate themselves, leading to a growing class of people who simply did nothing but stayed at home and consumed entertainment, content to live a life of minimalism within the means provided to them by the Basic Living Income.

Only those who wanted larger homes, luxuries, nanite treatments, and meaning beyond simple consumption worked to re-educate themselves.

But if that wasn't enough, the Millennials who already have all the engineering and science jobs aren't retiring, I thought while rubbing my face, feeling the familiar frustration my generation had grown up with surge through me. *Leaving us clutching at straws with nothing productive to channel our energy into.*

"I guess that's why Ascend Online worked out to be so popular," I said with a weary shrug.

"It's given everyone a better escape than sitting at home and consuming all the crap they put on the TV," Peter agreed, pushing himself off the wall as the elevator doors slid open to our floor.

"Hang on. Aren't we on TV now?" I asked, following Peter out of the elevator.

"Damn, I'd already forgotten about that," Peter whispered softly before barking a short laugh. "We should watch ourselves! That'll be hilarious!"

"Ha! I wonder if everyone's logged out yet," I asked with a chuckle as we walked down the hall towards our suite, my stomach rumbling loudly as the smell of food filled the air. "That smells great; I can't even remember the last time I ate."

"That makes two of us." Peter snorted, waving his metal bracelet in front of our door's sensor, then pushed it open.

"Hey, they're back!" Zach's voice greeted us the second that we stepped into the suite, followed by a powerful aroma of food. "About time! We thought you guys forgot about us!"

"Well… if we'd known there was food waiting for us, we'd have come back sooner," I replied, my eyes growing wide as I saw the massive amount of food that had been ordered. "Did you guys get—"

"Pizza, chicken wings, *and* Chinese food?" Misha cut in, holding a massive plate of food in both of her hands as she carefully walked from the kitchenette to the table everyone was seated at, trying not to spill anything from her pile. "Yes, yes, we did."

"Mish, that plate's bigger than you are…" Peter trailed off as the petite woman gave him a dangerous look.

"Choose your next words carefully, Peter."

"Uh…" Peter coughed. "*Bon appetit?*"

Misha's expression smoothed into a smile as she sat down at the table. "*Good boy*. There's hope for you yet."

Quickly shedding my winter jacket and hanging it in the closet, I fixed myself a plate and found a place at the table, Peter following close behind me.

"So, how'd it go?" Deckard asked us eagerly, causing everyone to turn their attention towards Peter and me. "Are we rich yet?"

"*Well*…" Peter began, drawing the word out for an unnecessarily long time, eventually prompting Heron to swat him on the arm.

"Quit it, you troll!" Heron grunted while waving a half-eaten pizza slice in my direction. "Let Marc tell it if you're just going to screw with us."

"But he has no sense of showmanship!" Peter complained, mockingly rubbing his arm in pain.

"A business report doesn't need showmanship," Zach added dryly.

"Of course, it does! Everything does!"

"We're doing really great," I said, shaking my head at Peter's antics as I began to explain the results of our meeting. Everyone stared at me intently as I outlined our success and the steps Peter and I had taken to make Virtus an actual business entity in the Real World.

"But that's not all either!" I teased as I wrapped up the day's events. "We're also going to be on GameTV tonight at nine! They're airing our entire series for everyone to watch!"

"That's amazing!" Misha shouted as the rest of the group broke out in cheers. "This is better than we could have hoped for!"

"We *have* to watch it!" Deckard said, clearly sharing the same sentiment that Peter had expressed in the hallway earlier.

"We'll also have to update Freya and the rest of the guild members," Misha told me, before cocking her head in thought. "And I'll have to get some of their real names too. I've been so dialed in lately, I can't believe I never bothered to ask."

"It's easy to forget about Reality when we're in Ascend Online," I told Misha. "Makes me wonder if they designed it that way on purpose."

"Maybe," Misha replied with a shrug. "Could just be how our brain tries to make sense of it all."

"Could be," I agreed before a slight frown crossed my face. "Wish they did a better job of helping us reconcile appearances though... my brain has been struggling pretty badly at getting used to how you all look again. I keep expecting to see you all either as your in-game avatars, or your pre-VR diet appearances."

"I'm glad to hear I'm not the only one struggling with that," Misha said slowly, running a hand through her short blonde hair. "I've found that slowing down and really *looking* at the person helps. It's the quick glances out of the corner of my eye that always causes me to scare myself, thinking that there's a stranger beside me."

Nodding slowly, I decided to give Misha's advice a shot and took a closer look at the friend I had known for nearly twenty-five years. At first, I didn't feel anything different, my mind still feeling as if there was something subtly 'wrong' with the person sitting before me. But the longer I looked, I started to see the familiar features that comprised my mental image of Misha.

Short blonde hair framed a face of obvious Slavic descent, a pair of green eyes accenting the already sharp features that had been magnified by the effects of the VR Diet. A familiar scar just under Misha's eye caught my attention, one that brought back memories of a playground mishap from ages past.

Something clicked in my brain as I refamiliarized myself with her appearance, leaving me nodding and feeling a little better about my mental state.

"Yeah, I can see that helping," I said slowly. "So how did the rest of the day work out after we left?"

"Pretty good overall, I guess," Misha replied with a non-committal shrug. "We got the tent up without any real issues and managed to get the Adventurers settled. Quite a few of them expressed interest in joining Virtus after our rather *daring* rescue this morning."

"That's great!" I said with a sigh of relief, mostly happy to hear that the town was still safe, but also excited to hear that we might have new applicants soon. "We'll have to hold tryouts once we're back online and see if any of them make the cut."

"I think a handful of them will," Misha said optimistically. "They're almost all lower leveled, but a few might have that *edge* we're looking for."

When we created Virtus, we decided that we were going to try and be as selective as possible in our recruitment criteria. We wanted to retain and recruit members that we could truly rely on, and that they would be able to carry their own weight from both a combat and out of combat perspective. We couldn't afford to have members that flinched in combat, and were afraid of getting hurt, or those who sat around and did nothing in their spare time.

Our goal was to build a group of self-motivated individuals that would stand up for one another, no matter what the game world threw at us.

"We also got Marlin settled in," Zach cut into the conversation with a wave of his dark-skinned hand, having been half listening to our conversation.

"Yeah? How's he making out?" I shifted my glance to look at Zach, going through the same process I had just gone through with Misha to refamiliarize myself with his appearance.

"Great!" Zach replied with a confident nod, causing his wavy jet-black hair to bob in the air as he looked at me with dark-brown eyes. "We managed to get his cart stored in the crafting hall, well out of the way where anyone would easily trip over it. We piled a bunch of our stuff that we had in storage on top of his cart too, so it's really unlikely that anyone's going to go digging through it all."

As Zach spoke, I couldn't help but notice that the wiry Italian man had lost a rather substantial amount of weight, likely as much, if not more, than Peter had. It left his face overly lean looking, the scraggly beard he had growing doing little to fill it out. "Thanks for sorting all that out, Zach."

"Hey, no problem at all!" he said excitedly, flashing a tooth-filled smile. "I'm excited to see what things we can come up with Alchemy-wise now that we have better tools to work with."

"Me too!" I agreed, looking forward to a chance when I could craft relatively uninterrupted.

The rest of the evening flew by as we slowly unwound from the day's events and collectively consumed a truly overwhelming amount of food; our bodies were desperately craving solid, non-intravenous nourishment. For me, it was the first meal I could remember eating in over a week, an experience I didn't realize that I missed having. With my in-game avatar not needing food to survive, I almost never bothered to eat, always working on the next item on my never-ending to-do list or finding something that needed checking on.

I was actually lost in thought, mentally reviewing that very 'to do list', while cleaning up after our epic feast, when Deckard's massive hand came down on my shoulder and pulled me back into the moment.

"Got a minute, Marc?" he asked, thumbing his other hand at Heron who was standing just behind him. "We have something to fill you in on."

"Yeah, sure." I tossed the towel I was holding down on the counter and turned around, craning my head upwards at Deckard's giant frame.

Well, at least there's a little bit of familiarity here, I thought, watching Deckard awkwardly shift himself to the side to allow Heron enough room to step into the tiny kitchenette. Built like a brick house, the VR Diet had probably had the least amount of impact on Deckard when compared to the rest of the group, only serving to further accent his already muscular form.

Finding a comfortable position leaning against the counter, Deckard ran a hand over his cleanly shaved head and fixed Heron with his steel blue eyes. "Alright, Heron. Tell him the same thing you told me."

Thankfully I was able to keep my head relatively level as I shifted my glance from Deckard over to Heron, the two of them being reasonably similar in height, if not body size. Where Deckard had a muscular and fit appearance, Heron was rail thin, appearing as if a stiff wind would be able to sweep him off his feet. Even more so now that the VR Diet had trimmed the little fat that had managed to somehow cling to Heron's overly lean body.

"Okay," Heron started slowly, uncharacteristically fiddling with a pop can in his hand. "So, I've noticed something with the new Adventurers."

"Oh?" I asked, curiosity blooming across my face. With how quickly Peter and I left after sorting out accommodations with Léandre, I'd barely had a chance to look at, let alone talk with any of the new Adventurers that we had rescued from the bandits.

"Well, first of all, I think the majority of them are *really* new to the game," Heron replied. "And I mean that they're still within the first or second cycle of play, so they haven't learned to be careful about what they let slip."

"They must be part of the second wave of players, after they added more pods," I commented with a nod.

"Yeah, I think so too. Anyway though, after talking with a bunch of them, I got the impression that bandit issues like we've faced today are pretty commonplace as soon as you leave Coldscar, if not as large a group," Heron continued, a nervous look creeping over his face. "Soon as you're outside the city limits, you're pretty much on your own, and if you're not travelling in a large group, chances are you're going to be going for a respawn before the day's out."

"Damn, it's gotten that bad?" I could hear the disbelief in my voice.

"Oh, you think that's bad? I'm just getting started." Heron grunted pessimistically as he shook his head, causing his dark, shoulder-length hair to swish side to side. "Pretty much every resource, be it a mine, forest, quarry or *something* that can be collected and used in crafting is either claimed by a guild or is being actively fought over by guilds."

"Oh, *damn,*" I echoed a second time, inwardly wincing at Heron's news. "So, it's basically a free for all out there."

"Yeah," Heron agreed. "But here's the icing on the cake. No one seems to care."

"What do you mean?" I cocked my head, not quite understanding what Heron was referring to.

"No one seems to care that the Adventurers are fighting! It's a complete shit show everywhere, with Guilds scrambling for whatever power they can get. From what I've been told, the Eberian Military is letting the Adventurers do pretty much anything they want, so long as it doesn't interfere with the development of Coldscar."

"Which tells me that the Military is busy dealing with something else that needs their full attention, which is likely the Holy Ascendency of Eligos," Deckard added. "Otherwise, they would be putting a stop to all the infighting between the Guilds."

"I'm surprised it hasn't broken out into a larger conflict, to be honest," Heron said, looking at the two of us with a grim expression. "You know that's how it'll end up. Maybe not soon, but eventually, someone's going to propose an alliance, and they're going to get enough people on board, after that..."

"Things will snowball, then escalate," I replied, completely agreeing with Heron. "Though what I want to know, is why did these Adventurers come out this way then? Seems like they would have enough opportunities filling the power vacuums that are forming and joining up with one of the guilds. Why go out to the frontier?"

"Do you think they know something we don't?" Deckard queried, crossing his arms over his chest while looking at me. "We really haven't had enough time to filter through all the settlers that arrived today. Maybe it's a simple case of just wanting to get away from the Player Versus Player combat?"

"Maybe," I said with a shrug. "Thinking about it though... Aldford isn't really in a strategically viable place, at least not in the short term. We're what, a four or five-day march to Coldscar? That's well off the beaten path."

"That's true too." Deckard rubbed the side of his face thoughtfully. "There's hardly enough of us out this way for anyone to worry about. I mean, even if all of the new settlers and Adventurers join Aldford, that'll only put us at about three hundred strong. Compared to the thousands of Adventurers that must have spawned in Eberia, in addition to NPCs, and even distant Adventurers that spawned within the Ascendancy."

"We're small fry." I breathed a small sigh of relief at the thought. I wasn't naïve enough to believe that we would completely be left alone if a major conflict broke out between the Adventurer guilds, or even Eberia and the Ascendancy, but we would definitely be a low priority.

"Maybe," Heron agreed, despite the worried look on his face. "But I'm concerned that one of the bigger guilds near Coldscar might decide to give up, or get driven out towards us. They may not be inclined to play nice."

"Nothing we can really do about that," Deckard grunted. "We have no easy way of keeping watch on Coldscar from five days away."

"The best thing we can do is to keep working on Aldford." I motioned for the guys to make their way out into the rest of the common room. "But while we're talking about this, we might as well take advantage of our time off to throw some plans around."

"For what exactly?" Heron asked turning back to look at me as we walked out of the room.

"*Survival.*"

Chapter 6

Sunday, March 10th, 2047 - 6:57 am
Aldford – The Foundry

As I logged back into Ascend Online, I felt my incorporeal body floating through nothingness, my vision swirling with a kaleidoscope of colors with a single line of text floating directly in front of me.

Loading, please wait…

Gradually, I felt my virtual self take shape as memories began flooding into my consciousness. In the span of seconds, I lived through another day, suddenly experiencing everything that my Avatar had done while I had been offline.

Images of weaving filtered through my mind as I remembered myself helping sew and adjust the rough squares of burlap that we had stored away in the Crafting Hall. The memories then shifted forward to when I helped set up the massive tent, working on whatever task that Léandre needed help completing. Then suddenly again, I found myself back in the Crafting Hall, carefully refining countless leather hides and bronze ingots.

My vision finally cleared as I completed the login process and found myself standing alone in the sweltering heat of the Foundry, dressed in a simple linen shirt and leather pants, having interrupted my Avatar in the middle of refining bronze ingots. A quick glance around me showed me that my armor was hanging from a rack nearby. Wiping a bead of sweat off my forehead, I noticed a system message appear in the corner of my vision.

Welcome back to Ascend Online! While you were offline, one or more of your skills have increased! Please check your Character Sheet for more details!

Oh, sweet! I gained a level in something! I mentally cheered as I dismissed the prompt, and opened my Character Sheet for what seemed to be the first time in ages, the information filling my vision. *I can't even remember the last time I took a solid look at my stats. Probably not since I hit level thirteen last week!*

Lyrian Rastler – Level 13 Spellsword

Human Male (Eberian)

Statistics:

HP: 726/726
Stamina: 660/660
Mana: 640/640
Experience to next level: 19287/27000

Attributes:

Strength: 53 (55)
Agility: 43 (49)
Constitution: 40
Intelligence: 48
Willpower: 18

Abilities:

Sneak Attack II (Passive) – Attacks made before the target is aware of you automatically deal weapon damage+35.

Power Attack II (Active: 50 Stamina) – You slash viciously at the target putting extra strength behind the blow. Deal weapon damage+25.

Kick (Active: 20) – You kick your enemy for 10-20 points of damage, and knock them back 1-2 yards. Depending on your Strength/Agility score, you may also knock down the target.

Shoulder Tackle (Active: 40 Stamina) – Stun enemy for 1-2 seconds with chance to knock enemy down based on Strength and/or Agility attribute.

Unarmed Mastery I (Passive) – All Unarmed attack damage is increased by 12.

Skills:

Magic:

Evocation – Level 13 – 56%

Alteration – Level 13 – 88%

Conjuration – Level 13 – 71%

Abjuration – Level 13 – 42%

Weapons:

Unarmed Combat – Level 13 – 21%

Swords – Level 13 – 75%

Axes – Level 11 – 35%

Daggers – Level 12 – 73%

Other:

Stealth – Level 11 – 12%

Wordplay – Level 11 – 81%

Perception - Level 13 - 75%

Tradeskills:

Blacksmithing – Level 13 – 12%

Carpentry – Level 13 – 51%

Cartography – Level 2 – 3%

Tailoring - Level 12 – 9% **(One level gained while offline!)**

Cooking – Level 5 – 54%

Herbalism – Level 11 – 4%

Leatherworking – Level 13 – 77%

Mining – Level 11 – 1%

Leadership Skills:

Increased Health Regeneration – Increase amount of Health Regenerated by 6.   (6/10)

Increased Mana Regeneration – Increase amount of Mana Regenerated by 5. (5/10)

Increased Stamina Regeneration – Increase amount of Stamina Regenerated by 6. (6/10)

Increased Movement – Increase mounted and unmounted speed by 7%. (7/10)

Spells:

Flare

Light

Blink Step

Shocking Touch

Lesser Shielding

Flame Dagger

Jump

Racial Ability:

Military Conditioning (Passive) *– All defenses are increased by 5%, and total hit points are increased by 10%.*

Traits:

Open Minded *– Accepting of racial differences and radical ideas, you have learned to accept wisdom and the opportunity to learn no matter what form it takes, allowing you to make intuitive insights where others would give up in frustration. Grants a substantial increase in learning new skills, and the ability to learn all race locked traits, skills, crafting recipes, and abilities that are not otherwise restricted.*

Re-Forge *– You have learned the basics of how to recreate a broken relic and are able to bring back some of its former glory. This skill will function across any and all Tradeskills you acquire.*

Improvisation *– Your study of goblin craftsmanship has given you the insight to make adjustments to standard and learned recipes by replacing required materials* *with something else. E.g., Replacing metal with wood in an armor recipe will create a set of wooden armor instead of metal. The higher your level in a Tradeskill, the more changes can be made and the fewer materials they will require.*

Ætherwarped *– Due to high exposure to Raw Æther, your body has undergone unpredictable changes! You have gained the following Sub-Trait(s) and Abilities as part of your condition:*

True Sight *– Your eyes have been enhanced by exposure to Æther to the point where they are able to pierce through natural darkness and all facets of magic to see things as they truly are. This ability replaces Arcane Sight and can be suppressed at will. When this ability is active, the player's eyes will visibly glow a bright blue.*

Mana Void *– Your body's hunger for Arcane Energy has become ravenous, turning your appearance gaunt as it desperately craves more and more mana in order to fuel your metabolism. For as long as you have mana, you do not require to eat or drink. However, if your mana reaches 0, your body will immediately begin to consume itself at a rate of one hit point for each second in mana deprivation state, per second, until mana is restored.   All mana regeneration is permanently reduced by 100%.* **Mana Leech** *– As a result of prolonged contact with an [Annulment Sphere] your body's hunger for mana is so powerful you are now able to leech mana from any object or creature that you come in physical contact with, regardless of intervening armor or clothing that is not specifically designed to block the flow of mana. When this ability is activated mana will be leeched at a rate of 35 mana per second, any mana leeched will be added to your current mana* *pool and any excess mana will be lost. This ability scales with Class Level and Intelligence.*

Familiar:

Name: Amaranth

Type: Ætherwarped Puma

Level: 13

Relationship: Fanatically Loyal

Familiar Abilities:

Mental Link – *The magical bond linking you and your familiar has created an intimate mental link between the two of you, allowing each of you to communicate mentally between one another for a distance of up to one mile, regardless of intervening objects. Magical wards, however, will block this form of mental communication.*

Soul Bound – *During the familiar bonding process, you have anchored the being's soul directly to your own. Should the familiar be slain in your service, you will immediately suffer a 10% penalty to all attributes and skills for the next 24 hours until the familiar is reborn. Should the familiar survive your death, it does not suffer any penalties but will be compelled to travel to your place of rebirth as quickly as possible.*

Looking over my sheet carefully, I spotted the level I had gained in Tailoring while I was offline, my newly gained memories matching the skill increase with preparing the burlap canvas needed for the temporary tent. I also noted small skill increases in both Leatherworking and Blacksmithing, a result of Léandre needing my Avatar's skills to help create rigging and fastenings to attach the canvas to the support timbers that held the entire tent aloft.

Before closing my character sheet, I couldn't help but glance over some of the other skills that I had learned and worked on over the last month, seeing just how much they had grown since my first play cycle, and how happy I felt to no longer be undertrained.

I was confident with several weapons now, having taken the time to train with both axes and daggers, in addition to maintaining my sword and unarmed skills. The extra effort spent learning the new weapon styles paid off almost immediately as I managed to learn the second rank of both Power Attack and Sneak Attack while training the two skills, without having to spend any precious Class Skill Points to unlock those abilities.

I'm so happy I lucked out on learning Unarmed Mastery too, I thought, seeing the Ability appear on my character sheet. I had learned the skill during a particularly desperate fight last week in the wolverine-infested plains to the south of Aldford, while the party and I were grinding our way towards level thirteen. We had spent most of the day clearing the vicious creatures from the plain when we accidentally walked past a burrow containing a level fifteen, Rare-ranked, Wolverine.

I still remembered its wicked howl as the massive beast suddenly launched itself out of the burrow, killing Constantine outright and slicing one of Sierra's arms clean off her body before Drace managed to get its attention. Everything after that was a blur of blood, terror and fur... at least until I found myself being held in the air, impaled on a set of razor sharp claws and desperately pummeling the creature's face as I tried to keep myself from ending up in its mouth.

Good times. I smiled to myself, remembering that the wolverine's silver fur was drying on a tanning rack, waiting for me to gain a few more levels in Leatherworking and a supply of potent alcohol before I tried cutting and tanning the hide, then hopefully crafting it into something useful.

Dismissing the sheet from my vision with the wave of a withered hand, I walked over to my armor, my eyes checking over the equipment that hung from the rack. I gently ran a hand over the *[Blackened Iron Chain Shirt]*, inspecting it for any broken links or damage from the battle with the bandits. Finding nothing, I called up the item stats, which appeared in my vision.

Blackened Iron Chain Shirt
Slot: Chest
Item Class: Relic
Item Quality: Good (+15%)
Armor: 100
Armor Type: Light
Strength: +3 Agility: +3
Durability 160/160
Under Layer: [Quilted Gambeson]
Weight: 3.5 kg
Favored Class: Martial
Level: 13

As much as I loved my old Webwood armor, this definitely provides better protection, I thought as I lifted the shirt off the rack, revealing a quilted gambeson that the armor was sitting on.

While Re-Forging the chainmail shirt, I discovered that Ascend Online had chosen to emulate a much more realistic and in-depth armor system than I had originally assumed at first glance by allowing players to wear special types of clothing under, or on top of their armor, via two special sub-slots called the Under Layer and the Over Layer.

These two new slots allowed for players to further customize or enhance the armor that they wore by wearing special types of clothing that provided minor benefits across a variety of equipment slots. In my case, I had chosen to wear an arming jacket, also known as a gambeson, as an Under Layer to provide an extra layer of defense and comfort while wearing the chainmail shirt.

As for the Over Layer. So far, I discovered that it was possible to wear a thick layer of furs, which I imagined would help prevent hypothermia from setting in while exploring colder environments, though given the rather warm weather we'd been having around Aldford of late, wearing a layer of furs on top of already sweltering armor was a great way to bring on a serious case of heatstroke.

The only downside to this feature was that not wearing an Under Layer wasn't a viable or comfortable option for those who wanted to wear heavier types of armor. Adding in a touch of realism, players who chose not to wear an Under Layer with heavier armor would quickly experience chafing, rashes and be generally miserable as the rough and heavy armor rubbed their skin raw.

Luckily enough, the statistical benefits of wearing an Under Layer was attractive enough on its own that the penalties rarely came into play. Setting the chain shirt down on a nearby empty rack, I reached for my gambeson, seeing its description fill my vision as I pulled it free from the stand and slipped it over my shoulders.

Quilted Gambeson
Slot: Under Layer - (Chest, Arms, Shoulders)
Item Class: Common
Item Quality: Fine (+10%)
Armor: 25
Durability 120/120
Weight: 1 kg
Favored Class: Any
Level: 13

Buttoning the jacket closed, I took the time to straighten it carefully before pulling the chainmail shirt over my head. Feeling comfortable with how the armor was hanging off me, I turned back to the armor rack, and with practiced ease, equipped the rest of my armor, checking each item for damage or wear as I put it on. Carefully reading their descriptions as they flashed by my eyes.

Blackened Iron Armguards

Slot: Arms
Item Class: Good (+15%)
Item Quality: Relic
Armor: 23
Armor Type: Light
Strength: +1 Agility: +1
Durability: 90/90
Weight: 1 kg
Favored Class: Martial
Level: 13

Blackened Iron Cap

Slot: Head
Item Class: Good (+15%)
Item Quality: Relic
Armor: 34
Armor Type: Light
Strength: +1 Agility: +1
Durability: 60/60
Weight: 1 kg
Favored Class: Martial
Level: 13

Blackened Iron Greaves

Slot: Boots
Item Class: Good (+15%)
Item Quality: Relic
Armor: 40
Armor Type: Light
Strength: +1 Agility: +1
Durability: 80/80

Weight: 2 kg
Favored Class: Martial
Level: 13

Blackened Iron Chain Gloves

Slot: Hands
Item Class: Good (+15%)
Item Quality: Relic
Armor: 23
Armor Type: Light
Strength: +1 Agility: +1
Durability: 70/70
Weight: 1 kg
Favored Class: Martial
Level: 13

Blackened Iron Chain Pants

Slot: Legs
Item Class: Good (+15%)
Item Quality: Relic
Armor: 57
Armor Type: Light
Strength: +1 Agility: +1
Durability: 80/80
Weight: 3 kg
Favored Class: Martial
Level: 13

Blackened Iron Shoulder Guards

Slot: Shoulders
Item Class: Good (+15%)
Item Quality: Relic
Armor: 28
Armor Type: Light
Strength: +1 Agility: +1
Durability: 80/80
Weight: 1.5 kg

Favored Class: Martial
Level: 13

Fur Mantle of Swiftness

Slot: Back
Item Class: Magical
Item Quality: Good (+15%)
Armor: 19
Agility: +4
Durability: 80/80
Base Material: Fur
Weight: 1 kg
Favored Class: Any Martial
Level: 12

With each piece of armor I put on, I felt my strength and agility improve, the minor bonuses of each item adding up.

Without a doubt, I probably have the best all-around set of armor in the Town. I couldn't help but smile with pride as I inspected my gear. Working from the seemingly endless pile of broken chainmail scraps and armor fragments we'd recovered from the Tower, I'd managed to cobble together a set of armor for myself, my friends, and Freya's group, giving all of us a rather substantial advantage over the other players in Aldford.

Which we thankfully haven't been forced to show, I thought happily, looking back on the last few weeks. *All the Players have been eager to help out and carry their own weight, plus the memory of Graves is still reasonably fresh in everyone's mind, so no one has tried to make a scene.*

I couldn't help but check over my Attributes one more time, after having equipped all of my gear. I always enjoyed seeing the contrast between my regular unarmored self and my fully equipped self.

Attributes:

Strength: 53 (64)

Agility: 43 (58)
Constitution: 40
Intelligence: 48
Willpower: 18

Almost two levels worth of stats added to both strength and agility, just from gear alone. I waved a hand to dismiss the character sheet information from my vision and turned back towards the forge, intent on cleaning up my mess before setting out for the day. *That's almost double what my old Webwood Striker armor set gave. Though, in fairness, this armor set is a tier higher in rarity in addition to being three levels hig- oh! That reminds me. I need to check on Razor!*

Pulling my trusty blade from its sheath, my heart sank as I realized that it had seen better days. The bronze metal no longer carried its old bright sheen, and numerous battle scars now adorned the length of the sword. I had done my best to repair the weapon, smoothing out chips and completely replacing the hilt and wrapping, but it was a losing battle at best. As much as I hated to admit it, it was only a matter of time before I was forced to retire Razor, in favor of a more durable weapon. Unfortunately, the core of the blade was simply too worn and damaged for me to melt down the blade and try Re-Forging it for a second time.

"Ho! Morning, Lyrian!" Jenkins's voice echoed through the Foundry, interrupting my thoughts. "Guess I'm never going to get an earlier start than you, eh?"

"Oh! Morning, Jenkins!" I turned to see the dark-skinned craftsman walking towards me. "Why on earth would you want to start early anyway? You have a pretty wife-to-be to stay in bed with!"

"I-uh…" Jenkins suddenly coughed in embarrassment, watching the grin spread across my face.

"It's about time you proposed to Shelia anyway!" I continued, watching the man break into a nervous smile. "We were all wondering when you'd finally get around to it!"

"Well...I-I mean, she wakes up with the sun for her morning prayers," Jenkins stammered before he managed to collect himself. "I try not to leave until she does."

I smiled knowingly at the man and nodded. "Have you two set a date yet?"

"Not yet to be honest," Jenkins replied, clearly happy to be on more familiar ground. "With all these new settlers... we aren't sure when we'll have a chance."

"We'll figure something out," I told the man while shifting my glance back to Razor. "We just need to get everyone settled in."

"True, though I'm happy to say that everything is going well so far!" Jenkins said enthusiastically before waving a hand at Razor. "Something wrong with your sword?"

"Wear and tear I'm afraid... I think its days are numbered." I sighed as I showed Jenkins the sword.

"It's certainly been well used." Jenkins nodded his expert eye looking over the blade. "As much as it pains me to say, starting fresh would be the best course. There isn't much left we could do to repair this blade. Smelting it down and re-forging it again would likely weaken the core too much for it to be trustworthy in battle."

"I know." I turned the blade over in my hand before returning it to its sheath. "We really need to get that new smelter working, so we can start smelting the iron we've recovered from the Tower."

"Do you really think that will make a difference?" Jenkins asked with a quizzical expression on his face. "I've worked with metals for nearly a decade and a half, and I've never seen iron behave the way that the scraps you've recovered do."

"I don't think it's just iron anymore," I replied motioning to the armor that I was wearing. "I think it's been...changed."

"Changed? You mean blackened?" Jenkins asked with a frown, waving a hand at my gear. "Like the armor you're wearing now?"

"No, not like that..." I paused, trying to think of a way to best explain my theory. "The armor I'm wearing now, I'm inclined to believe, was made with regular iron and had a pigment added to it, hence the blackened tint, then given a simple enchantment for strength and agility."

"The scrap we've recovered from the pillar of iron in the Tower, on the other hand, is different. Despite being blackened in the same way." I pulled a forearm long shard out of my inventory, holding the dark metal to the light. "The other day, I tested this very piece in the heart of our forge for hours, along with a scrap of leftover armor, the armor completely melted, but the shard didn't. In fact, it was completely cool to the touch once I pulled it out of the forge."

"*Really?*" Jenkins looked intrigued, "I hadn't thought to touch it... but then again I'd *really* rather not have lost my hand if I were wrong."

"Why does everyone think I touched it with my hand?!" I gave the smith an exasperated look, having heard the same thing when I had mentioned it to my friends.

"You... um, have a bit of a reputation for... touching things that shouldn't be touched," Jenkins managed to cough out, giving me an embarrassed look.

"Oh, come on!" I exclaimed while rolling my eyes. "You touch *one* magic crystal that happens to unfreeze several hundred spiders frozen in time and everyone thinks you have a problem!"

"Didn't I hear that you also singed your hand touching Donovan's rod too?" Jenkins asked pointedly.

"You want to think about what you just said?" I shot a raised eyebrow back at Jenkins. "Because that didn't sound right to my ears."

"What? I have no id—*oh!*" Jenkin paused then barked a short laugh at his verbal slip up. "*Anyway*, the shard was cool?"

"It was, and I have no idea why," I explained while indicating the open-hearth forge that was under construction at the center of the Foundry. "I'm hoping that this new forge will be able to melt the shards, and eventually, large pieces of the iron pillar we found - if we can ever get it back to Aldford."

"Well… we certainly have the manpower for it now." Jenkins waved a hand to indicate the rest of the town. "Never thought I'd see so many people in Aldford so soon; I can't believe how quickly we've grown!"

"It's coming together." I nodded happily at Jenkins. "Hopefully, this group of Adventurers will be as well behaved as the others."

"So far so good," Jenkins replied optimistically before his face took a slightly concerned look. "The Adventurers did bring quite a few… *odd* things with them though, Ritt and Bax have been forced to set up a quarantine for a few items."

"Hang on." My eyes shot wide open at that statement. "A quarantine? What exactly did they bring?"

Jenkins snorted and rolled his eyes. "What *didn't* they bring? I wish I knew what crossed the heads of some of these Adventurers."

"Uh, I should probably check this quarantine out," I said, feeling suddenly nervous. "Where is it?"

"Probably not a bad idea," Jenkins agreed. "It's just outside of the Town Hall for the time being. Léandre was pretty adamant about keeping it far away from the Crafting Hall."

"Oh, *fantastic!*" The nerves that I was experiencing intensifying at the news. If it was bad enough that Léandre didn't want anything to do with it, then I knew it was serious. I waved at the Smith and began to move towards the Foundry entrance. "See you later, Jenkins!"

Whatever reply he had was drowned out by the sound of my running feet.

Chapter 7

"Can you describe the snake to me?" Bax's voice was the first thing I heard as I jogged up to the quarantine, spotting him, Ritt, and a swaying half-orc Adventurer standing around a crate of boxes.

"Yeeaah…" the half-orc's speech was slurred as he replied to the scoutmaster. "It looked like… an angry rope."

"How is that even helpful?" Ritt's voice demanded angrily, his temper already shot for the morning.

As I approached the trio, I could see that the Adventurer was clutching his arm and his grey-green skin was extremely pale.

"It's a Rope Snake. It really does look like a length of rope. Bought it from a mage's lab, back in Eberia," the Adventurer replied, slowly shaking his head. "I think he may have been transfigured from a garden viper or something, but he's not normally so bitey. All the people around here are making him nervous."

"You fucking Adventurers are making me nervous!" Ritt practically yelled at the Adventurer. "What the hell possessed you to take a snake that looked like a rope with you?"

"I-I thought he looked coooool." The half-orc swayed on his feet drunkenly as he took a step back from Ritt's verbal assault. "I was hoping to bind him as a familiar one day. His venom is p-p-pretty potent."

"Yeah, I can tell." Bax was looking at the Adventurer with growing concern. "You should go see Shelia and get her to purge your system; you look awful."

"Oookay, yeah… I think I'll do that, I'm… really not feeling that great." The Adventurer slowly turned his body towards the Town Hall, looking increasingly unsteady on his feet with every second that passed. "Please let me know if you find Noodles… I know he didn't bite me on purpose. I just want him back in one piece."

"You named your snake *Nood—*" Ritt began to say with exasperation before the scoutmaster interrupted.

"*If* we find him, we'll let you know," Bax replied gently, shaking his head as the Adventurer stumbled away from us.

"Uh, morning guys," I greeted the pair hesitantly, my eyes looking over at several stacks of crates that had been grouped together, almost all of them had bright red lettering on them stating 'DO NOT OPEN - DANGEROUS'.

"Morning, Lyrian." Bax was the first to greet me, the muscular half-elf giving me a cheerful wave as I approached.

"How is everything working out?" I asked cautiously, noting the contrast between the frazzled looking Ritt, and the calm, relaxed demeanor that Bax projected.

"Not too bad, all things considered," the white-haired scoutmaster replied evenly, wiping his hands on the sleeveless leather tunic he wore. "We only have a few crates left that have been unclaimed. Likely belonging to those who didn't survive the bandit attack, and a handful more that just need to be stored in a secure area before we release them back to the Adventurers that own them."

"*Lyrian,*" Ritt's voice sounded like it was on the verge of becoming unhinged. "These Adventurers… they're bringing *creatures* into the village! That man's snake is the least of our worries!"

"Creatures?" I asked, looking over the crates one more time. "What sort of creatures?"

"All kinds!" Ritt exclaimed, slapping his hand down on a crate, which started buzzing angrily. "I think there is a hive of *bees* inside this one, and in at least three others! For what purpose someone would want bees, I don't know."

"Honey, maybe?" I offered, my eyes going wide as other boxes began to buzz in sympathy with the crate Ritt had slapped.

"If that's the only reason, I'm still inclined to throw the crates into Crater Lake and let them sink!" Ritt scowled at me. "I don't need to deal with this!"

"Could always make mead with the honey," Bax suggested as he crossed his heavily scarred arms over his chest. "I'm sure some of the farmers outside the town would be happy to buy the hives too. Could be worth a fair bit of money."

"I'll think about it." Ritt grunted, his avarice clearly not allowing him to turn down the opportunity to make a profit. "As long as I'm not the one who has to worry about moving them!"

"But that's still not all I have to worry about!" Ritt motioned for me to follow him to yet another a pile of crates that had a thick tarp thrown over them, and had been roped off preventing easy access. As we got closer, I couldn't help but notice that the tarp had been pinned down to the ground by rather heavy looking stones. "Another one of these lunatic Adventurers, brought cages filled with cockatr—*ah!*"

Ritt let out a loud yelp as he suddenly spotted Amaranth sitting on all fours behind the piles of boxes, staring at something moving beneath the tarp. Almost immediately Amaranth's eyes fixated on mine, and his cool voice filtered into my head.

<There is something delicious under this covering,> the cat said without any preamble. *<Command this man to give me whatever is stored within. I am hungry.>*

"Uh, Ritt," I turned to look at the distressed merchant. "What exactly is under there? Amaranth wants to eat it."

"Shit! Sorry. The cat scared me! I thought something had gotten *loose*!" Ritt took a deep breath to help steady his nerves. "In these cages are half a dozen cockatrices. You know, those half-chicken, part-bat, part-lizard things that can paralyze you with a glance and poison you with the barb on their tail?"

"Y-yeah?" I couldn't help but stutter at the final part of Ritt's description. "Do you know who brought them into the village?"

"Oh, of course, I do!" Ritt moved over to a second tarp an arm's length away from the cockatrice filled crates and pulled the covering free, revealing a paralyzed dwarven Adventurer lying flat on the ground, his arms splayed out before him. "I told him to move these stupid chickens outside of Aldford, but the idiot *had* to peek into the cages and got caught full blast by the glare of all six of the birds, *ten hours ago.* I covered him with a tarp in the hope he could still sleep while paralyzed."

"Ritt! Why didn't you get Shelia to try and cure him?" I practically shouted at the young merchant.

"Because he brought six fucking birds that could paralyze half the town while they died of poison! He needed a *lesson*!" He pointed a finger at me angrily, before waving at the Town Hall. "The only reason I haven't gotten Constantine to set these boxes on fire is because, despite the threat that these stupid cockatrices pose to the town, their eggs are *delicious,* and literally every Adventurer in Aldford has offered me a fistful of coins if I can get them a dozen eggs or more."

"Wait, they lay *eggs?*" I felt myself falling behind in the conversation, having momentarily panicked when Ritt mentioned 'Constantine' and 'Fire' in the same sentence.

"Yeah, in fact, I have a hard boiled one right here." Without breaking stride, Ritt pulled a large speckled egg out of a pouch on his waist. "Ragna just boiled a handful for me less than an hour ago, should be fresh."

"Uh, thanks." I took the egg from Ritt calling up the food's stats in my vision, my eyes instantly widening in surprise.

Hard Boiled Cockatrice Egg - *Food – Meal*

 Benefit: Satiate Hunger for 3 Hours

 Regenerate 3 health every 5 seconds for 3 Hours when not in combat

 +1 to all Attributes for 3 hours

 Part of a balanced breakfast

<Is this for me?> Amaranth sprang up from his position near the hidden cockatrices and moved to sit in front of me, licking his chops in preparation.

"Uh... sure," I replied looking down at the massive cat and cracked the shell of the egg on my knuckles before beginning to peel it. "I can see why Adventurers would want to have a ton of these! They also seem to be well loved by Ætherwarped Pumas too!"

"It wouldn't be too difficult to set up a farm to breed them," Bax spoke up, clearly more open-minded to embrace challenges than Ritt was. "We can fashion a hood to take their paralytic glare away, and cut the barb out of their tails. Besides, this type of cockatrice is much more manageable than their Greater Cockatrice cousins, whose glare can turn you to stone instead of just paralyzing you."

"If you can make it work, I'd say to go for it." I nodded at the scoutmaster and an increasingly pale looking Ritt.

"A cockatrice... *farm?*" Ritt whimpered nervously, "We'll see what the dwarf says about that when he wakes up."

"Fair enough," I said as I finished peeling the cockatrice egg and gave it to Amaranth, watching it vanish down the cat's throat in a single bite.

<Delicious indeed,> the azure-furred puma purred.

"Is there anything else that I should be worrying about?" I asked, feeling reasonably confident that if Ritt became overwhelmed, Bax could step in and take over the quarantine duties.

"Not really, at least assuming nothing gets loose," Bax replied with an easy shrug as he waved at the pile of crates. "So far, the strangest things we've found is a glass box of what I *think* is part of a gelatinous cube, or maybe the entire creature, never can be completely sure with them. After that, there was a crate completely filled with *bones* if you can believe it, with a separate box containing half a dozen skulls to match. Plus, a crate full of unlabeled plants, powders and something that might be an acid that we want Marlin to look at before we figure out to do with it. Oh, and a small box of really strange mushrooms that start shrieking whenever they're exposed to light."

"Don't forget about that Rope Snake," Ritt added, clearly not sharing Bax's easy assessment.

"Eh, it'll turn up, and everything will be okay… or it'll bite someone else, and they'll just kill it out of hand." Bax shrugged indifferently. "Either way, the problem will solve itself."

"With my luck, it'll bite *me*," Ritt snorted pessimistically.

A burst of noise and footsteps coming from the Town Hall had all of us turning as a fairly large group of Adventurers left the building and made their way towards the southern entrance. Despite the early hour, all of them looked to be rather excited and moving with purpose, a handful even waving in our direction as they passed.

"That's the *Hallowgarde* guild," Bax told me, motioning towards the group. "They've asked Aldwin for permission to start their own settlement about a day's travel to the north, on the edge of the plains up there and he's allowed it, seeing how we don't have any eyes that far from the town. They might actually succeed at it too since they actually stopped to ask and then *listen* to what some of the other Adventurers and myself had seen out that way."

"That's good I guess." I watched the departing group with slightly ambivalent feelings. On the one hand, I was happy that we had managed to get a decent group of motivated individuals out into the region, but on the other, I was a little disappointed that they had decided to leave Aldford to strike out on their own. Finding motivated and self-driven people was hard enough out here, and seeing twenty of them leaving when we could definitely use their help was a little frustrating.

But it's not like we won't see them again, I thought optimistically. *A day isn't that far to travel, and if they do succeed, we'll be a prime trading partner. It's better to make sure that they know we're nearby to help if they need it.*

"We'll have to send some people to check up on them in a few days and see how they're doing," I said, making a mental note to follow up later on in the week.

"Maybe we can give them these bees!" Ritt added hopefully, nodding at me in agreement. "That'd be plenty far enough away for my tastes!"

"I can check on them lat—oh, heads up, Lyrian." Bax cut himself off as three more people emerged from the Town Hall, this time turning directly towards us, moving quickly and with purpose.

Crossing the short distance between us and the Town Hall, I had just enough time to identify two of the people as being Samuel and Quincy, the two Eberian mages we had rescued from both Graves and the Goblins in the Tower's underground chamber. The third man in front of them, however, I had never seen before today.

Dressed in a dark, form-fitting robe with golden trimmings around the edges, the grey-haired man halted a short distance from the quarantine and looked over us with a scornful eye as he ground a crystal-topped walking stick into the dirt.

"*Baxter*," the sharply dressed man greeted the Scoutmaster with a curt tone. "Samuel, Quincy and I were just discussing the events that led up to the Expedition's loss, along with the seizure of a Nafarrian Ruin and Irovian Tower. We will need your statement to provide to the Justicar."

"Stanton." Bax's voice took on a very flat tone as he cast a glance towards me. "As I've *told* both Quincy and Samuel, the Expedition's loss was beyond our control, and as far as I'm concerned there was no seizure of anything, both the ruins were legally claimed by Lyrian and his guild, Virtus."

"There are matters of Kingdom security that have arisen that put those claims into question." Stanton's voice took on a noticeably hard tone. "And I would *remind* you not to forget your contract with the Expedition."

Bax waved a hand dismissively, "What Expedition? Out of the twenty of us that left Eberia, there are only five us still breathing, and even then, it's a miracle that we're alive. Far as I'm concerned, I've fulfilled my end of our agreement and the Expedition is dissolved."

"I disagree," the man's eyes narrowed. "Our contract is in force until the dates specified."

"I don't want to work for you anymore, Stanton. Nor do I feel *safe* doing so. If you have any complaints with that, take it up with the Justicar," Bax spat, pointing at Samuel and Quincy. "Because I'm sure once I tell him how your two men there disregarded or overruled every single one of my *basic* security precautions, and brought about the end of the Expedition, he'll side in my favor."

"You are not privy to all—"

"*Hold up.*" I'd been caught off guard by how quickly the conversation had unfolded, but I really didn't like what I was hearing. "What's going on—"

"*I do not like being interrupted,*" the older man said flatly, shifting his dark grey eyes onto me.

"And I don't like what I'm hearing." I stared back at the man as Amaranth interposed himself between me and Stanton, a low growl echoing from his throat. "We claimed those ruins through blood and sweat. If it weren't for us, the Expedition would have been lost with all hands."

"You and your guild's effort in rescuing the remaining members of the Expedition is acknowledged," Stanton stated emotionlessly. "However, those ruins cannot remain in your possession."

"Why the hell not?" I asked angrily. "We intervened to prevent *two* major catastrophes that *your* Expedition indirectly caused while poking around in those ruins! I'm going to need one hell of a good reason to even *consider* releasing them to someone!"

"You will not speak to Lord Stanton with such disrespect!" Quincy barked, moving to flank the older man, "He—"

"Enough, Quincy!" Stanton raised a hand, cutting off the red-haired mage's tirade. "As much as it pains me to admit... he is correct, and his guild has proven itself to be competent. We will require their cooperation if we are to succeed in our mission."

"Wait. I am? You do?" I frowned at the man, not having expected his sudden change of heart. A small notification appeared in the corner of my vision informed me why.

Your Renown in the region has greatly affected your standing with [Lord Adrian Stanton]!

Your skill in Wordplay has increased to Level 12!

So that's what Renown does! My heart leapt as I read the notification.

"I have arranged a meeting with the Justicar and Sir Aldwin to explain the situation, and to inform them of events that have transpired in Eberia," Stanton continued, completely oblivious to my discovery. "You *will* make yourself available to attend."

"Meeting?" I felt off balance with how fast the conversation had moved. In seconds, we'd gone from having our claims stripped from us to now being involved in whatever was going on. "I'm sorry, but just who are you exactly?"

The man fixed me with an unreadable expression. "My name is *Lord Adrian Stanton of House Denarius*. I am here representing the *Dowager Queen, Emilia Denarius* in a matter regarding the Kingdom's security."

He motioned to the Town Hall. "The meeting begins in ten minutes. *Don't be late.*"

Chapter 8

"Lyr, we've barely been logged in for longer than twenty minutes, and the rest of the group just left to go hunting for food!" Sierra exclaimed in disbelief as she entered the room and circled the massive table in the center, sitting down beside me. "What did you do?"

"I'm still trying to figure that out," I told Sierra, shaking my head slowly. "I was just ambushed by a 'Lord Stanton' from House Denarius just right outside of the Town Hall. He's said that he's here due to a matter of Kingdom security, which would trump our claim to the Hub and the Tower. I talked fast and somehow managed to get an invite to the meeting."

"*Kingdom security?*" Sierra repeated, looking at me with a confused expression, "Aldford is independent. Anything to do with Eberia doesn't concern us. What do you think is going on?"

"Not even the faintest idea," I said with a shrug. "He did say he was representing the Dowager Queen though, and not the King."

"I wonder what that means." Sierra shifted in her seat, clearly unsettled. "I don't know how much power an ex-queen retains… especially based on what you've told me about her."

"There has to be something that we're missing," I whispered as the door burst open and a pale looking Aldwin rushed in, slamming the door behind him.

"Lyrian, Sierra!" Aldwin exclaimed while scanning the room, finding that we were the only two people inside it. "Stanton just told me that he invited you to the meeting."

"What's happening, Aldwin?" I asked, having never seen him so worked up. "You don't look that great."

"Eberia is not doing well," he replied gravely. "I've only spoken once with Stanton since his arrival, and what he has told me so far has me greatly worried."

"Who is he exactly?" Sierra whispered, lowering her voice as footsteps began echoing through the hallway outside.

"He's the Que—" Aldwin's mouth shut with an audible snap as the door opened, and Stanton walked in, followed closely behind by Samuel and Quincy.

"Ah good, Fredric. You're already here." Stanton inclined his head in greeting to the Knight, his stoic expression at odds with the stress lining Aldwin's face. "The Commander and the Justicar are just moments behind us, along with Donovan and the Scoutmaster."

"Hold on. There's a *Commander* here too?" I couldn't help but ask as the trio took their seats at the table. Aldwin taking a seat on my left-hand side, sudden confusion blooming on his face as well.

"Yes, I've asked her to join us," Stanton replied, as the door swung open once more, revealing a tall, brown-haired Eberian woman and Dyre half a step behind her. "Ah, here she is now."

"Lord Stanton," the sharp-faced woman greeted the noble with a curt nod as she strode into the room, the heavy scale armor she wore jingling as she moved. As she sat down at the table, I noticed that her eyes had fixated on Aldwin, not even bothering to glance in Sierra or my direction. "*Sir Aldwin.*"

"V-Veronia? I didn't know you were here! I-I—" An unsteady look crossed Aldwin's face as the woman stared intently at him. "*Erm*, excuse my informality, Commander Tarius. Allow me to introduce Lyrian Rastler, the Guild Leader of Virtus, and his guildmate, Sierra Rain."

"I am aware of them." The woman's green eyes momentarily shifted to glance at Sierra and me, before settling back onto Aldwin. "Introductions are not necessary."

Who is this woman? Is there something between her and Aldwin? I glanced at Sierra, raising an eyebrow at her in silent question, only to have her nod ever so slightly in response. *What the hell have we just been dragged into?*

"Please be seated, gentlemen," Dyre spoke from the head of the table, having once again displayed his uncanny ability to move silently despite the heavy armor he wore, his eyeless gaze looking towards Donovan and Bax who had just entered the room.

Once the pair were finally seated, Dyre shifted his head towards Stanton. "This is your meeting, Lord Stanton. Please proceed."

"Thank you, Justicar." The older man stood as he looked around the table, making eye contact with everyone as he spoke. "This information is considered privileged, and I would ask that you not disseminate it without the approval of the Commander or myself."

Stanton paused, his stony demeanor landing on me as he continued. "I am afraid that I must inform you all that the Kingdom of Eberia is not well. We have been faced with numerous challenges over the last six weeks that have only served to intensify tensions already existing within both the nobility and military. As of right now, Queen Emilia considers Eberia to be in the first stages of Civil War."

I heard a collective gasp echo around the table as everyone absorbed Stanton's statement.

"The majority of these complications have arisen due to King Swain's actions... or lack of them," Stanton continued. "He has begun shirking his duties in the extreme, and he has not been seen publicly in over three weeks. Nor has he been accepting visitors."

"What is he doing with all his time then?" Sierra asked hesitantly.

"As far as we can tell... he has been spending the majority of his time in prayer and isolation with a favored priest," Stanton replied with a frown, the first sign of emotion that I had seen cross his face. "A priest belonging to a new sect that has recently splintered off from Nil, the God of Vengeance."

"I'm not familiar with that god," I said, casting a quick glance around the table to see that I was not the only one.

"I am not surprised," Bax spoke, leaning heavily on the table so that he could see everyone. "Nil is not the temple sort of god, with grand structures reaching into the sky. He's a god commonly worshiped by the poorest of the poor, or those who have been wronged by people with malice in their hearts."

"Nil works without regard to Law and Order, focusing simply on vengeance," Dyre stated from the head of the table. "Would all follow his teachings; the world would quickly become blind. His work often makes Mithus's harder."

"Be that as it may, Justicar, I would welcome the original teachings of Nil with open arms over the perverted teachings that this new... *cult* is filling the King's head with," Stanton said brusquely. "These new teachings no longer enshrine vengeance for actual wrongs, but now encourage active, *violent*, revenge, even for perceived slights. A trait grossly unbefitting any King, let alone one like Swain."

"Why the sudden interest in faith?" Aldwin asked. "I watched the boy grow up his entire life without giving a priest the time of day. What changed?"

"What else could cause a man to change so drastically?" Stanton shook his head with a bitter scowl. "The King has found a woman he wishes to wed. However, she requires him to share the same faith as her before considering his proposal. To that end, she has granted him access to her own personal priest, and he now spends almost every waking moment studying the tenants of this perverted faith in order to please his bride-to-be."

"And, of course, the King takes no counsel but his own," Aldwin grunted matching Stanton's scowl.

"In the King's best interest, we tried to have a detachment of knights remove both the priest and his mistress," Veronia spoke up for the first time, turning to look at Stanton as she spoke. "However, the King ordered the Royal Guard to intervene. It was nearly a bloodbath."

"After that, we lost all visibility into the palace," Stanton explained. "Swain has forbidden all but the Royal Guard to be present in the palace, and has ordered nearly the entire military out of the city, likely fearing that a coup was imminent."

"He's left Eberia undefended?" I couldn't help but blurt out in surprise.

"Not entirely," Veronia declared in what I was beginning to learn was her only tone of voice.

"The King is clearly not in the right mind to be making decisions at the moment." Sierra chopped a hand through the air with frustration. "Why did the military obey that order?"

"It didn't," Stanton answered with a grimace on his face. "At least not until Queen Emilia endorsed it."

"The Queen is not in the chain of command," Aldwin cut in, his expression one of concern as he scanned both Veronia and Stanton's faces for cues. "The military, *the*

Commander's father, should not have obeyed any command she gave."

Veronia's father is in the Military? I exchanged a quick glance of surprise with Sierra. *Sounds like he's pretty high up too.*

"You begin to understand the scope of our problems then," Stanton replied as Veronia simply stared at Aldwin silently. "The Queen has no *interest* or *right* to rule in Eberia, yet she and Marshal Tarius find themselves holding the reins of power until Swain comes to his senses."

"You can't be serious!" I exclaimed, not believing what I was hearing. "You'd give Swain back control? He's clearly shown that he can't handle the responsibility of actually running the Kingdom! Why don't you just elect another Noble to be King?"

"And fully invite the Civil War we are trying to avoid?" Stanton asked rhetorically, his expression one of frustration. "Events in Eberia have already escalated to the point where the Noble Houses are killing one another in the streets as they brutally trim one another's family trees of excess sons or daughters. Attempting to get them to agree on a candidate to replace Swain would require a small ocean of blood, and would almost certainly ensure Eberia's destruction when the Holy Ascendancy of Eligos comes calling at our door, *again*."

The room fell completely silent at Stanton's last words. Everyone, including myself, too stunned to reply.

"If our problems were not serious enough, negotiations with the Ascendancy have deteriorated beyond repair. Our latest terms were rejected with such vehemence that we feared military action was likely to follow," Stanton went on to explain after his words had a moment to sink in. "Which is why Marshal Tarius was forced to approach the Queen to clarify the scope of his orders after the King ordered him out of the city.

"Unfortunately for us, we had assumed that any attack by the Ascendancy would have begun through Coldscar and sought to reinforce it as soon as possible," Stanton said, pausing for a moment to look at all of us. "However, we were wrong."

"*Wait, Eberia was attacked?*" Aldwin exclaimed, glancing between Stanton and Veronia as he waited for an answer.

"*Nearly*," Stanton replied with a curt nod. "The invasion was thwarted by the slimmest of margins, thanks to a group of Adventurers that were caught up in the midst of a conspiracy designed to sow chaos in Eberia."

"A conspiracy?" I echoed in disbelief. "What happened?"

"The details of the event would take some time to recall, and only the Adventurers involved know the true extent of what happened," Stanton told me as his face turned into grimace. "I would advise you to ask them directly, but I do not anticipate that they will be forthcoming with many details."

"The Adventurers came with you?" Sierra perked up in surprise as she looked around the room. "Why aren't they here now?"

"They...*declined* to join the meeting," Stanton answered in clipped tones. "The terms of their service have made them rather difficult to work with, even if they have agreed to aid the Queen in this matter."

"And *what* matter is this exactly?" Aldwin asked pointedly, glancing between Stanton and Ronia. "I cannot begin to understand why Aldford would be anyone's concern, given the scope of the problems back in Eberia."

"That is far from correct," Stanton replied while leaning forward and focusing intently at Aldwin. "At the moment, the Queen considers Aldford one of the most, if not *the* most important strategic asset in the region."

"*She does?*" the Knight asked, clearly dumbfounded.

"Because of the ruins?" I queried, remembering how I had been dragged into this conversation.

"After a fashion, yes, but also no," the silver-haired noble replied while motioning to the Expedition members sitting at the table. "It is because of what was found within those ruins specifically."

"*Æther*," Donovan spoke up with a tinge of anger coloring his voice, carefully looking at the expressions of Stanton and the other two mages. "You three already *knew* that the ruins out here were likely Nafarrian in origin, didn't you?"

"We had strong evidence to believe that was the case," Samuel replied quietly, reminding me that I had rarely heard the dark-skinned mage's voice over the last month. "But we weren't certain until the events in the Tower."

"Why didn't you tell me?" Donovan demanded, staring directly at Stanton. "I was in charge of the expedition! I should have known! I would have done things differently!"

"You were not fully informed because your political reliability was unknown." Stanton returned Donovan's stare without even blinking. "You have risen through the Mages Guild ranks bereft of any patron guiding your path, and you are not affiliated with any of the Houses, nor have you ever shown any inclination to ever be involved with one. Should the Expedition have successfully discovered Æther in one of the ruins, Samuel and Quincy would have briefed you accordingly."

"Nearly the entire Expedition died because you withheld that knowledge from me!" Donovan practically shouted.

"A decision that the Queen and I were forced to make based on the political situation back in Eberia when we first organized the expedition," Stanton replied stoically. "It may not have been a *good* one, but it was the least *bad* one available to us."

"Why is the Æther so important?" Sierra intervened, glancing between Donovan and Stanton before the argument escalated.

"Because it can be used to power ancient Nafarrian technology," Donovan declared, shifting his glance towards Sierra and me. "We have discovered countless Nafarrian artifacts as we've excavated and explored the ruins that Eberia was founded on, all of them inert and harmless. At least until a spark of Æther is applied, something we have precious little of available to us.

"Based on our research, we've long since theorized that ages ago Eberia was once connected to a vast network of Ley Lines that spanned the entire continent, drawing Æther from the ground to use in all kinds of devices," Donovan continued explaining. "But during the war with the Irovian Dynasty, the Ley Line to Eberia was somehow severed, and the Nafarr that once inhabited the city were quickly overrun and slaughtered when their magical defenses failed."

"Almost their entire culture and way of life depended on Æther, and the devices they had built to use it, from the mundane sort, like heatless lamps to light the city streets, to truly useful ones that could move mountains of earth in a heartbeat, to—"

"To weapons that could turn the tide of a war," Veronia finished, turning her head to look at Donovan. "Or serve as a deterrent to prevent one altogether."

"I won't pretend that we have altruistic motivations for the use of Æther," Stanton said, nodding with Ronia's statement and ignoring Donovan's scowl. "But with the inevitable conflict between Eberia and the Ascendancy building, we need to secure every single advantage we possibly can, and restoring Eberia's access to the Ley Line network would be an incalculable benefit to either avoiding the war or giving us enough of an advantage to survive it."

"Fate, however, is a cruel mistress, and despite the seriousness of Eberia's situation there is a much more immediate and pressing concern that I have come to warn you all about that directly concerns Aldford," Stanton held up a hand to hold any questions. "Approximately one month ago, the Mages Guild began detecting a gradual, yet consistent, increase in the Ætheric energy permeating the surrounding region. The timing of which, I have just recently learned, coincides with the removal of an *Irovian Annulment Sphere* from a well set into the Ley Line."

"What does that mean exactly?" I asked, seeing the same expression of confusion on Sierra's face that I had on mine.

"It means that in addition to whatever its original purpose was, the Annulment Sphere has been serving as a stop-gap measure to keep the ruptured Ley Line in check." Donovan's face had turned pale. "The moment that it was removed, the Æther began flowing once more, at least up until whatever point where the Ley Line had ruptured."

"Then what would happen to it?" Aldwin demanded, his voice breaking as he glanced between all the mages at the table, including me.

"It would just continue flowing," Donovan replied. "Perhaps if the ground were soft enough, it would sink deeper into the earth and eventually dissipate, but it if wasn't…"

"It would accumulate, and continue accumulating until the Ætheric energy reaches a critical mass," Stanton explained, staring directly at me as he spoke. "It is imperative that we determine where the rupture is, and attempt to seal the Ley Line and redirect it back towards its normal channels it as soon as possible, lest it ignites."

"What would the damage be if it did?" Aldwin whispered, his voice colored with disbelief.

"Impossible to tell accurately," Stanton answered quietly. "But I am certain that Aldford and the surrounding region wouldn't survive it, and by extension, neither will Eberia."

Once again, silence took over the room, everyone looking at one another blankly as they absorbed Stanton's latest bombshell. Sierra and I traded nervous looks, before nodding at one another in silent agreement.

"We know where the rupture is…" Sierra broke the silence, all eyes focusing on her.

"…it's right here," I finished while putting a hand across my face. "It's right under Aldford."

Chapter 9

"Based on what we've been able to determine from exploring the area, we think that there once was a Nafarrian city where Crater Lake is now," I told Stanton and all the mages as we left the Town Hall and walked towards the Ætherwarped oak tree, outlining the damage that we had seen in the outlying regions surrounding Aldford. "And that it was catastrophically destroyed during the war with the Irovian Dynasty, wiping out nearly every trace that a city once stood here. All that we have been able to find so far are a pair of collapsed ruins, left buried under stone."

"I pray that whatever magic or technology their ancestors had that allowed them to create such destruction has long since been lost, and not inherited by the Ascendancy," Stanton said with a worried note in his voice. "Else we might find ourselves looking at Eberia or Coldscar in a similar state one day."

"Hopefully," I agreed wholeheartedly. The last thing we needed was having magic capable of destroying cities in the hands of Adventurers, the majority of which wouldn't even hesitate to use it. "Given the extent of the devastation to the landscape, I'm fairly certain that whatever event destroyed the city, also caused the Ley Line to rupture."

"I agree with your logic," Stanton replied his voice tinged with awe as he craned his head upwards while we approached the massive Ætherwarped tree. "In all my life, I have never seen, or read of anything like this. The wood at the base of the tree almost appears to be… crystalline, yet the further I look up the tree, the more it resembles natural if azure colored wood."

I nodded at the man while following his gaze towards the tree. It had come a long way since the tiny sapling that had sprouted from the glowing ichor of the Webwood Horror that had invaded the town several weeks ago, having grown easily seventy feet tall as it clawed its way into the sky, still continuing to grow a handful of inches every day that passed.

More recently, a noticeable change began to take hold of the tree as it grew, its base gradually beginning to lose its wooden texture, appearing smoother, and as Stanton mentioned, almost crystalline in appearance. We had no frame of reference of what to expect during the tree's lifetime, nor any idea if it would ever stop growing, but for the moment, it had become a very much-loved feature of Aldford, its constant azure glow a beacon of rest and safety.

"Several weeks ago, I used an Eberian Ætherscope to look at the tree in the magical spectrum," I told Stanton as Donovan opened a familiar looking case and pulled free two lengths of bone, offering one to both Stanton and myself. "I managed to see the tree's entire root system, and the barest glimpse of the Ley Line, before the Ætherscope burned my hand to the bone."

"*Really?*" Stanton accepted the bone Ætherscope with great interest, looking over the intricate carvings carefully. "It should not have done that."

"He said the same thing," I replied, motioning to Donovan with a thin smile.

"Lyrian's...*Ætherwarping* has given him a greater sensitivity to magic, and he is somehow able to push the boundaries we once thought were immutable," Donovan explained to the other mage. "Unfortunately, that somehow created a feedback loop in the iron Ætherscope causing mana to build up in the device, until it quite literally seared the flesh from his hand."

"Interesting." Stanton shifted his glance from the Ætherscope to me. "Samuel and Quincy had mentioned to me that your condition was the result of overexposure to Æther, the same with your familiar."

"There were...extenuating circumstances to both situations." I didn't quite know how to reply to Stanton's statement. His direct approach to my warped appearance not something that I had been expecting.

"*Both situations?*" The noble's eyes widened in surprise. "I would like to hear how exactly they came about when the time presents itself; it seems I have not heard the full story of your adventures."

"Sure," I replied hesitantly, still not trusting the man and how quickly he had swooped into Aldford with his vague warnings.

Despite everything that Stanton has told us, I feel like I'm missing something out of the big picture, I thought.

"Excellent! Now, what of this bone Ætherscope I'm holding?" Stanton indicated the wand in his hand. "This is Irovian in origin, no?"

"It is," I replied, happy to be on more familiar ground. "We found them in a storage room within the Tower's underground chamber, and it appears that they have an ever so slightly better range than the Eberian Ætherscopes, and do not overheat while being used."

"Useful," Stanton commented while pointing the wand towards the base of the tree. "The image appears slightly more distinct too."

"It does," Quincy agreed, having been offered a wand by Donovan while Stanton and I spoke.

"This is quite remarkable," I heard Samuel whisper from behind me. "We should have thought to use these earlier..."

Turning towards the tree, I gripped the Ætherscope tightly and pointed it towards the ground. Taking a deep breath, I activated *True Sight*, instantly watching the shadows of the world vanish as my vision shifted into the magical spectrum.

Canting my head towards the ground to avoid the bright glare of the tree, the root system bloomed to life as snaking white lines appeared in my vision, gradually transitioning to a deep azure tint the deeper into the ground they descended. Eventually, it became impossible to determine the individual strands of roots, only seeing a single faint line as the roots began to blur together.

As the Ætherscope began to reach the edge of its range, the Ley Line I remembered seeing before appeared. However, this time, it was thicker and brighter than I recalled, and now had a small kidney-shaped blob appearing just beside it.

The rupture, I realized, swallowing hard as I compared its brightness to the Ley Line. *It doesn't look too bright just yet.*

"There is something just on the edge of my vision," Stanton whispered, kneeling on the ground in the hope that the extra few feet would make a difference. "I can see the faintest hint something is there… just beyond the Ley Line."

"It's there," I told the group while deactivating *True Sight*, noticing that all the other mages had followed Stanton's lead in kneeling to the ground. "I saw the rupture. Not as bright as the rest of the Ley Line, but it's there."

Everyone's heads snapped towards me and they quickly stood up from the ground, crowding around me.

"Tell us exactly what you saw," Quincy demanded, the concerned expression on his face doing much to alleviate his harsh tone. "Leave nothing out. It may be important."

"U.," I took short step back as all the mages clustered around me, then attempted to explain what I saw. "...then there was this little *blob* just offset from the side of the Ley Line."

"You're *sure* it was from the side of the Ley Line?" Stanton asked, watching my eyes intently as he asked the question. "Not the front of it?"

"Hmm? Yeah, definitely the side," I replied with a confused expression on my face. "Why does that matter?"

"Because the channel the Ley Line used to travel may still be intact," Samuel answered excitedly. "If it's only ruptured on one side of the channel, then it may be possible to somehow patch it and allow the Æther to flow naturally once more."

"And if I'm wrong, and the channel has been destroyed?" I asked, seeing a look a panic cross everyone's face.

"Then we might as well flee back to Eberia, commandeer the fastest ship still floating in the city's decrepit harbor then sail north around the coast," Quincy answered bitterly.

"There is no way of truly knowing until we see the Ley Line ourselves." Stanton shot an unreadable look at Quincy, who winced in silent rebuke. "But since the rupture does not appear with the same intensity as the rest of the Ley Line, it seems that time may yet be on our side."

"How are we even going to get down to it?" Donovan asked, glancing between everyone. "Somehow swim through the Ley Line until we hit the rupture?"

"Having already fallen into a Ley Line, I highly recommend against the swimming approach." I couldn't help but shake my head at Donovan's suggestion, remembering the unending, searing pain I had experienced when I had fallen into the Ley Line. "You would be praying for death within seconds of entering the stream."

"And even if you somehow survived with your sanity intact," I waved a hand to indicate my appearance. "You would likely end up *warped* like I was."

"It is clear that we need more information before we can decide on a course of action," Stanton stated as he turned to face me and indicated the Ætherscope. "Would you allow us to examine the two Nafarrian ruins in the area? Perhaps we can discover a better way to approach this."

"Alright," I replied slowly while nodding at the mage, hearing the now familiar quest alert chime echo in my ears. "Both of the ruins are fairly damaged. Do you really think you'll find something in them?"

New Quest! The Ruptured Ley Line! (World Event) (Multi-Group) (Evolving Quest)

Lord Adrian Stanton of House Denarius, has arrived at Aldford bearing dire news that Ætheric energy is building up in the region due to a rupture in the Ley Line. He predicts that if something isn't done to repair the Ley Line, the leaking Æther will eventually ignite and catastrophically destroy the region. Help Stanton find and seal the Ley Line before time runs out!

Escort Stanton to the Ancient Transport Hub: 0/1
Escort Stanton to the Crater Lake Ruins: 0/1
Ley Line Sealed: 0/1
Difficulty: Legendary
Reward: Experience & Renown
Penalty for Failure: Aldford and the surrounding region will be destroyed.

As if we needed more problems to deal with! I mentally cursed while scanning over the quest details as they appeared in my vision, my heart tightening as it read the penalty for failing the quest and there being no clear timeline visible. *I should have been more careful in what I wished for when Peter and I visited Ætherworld*

Productions. I wanted something reasonably exciting, not a complete catastrophe in the making!

"It is too early to say—" Stanton began to reply when several loud shouts of anger echoed through the morning air.

As we instinctively turned our heads towards the noise, I saw a flash of pale light just outside the Town Hall, the sign that an Adventurer had just respawned. The shouting began to grow louder, and I immediately realized it was coming from the direction of the Training Grounds, where we were holding tryouts for Virtus.

"*Oh fuck,*" I gasped, already moving towards the noise.

Someone had just killed another person in Aldford.

The shouting continued to grow in volume as I jogged towards the Training Grounds, not wasting time to stop and talk to the respawned Adventurer. While running, Amaranth and several other Adventurers joined me to find out what all the commotion was about.

As I approached the Training Grounds, I saw dozens of Adventurers crowding together, blocking the drilling yard from sight. Wheeling my way around the bulk of the crowd, Amaranth and I pushed our way through the thinnest section of the group, the Adventurers moving out of the way the moment they saw me.

Stepping out onto what we had begun to call 'The Arena', a twenty by twenty field of loosely packed dirt designated for drills and training, I wasn't quite prepared for the sight before me.

Blood was splattered everywhere across the center of the Arena, still soaking slowly into the ground. A glance around the field told me that the body the blood belonged to had long since dissolved, part of the game world's way of cleaning up after the dead.

An unfamiliar group of five Adventurers stood defiantly a short distance away from the carnage, all of them holding their weapons in hand. A dark elf Adventurer dressed in tan leather armor, stood a half a step ahead of the group, his dark skin shining with the sweat of recent battle. In his hands he held a gleaming iron sword, dripping with blood.

In the center of the field, facing the group, were the two familiar forms of Freya and Theia, the former's sharp voice piercing through the angry murmurs echoing out from the crowd.

"—for the last time, Mozter, you *killed* an applicant!" Freya roared at the man holding the bloody sword as she gripped her own weapon, a spear, tightly. "You are *disqualified,* now get off the field!"

"You still think I'm here for that bullshit?" Mozter smirked while glaring at Freya. "I, *we*, never had any real intention to join your guild."

"Then you have two reasonsss not to be on this field," Theia growled angrily. "Now be gone, before we have you removed."

"I would like to see you try, *Lizard*," I heard Mozter snort as I stomped out onto the field, his blood red eyes snapping onto me. "Ah, *finally*, the Guildmaster shows his face!"

<These Adventurers have the stance of predators,> my familiar warned me as he let out a low growl. *<Be wary.>*

"What is going on here?" I called out as Amaranth and I crossed the field, murmurs breaking out throughout the watching crowd as they recognized who I was. Stopping beside Freya, I exchanged quick glances with her and Theia before turning back towards Mozter.

"This group is trouble, Lyr," Freya shifted closer to me, whispering softly. "I don't know what their goal is, but they've been pushing the boundaries ever since they got here. Now they just crossed it."

"Now, now! There's no need for whispers among friends!" Mozter's face pouted as he saw the blonde-haired woman lean in close to me. "I can't have you telling him lies about me and ruining my first impression!"

"Oh, I don't think that will be a problem," I said bluntly letting my growing annoyance seep into my voice, the Dark Elf's eyes never leaving mine as I spoke. With the news that Stanton had just brought now hanging over my head and the sheer quantity of work I already had to do, I didn't have the time, or desire, to be dealing with troublesome Adventurers. "Tell me why the hell you thought it was a good idea to kill one of my applicants, so I can proceed straight to telling you to go fuck yourself."

"I understand that you're angry, Lyrian," Mozter's smile widened as he spoke. "But, you see, I had no other choice. Killing that Adventurer was the only way to get your attention."

"My attention?" I looked at the Dark Elf incredulously. "You could have found me and tapped me on the shoulder. This wasn't necessary."

"I thought about doing that…" Mozter replied, nodding thoughtfully. "But you see, I didn't think it'd provoke the same response, considering what it is I'm looking to ask you."

"Ask me?" I repeated, completely caught off guard by the sudden shift in conversation. "You needed to kill someone, just to ask me a question?!"

"Of course!" Mozter exclaimed. "I had to do it publicly too, to make sure you wouldn't be able to refuse without losing face either."

My eyes narrowed at the Dark Elf's statement. "What do you want, Mozter?"

"To challenge you to a duel!" The elf exclaimed, his expression taking on a feral smile. "To the death of course."

The crowd surrounding us immediately began murmuring excitedly, a powerful voice from the crowd shouting out, "Do it, Lyrian. Kill this fucking coward and hang his head on a spike!"

"You did all of this for a *duel*?" I exclaimed angrily, waving my hand at the drying pool of blood as Amaranth echoed my displeasure with a growl. "Why the hell do you want to duel me?"

"Because you are the greatest challenge I could find," Mozter replied, his eyes burning with a fire I hadn't seen a moment ago. "Ever since I watched your feed with Graves I've wanted to cross blades with you... but I was forced to wait until a spot in Ascend Online opened up, and I could get myself here."

<He seeks to usurp your status, instead of seeking out his own,> Amaranth observed, his mental voice taking on a harsh tone. *<A scavenger seeking to feast on another's kill. Pitiful.>*

I was wondering how long it would take for this to happen, I thought while gritting my teeth, silently agreeing with my familiar. Staring at the dark elf intently I used the silence to carefully inspect the murderous Adventurer and his companions. *Paul warned me that just because we're in the top thousand, there was a risk that we were going to start attracting crazies because of our popularity.*

I just didn't expect for it to happen so soon.

Shifting my glance to his companions, my eye first landed on the half-orc that loomed directly behind Mozter. A veritable mountain of green flesh, the half-orc wore a crudely crafted iron breastplate that strained to keep itself buckled against his massive bulk. The half-orc, likely a warrior, held a massive double-sided axe as he stared back at me, his expression shifting to scowl when he realized I was looking at him.

Keeping my face impassive, my gaze continued to roam, spotting a thin, and unnaturally pale high-elf standing beside the warrior, dressed in simple brown robes. A symbol I was unfamiliar with hung around the elf's neck on a long necklace, partially obscured by a long cascading wave of bright blonde hair. Feeling my gaze on her, the elf blew me a single kiss, before winking at me seductively.

Keeping my face steady, I shifted my glance and found myself staring into a pair of green feline eyes that bored into me with an almost feral intensity, causing my eyes to widen in surprise. Pulling my gaze downward, I saw that the tiger striped Tul'Shar wore only a single woolen shirt and plain leather pants, for some reason not wearing a single stitch of armor whatsoever. Puzzling over his choice of attire, a subtle motion caught my eye, as the cat-man continuously flexed and unflexed the vicious claws his race carried in their hands.

Continuing my inspection to the final member of the party, I spotted a burly looking dwarf dressed in heavy brown leather armor, gently swaying from side to side as his hand rested on a single short sword hanging from his waist, the other holding a thick wooden shield. A red-haired top knot bobbed at the top of his otherwise cleanly shaven head as he moved, his bright eyes looking outward towards the crowd instead of me.

"What exactly do you see your end game being here, Mozter?" I asked the dark elf as I shifted my eyes back to look at him. "Even if you somehow manage to beat me, everyone here will simply kill you afterward."

"Ah, that's where the terms of our duel come into play," Mozter grinned. "You see, it's not just any kind of duel, but a *Ranked Duel*. There are rules and formalities to be observed."

"A Ranked Duel?" I repeated as I narrowed my eyes at the dark elf while trying to remember if I had heard anything about it in the past and coming up blank. Turning my head to look at Freya, I raised an eyebrow at the blonde woman to see if she knew what Mozter was talking about.

"No idea," she replied shaking her head with a whisper. "Maybe it's something like ladder matches from strategy games?"

"Sounds like it," I said somewhat distractedly as I mentally brought up a menu and began urgently paging through it hoping to find what exactly Mozter was talking about. It took me several seconds to navigate through all the options, eventually finding a submenu nested under the 'PvP' menu labeled 'Ranked Duels'. Mentally opening the menu, a wall of information filled my vision, causing me to blink unexpectedly as I scanned its contents.

Ranked Duels

Congratulations! You have taken the first step in ensuring that your name will be spoken in all corners of the world as you fight for blood and glory under the gaze of the gods!

Ranked Duels are god-sanctioned competitions where Adventurers or teams of Adventurers fight against one another in a battle to the death, with the winners being rewarded with Glory Points (GP) and increasing their own Personal Rating (PR). In addition, Adventurers may wager gold, items or even Glory Points between one another before the fight, to be awarded to the winner!

Glory Points may be used to unlock special PvP related character abilities and traits pertaining to Player versus Player combat, further honing their deadly skills and reflexes.

Personal Rating is used to determine your overall ranking for all the Adventurers in your current region (updated weekly) and may be used as a benchmark to determine your eligibility for tournaments and other special events.

This is a whole new subsystem to PvP, I realized as I finished reading and dismissed the text, only to have more appear in my vision afterward.

Ranked Duel Statistics:
> Current Title: Neophyte
> Regional Rank: Unranked
> Global Rank: Unranked
> Glory Points: 0
> Personal Rating: 0
> Wins: 0
> Losses: 0

Current PvP Skills Available for purchase:

Increased Health – *Increase total health by 0.5%. 0/5 (200 GP)*

Increased Stamina – *Increase total Stamina by 0.5%. 0/5 (200 GP)*

Increased Mana – *Increase total Mana by 0.5%. 0/5 (200 GP)*

Additional Skills will be unlocked once 10 skill ranks have been purchased.

"Have you had a chance to catch up now?" Mozter's smug voice called out just as I finished reading the newest wave of information. "I can see your eyes reading."

"I have," I finally said, breaking the uncomfortable silence that had steadily built over the last few seconds and focused my attention back on Mozter and cleared my vision.

"Good." Mozter grinned as a bright red message flashed in my eye. "Then we can get right on with this."

Mozter has challenged you to a Ranked One-on-One duel!

Terms:

Loser forfeits all of their weapons and armor to the victor.

All personal grievances are absolved.

Do you accept this challenge? As the challenged party, you may propose your own counter terms.

"I see what you're after now," I said in sudden understanding as I read the terms that Mozter had proposed, despite my eye suspiciously focusing on the second term. "You just want my weapons and armor."

The words were barely out of my mouth before a cry of anger erupted from the crowd around us, the assembled Adventurers shouting out at the dark-skinned elf, Amaranth, of course, being no exception either, the large cat hissing loudly.

"Of course, and I offer you the same for me, should you win of course," Mozter replied, ignoring the crowd around us. "I firmly believe that the greater the risk, the greater the glory afterward."

"Frankly, Mozter, I don't care what you think," I grunted while looking at the armor that he was wearing. "If you think your equipment measures up anything close to mine, you are sorely mistaken."

Freya: Lyrian, wait. We might be able to use this to our advantage.

I kept my face impassive as I saw Freya's private message appear in the corner of my vision, composing a reply before Mozter continued speaking.

Lyrian: What do you have in mind?

"Then propose a counter offer," Mozter said, slicing his bloody sword through the air impatiently.

Freya: To make a bloody example of them. Challenge them to five on three with Amaranth and me as your seconds. They can't refuse without looking even worse than they do now.

I turned to look at Freya in surprise, the blonde woman giving me a grim smile as she saw my expression. I heard Theia let out a low chuckle, Freya no doubt informing the lizardwoman of her plans simultaneously.

Lyrian: Are you sure you want to show everyone what we're really capable of so soon?

Freya: I think we need to. One of our applicants was just killed in front of everyone. We need to show that we won't tolerate attacks like that under any circumstances. The recruits need to know that we'll have their back if things get rough.

Pausing for a moment to think over Freya's logic, I couldn't help but agree, turning to look out into the crowd of Virtus recruits and seeing their eyes focused intently on me, waiting to see what I would do.

"Alright," I said loudly, coming to a decision as I modified Mozter's duel terms and sent it back to him, purposefully removing the second term that he had included before. I had a sneaking suspicion of why he had included it in the first place, and I wasn't about to let the dark elf off so easily. "Here is my counteroffer, that I think better reflects the disparity between our gear and skill. Freya, my familiar and I will fight all five of you. The winner taking everyone's weapons and armor."

You have sent a counter-duel offer to Mozter, challenging him to a Ranked Five-on-Three duel!

Terms:

Losing team forfeits all their weapons and armor to the victors.

"Ooooh." The crowd of Adventurers couldn't help but comment on my challenge as they excitedly waited for Mozter's reply.

Face frowning in a scowl, Mozter glared at me. "This isn't what I meant by a counteroffer. I wanted to fight you one-on-one with no other interference. It won't look the same in the feeds if I beat you while you're outnumbered."

"Why does it matter to me how it looks in the feeds?" I replied idly while putting my hand on the hilt of my sword. "You're the one who decided they wanted a fight and killed one of my applicants to get my attention. *Well*, you have it now. Take *my* terms or get the fuck out of Aldford and pray no one hunts you down tonight."

Suddenly unsure at my display of confidence, Mozter glanced over at the jeering crowd for a few seconds, before gripping his sword tightly. "*Fine.* I accept."

Mozter has agreed to your terms!

Prepare yourself! The match will begin in thirty seconds!

Without needing to say another word, the rest of Mozter's party drew their weapons as they formed a line of battle, the massive half-orc taking the center position of the group with Mozter on his left and the nervous dwarf on the other side. Standing half a step away on Mozter's other side was the feral looking Tul'Shar with the elven woman taking cover in the rear ranks.

Drawing Razor, I activated True Sight, causing my eyesight to brighten as the ability banished all the shadows from my vision, giving me completely perfect clarity of the battlefield. Raising my hand in the air, I mentally selected one of the newer spells that I had only used a handful of times since learning it and cast it upon myself, feeling a tingling sensation play across my skin as an invisible shield of magic took shape around me.

You cast [Lesser Shielding] on yourself!

You have gained +45 to armor and +7% Spell Resistance for 60 minutes!

Not wasting time during my preparations, both Freya and Amaranth had positioned themselves by my side. Growling with anger, Amaranth dug both his front paws in the ground, causing his large claws to extend as he readied himself to leap forward at my command. Standing calmly by my side, Freya twirled her spear, lying it flat against her arm as she pointed the tip towards the sandy ground of the arena.

Freya: Battle plan?

Lyrian: Steamroll them hard and fast. I'll rush ahead first to draw their attention and force them to commit. If I can get a chance to take out the elf I will. She looks like a caster. The rest appear to be all melee oriented.

Freya: Sounds good. I'll take the Dwarf. What about Amaranth?

Lyrian: I'll send him straight at the half-orc. I don't care how strong he is, seven hundred and fifty pounds of angry cat should be enough to ruin his day.

Freya: Hah, yeah, I bet it will. Will you be okay managing Mozter and the cat man until one of us are free? I have no idea what class either of them has chosen. We didn't get that far in recruitment process yet.

Lyrian: Yeah, I should be fine. I'll keep them busy and wear them down if I can. If I need help, I'll call out.

Freya: Alright, be careful though. We have a ton of eyes on us for this.

<Amaranth,> I nodded at Freya while mentally calling my familiar as the timer steadily continued to tick down. *<I want you to go after the half-orc. Kill him or make sure that he can't contribute to the fight. He will likely be tough and strong to take down.>*

<Good!> The cat snarled in acknowledgement, his azure eyes darting up to look at me momentarily. *<I will rend him to shreds and leave him begging for a mercy kill!>*

Conscious of the time ticking down, I checked my armor and weapon as the growing murmur from the crowds surrounding us began to grow in pitch and excitement. Bright red numbers ticked down in my vision, filling me with anticipation as my heart began to race.

Match begins in:

5...

4...

3...

2...

1...

FIGHT!

Chapter 10

Leaping forward the moment the countdown finished, I shot ahead of Freya and Amaranth, sprinting directly towards Mozter and his feline companion, who both stood completely still as the battle began. Cautious on why they would remain in place instead of using their numerical advantage against us, I slowed for half a step, just as a wall of force flared ahead of me. Mozter and the nameless Tul'Shar immediately turning to sprint around the shield in one direction, with the half-orc and the dwarf doing the same in the other. Standing with her arms outstretched, my earlier suspicions were confirmed as I saw the elf caster channeling the spell.

Ah, I thought to myself as I recognized the tactic, hearing Freya call out to Amaranth behind me as they shifted their assault. *They want us to slow down and meet them on the edges of the shield, where they'll then try to overwhelm and pin us against it. Not a bad idea against a regular group of opponents.*

Too bad for them we're not regular opponents.

Ignoring Mozter and his companions flanking efforts, I instead increased my pace, feeling my feet kick up sand as I sprinted across the arena, focusing my attention on the elf mage as I ran directly at the *Force Shield* before me. I saw a confused expression cross her face as I cast yet another spell on myself, feeling my body become even lighter. With a gentle leap, I soared up into the air, just barely clearing the edge of the *Force Shield* before I canceled the spell and triggered *Blink Step*, my world blurring in a maelstrom of colors before appearing right in front of the elven mage, practically standing between her outstretched hands.

Eyes widening in sudden terror, the mage managed a single yelp of surprise at my arrival, flinching backward as I used my momentum to swing Razor in a short-overhanded chop, the blade biting deep into her neck. Planting my foot on the ground, I continued my charge, driving Razor deeper into the wound as I slammed my shoulder into her chest and knocking the mage off her feet. Pulling my blade free as she fell, I stepped over the fallen woman who instinctively reached up to clench the massive wound in her neck and stabbed her in the heart, seeing her body instantly go limp as I glanced at my combat log in the corner of my vision.

You critically [Power Attack II] [Unknown Elf] in a vulnerable location for 248 points of damage!

You [Shoulder Tackle] [Unknown Elf] for 23 points of damage!

You critically [Power Attack II] [Unknown Elf] in a vulnerable location for 395 points of damage!

You have slain [Unknown Elf]!

You have gained Experience!

You have gained Renown!

That's one down, I noted to myself, having gotten into the habit of checking my combat log during a battle to make sure that I had actually killed my target and that it wasn't feigning death.

Spinning from the dead elf, I turned to face the direction where I had last seen Mozter and the Tul'Shar, the cheers from the crowd of Adventurers ringing in my ears as they saw the elf's body dissipate into nothingness behind me. I spotted the pair scrambling wildly as they tried to get themselves back into position to attack me, Mozter's expression failing to hide the surprise at how effortlessly I had killed one of their groupmates.

Glancing to my right as I waited for the dark elf and his companion to approach, I saw the tip of Freya's spear dart in front of the half-orc's upraised axe, catching the weapon by the haft moments before he began his downswing towards the charging form of Amaranth. Stalling his attack for a heartbeat, the half-orc's timing was completely thrown off, allowing my familiar to pounce on him with a savage growl and sink his teeth into the man's shoulder. Stumbling backward in a desperate attempt to keep his balance, the half-orc flailed uselessly with one free hand, doing little to dislodge the angry cat as he refused to let go of his weapon.

Turning my attention back towards my end of the battle, I shifted Razor into a defensive stance as Mozter and the tiger-striped Tul'Shar entered melee range. Eager to strike the first blow, Mozter lunged forward, his sword slicing out towards me and ringing harmlessly off Razor as I easily deflected the blow.

He's not as strong as I thought he'd be, a part of my mind told me, analyzing Mozter's opening attack, as I easily deflected a second cut with his sword while simultaneously evading a pair of claw-filled swipes from his companion. *Gear notwithstanding, he seems to be only level eleven or twelve and hasn't put that many points into strength*.

"You're weaker than I thought you'd be and I'm not exactly a juggernaut myself," I said, taunting the dark elf as I purposefully hammered two heavy strikes into Mozter's guard, forcing him to stagger under the attacks while simultaneously sending a short snap kick in the Tul'shar's direction to buy myself some space. "Do you even know how to spend your stat points?"

"Don't get cocky just because you've killed the weakest of us, Lyrian!" Mozter spat as his free hand unexpectedly flickered with magic, causing a spark of electricity to crackle along the edge of his sword.   Eyes widening in surprise as the dark elf slapped his blade against mine, I felt a wave of burning heat shoot up my sword arm, causing me to involuntarily flinch as my muscles contorted in shock. "How do you like that?"

Mozter hits you with [Shocking Touch] for 42 points of damage!

"You're a Spellsword too." I stated while reflexively dancing backward from Mozter's follow up slash, putting some space between me and the pair.

"Just like you." Mozter looked at me with a grin as he and the Tul'Shar rushed forward to follow me. "I was inspired by your fighting style while I watched your feeds. I've watched them so many times; you could say that I've learned everything that you've ever shown."

"Is that so?" I said, careful to keep my voice steady as I absorbed what Mozter had just told me, suddenly noticing the way that he held his sword and carried his weight.

His style was completely identical to my own.

"So, you're a copycat?" I asked while wracking my memory of all the fights that had been released to the public. *I never considered that I would have to hide my own fighting style in the feeds!*

"Oh, I'm doing more than just copying, Lyrian!" Mozter replied as he and the Tul'Shar renewed their attacks, forcing me to continuously move backward or be overwhelmed. "You may have a few tricks I haven't seen, but I've worked hard to improve on your build! Granted, I don't have the levels to show it all off just yet."

"Sounds to me like you're already making excuses!" I goaded the dark-elf for a second time, as I dodged another one of his attacks and sliced a deep wound along the Tul'Shar's knee, causing the limb to buckle and sending the cat man to the ground. Reacting at the speed of thought, I sidestepped around Mozter, shifting our battle until the wounded Tul'Shar was directly behind Mozter.

Does that mean that he's also learned the same spells that I have? I know I haven't shown everyone some of the new ones I've learned. I asked myself as an idea bloomed in my mind. *Only one way to find out, I guess.*

Stopping hard on my heels, I stopped my gradual backward retreat and launched myself at Mozter, using a simple four-stroke combination that I had used a thousand times before. Reacting instinctively to my attack, Mozter easily caught the strikes on his blade, a wide smile forming on his face as he stared into my eyes.

"I *told* you, Lyrian, I know all yo—" Mozter's boast was cut short as my fist smashed into his face, cutting his words short.

He's too focused on my usual patterns, I observed with a savage grin, following up my punch with a heavy kick to the stomach which caused Mozter to stagger backward and stumble as he bumped into the wounded Tul'Shar. *He's just fighting by rote based on what I've done before.*

Seizing the advantage, I raised my sword for a killing stroke and slashed down at Mozter's head, hoping to put the man down once and for all. Only to have it swish harmlessly through the air as Mozter vanished from before me, instantly appearing a short distance away, clutching a broken nose.

It looks like he can Blink Step too, I thought as I looked down at the bleeding Tul'Shar, who glared back at me with surprise in his eyes before launching himself upwards on his uninjured leg, clawing at me viciously.

Taking half a step back, I evaded one sweeping paw while the other harmlessly scratched itself off my armor, giving me an opening to draw Razor along the Tul'Shar's chest, cutting through the feeble tunic he wore and into the flesh underneath. Blood welled through the cat man's clothes, causing him to growl wildly as his attacks increased in speed and intensity, forcing me to give ground under his assault.

<Watch your step!> Amaranth suddenly shouted in my head, his growl echoing through the air directly behind me. *<You are almost upon us!>*

<Shit!> I cursed, silently thankful for my familiar's warning as I ground to a halt and swept Razor out in front of me, targeting the Tul'Shar's claws, forcing the man to reflexively pull them backward. Lunging forward, I pressed my advantage and landed yet another shallow cut along the Tul'Shar's body, the under-leveled Brawler grunting in pain as he staggered away from me, breathing heavily as the multitude of wounds began to take their toll.

Free from immediate danger and with a moment to spare, I chanced a glance behind me and saw the prone body of the half-orc as Amaranth straddled the man less than an arm's length away from me. With one hand wrapped around Amaranth's throat, the half-orc visibly strained to keep the cat at bay as his other hand desperately sought to bring a short sword to bear, only to have one of my familiar's paws push against the arm that held it and pin it to the ground.

<Do you need a hand?> I asked Amaranth as I turned my attention back towards the wounded Tul'Shar and Mozter, spotting the dark elf just as he began rushing towards me.

<I can continue this all day!> Amaranth reassured me. *<His metal tooth does not concern me; he will tire long before I do!>*

<Call out if you change your mind,> I told the cat as I lifted my sword in preparation to receive Mozter's charge, only to see him vanish midstride.

Shit! The thought barely had time to form in my mind as I instinctively threw myself to one side, just as Mozter's sword swept through the spot where my head had just been, instantly appearing on my flank. Using my momentum, I rolled on the ground and sprang back up to my feet, just as Mozter closed back in on me, his sword blurring through the air.

"I knew you were good, but you're even faster on your feet than I expected, Lyrian!" Mozter shouted at me, smiling through his blood covered face. "You played me completely! I'll have to try and remember that for the future!"

"Uh, thanks?" I answered, not having expected the man to compliment in the middle of combat as the two of us did our best to kill one another.

"No, thank *you*, Lyrian," the grin on Mozter's face seemed to be plastered there as we fought, the dark elf's free hand beginning to glow with a dull blue light. "But I think it's time we started to wrap things up here! The rest of my party doesn't look to be doing too well!"

Throwing his hand forward, a blast of freezing cold energy burst free from Mozter's hand, washing over me before I could react, blinding me as layers of frost and ice suddenly built up on my armor and body. A trail of messages appeared in my vision, followed by an unbelievable cold that reached into my very core.

Mozter activates [Multi-Cast]!

Mozter hits you with [Cone of Frost] for 98 points of cold damage!

Mozter hits you with [Cone of Frost] for 102 points of cold damage!

Mozter hits you with [Cone of Frost] for 99 points of cold damage!

What the fuck?! My mind reeled in panic as it suddenly became my turn to *Blink Step* out of combat, choosing to teleport away to the very edge of my ability's range, on the opposite side of where Amaranth and Freya were fighting. Scanning my combat log, I noticed that it listed an ability I hadn't seen before. *He just chained three spells in a row using Multi-Cast.*

"Lyr, you okay?" Freya called out to me, sensing my sudden shift on the battlefield as she rapidly stabbed out at the now unarmed dwarf who desperately cowered behind his scarred wooden shield, bleeding from half a dozen cuts and puncture wounds across his body as he did everything he could to stay ahead of the blonde woman's spear.

"Yeah," I replied through chattering teeth as I forced my body to move, causing the layers of ice and frost on my armor to crumble and fall to the ground. "He surprised me, that's all."

And took off nearly half my health in a single attack, I added silently as I checked my stats, to see just how far my health had fallen.

HP: 385/726

Stamina: 478/660

Mana: 340/640

Where the hell did he learn that ability? I took a halting step forward as I rushed forward to join Freya in taking down the stubborn dwarf - if only to free her up so we could focus both of our attention on the rest of Mozter's group. With his latest display of power, I mentally increased the threat he posed, silently realizing why his strength and agility was much lower than it should have been for someone his level. *Depending on how the ability works, he has to have a large mana pool to afford to be able to chain that many spells after one another, so he's been spending his attribute points on Intelligence rather than his physical stats.*

As I closed with the dwarf, I spotted Mozter and the limping Tul'Shar rush around Amaranth, giving the fallen half-orc and puma a wide berth as the pair crossed the battlefield in search of me. Eyes landing upon mine, Mozter looked surprised to see me still standing, but didn't hesitate in rushing forward towards Freya and me.

"Heads up!" I warned Freya as I moved to flank the unarmed dwarf, forcing him to split his attention between the two of us. Attacking, I feinted a thrust with Razor towards the dwarf, looking to split the man's defenses and give Freya a chance to kill or maim him further before the rest of his party arrived.

Panicking at my sudden appearance, the dwarf practically leaped backward to get away from both Freya and me, stumbling over the half-orc's fallen axe that was lying on the ground behind him. Taking advantage of the mishap, Freya's spear sailed through the air towards the dwarf's chest, only to be knocked aside at the last second as Mozter and the Tul'Shar entered the fight. Darting forward, Mozter's outstretched sword just barely caught the tip of Freya's spear, deflecting it just enough so that it sliced through the dwarf's side, instead of burying itself in his heart.

"So how did you like my ability?" Mozter asked as he sidestepped away from the scrambling Dwarf while evading a retaliatory attack from Freya, the five of us crashing together in a flurry of metal and claws. "Pretty awesome, isn't it?"

"It certainly was flashy," I told the dark elf as our blades crashed into one another again, sparks flowing from them as Mozter sent another *Shocking Touch* into my body, causing me to flinch as electricity coursed through my body. "I bet it takes a lot of mana though."

"Something that I have in ample reserve!" Mozter replied with his trademark grin wide on his face.

That's good to know, I said to myself silently as Freya and I fell into our familiar battle patterns, the long hours that we had spent drilling together showing as we began to steadily force Mozter and his party backward. Exhausted and wounded from the earlier fight, the Tul'Shar Brawler struggled to keep up with the flow of combat, his once frenzied pace having slowed as he constantly sucked in deep, labored breaths in order to stay on his feet. The dwarf on the other hand, with only a shield to bear, was hard-pressed to make a meaningful impact on the battle, doing his best to shield himself and Mozter, the man clearly not having spent the time to train his unarmed skill or bothering to carry a spare weapon at hand.

Not that it's going to make a difference for much longer, I noted as Freya and I worked through a sequence that the two of us had practiced endlessly.

Swinging Razor in a powerful overhand blow, I brought my blade down onto the edge of Mozter's sword, seeing his face wince as he absorbed the blow, while simultaneously delivering a *Shocking Touch* to the Tul'Shar with my free hand. Coming in under my guard, Freya's slow-moving spear darted towards Mozter's exposed stomach, causing the man to panic and pull back from our exchange. Taking a step backward, Mozter reflexively swept his blade downwards in an attempt to knock the spear away, only to find that Freya had already pulled it backward.

But not before using the attack as a distraction to hook the wing of her spear on the edge of the dwarf's shield, who had moved closer to Mozter in an attempt to defend him. With a powerful yank, Freya pulled the dwarf's shield out of position, exposing the entirety of his body to me just as I whipped my left hand forward and threw a burning dagger of fire directly into the dwarf's throat.

You hit an [Unknown Dwarf] with a [Flame Dagger] in a vulnerable location for 213 points of damage!

Eyes bulging from the unexpected attack, the dwarf's hand instinctively reached up towards the cauterized mess that was now its throat, only to have Freya's spear dart out and bury itself deep into the dwarf's eye. Standing in shock for a heartbeat, the dwarf let out a faint whimper before falling like a puppet with its strings cut, collapsing to the ground lifelessly.

"Damn it!" Mozter's curse was partially masked by the crowd's sudden cheer as they saw the dwarf fall, the dark elf and his companion taking two long strides backward as Freya and I advanced on them.

"Your teamwork leaves much to be desired," I told Mozter as he and the Tul'Shar steadily retreated. "You all fight like individuals and nothing like a team."

"I'm not done yet!" Mozter growled as he held up his hand before him and began to conjure a familiar blue light in his palm. "I still have more than enough in me to take you all on!"

"Not this time, Mozter!" I exclaimed as I shot forward, mentally triggering *Blink Step* to cross the short distance between us. "I think it's time for me to show you one of *my* tricks."

My vision blurred for the faintest of moments as I teleported just inside Mozter's guard, thrusting Razor forward and pinning Mozter's sword against his body. I felt the Tul'Shar's claws run uselessly along the back of my armor as I reached out with my free hand and grabbed hold of the dark elf's glowing palm, feeling an unearthly cold shoot up my arm as I grasped the spell that was still taking shape. Inches away from Mozter's face, I saw his eyes widen in shock as I began to absorb the mana that he was feeding into his spell, a handful of messages appearing in my vision as I tightened my grip.

Your [Mana Leech] drains 35 mana from [Mozter]!

Pushing against the man, I was readily reminded that the weight of my Ætherwarped body was insufficient to knock the dark elf to the ground, so I took yet another step into Mozter's guard and smashed my forehead into his already broken nose.   Yelping in pain, Mozter flinched and staggered backward, giving me the opportunity to hook my foot around his ankle and take him down to the ground.

Trusting that my armor would protect me from falling on top of both our swords, I maintained my grip on Mozter as he fell, the two of us slamming into the sandy dirt of the arena beneath us. Letting go of Razor, I grabbed hold of the wrist that held Mozter's sword, seeing Freya's feet appear on the edge of my vision, her shout echoing through the air as she attacked the still standing Tul'Shar behind me.

"What are you doing to me?" Mozter gasped as he tried to fight against my grip, but was unable to match my superior strength and positioning.

"Your mana pool is the only thing that makes you dangerous," I told Mozter as I shifted my body to straddle the fallen dark elf while twisting the hand that held his sword, gradually twisting the blade in his grip so that the tip pointed straight up at his chin. "So, I'm taking it away from you."

"*No!*" Mozter thrashed in my grip in panic as he desperately tried to escape from my grasp. With his eyes staring up at me in panic, I felt a wave of mana shoot through his arm as he tried to cast another spell, only to have it fall apart as my *Mana Leech* ability absorbed the energy before it could be put to use. "You aren't supposed to be able to do that!"

Several messages appeared in my vision as a gurgling cry of pain rang out into the air, followed by the sickening crunch of bone.

Freya has slain [Unknown Tul'Shar]!
You have gained Party Experience!
You have gained Party Renown!
Amaranth has slain [Unknown Half-Orc]!
You have gained Party Experience!
You have gained Party Renown!

"Looks like you're all alone now, Mozter," I said to the dark elf while dismissing the notifications, feeling the last dregs of mana drain away from his body as I forced the tip of Mozter's sword upwards, poking it into the soft flesh underneath his chin, causing a small drop of blood to spill forth. "And out of mana too."

"Lyrian, *wait!*" Mozter's eyes widened in terror as he struggled to pull his sword out of my grip. "Look, you don't have to do this, I'll concede, *I conce—*"

"*Shhhh,*" I said to the dark elf, soothing him as if he were a small child while I increased the pressure on his sword. "You're the one who wanted a fight to the death, Mozter, and if nothing else, I am a man of my word."

"*Please don't!*" Mozter shouted as he thrashed in my grip wildly. "I'm—"

"Smile for the camera, Mozter," I said to the dark elf, pausing for a heartbeat before I drove the point deep into his throat. "Everyone will be watching this."

Chapter 11

The crowd cheered wildly as I pushed myself up off Mozter's body and onto my feet, managing a single glance at the dark elf's corpse before it dissipated into nothingness, to be replaced by a loot sack containing all of the man's equipment.

Serves him right, I thought to myself savagely as I flicked the blood off Razor, noticing four similar sacks marking the spots where the rest of Mozter's party had died. Before I could take a single step forward, a flashing notice appeared in my vision, updating me on the duel's outcome.

You are victorious!

You have gained 20 Glory Points!

Ranked Duel Statistics:

  Current Title: Neophyte

  Regional Rank: Pending Weekly Update

  Global Rank: Pending Weekly Update

  Glory Points: 20

  Personal Rating: 1537

  Wins: 1

  Losses: 0

I don't have time to deal with this, I told myself mentally as I dismissed the notification from my vision and looked at the crowd, all of whom looked satisfied with the battle's outcome. *Maybe in a few weeks once everyone's settled I can have a few fun duels. But first, I need to make sure that no one ever decides to pull something like this again.*

"Are you alright, Lyrian?" Theia asked softly, her voice barely carrying over the cry of the crowd as she crossed the Arena and came to a stop before me. Drawn by her voice, Freya and Amaranth moved away from their kills and stood beside the tall Arakssi. "You really took a solid hit from his spell."

"Spells, actually," I whispered back to her, glancing between Amaranth and Freya to see if either had suffered any injuries during the fight. From what I could tell, both of them appeared to be uninjured, though Amaranth's bloody maw and paws made it difficult for me to be completely sure in his case. "He has an ability that lets him chain cast the same spell three times at once."

"Damn," Freya replied with a wince. "That's probably what made him so cocky."

"Yeah," I said in full agreement, mentally playing back the fight. I had been too focused on my own levels and gear when confronting Mozter and had forgotten just how new everything in Ascend Online was. Even with the game being out a month already, we had barely scratched the surface of what skills or abilities that were available to be discovered.

Something that often led to the same kind of surprise that I had just experienced. One that could have cost me dearly if I hadn't been able to negate Mozter's spellcasting ability.

"Anyway, we're not done just yet," I said while inclining my head towards the Town Hall. "Time to drive our point home and make sure that Mozter or anyone else doesn't try something like this again."

"A moment," Theia said as she muttered an incantation under her breath and reached out to touch my chest with a glowing hand, causing a healing wave of energy to shoot through my body and repair the damage that Mozter's spell had wrought. "There, that's better."

"Thanks, Theia." I smiled at the older lizardwoman, instantly feeling better as the lingering pain faded away.

"It is nothing," she replied with a shrug. "Go sort out what you must with Mozter. I will run herd on the recruits until one of you return. I daresay many will follow you to see what sort of punishment you will deal out."

Leaving the Arena behind, the three of us easily passed through the crowd of watching Adventurers, all of them shuffling to open a path before us as we moved with purpose directly towards the Town Hall.

"What are you going to do to him, Lyrian?" Freya asked, her tone clearly indicating who she meant.

"Right now, I have half a mind to bury him neck deep in the ditch surrounding the village for a week," I replied as several other ideas came to mind, none being any kinder. "Maybe with a bucket on his head to make life more difficult."

<A worthy punishment that will go a long way to ensuring that none dare challenge your status,> Amaranth's mental voice said approvingly as his azure eyes flicked up to meet mine. *<Perhaps the same for the rest of his pride?>*

"Maybe," I replied to the cat with a thoughtful smile before looking to Freya. "Amaranth thinks we should include the entire party as well."

"Now there's an idea," Freya snorted in amusement as we spotted Mozter and his party standing in front of the Town Hall, looking slightly dazed and confused as they all looked around, missing all of their weapons and armor. A short distance away from them stood a tall human Adventurer that I didn't recognize, who was glaring angrily at the group, no doubt being the person that Mozter had killed a few minutes earlier.

"Give us some space," I told Amaranth and Freya, not slowing down as I approached the dark elf and his companions standing in front of the Town Hall entrance, making a beeline towards Mozter. Looking up, his eyes widened in surprise a moment before I planted a hand on his chest and shoved him backward, hard.

"Huh, he—" Mozter yelped, staggering awkwardly away from me in an attempt to keep his balance, catching himself on the wall of the Town Hall as Freya and Amaranth rounded on the rest of his companions, giving the would-be duelist and me some semblance of privacy. "What the fuck, man? I con—"

"*Shut up, Mozter*," I spat at the dark elf as I grabbed his arm and brutally twisted it, spinning the man until I had him pinned against the wall face first. "Now that we have your bullshit challenge out of the way, we can move on to the fact that you killed one of my applicants in cold blood."

"What? You can't do anything about that," Mozter gasped in pain as he tried to pull himself out of my vicious grip, the loss of his gear further weakening his already less than impressive strength. "That was buried in the duel ter—"

"No, Mozter, that was in *your* duel terms," I told the dark elf, watching his face go pale as I spoke. "You thought you'd be able to avoid punishment for what you did, but I saw straight through you."

"*No!*" The one eye I could see went wide as he no doubt reviewed the terms of the duel. "That can't be right! I wouldn't have accepted it if—"

"I hope you don't have anywhere to be for the next week," I said as I pulled Mozter free from the wall, grabbing hold of the back of his neck. "I think you need some time for some quiet reflection."

But no sooner did I turn around, did I feel a cold metal hand grab hold of my arm, Dyre's steely voice filling the air as he suddenly appeared in the Town Hall's doorway with Sierra a half-step behind him before I could pull Mozter away.

"Lyrian, what is going on here?" the Justicar asked in a flat, no-nonsense tone. "Why are you assaulting this Adventurer?"

"Let go of me, Dyre," I told the Justicar, trying to pull my arm free, but finding it impossible to budge. "You missed your window to intervene."

"Guys, what happened?" Sierra asked, glancing between Amaranth's bloody maw and the tip of Freya's spear. "We heard a bunch of commotion and were on our way…"

"This man killed one of our applicants a few minutes ago in a misguided attempt to get to challenge me to a duel," I told Sierra, seeing her face shift into a hard expression. "I am going to make sure that he understands the consequences of his actions."

"You will do no such thing, Lyrian," Dyre stated harshly, his steel-like grip tightening around my arm. "You no longer have the authority, or reason, to take the law into your own hands now that I am here."

"Yet I find myself forced to," I said, staring at Dyre as I spoke, silently gritting my teeth as the pain from the Justicar's hold on my arm began to build. For a moment, I considered to try and pull my arm free of the man's grip, but was alarmed to see a tag appear in my vision, causing me to second guess my decision.

[Joseph Dyre] – Justicar of Aldford – Level Unknown

His level is masked, I realized, begrudgingly choosing to let go of Mozter as I regarded Dyre in a new light. *I didn't even know that the game hid levels from players.*

"I understand your anger," Dyre stated in his typical expressionless voice as Mozter flinched away from me and moved to stand beside the Justicar. "But it is my duty to ensure that justice is served *exactly* as the Town Charter proscribes and in accordance with Mithus's Will."

"Now, explain to me what happened," the Justicar asked, his head shifting his faceless gaze between Mozter and me.

"I wasn't there for the whole thing," I began, motioning to Freya who had circled around the Justicar with the Adventurer I had seen earlier.

"As part of our recruitment process, we were conducting sparring matches to determine everyone's skill level, specifically *non-lethal* matches," Freya told the Justicar, not missing a beat as she nodded towards the blonde-haired Adventurer beside her. "On three separate occasions, Theia or I were forced to tell Mozter to restrain himself due to the wounds he was inflicting."

"As the matches progressed, he became more and more violent, and I decided to pair him against some of the better recruits, hoping that they would knock some sense into him," Freya continued speaking, glancing over at the dark elf. "At least until he took a cheap shot after the match had been called."

"Not my fault they couldn't keep up with me," Mozter cut in somewhat petulantly, waving a hand at the Adventurer that he had killed. "In combat, you have to be ready for anyth— *ah!*"

Mozter flinched as a gob of spit hit him directly in the eye, followed closely behind by the blonde-haired Adventurer's fist as he stepped in front of Dyre, the unexpected blow completely knocking the dark elf off his feet.

"*Keep up with you?*" The man shouted, struggling to pull himself forward as Freya belatedly reached to grab him from behind. "I fucking paid attention to the rules, you fucking—"

"ENOUGH!" Dyre's voice boomed as he recovered from the Adventurer's unexpected attack, slashing a hand through the air that erupted with magic. Faster than the eye could follow, a golden chain wrapped itself around the man's body, immediately stopping him in his tracks. "You will cease your violence, or by Mithus's will, I will charge you with assault as well!"

Dyre can use magic? I noted with surprise, seeing similar expressions written on everyone's face.

Struggling against the bonds, the man gave Dyre a dirty look, moments before it was replaced by a grim smile. "Very well, *Justicar*. While I appreciate the guild master standing up for me, I felt I needed to make my own point."

"Do not test me, Adventurer," Dyre replied in clipped tones as an unseen mental action caused the golden chains binding the man to constrict painfully. "Mithus sees that you have been wronged, and for that reason alone he is willing to let your transgression slide, *this once.* Strike someone in anger before me again, however, and you *will* regret the consequences.

"*Understood?*"

"Ugh—" the Adventurer managed to gasp in pain. "Yes."

"Good." Dyre grunted, the golden chains dissolving from around the Adventurer's body. "Now—"

"Are you fucking kidding me?" Mozter whined from his position on the ground as he clutched his eye. "He pops me one and gets nothing?"

"*Quiet!*" Dyre snapped at Mozter. "Every word you have spoken thus far rings of falsehood to Mithus's ear and your aura is tainted with Discord. I do not expect any ruling I make to be in your favor. Do yourself a favor and remain silent."

"Should have been prepared for anything, Mozter," I told the dark elf as he slowly pushed himself up back onto his feet, momentarily revealing that the Adventurer's single blow had broken his cheekbone and completely ruined his left eye. While it would regenerate in a few minutes, I couldn't help but savor the man's pain given how much aggravation he had caused me in the short while that I had known him.

Mozter made a rude gesture in my direction, though I could see the worried look in his eyes as Dyre spoke again, this time to me directly.

"How did you get involved in this, Lyrian?" Dyre asked. "I expected you to be with Stanton for a while yet."

"I was," I told the Justicar with a nod. "However, the commotion from the Arena drew my attention, and after seeing someone resurrect by the Town Hall, I assumed the worse."

"I see," Dyre replied. "And when you arrived at the scene?"

"I was met by Theia and Freya, who had just begun to confront Mozter," I continued, my eyes flicking over to the Adventurer as I spoke. "From there, Mozter openly admitted that he had killed…"

"Alistair," the man supplied helpfully.

"That he had killed Alistair," I repeated, nodding my thanks to the Adventurer that I had yet to formally meet. "In order to get my attention and challenge me to a ranked duel. Twisting the terms of the duel so that he would escape any punishment for his actions."

"Which you accepted?" the Justicar asked, a note of hesitation appearing in his voice for the first time.

"Not before removing those terms," I replied, keeping my attention focused on Dyre.

"I see," he replied thoughtfully looking over at Mozter. "Then I believe sentencing is in order."

"What?" Mozter barked incredulously as his one working eye darted towards his party, all of whom who remained silent. "I don't even have a chance to defend myself?"

"Every word you have spoken thus far has been filled with nothing but false pride and lies," Dyre stated as he turned his faceless gaze over to Mozter. "Can you state in complete honesty that you were not the instigator of the events that just transpired?"

"Uh…" Mozter looked at the Justicar with hesitation. "I didn't—"

"Enough," Dyre spat, looking at Mozter with disappointment. "Mithus sees all, and through him, so do I. The lies you spin in your head will not work on me, for I have heard enough to pass *Judgment.*"

My heart leaped as Dyre spoke the final word of his sentence, his voice taking on a deeper tone as he leveled his gaze on Mozter.

"Mozter, for the crime of slaying an Adventurer in cold blood within Aldford," Dyre stated. "I find you *guilty.*"

"For the crime of instigating Discord within Aldford, I also find you *guilty*," Dyre continued, watching Mozter intently, who flinched at the two guilty verdicts. "In accordance with the Town Charter and the laws laid down within it, I *banish* you from Aldford for a period no less than a year and a day."

"Furthermore," the Justicar stated, keeping his faceless gaze on Mozter as he spoke. "Mithus has moved your Soulbinding from the town of Aldford back to your city of origin. Should you die again, you will find yourself far away from this town, lest you find another location to anchor your soul."

"What?" Mozter gasped, looking terrified. "You can do that? That's not fair! There's nowhere even close to here to bind my soul again!"

"That is not my concern," Dyre stated emotionlessly. "Perhaps it will serve as a valuable lesson to you for the future."

"Hang on," I said, having watched the exchange between Dyre and Mozter quietly until now. "Banishment is a fine final punishment, but it's not enough for what Mozter has done. We need to make it clear that Aldford won't tolerate the shit that he just pulled."

"Oh, fuck you, Lyrian," Mozter spat. "Haven't you done enough already?!"

"And what do you believe would make his punishment fair?" Dyre asked me, ignoring the dark elf's reaction.

"Imprisonment, at least for a week," I stated without hesitation. "*Then* banishment."

Dyre stared at me for a moment, processing my statement before he shook his head. "That will not be possible. There are no clauses for imprisonment within Aldford's Town Charter. Any punishment is limited to Fines, Death, Exile or Banishment."

"Are you serious?" Freya cut in, asking the Justicar with a note of disbelief in her voice. "We can't imprison anyone in Aldford *at all?!*"

"The laws of this town were written with the frontier in mind," Dyre stated, shifting his gaze to the blonde-haired woman. "It was not anticipated that resources would be spent building a prison, not when banishment to the wild almost guarantees death."

"Well, that's a big gap that we're going to have to fix." I couldn't believe what Dyre was telling me. "Just banishing Adventurers isn't enough of a deterrent!"

"The laws of Aldford is something that you will have to bring up with Aldwin. He is the only one with the legal right to adjust them or create new ones," Dyre told me as he reached out to grab Mozter by the arm. "In the meantime, however, I will continue to enforce them as they have been laid down."

"Hey, wait!" Mozter yelped as Dyre practically yanked him off his feet. "Don't I get an appeal either?"

"You may appeal your sentence directly to Mithus after a term of six months of good behavior," Dyre replied as he pulled Mozter away from us, taking a path directly towards the southern section of Aldford. "Should you have sincerely attempted to mend your ways, Mithus will commute your sentence at that time. However, should you be found wanting…Mithus may see fit to increase it instead. I suggest that you weigh your actions carefully before appealing to the God of Justice."

Moving to keep pace with Dyre, all of us, including Mozter's party, followed the Justicar as he dragged the dark elf to the bridge that spanned the river and marked the edge of Aldford's official boundary. True to Theia's earlier words, I then realized just how many Adventurers had followed us from the Arena, or had been drawn by the commotion surrounding the Town Hall as nearly two dozen of them eagerly waited to witness the punishment of the would-be duelist.

With little ceremony as we approached the bridge, Dyre shoved the dark elf forward, causing him to stumble across the rough stone, the rest of his party following wordlessly behind, joining in on their leader's banishment with barely a word or hesitation.

I have no idea where Mozter found these people, but damned if they are loyal to him, I thought as I watched the completely unarmed and unarmored group cross the bridge and form up behind him. *But I'm sure they know that they wouldn't be welcome, or necessarily even safe within Aldford anymore. Leaving quickly with Mozter is probably their best bet to stay together as a group before somebody tries to jump them with vengeance on their mind.*

"I won't forget this, Lyrian," Mozter growled as he shifted his hate-filled glare from Dyre and onto me. "I'll be back—"

"I'm sure you will, Mozter," I interrupted the man with a dismissive wave of my hand. "I've heard the same thing from far better people, and let me tell you something.

"*I'm still here.*"

Spitting at my feet, Mozter scowled in anger before he and his party turned away from us, slowly walking out into the wild. The tension of the situation diminishing with every step that they took.

<Do you wish for me to hunt them down tonight?> Amaranth asked me with a bloodthirsty tone in his mental voice. *<I can shadow them during the sunlight and fall upon them the moment they lay their heads to rest.>*

<I can't tell you how tempting that is,> I replied to Amaranth, the urge of ordering him to kill the party nearly overpowering my better judgment. *<But no. Let's hope they've learned their lesson for the time being. We have enough problems as it is without creating permanent enemies for the future. I also don't know how Dyre would react to that either. The last thing we need is trouble from him in our own Town.>*

<As you wish,> Amaranth replied with a tinge of doubt as he slowly walked onto the bridge and turned to look towards me. *<Regardless, I will follow them for a distance to ensure that they take your benevolence to heart. True predators like them will find it hard to accept your mercy. Until they fully accept you as their better, they will constantly test the boundaries you are willing to give them.>*

"We will see," I told the puma as he moved to stalk after the party without another word. "Be careful."

Turning away from Mozter's departing figure, I faced the crowd of gathered Adventurers, recognizing the majority of them from my duel with Mozter and his party. Their gaze landed on me immediately, causing me to pause for a moment, once again surprised to see how many had followed us during the altercation.

"They are looking to you for guidance," Dyre whispered to me in a soft voice that made me doubt if he had even spoken at all. "What you say now will set the tone for any future incidents. Choose your words carefully."

Eyes widening in surprise, I looked towards Dyre, only to see him already shifting away from me and walking back towards the heart of Aldford, circling the group of Adventurers without another word. I watched the Justicar thoughtfully for a moment before turning back towards the gathered Adventurers.

"Today, a man was murdered for the sole purpose of getting my attention," I began, casting a glance at Alistair before looking out towards the crowd. "And as you all saw, he has been dealt with harshly. Stripped of all his gear and banished."

I paused for a moment as I collected my thoughts.

"Aldford is young," I said. "And all of us right now have the opportunity to shape it into the town, and one day I hope, the city that we want it to be. I for one want it to be a place where we can all let our guard down and enjoy the comforts of civilization without worry of being assaulted, killed, or challenged unjustly. Something that I know is not easily found close to here."

A low rumble of agreement reached my ears, the newest arrivals to Aldford clearly sharing my sentiment of safety.

"With those words in mind, I have one promise and a warning to share with you all," I continued, nodding in sync with the adventurers before me. "If *anyone* repeats Mozter's actions, they will be dealt with just as harshly, if not even more, as our own laws develop and mature. It is up to us to set the standard as more Adventurers join our settlement, and it is my goal to make it one filled with honor and companionship, rather than one filled with distrust and conflict. Keep that in mind as we go forward in the coming days and weeks, for there will be no other warnings."

It wasn't my best speech by far, I knew without a doubt in my mind, but there was a low echo of approval from my statement as the Adventurers slowly began to disperse. Many of them heading towards the Arena with growing excitement in their voices. Scanning the crowd, I couldn't help but note that there were several more Adventurers heading back to the recruitment grounds than I had seen originally, something I silently hoped translated into an even larger application pool for Virtus. As it was, we had more than enough work to go around and not enough bodies to handle it.

"Any reason why we shouldn't restart the recruitment process?" Freya asked me, her smooth voice jarring me out of my thoughts.

"No," I replied empathetically, meeting her eyes as I spoke. "If they can't handle the sight of blood or something unexpected like this coming up, they aren't what we're looking for anyway."

"Damn right," Freya replied with a crooked smile before nodding her head towards the departing swarm of Adventurers. "We could use your help in getting everyone sorted though. Based on my rough count on everyone heading back towards the Arena, we're going to need more help managing the applicants. And, given everything that just happened, it's better that you're seen with the guild as much as possible."

"I'll be there," I told Freya. "Just give me a few minutes to fill Aldwin in. I'm not sure where he is, but he should definitely know what's happened here, at least before he hears it second hand. If you see the others before I do, will you let them know what's happened when they get back from hunting?"

"No problem Lyr, and it's probably a good idea to fill Aldwin in," Freya said. "I'm pretty surprised that he isn't here already to be honest, all of this commotion hasn't exactly been quiet."

"I can cover in the meantime," Sierra offered. "Aldwin was just in his office with '*Ronia*' before Dyre and I left."

The red-haired woman paused to shake her head before continuing to speak. "They have some sort of history between one another, and not all good from what I could tell. Aldwin may appreciate the rescue if nothing else."

"Fantastic," I replied with a weary tone, wondering what Stanton and the other Adventurers would think of everything that had just happened. There was no way that they could have missed Mozter's challenge or the fight between us. "Let's hope it's something simple."

"Ha!" Sierra commented with a snort as she and Freya moved to follow the group of departing Adventurers. "When was the last time something was simple for us?"

"Probably not since we logged on for the first time," Freya said wistfully, giving me a wink as she left to follow the group of Adventurers.

Sighing silently, I found myself unable to disagree with either woman's statement, wondering when the game had taken the turn from something fun to play with my friends, to being in charge of a budding virtual society with competing interests and personality conflicts.

This is a far cry away from my old life, I realized as I looked out towards the crowd, wondering just how many would end up making the cut to Virtus. *But would I really want it back?*

Shaking my head at the thought, I made to move forward and walk towards the Town Hall in search of Aldwin just as an unfamiliar voice called out to me.

"If this is how you handle all your problems, Lyrian, I think we're going to get along perfectly."

Caught off guard by the use of my name, I couldn't help but flinch as I shifted my glance towards a nearby elf standing off to the side, leaning nonchalantly against a nearby building far away from where everyone else had been standing. Clad in dark leather with an ornate metal cuirass covering his chest, I was surprised that I hadn't noticed him earlier. Judging by the quality of the gear that the man was wearing, he had to be somewhere close to my level, if not higher. Something that I always made a point to keep an eye out for.

He's not just an elf, I mentally corrected myself after staring at the bald, clean-shaven man for a moment, realizing that his figure was far too broad and muscular for a pure-bred elf. *He has to be a mix of something else…maybe human or half-giant?*

"What are you talking about?" I asked while watching the man carefully, wondering where he had just come from. It wasn't exactly hard to find out what my name was after spending some time in Aldford, but I still found it rather unsettling not to know who I was talking to. "And how exactly do you think that we are going to be working together?"

The man let out a bitter chuckle while shaking his head at me. "I saw you talking to Stanton, and I'm sure he's told you about the reason why he's here."

"And if he has?" I replied, slowly walking towards the man, my eyes scanning my surroundings. The day may have just started, but I'd already had far too many surprises for my liking.

"Then whatever he's told you is a complete lie," the man stated as he beckoned me closer, casting a wary glance at the departing Adventurers. "Or close enough to make no difference."

"How would you know that?" I asked, indulging the man and closing the distance between us, coming to a stop a few feet away from him, my hand moving to rest on Razor's hilt.

"He's the reason why my friends and I are here," man replied, taking no notice of my hand's placement as an angry expression momentarily crossed his face before vanishing into a forced smile. "If I had it my way, we'd still be in Eberia. Not out here in the middle of nowhere."

"Are you following him?" I cocked my head at the Adventurer, suddenly wondering where exactly this conversation was headed as I inspected him more intently.

"Ha!" The man snorted, shaking his head again. "No. Not voluntarily at least."

"I am actually his prisoner, in a manner of speaking."

"His...*prisoner?*" I repeated while frowning at the man's unexpected reply. Staring at him for a moment in surprise, a thousand questions clamored for attention in my mind until I chose the easiest of them as I collected myself and tried to mask my astonishment.

"Just who exactly are you?"

"Here I thought you'd never ask," the muscular elf replied, a wide grin forming on his face. "My name is Lazarus Cain."

Chapter 12

Moving away from the bridge, I followed the strange elf as he led me behind the building that he had been leaning against and further into Aldford, silently replaying his last words in my head.

Stanton mentioned that the Adventurers he brought with him were uncooperative, I reminded myself, keeping my eyes focused on Lazarus's back as he avoided the main road through the town, and careful of signs of betrayal despite noting that the man wasn't carrying any visible weapons on his body. *But he didn't say anything about them being here against their will.*

My spinning thoughts came to an abrupt end as two other male Adventurers came into view, the pair standing side by side as they waited nervously behind a house that had been built long before I arrived in Aldford. One was an olive-skinned human dressed in bright-red leather armor, the other a tall half-orc wearing a tight-fitting linen jacket with dark brown pants. They were clearly on edge as their attention immediately focused onto Lazarus and then onto myself as we approached.

"What took you so long, Lazarus?" the man dressed in the leather armor demanded the moment that we came into range, his long, dark hair swaying side to side as he looked between the muscular elf and me. "We've been waiting for ages! Someone is bound to realize that we're missing by now! If Stanton finds out..."

"And what is he exactly going to do about it, Sawyer?" Lazarus replied indifferently. "Make our lives even more difficult than he already has? He can't expect us to stay cooped up in the tent the entire day now that we've finally arrived."

"We shouldn't test him too much, Lazarus," the half-orc spoke as he inclined his cleanly shaven head towards me in greeting, his bright hazel eyes inspecting my gear. "If we push him too far..."

"I'm well aware of the stakes we're playing with, Ransom," Lazarus replied harshly before his expression softened and he waved a hand in my direction. "*Anyway*, the reason why it took so long was that Lyrian here was busy putting the beat down on Mozter and his crew. Pretty damn well if I may say so myself."

"That's what all the commotion was?" Sawyer asked, his dark eyes shifting to look at me with approval. "What happened?"

"He killed one of the applicants to my guild," I replied, feeling that the information would become common knowledge around Aldford within the hour. "He wanted to lure me into a ranked duel and to steal my weapons and armor. I turned the terms around on him and took his gear instead, before the Justicar banished him from Aldford."

"Damn, that's cold," Ransom said with a smile on his face. "Couldn't have happened to a better guy."

"You knew Mozter and his group?" I couldn't help but ask, realizing that they must have spent the last few days travelling with the man just as the words left my mouth.

"He tried challenging us back in Coldscar," Sawyer explained with a nod. "*Well*, more specifically, that huge half-orc tried to challenge Lazarus. What was his name again? Thar, Thad, or something similar?"

"Thra," Ransom replied with a shrug. "Regardless, it didn't turn out too well for him in the end."

"What happened?" I asked, my curiosity getting the better of me.

"I found out where he was sleeping and fed him a brick," Lazarus replied idly. "He got the message that I wasn't interested after that."

I paused for a moment as I considered Lazarus's reply, realizing after a heartbeat that he wasn't joking and had no qualms about brutalizing an opponent in order to make a point, something I knew all too well given my last interaction with Mozter and Graves before that.

Sometimes a vicious example just had to be made.

"Huh," I grunted, breaking the momentary silence that had fallen around us. "Anyway, what was it that you wanted me for? Lazarus told me that you were all Stanton's prisoners, but I find that hard to believe if you're running free in town."

"We aren't *exactly* his prisoners… but we're not exactly *free* either…more like indentured servants with a death sentence over our heads…" Sawyer answered as he cast an annoyed glance over towards Lazarus. "My name is Sawyer by the way. Since it doesn't look like Lazarus is going to formally introduce us."

"You're all grown-ups. Introduce yourselves." Lazarus grunted. "What am I? A nursemaid?"

"You're *something* alright," the half-orc muttered under his breath as he met my eyes. "I'm Ransom, and we're all unfortunately stuck with him for the foreseeable future..."

"I see," I said slowly, my tone indicating the exact opposite.

"You don't, at least not yet," Lazarus replied with a sigh. "The reason why I asked you here is that we wanted to cut through all of the bullshit that I bet Stanton just laid onto you, along with everything that's happening in Eberia and this *Æther* business that caused the three of us to be dragged out here."

"And how exactly do you know what sort of 'bullshit' Stanton might be telling us?" I asked, trying to mask the sudden increase in my heart rate and keep my expression even as I met Lazarus's gaze. "According to him, you declined to even show up to the meeting."

"Is that what he told you?" Lazarus asked with a scowl. "We didn't decline to go to the meeting. We were *barred* from attending."

"Barred?" I echoed with a note of disbelief, my eyes narrowing at the man. "Why?"

"Because for as much as he needs us, he doesn't *trust* us," Ransom answered softly. "And he knows we don't trust him. I'm sure he was concerned that we'd contradict him in front of everyone and throw off whatever he's planning."

"That doesn't really answer the question," I said, letting a bit of annoyance color my voice. With how slow the conversation was unfolding, I was going to be here all day, and I didn't have the time to waste.

"I know what he told you because I overheard him and Commander Tarius rehearsing their story while we were on the road," Lazarus stated, while motioning to his elven ears. "I may be a half-giant as well as an elf, but these just aren't for show, you know."

"That's easy to *say* and hard to prove," I replied with a shrug, despite being silently happy to now know the other half of the man's racial makeup. "Give me something specific."

"Well, for one, they talked about their long-term plan to have Eberia annex Aldford once they have control over something called a *Ley Line*," Lazarus said, refusing to be intimidated. "Then Stanton went on about House Denarius technically *owning* this settlement, then mentioned a disgraced knight named Fredric Aldwin being a bad political choice to remain in control of the region."

"They want to annex Aldford?" The words leapt out of my mouth before I could regain my composure.

"*Ah!*" Lazarus's eyes widened at my reaction. "I knew that would get your attention."

"Don't be crass, Lazarus," Sawyer interjected as he cut a hand through the air and gave me an apologetic look. "We want—*need*, to work with Lyrian and his guild if we're ever going to get back to Eberia in a decent timeframe, especially with *The Ascendancy* on its way."

"Stanton mentioned that they tried to invade Eberia," I said, feeling off balance as I shifted my glance towards the red-armored Eberian. "And that you three stopped it. Is that actually true?"

"In a manner of speaking...*yes*," Ransom acknowledged as a pained expression crossed his face, and he looked over towards Lazarus. "But that is a rather complicated story."

"That we don't have the time to tell right now," Lazarus said somewhat forcefully to Ransom before looking back towards me. "But in either case, Sawyer is right. First and foremost, we need your help, which is why we're warning you about Stanton and what he's planning in an attempt to build some goodwill between us."

"*Okay,*" I replied uneasily, still feeling like I was missing a substantial part of the bigger picture. "And what exactly would my help entail?"

"We need you and your guild's help to fix the Ley Line and restore the flow of Æther to Eberia, like Stanton no doubt asked you," Ransom said. "After all, that is the reason why we were sent here to support him."

Ransom paused for a moment, looking briefly at Lazarus and Sawyer before continuing, "But we need you to do it in such a way that doesn't force Stanton to order *us* to try and take control of the town from you."

"*Are you crazy?*" I exclaimed while staring at Ransom numbly for a moment as I tried to process what he had just told me. My eyes then shifted towards Sawyer and Lazarus, seeing them both staring at me expectantly. "My own ego aside, none of you would survive attempting that. You are all simply far outnumbered."

"Then you understand our problem," Lazarus said grimly. "We've been here long enough to hear what you did to some guy named Graves and the last thing I want to do with my time is be stuck in a meaningless territory skirmish on the edge of the frontier when I could be back in Eberia."

"Actually, I'm not so sure that I do." I looked at the man with confusion, his candid nature at odds at what I was expecting from a clandestine meeting such as this. *Why is he so set on getting back to Eberia? That's the second time he's mentioned it now.*

"The three of us need to keep Stanton alive," Sawyer told me, keeping his attention focused on Lazarus as he spoke. "He and his...*mistress*...have hostages back in Eberia and have arranged some sort of magical dead man's switch. If we don't fix whatever this Ley Line *thing* is and bring Stanton back to Eberia in one piece..."

"Then some of our friends will die," Lazarus finished. "And others will be...*lost* to us, possibly for a very long time, if not forever."

"His mistress?" I queried while making a mental note of what Lazarus had just told me regarding hostages. "You mean, Emilia Denarius?"

"Yeah," Lazarus replied with a nod as a scowl came across his face. "*That bitch.*"

"I've heard Aldwin refer to her the same way," I replied dryly as I slowly began to understand the trio's motivations for making contact.

Had Stanton and Veronia actually tried to annex Aldford by force, they'd have to deal with several dozen angry Adventurers who wouldn't even hesitate to put a dagger in one of their eyes if it meant keeping the town free of an outsider's influence. Not to forget the other Adventurers that had arrived with Stanton who would leap to our assistance over the prickly nobleman.

"Nice to know it isn't because of my charming personality," Lazarus said flippantly before schooling his features back into a serious expression. "I'm going to be honest with you, Lyrian. Reaching out to you wasn't our original plan, or our backup plan, or our backup-backup plan. Based on everything that Stanton had told us, we were expecting to find a small village barely eking out an existence out here, starving for supplies and ready to cave the moment we arrived, not a fortified settlement that has more manpower and resources than the majority of the Guild Estates surrounding Coldscar."

"So, you were ready to just take over the village on arrival?" I queried, meeting Lazarus's eyes unflinchingly and seeing him nod in response.

"Stanton told us to prepare for that option," he admitted. "That or simply burning it to the ground and rebuilding on top of it."

"You should be telling Aldwin this," I said through gritted teeth. "He thinks that Stanton is here as an *ally,* not as a would-be conqueror."

"It was hard enough finding a chance to talk to *you* without anyone listening in, let alone sneaking into the Town Hall without Stanton seeing," Lazarus told me pointedly while waving a hand dismissively at my suggestion. "Besides, we've only been here for a day, and after asking around town, it's clearly obvious that you and your Guild are the ones that are really in charge here, even if Aldwin is *technically* the leader."

I instinctively readied a reply to correct Lazarus but found myself unable to completely disagree with what he was saying. Every single major decision that had been made within Aldford over the last few weeks had gone through both Aldwin and me, the two of us effectively guiding the town's development. Thinking about it in hindsight, however, I suddenly realized just how much Aldwin had begun deferring to me, trusting me to keep the settlement's best interests in mind.

"Fair enough," I replied slowly, still trying to wrap my head around what exactly Lazarus and his friends wanted me to *do*. Keeping Stanton from even *attempting* to annex Aldford was going to be a difficult prospect, considering that I didn't know the full scope of his plans or his motivations.

Assuming I even believed what they were telling me.

Taking a moment to consider my words carefully, I slowly scanned the group, meeting everyone's eye in turn before speaking. "Let's say for a moment that I believe what you're all telling me, and that Stanton has plans to seize Aldford for Eberia. I still don't fully understand *why*. Sure, he mentioned that *The Ascendancy* is breathing down Eberia's neck, which you three have confirmed, and that restoring access to the Ley Line would help with the coming conflict.

"But that doesn't seem enough to me to warrant annexation. If war breaks out, Eberia will be cut off from the rest of the continent and Aldford will wither on the vine."

"It's politics from what I understand," Ransom replied. "The noble houses in Eberia are currently...having a few...*disagreements* with the King—"

"Don't sugarcoat it, Ransom. Lyrian needs to know the unvarnished truth if he's going to even have a chance at helping us," Sawyer interrupted before glancing at me. "The noble houses are inches away from a flat-out rebellion against the King and open warfare between one another. As it is, they haven't paid their taxes in weeks and have split up the city districts into their own fortified camps, patrolled exclusively by House Guards and not the Eberian Military. The city is a powder keg ready to go off at any second. Assuming it hasn't already since we left."

"And somehow annexing Aldford is going to stop that from happening?" I asked, unsure of how a frontier town a week's travel away figured into that equation.

"*Not* annexing Aldford might set everything off," Ransom told me. "You know just how...*unpopular* Aldwin is back in Eberia...don't you?"

"I have a vague idea...based on what he himself has told me," I told Ransom with a shrug, despite feeling a sense of worry bloom in my gut. I had known that Aldwin's past could have posed problems with Eberia down the road, but I hadn't expected for it to be this big an issue. "From what I understand though, that shouldn't be a problem. He's been out of the public eye for a while and out here for the last few months."

"That's not what I've overheard Stanton and Veronia say," Lazarus told me. "The way they talk about Aldwin..."

The half-giant paused to shake his head. "They believe that the moment that the rest of the Nobility learn that he controls all of Eberia's Æther, they'll do something reckless, thinking that one of the other Houses is holding an unfair advantage over the other..."

"So, Emilia thinks that the best way forward is to remove him from power," I finished bitterly, a bad taste filling my mouth as I spoke. "That is nothing but bullshit! *She* is the one who exiled Aldwin out here anyway."

"I agree, Lyrian," Lazarus told me with a shrug. "But this is the reality of the situation back in Eberia."

"So, what exactly is the endgame here for Emilia?" I asked, feeling a surge of anger shoot through me as I began to realize that Eberian politics had finally reached far enough to affect Aldford and that there was going to be no easy way to escape them. "Based on what I've heard about her, I didn't expect for her to be one to try and play the mediator in this situation or even care what the other houses do.

"Besides, if everything is as dire as you say it is, what is she going to do when the next situation arises? Today it might be Aldwin being in control of Aldford, tomorrow the sun might cast a shadow on the wrong noble house. What will happen then?"

"This is a shitty situation for all of us, Lyrian," Sawyer replied. "But we're hoping that we can work together in some capacity to keep everything from falling apart."

"That's where *I'm* stuck at," I said as a group of loud voices on the opposite side of the building began to draw closer, causing the three men to look around nervously. "In order to work together, we're going to need to *trust* one another, and I'm not quite there yet. For all I know you could be working towards your own ends, telling me exactly what I need to hear to do something rash."

"Has Stanton told you *specifically* how he found out about the Ley Line's rupture?" Lazarus asked me, brushing my statement aside as he made a sudden motion with his hand, indicating that we should all move away from the building and whomever was walking by.

"No," I replied in a neutral tone as I moved to follow the group. "Only that the Mage's Guild found it."

"Like *fucking hell* they found it," Ransom spat, drawing a grunt from Lazarus due to the volume of his voice.

"He's not wrong," Sawyer added a heartbeat after, meeting Lazarus's eye unflinchingly as the big man shifted his gaze.

"What is it?" I pressed, starting to become concerned by Lazarus's lack of response.

"The Mage's Guild sure as hell didn't find it," he replied meeting my eyes as he spoke. "And the fact that Stanton isn't being completely honest with you on at *least* that basic level, should worry you, a lot."

"That doesn't prove—" Before I could finish replying to Lazarus's statement, the man held up a hand and shook his head.

"Look, Lyrian, we don't expect you to trust anything that we've told you right away, and frankly we wouldn't believe you if you said you did," Lazarus told me while inclining his head in the direction of the tent we had set up outside Aldford for the new arrivals. "We need to get back to our minders and reassure them we haven't flown the coop, but take some time to think about what we've told you and pay attention to just how much Stanton *doesn't* tell you over the next few days. The three of us need to take our rest cycle tonight anyway, so we'll be out of touch for a day or so. But if things don't start adding up by the time we're back, then send one of us a message, and we'll go from there."

Without giving me a chance to even acknowledge his statement, Lazarus and his companions turned on their heels and sped away from me, ducking behind the Crafting Hall as they avoided the main street that cut through the center of Aldford, vanishing from sight almost immediately.

"What the hell have I just gotten myself involved in," I asked myself while letting out a heavy sigh and checking the in-game clock. "I've only been logged in for what... two hours so far? The way today's going, I'm going to need a shot by the time the day's over."

No sooner did I finish my statement than an all-too-familiar chime echoed in my ear, causing my heart to skip a beat as a wall of text appeared in my vision.

New Quest! Statecraft, Deception and Veracity! (Evolving Quest) (Espionage Quest)

After meeting a trio of Adventurers who claim to be working with Lord Adrian Stanton of House Denarius, you have been warned that he and his companion, Commander Veronia Tarius, have come to Aldford with less than altruistic motivations, seeking to annex Aldford in Eberia's name, rather than honoring the contract originally signed by Aldwin and House Denarius. The Adventurers have provided you with a great deal of information that Lord Stanton has yet to reveal to you, assuming he will at all.

Going forward, will you trust what Lord Stanton has already told you? Will you expose the Adventurers to him? Or will you listen to the Adventurers who have approached you for help?

Collect more information before making a decision!
Evidence supporting the Adventurers' story: 0/?
Evidence supporting Stanton's story: 0/?
Difficulty: Very Hard
Reward: Unknown
Penalty for Failure: Unknown

My mouth dropped open as I scanned through the new quest, feeling a heavy stone of stress and anxiety sink deep into my stomach.

On second thought, forget just a single shot. I'm going to need an entire bottle.

Chapter 13

Walking into the Town Hall, I passed through the main room of the building with barely a second glance at all the people seated at long tables sharing meals with one another. Many were putting together their plan for the day or simply sat together, enjoying a moment of rest before beginning on their next task. My feet carried me into the back corner of the large hall and up a flight of stairs that led to Aldwin's study, where I was hoping to find the man so that the two of us could begin to make sense of everything that Lazarus had just told me.

I hope Aldwin has a few ideas on how to deal with all this political shit that just landed in our lap, I thought fervently while mentally replaying everything that Stanton had said in the meeting just a short while ago and re-examining it in a new light. *I don't even know if I'm going to be able to look at Stanton or Veronia in the eye without appearing suspicious as hell. If it were as simple as fighting a battle, I'd know better how to deal with all this. But figuring out who's lying and telling the truth...I don't even know where to start!*

Leaving the clamor of the Adventurers behind, I finally reached the top of the stairs, enjoying a brief moment of silence before a familiar feminine voice erupted from Aldwin's office on the far side of the hall ahead of me.

"It's your fault he left, Fredric!" Veronia's voice barked. "It's your damned fault all of this happened!"

"Shit, Ronia! How many times do I have to tell you? He saved *my* life!" I heard Aldwin shout back as I crossed the hall, hearing a loud thump as something was knocked over in the room. "I was ready to die! Hell, I *should* have died! He pulled me back from the brink and practically dragged me back to Eberia after the battle! I was as heartbroken as you when he vanished!"

"Damn you, Fredric, don't tell me anything about being *heartbroken*!" Veronia's voice echoed back once more just as I placed my hand on the door and pushed. "I was the one engaged to him!"

Swinging with a creak, the door opened, revealing Aldwin standing behind his desk as Veronia leaned over it from the other side, the chair she had been sitting on lying on the floor behind her. Sensing my intrusion, the pair whipped their heads to look at me, Aldwin's face shifting to one of relief, whereas Veronia's remained angry.

"Lyrian—" Aldwin began to speak before Veronia's reply drowned him out.

"*Get. Out.*" The armored woman snapped at me, her voice dripping with venom, a far departure from her earlier emotionless behavior during our meeting with Stanton.

"I don't think so," I retorted, matching her stare unflinchingly as her face turned red with rage. "I can hear you from down the hall, which means everyone downstairs can hear you as well. What the hell is going on here?"

"That doesn't concern you, *Adventurer*," Veronia spat while slashing her hand at the door. "I'm telling you—"

"I beg to differ," I interrupted the angry woman. "You are making a scene, *and* you are screaming at my friend—"

"The *Kingkiller* doesn't have friends," Veronia stated, casting a hard look at Aldwin who winced as if struck, then turned to look back at me. "Only victims. I strongly suggest that you reconsider *any* affiliation that you have with this man."

"I think you need to leave, *Commander*," I said, feeling a cold sensation sweep over my body as I glared at Veronia, barely containing my anger. "Before you say something you can't take back or something that I won't be able to forgive."

Veronia glared at me for a moment before shifting her gaze towards Aldwin, "I will *never* forget, or forgive what you've done or what you've cost me."

"Ronia...*please understand*," Aldwin managed to grind out, his voice heavy with emotion as Veronia pushed herself off the table and turned her back on him. "I—"

"I understand everything that I need to, *Fredric*," she replied firmly while stalking across the room towards the door that I held open and passing through it with an angry glare at me before I closed it behind her.

Barely a second after the door was closed, I heard Aldwin practically collapse in his chair with a loud sigh, followed by several curse words I couldn't make out.

"Are you okay?" I asked as I crossed the room and picked up the chair that Veronia had knocked over during their argument and righted it. "That sounded...*bad*."

"It is nothing I haven't heard before," Aldwin replied, despite the heaviness in his voice. "Though this is the first time I've heard the word '*Kingkiller*' coming from her lips."

"Is that what they called you, back in Eberia?" I asked the man gently as I took a seat in front of his desk and for the first time noticed the tears in Aldwin's eyes as he stared up at the ceiling.

"That's what they called all of us back in Eberia," Aldwin said with a bitter note in his voice. "*Kingkillers.* The survivors of Rainier and Cyril's death. I just happened to be the only one who stayed around long enough to be associated with the title."

"I'm sorry about that," I told the knight, who simply shrugged in response.

"It isn't the first time that Veronia and I have had that argument," he stated. "I had hoped some time would have cooled her emotions. I was wrong."

"What was the argument about?" I asked carefully, not wanting to pry any more than Aldwin was willing to reveal. "If you don't mind me asking, that is."

"It was about her husband to be, Myles Grayson. She *still* blames me for his 'disappearance'," Aldwin replied as he raised a hand to rub his eyes while waving my concerns away with the other.

"Who was he?" I asked. "And why would she blame you?"

"Myles was my second in command when I was in charge of the Prince's protective detail," Aldwin replied. "The two of us, *three of us*, if you included the prince, were like brothers, even beyond the call of duty."

Looking down from the ceiling, Aldwin fixed me with a steady gaze before he continued speaking. "He was the one who saved me after the ambush where the prince was killed when by all accounts I should have died."

"You never mentioned what happened during the ambush," I said slowly, not wanting to push the knight into reliving a bad memory if he didn't want to.

"We never saw it coming," the older man grunted, his face grimacing as he spoke. "One moment we were cutting our way through a routed horde of orcs and goblins, then the next thing I knew…I had taken four arrows and was desperately trying to get to the prince's side."

Aldwin paused to tap two spots on his chest, one under and one above his heart before touching his stomach and side, marking the spots where the arrows had hit him. "I knew I was too far away to make a difference after he fell, but I was beyond reason. I *had* to get to his side. I felt that the least I could do was die beside him to somehow make up for not being able to save him."

"But before I could even cross half the distance towards him, my body failed me, and I collapsed." Aldwin clenched a hand over his heart as his eyes glazed over. "My memories of the time afterward are faint and fragmented, but I remember Myles dragging me free from the chaos and speaking to me as he pulled the arrows from my body and healed my wounds. At one point, I passed out from the pain, and by the time I awoke again, I was back in Eberia, and Myles was nowhere to be found."

"He was one of the survivors then too," I stated, remembering what Aldwin had told me several weeks ago in this very study, that there had only been six survivors from the ambush that had claimed the prince's life.

"Yes," Aldwin affirmed. "After the battle, he vanished...in as much that we never found his body to prove that he may have..."

"Committed suicide," I finished, seeing the Bann nod sadly at me.

"According to what I was told, he disappeared barely an hour after bringing me back to Eberia," Aldwin said. "He left no note, or took anything of his with him...I have always thought that he climbed one of the bluffs and cast himself into the ocean...to escape what had happened."

Survivor's guilt, I thought as Aldwin and I lapsed into a momentary silence, the older man turning his head to stare out the window. *They fought for decades to end The War and the moment that it did, they lost the two symbols that kept the nation unified.*

"How do you know Veronia?" I asked, changing the topic and finally breaking the stillness that had come over the room. "From what I overheard in the meeting, her father is in the military too?"

"Her father, Marshal Abraham Tarius, *is* the Eberian military," Aldwin replied with a tone of reverence. "He is in charge of the army and the reason why Eberia survived *The War.* Before he took command of the military, nearly thirty years ago, we paid dearly in blood to hold onto *The Bulwark* and keep Eberia from being overrun by the Orcs. His leadership and example saved countless lives, and over three decades eventually shifted the war in our favor."

"I see." I nodded in understanding as pieces began to fit together in my mind. "You must have worked with him closely to watch after the prince."

"We did," Aldwin affirmed. "And that is how Veronia met Myles. She was her father's protégé and spent most of her career learning at his side. Naturally, the prince worked closely with the marshal, and by extension so did the Royal Knights. The constant proximity allowed for Ronia and Myles's love to bloom as the years passed."

"But ever since Myles vanished, no...*died*," Aldwin corrected himself, revealing what he truly thought happened to his old friend. "Veronia hasn't been the same. She has been consumed by a cold rage that even her father hasn't been able to put out, and has pushed everyone close to her away. I of all people am no stranger to what grief can do to a person, but the burden she carries on her heart has twisted her from the woman I once knew."

Aldwin let out a deep sigh as he leaned back in his chair and rubbed his face once more. "Seeing her again for the first time brought back memories I hadn't thought about in ages...and wounds I had thought healed."

There was a long pause as Aldwin collected his thoughts one last time.

"At any rate, however, I appreciate your timely arrival, Lyrian. That argument would have only gotten worse from there," Aldwin said to me as he leaned forward onto his desk and clasped his hands together. "Is there something that you needed me for? I don't suppose you saw or heard whatever noise pulled Sierra and Dyre away from our meeting on your way up?"

"Actually, I was involved in that noise," I admitted to Aldwin without any hesitation. "There was an incident with a group of new Adventurers, and I'm not so sure that Dyre resolved it appropriately or was *able* to resolve it appropriately."

"I suppose a day was longer than I expected before an incident involving the new Adventurers occurred," Aldwin said with resignation, casting me a curious look at the last part of my statement. "What happened exactly and how did you get involved? I expected you to be with Stanton for quite a while longer dealing with the...*news*...that he had brought us."

"So did I. But we were interrupted..." I began as I then went on to explain everything that had happened with Mozter, describing the dark elf's challenge, our duel, and Dyre's subsequent punishment.

"It sounds to me like Dyre did his job adequately," Aldwin told me as soon as I finished my story. "This...Mozter fellow has been punished, and now that he's banished, he is no longer our problem."

"I feel given the scope of his crimes, he needed to be made an example of, and *then* banished," I stated. "Dyre let him off far too easy for my tastes."

"I'm not so sure he did, Lyrian," Aldwin said flatly. "By your own words, you killed Mozter yourself during your duel, brutally from the sounds of it, and claimed his equipment. Anything more than that, on top of his banishment would seem...excessive, if not tyrannical. As it is, it's not as if the death penalty means anything for you Adventurers."

"That's exactly what I mean," I told Aldwin empathetically. "You don't punish an Adventurer by killing him, inflicting pain, or taking his equipment away. You punish him by taking his time away."

"Time?" Aldwin looked at me with confusion. "Why does that matter?"

"Because that's all that we have that's valuable to us," I said. "Think about it. Death means nothing. Pain fades away into memory. Equipment can be replaced. But *time* is something that we can never get back. Killing him and humiliating him were good first steps, but keeping him and his group prisoner for a few days would have driven the point home."

Aldwin looked at me thoughtfully as he stroked his beard, his expression looking hesitant, "I think I understand what you're getting at a little better, Lyrian."

"But we simply don't have the resources to manage to build a prison for Aldford just yet. As it is, we have our hands full trying to build enough housing for the new arrivals, let alone finish the Crafting Hall, palisade or any of the other buildings we need!"

"It isn't that we need a formal prison," I countered while trying to get my thoughts straight. "At least not yet. If we truly needed to imprison someone we can take a few shovels and a fistful of leather straps and simply bury the offender in the ground up to their necks."

Aldwin stared at me in disbelief at what I was proposing, "Lyrian...I don't even know where to begin with that! We treated orc and goblin prisoners with more dignity and honor than that! And they threatened to completely wipe us out to the last woman and child!"

"Then how else do you punish an immortal?" I asked Aldwin pointedly while waving at myself. "Because that's what we Adventurers are. Granted my example may be a little unusual, but taking away our time is the most meaningful punishment that I can think of to serve as a deterrent for future incidents. Right now, it isn't about having a prison in Aldford. It is the way that Aldford's laws are written and how Dyre is enforcing them."

"When the incident with Mozter arose, Dyre told me that we are unable to detain *any* adventurers that may break the law in the town, simply because we have no laws that *allow* for him to do that, regardless if we have a place to put them."

"I think I begin to see your point," Aldwin said while appearing deep in thought. "The laws I included in the Town Charter during the founding of Aldford are basic guidelines at best. I hadn't anticipated ever having to write them with a Justicar in mind or growing so quickly. But if we are fortunate enough to have one here to enforce the law, then we need to make sure that the most appropriate laws are in place to ensure that Dyre is able to do his job adequately and as best suits Aldford."

"*Exactly*," I told Aldwin with a firm nod. "And as Bann of the settlement, those laws have to come from you. The sooner we can tell the Adventurers what to expect, the better Aldford will grow for the future. We need better assurances than simple *Frontier Justice* to those that are wronged, and real consequences for those that break them."

"I understand better now, Lyrian," Aldwin replied, though the hesitant look on his face was at odds with his words. "But isn't all of this a bit...*trivial*, given the danger that lurks beneath us? As much as it pains me to say, perhaps we should be preparing to evacuate Aldford until it is resolved? Assuming it can be at all."

"I don't think we're at that point just yet," I said, feeling my heart twist at the thought of abandoning Aldford. "Nor do I think we should let word about the Ley Line spread to the rest of the town."

"You want to keep it secret?" Aldwin looked surprised at my statement. "Why? It seems to me that we could use any and all help if we are going to have a chance at finding a way underground to where the Ley Line sits."

"Because I am not so sure I entirely believe or trust what Stanton has told us," I said while trying to find a gentle way of breaking the news that Lazarus and his friends had told me and the suspicions that I now carried.

"What you mean?" Aldwin immediately looked worried. "Do you believe that he's lying about the rupture? To what end?"

"I don't believe he's lying about the rupture, considering that I have seen it with my own eyes through an Ætherscope. But I also don't believe that he's being completely honest about his motivations either," I replied. "Tell me, just how well do you know Stanton? Did you ever have dealings with him before?"

"Nothing formal," Aldwin said as he considered my question. "I've only met him a handful of times in my life, and even then, only during social events where I was attending the Prince. He is a cousin of some sort to the Queen, though I'd have to consult a family tree to know exactly *how* they are related to one another. Why do you ask?"

"Because, shortly after the incident with Mozter occurred, I was approached by the group of Adventurers that Stanton brought with him. The ones he claimed *declined* from attending the meeting." I saw Aldwin eyebrow rise in curiosity as I spoke.

"And?" he prompted.

"They didn't decline to attend the meeting; they were barred from it," I stated. "Citing that Stanton didn't trust them to support his story during it. Furthermore, they considered themselves here against their will."

"And do you believe them?" Aldwin asked. "During the meeting, Stanton did mention that they were uncooperative and if he told outright falsehoods, Dyre would have made a note of that."

"Wait, Dyre can do that?" I looked at Aldwin, feeling caught off guard, suddenly remembering what Dyre had said while speaking to Mozter. "He can just tell when people are lying?"

"Of course," Aldwin replied with an indifferent nod. "All Justicars can. It is what makes them so effective and sought after."

"I didn't know that," I said quietly, as I absorbed the implications. I had assumed that Dyre saw through Mozter's lies due to practiced skill and the evidence against him, not because of divine aid.

If Stanton lied through omission and not deliberate falsehoods, then Dyre wouldn't have picked anything up. A growl escaped my throat as a new wave of frustration swept over me, realizing just how far out of my depth I was. *But at the same time, if Lazarus is telling the truth, that means Stanton was then able to manipulate the whole conversation even with a Justicar present to evade letting anything slip.*

Yet, what if Lazarus has his own goals though and is trying to make me second guess everything Stanton told us? Stanton might very well be the honest one in this situation and Lazarus not. Or Stanton may have sent Lazarus to us...

"Are you okay, Lyrian?" Aldwin said with concern, looking at me with surprise. "Did I say something to upset you?"

"It's not you," I replied, shaking my head as I leaned forward in my chair and ran my hands through what remained of my hair. "I am going crazy in my head trying to make sense of everything that's happened today, and I'm realizing now that I have no idea what to do or who to trust."

"I'm not sure I'm following, Lyrian," Aldwin said. "What exactly did the Adventurers tell you that has you so worked up?"

"Are you sure you want to know?" I asked Aldwin, giving him a serious look. "If I do, you might not be able to look at Stanton or Veronia the same way again."

"That bad?" Aldwin commented, before shaking his head and sighing deeply. "Tell me everything. You are the only reason why Aldford still remains free and standing. As long as I am alive, I won't allow you to carry your burdens alone."

"Thank you." I breathed with relief, a part of me worried that Aldwin might have taken me up on my offer. "The Adventurers told me that Stanton and Veronia were planning to annex Aldford for Eberia, and to remove you from your position as Bann."

From my opening words, Aldwin stared at me in stunned disbelief as I then went on to explain everything that Lazarus and his friends had told me, leaving nothing out. At first, Aldwin's expression began with sullen resignation, before gradually shifting into anger as I finished my story.

"That's why *she* pushed so hard to get a garrison up here in the town," Aldwin said, his knuckles white as they clutched the edge of his desk. "It isn't enough that they *exiled* me out here and now they want to depose me! Haven't I given *enough* for Eberia?"

"Who, Veronia?" I asked numbly, feeling deflated after sharing my story. "She wanted to put soldiers up here?"

"*Yes*," Aldwin spat while letting go of the desk and clasping his hands together. "Before our conversation...*deteriorated*. She mentioned that her father would want to send protection here as a gesture of goodwill after the incident with the Bandit Adventurers and to ensure something like that never happened again. I refused her, citing their impending conflict with The Ascendancy and not wanting to be drawn into it, but she became more insistent...it didn't go well after that."

"So, you believe that the Adventurers may be telling the truth?" I queried, watching Aldwin shake his head in response.

"*I don't know*," Aldwin grunted harshly as he continued to work through his anger. "But this stinks of *politics*. For one, when *I* asked for an escort to lead us out here during the founding of Aldford and to protect us for a time, I couldn't get so much as a vague promise for assistance out of the military. But now that Aldford has something valuable, Veronia is trying to practically force a company of soldiers down my throat."

"Which would answer to someone Eberian, not someone from Aldford," I pointed out.

"And give her the manpower to remove me physically," Aldwin stated bitterly while nodding at me. "Which would cause a bloodbath if Adventurers like yourself decided to stand against them. While I would personally find it hard to raise arms against an Eberian soldier, I daresay many of you wouldn't."

"No," I admitted, knowing that if Aldford was under attack by *anyone*, regardless of their origin, I wouldn't hesitate in fighting them. "But would you want us to?"

Aldwin gave me a sharp look. "What I want is Eberia to leave me *alone!* I have given them my entire adult life in service, forgone marriage and children to duty, even willingly accepted *exile* to ensure that the nation wouldn't tear itself apart due to my presence! Now they seek to take the last thing I have left to my name!

"I have had enough!" Aldwin said forcefully, slamming his fist on the desk. "I don't *know* what Emilia sent Stanton here to do, or how Veroina has become involved in this all, *or* what these Adventurers could possibly want, but I will not risk even the slightest chance of being ejected from my new home."

"Then what are we going to do?" I asked the Bann with frustration in my voice, hoping he had a better insight into what our next move was. "Assuming Stanton isn't lying about the Ley Line, we will have to find a way to address that or Aldford will be destroyed. But then if we do somehow figure out a way to repair the Ley Line, we will be exposed to whatever they're planning, *if* they're planning something. We still don't know for sure."

"Stanton is an Eberian noble," Aldwin said bitterly. "Plotting and intrigue is second nature to their kind. Truthfully, I was prepared for him to do *something* when I had heard he had arrived. However, I merely expected him to demand early repayment of the debt that I owe House Denarius and cut his losses."

"And can they force you out based on that debt?" I queried, trying to think of any *legal* ways Stanton or House Denarius could take control of Aldford.

"Not easily," Aldwin answered without hesitation. "I would have to consult Ritt for the full details, but I believe with the tax collected from the Adventurers so far, I can make a substantial payment and offer them the rest in resources."

"Or you could just pay them in Æther," I told Aldwin thoughtfully as a germ of an idea slowly began to form in my head. "We could make a fair argument that it is worth *more* than raw coinage."

"Aldford *technically* doesn't possess any Æther though," the Bann replied pointedly. "Only Virtus does, through its claim on the Hub. Stanton may use that point against me and refuse to allow you to effectively buy out my debt."

"And if I were to sell a vat of Æther directly to Aldford in exchange for food or supplies?" I countered, waving Aldwin's concerns away. "For say...a low price of a copper a liter? There's not exactly a thriving market for it out here outside of me and handful of the other mages."

"That could work," Aldwin allowed, speaking slowly as he considered my offer. "But Stanton will know exactly what you did."

"So what?" I grunted. "He has already threatened to dispute our claim to the ruins we've found. Assuming he still even wants to now that we have a rough idea of where the rupture is."

"I'm sure he will, eventually, if not right away," Aldwin said confidently. "From their perspective, if Aldford controls the Æther to Eberia, then they will see themselves effectively at our mercy. Regardless if Stanton is telling the truth and sincerely wishes to help us right now, Emilia will never let that stand long term, neither will the King or the other nobles. Especially with the threat of war looming over Eberia."

"Then we need to join the game and start building our powerbase right now," I told Aldwin excitedly as a wave of inspiration struck me.

"You have an idea?" Aldwin asked. "What can we possibly do to stand up to the might of an entire Kingdom?"

"We use the coming war to our advantage," I replied, feeling my earlier stress fade away as my thoughts began to race. "Currently the military is fortifying Coldscar and preparing to meet *The Ascendancy* head on. Once the war starts, Eberia won't be able to send forces up to Aldford without attracting attention from The Ascendancy and risking it being intercepted. They'll be cut off from the continent by all except the fastest and sneakiest scouts."

"That would cut *us* off as well," Aldwin noted. "If The Ascendancy realized that we were the source of all Æther for Eberia, we would be doomed to stand against them."

"I don't disagree," I acknowledged with a nod. "But we have a wild card that can tip the scales in our favor, even if we are isolated."

"We d—" Aldwin's expression shifted rapidly from confusion to realization as he cut his question off before he could fully ask it. "*The Adventurers.*"

"Exactly," I said with a knowing smile. "The first thing that is going to happen when The Ascendancy and Eberia go to war is all of the Adventurers and guilds surrounding Coldscar are going to be destroyed or forced to flee."

"And you want to offer them safe haven and absorb them," Aldwin finished, resting a hand on his chin in thought. "That may work, but would bring problems of its own depending how many joined us."

"I think we can deal with Adventurer problems much easier than the political one Stanton represents," I said confidently. "If only for the fact that if we reject them, they will have nowhere else to go. As it is, Adventurers are fiercely territorial, and we have more than enough space to spare if they're willing to play by our rules. If The Ascendancy or Eberia decide to move on us in the future, we'll have enough manpower to make them regret it."

"Lyrian, what you're proposing is more than just using the Adventurers as a deterrent," Aldwin said with concern. "You want to turn Aldford into an Adventurer City."

"Bigger than that, Fredric," I replied, mentally readying myself for the genie I was about to unleash.

"I want to turn Aldford into the heart of an Adventurer Nation."

Chapter 14

CTI Player Housing Complex

"Hey, Marcus!" A smiling blonde-haired woman greeted me as her face appeared on one of the large screens before me. "It's nice to finally see the *real* you after all this time!"

"Likewise, Sonia!" I replied with a genuine grin as I finally saw the real person behind Freya's Avatar and found her startlingly similar to her in-game appearance, save for her having slightly longer hair in reality and sharper Scandinavian features. "We've put this off for too long!"

"Hey, is that Sonia?" a familiar voice called out as an older, bearded man's face appeared on the screen beside the one that held Sonia's, having not been in view of his camera's pickup. "Nice to finally see you too!"

"Hello, Thorne!" Sonia started to give the man a small wave before realizing her slip up. "Ah! I suppose I should call you George out here!"

"Oh, don't worry about that!" George replied with a chuckle. "I've done that at least three times now going between Marcus and Peter. It takes a bit of getting used to!"

"That it does," Sonia agreed wistfully.

"It's not like we spend all that much time in Reality anymore!" Peter chimed in from behind me as he, Zach and Deckard made their way over from the table and fell into the couch beside me, each of them carrying a drink in hand. "We hardly even use our real names now."

"Did any of the others say if they're going to be coming to the meeting?" I asked, wondering if I'd have a chance to see Cerril, Huxley, or any of the other Thunder Lizards for the first time.

"No, not this time," Sonia shook her head, causing her long blonde hair to sway from side to side. "Léandre needs all the help he can get right now, so they all stayed behind to help him out with crafting and raising the framework for the newest longhouse, along with managing our new recruits. They said they're happy with whatever we decide."

"Alright," I said with a nod, understanding their choice all too well. Even as we spoke, our virtual avatars were likely working right beside them as they worked to settle all the new arrivals in their new home, as well as serving as a warning system to alert us if something happened in game. Turning around to the apartment behind me, I called out to the two missing members of the group. "Are we ready to start? Hopefully we can sort out a plan without it taking too long."

"We're ready," Misha's voice echoed out from the kitchenette a moment before she and Heron appeared and made their way over to us, grabbing a pair of chairs from the table as they joined us.

"Okay," I began, shifting myself around to look between Sonia and George displayed on the screens before me. "So, today turned out a bit more...*exciting* than any of us had anticipated, and I think we need to regroup and make sure that we're all on the same page."

"*I'll say*," Sonia agreed enthusiastically.

"You mean the page where there's a giant Ley Line under Aldford that may explode at the drop of a hat? Or the page where you told Aldwin that you want to found an entirely new nation and give us even more work to do?" Peter asked sarcastically clearly enjoying the opportunity to give me a hard time. "Because forget *page*, I don't think I'm even in the same *book* as you!"

"Peter is right here, Marc. We were barely gone for *three hours,*" Deckard chimed in, leaning forward on the couch so he could see me as he spoke. "Couldn't you have waited a few weeks before giving us *two* impossible tasks and embarking on a path to piss off a neighboring nation on the edge of war?"

"We were blindsided," Misha replied, coming to my rescue. "Stanton just *appeared* and roped us into his meeting, as it was, it was lucky Marcus was in the right place to even meet him."

"Unless his timing was calculated *to* include Marcus," Heron added, having heard all my suspicions of Stanton's honesty.

"God, thinking like that is going to give me grey hair," Zach commented with a sigh. "Or give me ulcers."

"I know a lot happened really fast," I said, shifting myself in my seat so I could look at the group while still seeing Sonia and George on the screens. "And maybe I overstepped with the whole nation idea, but in the span of a day, our original plan of '*Let's settle the newcomers and build up Aldford*' turned into '*Hey, there's a magical time bomb under your town, and by the way, a war is coming. Oh and also your town may be annexed if it doesn't explode first*'. We need to come up with a better long-term plan and assume the worse."

"And the best way to do that is to figure out what Stanton's real motivations are," Sonia suggested confidently. "If he's hiding stuff from us, either about the Ley Line or his plans for Aldford, confirming that will go a long way to helping us to do what needs to be done."

"Well, I don't think we'll be able to trap him in wordplay or get him to contradict himself," I said considering Sonia's idea. "He's too crafty for that."

"You're thinking about it the wrong way, Marcus," Sonia replied with another shake of her head on the big screen. "The Adventurer you met, Lazarus, told you that Stanton isn't telling the truth. Make *him* prove it. Tell him to send us his raw feed of what he said about Stanton. It's impossible for someone to forge and CTI has no restrictions about sharing it after the time limit is up."

"*There's an idea!*" Peter replied enthusiastically.

"I hadn't considered taking a meta approach to getting Lazarus to prove what he said," I commented thoughtfully as I reached out to grab a tablet that was sitting on a nearby end table and brought up a search. "Maybe we can see if he's posting his feed anywhere right now and save us some time..."

"While Marc does that, I want to talk a bit more about this whole 'founding a nation idea' that he had," Heron stated.

"As great as it would be. It seems a bit beyond our reach right now," Peter jumped in immediately. "I mean as it is we're struggling to find a place to house anyone, let alone let more people in."

"Actually, that's my point, I kinda think it is within our reach," Heron said, looking around the group as he spoke. "Sure, we're nowhere near ready to elect or crown someone and declare ourselves a sovereign state, but we can at least start preparing the groundwork to do so."

Heron paused to collect his thoughts and nodded his head towards Deckard and Zach. "Remember when we passed that *Hallowguard* guild in the wild today? They were off on their way to carve out their own settlement somewhere towards the North East, far away from Aldford."

"Yeah, I remember them," Deckard replied. "Wish they stayed with us; they actually knew what they were doing.

"They did seem like a decent bunch, smart too," Zach agreed with a nod. "But what does that have to do with anything?"

"It has *everything* to do with it," Heron stated. "If they manage to survive and form their own settlement, then we'll be in a position to support one another, trade goods and have mutual protection if something comes to threaten the area. Marcus's idea to invite more Adventurers into the area will only cause other settlements to spring up, or give the existing settlements more manpower to expand."

"If we can get enough Adventurers up here, then their presence in the area will make Eberia or The Ascendancy think twice before coming to poke us with a stick. With enough time, we can get enough of us working together to declare ourselves completely independent from either nation."

"I can see inviting more Adventurers working in some cases," Peter said. "But I think you're being really optimistic with the quality of Adventurer that we're going to get. There are going to be a ton of people who aren't going to play along. Look at what happened with Graves and Mozter. We're going to be inviting a hell of a lot of trouble right into our backyard."

"More trouble than Eberia or The Ascendancy?" Heron queried. "Let's face it, guys. As soon as that war starts, we're going to be completely cut off from Eberia for who knows how long, and while we're far away, there's nothing stopping The Ascendancy if it decides to keep going westward at some point. The way I see it, we either start trying to make ourselves look too tough to risk bothering, or we pull up stakes in Aldford and try resettling somewhere else even deeper in the wild."

"Which would mean giving up our claim to the Nafarrian Ruins in the area," I added having been following the conversation while browsing for Lazarus's feed on my tablet. "And by extension our Æther supply. The chances of us finding something similar would be slim to none."

"That's why I think we should seriously look at digging in and seeing if we can get even more Adventurers out this way," Heron repeated, his eyes darting between Deckard and me. "Look, I know that I painted a pretty bad picture of Coldscar the other day, with all the infighting and banditry. But I took a quick scan of the newest feeds coming out of the major guilds in that area this last afternoon and a handful of them have mentioned that they are considering abandoning their holdings since they already know that The Ascendancy is coming. Don't forget, them thinking that was ten days ago. The situation may have gotten worse by now."

"A targeted...invitation would be a better approach than just announcing ourselves online or in our feeds," Peter agreed, still not clearly sold on the idea. "Have you seen any feeds from The Ascendancy's point of view? What are they doing? They have to have their own Adventurers too."

"There's a fair bit I saw, but not all of it useful," Heron replied. "A handful of Ascendancy guilds have set up their own settlements on the edge of their westward frontier and have focused around town development like us. There are also a few Ascendancy guilds that are actively raiding Eberian guild settlements, which then, in turn, do the same thing back to one of their settlements. It's hard to say what's really happening since there are just *so many* feeds to sift through. I could spend all day searching and not find anything useful."

"I'll say," I chimed in while scowling at my tablet, using my thumb to scroll downwards. "Apparently you can have multiple people with the same name in Ascend Online, and there are currently one-hundred-and-forty-nine different '*Lazarus Cains*' that are currently playing right now and posting their feeds."

"Anything from our incarnation of the name?" George's voice called out from the screen.

"I haven't been able to find anything that matches what I remember of him," I replied with resignation, turning the tablet off and putting it in my lap. "I managed to filter the list down by location, and it still didn't come up with any results."

"It was worth a try," Sonia said, her pale shoulders appearing briefly on the screen as she shrugged at me. "I think Peter has a good idea though with inviting guilds that have indicated they want to leave the Coldscar area. At any rate, they may seem the most likely to take us up on our offers."

"I meant that invitation more as an offhand comment," Peter said hesitantly. "I'm still not sure if this is the best idea for us. We've survived for the most part by being off the beaten path and hidden. If we invite a huge crop of guilds out our way, what's to stop the whole situation surrounding Coldscar to repeat itself? I watched the same feeds Heron did, and some areas are a few steps shy of a warzone there. We don't need that up here near Aldford."

"What you've seen are only snapshots of the area, Peter, so you probably don't know *why* it turned out the way it did," George said, a hand coming up to scratch his beard as he spoke. "I was there with the first wave of players and a lack of space combined with the terrain is what's causing all the conflict that you're seeing now."

"What do you mean?" Peter asked, cocking his head to the side. "I didn't notice anything particular with the terrain when I watched. It was mostly flat too."

"The outlying regions are flat, but how much of the area surrounding Coldscar did you see?" George asked. "Because the approach to the actual city is very hilly, and there are only a handful of safe routes to reach it, unless you fancy climbing straight up an escarpment.

"During the early days when the first guilds settled the area, they settled on top of the best routes that led to and away from Coldscar, which in turn forced newer guilds to settle further away from the city, or to find a new path through altogether. Some of the guilds decided that they didn't want anyone passing through 'their' domains," George continued to explain. "That led to really long travel times to and from Coldscar, if not cut it off entirely if a guild decided to close a route for a time."

"Which builds resentment and eventually causes things to snowball," Peter finished with a slow nod of understanding. "Okay, that does make sense."

"If Eberia policed the routes and ensured they stayed open, it might have ended up being a peaceful area," Sonia added. "But the moment you passed the city limits, they just didn't care and let the Adventurers run wild."

"We wouldn't have that problem in Aldford," I said. "The area surrounding us is flat and lush for miles, if not further. There's plenty of room for everyone to expand."

"Which again gets us back to the question of how we're going get the right sort of people to move up into our area," Deckard pointed out. "If we can get more people like those from *Hallowguard*, I'm on board, but I'd want it targeted to a select few. As it is, once entire guilds start moving out towards us, people are going to notice."

"I think you've lost me," Zach interjected. "How are we even going to convince people to come up here? Just cold call them? They won't know us from a hole in the wall."

"I'm not so sure, Zach," Misha responded. "You forget that we're ranked eight-hundred-and-ninety-ninth on the feeds. If we approach any serious guild and tell them that there's opportunity out here if they want to play by the rules, they'd be idiots not to take us seriously."

There was a brief moment of silence as Misha's words resonated with the group, everyone turning to look at her.

"Misha," Sonia was the first to speak, her eyes widening as she looked out from the screen. "That's brilliant!"

"Damn I forgot about that!" Zach exclaimed while rapping his knuckles on his forehead. "I keep looking for an *in-game* solution to all of this."

"We spend so much time playing, Zach, that it's only natural to," I replied, completely understanding his perspective. "I mean we've spent what? Maybe four days out of the last month in Reality?"

"If no one has any objections, I can put a list of guilds together that we could reach out to over the next few days or weeks then?" Heron asked while glancing between everyone.

"No problem with me," Deckard answered as everyone chorused in behind him.

"Well, I guess that solves our long-term problems," I said, feeling a bit better to have a plan in place. "What about dealing with Stanton and Lazarus in the short term?"

"First thing's first, we should do what Sonia recommended and get him to send us his feed," Misha replied without hesitation. "That way we can be *sure* about what Stanton is telling us, and just how much we can or should bring Lazarus into our planning. But in the meantime, I think we should just play along with whatever Stanton wants, but to also be sure to reinforce our independence."

"And if this Lazarus guy refuses to share his feed?" Peter asked. "Or if the time delay prevents him from being able to?"

"Then we keep them both at arm's length and do what's best for Aldford," Sonia suggested. "We still have a *ton* of work to do around the town, on top of training the recruits."

"There's also the quest I got from Stanton, wanting us to escort him to the Hub and Lake Ruins," I added. "If we show him the ruins, we might be able to get a better insight into what his plans are, depending on how he reacts to them. We're also stuck waiting a day for Lazarus and his group to log back in since they're taking their rest break tonight."

"If nothing else that'll give us a day to get more stuff finished around Aldford," Deckard said wearily while nodding his head at me. "Before we left, Marc, Léandre mentioned that he could use our help for the day tomorrow, he needs us completely dedicated to planning and crafting if we're going to get everything finished before his rest cycle comes up in a few days."

"That's fine," I acknowledged, silently happy that Léandre was so willing to take over so much of the building and development in Aldford. "I need to talk to him about getting the new forge and smelter in the Foundry finished too. He's the highest level stonemason we have, and I honestly don't have time to pick up a new tradeskill to catch up."

"You really want to try melting that mystery metal from the Tower, don't you?" Deckard commented, well aware of the troubles I had trying to smelt it.

"It'd be nice to," I said with a sigh. "We need metal badly as it is. I'm just hoping that with all the trouble it's giving me, it'll be worth it."

"Hopefully," the big man agreed.

"So, with all that stuff about Stanton and guild recruitment out of the way, is there anything else that we need to talk about for the night?" George asked from the screen, sensing that the meeting was starting to digress. "If not, I may go see about getting myself something to eat before our show starts."

"Oh, I forgot about that!" Sonia called out from the opposite screen, her expression becoming excited. "We're on again tonight too!"

"I think that's everything for now," I replied back to the pair, everyone else near me exclaiming their excitement for the upcoming show. "We can regroup once we have a list of guilds to reach out to, or get in touch with Lazarus."

"Sounds good to me! Have a good night, everyone!" George said giving us a goodbye wave before disconnecting.

"Same from me! Good night, everyone!" Sonia joined in as her eyes shifted to find me. "See you tomorrow, Marcus!"

"Good night, Sonia!" I called back with a smile just before she disconnected and vanished from the screen.

"We have thirty minutes before it starts!" Peter called out without missing a beat as he switched the channel to GameTV. "Get yourself sorted!"

Without another word, Zach, Deckard and Heron practically leaped off the couch as two of them rushed towards the washroom and another towards the kitchenette, leaving Peter, Misha and I staring at two men dressed in over-the-top, stylized armor, one being painted blue and the other red.

"Oh, I love this show!" Misha said as she leaned back on the couch and pulled her legs in close just as Peter turned up the volume.

"Good evening, gamers!" The man in red armor announced. *"Welcome to our second ever Ascend Online segment of 'Xtreme Deaths of the Week'! My name is Kenneth Spank N'Tank and this is my partner Vincent The Faceroller! We have an awesome show prepared for you tonight!"*

"Right you are, Ken! I really don't think our viewers are going to be disappointed tonight!" The blue armored man picked up seamlessly from his partner. *"For those of you joining the show for the first time tonight, get ready to experience the heaviest, bloodiest, and most 'Hydra-ist' compilation of deaths we've managed to find this week!"*

"That's right!" Kenneth exclaimed as he drew a large foam sword from his side and held it in the air. *"For our first hapless Adventurers of the week, we're off to the dark marshes of the Demon Wood! I bet this group wishes they paid more attention to that name now!"*

"Their loss is our gain, Ken," Vincent quipped as the scene shifted into someone's feed, revealing a pitch-black bog in the middle of the night.

"Hey, Misha, Marc, you want a beer?" Deckard's voice called out from behind me a heartbeat before a loud roaring sound filled our small apartment.

"Yes, please!" Misha answered, not taking her eyes off the screen.

"Yeah!" I shouted back, trying to make myself heard as a flash of scales appeared on the screen, followed by a wave of fire and screaming. "On second thought, bring me *two* beers!"

"I think I'm going to need them after watching this!"

Chapter 15

Tuesday, March 12th, 2047 - 9:57 am
Aldford – The Arena

"Hah!" Alistair grunted as he swung his axe in a vicious swing towards me, giving me barely a second to react to the attack as Helix's sword slammed into Razor's edge and held it firm, trapping the blade on the opposite side of my body.

No chance to avoid this, I mentally noted as I reached up towards Alistair's descending axe while simultaneously preparing myself for the pain that was about to come. My hand caught the haft of the Adventurer's axe and pushed against it, slowing Alistair's attack before it could build enough momentum to completely ruin my day.

With a flash of searing pain, I felt the cool edge of the axe graze my shoulder, carving through a layer of flesh and muscle as it bit through my exposed skin, instantly making me regret that I agreed to this bout without my armor.

"Damn it!" I couldn't help but curse softly through clenched teeth, forcing myself to focus as I yanked sharply on Alistair's axe while simultaneously lunging closer towards him.

Forced to step forward or lose his weapon, Alistair chose to doggedly hold onto his axe as my grip pulled him off balance and towards me, giving me the opportunity to twist away from Helix and sink my knee deep into his stomach. The blow left him gasping, allowing me to easily step around him and shove him into the tall Arakssi, who called the match, after seeing that his sparring partner was unable to continue.

"Hold!" Helix called as he shifted his weight to catch the now retching Alistair, who clutched at his stomach.

"*Hold,*" I echoed meeting Helix's eyes, signaling that I understood that the match was over. "That was pretty good this time around, Alistair!"

"That was pretty good!" Cerril's voice shouted from the edge of the Arena, prompting me to look up and see that both he and Huxley had been watching the sparring match.

"Should have let go," the blond-haired man wheezed in Helix's grip, before descending into a coughing fit.

"Here," Helix offered a moment before muttering under his breath and touching Alistair with a glowing hand. "Better?"

"Loads, *thanks*," the Adventurer acknowledged as he straightened his stance and looked towards me. "I tried for too heavy a hit and should have let you have my axe after you caught it."

"Maybe," I replied while slowly flexing my wounded shoulder. "If you were a bit stronger, nothing I did would have mattered. Your timing on the attack was near perfect."

"Lyrian sspeaks the truth," Helix told Alistair, nodding empathetically. "Your ssskills have come a long way in a short amount of time, plus, unlike many, you have no fear of being hurt. It is often the mossst difficult thing we need to teach recruits."

"Pain is an excellent teacher," Alistair stated with a knowing nod, before indicating his armor, the very same that Mozter was wearing two days earlier. "But I am still fighting against you being fully geared out, while you're in a pair of pants and bare-chested."

"And you're a Priest with a melee build," I replied to Alistair despite knowing where he was coming from. Scoring a hit in a practice bout didn't mean much when your opponent was practically naked, but at the same time, it was the only way to keep the fight as fair as possible while I was personally training the newest member of Virtus. "Plus, Helix wasn't allowed to do anything more than mess with my guard. If it were a no holds barred fight, the two of you working together would have put me down easily."

Given what had happened with Mozter, I felt that personal training was the least I could do for Alistair, going as far to give him the Spellsword's armor that I had won after making a few of my own adjustments to it, and crafting him a brand-new axe to go with it.

"In any case, you should have a chance to catch up today while we're out and about," I told the man as I motioned for him and Helix to step off the Arena grounds towards where Cerril and Huxley were standing, seeing that there was another group of Adventurers lining up for their own match. "Assuming Stanton and his pet mages ever get their asses moving…"

"They *are* remarkably late," Helix agreed as he turned to look towards the Town Hall. "Of coursssse we are just lowly commoners and cannot presume to tell our betterssss what to do with their time."

"*Right*," Alistair snorted.

"Hey guys!" Huxley greeted us as we came off of the sandy field, the man's face in a wide smile. "I'm surprised to still find you all here! I'd thought you'd have left hours ago!"

"That was our plan," I grunted as I waved a greeting at the two guild members. "Apparently Stanton likes his bed much more than he likes being productive in the morning."

"So it seems," Cerril replied, before giving me a shrug. "But in either case, we're happy to have caught you. I was hoping to bug you about our new crop of lowbies."

"Oh?" I asked, suddenly concerned. "What's going on? Is there a problem?"

"Nothing too critical," Huxley replied. "But a bit of a long term one we're going to need help with, especially if we're going to bring them up to speed and have them contributing to the guild sooner than later."

"They need new gear badly Lyr," Cerril told me. "The higher leveled players that you, Freya and the others are minding don't have it as bad, since they've been playing longer and have had a chance to upgrade their stuff. But the majority of the people Hux and I are minding are still using their starter gear, minus whatever scraps we've been able to pull together from the guild spares."

"Damn," I replied, reaching up to rub the sweat off my face with a hand. "I didn't realize it was that bad, will that affect your training today?"

"Well, we've tried to account for it, so it shouldn't," Huxley answered. "But once everyone starts getting their Base Classes and pushing past level ten, it'll start becoming much more noticeable."

"And slow us down," Cerril added.

"Alright," I said with a sigh, adding another item on my endless 'to-do' list. "I'll try and sort that out in the next day or so then. I have some stuff that I've been working on that I can hopefully find the time and materials to finish."

"We'll be sssure to contribute whatever we find today to the guild stores," Helix said to me. "*Assuming* we ever depart."

"Speaking of that, I think we've waited long enough," I stated, glancing up briefly at the rising sun, agreeing with the lizardman's sentiment as I turned to walk towards the newly built stands where I had left my armor for the morning. Amaranth being more than happy to guard it as he dozed nearby, lying in the morning sun. "I'm going to clean up, then go check on Stanton one more time. If he's not ready to leave, we'll get our groups together and go out for the day without them."

"Sounds good to us Lyrian." Cerril said, giving me a wave as I departed. "Good luck!"

The three of us, specifically, Helix, Alistair and myself, had thus far wasted the better part of the morning waiting for Stanton and the others to finally show up for their tour to the Hub and Lake Ruins, despite being told that we were intending to leave first thing in the morning.

I had hoped to get a nice and early start to the day, *three hours ago,* so that we could make the best use of daylight and still have time to do something once we got back. But it seemed that neither Stanton nor Samuel or Quincy were inclined to get moving this early in the day. With a sigh, I walked past the stands and my sleeping familiar to where a large bucket stood and took the time to scrub the dried blood off my nearly healed shoulder before turning back towards the stand to dress myself.

As useful as it may be to train the new recruits, standing around here is a waste of time in the big picture. I couldn't help but scowl in frustration as I pulled on an undershirt, followed by my gambeson. Drace and I spent nearly eighteen hours crafting yesterday to make sure Léandre had enough building materials for the day today, and the two of us could easily put in another eighteen hours today just to keep up with the fervent pace of construction going on in Aldford. Not to mention the gear that Cerril and Huxley needed for our lowest leveled recruits. *But even if Stanton drags his feet in visiting the ruins today, we have to go out anyway… we're getting damned close to running out of food.*

An unfortunate side effect of tripling our population without adequate preparation or forewarning of their arrival was its impact on our food stores. In the handful of days since the new settlers had arrived, we had practically devoured the entirety of our stores and were in danger of not having enough to go around if there was an emergency.

In hopes of solving that, we had decided to split the Adventurers that had been recruited to Virtus into three groups and lead them out into the wild to replenish our supplies. All the while putting them through their paces and throwing them into the most vicious creatures we could find.

The plan was for my group, plus Freya, to take two of the higher leveled groups of Adventurers with us to an area north of the Hub, while Helix, Cerril, Huxley, and a handful the other guild members took our lower leveled recruits to the wolverine filled plains far to the south of Aldford. With any luck, we would be able to bring back a decent amount of meat and herbs to replenish the village stores.

But if we can get Stanton to come with my group while we do that, we can save ourselves half a day in travelling and hopefully show him how we fight. Maybe it'll make him reconsider any attempt at using force to annex Aldford.

Deep in thought, I picked up the last piece of my armor without looking at it, causing a copper ring and a length of chain to slide off it and spin in the air, before landing in twin puffs of dirt before me.

"Crap," I cursed softly to myself as I put the armor back on the stand and reached down to pick up the ring, placing it on my finger and feeling a surge of strength course through my muscles. "Still not used to having these."

It had taken me a while to bring myself to sort through all the loot that I had gained from the duel with Mozter, a part of me having subconsciously written off all the gear that he and his party had been wearing as being worthless when compared to my better quality weapons and armor. By the time I had finally got around to checking it, I was standing in the Crafting Hall preparing myself to salvage the pieces outright for scrap. After finally looking through it, I was surprised to find that two pieces of jewelry had been included in the spoils that Mozter and his companions were forced to hand over after his ill-fated duel.

After sifting through the bag, I discovered that there was a single copper ring in the collection of loot, along with a single bronze chain necklace, but it wasn't until I took a closer look at each of them that I realized that they had been enchanted. Picking up the fallen necklace, I shook the dirt off it and brushed it clean before hanging it around my neck, calling up the item's stats as I fastened the clasp.

Necklace of Physical Prowess

Slot: Neck
Item Class: Magical
Item Quality: Good (+15%)
Strength: +1 Agility: +1 Constitution: +1
Base Material: Bronze
Weight: 0.0 kg
Class: Any
Level: 12

If I can ever find some time for myself, maybe I could find out how to learn the Enchanting tradeskill, I thought idly while looking down at my hand and playing with the ring on my finger as I checked its stats as well. *I have seven more ring slots free, plus two earrings and two wristbands. If I managed to fill up each of those slots with similar items like this…I could end up being really overpowered for my level. Hell, we all could. But I remember Caius ages ago mentioning that Enchanting was an Advanced Tradeskill…whatever that means.*

Ring of Strength

Slot: Ring

Item Class: Magical
Item Quality: Good (+15%)
Strength: +2
Base Material: Copper
Weight: 0.0 kg
Class: Any
Level: 12

<Is it time to hunt?> Amaranth queried sleepily while opening a single eye to look in my direction, his mental voice clearly unhappy to be awoken.

"We've waited long enough," I told the cat as I equipped the final pieces of my armor and tightened the straps, ensuring that it would stay in place. "We're leaving either with Stanton and the others or without them."

<Finally!> My familiar stated, standing up from its curled position on the ground and arching its back into the typical feline stretch, his massive claws digging deep into the ground in the process. *<I was beginning to become concerned that I would spend the entire day asleep.>*

"You mean looking forward to it," I teased Amaranth as I looked back towards the four Adventurers, the group having turned to watch a ranked duel between two teams of three Adventurers that had taken the field in our place.

Despite the negative aspect to Mozter's antics the other day, the spectacle that he had put on had given birth to what was shaping up to be a very competitive dueling culture between the Adventurers in the town. Something that I approved of wholeheartedly, seeing that it had already led to several improvements around the training ground with a group of Adventurers having created several stands to watch the fights from. I had even heard of a handful of them talking about approaching Léandre to create a proper stadium to hosts large scale fights and duels one day.

<Perhaps. The sun is quite warm this day,> Amaranth admitted, my earlier quip completely going over the puma's head as I heard him sniff the air. <However, there will be rain coming today. I can smell it in the air already.>

"In that case, we really need to get moving," I said, accepting my familiar's prediction without hesitation as I tore my eyes away from the duel and began walking towards the Town Hall, Stanton having moved into one of the three rooms on the second floor.

Moving away from the Arena, Amaranth and I crossed the length of Aldford, watching countless other Adventurers and settlers rushing about the town as construction proceeded at a breakneck pace, all the newcomers eager to have a place of their own to get out of the massive tent.

If they keep this up, we might actually be able to get the majority of the buildings done by the end of the week, I noted hopefully, spotting Léandre's familiar form in the distance as he directed a group of Adventurers towards the newest building site, each of them carrying various building materials and supplies.

Continuing our walk through the heart of Aldford, we eventually passed by the now giant Ætherwarped oak tree that reached up far into the sky above, its azure branches and leaves almost perfectly blending in with the sky above. A large ladder stood leaning against the tree with a pair of Jenkins' helpers keeping it steady as they craned their heads upwards.

"Oh boy," I whispered to myself, following the ladder upwards and seeing Jenkins high up in the tree, leaning on a relatively low hanging branch. Shifting my route towards the ladder, my approach caught the eye of one of the men holding it steady.

"What's going on here?" I asked, hearing Jenkins curse from high above us as a tool slipped from his grasp and fell to the ground harmlessly several feet away from us.

"Trying to trim the tree," the man replied with a resigned look before wincing at the fallen tool. "But she doesn't want to be trimmed."

"Trim it?" I looked back up at the branch Jenkins was leaning against and noticed that it had grown long enough that it would start pressing up against the side of the Town Hall any day now. "What do you mean?"

"Take a looksee at the tool that Jenkins tossed," he said, just as a second tool came falling from the sky. "Or that one. You'll understand."

Giving the man a curious look, I decided to indulge him and walk over to the spot where I had seen the tools fall, keeping a mindful eye up above in case more came raining down on my head. A few seconds later I found myself holding a shattered hand axe, its edge completely gone and the metal dangerously close to completely fragmenting.

<It appears…shattered,> Amaranth said, looking at the axe curiously before pawing at the second tool that fell, revealing a bent saw whose teeth had been worn down to mere nibs. *<This too is damaged.>*

<It does,> I agreed, glancing upwards at Jenkins and seeing that he had abandoned his attempt to cut the branch and was climbing back down the ladder. *<Let's go see what's going on.>*

Grabbing the two broken tools, we returned to the base of the ladder just as Jenkins stepped off it, shaking his head at me.

"So now you see my latest problem," he began without any preamble, waving a hand at the tools I held. "I've broken seven different sets of saws and axes on the tree, trying to get that low hanging branch before it carves through the roof of the Town Hall."

"Damn," I replied with a wince. "You can't cut it at all?"

"Barely anything," Jenkins said with a sigh. "I could have sworn I managed an inch last night before breaking everything I had on me, but by the time I climbed up this morning, the tree had somehow *healed* itself, and I was nearly starting fresh."

"Really?" I exclaimed, looking over at the tree with curiosity. "That's interesting. I didn't know it could do that."

"Hrm," Jenkins grunted, clearly not sharing the same sentiment as me. "My last resort is to try and use the stonecutting tools I have on the tree, but if that doesn't work...I'll have to tell Aldwin that we're going to have to open up the roof of the Town Hall and give the branch a path through the building. It'll be less work for me to do that, than to forge a mountain of axes and saws to get through the tree, assuming I could find enough metal for it."

"Hopefully that'll do the trick," I told Jenkins. "If you need any—"

<The sleeping bear has awoken, and he approaches this way,> Amaranth interrupted as he turned his body away from me, at the same time making a raspy cough at the back of his throat.

Cutting off my conversation with Jenkins, I turned my head towards the Town Hall and spotted Stanton walking down the path and in our direction, with both Samuel and Quincy close behind.

"Sorry, Jenkins. I have to go. I've been waiting on him all morning," I said, seeing the man nod understandingly.

"Better you catching him now than him catching me while I'm trying to carve a length off the tree," Jenkin stated as he motioned for the men holding the ladder to take a break and took the tools I was carrying from me. "I've yet to meet him myself, but based on what others have said, I'm happy to postpone that indefinitely."

"If only," I replied, letting envy seep into my voice as I gave the man a wave goodbye. "I'll catch you later, Jenkins. Good luck with the tree in the meantime."

Pulling myself away from the smith, I moved to intercept Stanton and his accomplices, the elder man spotting as I approached and giving me a curt nod.

"Lyrian, I apologize for the lateness of the hour," Stanton told me in a thin voice as he leaned heavily on his walking stick. "An old...*injury*, flared up this morning and I found myself unable to rise for longer than I had hoped."

<He smells of sweat and fever,> Amaranth told me silently from my side. *<He hides how much discomfort he is truly in.>*

"Are you going to be able to travel today?" I asked, surprised by Stanton's rather ragged condition. True to Amaranth's words, the noble's brow was covered in sweat, and his balance seemed precarious at best. Either the man was a brilliant actor, or there was something indeed wrong with him.

"I will be fine," Stanton assured me. "A bit of movement is all I need to get myself back into form."

"A *bit* of movement is walking to the river and back," I told Stanton. "We are going on a hike for the better part of a day; we will be walking several *miles* before the day is out. You look like you're about to fall down."

"Perhaps a horse would be better, my lord," Quincy interjected, causing Samuel to nod in agreement.

"You cannot walk the terrain towards Crater Lake, or the forest beyond, in your current state," Samuel added. "We know from experience."

"If that is the case, I will take a horse," Stanton said, turning his head to glare at the two mages before looking back at me. "I trust we are ready to leave shortly?"

"I can have everyone ready within ten minutes," I replied while sending off a private message to Sierra, telling her that Stanton had finally woken up and was ready to leave. "But we can also take you another day if need be."

"Today will be fine," Stanton answered curtly. "I dare not waste time because of my own frailties."

"Quincy, while Lyrian readies his guild to leave, please inform *our* Adventurers that I wish for them to accompany us on our trip," the older noble continued. "They should be a part of this investigation as much as anyone else."

"Certainly, my lord," Quincy replied with a nod. "I will see to it."

"In the meantime, Samuel, would you fetch me a horse?" Stanton looked towards the other mage.

"Of course," the younger man acknowledged.

He's inviting Lazarus and his group to come with us? I tried to hide my surprise as I watched the pair scurry off to fulfill Stanton's orders. *We didn't discuss that earlier; it was supposed to be just Virtus escorting him. Unless he's finally realized just how outnumbered he and Veronia are...*

"We'll be leaving through the northern entrance, so we might as well start heading that way," I told Stanton. "Everyone else will meet us there."

"Excellent," Stanton acknowledged, taking a shaky step forward with his walking cane. "Let's be about it then."

<Bizarre how one who you believe is working against you sends his companions away and openly walks with you, despite being sick and lame,> Amaranth told me as we slowly walked through Aldford and towards the opposite end of the town. *<Should you wish to take his life, we could*

do so at a moment's notice, and he would be powerless to stop us, even armed with sorcery.>

<But we aren't sure that he is working against us,> I replied to my bloodthirsty familiar, realizing that he was still struggling to fully understand the concept of morality and how one couldn't, or at the very least, *shouldn't* simply kill anyone that annoyed him. *<If we killed him without proof or cause, the Justicar would become involved and punish us dearly.>*

<The Scentless One is concerning indeed,> Amaranth told me. *<He moves unlike any other predator I've seen, beyond what even you Adventurers are capable of. There is something...unnatural about him.>*

<He is blessed with the power of his god,> I said, happy to have steered the cat away from cold-blooded murder. *<He is supposed to ensure that all remains in balance and that any disputes are handled fairly.>*

<Blessed? God?> Amaranth queried, casting a look up at me as the three of us walked, Stanton completely oblivious to the conversation passing between us. *<These are new words to me. What do they mean?>*

<That's complicated to explain...> I told the cat while letting a small smile cross my face at his curiosity.

I did my best to explain the concept of divinity to Amaranth as we escorted a slow-moving Stanton towards the northern half of the village, the walk taking several times longer than it should have due to the lame noble's pace.

Thankfully he's taking a horse! I exclaimed mentally the moment that we arrived, seeing that Sierra had already organized our group, Donovan, and the Virtus recruits we were taking with us. *If he were walking on foot, we'd barely make it to Crater Lake by nightfall!*

"Hey, Lyr," Sierra greeted me with Constantine and Freya following closely behind her as Stanton limped off on his own towards Samuel, who already had a horse waiting for him. "What's up with Stanton? He looks a bit...*rough*."

"I'd say hungover," Constantine added quietly. "But Marlin hasn't managed to make a drop of alcohol yet."

"He said it was an old injury," I replied with a shrug, letting them know what I thought of that.

"*Sure,*" Constantine whispered sarcastically.

"We still up for our...*plan?*" Freya asked, raising an eyebrow in Stanton's direction as he mounted the horse. "We need to get the recruits used to our way of doing things and..."

"Yeah," I said with a nod, keeping my face steady as I glanced between each of them, our plan to show Stanton just what Virtus was capable of fresh in my mind.

"Good," Freya replied with a nod.

"One wrinkle though," I said to the group as I spotted Lazarus and his companions enter through the northern entrance of Aldford, escorted by Quincy. "Stanton invited Lazarus and the others to come with us."

"We knew that was a possibility when we planned this," Sierra replied as we all watched Stanton say something sharp to the trio before kicking his horse and trotting over towards us. "We still have them badly outnumbered though."

"We do," I finished, looking up towards Stanton as he came into range.

"My group will watch our rear as we travel, with your guild in the front," Stanton stated without any preamble. "Let us be off quickly. We've lost enough time for the day."

Giving orders already? I thought while looking at up at Stanton. *Maybe he isn't so sick after all.*

"Let's get moving," I said not answering Stanton directly while turning my head towards my friends and rolling my eyes where he couldn't see. "We *have* lost enough time for the morning already."

Stepping around Stanton's horse, I couldn't help but shake my head in resignation as I heard everyone sigh quietly.

"*Here we go,*" I whispered to myself.

Chapter 16

"So, I haven't had a chance to fill you in yet, but I checked out some of the feeds coming out of Eberia last night," Constantine said as we gradually descended towards Crater Lake, everyone having formed into their own clusters as we travelled, giving us some semblance of privacy from everyone else. "And one thing that Stanton and Lazarus have mentioned *is* true, Eberia is in pretty rough shape. If anything, they're both *understating* just how bad it actually is back there."

"What's going on exactly?" I asked as the rest of the group drifted closer to hear Constantine's reply.

"The whole city is practically on lockdown and at one another's throats," Constantine replied. "Each of the noble houses has set up checkpoints throughout the city and have outright banned other houses from entering certain districts. Regular citizens have to be searched before passing through a checkpoint, and they *really* don't like that."

"Damn," Halcyon commented from beside me. "What the hell happened?"

"I don't know for sure," Constantine said with a shrug. "From what I've been able to piece together from multiple feeds, there was a massive street fight about two weeks ago between three of the noble houses, which only happened because the heir of one house killed the two heirs belonging to the others in a separate incident."

"But with that being said, I can't find any stream that shows what happened between the heirs," he continued. "Nor anything else that details the lead up to the conflict. It was just as if it all happened at once. Plus, there are wild rumors of demons or devils being seen in the city, but nothing to back it up."

"With that many Adventurers in the city, it was probably a warlock just fucking around with people," Caius interjected.

"As it is, I can't imagine that there would still be that many Adventurers hanging around Eberia to see everything that's going on, let alone bother to post their feed," I said, understanding Constantine's frustration. "With all the action happening in Coldscar or further out in the wild, staying in the city is a waste of time."

"Lazarus and his group stayed in the city," Freya pointed out, her voice coming from behind me. "I've seen their gear, and it looks pretty good. I think they have to be around level thirteen or fourteen."

"I wonder what they did to level so close to the city then," Drace commented. "There was hardly anything higher than level four in the wild when we were out there."

"Who knows?" Constantine replied. "Maybe we'll get a chance to ask them today if Stanton ever strays more than ten feet from them, or through private messages later tonight now that they're logged in again."

"Let's just see how the day goes," I said as we finally reached the tree line and left the forest surrounding Crater Lake. "We haven't even reached the Hub yet, let alone seen how Stanton reacts."

Scanning the shoreline reflexively for threats as we left the cover of the woods, I was happy to note that nothing of interest caught my eye. Over the last couple weeks, there had been countless Adventurers passing through the area as they made their way to the Webwood to hunt, which had a fortunate side effect of thinning the population of creatures that once infested the area. Glancing upwards, I checked the trees high above, seeing that they had successfully recovered from the temporary spider invasion that had left them coated full of webs when hordes of spiders had fled from the Webwood, fleeing from their Ætherwarped cousins.

Satisfied that we could keep walking towards the Hub, we continued our journey around the lake's edge and eventually turned north to cut through the gradually shrinking Webwood, which while still infested with countless spiders, was no longer spreading out of control and in danger of strangling the entire forest.

"The memories in these woods will take a lifetime to forget," Donovan commented wistfully as we carefully negotiated our way through the forest, only spotting a handful of spiders that the new Adventurers eagerly dispatched.

"That they will," I heard Samuel add, his voice sounding remorseful as he spoke. No doubt remembering the rest of the Mages Guild Expedition that had been kidnapped by goblins.

With those memories now at the forefront of everyone's mind, the rest of our trip to the Hub proceeded in silence, save for the new Adventurers and Alistair that excitedly commented between one another as they explored the area for the first time.

"This is the first ruin we're stopping at," I announced after a while, turning to look back at Stanton who gazed up at the weathered statues that flanked the rocky entrance in awe. "Are you going to be able to make the climb up?"

"I will be fine," Stanton assured me as he moved to get off his horse, Quincy rushing to his side to aid him.

<He appears to have recovered rapidly,> Amaranth told me as we all watched Stanton slide off his mount as if born to the saddle, landing on the ground with a faint wince.

"It is a long way up *and* down," I warned the noble, despite turning my attention towards Drace and Sierra as I spoke. "Freya, Amaranth and I will show Stanton and the others around the ruin, while the rest of you get started on hunting. We'll catch up when we're done."

"Sounds good to me." Sierra nodded, her eyes shifting towards the two groups of Adventurers that stood nearby. "We'll be sure to put the recruits through their paces too."

"That sounds worrying," I heard Alistair's familiar voice mutter from somewhere in the group of Adventurers.

"*It should be*," Drace affirmed, flashing a devilish smirk towards the recruits who had formed two loose groups beside one another.

"Hunting?" Lazarus queried as he, Sawyer and Ransom formed up beside Stanton.

"For food and practice," Constantine replied. "We weren't prepared for all of you newcomers to arrive so suddenly and didn't have a chance to stockpile food. If we don't get more soon, we're going to start having problems feeding everyone."

"Ah," Lazarus said with a nod as understanding came across his face. "Makes sense."

"Indeed," Stanton added curtly while glancing sharply at Lazarus then back at Sierra. "Do not wait to begin your hunt on our account. We aren't certain how long our inspection of the ruin may take."

If that wasn't a dismissal, I don't know what is. I forced myself to keep my face impassive and turned to look towards Sierra. "Might as well get on it then. We'll see you all in a couple hours."

"See you then," Drace stated simply, before motioning to the North East with a big hand. "Let's get moving everyone! We have another walk ahead of us!"

A handful of groans filtered into the air as the two groups of Adventurers shifted away from us and began their journey away from the ruin.

"Oh no! Are those groans I hear?" Sierra called out to the two groups in mock anger. "Well, it looks like our nice walk just turned into a *run!* Let's go! Move your feet!"

"Poor bastards." Sawyer couldn't help but laugh as the two groups of departing Adventurers suddenly launched into a jog at the red-haired scout's urging.

"Just wait until you see what we have planned for them," Freya replied, giving Sawyer a knowing look.

"What—"

"There will be time for talking later," Stanton interrupted as he motioned towards the Hub entrance and began walking towards it, tossing the reins of his horse to Samuel. "Let us get a move on into the ruin. Samuel will secure my mount and join us when he can."

"Of course," Samuel replied, his voice clearly carrying a tone of annoyance with the task that Stanton had saddled him with.

I guess everyone has their limits, I noted as Samuel gently led the horse to a nearby tree where he could tie him up with a scowl on his face. *I suppose being used as a personal valet is his.*

"I will lead the way," Donovan stated firmly as he rushed ahead of Stanton. "The entrance is warded by my key."

"Warded?" Ransom asked as we all began to climb up the avalanche of rocks that led to the entrance's mouth. "Why did you have to ward it?"

"Because there is an exposed section of the Ley Line in this ruin," I replied, looking over at Ransom. "And we don't want to risk a wandering critter having a chance of falling into it...again."

"Wait, something fell into it before?" Ransom asked just as we reached the mouth of the entrance and Donovan began to unravel the protections that he had laid down several weeks earlier. "What was it? What happened?"

"A spider," I replied, seeing that everyone was looking at me with curiosity, including Stanton. "As for what happened, well, that's a long story…"

"This…this is amazing," Stanton's voice echoed through the massive domed chamber that formed the heart of the Translocation Hub, everyone else save Donovan, Amaranth and I echoing wonders of amazement as the four mages directed several glowing balls of light through the air.

"This place is huge," Sawyer said, glancing between me and the wide-open room. "Do you have any idea what it may have been used for in the past?"

"Not really," I lied, sticking to the story that we had agreed on, deciding against telling Stanton or any of the others the true nature of the Nafarrian ruin. "Save that it was something that drew directly on the Ley Line and was an important part of the city that was once here."

"I see…" Stanton said numbly. His attention still focused on the chamber around us.

"Given the strange magics we faced after Lyrian unfroze me, I have one theory that this place may have been a research lab of some sort," Donovan stated. "But, it could have very well been a gladiatorial ring, given the nature of the battle we had. It is impossible to say with certainty."

"There is nothing like this chamber in Eberia. At least, nothing that we've discovered," Stanton told us, fixing his intense gaze on me as he spoke. "There is so much that we have yet to discover, that has been ignored due to *The War* and a lack of Æther to conduct proper research."

"This place is certainly Nafarrian in origin," Quincy added as he looked up at the smooth stone above us. "I recognize some of the similar architecture...yet there are some...cultural differences perhaps? Not all of it is completely the same."

"Eberia...or whatever the Nafarrian city that is now Eberia is quite far away from here," I said, despite barely knowing anything about the Nafarr. "It's not surprising that their culture would be different."

"True," Samuel agreed. "However, we have some evidence to suggest that the Nafarr were able to communicate over vast distances. Something that allowed them to coordinate their forces against the Irovian Dynasty to great effect...even if it didn't allow them to win the war."

"Had they not lost access to their supply of Æther, they may have," Donovan said. "Whatever cataclysm befell the area here, spelled the end for the Nafarr back at Eberia. All of their technology depended on having access to the Ley Line. The moment it dried up, so did their chances of survival."

"Pity that the first moment we have an opportunity to study more of our city's history, another war looms to threaten our way of life," Stanton whispered bitterly, his sour tone sounding surprisingly genuine to my ears.

Stanton paused for a moment as he glanced around the chamber, his eyes following the floating balls of light as they illuminated the chamber, revealing the setting where the large crystal we'd been forced to destroy once was. With a loud sigh, he tore his gaze away from the sight, motioning towards me as he spoke.

"You mentioned that there were other chambers here," he said. "Was there anything left behind? Anything at all?"

"Nothing that we could find," I replied to Stanton as I motioned for us to slowly start making our way towards the far end of the chamber and down the incline that led to the lower levels of the Hub. "There are a number of hallways on the upper level that collapsed, likely due to whatever blast destroyed the city. It may be possible to excavate them in the future, but we haven't had the time or reason to do so just yet."

"As for the lower level rooms that were left intact, we didn't find anything of interest inside them, save for the Ley Line at the very bottom. Whatever Nafarr survived the destruction of the city, must have stripped the place before abandoning it...or the invading Dark Elves did afterward," I continued, indicating the collapsed hallways as we slowly began to descend deeper into the ruin.

"I wonder how large the Nafarrian city here was," Lazarus said, speaking up for the first time since entering the ruin. "If you dropped the city of Eberia where Crater Lake is, I think it would sprawl wide enough to include this place within its limits."

"I would give much to find out myself," Donovan added, nodding along with Lazarus's statement. "The little we've been able to piece together from the records and maps in Eberia, is that the Nafarr had three major cities across this region, with the other city much, *much*, further north. I can't help but wonder if it escaped the war unscathed."

"It may be worth a journey one day to see," Freya commented, sharing Donovan's excitement. "But it'll have to wait until we're settled, and Aldford is more established."

"Agreed," Donovan stated. "Though at the rate things are proceeding, that may end up being sooner rather than later."

We continued to talk amongst ourselves as we slowly descended deeper into the ruin. Stanton and the other mages commenting excitedly on everything around us, leaving both Freya and myself slightly taken back by their reaction. I didn't know what had exactly come over Stanton since entering the ruins, but his haughty and abrasive demeanor had vanished, replaced with a genuine curiosity of what this place once was and the people who had lived here.

I suppose you can have ulterior motives and still share an interest in something, I thought, keeping a subtle eye on the man as we reached the final approach to the Ley Line below, the air before us humming with magic. *But I suppose seeing the ruin may make him even more inclined to try and take it from us.*

"Hold up," I called out to everyone, bringing everyone to a stop just before they crossed over into the magic-filled area. "Past this point, you are going to be affected by Æther Sickness, and you won't be able to stay here long without risking your health. If you want to see the Ley Line, you'll have a couple minutes at best; then you should get back here to safety."

"And if we don't?" Lazarus asked from behind me.

"Then you risk being transformed into a ghoul," Quincy said softly, his gaze landing on me as he spoke. "Or…"

"You end up looking like me," I finished, meeting the mage's eyes without flinching, knowing exactly what was going through his mind. "And I assure you, how I look is the absolute *best-case* scenario that prolonged contact with Æther will get you."

"*Noted*," Lazarus replied, his gaze dropping down from my face as he looked at my withered body.

"Let us see," Stanton said eagerly, taking a step forward down the final ramp. "I have come too far to leave without seeing the Ley Line."

"I pray that is all we see," Donovan muttered as we all moved to follow the noble. "And that no new horror is waiting for us. I still find my dreams plagued by nightmares about what we found here before..."

Moving in silence we descended into the bottommost room of the ruin that housed the Ley Line, everyone save Amaranth and I audibly grunting as we entered the Æther filled area, causing their stomachs to clench with nausea.

<*I had forgotten how pleasant this energy was,*> Amaranth told me while purring contently as we all walked towards the Ley Line. <*If I did not know better, I would think I was lying out in the sun.*>

<*It certainly feels better than the last time we were here,*> I admitted to the cat, feeling my body begin to subconsciously draw on the Æther in the room, causing my skin to tingle underneath my armor. In the time it took us to cross the room, I felt the exertions of the day fade away, leaving me staring down at the Ley Line as if I had slept for the entire night, my body practically trembling with energy.

"So, this is it," Stanton stated in a weak voice, his free arm curling itself around his midsection as he spoke. "A Ley Line, and more Æther than I have ever seen in my life."

"All the Æther ever created in Eberia would not match what courses through this river every second," Donovan said in a tight voice, clearly feeling the effects of Æther Sickness as we all looked down at the azure river that had carved a channel through the floor.

"This—oh!" Samuel's words died in his throat as he looked up towards me, then flinched in surprise, his eyes going wide. "Lyrian, what are you doing?!"

"What?" I looked at the mage with confusion, seeing that everyone else was staring at me, their eyes wide. "I'm not doing anything, just standing here."

"Lyr, your eyes...the veins on your face," Freya whispered worriedly. "They're all *glowing*."

"*Oh*," I breathed, feeling slightly embarrassed as I suddenly understood everyone's reaction. As it was, my gaunt appearance was enough to unsettle someone, let alone have everyone see the veins under my skin begin to glow. "Another side effect from my Ætherwarping, I guess."

"Does it hurt?" I heard Sawyer's shaky voice ask as he took a step away from the Ley Line to get a better look at me.

"No," I replied, shaking my head. "I feel fine. *Great* even."

"A curious affliction," Stanton said while inclining his head away from the Ley Line to look at me. "But perhaps we should heed Lyrian's earlier warning and retreat from this room before the sickness affects us any further."

A chorus of assent rose from Stanton's statement, everyone happy with their momentary glimpse at the river of Æther.

"I'll be right behind you all," I called, remembering something I wanted to do the next time I visited the Ley Line and turned my attention back to the river of Æther, Amaranth moving to join me by my side. "I just need to do something first."

Hearing everyone leave behind me, I raised my hand and slowly pulled the gloves I was wearing off, immediately being greeted by a spidery network of glowing veins that crisscrossed my palm.

I can only imagine how my face looks, I couldn't help but think as I clenched my hand into a fist and relaxed it, trying to force myself past a familiar wave of self-consciousness due to my warped appearance. Focusing on what I had come here to do, I reached into my inventory and pulled out one of the several [Large Bronze Jugs] that I had crafted late last night and knelt down towards the Ley Line, keeping a tight grip on the jug's handle.

"Hopefully this works," I whispered to Amaranth, who watched me curiously as I plunged the bronze vessel into the Ley Line and watched it fill full of the azure liquid.

It only took a few seconds for the jug to fill itself, before I pulled it out of the Ley Line and set it down on the ground beside me, a small tag appearing in my vision as I focused on the now full container.

Ætherfilled Bronze Jug
   Quantity: 1
   Item Class: Magical
   Item Quality: Average (+0%)
   Durability: 0/0
   Weight: 3 kg

"Doesn't look like it's going to melt or explode so far," I whispered to Amaranth, and I watched the Ætherfilled jug carefully, ensuring that it didn't do something strange before I put it back into my inventory.

<Were you expecting it to?> Amaranth questioned, regarding me warily with an azure colored eye as he backed away from the jug.

"Maybe," I replied with a shrug as I pulled out a cap and screwed the jug shut tightly, then pulled a similar jug from my inventory and repeated the process a second time. "I don't know. It seems like it is going to be fine."

<I believe I will wait for you from a distance,> my familiar said in a nervous voice, putting even distance between me and the Ley Line. *<Death may not hold sway over me any longer, but I am loath to repeat the experience once more.>*

"Stop worrying," I told the cat as I set the second jug down beside the first and capped it, pulling out a third from my pack. "I'm almost done."

<Just how many of these vessels are you filling?> Amaranth asked, a worried croak coming from his throat as I finished filling the third jug and pulled out a fourth. *<I must know how wide a berth to give you for the rest of the day, in case you erupt.>*

"Just one more, *scaredy cat*," I told Amaranth with amusement as I filled the final jug and capped it. Standing up from my crouched position over the Ley Line, I turned to look at the four large containers that I had filled with Æther, each of them standing on the ground without any visible reaction. "That should hopefully be enough for what I'm planning."

<And what would that be?> The azure-furred puma asked me from his sitting position halfway across the room.

"My next crafting project."

Chapter 17

It was late afternoon by the time Stanton, Quincy and Samuel had had their fill of exploring and searching through the Translocation Hub, the trio having gone through nearly every inch of it with the new Irovian Ætherscopes. For hours, the three were completely enthralled with researching the ruin, and just as I was starting to get concerned that we would have to make the trek back to Aldford in the dark, Stanton called an end to their initial survey, citing that as interesting as the ruin was, he didn't believe that it had anything to do with the Ley Line rupture, and that any further exploration would have to be done at a later date when they had more time and less pressing matters to attend to.

"Almost done," Donovan said to me, bringing me back to the present as Freya and I stood at the mouth of the Hub's entrance, watching him weave another ward into being, sealing the place from uninvited visitors.

The last thing any of us needed was having another creature falling into the Ley Line and getting warped into some sort of monstrosity that would terrorize the countryside.

"No rush," I replied to Donovan as I scanned through a pair of quest updates that had appeared in my vision a few moments earlier.

Quest Update! The Ruptured Ley Line!

You've shown Lord Stanton and his retinue the Ancient Transport Hub and allowed them to explore it freely. However, based on your suspicions from [Statecraft, Deception and Veracity] you have decided to keep its true purpose hidden from him and his group.

With one ruin explored and nothing that could help you pinpoint the ruptured Ley Line, Stanton has now requested for you to take him to the Crater Lake Ruins.
Escort Lord Stanton to the Ancient Transport Hub: 1/1
Escort Lord Stanton to the Crater Lake Ruins: 0/1
Ley Line Sealed: 0/1
Difficulty: Legendary
Reward: Experience & Renown
Penalty for Failure: Aldford and the surrounding region will be destroyed.

Quest Update! Statecraft, Deception and Veracity!

After showing Lord Stanton the Ancient Transport Hub, you've noticed that Stanton shares a genuine interest in Nafarrian lore and history. But despite that, you've noticed him bearing an abrasive and abrupt attitude towards Lazarus and his other companions.

It is clear that there is more going on under the surface than first glance would suggest.
Collect more information before making a decision!
Evidence supporting the Adventurers' story: 1/?
Evidence supporting Stanton's story: 1/?
Difficulty: Very Hard
Reward: Unknown
Penalty for Failure: Unknown

Dismissing the two updates from my vision, I couldn't help but feel frustrated with the second quest's update and its relative lack of substance. During our time exploring the ruin, I had hoped that an opportunity would present itself to leave the mages to their own devices and speak with Lazarus or one of his companions privately about obtaining their feed. But no matter what we did, one of the mages always seemed to be within earshot or needed to ask me a vague question I couldn't possibly answer.

It's almost as if they're purposefully trying to keep us apart or monitor our conversations, I thought, shaking my head as I watched Donovan complete the ward around the entrance.

"There, that should do it," Donovan announced, turning to face me with a weary expression and lowering his voice. "I've included a few…*tricks* in the ward this time around, should *someone* try to break it. No matter what they do to disenchant the main ward, there are other small wards that will ensure that we are alerted immediately."

"Good," I replied, nodding at Donovan before shifting my glance to Stanton and the others who were waiting at the base of the rockslide. "Hopefully, we won't need them."

"*Hopefully,*" Freya echoed as she shifted her spear in her hand and moved to start climbing down the rocks.

<The air has become heavier out here,> Amaranth told me as we moved to rejoin the group, the cat's eyes staring upwards. *<And the sky darkens in the distance. The storm tonight will be vicious.>*

Following my familiar's gaze, I saw the dark clouds on the northern horizon as they passed over a distant pair of mountains, remembering his earlier prediction for the day.

"It looks like there's a storm on its way," I told everyone as we reached the base of the incline, focusing my attention on the older noble who was looking in much better shape than he had earlier in the morning. "We need to regroup with the rest of the guild and start heading back before long. The other ruins are back by Crater Lake, and I'd rather not be caught out this far from Aldford in the middle of a storm."

"Having traveled through more than one thunderstorm on our way up here, I second that," Ransom said, watching the distant clouds.

"I agree," Stanton replied, his gaze wandering to the coming storm then back to me. "Your guild will take point once more and we will follow close behind."

Without another word, the ten of us split into our own groups once more, Freya, Amaranth, Donovan and I taking the lead as we used our Party Sense to navigate our way to the hunting ground that Sierra had picked out, with Stanton and the others following a few dozen paces behind.

"They like to make it clear that we're not part of their circle," Freya whispered to me after we'd been travelling for a while. "Close enough to work together, but not close enough to hear what they're saying."

"Yeah," I replied, casting a subtle glance over my shoulder, pretending that I was making sure that everyone was still accounted for. "Allies of convenience, I guess."

"Those are the only allies a noble like Stanton can ever have," Donovan said pessimistically, the man having been uncharacteristically quiet all day. "Why do you think I worked so hard *not* to be affiliated with a House? I've seen firsthand what happens when a patron pulls their support from someone they no longer need, and I wanted no part of it."

"I can imagine," Freya stated, her demeanor suddenly getting sharper as she scanned the forest to our right. "We have to be getting closer to where they stopped to hunt; I'm starting to see creatures on the tree line."

"They should be somewhere North East of us," I said, following Freya's eyes and spotting a pair of brown furred shapes running about the edge of the forest, a tag briefly appearing in my vision and pointing to the creatures.

[Greenwood Badger] – Level 14

Level fourteen?! My eyes couldn't help but open wide in surprise as I saw three more badgers bound into view, their heads popping up to look in our direction warily before scampering off out of sight. *This area looks to be even more densely packed and higher leveled than the wolverine-filled plains closer to Aldford!*

"I wonder how the rest of the guild is doing," I commented as we gave the badger-filled tree line a wide berth. "I'm a little jealous they had half the day to hunt, while we were busy standing around with Stanton. I feel like I'm behind again in levels."

"I hear you," Freya said with a note of amusement in her voice. "But we still do have *something* to look forward to once we get there."

"That's true," I replied with a smile. "I wonder how Stanton and the others will react."

"React to what?" Donovan asked, having not been filled in on what we were planning once we rejoined with the rest of the guild. "Is something going on?"

"We're hoping to put on a show for him and the other Adventurers," Freya told the man vaguely, sharing the same smile I had on her face. "To see just how far we can trust them in a pinch."

"A show?" Donovan repeated, a worried look coming over his face. "Lyrian, Freya, what are you going to do?"

"Don't worry about it, Donovan," I soothed. "Just be sure to have your wand handy for when it starts."

"When *what* starts?" the man asked, doing his best to keep his voice down.

"You'll know it when you see it," Freya replied unhelpfully.

"*Lyr—*" Donovan gasped in exasperation just as I cut him off.

"Oh, I think I see them!" I announced loudly, drowning out Donovan's growing protests as the forest beside us began to recede, revealing several people sitting around a large rock in the distance.

Moving with renewed purpose, Freya, Amaranth and I practically left Donovan behind as we put on a burst of speed, eager to rejoin the rest of Virtus. Scrambling, Donovan was forced to abandon his line of questioning in order to keep pace with us, but I couldn't help but notice that he had taken my words to heart and was now holding his wand in his hand, his knuckles clenched white as he glanced around nervously.

"Hey! You guys made it!" Constantine greeted us cheerfully as we approached, both he and Sierra sitting on top of the rock without a care in the world while six bloody, dirty and exhausted looking Adventurers lay in the grass surrounding it. "We were wondering if you guys would ever show up."

"It took longer than we expected," I replied with a shrug, seeing that Alistair was among the Adventurers resting, his armor badly scratched and even rent apart in places. "I see you're all having a productive day getting the new recruits in shape."

"*Ha*," Alistair grunted dryly while sitting up from his prone position after hearing my voice. "You may call having to deal with giant snakes falling from trees right on top of you, and vicious badgers popping out of holes in the ground to bite your ankles, *productive*, but if I didn't know any better, I'd call it *hazing*."

"It can be both," Constantine replied without missing a beat, his gaze shifting past me as Stanton and his group approached. "What level was your Perception skill when we started?"

"*Zero*," Alistair answered with resignation.

"And now?"

"Nearly level twelve."

"If that's not productive, may the gods strike me down!" Constantine declared mockingly, raising hands to the sky.

"And when you fed us those mushrooms?" Alistair asked as he forced himself up onto his feet, turning to look up at the rogue. "You said they were *fine* to eat."

"I said I *thought* they were fine to eat," Constantine replied, rolling his eyes. "And I was right, the red ones were."

"Only after everyone who ate a purple or green one vomited," Sierra added as she hopped down from the rock and down to our level, holding a fist-sized mushroom in her hand.

"You're not helping, Sierra," Constantine grunted as he followed her down from the rock.

"Not trying to help," she replied with a shrug, before turning her attention towards me and tossing the mushroom in my direction. "The forest here is filled with these red mushrooms, along with a few other types that aren't edible."

"That should definitely help with our food problem," I said with relief, catching the mushroom and bringing up its description. "How many have we found so far?"

Red-Speckled Mushroom
   Item Class: Herb
   Benefit: Unknown - Herbalism skill too low to identify
   Weight: 0.1kg

"At least two hundred in our group so far," she replied, waving a hand in the direction of the forest while giving me a sharp glance with a single raised eyebrow. "Plus, whatever the others end up bringing back."

"That's great!" I said enthusiastically, nodding to Sierra as I spoke. "That'll solve our food problems in the short term. Hopefully, the other group was just as lucky."

"They have been out there a while," Constantine chimed in, just as Sierra dropped from our party, sending our prearranged signal to the other members of our group that were deep in the forest. "Hopefully, they won't be too much longer."

"Is our food supply that dear of a concern?" Stanton asked, finally deciding to join the conversation as everyone spread out around us. "I have never seen a land as lush as this region...surely it would be easier to raise crops?"

"One day it might be," Constantine replied. "But growing our own food takes time. Time that we don't have after everyone arrived."

"Hunting is how we survive out here," I added as I re-invited Sierra to our group and watched the forest's edge, waiting for the rest of the party to appear. "We've made great strides so far, but it's going to be a while until the farms are up and running, then even longer until we're able to reliably grow things without a wandering creature threatening the farmers working the field and eating the crops."

"I see," Stanton said as if the realities of frontier life were new to him. "I didn't realize."

"There's a big difference between living in the city and out in the wild," Sierra stated. "We're truly on our own out here."

"It doesn't seem too bad to me," I heard Sawyer's voice say from behind me. "It's peaceful out here compared to the crush of the city. Not as many people around and rushing about."

"Maybe for you guys," I said, taking my eyes off the forest for a moment to look at Sawyer. "But from our perspective, our population just *tripled*. We—"

<*I hear shouting from the woods and many running feet,*> Amaranth's sudden mental intrusion coupled with a warning croak caused me to lose my train of thought as I processed what he had said and turned to look at my familiar, seeing that he had pressed himself close to the

ground with his ears flat on his head. *<Something very large is moving through the forest behind them.>*

"What's wrong—" Lazarus began to ask, a heartbeat before several thunderclaps of magic echoed from the forest, sending a rush of countless birds fleeing into the sky and out of the forest. "*Shit*, something must have happened."

"Looks like it," I replied slowly, watching the forest worriedly as several balls of magic erupted from underneath the canopy before vanishing into the sky.

Shit! I told them to pull enough creatures to stage a good fight in front of Stanton, not to annoy the entire forest! I felt my heart begin to race as the resting Adventurers all shot to their feet and formed into a group beside me. As Lazarus and his friends moved to surround Stanton, his horse began to whinnie nervously.

"What's going on?" I heard Samuel shout from behind me.

"It looks like the other group bit off more than they could chew!" Constantine called out as the shouts from the forest finally began to reach our ears.

"W-what are we going to do?" Quincy asked worriedly, his voice breaking as he spoke.

"What else is there to do?!" Freya spat as she fell in on my right-hand side. "Get ready to fight! They're coming our way for help!"

"They're coming *here?*" Quincy gasped as a single Adventurer carrying a bow rushed out from the forest ahead of us, immediately angling his flight towards us. "No—"

"*Shut up and draw your weapon, Quincy!*" Lazarus's bark from behind me silenced the mage's protests.

Springing with long, rapid strides, the Adventurer closed the distance between us, his voice arriving barely seconds ahead of himself.

"*Giant Snake incoming!*" he managed as he bent himself double, desperately gasping for air to fill his lungs. "We didn't know…"

"*Breathe,* Ameron," Sierra said as the elven Adventurer descended into a coughing fit as he tried to inhale and speak at the same time. "Slow down and breathe. Tell us what happened. There are snakes coming?"

"Big snake," Ameron managed while sucking in a deep breath, waving a hand in the air. "*Really big.*"

"How—" I started to ask, just as a flurry of activity from the tree line caught my eye and caused the words to die in my throat.

Bursting from the forest in a panicked mass, I saw the missing members of Virtus sprint out from the foliage, Drace's massive form leading the way, with both Caius and Halcyon on either side of him and the other Adventurers fanning out, half a step behind. No sooner did the group cover more than ten paces from the forest's edge, did a massive, twenty-foot-long emerald scaled snake launch itself out from the trees, hissing wildly as it chased the fleeing group of Adventurers.

"*Oh fuck!*" Sierra swore, moments before Halcyon's words reached our ears and made everything worse.

"*Shit! There are two of them!*"

Chapter 18

No sooner did we have a chance to process Halcyon's words than a second, grey scaled snake, even larger than the first charged out of the forest. The sudden appearance of the creature freezing all of us in place. Hissing with rage, the gargantuan, twenty-foot-long snake rushed after the fleeing Adventurers with blinding speed and charged ahead of them, effectively cutting them off from reaching us. In the span of seconds, a relatively peaceful glade had been filled with two absolutely monstrous sized snakes, both rising up high on their tails as they regarded their now captured prey.

"Ranged attackers, focus on the grey one!" Sierra shouted, recovering from the shock of the second snake first and seeing both snakes begin working in tandem as they corralled Drace and his group into a circle. "Give our guys a chance to regroup!"

With Sierra's voice snapping them out of their surprise, a ragged volley of arrows and magic sailed through the air and splashed against the grey snake's scales, causing the creature to recoil in pain and twist its sinuous body in our direction. A massive forked tongue flicked through the air as the snake then pressed itself against the ground and shot forward towards us, leaving its mate behind to deal with Drace's group.

"Melee forward!" I called out, Sierra's shout helping me push through my own initial wave of shock as I stared at the snake charging towards us and began issuing orders while drawing Razor. "Try to keep the snake's attention on you and buy time for the ranged attackers to wear it down!"

With no better plan for the moment, I decided to lead by example, taking the first step forward towards the oncoming snake, reflexively casting *Lesser Shielding* on myself as I desperately tried to figure out what I was going to do when the snake came into range. Focusing on the two massive creatures in hopes of getting a better idea of what we were up against, I saw two tags appear in my vision.

[Emerald Moss Snake] – Rare Boss – Level 14

[Grey Moss Snake] – Rare Boss – Level 14

They brought back Two Rare Boss creatures? I couldn't help but mentally curse at the other group, praying that we would be able to find a way to kill the pair without our whole group being killed, or more importantly, one of the NPCs who wouldn't come back to life afterward. *They were just supposed to pull a dozen or so creatures for us to fight! Not risk a complete wipe!*

As we sprinted towards the rapidly approaching grey scaled snake, a risky plan snapped into my mind, one that relied on split-second timing and one that I only had seconds to try and pull off before the opportunity passed.

"Doing something stupid!" I informed Freya at the same moment that I conjured and threw a weak Flare spell at the oncoming snake's face, immediately going on to cast *Jump* a heartbeat afterward. Sailing through the air with precision, my tiny fireball splashed against the grey snake's face, the spell too weak to do anything but get its attention.

Which was exactly what I wanted right now.

Wasting no time after seeing the snake's eyes fixate on me, I leaped high into the air, hearing Freya shout something I couldn't make out. Soaring through the sky, I felt nearly weightless as my spell practically negated gravity's hold on me, giving me the opportunity to look down at the snake and see the muscles in its body coil as it prepared to snap out at me.

Take the bait, I urged the snake as I felt myself reach the highest point of my jump before beginning my descent downwards. *Take the bait...*

Exploding with near blinding speed, I almost reacted too late as the snake launched itself up off the ground and into the air, its mouth opening wide as it sought to catch me in midair. At nearly the last possible moment, I triggered *Blink Step,* choosing a space in the middle of the air just above where I was now.

My world blurred into a spray of colors just as a loud snapping sound filled the air, leaving me staring directly into the snake's surprised eyes as I canceled my *Jump* spell and landed directly on top of its head, my free hand grabbing a length of bony ridge above its eye socket.

I can't believe that worked! The thought pounded through my head as the snake recoiled in rage after realizing what I had done and began to thrash wildly.

"Crap, on second thought, I didn't quite think this through," I wheezed as my chest slammed into the snake's head and knocked the wind out of me as I desperately tried to keep myself on top of the snake, refusing to let go of Razor in my other hand as it tried to shake me loose. "Can't hold on like this much longer."

Careful not to stab myself, I shifted my grip on my blade and thrust it downward into the snake's skull, hoping to either create a second anchor point on the creature's head so I could maintain my position or be enough of a distraction so that those on the ground could close without worry. Unfortunately for me, however, the snake's skull proved to be too strong for Razor to pierce, the tip of the blade skipping off the bone and carving a long bleeding gash in the process.

Cursing at my ineffectual attempt, I struggled to maintain my grip on the snake's eye socket and raised my sword for another attempt. But before I could bring my blade down, I felt the entire body of the snake recoil as something heavy charged into it from below, a savage feline roar reaching my ears, followed by the shouts of several Adventurers.

Spitting in pain at the attacks, the Moss Snake's head shot downwards as it attacked the tiny creatures causing it so much pain, forcing me to abandon my efforts at stabbing the snake's head, in favor of trying to maintain my grip. With blinding speed, the snake's attack brought me back practically to ground level, leaving me staring into Freya's surprised eyes as she spotted me holding onto the snake's head.

"*Lyrian!*" she managed to shout just before the snake rushed forward, forcing her to dodge out of the way or be overrun as it circled away from all the Adventurers crowding around it and rushed back towards its mate.

Clinging onto the snake as it retreated from Freya and the others, I found myself with a perfect view of Drace's side of the battle, seeing the emerald Moss Snake's head shoot forward with a burst of speed into the mass of Adventurers swarming around it, catching an unfortunate guild member in its maw. In one smooth motion, I saw it toss the now screaming man high into the air behind it before returning its attention to the group, leaving the Adventurer to windmill his arms uselessly in the sky then land with a bone shattering crunch.

"Oh damn!" I exclaimed in between breaths, not seeing the Adventurer rise from the snake's attack and feeling a growing numbness in the hand that clung to the snake's head.

I need to slow this guy down from rejoining its mate and give everyone else a chance to catch up, I told myself while pulling my body forwards towards the snake's brow and gripping Razor tight, another idea on my mind. *But I have a feeling this one is going to hurt...*

Before I could talk myself out of my decision, I pulled myself forward and swung my body over the snake's brow, looking down to see a large yellow eye gazing up at me.

"Forgot about me, did you?" I said to the snake, a heartbeat before I stabbed a crackling Razor into the snake's eye, managing to bury the tip of the blade into the creature's head before discharging a *Shocking Touch* into the snake, seeing a pair of notifications appear in my combat log.

You critically hit a [Grey Moss Snake] in a vulnerable location for 298 points of damage!

Your spell [Shocking Touch] critically hits a [Grey Moss Snake] for 102 points of electricity damage!

Screaming beyond pain, the Moss Snake recoiled, whipping its head so viciously that my tenuous grip on the snake finally gave up and I found myself flying through the air, before brutally crashing into the ground and bouncing through tall grass, hearing the sickening snap of bone as my elbow hit something hard and unforgiving. Vision blurring with pain, I let out a brief yelp as I came to a stop, reflexively cradling my shattered arm in close to my chest, the movement only serving to intensify the agony.

"Shit that hurts!" I breathed, the smallest motion of my left arm causing a wave of nausea to grip my stomach. Wincing in pain, I forced myself to take a deep breath and collected myself, seeing a warning alert appear in the corner of my vision, followed by an alert in my combat log.

You have fallen for 234 points of damage!

You have suffered a [Broken Arm], and the affected limb has been disabled!

"*Great*," I seethed through clenched teeth as I dismissed the alerts then forced myself up and into a sitting position, seeing Razor lying in the grass beside me and suddenly being thankful that I hadn't lost or fallen on top of the blade as I landed.

After sitting for a few heartbeats, I felt the pain of my injured arm fade from the forefront of my mind, giving me the clarity to look around the battlefield once more and see the two battles unfolding around me.

A glance to my right, showed the Grey Moss Snake a fair distance away from me as it continued to thrash wildly in pain, Freya and the others were on the verge of catching up with the creature, which was beginning to look worse for wear, with blood streaming from countless broken scales and wounds. Focusing past the snake, I caught a brief glimpse of Stanton, Samuel and Quincy all standing where we'd left them, watching the battle unfold completely frozen in place.

I guess that tells us everything we need to know about them, I thought with a scowl as I shifted my head in the other direction, seeing that the battle with the Emerald Moss Snake wasn't proceeding as well in comparison. I saw several unmoving bodies in the distance, with the smaller and agiler serpent having coiled itself around a distant figure and had begun squeezing the life out of it while lashing out at any Adventurer that drew within range.

Shit, that's Drace! I realized as my eyes recognized the familiar armor in the middle of the snake's coils. *Have to see if I can help them before it's too late! The others seem to have the grey snake under control for the time being.*

Pushing myself up onto my feet, I rushed towards Drace and the Emerald Moss Snake, each and every step causing my arm to flare with pain. As I approached the battle, I saw both Caius and Halcyon standing on either side of the snake, the pair throwing balls of magic at the creature with little effect, with several of the other recruits trying to close into melee range but unable to get past the nimble creature's hissing head.

"Lyr!" Caius called out without looking at me, sensing my arrival via Party Sense as he threw another ball of fire at the snake. "Watch out; it's venomous! It'll paralyze you if you get bitten, we've lost at least four to the venom already!"

"Damn, okay!" I called out, understanding now why everyone was hesitant to close with the creature. Raising my voice to the hesitating Adventurers, I barked out an order and continued my charge directly towards the snake. "I'm going to distract it! Rush the creature when you can!"

Not waiting for any acknowledgment from the recruits, I looked up at the Emerald Moss Snake's head as I sprinted, seeing its eyes fixate on me and mouth open in preparation to strike. Not trusting myself to get the timing right this time around, I decided to pre-empt the snake's attack and triggered *Blink Step*, the spell thankfully not needing a free hand to cast. With a familiar blur of colors, I teleported inside the snake's guard, my feet coming down on smooth scales as I reappeared just a few feet away from Drace.

"Lyrian!" The warrior gasped in surprise, his face completely red as the snake's muscular body attempted to crush him, the big man straining desperately to keep the creature at bay. "I could use a hand—*shit, what happened to your arm?!*"

"Don't worry about it!" I shouted back to the warrior as I stabbed Razor deep into the Moss Snake's coiled body that held Drace, throwing my hip against the hilt of the blade to drive it in as deep as possible. "Just be ready to move when it lets you go!"

"Don't have to tell me twice!" Drace yelled back at me as the creature spasmed from my attack and a loud hissing filled the air. "Oh fuck, Lyr! Dodge left!"

Taking Drace's warning to heart, I reacted at the speed of thought and threw myself to the side, yanking Razor free as I moved, barely a heartbeat ahead of the snake's snapping maw. Twisting to look behind me, I found myself barely more than an arm's length away from the bright yellow eyes of the Emerald Moss Snake as it rushed to attack me, its mouth opening once again to strike. Not wanting to end up as a meal, or even suffering a paralytic bite from the creature, I reflexivity swept out with Razor, catching the snake across the snout with the tip of the blade and slicing open a line of scales in a spray of blood.

Jerking its head away from me in pain, the snake aborted its attack, allowing me the opportunity to sidestep away and take cover behind the bulk of its body, slashing out with Razor as I ran, doing my best to make sure that the creature never had a clear view of me. Frustrated by my speed, the Moss Snake twisted the length of its body in an attempt to catch me, but was forced to abandon its efforts as the rest of the Adventurers finally arrived, their weapons landing punishing blows as they stabbed and sliced deep into the creature.

The battle then dissolved into chaos, as half a dozen guild members swarmed over the snake's coiled body, turning its pristine emerald scales into a patchwork of blood and gore. All I heard was magic thundering through the air as balls of fire seared into the snake's flesh, while axes, swords and spears flashed through the air, turning the ground crimson. However, for as much damage as we did, we weren't all able to escape the snake's wrath indefinitely.

Twice the snake managed to catch Adventurers too slow to move out of its path or pay sufficient attention to where its head was looking, resulting in one being bitten and left lying on the ground as the venom paralyzed her, the other being swallowed whole, vanishing down the massive creature's throat before any of us could react.

"It's getting ready to run!" I heard Drace's distant shout filter into my mind as I carved yet another line into the wounded snake, keeping my eyes focused straight up at its head. "Lyrian, *watch out!*"

With the exhaustion of battle weighing upon me, Drace's warning took too long penetrate my brain, leaving me glancing away from the snake's head just in time to see its massive tail sweeping across the ground, seconds before it hit me.

For the second time in the day, I felt myself sailing through the air, reeling from the snake's powerful blow as I numbly considered my combat log, confused by the latest entry that had just appeared.

An [Emerald Moss Snake] kicks you for 155 points of damage!

The snake...kicked me? The weak thought floated through my confused mind a heartbeat before I crashed back into the ground, bounced twice, and slid to a stop once more, leaving me lying stunned for a moment as my vision blurred from the pain of the landing.

"Shit! Lyrian!" Caius's voice called to me what seemed ages later, his face appearing directly over me. "Your arm!"

"B-broke it earlier," I told the dark elf weakly as I tried to sit up, only to be forced back down by a steady hand on my chest.

"Hold on a second, Lyr," Caius ordered, taking a deep breath and moving his hand to touch my arm. "You don't look so great. Let me heal you a bit first."

"Sure," I said to the man dizzily as I felt a wave of energy shoot through me and the pain in my arm recede to a dull throb, the bones forcefully realigning themselves with a disturbing crack. "Thanks, Caius."

"N-no problem," Caius replied wearily, suddenly sounding exhausted as he spoke. "That's the best I can do right now. I don't like my chances of getting close to lifetap one of the snakes."

"I don't blame you," I told the warlock, feeling much better as I sat up. "I have been in close and got creamed twice."

<Where are you?> Amaranth's voice suddenly rang in my head. *<Their wounds are grave and they rally to one another for a last stand! Now is the time to strike at their throats and put an end to them!>*

<I'm on my way!> I told the cat mentally while pushing myself back up onto my feet, glancing at my stats as I stood.

HP: 487/737

Stamina: 249/670

Mana: 30/640

Damn, I'm running out of mana, I thought, just realizing now how fast I'd been burning through it. *Not being able to regenerate anything at all is proving to be a colossal pain...*

"Let's get back to it," I told Caius as I twisted towards the sounds of battle, seeing that both of the snakes had broken free of their respective engagements and were now fighting side by side a short distance away from us as the surviving Adventurers rushed to form a loose circle around the pair. "Looks like the snakes are just about done."

"I hope so," the warlock replied wearily as he hefted his skull-tipped staff in the air. "I'm just about out of mana."

"Me too," I told Caius as we broke into a run, seeing his worried look out of the corner of my eye. Everyone in the party knew what would happen to me if I happened to run out of mana. "Should be fine though."

The two of us rushed closer to the battle, which had fallen into a momentary lull as everyone adjusted to the snakes positioning, only a handful of arrows and spells flying through the air. The two snakes hissed angrily, their heads whipping through the air as they snapped at the closing ring of Adventurers, slowly realizing that they had bitten off more than they could handle, their scales now covered in countless wounds and blood.

"Freya!" I called out as Caius and I rejoined the group, relieved to see that the blonde-haired woman appeared to be relatively unscathed, standing beside Lazarus and Sawyer. "How are we doing?"

"We've lost three so far, with two more seriously injured. I just sent Alistair to heal them and get them back on their feet." Freya wasted no time in replying, a note of relief evident in her voice as she turned to look towards me, blood and dirt covering her face. "The grey one may be slow, but he hits *really* hard."

"The green one has a paralytic bite," Caius informed. "We've lost one for sure, with four bitten, we won't know for sure if any of the bitten ones have survived until after the battle."

"*Great*," Lazarus spat, turning to look at me with a hard expression and waving a rather impressive looking glass greatsword at the two snakes. "We need to take them down, *now*, before this gets any more out of hand."

"No argument from me," I replied while scanning the area and seeing the rest of the party and a handful of the still standing recruits spread out loosely around the two serpents. "Looks like everyone is as ready as they're going to get. Let's go finish this."

"Wait," Sawyer interrupted as Freya and I took a step forward. "That's it? We're just going to charge them and hope for the best?"

"You have a better idea in mind?" Freya asked impatiently.

"Literally anything less suicidal maybe?" He grunted.

"Enough, Sawyer," Lazarus growled as he stepped up beside Freya and me. "It's not like this will be our *first* suicidal charge."

"*I know!*" the red-armored man exclaimed. "Why do you think I'm trying to avoid another one?!"

"You lived through the last one," Lazarus said dismissively as he glanced over at me. "Let's go."

"*Right*," I replied taking another step forward as I broke into a sprint, mentally shaking my head at the pair.

Leading the charge into battle for the third time, I felt a familiar calm descend over me as I focused on the two Moss Snakes, seeing their heads snap in our direction as they spotted us.

"Spread out!" I shouted, the four of us quickly putting distance between one another in hopes of forcing the snakes to choose between two of us to attack, giving the other two a chance to close with the creatures unmolested.

Fortunately for all of us, it worked. Though unfortunately for me, it was because they both decided that I was the most appealing target amongst the charging attackers.

Oh shit! My mind raced in panic as I instinctively threw myself forward into a somersault, diving under the green snake's sweeping maw and rolling back up onto my feet, only to find myself staring point blank into the open mouth of its mate.

My mind blanked as I tried to turn and twist my body out of the way, reflexively casting *Blink Step* in an attempt to get away. But instead of seeing a blur of colors as I shifted locations, a bright red message appeared in my vision, followed by a sad chime.

You do not have enough mana to cast this spell!

I'm screwed, I realized with a sickening sensation, time slowing down just enough for the thought to cross my mind, my foot coming down on the ground as my momentum continued to carry me forward. *There's no way I can dodge in time.*

But despite the futility of my situation, I still tried, awkwardly planting my other foot on the ground in an attempt to sidestep my impending doom, only to see the gargantuan snake adjust to follow me, causing the little hope I had in my chest begin to die. But, a heartbeat before I was about to accept my fate, a streak of azure caught the corner of my eye, racing across the ground faster than I could follow. With a feral roar filling the air, I caught a single glimpse of Amaranth as he left the ground and slammed into the snake, the impact of nearly eight-hundred pounds of angry puma causing its head to snap awkwardly to the side, succeeding in only clipping my shoulder, before slamming into the ground with a crash.

<You run about like a blind kitten who wishes to be eaten!> Amaranth's mental voice thundered through my head as I spun from the snake's glancing blow. *<Assist me before it regains its senses!>*

Stumbling wildly, I struggled to maintain my balance as I ground to a halt, wincing as pain flared from my shoulder. Glancing upwards towards the snake, I spotted Amaranth on the side of the snake's head, having sunk all four claws into the creature's face as he brutally rent apart scales and flesh, going as far as to expose bone in places.

<Thanks, Amaranth!> I called to my familiar, and I forced myself to move, not wanting to waste his timely intervention that would have surely seen me respawning back in Aldford.

Rushing in close to the panicking snake as it began to thrash under Amaranth's vicious assault, I took advantage of the cat's distraction, thrusting my blade deep into the base of its head, just under its jaw as it swung towards me.

Aided by the snake's motion, I felt Razor grate against bone as it pierced through scales and sunk into flesh, stopping only when the hilt wouldn't allow it to go any further.

Freezing in surprise from the attack, the snake let out a strangled cry before desperately trying to lift its head further away from the ground, burdened by the oversized puma still latched onto its face. Unable to pull Razor free, and too stubborn to let it go, I found myself lifted off the ground as the snake rose to nearly its full height, the motion forcing me to grab the hilt of my sword with both hands to keep myself from falling.

This wasn't exactly what I had in mind for today. The stray thought crossed my mind as I hung high in the air, holding onto my sword with my legs dangling in the air, feeling the flesh surrounding the blade begin to rip and tear, unable to support my weight indefinitely.

"*Damn it, Marcus!*" I cursed myself as I looked down at the ground and found it further away than was comfortable. "You just taught Alistair this morning about when to let go of his weapon, and now you're hanging from a giant snake's throat because—"

I shut my mouth with a snap as I looked up at the snake, realizing just where I had buried my blade.

"That might work…" I told myself softly as I turned to look back down towards the ground with a grimace. "I suppose a little bit more falling damage won't kill me, *hopefully…*"

Taking a heartbeat to gather my courage, I gently pulled myself up, gripping Razor tightly until I was almost level with the hilt protruding from the snake's flesh. Taking a single deep breath, I then let my weight drop, yanking the blade with all my strength as I fell, the motion causing Razor to slice deep into the snake's flesh from within.

Almost instantly the snake roared in pain, its body trembling from the unexpected attack as the blade wreaked havoc to its throat. Wasting no time, I repeated the motion a second time, feeling Razor shift as it sliced through the flesh that kept it in place, a thick spurt of blood spilling from around the wound and onto my hands and face.

One more time, I thought, spitting out a mouthful of blood that rained down from above me, silently praying that I wouldn't lose my grip on my now slick blade, the snake now desperately shaking me side to side as it tried to dislodge me, to no avail.

Heaving one final time, I felt my blade carve through the final layers of flesh and scale as I split open the snake's throat, a torrent of blood raining down on me as I fell to the ground. Landing feet first with a heavy crash, I felt something snap in one of my ankles as I fell to the ground in a heap.

"Can't believe that worked," I muttered to myself, my hand instinctively gripping what had to be a broken ankle as I glanced upward, seeing the Grey Moss Snake flailing wildly in the air as it began its death throes. A torrent of blood gushed from its throat as it swayed drunkenly in the air, teetering from side to side before it finally lost its balance and collapsed to the ground with a thunderous crash.

<You slew it!> Amaranth called to me in a triumphant voice, the cat having jumped off the falling snake from an angle I couldn't see. *<Only one remains!>*

Before I could reply to Amaranth, a screeching cry ripped through the air, causing me to twist my head and look in the direction of the noise, spotting Lazarus standing on top of a length of the Emerald Moss Snake's body, his translucent sword cleaving a massive wound through its flesh. With something critical being damaged in the attack, the lower half of the snake's body immediately went limp, causing its bulk to collapse to the ground lifelessly. Flailing off balance, the upper half of its body swayed perilously as severed nerves refused to respond, sending the creature's head dipping towards the ground.

Sensing that the battle was nearly at its end, I heard a cheer rise up from the surviving Adventurers as a renewed wave of magic and arrows reached up to scour the mortally wounded snake, its body contorting wildly in an attempt to shield itself from the onslaught. As the ranged attackers continued to damage the massive creature, I saw a familiar blonde-haired figure race up the snake's drooping body, before leaping powerfully into the air, a gleaming spear fully outstretched before her.

With a wordless battle cry heralding her attack, Freya then slammed into the snake's descending head, her spear piercing through the creature's skull and deep into its brain, sending it crashing into the ground with a sickening finality, the rest of its body joining it a heartbeat after. Holding back my relief, I glanced at my combat log, looking for confirmation that the battle was over.

You have slain a [Grey Moss Snake]!
You have gained Experience!
Freya has slain an [Emerald Moss Snake]!
You have gained Party Experience!
That was too close! I breathed silently as the adrenaline in my body began to fade and was slowly replaced with the gnawing ache of countless bruises and broken bones. *That could have been much worse. As it was, we lost a good number of our recruits.*

"We did it!" A voice that I didn't recognize shouted from somewhere on the battlefield as the two massive corpses dissolved into nothingness, leaving a single large loot bag behind in their place.

A weary cheer rose briefly into the air before Sierra's words cut it off and brought everyone back to the present.

"We're not done just yet, Virtus! We have wounded still on the ground!" She called out to the surviving recruits. "Find and bring any injured to your group's healer and get everyone back on their feet! Then we'll have a reason to cheer!"

Barely seconds after Sierra's shout, I heard footsteps rushing behind me with Alistair's voice calling out to me as he approached. "Hey, Lyrian! I saw you take a nasty fall, are you okay?"

"Mostly," I told the priest, waving at my foot as he came around me. "Fucked up my ankle when I landed though."

"Well, I can fix that easily enough," he replied, reaching out to touch it with a glowing hand and channeling healing magic into it. "Anything else? I can't tell if that's your blood or one of the snake's."

"The snake's," I said while shaking my head at the offer for more help and slowly rising to my feet, seeing both Freya and Amaranth crossing the field in my direction. "But I'm fine otherwise, just a few bumps and bruises that'll fade in a few minutes. You should go check out the area where Drace's group fought the Emerald Moss Snake though, it had a bite with paralytic venom, so we may still have wounded survivors out that way."

"Shit! That's nasty!" Alistair acknowledged, grimacing at the mention of the venom. "Alright, I'll go take a look right now!"

Turning on his heel, the priest sped away from me and rushed out of sight, just as Freya and Amaranth came into range, the blonde-haired woman giving me an exasperated shake of her head as she met my gaze.

"Well, that was more than we bargained for," she said with a whisper, her eyes looking over my blood-covered face and armor. "You look like something out of a bad movie production."

"I can imagine," I replied dryly, feeling the sticky blood starting to thicken as it seeped deeper into the chainmail and gambeson underneath. I already wasn't looking forward to cleaning my armor when we got back to Aldford. "We were lucky this didn't go bad for us."

"It was a near thing," Freya agreed, her eyes meeting mine meaningfully. "But we did learn *something* useful out of it all."

"Yeah," I said, knowing that she was referring to Stanton's lack of participation in the battle. "We certainly did."

<He did not even attempt to raise his paw in defense of the group,> Amaranth stated with disgust as he began to lick a line of blood from his fur. *<However, we were still victorious. That is all that matters at the moment.>*

<I suppose so,> I replied to the cat, appreciating his simple perspective.

"At least there's one good thing about two rare boss creatures," Freya said, changing the subject as she inclined her head towards the loot bag that sat on the ground.

"Experience *and* loot," I answered, meeting her eyes with a smile.

"Everyone does seem to be fairly preoccupied at the moment," Freya noted, taking a step towards the bag. "We should probably go sort through it, so we're just not standing around while everyone works."

"I think that would be the fair thing to do," I said, following the woman towards the loot bag, the two of us wasting no time in taking a look what was inside.

Giant Snake Meat
   Quantity: 140
   Item Class: Common

Item Quality: Good (+15%)
Weight: 140 kg
Giant Snake Scales
  Quantity: 120
  Item Class: Common
  Item Quality: Good (+15%)
  Weight: 60 kg
Giant Snake Eye
  Quantity: 3
  Item Class: Common
  Item Quality: Good (+15%)
  Weight: 2 kg
Giant Snake Fang
  Quantity: 2
  Item Class: Common
  Item Quality: Good (+15%)
  Weight: 2 kg
Giant Snake Venom Gland
  Quantity: 2
  Item Class: Common
  Item Quality: Good (+15%)
  Weight: 2 kg
Giant Snake Bone
  Quantity: 80
  Item Class: Common
  Item Quality: Good (+15%)
  Weight: 80 kg

"Well, it looks like our food problems have been solved for the next little while," Freya commented as she looked through the bag. "What are we going to do with eighty pieces of snake bone though?"

"Hell, if I know," I replied with a shrug. "I might be able to use some pieces for crafting...but I think it can be used as fertilizer too."

"The item quality for all of this stuff is pretty high," I added, with a note of excitement as I continued to read over the items. "I should be able to craft some pretty high-quality gear with the scales and maybe the fangs—"

"Hey! You two are going through the loot already?" Constantine's voice echoed out from behind me causing both Freya and I to spin, seeing the rest of the party approaching. "What happened to waiting for us?"

"You guys were taking too long," I grunted, waving my hand dismissively as my eyes focused on Drace, Caius and Halcyon, the three of them flinching under my gaze, already knowing what I was going to say. "But now that you're all here, I have a few *questions*..."

"It wasn't our fault," Caius said immediately.

"We had to do it," Drace stated.

"We were pretty sure there was only one!" Halcyon exclaimed.

The three paused to glare between one another with blank expressions, then back towards me.

"Three different answers," I replied thoughtfully, my hand rubbing my chin as I regarded the trio with a smile on my face. "But something tells me that each of those responses is true."

"They are—" Drace started to reply as a loud clatter of hooves interrupted him, followed by Stanton's sharp voice splitting the air.

"*What is the meaning of this?! Are you trying to get us all kill—*" the noble's harsh words died in his throat as we all turned to look towards him, glaring intently at his sudden intrusion. Scanning our faces, a visible wave of fear passed over his face, before vanishing under an impassive mask.

"How nice of you to join us, Stanton," I greeted the man loudly, savoring the man's discomfort. "We missed you during the battle."

I let a pause hang in the air as I watched my words cause Stanton's lips to tighten, the implication behind my statement obvious to everyone within earshot.

"My friends here were just about to inform us what happened in the woods, and how they caught the snakes' attention," I continued, waving a hand in Drace's direction. "I'm sure you're curious to hear as well."

"Of course," Stanton replied in short, clipped tones that failed to hide the anger underneath as he kept his gaze locked onto mine.

"We were deep in the forest hunting with our recruits," Halcyon began, catching my unspoken cue as his eyes shifted to Stanton. "You know, teaching them the value of looking up for snakes hidden in the trees, while also making sure not to step onto a badger den at the same time."

"Basic stuff," I acknowledged, everyone in the circle, save Stanton nodding in sync with me.

"Right," Halcyon continued. "So, we had just finished carving through a batch of creatures when one of our scouts, Ameron, found a beaten path cutting through the brush. We thought that it would be something interesting to follow, and we did, up until the point where it led us to this massive nest."

"*A nest?*" Stanton queried hesitantly, his anger vanishing and slowly being replaced with concern.

"A snake nest," Halcyon clarified. "*Full of eggs*. Easily over two dozen of them piled high, with the Emerald Moss Snake perched high in the trees above it..."

I struggled to keep my face impassive as Halcyon continued to explain his group's adventure through the forest, watching Stanton's face grow pale the longer that the mage spoke.

Maybe this didn't turn out so bad after all, I thought with a thin smile, seeing a brief look of horror cross Stanton's face as Halcyon's story went on to outline their decision to steal the eggs from the snake's nest.

Not bad at all.

Chapter 19

The clap of thunder followed by a near torrential downpour of rain heralded the end of any meaningful adventuring for the day, the heavy deluge having thankfully waited until we reached Crater Lake to start. After recovering from the battle with the snakes, we found ourselves down four Adventurers on our return journey back to Aldford, a much lighter casualty count than I felt we deserved, given just how badly we were taken by surprise.

In the end, our numbers saved us, I told myself as Constantine, Amaranth and I led our soggy group in the direction of the tree line where the entrance to the Crater Lake ruin lay. *Something that I'm sure hasn't been lost on Stanton.*

"I'm convinced that this region only has two types of weather," Constantine muttered from beside me. "Heavy thunderstorms or crippling heat waves."

"Still better than Reality," I replied, rubbing a waterlogged glove across my face to clear my vision from all the rainwater pouring down. "We're supposed to get another snowstorm this week."

"Fuck, I can't even think of snow right now. Spring is supposed to be around the corner!" he grunted, his head perking up as he saw something ahead of us. "Finally! I think I see the entrance to the ruin! I take back all of my complaining when you got us all to dig it out."

"Hiding from a thunderstorm wasn't exactly what was on my mind when we did that," I started to tell the rogue, only to have him pull away from me as he rushed to get inside the now-exposed tunnel that led into the lakeside ruins. "Though I won't say I'm not eager to get out of this rain…"

<That makes for two of us!> Amaranth said to me as he bounded past, running after Constantine.

Trudging forward through the downpour, I watched Constantine and Amaranth vanish into the freshly excavated opening that protruded from the hillside, before turning around to look behind me. Travelling closely behind, I saw the rest of our entourage, their expressions one of relief as they too sighted respite from the rain.

"You'll have to walk your horse through the tunnel," I called to Stanton as the Adventurers slowly filtered their way into the tunnel, their voices echoing from the passage. "He should hopefully be able to fit without too many problems."

"Hrm," Stanton grunted in acknowledgment, the man having said little to me since the battle with the snakes, his bad mood going as far as to infect the rest of his group. But nevertheless, he motioned for Samuel to hold the animal steady before dismounting, his boots landing on the wet ground with a squish. Not giving any of us a second look, the silver-haired noble left the reins in Samuel's hands and waited his turn to enter the passageway, motioning sharply for Lazarus and his friends to join him in line.

Content on waiting patiently for everyone else to enter the tunnel ahead of me, I ran a hand through my hair in an attempt to wring the excess water from it, watching both Samuel and Quincy lead Stanton's reluctant mount forward. Finding myself at the back of the line, I finally stepped into the tunnel behind the horse, keeping a fair distance behind it, lest my presence spook it. The last thing I wanted at this point, was to be kicked by a panicked animal in close quarters.

It feels like ages since the first day I fell into here, I thought as I slowly moved deeper into the ruin, my fingers tracing over the scars on the wall. *Has it already been over a month since I started playing this game?*

Lost in thought, I lost track of time as we crept forward, knowing that the Adventurers ahead of me would be busy admiring the small, decrepit ruin before filtering up the switchbacks and up towards the higher elevation. After steadily moving for a time, I eventually reached the shattered remains of the doorway and stepped into the long rectangular room, seeing my friends standing on one side of the room, with Stanton and his retinue on the other. The air was thick with tension as the two groups regarded one another warily, Lazarus and his friends having been watching us with guarded expressions ever since the battle.

"I can lead the horse up the switchbacks while you all look around," Sierra offered to Samuel, breaking the awkward silence that had filled the room, save for the agitated whinnies coming from Stanton's mount as it became more and more irritated by being underground. "He's starting to get a bit nervous."

"*Ah!* I think that might be a good idea," Samuel replied, dodging the animal's half-hearted attempt to bite him before offering the reins to Sierra. "Here, and thanks."

"No problem," Sierra said, accepting the reins and slowly leading the horse towards the far end of the room and into the passageway that led towards the switchbacks. "I'll wait with him by the entrance up top."

"So, if you haven't guessed," I began, motioning to the room around me. "This is the second Nafarrian ruin that we found."

"It certainly isn't as well preserved," Quincy commented pessimistically as he looked around the room. "And the damage to it is rather considerable."

"That's because it was nearly in the center of whatever destroyed the Nafarrian city here," I said, motioning to the doorway that we had entered. "I believe that when the city still existed, this chamber, *and* the tunnel that we just passed through, was once far under the city."

"Which certainly fits what we know of the Nafarr," Donovan agreed. "The sewer system in Eberia, for example, goes quite deep."

"You have no idea," Lazarus muttered. "Runs nearly the entire length of Eberia too."

"Was there anything of interest in this ruin when you first entered it?" Stanton asked, his expression markedly less excited than when he had visited the Hub.

"Actually, yeah," I replied with a nod, motioning to Razor on my waist. "There was an undead skeleton trapped in here, for ages based on my guess. When I first entered the room, it attacked me, but I managed to kill it and recovered a relic from it that I used to create my sword."

A spark of excitement surged through all the mages at my mention of the skeleton, their bored expressions suddenly focusing on me with a laser-like intensity.

"Lyrian, you didn't mention *anything* to me about finding a risen skeleton in here!" Donovan exclaimed.

"Hmm?" I grunted in surprise, turning to look at Donovan, then back towards the others. "I didn't think it that important to mention. It was just a skeleton."

"*Just a skeleton?*" Stanton gasped, his face turning red as his hands reached out towards me, all the other mages sharing a similar look on their faces. "You really have no idea, do you?"

"Idea of what?" I asked, glancing towards Lazarus and my friends, seeing confused looks on their faces as well. "I don't understand."

"That skeleton," Donovan began, "may have been the first physical proof of the Nafarr that we have ever even *heard* of. In all our time in Eberia, we have never as much as uncovered a shard of bone to *prove* that they truly existed."

"Oh," I replied, the revelation causing me to pause. "I had no idea..."

"We only have their creations to base any of our theories off," Samuel added. "The structures they left behind, artifacts, collections of weapons and armor. But nothing to indicate how they may have looked."

"We saw the Slave King," Constantine interjected, glancing sharply at Samuel and Quincy. "Was that not a good enough look?"

"The Slave King brought himself into existence by forming his body out of Æther," Samuel replied shaking his head. "For all we know, if he truly wanted to, he could have formed himself to appear as a dragon."

"What did it look like?" Donovan asked. "Did it look any different than a human or elvish skeleton?"

"Uh, I really didn't think to pay attention to that sort of detail," I replied uneasily, feeling everyone's attention on me.

"You have to remember *something*!" Quincy demanded.

"Well, it was pretty dark, and it was trying to kill me," I stated a bit defensively as I scanned the room, trying to remember my battle with the Decaying Commander. "But I think that the skeleton was about my height, or at least would have been had he not been missing pieces of his arm and leg. It looked like he'd been killed by burns all over the one side of his body...*well*, at least before he rose once more."

"As for *how* he looked," I continued, wracking my memory for any shred of detail that I could recall. "I don't *think* it looked too different to how a typical human skeleton would. The skull may have been a little differently shaped, but it also wasn't in the best condition. It may have just been decay."

"I see," Stanton said with disappointment, the other mages echoing his sentiment. "There was nothing else in this chamber?"

"Nothing," I affirmed, waving my hands around at the debris that still filled the room. "I picked through the debris that you see here and didn't find anything interesting. Just shards of metal from the broken door and some other scraps that may have once been furniture ages ago. That's about it."

"No one would have gone through the trouble to dig and carve this room out without *some sort* of purpose," Quincy commented as he finished his inspection of the area. "Did you detect anything of interest with an Ætherscope?"

"Uh, actually, I never thought to scan the area," I said, looking over at Halcyon and Caius, knowing that it was Donovan's first time in the ruin. "Did you guys?"

"I didn't," Halcyon replied, shaking his head.

"Didn't cross my mind either," Caius admitted with a shrug.

"Well, no time like the present I guess," I said as Quincy reached into his pocket and pulled out an Irovian Ætherscope.

The room fell silent as all the mages, myself included, followed the man's lead and drew their own Ætherscopes, spreading out around the room, trusting in the wand to draw attention to any stray sources of magic that lingered in the area.

Holding the length of bone firmly in my hand, I activated *True Sight*, instantly seeing the lingering shadows in the chamber fade away as my augmented vision pierced through the darkness. Walking slowly, I then scanned the room carefully, seeing nothing of interest appear in my vision at first glance, my feet eventually leading me towards the switchbacks and standing between the collapsed route leading downward and the other leading to the surface when something finally appeared in my vision.

"Huh," I grunted in surprise as countless dark blue wisps appeared in my vision, the color indicating that whatever I was seeing was far away and nearly at the edge of my range. "I see something from over here!"

"You do?" Stanton's voice was the first to answer as everyone rushed to join me at the base of the switchbacks, their eyes focused intently at the wall straight ahead of us.

"I just barely see something too!" Quincy added with excitement in his voice. "I…am not certain what it could be, however, it is very faint…"

"It is too scattered and small to be the Ley Line," Halcyon said as he slid beside me. "Too faint as well…it's hard to tell exactly what it could be."

"Ah! I saw something move!" Samuel's sudden shout caused all of us to flinch in surprise and look back at him, seeing him staring downwards at the collapsed route.

"What do you see?" Donovan queried as we all followed Samuel's gaze, canting our heads towards the ground when the speechless mage didn't reply.

Almost immediately after shifting my vision, I saw several bright blue and white wisps appear in my vision, their position slowly moving beneath us. Judging from the brightness of the signatures, whatever they were, they were much closer to us than the fainter signatures we had just seen seconds earlier.

"There is something beneath us," I said excitedly while continuing to gaze downwards, some of the wisps blurring together into one indistinguishable blob of magic as they moved further away from us, towards the other signatures in the distance.

"There must be another chamber deeper underground," Quincy whispered while pointing at the blocked passage.

"Possibly a lower level that was part of a larger network?" Samuel suggested, his eyes widening in excitement as he twisted to look back at Stanton and Quincy. "That would explain the signatures that we saw further away and the ones moving."

"Maybe," I replied, shifting my glance between the bright sources of magic beneath us and the fainter sources further away. "But what could it be?"

"Possibly a route towards the Ley Line?" Samuel offered eagerly. "If the city once sat where the lake is now, then practicality would demand that the Nafarr access the Ley Line where it passes under Aldford, instead of miles away at the other ruin."

"How could you possibly know that?" Donovan interjected, dampening Samuel's excitement. "We hardly know enough about the Nafarr to comment what was or wasn't practical for them, let alone *how* they used the Ley Lines in the first place to power their technology."

There was a pause as Samuel and Quincy turned their heads towards Stanton, the elder mage shaking his head slowly.

"That statement is not entirely accurate," Stanton said slowly, clearly choosing his words with care.

"I don't understand," Donovan replied flatly, suspicion evident in his voice. "What part of it exactly? Has there been a ground-breaking discovery about the Nafarr since I departed Eberia?"

"No," Stanton stated evasively but didn't elaborate any further.

"Then what the hell are you talking about?" Halcyon cut in before Donovan could reply, all of us shifting our attention away from our Ætherscopes and onto the noble. "You know something that you're not sharing."

"Understatement of the fucking century there," Sawyer muttered loud enough for everyone to hear.

"*Quiet,*" Stanton demanded, turning his head to look at the red-armored warrior out of the corner of his eye. "I don't—"

"No, I think we've been *quiet* enough, Stanton," Lazarus interrupted harshly. "We've just made a *major* discovery here. Be fucking honest for once in your life and tell them what they need to know."

"You are in no position to dictate anything to me!" Stanton growled, glaring at the man as he spoke. "The sooner you remember—"

"*But I am,*" I interrupted forcefully as I watched the argument unfold before me. "And I am curious to hear the answer to Donovan's question."

Head spinning in my direction, Stanton's eyes narrowed as they landed on me, his words coming out in short and clipped tones, "That information is privileged."

"We're in the middle of an underground ruin on the edge of the frontier for fuck's sake!" Constantine practically yelled, taking the words right out of my mouth. "Who the hell are we going to tell?"

"Regardless of *where* a secret is unveiled, the moment that it is let loose it no longer under your control," Stanton countered, glaring at Constantine's profanity.

"That's a bullshit answer, Stanton," I growled, tired of the man's evasiveness. "Remember, you're the one who came to *us* for help, and it's obvious that you know *something* that could make sense of what we all just saw. So, either you tell us now, or we find out once we dig our way down there."

Silence fell over the room as all our attention focused onto Stanton, the noble staring back at me with half of a scowl on his face as he weighed my words carefully.

"What I am about to tell you does not go beyond this audience," he ground out, meeting the eyes of everyone he could in the cramped hallway. "Is that clear?"

"Like crystal," I answered, hearing a chorus of weary acknowledgments around me.

"Some time ago, a chamber, a *massive* chamber, was discovered in the depths below Eberia by my House," he began, speaking as if every single word he said caused him physical pain. "After studying the equipment recovered from it for a time, we believe that we have a theoretical understanding of how the Nafarr drew Æther from the Ley Line."

"*Some time ago?*" Donovan repeated as he pushed past Halcyon beside me, and took a step forward towards Stanton, his voice hardening with anger. "How long is '*some time ago?*'"

"A decade. Perhaps longer by now," Stanton answered with a dismissive shake of his head. "I am not certain."

"House Denarius has hidden such a monumental discovery from Eberia for a *decade*?" Donovan spat, his arms trembling as if he wanted to physically strike the noble. "You bastards! You have no right to—"

"Watch your tongue!" Stanton snapped, his voice taking on a dangerous tone as it echoed through the tunnel we'd crammed ourselves in. "Do you think the *other* Houses aren't doing the same with their discoveries? Do not be so naïve!"

"That doesn't make it right!" Donovan exclaimed.

"'Right' and 'wrong' belong in the province of Justicars and Magistrates!" Stanton spat back at the mage. "They are foolhardy things to cling to when your nation's existence is at stake!"

"Goddamn you nobles—" Donovan began to snarl, his anger starting to get the better of him.

"Donovan, now is not the time!" I called his name loudly, reaching out to grab the man by the arm despite understanding his anger and pulled him behind me before he did something rash. Giving the mage a sharp look, I turned my attention back towards Stanton and continued to press him for answers.

"How did the Nafarr tap the Ley Line?" I asked in a sharp tone that I hoped would make the noble reconsider an evasive answer.

"Physically," Stanton replied. "By sinking large poles of an Æther conductive metal into it, which we believe drew the Æther into reservoirs for storage and transport. The scale of their work in that chamber dwarfed anything that we had ever seen before."

"So, they could have done the same here as well," I said, watching Stanton's face carefully for any sign that he may be hiding or evading the truth.

"I am certain they did," Stanton stated. "Based on the signatures that we all saw through the Ætherscopes, I believe there is a lower section to these ruins that continues southward in the direction of the Ley Line. With luck, it may still be intact, at least up until the point of the rupture."

"You think that the rupture happened where they tapped it," I stated, catching on to the words left unsaid by the noble.

"It is likely," Quincy acknowledged, answering for Stanton. "Whatever event that destroyed the Nafarrian city here would have been cataclysmic, enough to cause the bedrock that surrounds us to shift. If whatever the Nafarr built into the Ley Line shifted as well..."

"It would have torn the Ley Line right open," I finished.

"We have no way of knowing until we see it with our own eyes," Stanton said, motioning with a hand towards the collapsed route deeper into the ruin. "We should begin excavation at once and with haste. If this happens to be a dead end or if we need to dig further..."

"Digging out a collapsed tunnel isn't something you rush," Drace interjected, already knowing that the project would fall to him to complete. "We'd be looking at several days, if not a week or more to clear a way down, and that's assuming that we don't run into any complications."

"Time is not on our side for this—" Stanton began to warn impatiently before Drace cut him off.

"Which is why we are going to do this *right*," the big man stated in an annoyed tone, refusing to back down. "You're not going to be the one who's swinging a pickaxe or carting stone away here, risking being buried alive if something goes wrong. A collapse because we rushed will set us back even further."

"Do what you must to ensure the integrity of the tunnel, but do it quickly," Stanton ordered, his face twitching at Drace's implication that he was of no help. "But we all know what is at stake here."

"We do," I agreed, feeling the same surge of annoyance as I knew Drace did. "But with that in mind, however, I think this is a good time to make a few points clear before we go any further."

"Oh?" Stanton asked, his feigned curiosity unable to completely hide the steel in his voice. "What may those be?"

"Uh..." I heard Lazarus grunt from behind Stanton's back as he shook his head at me.

"First and foremost, going forward, you are going to stop spouting orders at us," I said, hearing Lazarus curse as I ignored his warning. "You are a *guest* in Aldford and have no standing whatsoever in this town beyond what people give you as a courtesy due to your rank in Eberia. A courtesy that you will find waning the more you continue to overstep your authority."

"*Overstep myself?*" Stanton seethed in between clenched teeth, his eyes widening in anger. "*You're* the one overstepping, Lyrian. You forget that my house *owns* Aldford, and I am here as its representative, without its investment this town wouldn't have ever even existed!"

"And without us, Aldford would have been raided by goblins, *or* destroyed by a horde of spiders, *or* captured by an army of Adventurers, *or* razed to the ground by a Nafarrian Slave King!" I retorted, holding my fingers up in the air as I counted each event. "Your House may have brought Aldford into existence with gold, but *we* paid for it in blood!"

"Your diligence in defending Aldford is appreciated," Stanton growled, his tone indicating the exact opposite. "But your actions buy you no claim to the town over House Denarius's."

"I disagree, but that would be a matter for the Justicar to decide, should you wish to take it that far," I answered, feeling my friends shuffle around me as Quincy and Samuel moved to flank Stanton. "But you bring up a good point about claims. Given that this ruin likely links to whatever is beneath us, Virtus will be extending its claim to it and anything else found under Aldford, *including* this portion of the Ley Line. In fact, until one of us says otherwise, I don't want you anywhere *near* these ruins, we'll manage exploring the ruins and the Ley Line rupture ourselves from here on out."

"*What?*" Samuel barked his face red with anger as he joined the growing argument. "You cannot be serious in barring us from the ruins when the safety of Eberia is at stake!"

"*You* may be worried about Eberia, but *my* concern is the future of Aldford," I retorted angrily. "We're the ones with the most to lose if the Ley Line erupts after all. I am just making sure that it remains in control of those most invested in Aldford's survival, and right now, I don't trust any of you further than I could spit."

"This is ridiculous," Stanton seethed, thrusting out a finger at me as he spoke. "Just who do you think you are? You cannot take a task such as this onto yourself single-handedly! You do not have the background to even begin to understand what is buried underneath here!"

"Virtus is hardly single-handed, Stanton, we are the largest guild in this region by far," I replied, waving at my friends behind me. "Besides, what right do you have to contest anything we claim?"

Staring at me silently, Stanton opened then closed his mouth, watching me closely as he processed what I said, his eyes narrowing as he stared at me. "Today was a show, wasn't it? The ruins, the snakes, everything."

"We wanted to show you what living on the frontier truly means," I replied matching the man's stare unflinchingly. "And to drive home that a person's worth is measured by their actions, not the titles that they have attached to their name. Today you couldn't even be bothered to raise your hand in our defense when the snakes attacked us, and that action alone told us all we need to know about you. I don't trust you to have my back going into this ruin, and until that changes, you're not going to step foot inside it."

"Are you calling me a *coward*—" Stanton's shout reached dangerous levels as he took a single rage-filled step towards me before Lazarus's big hand slammed into the noble's shoulder and gripped it tightly.

"*That is enough!*" Lazarus shouted, effortlessly swatting Stanton's flailing hands away as Sawyer and Ransom forced themselves past Quincy and Samuel to stand before me. "I'm putting a stop to this before someone else does something even *more* stupid! Get out of our way; we're leaving!"

"*Let go of me, you filthy criminal!*" Stanton shouted as Lazarus pushed him forward and towards the switchbacks, whispering something in his ear that had him fall immediately silent.

Criminal? Stanton's choice of words caused my eyebrow to rise, seeing a momentary wince pass over both Sawyer and Ransom's faces as we stepped out of their path, allowing them a clear passage up the switchbacks.

"*What the fuck, Lyrian?*" Lazarus spat, giving me an angry glare as he passed me before leading Stanton up the switchbacks and up to the surface, the two mages following close behind.

The sound of angry feet slowly faded away as the group turned a corner and continued their rush upwards, leaving us staring at one another in silence until Constantine's words filled the air.

"I think they took the news pretty well, all things considered."

Chapter 20

A roaring clap of thunder rolled through the air, followed by several flashes of lightning that lit up the sky, jagged lines of electricity filling my vision. Blinking the after images away, I pulled my attention away from the raging storm overhead and looked down at Crater Lake below me, the very same ridge line that I had once jumped off inches away from my feet. The lake rippled with the impact of countless droplets, the heavy deluge only having intensified as the evening progressed.

<Is it wise to be standing out in the open?> Amaranth asked me from his position in a tree behind me, having found refuge on a branch. *<You may be struck by a bolt of light.>*

<Probably not,> I admitted to the cat from my position in the rain, now completely soaked to the bone. *<But I'm wet anyway and sitting out in the rain is relaxing in its own way.>*

<If you say so,> he replied doubtfully, his mental voice trailing off as the two of us then sat in silence for a while.

Lazarus is sure taking his sweet time in getting here, I mused as I shifted my gaze from the lake and onto the distant horizon. *If he's not here soon, I'll head back and call it a night.*

After our argument with Stanton and his subsequent removal from the lakeside ruin by Lazarus, we had returned to Aldford in two separate groups, wondering if the noble was going to press Aldwin or Dyre about our claim straight away. But to our surprise, we learned that after arriving back at the Town Stanton had immediately stormed up to his room in the Town Hall and locked himself in, Veronia eventually joining him after a time.

None of us had any idea what to make of the noble's reaction, but decided it was best to let both Aldwin and Dyre know what happened, in case Stanton tried to do something sneaky behind our backs. No sooner than I had finished my meeting with the Bann, however, did Lazarus send me a rather curt private message, asking me to meet him privately, one-on-one, somewhere outside of Aldford.

Which is how I ended up here, feet now dangling over the edge of hundred-foot drop and watching a summer thunderstorm sweep through the land.

I wonder what Stanton's next move will be, I thought while bringing up my quest log and reading through the latest quest update that I had received after we had left the Crater Lake ruins. *He should have known we're not going to give up our claims on the ruins, and he badly needed an attitude adjustment before he mouthed off to an Adventurer with less patience than us.*

Quest: The Ruptured Ley Line!

After escorting Lord Stanton and his retinue to the Crater Lake Ruins and exploring the area, you have discovered that there may, in fact, be a lower level buried deeper underground. During the excitement of the discovery, Stanton revealed that the Nafarr have been known to excavate underground chambers in order to reach and tap the Ley Line. Based on his experience he believes that there is a good chance that an underground ruin stretches far enough to reach the Ley Line.

Your next step now is to try and excavate the collapsed passage leading deeper into the ruins.

Escort Lord Stanton to the Ancient Transport Hub: 1/1

Escort Lord Stanton to the Crater Lake Ruins: 1/1
Attempt to excavate the collapsed passage and see where it leads: 0/1
Ley Line Sealed: 0/1
Difficulty: Legendary
Reward: Experience & Renown
Penalty for Failure: Aldford and the surrounding region will be destroyed.

<I hear footsteps,> Amaranth warned me, causing me to dismiss my quest log from my vision and push myself up onto my feet. *<It seems he has come alone.>*

<Good,> I replied to my familiar. *<Let me know if anyone else approaches, but don't interfere between the two of us. I'm expecting him to be angry.>*

Turning to face the forest behind me, I activated *True Sight*, watching the dark shadows fade away as I spotted Lazarus force himself out of the woods, his eyes immediately landing on me.

"You picked a goddamn far enough place to meet," he spat as he stalked out of the woods and into the rain.

"You wanted a private place," I replied, spreading my hands out wide and indicating the edge of the ridge. "This is about as private as it gets around here."

"*Good*, because we're about to have it out right fucking here," Lazarus growled as he walked towards me, cracking his knuckles ominously. "Your fucking stunt could have killed Stanton today and cost the three of us *everything*! What the hell were you thinking? I *told you* that we need to keep the fucking prick alive!"

"Oh, he seems in perfectly fine health to me," I replied to Lazarus, unfazed by the amount profanity coming out of his mouth or his threatening advance. "In fact, I'd be surprised if the man got close enough to the battle to even tell what color the snakes were."

"That doesn't change the fact that you fucking pulled them on purpose!" Lazarus shouted as he loomed over me and thrust a finger into my face. "What the fuck made you think that was a good idea?"

"We needed to see what you were all made of," I said evenly, looking up at the half-giant's angry expression. "And if we could count on you if the shit hit the fan."

"That's it?" Lazarus exclaimed, taking a step back from me and clenching his fist. "You risked everything just to see if we'd *fight*?!"

"And it paid off," I stated, waving my hand over the man's shoulder, indicating his sword. "You, Sawyer and Ransom fought, while Stanton, Samuel and Quincy cowered. If they had any shred of courage on them, they would have figured out some way to contribute to the battle. Stanton is a mage on a horse for fuck's sake! He could have run circles around those snakes!"

"Stanton may be a colossal fucking ass, but the only damn thing I've been able to get him to agree on is not to put his life in needless danger!" Lazarus countered. "It is *our* job to take care of shit that could kill him, because if he dies—"

"Then your hostages die," I interrupted, watching Lazarus's face shift into a scowl. "Yeah, I remember what you told me."

"And it didn't even make you think twice about what you planned to do?" He barked back at me. "If he died…"

Lazarus paused for a moment to shake his head, a dark expression coming over his face. "As if that wasn't enough, you then fucking shoved your claim down his throat at the ruin *and* banned him from the site,! You had to know he would take that badly!"

"Of course, I knew that! That's why I picked my timing so carefully," I replied to Lazarus. "But what other choice did I have? Stanton kept us all waiting for the entire morning, ordered us around all day and refused to share even the barest shred of information with us until it was pried from his jaw. He needed to know where the line was. You and your friends may be under his thumb, but we sure as hell aren't."

"Goddamn it, Lyrian. Stanton, and by extension, *Emilia*, isn't someone you can fuck around with this way," Lazarus said. "There has to be more to Stanton than either of us have seen so far, and as for *that bitch,* she wields *actual* power back in Eberia, and can make your life miserable in more ways than one."

"Eberia is about to be drawn into a long and drawn out war with The Ascendancy, which is going to leave Aldford out here completely alone and cut off," I stated, seeing Lazarus's eyes narrow. "I couldn't care less about what *either* of them can do, and more about being dragged into a war that we couldn't possibly survive. Not yet anyway."

"So, is this is your response to our warning then?" Lazarus questioned his eyes burning with anger as they focused on me. "Thanks, but no thanks?"

"It's your damned warning that brought all of this on!" I exclaimed acidly. "You swoop in and tell us things that we couldn't possibly verify, then expect things to fall into place? No, things don't work like that. You want us to trust you? Send us your feed. All of it. Completely uncut. Then we can start talking if what we see matches up to what you've told us."

"Out of the fucking question!" Lazarus snapped angrily. "I don't trust you with my feed after what you did today!"

"Are you sure it has anything to do with what happened today or is it because there is something you don't want us to see?" I shot back, matching the man's tone. "Stanton called you a criminal earlier today, just before you pulled him away. I wonder what he meant by that?"

"Keep wondering," he spat. "That's none of your business."

"Then I think we're done here," I said dismissively, moving to step around Lazarus. "You want my help? Then your feed is my price. Come find me when you're ready to deal."

"*No*," Lazarus growled, his hand reaching out to grab my arm as I passed by him and gripped it tightly. "I have too much on the line to deal with this shit."

"*Let go of me, Lazarus*," I said dangerously as I turned to face the half-giant. "*Now.*"

"I'm sorry, Lyrian, but I can't do that." Lazarus's grip tightened on my arm until I felt the chainmail links begin to dig into my skin. "If you're not going to help me willingly, then I'm going to have to do something rash."

"Like kill me?" I asked, feeling adrenaline shoot through me as I prepared myself for a fight. "You know that won't change anything. Death doesn't matter to us."

"Not to us, no," Lazarus agreed. "But to some of the other people in town? Death is rather *permanent.*"

"You wouldn't *dare*," I snarled as I yanked hard on my arm and tore it free of Lazarus's grip, taking a step back.

"With what I have on the line..." Lazarus replied wearily as he moved to follow me, his hands balling themselves into fists. "I wouldn't even hesitate."

"This isn't going to end well for you, Lazarus," I warned as I shifted into a ready stance, hands hanging loosely by my side. "Stop this while you still can."

"We're past that point, Lyrian," Lazarus said, shaking his head a heartbeat before he lunged forward, a fist sweeping through the air where my head had just been.

<Lyr—> my familiar's concerned voice rang through my head before I cut it off with a mental shout.

<Don't interfere!> I sent to Amaranth as I backed away from the half-giant's sudden assault. *<We need to work this out ourselves!>*

Putting Amaranth's reply out of my mind, I dodged another heavy punch, then sidestepped a snap-kick aimed at my leg, that would have surely sent me crashing to the ground with broken bones. Careful to keep my balance on the slick mud and stone beneath my feet, I focused my attention on Lazarus who wasted no time in pressing his attack.

He's stronger and faster than me, I noted as his rapid assault had me entirely on the defensive, forcing me to give up ground, lest I get caught with a flurry of blows I couldn't hope to recover from. *But he's all offense, with barely a second thought to his guard or form. I think I have a skill level or two on him at the very least.*

Analyzing Lazarus's timing, I abandoned my steady retreat and stepped forward into his latest attack, ducking under a flying fist as it passed over my shoulder. Darting into his guard, I lashed out with my own punch, catching the half-giant high on the cheek before slipping past him and reversing our positions.

"Fighting me isn't going to solve anything!" I called out to the man as a crash of thunder echoed from the sky, drowning out my words.

"Like hell, it isn't!" Lazarus barked angrily as he whirled around to face me, barely noticing that my blow had split his cheek.

Rushing forward, Lazarus continued his relentless assault, his fists and feet blurring through the air with more anger than skill, forcing me to dance around the man's attacks. The storm raging above us soon faded from our conscious thoughts as our worlds shrank to one of moves and countermoves, water flying through the air from timely blocks, a sharp gasp of air marking a blow that one of us were too slow to intercept or avoid.

The slight skill advantage I had over Lazarus in unarmed combat allowed me to mitigate his physical prowess, but not enough to remain unscathed forever. My body ached from more than a dozen heavy blows that I was forced to absorb, the worse amongst them emanating from my side, leaving me taking sharp, pained breaths from what could only be a trio of cracked ribs. In comparison, Lazarus's face was almost unrecognizable, one eye completely swollen shut and his nose plastered to one side. The heavy cuirass that had covered his chest had forced me to focus my attacks on the exposed portions of his body, lest I break a hand punching solid metal.

Thankfully, my Unarmed Mastery ability lets me land heavier hits than my strength would normally allow, I thought with a grimace as I accepted a glancing blow across my ear while stepping deep into Lazarus's guard and landing a punishing knee into the side of his kidney, where his breastplate didn't protect. *Otherwise, I'd be in real trouble.*

Gasping from my attack, Lazarus's balance finally faltered, causing him to fall to one knee and clutch at his side, a bitter curse filling the air.

"Fuck!" he slurred angrily, his one open eye looking up at me with rage as a red aura of magic suddenly bloomed around his body. "*ENOUGH!*"

"What the hell are you doing, Lazarus?" I shouted back at the man, reaching for Razor's hilt, completely surprised to see a wave of magic surge through the half-giant, not having pegged him as a spellcaster. "You do *not* want to escalate this!"

"Maybe I do!" Lazarus roared as his hand began to reach up to the greatsword strapped to his back.

"Damn it, Lazarus!" Not waiting for the man to draw his sword, I lunged forward with my hand outstretched, triggering *Blink Step* as I moved, intending to put an end whatever spell he was weaving. "*Stop!*"

My vision blurring as I teleported, I reappeared practically on top of Lazarus at the same moment a bolt of lightning crossed the sky, leaving me staring down at the soaked half-giant's face. My hand followed a heartbeat afterward, gripping Lazarus by the side of the throat and immediately began to drain his mana.

But instead of the cool refreshing flow of mana that I expected, I felt a lance of fire shoot up my arm, causing my body to burn from within as if my blood had become liquid metal.

"Aaah!" I had no idea who the scream came from as my hand clenched down around Lazarus's throat, refusing to let go.

The burning energy continued to pour into my body, causing my vision to turn crimson as an unfathomable torrent of anger swelled from somewhere deep inside me. Reeling from the unexpected wave of emotion, I looked down at Lazarus as if I stood somewhere outside of my own body, seeing his flailing arm knock my hand free of its grip around his throat.

Immediately I felt the searing rush of fire vanish from my arm, leaving only the energy that I had already absorbed roiling inside me, causing my veins to burn as it looked for a way out. Staggering half a step away from Lazarus, I saw red letters appear in my vision notifying me of my new condition.

You have absorbed energy from a [Sigil of Rage]!
You have gained the temporary buff [Sigil of Rage]!

You gain +10 to Strength and Agility, but will suffer 10 points of damage per second for the next 15 seconds!

What the hell did I just absorb? I asked in a mental panic, trying to make sense of what was happening to me as the energy raging twisted inside me, a crimson veil falling over my vision.

A shout from Lazarus brought me back to the present as the half-giant shot to his feet and lunged forward, the red aura surrounding him intensifying. Moving faster than I thought possible, I rushed to meet his attack, any thought for strategy lost in the haze of rage that now consumed me.

I felt Lazarus's fist smash into my face as we collided into one another, the blow causing my head to twist awkwardly to one side while I simultaneously drove my knee into his groin. Pain was strangely absent as I recovered from the attack and swung my head back towards Lazarus, my fist coming up in a savage uppercut, catching him on the chin, only to have him shrug it off and backhand me away.

Fighting like savage animals, we pummeled one another wildly, both of us lost in the grip of an all-consuming rage. The booming echo of thunder overhead drowned out our cries as anger fueled fists bruised flesh and in more than one case, cracked bone. Anyone who had looked up from Crater Lake at that moment would have seen the two of us, fighting at the very edge of the ridge, where one misstep could send someone plunging down into the lake below.

But despite the energy that coursed through us, our bodies still had limits, and before long, the two of us found ourselves pressed right up against them, the burning rage that had consumed us fading away, leaving us both collapsing down to our knees in pain.

"Had enough?" I wheezed, spitting out a mouthful of blood as the haze that had filled my vision faded away, leaving me feeling completely spent and wondering what had just come over me.

"*Never*," Lazarus gasped as he tried to force himself back up onto his feet but failed. "As long as I'm alive, I'll still fight."

"You don't need to fight me, Lazarus," I replied, grimacing in pain as all the injuries from our brawl reasserted themselves now that the strange energy I had absorbed from Lazarus was gone. "What the hell is a Sigil of Rage?"

"A curse. A gift," the half-giant said vaguely as he attempted to push himself off the ground for a second time, this time managing to rise shakily to his feet. "It's what started all of this, in a way…"

"What do you mean?" I asked, struggling to get up off the ground as Lazarus took a step towards me, his feet sliding dangerously close to the edge of the ridge.

"It doesn't matter," he answered with a shake of his head as he continued to stagger forward. "I'm sorry about this, Lyrian, but I really don't have a choice."

"So am I, Lazarus," I said, watching the man's step as he advanced towards me, my muscles slowly tensing for action. "You do what you feel you need to do, but there's one thing that you should keep in mind."

"I'm all ears," he grunted half-heartedly as he raised his fists once more.

"If I go down…" I began, watching Lazarus's one working eye widen in surprise as I suddenly sprang forward at him. "I am damned going make sure I take you with me."

"What—" Lazarus managed a single gasp as I ducked under his reflexive punch and leaped on top of him, wrapping my arms around his neck.

Moving faster than he could react, I used the momentum of my leap to swing my legs past the half-giant and pull him off balance, causing his feet to slide out from under him.

The two of us plummeted off the ridge.

I barely had enough time to process my second fall into Crater Lake as Lazarus flailed wildly in my grip before the two of us hit the water with a thunderous splash. Tangled up in one another, we immediately began to sink, the faint light around us vanishing. Thrashing desperately in an attempt to break my grip, Lazarus's head spun to face me, his one eye wide with shock as I grabbed hold of his hands and wrapped my legs around his chest allowing our combined weight to take us down into the depths of the lake.

I'll drown us both if that's what it takes. I stared back into Lazarus's eye without blinking as he began to struggle harder and harder the deeper that we sank. I felt myself being thrown around as he twisted under me, unable to find the proper leverage to break free, his motions gradually working up into a frenzy. Hanging on for dear life for what seemed like ages, I eventually saw a flashing notification appear in the corner of my vision, alerting me of just how much air I had left in me.

Oxygen Remaining: 49/100

Not much longer left, I thought as the number slowly began to tick down, and my lungs began to burn. Seconds later, I felt Lazarus go slack in my arms, all fight suddenly going out of his body, causing me to look down at him in surprise.

Staring back up at me in resignation, I saw the defeated gaze of the half-giant meet my eye, then shake his head before motioning up to the surface with his chin. Wary that he might be trying to trick me, I looked back at him blankly for several heartbeats, only to have him blink twice at me, before closing his eye in acceptance.

Sinking through the water peacefully, Lazarus and I continued our slow descent towards the bottom of the lake as I weighed his sudden change in attitude, the man having completely given up on resisting.

Don't make me regret this, Lazarus, I thought towards the man as I let go of his wrists and saw his eye open in response. Pointing upwards towards the surface with one hand, I untangled myself from the man and kicked myself away from him before starting the ascent.

Racing against time, I then turned my attention away from Lazarus and clawed my way upwards, my vision beginning to narrow as my lungs used up the last bits of air stored inside them. Every stroke brought me closer to the surface until it seemed like it was only inches away, a last-ditch kick propelling me the final distance, my head breaking free of the water.

Sucking in a deep, life bringing breath of air, I felt my head spin as I filled my lungs, my cloudy vision restoring itself with every gasp I took. Splashing wildly as I trod water, I saw Lazarus's head break the surface a short distance away from me, his cough echoing over the water.

"*Fine,*" he panted after he had a chance to regain his breath. "You can have it."

"Your feed?" I asked, swimming closer towards him.

"Yeah," Lazarus clarified, resignation clear in his voice. "My feed."

"*All of it?*" I couldn't help but confirm, despite feeling a sense of relief shoot through me. "Including what you told us about Stanton."

"All of it," Lazarus confirmed. "But Stanton's portion is still locked for a few more days…"

"That's fine," I replied, having already expected that to be the case. "We can wait."

"There's something else you should know too, Lyrian," Lazarus said to me. "Before you watch the feed, so you're not surprised…"

"What is it?" I queried, feeling a sense of unease at Lazarus's words.

"Sawyer, Ransom and I are all members of a Thieves Guild in Eberia," he told me, his head barely bobbing above the surface as he spoke. "And everything that's happened in Eberia is our fault."

"W-what do you mean?" I questioned, taken aback by Lazarus's revelation. *There are Thieves' Guilds in Eberia?*

"The Noble Houses being at everyone's throats, the chaos in the city, all of it," Lazarus said, his eye staring at me intently as he spoke. "All of it is our fault.

"We caused it."

Chapter 21

"Oh, damn it!" I cursed angrily as I looked down at the ragged length of snakeskin that I had just ruined, my mind having slipped away from the task at hand for the briefest moments. "That was the last piece too!"

With a sigh, I set down my knife and reached out to grab the ruined mass of leather and threw it into my inventory without a second thought. *I'll deal with that later when I don't constantly have yesterday on my mind.*

Closing my eyes for a moment, I brought up my hands and rubbed my face, admitting to myself that the bombshell that Lazarus had dropped on me had left me unsettled, going as far to infect my mood this morning, leaving me making silly mistakes. For what had to be the hundredth time, I brought up my quest log, reviewing the latest update that had appeared after my savage brawl with Lazarus.

Quest Update! Statecraft, Deception and Veracity!

After showing Lord Stanton both of the Nafarrian ruins in the region, you decided to confront him about his arrogant behavior and to reinforce your claims to the ruins. This prompted an argument between the two of you, resulting in you banning Stanton from the ruins, which eventually forced Lazarus to intervene and escort Stanton away before it escalated even further.

Several hours later, on Lazarus's request, you met up with him on the outskirts of Aldford, where the two of you had heated argument of your own which eventually descended into violence. After a vicious brawl, you managed to subdue Lazarus, which prompted him to reveal to you that he and his companions are criminals belonging to a Thieves Guild and are directly responsible for the unrest that has gripped Eberia.

With this latest revelation you understand a bit more of Stanton's treatment of Lazarus and his companions. However, you can't help but question just how truthful either of them are being anymore.

Collect more information before making a decision!
Evidence supporting the Adventurers' story: 2/?
Evidence supporting Stanton's story: 2/?
Difficulty: Very Hard
Reward: Unknown
Penalty for Failure: Unknown

Lazarus might have been lying for all you know, a cynical part of myself said as I dismissed the quest update. *You won't know for sure until you actually get the feed, and that won't be until Sunday. He might just be stalling.*

Yeah, and all the references to the devils Constantine mentioned the other day? Another part of my mind countered, rehashing the very argument that had caused me to ruin the snakeskin. *But what he said made sense and pieced together a lot of things we couldn't find out on any Eberian feeds. Also, why would he openly admit to causing problems in the city if he really hadn't?*

Sure, but— my sub-consciousness wasted no time in replying before I shook my head viciously, my voice echoing through the empty crafting hall. "Ugh!"

Taking a deep breath, I did my best to keep my mind blank as I cleaned up my workspace and turned to leave the portion of the Crafting Hall that had been dedicated to leathercrafting, deciding that what I needed the most right now was a walk to clear my head before I attempted to craft anything else. Damaging or ruining several pieces of the high-quality snakeskin when I was trying to fashion it into armor would definitely not improve on my mood.

Leaving the room, I walked through the quiet Crafting Hall, none of the new arrivals to Aldford so far sharing my habit of waking up early to get to work. Though to be fair, there had been a handful of Adventurers that had still been awake and working on their own projects when I had arrived at the hall, just before five in the morning.

On second thought, scratch that. I think someone's in the Foundry, I corrected myself as a repetitive banging sound echoed from an adjoining hallway that split off from the main building.

Curious to who might be up this early, I decided to follow the sound of the noise and changed my direction towards it. The sound gradually grew in intensity as I approached the Foundry and pushed the large doors leading into it open, revealing the familiar form of Jenkins, sitting at the forge already covered in a heavy sweat from his work.

"I should have figured that if anyone was here this early, that it would be you," I called out.

"Eh?" Jenkins grunted, turning around to look at me with an odd expression. "Should be no surprise that I'm here, I stopped in nearly an hour ago to say good morning while you were carving all that leather."

"Uh," I looked at the man sideways, a confused expression on my face. "You did? I don't even remember..."

"Explains why you didn't reply then," Jenkins replied with an idle wave of the hammer before turning back towards the forge.

"Sorry, Jenkins," I said as I crossed the room. "I'm distracted and have a lot on my mind lately."

"Figured as much," the man acknowledged as a rhythmic pounding sound filled the air again. "You walk around like the whole town sits on your shoulders."

"Perhaps a certain noble who was seen storming back into town yesterday evening is the source of your distraction?" Léandre's voice echoed out from inside the new forge that sat in the center of the room, causing me to flinch slightly in surprise.

"Léandre! I didn't know you were here too!" I exclaimed, while turning away from Jenkins and moving towards the Tul'Shar's voice, eventually spotting him lying inside the nearly completed forge with a heavy chisel in his hand.

"Where else would I be?" he questioned. "Still asleep maybe? Pah! I am an old man! Even in this world, anything more than six hours is a blessing."

"Old or not, you still work more than anyone else here," I replied.

"Work is life," Léandre stated. "The day that I stop moving is the day that I die. Besides, I am curious to see if your idea for the forge here will bear fruit."

"Heh, too true," I agreed with a chuckle, knowing exactly how the man felt. "But to answer your earlier question. Partly. The rest of my worries belong to the Adventurers that he brought with him."

"Worries that will lead to troubles?" Léandre asked, a note of caution in his voice.

"More like worries that raise uncomfortable questions, which in turn bring troubling answers," I said seeing Léandre start to crawl his way out of the forge.

"*Ah*," the Tul'Shar replied with sudden understanding. "Then perhaps I can take your mind off your troubles with some good news?"

"That would be wonderful!" I said excitedly as Léandre finished extricating himself from the forge and pulled himself up to his full height.

"Well, first thing," the lion-headed man began with a dramatic wave at the forge. "I proclaim this new forge ready for use! All we need to do now is stoke it...and see if your idea proves to be fruitful."

"That's great!" I exclaimed, clapping my hands together as I looked over the forge. "I can't wait to try it out!"

"I do hope it works," Léandre told me with a momentary look of worry. "Metals are starting to become a growing concern. Despite the quantity that we've managed to stockpile so far, the amount we are finding has dropped drastically. Unless we discover a more reliable source in the coming weeks, we are going to start experiencing shortages."

"I know," I said with a nod, understanding the architect's concerns all too well. "Hopefully this new forge will be able to smelt the metal we've recovered from the Tower. Gods know we have enough of that lying around."

"It may end up a case of using golden nails depending how valuable the metal ends up being," Léandre commented, turning to look at Jenkins as he walked over towards us. "But better for us to do that than to have the town's construction stagnate."

"Metals aside, Léandre told me earlier what you're planning to do with the forge...and I have to ask, do you think it'll really work?" Jenkins asked me uneasily. "I don't know anything about all this Æther that you've found, but do you really expect cutting a few channels in the forge and letting it mix with the coals to do anything?"

"I don't know, to be honest," I told Jenkins with a shrug. "If anything, I expect it to react violently and possibly explode."

Jenkins stared at me with his mouth slightly agape, "*What*?"

"I've already tried bringing the original forge to as hot as it could possibly go, and truthfully, I'm surprised I didn't cause it to crack from all the heat," I told the smith with a shrug, motioning towards the smaller forge that he had just been working on. "I figure scaling this one up to be larger and hotter can't hurt, but really at this point, I'm just throwing ideas at the wall."

"So...as I understand it, you're going to pour pure highly concentrated mana into the roaring fire and see what happens?" Jenkins repeated incredulously.

"Pretty much," I said with a shrug. "I'll start with a small amount and see what happens first."

"*Great*," Jenkins replied, completely deadpan.

"When in doubt, add Æther," Léandre chimed in with amusement before a thoughtful expression crossed his face. "But not to the wood. We've found that doesn't work well."

"What do you mean?" Jenkin asked, looking at the Tul'Shar with confusion. "Why?"

"It causes the wood to explode, unfortunately," Léandre replied wistfully and shook his head. "Ruined my favorite apron that day, I was never able to get all the blood out of it. Perhaps I added too much? I will have to try again another time..."

Jenkins glanced between Léandre and me, clearly struggling to keep his expression under control. "Remind me to go stand behind the doors when you start adding Æther to the forge. As curious as I am to see if your idea will work, I won't come back to life if I'm blown to smithereens like you two will."

"Plus, it would upset Shelia if she had to put you back together again," I offered to Jenkins as Léandre began to prepare the forge for lighting.

"She frets enough from the scrapes and scratches I get while working," Jenkins said with an exasperated look. "I would never live it down."

"Now that I think of it, I haven't seen much of your bride-to-be in the last few days, at least not since my assistants have learned to heal themselves from their mishaps," Léandre added, pausing from his work at the forge for a moment to look over at Jenkins. "She is keeping busy I trust?"

"She is," the man acknowledged as we moved to help the Tul'Shar in getting the forge lit. "She has started up a small chapel in town with a handful of Adventurers that want to become acolytes of the Dawnfather. There is quite a bit of study involved, both mystical and scripture."

"I can imagine," Léandre replied as he lit the forge and waited for the coals to start burning. "Hopefully though we won't be needing her or any of her acolytes' services today."

"Hopefully," Jenkins echoed in complete agreement.

We continued to chat amongst ourselves as the forge slowly began to build in heat, the temperature of the room rising in sympathy. The easy comradery between us quickly had the stress of Lazarus's news fading off my shoulders as I eagerly watched the intensity of the now blazing forge increase, until I finally deemed it ready.

"That should do it," I said, casting a warning glance at Jenkins as I pulled a jug of Æther out of my inventory and began to unscrew the cap. "If you were serious about putting some space between us, now's the time."

"To be safe, I think I will," Jenkins replied quietly, every inch of his expression showing that he wanted to stay beside Léandre and me. "Just in case this gets out of hand, and we need to react quickly."

"It *should* be fine," Léandre offered with an understanding nod. "Maybe. *Hopefully.*"

"We will see," Jenkins said, shaking his head at the Tul'Shar before stepping away from us. "Fingers crossed, right?"

"Right," I affirmed as I lifted the jug and motioned for Léandre to show me where he wanted the Æther. "Let's try a little at first and see what happens."

"Of course," he replied, guiding me towards a channel cut into the side of the forge. "Pour slowly and let it drain through the channels."

Following the man's instructions, I held my breath while I lifted the jug and began to pour out the Æther stored inside it into the forge. I saw the familiar glow of the Æther briefly as it left the jug and vanished into the stone channel that Léandre had carved. Watching the Tul'Shar for a sign to stop, I poured nearly half of the jug into the forge before his hand sliced out, warning me to stop.

"Do you see anything?" I asked, capping and putting the jug back into my inventory to free my hands.

"A moment," he replied, motioning for me to follow as we walked around to the mouth of the forge and peered inside, seeing the blazing red-hot coals. "It may take time to react, assuming it even does at all."

Waiting in anticipation, the two of us stared into the forge nervously, waiting for some sort of visible reaction to show that the Æther had taken effect, be it either a violent explosion or something else. The seconds ticked away slowly as the two of us continued to stare, disappointment slowly building until well over a minute had passed.

"Perhaps we could add more?" Léandre suggested. "We may have not—*oh!*"

Almost as if they had heard the cat-man's words, all of the flames inside the forge suddenly intensified with a loud rush of air and turned a bright azure color, causing Léandre and me to cover our eyes from the brightness. Blinded from the searing wave of light, I raised my arm to protect my face just as I heard a chime of triumph, followed by a message appearing in the center of my vision.

You are the first settlement to create an [Ætherfire Forge]! Congratulations!

You have gained 500 Renown!

"It worked!" I shouted, opening my eyes as the intensity of the Ætherfire forge began to dim, eventually evening out to a brightness that was bearable to look at. I heard Léandre exhale in relief before clapping his hand on my shoulder.

"We were first too!" he said excitedly, having seen the same notification that I had.

"You guys did it!" Jenkins shouted from across the room as he jogged his way over towards us, his face completely in awe as he stared at the azure-tinted fire in the forge. "It looks stable too!"

"It does," I agreed while watching the flames carefully for any sign of a runaway reaction that would be cause for concern.

"What are you waiting for, Lyrian?" Léandre asked me, his voice sounding impatient. "Try to smelt the shard that you recovered; we have no idea how quickly the forge will burn the Æther!"

"Right!" I replied, tearing my eyes off the azure flames as I reached into my inventory and pulled out the foot-long shard of metal that I had taken from the Irovian Tower. "Let's see if this does the trick!"

Grabbing a crucible, I tossed the shard inside and gently pushed the ceramic container into the mouth of the forge with a long pole, careful not to knock it over in my haste. Waiting patiently, I focused on the tip of the shard that was protruding from the top of the pot, silently praying for it to melt. If this new forge was unable to smelt the strange metal, then I had no idea what I was going to do.

Minutes passed as heat bore down into the crucible, and by extension the shard within, all three of us staring at it in anticipation, oblivious to the sweat that poured down our faces. Little by little, the shard took on a glassy sheen, losing its dark coloring as it slowly turned grey, eventually beginning to sag, its tip vanishing into the pot as it began to melt.

"It's melting!" I exclaimed, feeling a second wave of excitement course through my body as both Jenkins and Léandre let out similar cries of joy.

"Now if only we can bring enough metal back from the Tower!" Jenkins said excitedly while wringing his hands together. "Then our metal problems will be solved for a while!"

"Let's see how easy it is to work with first," Léandre cautioned, motioning me to pull out the crucible. "Try crafting it into something."

"Any suggestions?" I asked as I reached into the forge with the pole and latched it onto the crucible, lifting the red-hot pot out of the head.

"Axe head," Jenkins suggested. "I'm going to take one last crack at the tree today before tearing the Town Hall apart; I'll need all the extra tools I can get my hands on."

"In that case, one axe head coming up!" I replied as I set about pouring the liquid metal into an ingot mold, surprised to see that it was a dull azure color when molten, a small tag pointing to it as it dripped free of the crucible.

[Æthertouched Iron Slag]

Æthertouched? I repeated to myself mentally, careful not to let any of the metal drip as I set the crucible back down. *Is that because of the Æther in the forge, or is that what it used to be before?*

Pushing my question aside for the moment, I focused on working with the still hot metal trying to shape it into the axe head that Jenkins had requested, immediately finding that the metal was extremely difficult to work with. Cooling rapidly and unevenly back to its dark tint, I found myself hard-pressed to keep up with the hardening metal as it refused to shape itself from under my hammer evenly, leaving the finished axe head uneven and oddly shaped.

"Damn," I cursed after a moment, realizing that the metal was no longer malleable. "This metal cools *really* fast; I barely had enough time for more than a handful of strokes before it hardened."

"If I hadn't seen it with my own eyes, I never would have thought it possible," Jenkins agreed, looking over my shoulder at the axe head. "Though for a first attempt with an unknown metal that isn't too bad."

"It seems that unless it can be kept nearly molten, speed is more important than form when shaping this…Æthertouched Iron," Léandre noted, his head slowly nodding in thought.

"Seems like it," I replied, noticing that the single, poorly crafted, axe head had raised my blacksmithing experience by nearly forty percent.

Blacksmithing – Level 13 – 38%

We need to get more of the metal at the Tower back to Aldford, I thought, my eyes widening as I inspected the axe head, seeing its description appear in my vision, followed shortly after by a second notification. *With how much experience that one axe granted me, I could end up* reaching level twenty in Blacksmithing by this time next week!

Æthertouched Axe Head

Item Class: Magical
Item Quality: Poor (-10%)
Damage: 13-23 (Slashing)
Strength: +2 Agility: +2
Durability: 120/120
Weight: 0.75 kg
Base Metal: Iron
Special: Æthertouched

You have discovered the Crafting Prefix: Æthertouched!

Æthertouched: *Items with this prefix have been suffused with raw Æther, granting it an increased conductivity to mana. All weapons, wands, or implements created from an Æthertouched substance gain increased effectiveness when used to channel or cast magic. All armor created from an Æthertouched substance gain increased resistances against hostile magic and increased mana reserves. The effectiveness of the increases is dependent on the crafter's skill level and any other materials used in the item's creation.*

Damn, that's perfect for me! I blinked in surprise as I read over the notification, immediately understanding its worth to spellcasters, and in my case, Spellswords. *If we didn't have enough of a reason to go back to the Tower to recover the metal that's there, this would be enough on its own! As it is, this axe is almost just as good as Razor, and 'poor quality' on top of it all. If I can work at leveling my blacksmithing skill so I could make a high-quality version of a weapon with this type of metal...*

"Looks like we're about to get even busier," I said, barely able to contain my excitement as I motioned for Léandre to take a look at the axe head's stats. "Even with my half-assed crafting, this metal is stronger and sharper than the bronze we've been working with and based on its prefix, it looks like every single caster in the region, hell, *continent*, since we're the first to create an Ætherfire forge, is going to want gear made from this."

Léandre's eyes widened for a moment as he inspected the hand axe, absorbing the same information about the Æthertouched prefix that I had just seen. After a few seconds, he shook his head and looked up at me, a wide grin crossing his face. "I agree! I think we need to put recovering metal from the Tower at the top of our list now that we have a way to smelt it and an inkling of its true value..."

"Definitely," I affirmed, my mind already shifting towards how we would be able to move that much metal back to the town. "I'll have to think of a way that we can do it. Maybe we can connect a handful of the wagons the settlers brought together to help bear the load..."

"That may work," Léandre agreed, his voice taking on a thoughtful tone. "They certainly aren't being used for much now that the settlers have arrived, nor are the majority of the horses they brought with them."

"I'm sure that won't last," I replied, my mind already considering ways I could modify the wagons that were sitting unused in the far corner of the town. "Hmm..."

"Well, since it looks like all the excitement here is over for the morning, I'm going to get back to work," Jenkins said, noticing that both Léandre and I had fallen deep into thought as we considered the problem of recovering the metal. "Won't say that I'm not excited about getting some of that new metal to play with, but unless I can sort out that low hanging branch from the Ætherwarped tree...I'm going to be spending all my time repairing the Town Hall while the two of you get to experiment."

"I hope it works out, Jenkins," I told the man while motioning to the deformed axe head. "You want to use that thing? You should be able to get a decent edge on it…"

"With how many tools I've gone through trying to cut through the branch, just having one more might make all the difference," Jenkins replied with a frustrated expression on his face. "If nothing else, we'll be able to see just how well this metal stands up against the tree."

"Good luck, Jenkins," Léandre said to the smith as Jenkins grabbed the axe head and wandered over to fashion a haft for it. "Can I have a moment of your time, Lyrian, before you set off as well?"

"Of course!" I replied, watching the Tul'Shar turn to face me. "I'm just going to head back to craft some armor for the guild. What's up?"

"I wanted to let you know that my rest cycle starts today at noon, but that I will likely be gone until Friday morning," Léandre stated, watching me carefully as he spoke. "My assistants and the foremen from the settlers know what's expected of them, but I'm going to need your help with some of the construction that will be ongoing while I'm offline. Some of the bracing and material that needs to be crafted are beyond their skill, and I won't have the time to get around to it this morning."

"That's not a problem at all," I acknowledged, having filled in for Léandre on more than one occasion. "Whatever they need I'm happy to sort out."

"Good, thank you," Léandre said slowly, taking in a deep breath as he spoke. "But there is something else that you should know…just in case I don't come back."

"Don't come back?" I exclaimed with alarm. "What do you mean? Do you think you're going to quit playing Ascend Online?"

"I hope not," Léandre said in a small voice as he clasped his hands together nervously. "But coming back may not be up to me, not entirely at least."

"I don't understand, Léandre," I replied, the man's worried expression at odds with everything that I had known about him. "What's going on?"

"When I log off today, I am going to be undergoing Age Regression treatment," Léandre told me, his eyes fixating on me as he spoke. "At my age...there is a more than even chance that I may not survive the procedure, but with the waiting lists so long...this is the first opportunity that I've had."

"You're going for Age Regression?!" I looked at Léandre in disbelief, never having met anyone rich enough to afford the intensive nano-treatments that could effectively peel decades of aging away from a person, leaving them looking and feeling as they once did in their prime. "Léandre, j-just how old are you? If you don't mind me asking that is."

"It is not a problem at all," the Tul'Shar replied with a smile. "In May, I will turn ninety-five."

"I had no idea," I said, staring at Léandre in awe. "The way you move, how energetic you are..."

"Is how I used to be," he answered, giving me a sad look. "Before the weight of time pressed down on my bones and diseases robbed me of my health. This game has given me a taste of what I once had when I was younger, and even with the odds against me, I find that even if it costs me my fortune and my life, I must try."

"You'll make it," I told Léandre firmly, still trying to wrap my mind around what he had just told me, realizing that he was rolling the dice for a chance to turn his body's clock back to my age, or possibly even younger depending on how he reacted to the treatments.

I couldn't help but wonder if I would do the same in his shoes. After all, who didn't want to have a second chance at life?

"We will see," Léandre said fatalistically, his mood improving instantly now that he had unburdened himself. "But now with that news out of the way, I should bring you up to speed with all the projects that I have on the go, just in case…"

"Alright," I nodded at the Tul'Shar as he motioned for me to follow him out of the room, unable to stop myself from wondering if this would be the last time I spoke with him.

"So, first thing," Léandre began. "I've crafted the framework for the third longhouse already, and it should assemble easily, all you need to do is…"

Chapter 22

"Hey Lyrian, Cerril said that you were looking for me?" I heard Ritt's voice ring out in the Crafting Hall as I worked to finish a stitch on the helmet before me, the last and final piece of armor in my day-long marathon crafting session.

"Yeah!" I called to the merchant, turning away from my work for a second to beckon him over. "I have a few armor sets that I want you to put up for sale. I figured it'd be easier to get him to call you in here to show you everything, rather than drag it outside."

"Fair enough—" Ritt started to say as his feet echoed across the room, his voice suddenly catching when he saw the fruits of my labor organized into piles on the nearby tables, sorted by the differences in their design. "*Lyrian*, there has to be two dozen sets of armor here! You made this all *today*?!"

"Well, not all of it," I told the man, tying off my stitch and tucking it behind a fold of leather. "The leather base for the armor I made a few days ago, I was just waiting until I found something I could use to reinforce it all. Thanks to the snakes we fought yesterday, I finally had something to work with."

"I heard about that," Ritt stated uneasily. "I had one of your Adventurers resurrect practically on top of me at the quarantine yesterday. He said something about being eaten..."

"That must have been Connor," I replied with a nod. "He zagged when he should have zigged. Didn't stand a chance."

"Ugh, I don't know how you can do it," Ritt said visibly shivering at my caviler attitude. "I can stand up to a goblin or an orc without even blinking, but if it's something that can eat me…my knees are all jelly."

"Everybody has their fears, Ritt," I told the young merchant understandingly. "Nothing wrong with that."

"Easy for you to say." The man shook his head. "You can't die, well, permanently at least."

"Doesn't mean we're all eager to experience it," I said, motioning for him to follow me towards all the armor that I had crafted, picking up the helmet that I'd just finished. "Anyway, want to see what I have for you?"

"Very much," Ritt said, a note of excitement entering his voice as he looked down at the helmet I was carrying. "Are you looking to sell *all* of this?"

"Unfortunately, no," I replied, shaking my head at the man and seeing his expression fall. "The majority of this armor is for Virtus members. Considering that they all helped us kill the snakes yesterday, it's the least I can do to make sure that they have a share in the spoils. Plus, I've already handed out a few sets to Cerril and our newest recruits, they all desperately need new equipment."

"Are you sure, Lyrian?" Ritt asked as we arrived at the first table, his hand going out to stroke an emerald scaled tunic. "There is a lot of demand for your work in the town…"

"The guild has to come first, Ritt," I said, watching him reach out to pick up the piece that he had just touched. "The new recruits aren't wearing anything much better than rags, making sure that they're protected and outfitted is more important than making a fistful of coin."

"I guess," Ritt agreed half-heartedly, his attention largely focused on the armor in his hands. "Is this *bone*?"

"Snake bone," I confirmed as I brought up the item description of the set that Ritt was holding. "We recovered quite a bit of it from the snakes, and I didn't know what else to do with it at first. But after some thought, I figured I could use some of the ribs for bracing and the heavier pieces to protect the wearer's spine, shins and forearms."

Serpentine Striker Armor Set

Slots: Arm, Chest, Feet, Hands, Legs, Head, Shoulders
Item Class: Magical
Item Quality: Mastercraft (+20%)
Armor: 245
Set Bonus: (7/7)
Strength: +7 Agility: +7
Armor Type: Light
Weight: 9 kg
Favored Class: Any Martial
Mana-Infused: +15% Arcane Resistance
Level: 13

"It's somewhat similar to that spider armor that you made before," Ritt observed as he carefully inspected the various pieces of armor on the table. "Though the craftsmanship of your work is nothing short of amazing…"

"No reason to change a successful formula," I replied, dismissing the item's description from my vision. "Though there's only so much I can do with only leather at hand, I used up all of the chainmail we recovered from the Tower making armor for my group and Freya's group. But I'm sure you'll be happy to know I've finally used up all of that glowing spider blood that was lying around."

"Thank the gods for that!" Ritt exclaimed as he set the armor back down on the table and walked over to the one beside it. "The number of times that I opened the wrong crate and caught sight of that eerie blood with all fangs and claws packed away with it…I can rummage without fear now."

"Well, the claws and fangs are still in the crate," I cautioned, despite smiling wide at Ritt's statement. "So, don't let your guard down too much."

"*Noted,*" Ritt said with a nod before looking over at the armor stacked on the second table. "This next set here looks thinner than the other one; I take it this set is intended for the spellcasters?"

"Yeah," I confirmed, checking over the item description one more time as Ritt inspected the pile.

Serpentine Adept Armor Set

Slots: Arm, Chest, Feet, Hands, Legs, Head, Shoulders
Item Class: Magical
Item Quality: Mastercraft (+20%)
Armor: 185
Set Bonus: (7/7)
Intelligence: +7 Willpower: +7
Armor Type: Light
Weight: 6 kg
Favored Class: Any Arcane or Divine
Mana-Infused: +15% Arcane Resistance
Level: 13

"Flawless quality too, though I never doubted otherwise," Ritt commented while looking over the second set. "I doubt I'll have to try very hard to sell this armor once word gets out. If anything, I'll likely end up breaking up fights between Adventurers as they fight over your stuff. How many of the sets are you putting up for sale and how much?"

"Three of each set," I replied, motioning for Ritt to take a look at the last and final armor set, which was notably heavier and substantially reinforced when compared to the other two. Taking a moment to consider Ritt's second question, I brought up the last set's description, reading it over carefully before making a decision.

Serpentine Defender Armor Set

Slots: Arm, Chest, Feet, Hands, Legs, Head, Shoulders
Item Class: Magical

Item Quality: Mastercraft (+20%)
Armor: 370
Set Bonus: (7/7)
Strength: +7 Constitution +7
Armor Type: Medium
Weight: 18 kg
Favored Class: Any Martial
Mana-Infused: +15% Arcane Resistance
Level: 13

"I want it run as an auction, starting at ten gold with a thirty-gold buyout for each armor set," I told the merchant, clearing the item's information from my vision. "I have no idea what the demand will be like, but you can adjust the buyout if it's not high enough."

"I think that is reasonable," Ritt replied turning away from the tables and giving me a thoughtful look. "Some of the new Adventurers have a fair bit of coin on them, especially those that have been taking odd jobs with Jenkins, Ragna or Léandre. The least we can do is try to make money back off them."

"It wouldn't hurt to improve on the guild coffers either," I added, knowing that Virtus collectively had a little less than two-hundred gold pieces to its name. "If the guild keeps growing as it has been, it won't take long before we need a guildhall of our own and that labor will certainly cost us."

"Just keep making pieces like these and money will be the least of your problems," Ritt told me, inclining his head at the armor on the table. "Mind if I start carting some of the stuff away now? It's still early evening and most of the Adventurers will start coming back to Aldford when the sun sets, I'd like to get these armor sets set up in the shop before they arrive, in case any of them feel like shopping."

"Works for me," I told Ritt just as the Crafting Hall door opened once more, letting Constantine, Thorne and Marlin into the room.

"Yo, Lyr!" Constantine greeted with a wave as the three of them approached me. "Figured this would be where you were hiding all day today."

"Armor doesn't craft itself," I answered dryly, returning the wave to the trio. "What's up?"

"We've just about finished setting up Marlin's lab," Thorne said. "But we've run into a bit of a problem that we were hoping that you could help us with. Crafting help specifically."

"Oh?" I asked curious about what the three may need. "What's the problem?"

"There are a series of val—" Marlin began to explain before Constantine cut him off.

"Fiddly-bits," he stated, lifting what looked to be a broken length of copper metal that had ruptured violently. "We need a bunch of fiddly-bits like this pipe made so we can finish assembling the alembics. Apparently, it controls the pressure of the system...along with a bunch of other stuff that I really wasn't paying attention about."

"It allows the solu—" Marlin tried to add before Constantine cut him off a second time.

"Lyrian doesn't need to know all the details, Marlin," the rogue said, putting a hand on the alchemist's arm. "He just needs to copy this, but make it so it doesn't explode under pressure."

"Uh, I may need to know a bit more than that..." I replied uneasily, motioning for Constantine to give me the pipe that he held. "You said something about valves?"

"To control the flow of the solution in the alembics," Marlin blurted out, clearly expecting Constantine to interrupt him a third time. "This valve system couldn't withstand the pressure and exploded."

"It looks to be made poorly," Thorne added as Constantine gave me the pipe he was holding. "Whoever made this was likely half-blind or drunk, possibly both. We didn't think to check it compared to the rest of the equipment. Zethus is giving it a look over right now in fact."

"Well, I can give it my best shot," I said, trying to sound confident as I inspected the broken pipe. "I haven't made anything like this before though."

"If it helps with your motivation, once the alchemy lab is set up, Marlin thinks he can use some of the mushrooms we found, along with our stash of Yellowthorn to create a healing potion of some sort," Constantine told me excitedly. "I can't tell you how useful *that* would be to have."

"No kidding!" I exclaimed, looking down at the broken mass of metal in my hands and giving it a more detailed look. "Okay, I'll see what I can do to fix this."

"Hang on," Ritt called out while lumbering over towards us while carrying a small mountain of leather armor in his hands, his head barely visible from behind the pile. "Did I hear something about turning mushrooms into healing potions?"

"You did," Thorne affirmed, looking at the overburdened merchant warily. "Assuming Lyrian can fix the valve though."

"Lyrian will fix it," Ritt affirmed as he turned sideways and turned his head, allowing his greedy eye to land on me. "*Right*, *Lyrian?* We can sell healing potions to the Adventurers by the dozen for *fistfuls* of coin, and they'll always come back wanting for more."

"Uh, I'll try," I said, taken aback slightly by Ritt's sudden enthusiasm.

"Reagents would be a limiting factor in how much I could produce..." Marlin cautioned. "The mushrooms can be quite difficult to find in bulk."

"Nonsense! Why would we go looking for them?" Ritt exclaimed, turning himself around once more to look at the alchemist. "Have you never heard of a mushroom garden?"

"I-I can't say I have," Marlin replied nervously.

"Oh, that may work!" Constantine said with excitement. "That way we could have a steady supply of everything we need to keep brewing more potions."

"Steady supply of horse...*poop* too," Thorne added dryly.

"Exactly!" Ritt said enthusiastically while motioning towards Marlin with his chin. "Say, while Lyrian fixes that fiddly-thing for you, why don't we take a walk together, Marlin? I'm curious to hear what other things you'd be able to brew for Aldford once your lab is up and running."

"Uh, I suppose," the alchemist said nervously, casting a look at Constantine and Thorne who both waved him on.

"Ritt's going to have to make a few trips," Thorne told the Alchemist. "Can't hurt to hear him out. We'll be here sorting out what exactly we need from Lyrian to fix the valves."

"Okay," Marlin replied, clearly once again overwhelmed at just how in demand his services were. "I'll be right back then.

The three of us watched Ritt and Marlin leave, the young merchant wasting no time in starting to fire questions at the alchemist, oblivious to the heavy load of armor in his hands.

"Good guy, that Marlin," Constantine said. "But if you give him an inch to talk, he'll wear you down with the minutiae of his craft. I tried to be polite once and lost an hour of my day listening to him talk about differences of shade-grown Dustweed verses sun grown...thankfully a weird looking rope-snake interrupted him and gave me an excuse to leave."

"Oh, you found Noodles?" I asked, taking my eyes off the shattered piece of metal in my hands. "I overheard that one of the new Adventurers lost a snake few days ago."

"Noodles?" Constantine repeated, giving me a confused look before shaking his head in negation. "You know what, never mind. That must have been why Bax was so willing to take it off my hands."

"He is a pretty big help," I said. "Though I really haven't seen him around the last couple days or had a chance to talk to him."

"He's always on the move and hard to pin down," Thorne agreed. "Last I heard, he and Natasha were helping a group of settlers' stake out boundaries for farms to the west of Aldford. Given how many creatures we have running around the area, that's not exactly an easy thing to do."

"They'd certainly have their work cut out for them," I said, hearing the doors to the Crafting Hall open once more as Drace's dust-covered form walked inside.

"Lyrian! There you are!" the man exclaimed with a dry cough, trailing a small cloud of dirt behind him as he walked towards us. "I need a favor."

"Shit Drace, what the hell happened to you?" Constantine asked before I could reply. "You look like you've been swimming through dirt!"

"Ha, very funny," Drace growled with annoyance. "This is how *real* work looks, in case you were wondering."

"Is that what it is?" Constantine sniffed before letting out a mock sneeze. "No wonder my allergies are coming on."

"What do you need, Drace?" I asked, joining Thorne in shaking my head at Constantine's antics. "Is everything okay? You spend the whole day digging out that passage?"

"Yeah, me and a couple of other volunteers," Drace replied, the cloud of dirt and dust around him settling as he stopped moving. "But the going is *slow,* and we've already shattered practically all the picks that I made. I need you to make more for me, preferably a dozen, maybe two. With how the tunnel collapsed, we're digging through massive pieces of solid rock."

"Damn, okay, but why do you need me to make them?" I asked, not opposed to helping out, but concerned of how much time the crafting would take. "Was there something wrong with the ones you made?"

"Durability and item quality," Drace told me. "I'm not skilled enough in blacksmithing to hit 'Mastercraft' quality yet, even making the lower leveled bronze picks, but you are. The mastercraft pick I had this morning lasted about four times longer than a regular quality pick."

"Oh damn," I noted with surprise. "That's a pretty huge difference."

"No kidding," Drace replied. "Since we have no idea how far we need to dig...I rather us try and conserve as much metal as possible, because once it's gone...we're kinda screwed."

"I understand now," I said, thinking more about how item quality played into the overall lifespan of an item. "Though our metal problems may not be so bad anymore. I managed to smelt that mystery metal from the Tower, turns out it's something called 'Æthertouched Iron' and gives bonuses to anything involving magic."

"Sweet!" Drace exclaimed, his weary face breaking into a smile. "That'll be perfect for you and the other casters!"

"That's what I'm thinking," I replied nodding enthusiastically. "It's a bit of a pain to work with, but I'm sure we'll figure it out in time. I was hoping to put a few wagons together and take the guild out to try and bring back one of the big pieces, though that may take a couple days until we're ready though."

"That's not a bad idea," Drace said. "Though you'll have to count me and a few others out of that unless you want to put the excavation on hold."

"That's not a problem," I answered. "The metal will be useful to have, but I don't think it's worth delaying the dig for a day. I was thinking to grind our way through the plains to break up the boredom, since, after our fight with the snakes, I'm only a stone's throw away from level fourteen now."

"I'm pretty sure that Helix and the others will be excited to come," Thorne added. "They've been working hard on bringing the new recruits up to speed."

"Then I think we're—" I started to say before a muffled shout from outside the room caused me to stop and turn towards the door.

"I did it!" Jenkin's excited voice called out. "Lyrian, I did it! I cut that stupid branch!"

"What is it with everyone needing you today, Lyr?" Constantine commented just as the door to the room slammed open, swinging wide on its hinges as it revealed an exuberant Jenkins, holding a long azure branch in hand.

"Lyrian! Your axe worked! It cut through the wood like an axe should have!" The man shouted with near maniacal laughter as he crossed the room, waving the still glowing length of crystalline wood in the air. "I should have used the stupid thing first! But I waited until I'd blunted all of my other tools…"

"That's great news, Jenkins!" I exclaimed, my eyes focusing on the Ætherwarped branch that he held. "That can't be all of it though…"

"No, no, it isn't," Jenkins shook his head as he handed me the branch. "I gave the axe to one of my assistants to cut the rest of the branch down. Now that we know we can cut it. We're going to have to bring it down in a more controlled manner."

"Fair enough," I said, accepting the branch, surprised to find that it was cool and very smooth to the touch. "This branch is almost cold."

"I noticed that too," Jenkins acknowledged. "It was warm when I first cut it but cooled quickly on the way over here. Though, oddly enough, it is glowing brighter now."

"Strange," I commented, looking at the Ætherwarped length wood and seeing a tag appear in my vision. "But what isn't lately?"

[Ætherwarped Oak Branch]

"Tell us about it," Constantine grunted, similar sounds of agreements coming from both Drace and Thorne.

"Until we get more of that metal left to fashion any tools capable of cutting it, I don't know what we're going to do with it," Jenkin said, waving a hand at the piece of wood. "But I don't have any use for it; you can just hang onto it, for now, Lyrian, or toss it into the firepit, I guess."

"I'll hang onto it," I replied putting the length of crystalline wood into my inventory. "It seems pretty durable; maybe I can make it into something useful when the time comes."

"We'll see," Jenkins replied with a shrug before motioning to the door. "In either case, I'm going to get back to it. I'm clearing out a place in the storage room where we'll store the rest of the branch as we cut it down."

"Works for us," I said, everyone echoing in assent.

"Wrapping up then, Léandre told you he's gone for the next day?" Drace asked me as Jenkins gave us all a wave and turned to leave the room.

"He did," I replied. "I'm covering for him with some of the construction going on in the town tomorrow."

"Good, then I have a few more things to add onto that since I'm going to be busy with the dig for the next little while," Drace said inclining his head towards the door. "Walk and talk to the Foundry? If I can get those picks today, we can keep working a bit longer."

"Sure," I answered hesitantly, starting to feel the walls around me closing in as more and more work was piled on top of me.

"Gotta crack the whip to make sure Lyr keeps moving," Constantine chimed in elbowing me in the side as we started to move. "There's too much to do to keep those crafting hands idle."

"God forbid you actually pick up a tradeskill to help out," I said dryly as the four of us left the room. "Then you might actually be useful to have around."

"Sure, but at what cost?" Constantine replied, his voice taking on a mock dramatic tone. "Then I'll end up like you, and everyone will want a piece of me! I won't have a chance to turn around without someone asking me for something!"

"Maybe I should make you help Drace dig out that tunnel," I retorted, seeing a look of panic cross the half-giant's face.

"Lyr, no," Drace said quickly. "He'll cause a collapse within an hour. He's a hazard to be around!"

"I'm not a hazard!" Constantine exclaimed. "Things just don't always work out for me."

"Don't work out?" Thorne scoffed. "You nearly set Marlin's lab on *fire* this morning!"

"Wait, what?" I said with alarm, glancing between Thorne and Constantine. "What is it with you and fire, Constantine?"

"How was I supposed to know that powder was flammable?" Constantine grumbled waving a hand at the dwarf. "It was in a plain box!"

"I *told* you it was flammable and not to leave it in direct sunlight! But what did you do..."

"How much is happening around here that I don't hear about?" I turned my head to look at Drace while the bickering between Constantine and Thorne began to escalate.

"Do you really want to know the answer to that, Lyr?" The half-giant gave me a pointed look as we rounded the corner towards the Foundry.

"You know, on second thought...probably not."

"Good," Drace replied with a morbid laugh. "You'll sleep better that way."

Chapter 23

Friday, March 15th, 2047 - 7:34 am

How does Léandre do this every single day? The thought pounded through my already exhausted mind as me and half a dozen people strained to lift the framework of the fourth and final longhouse, the rope digging deep into my hands. Forcing myself a step forward, I felt Abaddon's elbow brush my side, the large Arakssi's muscles bulging as he bore down on his own rope. *I still feel wiped out from all of yesterday's work and today has barely even started!*

"A little bit more!" Jenkins' voice called out from behind us as we all continued to claw our way forward, grunts and curses filling the air. "There! That's enough. Stop! Second team, hold the frame steady while we fix it in place!"

"Finally!" Abaddon gasped as the rope in both our hands went slack, and we turned back to look at the fruits of our labor. "All done!"

"That felt like the heaviest one yet." I breathed, the sound of hammers filling the air as Jenkins and his assistants rushed in to stabilize what would become the entire side of the longhouse.

"We saved the biggessst house for last," the lizardman breathed. "I feel our trip hunting today will be the easier part of our day."

"Hah," I couldn't help but chuckle in agreement, my eye reflexively scanning all the settlers and Adventurers as I searched for a very specific Tul'Shar. "*Hopefully,* but you can never be sure with Léandre. By the time we come back, he might decide that we need to throw a fifth house up for good measure."

Assuming he comes back, I added silently to myself as I didn't see the man nearby, meaning that his avatar was likely still back at the Crafting Hall, working on the automated tasks that Léandre had assigned himself before logging off.

"Hrm, maybe," Abaddon grunted as he rolled his shoulders. "But by then we should hopefully have more hands to go around."

"Hopefully," I said, Jenkins's beckoning arm catching my eye as his team finished securing the framework. "Looks like I'm needed elsewhere. I'll be back."

"Sounds good," Abaddon called, the large lizardman turning to walk towards a cluster of Adventurers and Townsfolk waiting for their next task. "I'm going to go sit for a moment. Call us over when you're ready."

Giving the Arakssi a grunt of acknowledgment, I jogged over to Jenkins, the man carefully inspecting the entirety of the framework, ensuring that it wouldn't fall over once we moved onto the next stage of construction.

"Everything is looking good, Lyrian," he told me the moment I came into range. "We can start moving in the rest of the smaller frames and start nailing it all together. I know you're set to leave to the Tower today, but can I borrow you and the lizards for a bit longer? We're going to need some muscle moving things around."

"That's not a problem, Jenkins," I replied, glancing over the partially assembled longhouse myself. "We still have plenty of time before we're set to leave and I'm hoping to catch Léandre before we do."

"Alright, great," Jenkins nodded, his eyes looking over the building and planning out his next steps. "Grab your team and start on the back half, I'll work away up here with mine, we'll meet somewhere in the middle."

"Works for me," I stated, before spinning on my heel and making my way back towards Abaddon and the others.

The next hour passed with a flurry of construction as we continued to work on building the longhouse, our enhanced strength and endurance allowing us to work faster and harder than any of us could have ever managed back in Reality.

Heavily muscled warriors carried massive planks that would have required a small crane to hoist, while deft rogues and scouts hammered nails with blinding speed and precision. Any injuries were swiftly mended by a pair of roaming priests, and more than one disaster was avoided by the timely intervention of a mage, catching a falling or shifting object with a *Force Shield*.

With the majority of the crew having already had several weeks of construction under their belt from other projects around the town, everyone knew what was expected of them, allowing the work to proceed steadily and without any serious complications.

We're moving along faster than yesterday, I thought, silently measuring our progress and comparing it against our previous day's effort, which to me already felt like a lifetime ago.

It had been an eye-opener for me to step into Léandre's shoes for the first time yesterday, realizing just how much work he had taken upon himself to develop Aldford. It seemed that the man had an uncanny ability to be in multiple places at once, while simultaneously multi-tasking at each location and giving direction to those around him. I had found myself hard-pressed to keep up with all the work that he had left behind for me to manage as we completed the third longhouse and began to prepare the ground for the forth.

I hope he comes back, I repeated to myself for what had to be the hundredth time as I helped guide a heavy beam into place from high on the framework, held up high by the trembling arms of Helix, Abaddon, and Cadmus.

"That should do it!" I called down to the trio, after getting a thumbs-up from Myr and Huxley indicating that it was secure from their side. "You can let it go now."

With a groan of relief, the three lizardmen gradually relaxed their grip on the thick length of wood that they had hoisted over their heads, each of them happy to see that it remained fixed firmly in place.

"Great! Now we just—" I started to say as I jumped back down to the ground, only to be interrupted by Constantine's grumpy shout.

"Hey, Lyrian!" he called out as he entered the construction area and walked towards us, his expression already bearing a tired and annoyed slant to it. "Sorry to interrupt, but do you have a minute?"

"Uh, sure," I replied as Constantine stepped in close to us and motioned for the Thunder Lizards to form a circle around us. "What's up?"

"Stanton's done his sulking and has called a meeting, *right now*, of course," he said. "I have no idea what it's about, just that he wants to discuss how we're moving forward after our...*disagreement* the other day."

"You think it's a ruse?" Myr asked, her and all the other Thunder Lizards having been kept in the loop with Stanton's antics.

"On some level, *probably*," Constantine said. "But this time he's invited Lazarus and his group to be part of it. I sent him a message asking him if he knew anything more about it, but apparently, he doesn't."

"*Great*," I replied as I rubbed the sweat off my forehead. "Do we have anyone else in the meeting already?"

"Sierra and Halcyon are there right now," he said. "Drace already left to go dig. Caius, Freya and the others are getting the wagon ready for our trip."

"Alright," I sighed, looking up at the rest of the group. "Can you guys manage here while I go sort this out? I'm really hoping that Léandre is going to show up soon..."

"We'll manage," Helix said confidently, giving me a toothy smile. "This isssn't the first house we've helped build you know."

"Thanks, guys," I acknowledged as I stepped out of the group with Constantine and started to pick our way out of the construction site. Making sure to catch Jenkins' attention as we left, I pointed to the Town Hall while mouthing Stanton's name, only to have him nod in understanding while giving me a sympathetic look.

"I have to wonder just how oblivious Stanton is to how everyone perceives him," I said to Constantine as we walked. "Even people who haven't met him know that he's an ass."

"Word travels fast in a small place like this," the rogue replied. "Plus, I'm sure everyone that had the pleasure of travelling with him probably got their fair dose."

"I guess so," I said half-heartedly while mentally trying to reach out to Amaranth and finding that he wasn't in range of our mental link.

Must still be out hunting, I realized with a mental shrug, knowing that the cat had grown bored sitting around while I had spent the last two days crafting and building.

Moving with urgency, Constantine and I made our way back into the Town Hall and rushed up the stairs into the meeting room, the both of us silently wondering what Stanton wanted now. Pushing open the door, the room was already silent as we stepped through it, everyone turning to look at our arrival.

"Lyrian, thank you for coming on such short notice," Stanton greeted with a calm aura of politeness that I would have never expected to hear from him, let alone after how we parted ways the other day. "I understand that you were busy this morning."

"There's always something to do," I replied, completely caught off guard by his amicable disposition as I looked around the large table to see who else had been invited to the meeting.

Sitting to Stanton's left was Veronia, with Lazarus, Sawyer and Ransom on the noble's right. On the opposite side of the table, Sierra and Halcyon sat near Aldwin, leaving two empty seats for Constantine and me directly across from the noble.

"What was it exactly that you wanted to meet about?" I asked, moving to take a seat at the table, unable to help but notice that none of the Mages Guild members or Dyre were present at the meeting.

"I wanted to discuss what happened the other day at the ruins and how we can move forward from our last...*conversation*," Stanton began, his bright eyes fixating solely on me as he spoke, immediately unsettling me with a piercing quality that I had never felt from the noble before. If I hadn't known better, I would have almost imagined that there was someone other than the Stanton I knew sitting before me. "But I believe that before we can do that, a confession, of sorts, is in order. Events have progressed far enough for you all to be brought into the fold."

"Huh?" I grunted with sudden confusion, glancing over at Constantine and Sierra on either side of me and seeing similar expressions on their faces. "What are you talking about, Stanton? Brought into what fold?"

"I will address that in a moment," Stanton replied, holding up a single finger to keep any further questions at bay. "But until our conflict a few days ago we weren't certain if you all could be trusted, and we needed to be sure where your loyalties truly were."

"You didn't trust *us*?" I exclaimed incredulously, unable to restrain myself after hearing what the man had just said. "That's rich coming from you!"

"What is the meaning of this, Stanton?" Aldwin growled from the head of the table. "What exactly have you two done?"

"What we were sent here to do," Veronia stated in a hard voice as she turned to regard Aldwin with an unreadable expression. "Ensure that Aldford stays free from any the other Noble Houses influence."

"The other Houses?" Aldwin repeated, his eyes glancing between the pair. "What do they have to do with this?"

"Please, Fredric. Did you think that House Denarius would be the only House that would have an interest in a settlement this far beyond Eberia's borders?" Stanton asked. "Or the only House with access to the Mages Guild to detect the ruptured Ley Line?"

"Ever since I was exiled from Eberia, I haven't thought about *any* of the Houses, Stanton. *Yours especially*," Aldwin spat viciously.

"*Clearly*," Stanton replied. "But you are foolish to think that they haven't been thinking about you, especially in light of what's happened in Eberia of late."

"Me?" Aldwin's eyes widened with surprise. "Why in the world would they give a damn about me?"

Veronia grimaced at the Bann, her voice sounding hard as she spoke. "You know exactly why they would give a damn about you, *Fredric*."

"You need to start explaining what the hell you're talking about," I interjected angrily as an all-too-familiar expression of resignation crossed Aldwin's face at Veronia's statement. "Because I for one am starting to lose my patience."

"That includes us too," Lazarus added from his side of the table, his voice matching mine as he twisted in his seat to look at the noble beside him. "What *more* have you been hiding from us?"

"Nothing more than you needed to know to play your part," Stanton replied, turning his head towards Lazarus and his companions. "And you have done well enough, all things considered."

"What does that—" Lazarus began to ask before Stanton cut him off, frustration finally entering the noble's voice.

"*Enough*," he announced sharply, raising his hand in the air to forestall any more questions. "Allow me to explain what I must first; then you can all ask the questions that are no doubt burning in your minds. These interruptions are doing nothing but wasting our time."

Closing my mouth at my own question, I pushed down on the confusion and anger that was coursing through my mind, trying to calm myself as Stanton began to speak.

"As you all know, when I first arrived I announced myself as a House Denarius representative, here to check on our investment and bring news from Eberia, a role that perfectly fits everyone's expectations of *Lord Adrian Stanton's* abilities," the man began to explain. "But what few people know, is that the original bearer of that name has been dead for over twenty years now, killed in a meaningless skirmish during *The War*."

The man that we had just known as Stanton regarded us for a moment, letting his revelation sink in as our mouths dropped open in shock.

"Instead of letting his name die, House Denarius chose to keep it alive and allowed me the opportunity to cultivate it into a personality suitable to pass unnoticed among high society, enabling me to conduct House business that would best not be made public, if you understand my meaning."

"So, let me get this straight," Constantine said slowly, shaking his head from side to side. "All this time you have just been *pretending* to act like a pompous dick? Like some sort of act?"

"That is an exceptionally crude way to describe that persona, yet not entirely inaccurate," Stanton replied inclining his head towards the rogue in acknowledgment. "People choose to see what they wish to see, and very few decide it worth the energy to look past an abrasive man such as Adrian Stanton."

The man paused, letting a small smile creep across his face. "Yourselves included."

"After all these years, you've been a damned *House-Spy*?" Aldwin accused, his voice sounding completely disgusted as he glared at the masquerading noble. "I can't believe I was so *blind*! I would have never let you within the same room as the Prince had I known! Though it truly doesn't surprise me to learn that Emilia has use for your kind!"

"As you no doubt know, Fredric. We prefer to be referred to as '*Agents*' in polite company," Stanton corrected, shifting his gaze towards the Bann. "And I wouldn't have been much of one if I allowed you to find out what I was in the few chance meetings we had."

"A clever name hides nothing, '*Stanton*'," Aldwin said, emphasizing the man's stolen name. "I am no fool. I know all too well what your kind is used for, and an inkling of the all of blood that has been shed in shadows over the years."

"Then you should be all too happy that the Queen has directed me to Aldford on your behalf," the man replied. "Because we have reason to believe that the other Houses have sent some of their agents to infiltrate Aldford...assuming, of course, that they hadn't already placed some in the original group of settlers."

"*Wait*," I interrupted, still trying to wrap my mind around the unexpected turn this meeting had taken. "You're telling us now that we could have *spies* in the town?"

"We believe there is a very strong chance," Stanton admitted. "Nearly a month ago we lost sight of a handful of known agents belonging to House Amberwain and House Phineas, last seen leaving Coldscar in an westbound direction. Furthermore, on our journey here, I made one House Wynbrandt agent as well, though...*fortuitously* perhaps, he fell prey to the bandits during the raid."

"Those other Agents never made it here," Sierra said casting a hard glance at Stanton as she spoke. "You and the other settlers are the first arrivals to Aldford in weeks. Either they went somewhere else, or they ran into the bandits ahead of you and were killed."

"Or perhaps they organized the bandits in the first place, attempting to cut Aldford off from Eberia," Stanton countered, drawing surprised stares from everyone at the table.

"They would do that?" Halcyon asked in a sharp tone. "The settlers are your own people! What could they possibly gain from killing your own countrymen?"

"To isolate us," I said, looking at the bandits we had killed in a new light.

I had assumed that they had set up shop near Aldford hoping to catch travelers unaware as they either left the town or were about to arrive, being motivated by greed.

But if what Stanton is saying is true, and greed wasn't the only factor...

'If' being the key word.

"I will remind you all that, all of this is conjecture at best—" Stanton continued to explain before my voice cut him off.

"How do yours and Veronia's plan to depose Aldwin and annex Aldford fit into this?" I asked, seeing everyone's head snap towards me as the words left my mouth, and then back towards Stanton after I finished. Lazarus's eyes were especially wide when he looked at me, but the angry expression on his face told me that he wanted to know just as much as I did. "Because right now, that's a more pressing concern than wherever these agents may be. Of course, *assuming* there are any agents in the first place."

Despite having everyone's eyes on him, Stanton appeared completely unfazed by my statement, giving me a slow nod as he clasped his hands in front of him.

"Very well, I suppose we can jump ahead to there if you are so impatient for me to explain my motivations," Stanton said with a slight sigh of frustration. "The plan to annex Aldford was my attempt to get any agents within Aldford to reveal themselves, namely by giving them an avenue to make contact with Lazarus or his companions. I had hoped to use their dissatisfaction with being pressed into my service as being a motivator. Unfortunately, no doubt due to your rather dramatic rescue of the caravan from the bandits, he chose to make contact with your guild. Something I hadn't anticipated when I had first laid the groundwork for the plan, nor something that I could easily counter once it was in motion."

"You *knew* I was listening?" Lazarus asked in disbelief. "You set *all* of this up just to see who we'd contact?

"Of course," Stanton stated. "In fact, I went through great pains to ensure that you would be. I have also been meaning to tell you that you aren't as stealthy as you think you are. How you even managed to survive as a thief is beyond me."

"God damn you, Stanton!" Lazarus snarled from his seat. "All we've been trying to do is keep you from getting *killed,* while you play your games and manipulate everyone around you!"

"Again, *that is my job*, and I won't apologize for using you as the blunt tools that you are," the agent replied, annoyance finally entering his voice. "And while I appreciate the sentiment of your protection, I assure you, I am *quite* capable of taking care of myself."

"This is fucking bullshit!" I exclaimed as I saw Lazarus open his mouth to yell at Stanton, the frustration around the table starting to build to unbearable levels. "I can't believe a thing that you're saying anymore, Stanton! Do you have a shred of proof to back up any of this?!"

"Of course, I do," Stanton answered, his hand reaching to his robe and pulling free a folded length of paper with a heavy wax seal, offering it to Aldwin. "We didn't know under what circumstances I may have had to reveal myself to Fredric, and as such, the Queen prepared a letter of introduction for me."

"Oh, come the fuck on!" Constantine exclaimed from my side. "You expect us to fall for that? Letters can be easily forged!"

"Not one from the Queen," Stanton said idly. "She has sealed it with magic, and Fredric is the only one here that can open it. Should anyone other than him break the seal on it, the letter will simply go up in flames."

"I left all this behind for a reason, Adrian," Aldwin growled, clearly familiar with the type of protections that

Stanton was talking about as he reached to snatch the letter roughly from the agent's hand. "I wanted to be free of Eberian politics for once in my life. To finally be away from the constant secrets and intrigues that plague the kingdom."

"I am sorry, Fredric, but that is simply just not possible," he replied, shaking his head. "Ignore it at your own peril, but Eberia's politics have begun reaching out to Aldford and refusing to play the game is no different to conceding."

Aldwin didn't reply as he turned the letter over his in hand, then broke the wax seal with one smooth motion of his finger. No sooner was the seal broken, did a tiny spark of magic flash in the air, vanishing as quickly as it appeared. Reading the letter intently, Aldwin's face turned into a scowl as his eyes darted from line to line, shifting into anger and finally outright surprise.

"The gods must laugh and laugh as they witness my life," he said with resignation, passing the letter onto Sierra and Halcyon. "There is no doubt that this letter is from her…"

It didn't take long for my friends to finish reading the letter before sliding it down the table towards me, leaving me staring down at a page with long and flowing handwriting.

To Sir Fredric Aldwin, from the hand of The Dowager Queen and Matriarch of House Denarius,

Fredric,

If you are reading this letter, then chances are that either you or my agent have irrevocably screwed something up and are in need of my words to either verify his mission or to keep you from killing him. Perhaps both.

In either case, I am disappointed in the both of you.

I had hoped that his mission would proceed with a minimal amount of exposure, but unfortunately, I must assume my agent had good cause to reveal himself. To that effect, I will reiterate what he should have told you: we believe that the other Houses have taken notice of Aldford, either having detected the presence of the Ley Line themselves and seek to claim it or have finally decided to pursue a personal vendetta against you.

However, with the political situation of Eberia having become what it is, I cannot afford to publicly rebuke them or continue to retain any formal ties with Aldford, or with you.

I am certain you rejoice at this prospect as much as I do.

*To that effect, I am hereby absolving you of any debts you may owe to my House, with the understanding that you will follow through with the mission that my agent brought to you in regard to the Ley Line. Eberia **needs** it restored if we are to put up a good show against the Ascendancy.*

As a parting gift and insurance against any foolishness on your part, I am assigning you my agent for a term not to exceed six months before you are to send him back to Eberia, war or not. He should be able to assist you in ensuring that your settlement is free of any of the other Houses' agents while providing training on how to avoid any future political entanglements.

Do with it what you will, Fredric, but it is my advice that you find yourself powerful allies to surround yourself with. Perhaps a legion or two of Adventurers if you can find enough of suitable temperament. Regardless to say, Eberia will not be coming to your aid should something befall your settlement.

It is my sincere wish that we never meet again, in this life or the next, though I doubt the Gods will be gracious enough to honor that request.

Yours truly,

-Matriarch Emilia Denarius

"Satisfied?" Stanton asked me as I finished reading the letter and passed it over to Constantine.

"The Queen has a rather particular way with words," I said slowly, still trying to process what I had just read and the future implications that it would have for Aldford. "But I still don't understand why the hell you went through all this trouble; you should have told us earlier!"

"As I said before, I didn't trust you earlier," Stanton replied. "Until *I* was sure that you yourselves hadn't been suborned by one of the other Houses, I couldn't take the chance. It wasn't until you banned us from accessing the ruins that I was confident you were working alone and that your loyalty lay exclusively with Aldford.

"Had you been working with another House, you would have likely continued to keep us close to determine the fullest extent of what I knew, then likely attempted to arrange an '*accident*' somewhere in the ruins."

"Is that what you would have done?" Constantine asked, having finished reading the Queen's letter.

"No," Stanton replied shaking his head at the rogue. "Accidents like that are hard to prove.

"I would have done it during the chaos of a bandit raid with no one else the wiser."

Chapter 24

"Rah!" I slammed Razor into the head of the giant beetle before me, the burning anger behind my attack cracking the tough chitin that comprised the creature's face. Dodging around a pair of snapping mandibles, I hefted Razor back again in the air and brought it down onto the creature's head a second time, a loud crunch sounding over the plains as the weakened chitin finally gave way in a spray of ichor.

Working itself up into a frenzy from the pain, the creature launched its large bulk forward to knock me off my feet, only to sweep through the empty space where I had just been standing. I had long since become familiar with these creature's tactics and fighting them had become a mechanical series of moves and counter moves.

Leaving me with all too much time to dwell on anger and frustration that I was carrying.

I caught a clawed leg on Razor's edge, gritting my teeth as the anger within bubbled to the surface, causing me to shove hard against the creature's limb. My anger driven sword, easily slicing straight through the chitinous leg at the same moment a burning dagger appeared in my free hand. Stepping past the beetle's now shortened guard as it spun to face me, I slammed the dagger into the creature's head, aiming for the very spot that I had weakened with my earlier blows.

Already cracked and bleeding, the beetle's natural armor was no match for my attack as the flaming dagger pierced straight through its exoskeleton and turned its brain to ash. Hesitating, the creature's mandibles twitched as it slowly registered what had just happened, its body then falling to the ground with a heavy crash.

You have slain a [Giant Plains Beetle]!

You have gained Experience!

Congratulations! You have reached Level 14!

The prospect of having finally gained a new level did nothing to soothe my foul mood as I shook the blood off Razor's edge and looked around the battlefield for any more beetles in my immediate vicinity, hoping that there was still something to take my anger out on. My eyes scanned over the fallen corpses of five other beetles, already barely remembering fighting them.

<That appears to be all of them,> Amaranth's wary tone filtered through my mind, unable to hide his worry at my mental state. *<The woman appears to be reasonably unharmed as well.>*

<Hrm,> I mentally grunted back at Amaranth as my eyes landed on the bald Adventurer that we had seen fleeing from the swarm of beetles a few minutes ago, looking only slightly worse for wear. I couldn't recall even seeing her during the battle after Amaranth and I had charged into the beetles, though judging by the ichor streaming from the mace she was holding, she hadn't been idle.

"Thanks." She breathed heavily, glancing between us as the bodies began to dissipate. "There was no way I could have survived that—hey, you're that guild leader guy from Aldford aren't you? I've seen you before in town."

"No problem, and yeah, that's me," I replied, no longer surprised that I was noticeable enough for people to recognize. "Do you have a group out here? You look a bit lost, and these plains aren't safe enough to travel alone."

"Not all who wander are lost," the Adventurer said philosophically, causing me to look back toward her with a blank expression. "...but I sure am."

"By yourself?" I asked for a second time.

"Yeah," she admitted with a deep sigh. "And I *really* have no idea where Aldford is anymore."

"Well, you're pretty far away from it," I said, motioning towards the South-East. "How long exactly have you been wandering out here?"

"Uh, well…" the woman replied hesitantly, clearly embarrassed. "Since Wednesday? I didn't think I went that far…but when I started to head back, I ended up coming across a lake, which I knew I never passed by before. Then when I climbed a rock to try and get my bearings, I ended up disturbing a bunch of lions and had to run away from them…at least until I fell into some sort of bug colony and was captured by some sort of ant—"

"I think I get the picture," I said holding a hand up to stop the Adventurer, unable to keep a chuckle from escaping my body, which had the fortunate side effect of dampening the anger that I had been holding onto. "Well, we're not headed back to Aldford just yet, but I have a group nearby that you can travel with for the day. We should be back in Aldford later on tonight."

"That would be perfect!" the woman exclaimed, relief crossing her features. "My name is Edanea by the way."

"I'm Lyrian," I replied before offering her the loot from the beetles that Amaranth and I had killed. I figured with the way her luck had been running, she could definitely use something to show for her efforts.

Shifting away from the battle scene, I turned back towards the south-west, relying on my Party Sense to guide me in the direction of my group, and by extension the rest of the guild as they slowly made their way towards the Tower. The meeting with 'Stanton' earlier this morning had taken up well over an hour before we all decided to take a break for the day and give ourselves a chance to digest everything that he had revealed to us.

That and to give Lazarus and his friends the time that they needed to yell at the agent in private since none of them were thrilled at the prospect of spending the next six months away from Eberia, nor happy with just how much he had hidden from them.

Something that I can't help but sympathize with, I thought, staring at the ground as I walked, feeling the distant anger and frustration still raging deep in the core of my being. Stanton's revelation had gone far to shatter any sense of control and understanding that I had begun to feel in handling him or understanding Eberian politics, causing me to berate myself for my naïveté. Everything had seemed so much simpler this morning when I had woken up having to only worry about finishing the next longhouse and hoping that Léandre logged back in.

Now, after Stanton's revelation, I couldn't help but look at everyone in Aldford suspiciously, wondering if they could be a double agent or there on behalf of one of Eberia's Noble Houses. What would I do if it turned out that Shelia, Jenkins or Ritt turned out to be a spy? Or any of the other founding settlers? Finding out that there was a spy within the town would destroy morale permanently, if not turn everyone on one another. Even the barest rumor could result in a witch-hunt that could end up hurting, if not killing someone who could otherwise be innocent.

And that didn't even include the bandits that we had killed several days ago. It was entirely possible that they may try to make their way back up towards Aldford for a shot at revenge. In addition, if one of the other Houses *did* send an agent in one of the caravans that had been destroyed by the bandits, they could very well assume that it was *us* that had killed them and decide to retaliate somehow.

God, I hate politics, I scowled before shifting my attention towards my character sheet in hopes of distracting myself, remembering that I had gained a level after the fight with the beetles. Scanning through it to take note of any changes, I then mentally added my five free attribute points to agility, instantly feeling my body become ever so slightly more limber.

Lyrian Rastler – Level 14 Spellsword
Statistics:
   HP: 792/792
   Stamina: 720/720
   Mana: 790/790
   Experience to next level: 43/29400
Attributes:
   Strength: 54 (68)
   Agility: 49 (65)
   Constitution: 43 (44)
   Intelligence: 51
   Willpower: 19
Skills:
   Magic:
      Evocation – Level 13 – 96%
      Alteration – Level 13 – 98%
      Conjuration – Level 13 – 85%
      Abjuration – Level 13 – 72%
   Weapons:
      Unarmed Combat – Level 14 – 38%
      Swords – Level 14 – 2%
      Axes – Level 11 – 35%
      Daggers – Level 12 – 73%
   Other:
      Stealth – Level 11 – 12%

Luke Chmilenko

Wordplay – Level 12 – 31%
Perception – Level 13 – 85%

I'm going to have to start specializing soon, I realized as I looked at my character sheet and noticed that my three main attributes, Strength, Agility, and Intelligence, were all reasonably balanced with regards to one another. I had done my best to try and keep them that way, at least for these early levels in the game, but with my next Class Skill Point available to me at level fifteen, I had to start thinking a bit more of how I was going to develop my playstyle.

I knew that no matter what, all three attributes would be important to me, but it was likely in my best interest to focus on one over the other. But with that being said, I had no idea which route appealed to me the most. Going a strength route would allow me to hit harder and wear heavier armor, but the tradeoff would have me sacrificing mobility. In comparison, going an agility route would raise my mobility to almost impossible to match levels, but would limit my raw damage output.

Then there was also the option of going into an almost pure caster build, and focusing on intelligence, like the one Mozter had shown. If I had a large enough mana pool, I could dump spells into people from near point-blank range and not have to worry as much about keeping up with them physically.

At least until I ran out of mana, I told myself grimly, remembering the nature of my Ætherwarping and unsure if I'd ever find a way to cure it. As useful as it would be to have a larger mana pool, if only for my own piece of mind, not being able to regenerate it naturally or being at risk of dying if I ever ran out didn't make that path as appealing to me.

I let my thoughts wander for a while as Amaranth, Edanea, and I walked slowly across the plains in silence, my mind bouncing between what my future playstyle could be and going over the one point that had largely been forgotten during the meeting with Stanton. In her letter to Aldwin, Emilia had effectively divested herself from Aldford and given up any claim to the settlement, essentially recognizing the town as an independent entity, which was something that we had all wanted, but something that also had the side effect of withdrawing whatever protection her house had been able to offer.

Before learning that there could be potential spies in our midst and other Houses moving against us, I wouldn't have even second-guessed her absolving Aldford of its debt and accepted it at face value. But knowing what I knew now, I wasn't all that confident anymore. With my cynicism and paranoia working in overdrive, I couldn't help but wonder if there was more going on behind the scenes than she was willing to tell us.

You have no frame of reference for any of this, Marcus, an inner voice tried to tell me. *It's not like you took 'Espionage 101' back when you were still in school. That's probably why the Queen assigned Stanton to us, likely to give us the basic grounding in what to look for and how to react.*

Which forces us to trust a professional liar and killer, I mentally countered, making a note to myself to pick up some real-world material about the spy trade and medieval politics the next time I logged off. I had no idea if anything I read would even come close to applying to our current situation, but knowing myself, I'd feel better if my mind was occupied.

Shaking my head to pull myself out of my reverie, I was surprised to find that I had unconsciously pulled up my quest log, specifically the portion of it pertaining to the espionage quest that I had become all too familiar with in seeing over the last few days. Once again it hovered in my vision, full of information that was questionably useful at best and downright aggravating at worse.

Statecraft, Deception and Veracity!

After a particularly tense confrontation, Lord Stanton has revealed himself to be a House Denarius Agent, a spy directly in the employ of Queen Emilia. Proving his credentials with a letter from his mistress, the agent then went on to warn you that the other Houses have taken notice of Aldford and either already have, or are looking to insert their own agents into the town.

Writing off his past actions and Lazarus's warning as an attempt to force any other agents to reveal themselves, Lord Stanton then went on to explain what he had learned of any other House Agents, mentioning that he has already detected and eliminated one during the bandit raid, but that the potential existed for there to be others hiding in Aldford.

Under orders from the Queen, Lord Stanton has been assigned to train those in Aldford in the arts of espionage and subterfuge, while ensuring that Aldford remains independent and free from any of the Eberian Noble Houses' control. You aren't sure what sort of politics is being played behind the scenes or if you can truly trust Lord Stanton and Queen Emilia, but for now, they appear to be on your side.

Or are they?
Discover any Agents in Aldford: 0/?
Pass Stanton's Training: 0/?
Difficulty: Very Hard
Reward: Unknown
Penalty for Failure: Unknown

I was fairly confident that I was going to develop an ulcer the further I progressed down this espionage quest chain, if not in game, then certainly back in Reality. I had no idea what Stanton's training would entail, or if I would be able to stomach what was bound to be a morally questionable experience. But for the sake of Aldford, I knew I had to try. Especially if I was serious in trying to follow through on my idea of founding an Adventurer led nation out here in the region. If I didn't get a good grip on how to play the political game now, while I still could, I was more than likely going to regret it later.

"Is that them?" Edanea's voice had me looking up from the ground I had fixated on, and spotting her hand pointing towards a slow-moving shape in the distance.

"That's them," I confirmed, following the woman's hand and squinting, seeing the blurry shape resolve itself into a long flatbed wagon being pulled by a team of horses with several other people walking alongside it.

"Whew, you certainly have a lot of people in your guild," Edanea replied with a note of surprise as we picked up our pace now that our goal was in sight.

"And always looking for more," I told the Adventurer in what I hoped was a good-natured tone. "Feel free to mingle about today and see if you're interested in joining. We have a pretty good group so far."

"Hmm, I may do that," Edanea said, thinking thoughtfully to herself as we covered the final distance between us and the guild, Constantine's waving hand signaling me from his standing position on top of the wagon.

Letting the now rescued Adventurer move away from me as she went to join Cerril's group walking alongside the wagon, I shifted my approach towards Constantine, seeing the rogue take a seat at the edge of the flatbed, his feet hanging over the side.

"Feeling better now that you've managed to blow off some steam?" Constantine asked me by way of greeting, stroking Amaranth as the big cat rushed past me and leaped onto the wagon, lying down beside the rogue and letting his paws hang off the edge. "Saw you picked up a stray too."

"She was lost on the plains for the last couple days," I replied, answering Constantine's second question first while angling myself to keep pace with the wagon as it continued its steady trek eastward. "As for your first question, no, not really."

"Can't say I blame you," Constantine said sympathetically while glancing over at Edanea, who had since struck up a conversation with Cerril. "Also, that's not bad for surviving out here alone."

I shrugged at my friend while giving him a serious look. "You ever get that feeling where you're over your head and just trying to stay afloat?"

"Pretty much ever since I fell out of my mother," Constantine answered crudely, despite matching my stare. "But that's a natural state for me. The moment I feel that I finally 'get' something, I'm instantly bored and start screwing around looking for something else to do."

"Hrm," I grunted back at the rogue, knowing all too well what Constantine meant. Having grown up with him, 'being bored' often precluded an event that almost always ended up getting him or the both us in trouble.

"I take you mean more about everything that Stanton dumped on us today?" Constantine went onto ask.

"That's a big part of it," I replied, despite shaking my head at the question. "Léandre hasn't come back yet either."

"He's only half a day late," Constantine told me in an understanding tone. "And like you said, he has a hell of a long way to wind back the clock."

"Assuming they were able to wind it back at all," I countered, remembering what the man had told me. "His odds of living weren't the best."

"As opposed to the one-hundred percent chance nearly everyone else has to die?" Constantine shot back with a raised eyebrow. "Don't borrow any more stress than you need to, Lyr. Sure Léandre may be late in coming back, but there could be ten thousand and one reasons explaining that. All of which still leave him alive."

"You're right," I said with a sigh before continuing to walk along for a while in silence. "This wasn't quite how I expected the day to unfold today though."

"Well, you should start adjusting your expectations then, Lyr!" Constantine exclaimed, waving a hand at our surroundings. "We're living in a fantasy world now! Who's to say what will come our way next?"

"Maybe Aldwin is really an ancient dragon in disguise," he said dramatically. "Or that tomorrow one of the moons will fall from the sky, or that Amaranth here will suddenly sprout wings and be able to fly."

<Wings would be a pain to clean,> Amaranth grumbled to me as he let out a snort. *<I would prefer to be faster if nothing else.>*

I couldn't help but laugh at my familiar's serious tone of voice while understanding what Constantine was getting at. "Amaranth says he'd prefer to have super speed over wings."

"*Smart*," the rogue agreed, moving to scratch the cat's back. "Flying's overrated."

"I understand what you were getting at though," I told Constantine. "We shouldn't expect things to stay the same all the time, and to know that the game will throw us curve balls from time to time."

"Exactly," he acknowledged. "Could be a blessing that we find out this way from Stanton now, instead of later. I figure with all the Adventurers we're looking to recruit, being a little cutthroat and manipulative may be the difference between getting our way and getting steamrolled."

"I had a similar thought earlier," I admitted. "I can't help but cringe at what Stanton's training is going to be like though. I'm not expecting it to be all roses and sunshine."

"I don't either, Lyrian," Constantine agreed while holding up a hand. "But there's one important thing to note."

"Oh?" I asked, suddenly curious. "What's that?"

"I'm not bored anymore."

Chapter 25

"Great job, everyone!" I called out while looking over all the exhausted and sweaty guild members before me, each and every person having spent the last four hours helping load the jagged, fifteen-foot-long piece of dark metal onto the flatbed wagon. "Take a few minutes to rest up, and we'll start the trek back."

It had been a long and laborious process as we extricated the broken length of metal from inside the fallen tower, with more than a few mishaps and one outright near catastrophe marking our day. But at long last, our first recovered chunk of metal was finally secured to the wagon and ready to be taken back to Aldford, where I was sure we would no doubt face an entirely new set of challenges in unloading it.

At the moment though, that was a problem for the future and one I would be happy to tackle solving, now that I had a way to smelt the metal.

"Well," Helix greeted me with a weary breath. "That was both harder, yet easssier than I was expecting."

"And as easy as it'll ever be," Freya added tiredly as both she and Thorne moved to join us. "The other pieces are going to be even worse to recover. They're buried too far into the ground to be easily pulled out. We'll have to come back with a team and spend a day or two just digging."

"I'm not looking forward to it either," the dark-skinned dwarf added. "But let's leave problems like that far off in the future; we can worry about them later. We still need to get ourselves back to Aldford first!"

"That we do," I said, unable to disagree with Thorne's sentiment. "Hopefully we can stretch this metal long enough so we won't need to make a second trip anytime soon. It's going to be one hell of a learning curve before any of us are able to craft things with it reliably though."

"We sshall see," Helix replied with a shrug of his large shoulders while inclining his head towards the solid hunk of metal sitting on the wagon. "We certainly have plenty to practice with."

First nodding at the lizardman, I then turned my attention towards the Tower, seeing the burnt-out shell of what was once its roof littering the ground before it. The fire that I had set what seemed like a lifetime ago, having done a number on the fallen tower, devouring all the wood that had once been present in the structure as well as crushing all of the goblin huts below it when it had fallen free.

"Might as well get moving," I said after a moment, my eyes landing on the blackened remains of the tiles that were once the roof of the Tower. "Hopefully we can be back before it gets too dark."

"And hopefully we don't get stuck," Freya added, her eyes glancing down nervously at the wagon's wheels. "This metal sure weights a lot."

"Here's to hoping," I agreed, motioning towards the front of the wagon. "I'll check on the horses, and make sure they're ready to go. Might as well start getting the rest of the guild ready to move in the meantime."

"I'll be sure to tell them that the sssooner we get back, the sooner they can eat a hot meal and go to bed," Helix replied with a chuckle. "They may just end up pulling the wagon themselves in hopes of getting back faster."

Parting with a laugh, the four of us then split up, each of us heading off to take care of our last-minute tasks before we set off back on our journey to Aldford. By some miracle, our combined efforts managed to get everyone to leave within the next fifteen minutes, all the newer Virtus members suddenly moving with renewed purpose, no doubt motivated by Helix's promise of food and sleep when they returned to the town.

Before long, we had left the Tower behind, taking a narrow route through the forest that we had discovered a handful of weeks earlier. No doubt cleared out by the goblins that had once inhabited the fallen tower to move their own wagons in and out of the forest. It was slow and careful going at best, given the oversized length of the wagon and the proximity of the trees   , but we managed to press through the woods gradually without getting stuck.

"I can see the plains up ahead," Thorne called back to me from his position driving the wagon. "We should be able to make great time once we get out in the open."

"Great!" I replied, from just behind the dwarf, sitting in a loose circle with Freya, Caius and Halcyon. The four of us shamelessly enjoying the perks of our rank within the guild and catching a ride on the wagon, while everyone else was forced to walk alongside it.

"We're making pretty good time all things considered," Caius said leaning back in his seated position, his skull bone staff sitting across his lap. "I was worried that we might get stuck on—"

Caius paused halfway through his sentence, a frown coming over his face as he looked out towards the forest, a worried expression coming over his face.

"I hear something," he said, his eyes suddenly widening. "*Shit!* A lot of somethings!"

"What?" Thorne gasped from ahead of us, his head whipping around to look behind him.

"Where?" I asked pushing myself up to my feet and looking out into the woods, realizing that Caius was referring to his Bloodsense ability, which allowed him to hear the heartbeat of anything that carried blood in its veins within a certain range.

"Straight ahead to either side of us," he replied, shaking his head as he followed my lead and stood up.

"An ambush?" Freya asked as she readied herself to stand up.

"Don't all move at once!" Halcyon exclaimed in a nervous tone, catching Freya by the arm before she could stand up. "If someone's watching us, you're going to spook them!"

"What do we do then?" Caius asked, belatedly turning the quick ascent to his feet into a stretch.

"We—" An arrow flying through the brush cut off my reply as it suddenly slammed into my shoulder, filling my world with a burst of pain and causing me to fall down onto my knee in shock.

"Oh, fucking hell!" Freya spat as she scrambled over towards me, her voice then splitting the air. "AMBUSH!"

Freya's shout barely had time to register in everyone's mind, before the sounds of screaming voices and rushing bodies began to echo from the forest ahead of us. Looking up in the direction of the noise, I saw the world shimmer, as Halcyon threw up a wall of force before us, catching a handful of follow up arrows before they could fall upon us.

"Shit!" Thorne yelped, flinching from the onslaught of arrows that bounced off Halcyon's shield, the mage thankfully having the foresight to include him within its protection.

"Lyrian, are you okay?!" Freya asked as both she and Caius turned to look at the arrow sticking out of me.

"I'll be fine," I replied, reaching up to pull the arrow free of my shoulder, wincing as I did so. "A little help, Caius?"

"On it!" Caius said, already moving before I could even finish the question, his hand lightly touching my shoulder and causing the wound to vanish.

Nodding at Caius in thanks, I motioned for us to get off the exposed wagon while simultaneously sending a message to Amaranth, the cat having gone scouting with Sierra and Constantine. *<We're under attack!>*

<We know! They just revealed themselves!> My familiar replied somewhat distractedly. *<We are moving to flank them now! Many are rushing towards the path! Be wary!>*

"Damn, we have incoming!" I said as Freya, Caius and I leapt off the wagon, Halcyon choosing to remain on top to protect Thorne and the horses pulling the wagon. If either of the two large draft animals pulling the wagon went down, getting the wagon back to Aldford was going to be next to impossible.

Assuming of course, that any of us survived this surprise attack at all.

Putting aside the question of *who* would be attacking us for the moment, I glanced around my surroundings, looking to see how the other guild members had reacted to the sudden interruption of our journey back home, half expecting my eyes to land on several clusters of shell-shocked Adventurers, staring numbly into the forest.

But instead of an array of frozen or panicked statues, I saw that they had all reflexively fallen into their assigned groups, each of them complete with a glowing shield of force shimmering around them as they rushed forward towards the head of the wagon, two of the groups rushing forward on the side opposite from us with the other moving directly towards us.   A wave of pride and relief flowed through me as I realized that all the new recruits had taken our lessons over the last week to heart and hadn't let panic overcome them.

Spotting Alistair's familiar face at the head of the group of Adventurers rapidly closing in on us, I waved for him to follow us, before turning my body and leading the way, shouting as I ran.

"Raiders attacking from the woods on either side!" I bellowed as I rushed towards the front of the wagon, seeing dozens of people burst free from the heavy brush ahead of us, rushing onto the path, some of them visibly stumbling as branches and thick plants impeded their progress.

I idly wondered if it was my movements that had forced the attackers to spring their attack early, or if Amaranth and the others had contributed in spooking them, but whatever the case was, it was readily apparent to me that we had only partially fallen into their ambush. With every second that passed, more and more attackers steadily streamed out of the forest ahead of us, clearly caught out of position from where they had planned to launch their attack.

Up to us to make the most of a lucky break, I thought, the wound in my shoulder already a memory as my feet continued to move forward, a plan forming in my head. *We're still a long way from being in control of this fight.*

The first rule that I had learned when surprised by a close ambush was to push past the instinct to hide and take cover, especially against one that had gone off halfcocked like this one. Staying put gave away the initiative, giving the enemy the opportunity to do whatever it was that they wanted. No, the best way to survive an attack like this, was to charge straight into it, taking away the time for the enemy to adjust and take control of the encounter.

Which is exactly what I planned to do.

"Charge them!" My voice rang out into the forest around us as I rushed past the now panicking horses at the front of the wagon. "Don't let them form up! Ranged attackers, let them have it!"

"You heard the man!" Helix shouted a heartbeat behind mine, his large scaly form visible as he and the rest of the Thunder Lizards rounded the other side of the wagon, moving to fall in on my right. "Melee in the front ranks!"

A roar of defiance rose up into the air as we all surged forward towards the raiders, the thunderous clap of spells beginning to ring out as mages on both sides began to unleash their arsenal from afar, before the clash of melee forced them to switch to more precise and targeted spells.

Despite the planning and tactics the attackers had shown, I couldn't help but notice that the leading edge of their ranks appeared to be caught off guard by our sudden rush into combat. Their movements faltering for a moment as some of their members took a step back, watching us as we closed the distance in surprise. Whoever these Adventurers were, it seemed that they lacked the edge that only hard training and experience could provide.

Who are these people? The thought couldn't help but cross my mind as I looked at the raiders ahead of me, seeing that some were covered in nothing better than rags, while others were clad in finely crafted leather armor. *Was there another group of Bandit Adventurers this way that we missed? Or have they made it back this way already?*

Time quickly ran out for my internal questions as we finally slammed into the raiders, the loud crash of bodies and metal overwhelming the earlier sounds of magic. A half-orc's face briefly filled my vision as the battle began, his expression shifting from angry defiance to horror as I batted the point of his sword away from me and plunged Razor into his unarmored chest. Without even hesitating, I continued forward with my charge, shouldering him hard in the chest and knocking him backward off his feet, aided by his desperate efforts to pull himself off my blade.

Flailing wildly, the half-orc crashed into a companion behind him, taking the pair of them down to the ground in a tangle of limbs. Without even a second's hesitation, Freya's spear shot out from beside me, reaching to stab the unlucky Adventurer in the throat with her spear, before snapping back to embed itself in the stomach of the man before her. Stepping forward, I moved to finish what I had started, thrusting my blade into the eye of the half-orc I had wounded earlier, and then immediately delivering a wicked slash to an attacker on my left, his attention keenly focused on Alistair, who had taken up position beside me.

Caught completely unaware, Razor sliced a long gash under the man's arm, causing him to flinch in pain and glance towards me, inadvertently giving Alistair the opportunity to bury his axe directly into the side of his head, sending him falling lifelessly to the ground.

It was hard for many to understand at first, but fighting in a line of battle like this was not a clean or honorable affair. The fights didn't unfold like personal duels played out on a grand scale like they did in movies, each attacker only striking at the one before them. A line of battle was in fact, pure chaos, a press of bodies so close that there was rarely enough room to swing your weapon, let alone have a clear and fair angle at a single opponent. Attacks could seemingly come from any direction at any time, and more often than not, any fatal wounds that landed weren't delivered by the person before you, but from the person on either side of them, taking advantage of an opening that you had no chance of defending against, let alone seeing.

That was the reason why I had gone through such pains in making sure everyone - my friends, the new guild members and even myself - had practiced intently in fighting together. Survival in a close battle such as this depended on having those beside you watching your guard and you watching theirs. Catching a blow that was meant for your partner on the left, meant that she was able to land a thrust of her own on another opponent, which then, in turn, created an opening for someone else, the action endlessly repeating up and down the entire line. Consequently, a single person falling out of line could result in several others taking injuries or falling themselves as several attacks of opportunities played themselves out from the momentary lapse, forcing the line to readjust itself in a hurry.

It was this hard-practiced skill, combined with our better equipment that allowed myself and the rest of Virtus around me to carve through the first few rows of raiders like they were nothing, their numbers only serving to get in their way as they scrambled to meet our assault, more than a few latecomers still trying to force themselves out of the heavy foliage that bordered the forest path.

"Gah!" I screamed in exertion as I chopped Razor into the shoulder of a poorly armored bandit, feeling his rusty sword grate harmlessly against my chest, the dull blade unable to damage the links that made up the armor.

Ignoring the man's pained scream as I pulled my weapon free, I shoved him hard away from me and saw him vanish in the press of bodies behind him as yet another Adventurer wearing a set of rags that could barely be called clothes, let alone armor, practically threw himself onto my sword in a rush to attack me.

What the hell is with all of these unarmored bandits? I thought as I pulled Razor free from my overeager attacker's gut and delivered a killing slash across his throat, sparing a moment to glance around the press of people. *Where are all the ones I saw wearing armor earlier?*

Taking in my small portion of the line in an instant, I felt my heart leap as I realized that I had lost sight of the overall battle and that in the chaos of fighting, the center of our line, driven forward by the Thunder Lizards, Freya and myself, had pushed itself too far forward. To my left, I saw Alistair and the rest of his group struggling to keep pace with their attackers, the majority of whom appeared to be the armored bandits I had seen earlier.

"Shit!" I breathed, immediately recognizing what the raiders had suckered us into doing. "Pull back! They're stacking the—"

<LOOK OUT!> Amaranth's mental shout tore through my mind at the same moment that four large balls of fire swept out from the woods on either side of us.

Moving faster than anyone could react, the fireballs streaked through the air directly towards us, burning effortlessly through the low hanging branches, before detonating in a fiery explosion all around us. Throwing my hands in front of my face in reflex, I felt my feet leave the ground as I was thrown backward from the blast, briefly catching a glimpse between my fingers that one of the fireballs had been far enough off target to land directly in the heart of the attackers in front of us.

Spinning through the air, I barely had enough time to process the searing pain that shot through my body before crashing back down onto the ground in a heap, a heavy weight landing on top of me just as something hard hit me directly in the forehead.

"Ugh," I reflexively tried to coil away from the pain but found myself unable to move, my head spinning wildly as a trio of alerts flashed urgently in my vision, sending cruel sparks of pain into my rattled brain.

Unknown's [Fireball II] hits you for 238 points of fire damage!

Unknown's [Fireball II] hits you for 112 points of fire damage!

Unknown's [Fireball II] hits you for 87 points of fire damage!

Freya hits you for 45 points of damage!

Shaking my head to dismiss the prompt, my eyes snapped open, only to find Freya lying directly on top of me, her free hand clutching the side of her helmeted head as she grunted in pain. A long mark of blood on the edge of her helmet making it readily evident to what had hit me in the head.

"*Freya,*" I managed to gasp as I felt something wet drip across my face.

"Shit, what—," Freya began to say, her eyes snapping open, widening as she saw my face and began scrambling to get off me. "Oh damn! I'm sorry, Lyrian!"

"It's fine," I replied, cutting her off as I moved to force myself up off the ground and tried to piece together what had just happened, feeling my head begin to spin. "W-we need to move."

Forcing myself through the pain as I sat up, I turned my head to scan the battlefield, finding that we had been far from the only ones to be affected by the blast. Nearly everyone, be it Virtus member or raider, had been staggered or knocked off their feet from the quartet of fireballs that had streamed from the forest around us, with the raiders seemingly having taken the worse of the damage due to the one rogue fireball that had landed in the heart of their formation.

Those who still stood amongst the raiders hesitantly glanced into the forest, their expressions a mixture of both worry and anger, while the stunned Virtus guild members struggled to pick themselves up off the ground and buy themselves some measure of space during the brief pause in battle.

"Fuck, Helix and Zethus just vanished from Party Sense," Freya told me just as I finished my scan around the battlefield, having already pushed herself up into a standing position. "They must have caught the fireballs point blank."

"Damn," I cursed while mentally reaching out to check on my groupmates, then flinching as I realized that both Sierra's and Constantine's presence was much further away than it had been a few seconds earlier. Whatever they had run into in the forest, had been more than they could manage, and they had both just respawned back in Aldford.

"Sierra and Constantine too."

"What the fuck is going on?" Freya snapped as she offered me a hand to get me back up on my feet. "I thought we cleared out all the bandits in the area!"

"So did I," I wheezed as I accepted her hand and allowed her to pull me up, sending a message to Amaranth as I rose. *<Hey! What's happening?! Are you okay?>*

<I killed one of them and wounded the other!> Amaranth's mental voice was pained and rushed as he spoke. *<I am coming to rejoin you! I require help!>*

<Who did you kill? What happened to Constantine and Sierra?> I asked my familiar, completely unaware of just what he was talking about, but not receiving a reply.

"Amaranth is coming," I told Freya urgently while taking a moment to cast *Lesser Shielding* on myself now that I had the opportunity. "He said that he needs help and he's not replying to me."

"We're about to have our own problems here, Lyr," Freya said, motioning towards the raiders who had steadily managed to pick themselves up off the ground during our interlude. "We need to form up and regroup back at the wagon—"

A loud feline roar intermixed with feral barking cut off the remainder of Freya's statement as Amaranth leaped out from the forest in a spray of leaves and broken branches, a large, translucent red wolf soaring through the air a heartbeat behind him. Moving faster than the cat could react after landing, the wolf leaped onto Amaranth and knocked him onto his back. Straddling the cat, the wolf savagely bit at my familiar, managing to land several bites before a vicious kick sent the ghostlike creature flying off him, the creature's body shifting eerily as it landed on all fours without any apparent effort.

<Are you okay?> I called out to Amaranth, moving to rush forward towards the creature that threatened my familiar, only to have it bound away from me at a blinding pace, a single tag identifying it in my vision. *<What the hell is that?!>*

[Malevolent Wolf Spirit] – Level 17

<I don't know,> Amaranth replied in a pained voice as he forced himself up onto all four paws, revealing a patchwork of bloody and burned fur across his body. Some of it being obviously someone or something else's, but a generous portion belonging to the cat himself. *<But it leaped upon Constantine before I could react and moves unnaturally like no creature I've ever seen.>*

"Would you look at that?" a familiar voice called out from across the battlefield, interrupting our conversation as a group of armored men dressed in heavy leathers walked out of the woods, opposite to the one that my familiar and the spectral wolf had just emerged from. "Seems that they like playing with one another."

The spirit wolf gave a snort of derision at the statement, giving Amaranth a hungry look before turning and trotting over to join the speaking man's side, its ghostly appearance making it hard for the eye to follow.

Tearing my attention away from the strange creature, I felt my blood go cold with anger as I recognized who the speaking man was, the large stag's skull on his head doing little to disguise his identity. It had been weeks since any of us had seen him last, not since everything had happened with Graves. We had just all assumed, *hoped*, that he had cut his losses and went elsewhere.

Clearly, we were wrong.

Glaring at the man, I tried to force down the rage that erupted in my chest, his name tearing itself out of my throat like a curse.

"*Carver.*"

Chapter 26

Silence fell over the battlefield as the name floated through the air, everyone staring numbly at the half-orc, taking in his new appearance, the man having long since shed the plain leather armor that we had all last seen him in, replacing it with a nightmarish collection of fur and hide.

Dressed from head to toe in a patchwork of blood-soaked leathers and animal fur, Carver's armor sent involuntary shivers down my spine as I spotted bits and pieces of flesh still clinging to the individual pieces that comprised it. The longer I stared at the armor, the more it appeared to be sewn together by a madman, with barely a care to appearance, unless one actively wanted to project fear and the capacity for violence.

Which knowing Carver, he most definitely did.

Completing the rest of his disturbing appearance was a cruel looking short spear bearing a serrated edge and a heavy wooden shield covered in similar bloody hides as his armor, the items serving only to enhance his already vicious image.

<Him!> Amaranth hissed audibly from my side, his ears going flat on his head as he pressed himself to the ground, ready to pounce. *<I remember this man from before…>*

"Lyrian, Freya," Carver called out joyfully, his stag-horned helmet dipping towards me in greeting before his eyes shifted ever so slightly to the blond warrior beside me. "It's been too long since we've last seen one another."

"No, Carver, it hasn't," Freya spat angrily as she whipped her spear into position before her, training its point on the half-orc. "In fact, you should have never come back here."

"Goodness I've missed you, Freya, your friend Thorne too," Carver replied with a chuckle, his gaze then focusing past us and towards the wagon. "It just isn't the same without you two anymore, you—"

"What do you want, Carver?" I cut the half-orc off, noticing that while the man was talking all the surviving raiders on the battlefield were regrouping behind him and the other men that he had exited the forest with, prompting me to motion for the rest of the guild to do the same, lest we get caught off guard a second time. "What the hell are you doing here?"

"Straight to the questions already, Lyrian?" Carver asked, shaking his head and making an all too familiar clucking sound with his tongue, his eyes shifting to watch the surviving members of Virtus carefully as they formed up around me. "No time to stop and catch up with an old friend before diving straight into business? Seems to me like plenty has changed with you; you look *rough*."

"*You aren't our friend,*" Freya spat from beside me.

"And we don't have *any* business together, Carver," I ground out through clenched teeth, feeling a hand touch my back and send a brief wave of healing energy through me, before Alistair appeared in the corner of my eye and doing the same for Amaranth. In the distance, I could hear the nervous whinnie of the horses pulling the wagon, along with the slow clop of their hooves as they drew closer. No doubt Thorne was concerned that more raiders could be prowling through the forest, attempting to circle us, and had decided to bring the vehicle closer to us.

"As wounding as your words are, they aren't entirely true, you see, at least not anymore," the half-orc replied, his voice taking on a scolding tone as he jabbed his spear in my direction. "I know we had a rather harsh parting the last time we saw one another, but I was willing to let bygones be bygones, assuming you all minded your own business. We all got swept up into Graves's crazy scheme after all, and were just trying to find a way to survive."

"But then several days ago, I get word that not only have you lot have been sticking your noses into places they don't belong," Carver continued, his expression hardening as he spoke. "But that you have managed to destroy one of my best-producing groups, root and branch."

There was a pause in the air as we absorbed what Carver had just said, several of the newer guild recruits calling out as they put the man's statement together.

"*The Grey Devils,*" Freya's scorn filled voice split the air. "They were *yours?*"

"They *are* mine," Carver corrected, his hand waving towards several of the unarmored Adventurers behind him who were now glaring at us with undisguised hatred. "You see...the little stunt you pulled, destroying their hideout and killing the lot, split them between Eberia and Coldscar, depending on where they last bound themselves, which you can imagine is more than a little bit inconvenient."

"I can't say that breaks my heart all that much," I said, allowing my eyes to slide off Carver and towards the unarmored Adventurers, my mind trying to make sense of the half-orc's admission and piecing it into what we had just learned from Stanton a few hours earlier.

If Carver was running the bandits, does that mean that there isn't any connection with the other House Agents? I asked myself. *He isn't the kind that would take orders from someone else willingly...unless of course, it inconvenienced someone he didn't like.*

Like us.

"Mine either," Carver replied with more candor than I was expecting, unaware of the flurry of thoughts passing through my mind. "I know now that they got greedy and were taking every single caravan or wagon that passed by. In hindsight, I should have caught that, given how much they were bringing in, but that doesn't matter anymore, does it? We're past that point now."

"No, it doesn't," I agreed, bringing my gaze back to Carver and banished my whirling thoughts, knowing that I was going to need to be present with what was coming next. "And because of that, you're here to send a message by repaying the favor."

"I knew you were a smart one when I first saw you, Lyrian," he said, his face breaking out into a genuine smile. "That's exactly what I'm doing. What I *have* to do if I'm to keep things nice and manageable on my end of things. I'm sure you understand."

"I do," I replied, tightening my grip on Razor's hilt as I spoke, mentally readying myself for the second round of this battle. "But regardless of how this turns out, now that I know that you're out here and setting yourself up as some sort of a Bandit King, I'm not exactly going to let that stand."

"A Bandit King?" Carver repeated, giving me an incredulous look before he broke out into a laugh. "Yeah, I suppose that's how you'd see it. On some days, I suppose it's not all that far from the truth either. As for letting it stand, I suggest *very* much that you do exactly that, Lyrian. This...*peace offering* of mine is a one-time thing."

"We know too well how any of your *offers* end up, Carver," Freya growled, the surviving Thunder Lizards grunting in sympathy. "With a knife in your ribs when you least expect it."

"Only if you step out of line again," Carver warned, before slicing his spear through the air and waving all the Adventurers behind him forward. "But on that note, I think it's high time we got this show on the road. Maybe if you're lucky, one of you might live long enough—"

"MOVE!" Thorne's bellow, accompanied by the pained sound of injured horses tore through the air, followed by the creaking rumble of hooves and wood.

"Wha—" Reacting instinctively, I moved to spin around and look behind me, my gut sinking as I thought that we were under attack from behind. But before I could complete my turn, Freya grabbed me roughly by the shoulder and dragged me off my feet as she leaped past me.

"Shit!" Freya cursed behind me as the two of us fell on top of a small bush that lined the path, just seconds before a pair of horses thundered through the spot that we had just been standing, the rest of the wagon following close behind.

Shaking off the impact, I craned my head upwards just in time to hear Thorne shout something incomprehensible as the wagon shot past us, directly towards Carver and the advancing Adventurers. No sooner did he finish, did a thunderclap of magic fill the air, followed by a shimmering wall of force appearing at the head of the wagon.

"*Oh damn,*" I gasped, realizing what both Thorne and Halcyon had just done as the wagon plowed into the horde of raiders with a loud crunch of flesh and bone, clipping or outright trampling all those who were unable to get out of the way in time, due to his timely *Pryoclap* and the press of bodies.

"Lyrian, let's go!" Freya yelled, slapping me on the back as she pushed herself off the now flattened bush. "They bought us a chance!"

"Right!" I called back while getting my feet under me and staring ahead at the chaos that Thorne and Halcyon had caused.

The large cluster of raiders that had been threatening us had been thrown into complete disarray, a gaping hole now in the middle of their formation as they desperately tried to pick themselves off the ground or continued to writhe in pain on the ground. Their numbers, plus the heavy foliage on either side of the path had worked against them, many of them unable to get completely clear of the charging wagon in time.

The few lucky ones that had managed to avoid getting hit by the wagon stared numbly away from us, watching the departing wagon rumble and bounce furiously as the panicked horses carried it away from us and onto the distant plains.

At least the wagon is safe for now, I thought as I glanced towards the surviving members of Virtus and noticed that a few of our own had also suffered glancing blows from Thorne's maneuver and were receiving healing from Theia. Something that I figured was a small price to pay for the damage that we had managed to inflict.

"Now's our chance!" I shouted as I gripped Razor tightly and took the first step forward towards Carver and his band of raiders. "Let's finish this or go down fighting! Virtus, attack!"

There was a moment of silence, my words taking a few seconds to register in everyone's head, allowing Freya, Amaranth and I to take several steps before a disorganized cry rose behind us, the rest of Virtus finally rallying to my call. An echo of footsteps filled the air behind me as I led the charge back into battle.   It was time for round two to begin.

The three of us slammed into the disoriented mass of Adventurers like a force of nature, Amaranth's flying form taking down a quartet of the raiders as he leaped into the fray with a savage roar, his claws and teeth flashing viciously, rending apart flesh everywhere they touched. A heartbeat behind my familiar, Freya and I followed in his wake, ruthlessly slashing out at the wounded still lying on the ground or taking advantage to attack those distracted by his rampage.

For the second time in the day, my world dissolved into chaos as the rush of battle consumed me. Blood and violence filled my vision everywhere I looked, screams of pain intermittently drowned out by thunderclaps of magic or Amaranth's primal roar as he threw himself onto yet another victim. I had thought that the first battle with these raiders had been a brutal affair, each of us fighting with the burning rage of being ambushed out of the blue, but with the way this second battle was evolving, it had been almost cordial in comparison.

Carver's presence struck far too many chords amongst the founding members of the guild, many of them having experienced his cruelty first hand. From the moment that he had revealed himself, this whole incident had gone from a simple ambush in the wild, to something very personal, something that would be impossible to stop until we were standing over his body.

Or he was standing over ours.

Swinging a crackling Razor in a powerful arc through the air, I bared my teeth in a vicious snarl as the blade connected with the side of an Adventurer's head, biting deep into flesh and bone. Feeling the sword anchor itself into the man's skull, I gave it a hard yank while simultaneously discharging the *Shocking Touch* I held, causing my attacker to jerk and twitch violently as he collapsed to the ground.

Wrenching my weapon free as the man fell, I angled my blade and stabbed it deep into the armpit of a man threatening Freya, before tearing it free and deflecting a scything axe that was aimed directly at my head. No sooner did I bat the axe away, did a single set of Amaranth's claws sweep along the midsection of my attacker, tearing through both armor and flesh as if it were paper, exposing soft and vulnerable organs.

With no time for a merciful stroke to end his suffering, I lashed out with a heavy kick at my attacker, catching the stooping man directly in the face as he reflexively bent down to stuff his exposed innards back into himself. The blow sent him reeling backward as he fought to keep his balance, eventually causing him to collide with an all too familiar shape behind him. Before the man could even begin to recover, a jagged spear tip burst free of his chest from behind, then vanished with a wet sucking sound as it was pulled free.

"Pitiful fool," Carver growled as he shoved the now dead man off himself and out of his way, fixing me with an angry glance, his stag bone helmet sitting awkwardly on his head, which was now missing a single antler, no doubt due to Thorne's reckless charge with the wagon. "Not even worth the energy to keep alive."

Bounding forward right at Carver's side was the crimson spirit wolf that I had seen earlier, its hungry, feral expression shifting eerily as it faded in and out of sight. I had no idea where Carver had managed to find or befriend such a high-leveled creature, but the cunning glint that I saw in its eye made me doubt that it was a simple spirit.

"Nice to see that you haven't changed, Carver," I greeted the man, noticing that all of the other raiders around us had suddenly given us a wide berth after seeing him brutally dispatch one of his own, allowing both Freya and Amaranth a chance to break free and fall in beside me.

"He was weak," Carver explained as he flicked the blood off his spear. "And if there is one thing I cannot tolerate, it's weakness in my followers."

"I missed my first chance to kill you, Carver," Freya spat, her body visibly trembling as she readied herself to lunge forward. "I'm going to enjoy burying my spear in your heart!"

"Oh, I would like to see you try, Freya. The both of you actually," Carver taunted, pulling his shield close towards his body as he glanced between Freya and me, waving his short spear through the air. "The last time that we met, you all had the levels on me, so I was forced to take a more...*conservative* approach. This time, however...I think the advantage is mine!"

Without another word, Carver suddenly thrust forward his spear and barked an incomprehensible word of power, causing a violet cloud of energy to shoot from the end of his spear and wash over Freya, Amaranth and I, immediately causing the three of us to hack and cough as a searing pain filled our lungs. A set of flashing alerts appeared briefly in my vision, before vanishing and leaving a single red icon in the corner of my eye.

You have been afflicted by Carver's [Sickening Miasma]!

Carver's [Sickening Miasma] hits you for 13 points of disease damage!

"Shit!" I exclaimed in between ragged coughs as Carver leaped forward after finishing his spell, his short spear jabbing directly towards my face. Caught completely off guard by the man's sudden display of magic, I barely swung Razor up in time to deflect the spear, only to have the edge of Carver's shield slam heavily into my side with enough force to crack ribs. "Ugh!"

"He's a Shaman!" Freya called out, voice sounding raw as she too continued to let out several pained coughs from

Carver's affliction, her spear darting in from the corner of my vision and forcing the half-orc to take a half a step backward.

No sooner did Carver step out of the way, however, did my vision fill with the blurred form of the crimson spirit wolf as it effortlessly dodged around Amaranth's attack and leaped towards me, its ghostlike paws slamming into each of my shoulders before I could even think of reacting. Landing with a heavy crash, I reflexively threw my free hand up into the air before me, just as an iron jaw clamped down on my forearm, filling me with both pain and a sickening draining sensation that I knew all too well.

No! My eyes widened in sudden terror as I felt the energy in my body begin to fade, a damning message that I had hoped never to see appearing in my combat log.

[Malevolent Wolf Spirit] bites you for 76 points of damage!

[Malevolent Wolf Spirit] drains you for 37 points of mana!

It's draining my mana! I felt my mind go into a panic as I fervently tried to pull my arm free of the spirit's maw and swung the arm that held Razor in an upward motion, hoping to stab the creature in the side. But before I could move my sword arm more than an inch, the wolf leaped off me, twisting my arm viciously as it evaded a savage swipe from Amaranth, who had since recovered from his missed attack just seconds earlier.

<It is too quick!> Amaranth snarled with frustration in my mind as he adjusted to the wolf's sudden movement and rushed to follow.

Not able to form a coherent reply to Amaranth from the panic that still consumed me, I instead choose to pull hard on the arm that was still trapped in the wolf's mouth as my mana steadily continued to drain out of my body. Feeling both flesh and armor give way under the wolf's teeth, I tore my arm free of the creature's mouth, just as Amaranth rushed past me and finally collided with the ghost wolf with an earsplitting cacophony of canine snarls and feline hisses.

<Leave the creature to me!> Amaranth ordered mentally amid the chaos of his fight.

Completely in agreement with my familiar, I scrambled along the ground in an attempt to put some distance between Amaranth and the mana devouring spirit, before forcing myself up onto my feet and turning towards the sounds of Freya and Carver, reflexively checking just how much mana I had left in the process.

HP: 562/792
Stamina: 436/720
Mana: 351/790

Fuck! The wolf stole over a hundred points of mana! I blinked away the update as another searing cough forced itself out of my body. In the excitement of the wolf's attack, adrenaline had allowed me to forget about Carver's affliction, but not completely ignore the damage that it did to my system.

Pushing aside the searing pain in my chest for a moment, I rushed to rejoin Freya and Carver, the two of them brawling viciously in our relative oasis of calm within the greater battle that continued to rage around us. In the few seconds that I had lost track of the battle, the tempo had notably shifted, becoming even fiercer, neither side willing, or able to spare anyone to intervene in our fight.

For all intents and purposes, we were on our own.

"So, Lyrian, did you like your first meeting with Valefor?" Carver asked me just as I re-entered the melee, disengaging momentarily from Freya and regarding the both of us warily. "I figured the two of you would hit it off; he has quite the taste for spellcasters!"

"What the hell is he?" I shot back, not truly expecting an answer as I lunged to attack Carver, Freya following me a heartbeat behind.

Given the level difference between Amaranth and the wolf spirit, I didn't expect him to be able to keep it off our backs forever, but hopefully long enough for Freya and me to put an end to Carver. Or at the very least, drive him off.

Assuming Freya and I even can. The grim thought passed through my mind as Carver whirled his spear through the air, deflecting or avoiding our attacks with ease. It seemed that he hadn't been lying about having a level advantage on us, which could have put him as high as level seventeen, assuming it was comparable to the wolf who seemingly followed his orders.

"A spirit wolf," Carver replied unhelpfully as he blocked Freya's spear with his shield and then thrust his own weapon towards me, the jagged tip piercing through the section of armor that protected my hip and drawing forth blood. "A *special* kind of spirit wolf though."

"Very helpful," I spat, burying the pain from Carver's attack and launching myself forward at the man, swinging a crackling Razor through the air as I decided to take a risk and use up some of my mana while I still had it. Without using magic to augment my fighting style, I was at best, a lightly armored warrior and given the level disadvantage that we already had; this wasn't the time to hold anything back.

Besides, I added silently as I finally managed to get Razor's electrified tip through Carver's guard, sinking it deep into the heavy leathers that protected his shoulder. *I can always return the favor and steal his mana like the wolf did mine!*

Grunting in pain as electricity discharged itself through his body, Carver flinched involuntarily, giving both Freya and I the faintest opening to press our attacks. With a cry of triumph, she drove her spear into the half-orc's side while I pulled Razor free of Carver's shoulder and used it to knock the rising point of his spear back towards the ground, reaching out with the hand that the wolf had bitten earlier.

Grabbing his arm roughly, I tightened my grip on Carver's arm and wasted no time in beginning to drain his own mana myself, watching his eyes widen in surprise as he realized what was happening.

"I happen to like spellcasters too," I repeated Carver's words to him as he reflexively pulled himself free of Freya's spear in his side and began to backpedal in an attempt to break my grip. However, I had expected the move and managed to maintain my mana draining grip for a couple more seconds, before a short thrust of his spear forced me to abandon my efforts or suffer another injury.

"Well, aren't you full of surprises, Lyrian!" Carver announced, his expression becoming unreadable as he regarded me in a new light. "Seems like I'm not the only one who's been busy over the last few weeks and learning new tricks to show off."

"You don't know the half of it," I replied as Freya and I resumed our attacks, not wanting to give Carver the opportunity to recover.

"It's a shame though you didn't spend more of it leveling though," Carver added mournfully, shifting his body to accept a glancing blow from Freya's spear while blocking Razor with an expert shift of his shield. Leaving his spear completely free as a sickly green orb of magic formed at its tip. "You might have just been able to stand up to *my* tricks."

Before I could react, the orb shot forward and slammed into my chest, instantly filling my body with a sickening sensation as a fever caused my internal temperature to soar. A second later, an aching pain filled all my joints, followed by a wave of muscle spasms and an overwhelming feeling of nausea. In the blink of an eye, I had gone from my regular healthy self to the sickest I could ever recall being, each and every cold or flu that I had ever experienced paling in comparison.

And then I felt Carver's spear bury itself into my stomach.

I gasped as a burst of pain exploded through my body, Carver savagely twisting his spear as he pulled it out of me, leaving me staggering backward away from him, trying to create some distance between us. Blinking numbly from the combined agony of Carver's spell and the brutal wound in my stomach, I was barely able to make out the list of messages that had rapidly appeared in my combat log.

You have been afflicted by Carver's [Insidious Fever]!

Carver's [Insidious Fever] hits you for 33 points of disease damage!

Carver critically hits you for 178 points of damage!

"Lyrian!" I heard Freya shout in concern as I tried to force myself past the near-crippling sickness that wracked my body, only to have Carver's voice drown her out.

"That is a pretty nasty spell isn't it?!" the half-orc taunted with glee. "Too bad it doesn't last that long though! But fortunately, I'm not done quite just yet! Valefor, *come!*"

Almost before the words finished leaving Carver's mouth, did the translucent form of the crimson spirit wolf suddenly appear in front of him, Amaranth's surprised shout entering my mind a heartbeat afterward.

<The creature vanished!> He shouted in a panic from somewhere behind me, the sound of his claws scratching along the ground reaching my ears as he tried to figure out what had just happened.

"Pretty neat, no?" Carver continued seamlessly as I reflexively flinched away from the wolf, forcing myself to bring Razor's point up high to defend myself despite the illness still coursing through my body. "Though it's this next trick that's the one really worth watching!"

Carver let his words hang in the air for a second, before barking out a harsh command.

"Valefor, *kill!*"

With a feral bark, the wolf's body partially shifted into an insubstantial state as it practically flew off the ground towards me, covering the distance between us at the speed of thought. Moving reflexively, I threw up Razor in front of me, hearing both Freya and Amaranth shout as the wolf slammed into me and took me off my feet for a second time, sending me crashing down onto my back.

Struggling to catch my breath from the fall as the wolf pressed down on top of me, I felt a hard pressure dig into my hand, Razor's hilt twisting awkwardly in my grip. Gazing upwards at the wolf, I saw that my quick reaction had forced my sword into the creature's ethereal maw and was the only thing keeping it at bay. I didn't know whether a spirit creature such as the wolf was a wholly corporeal or incorporeal entity, but given that my sword had stopped it, at least temporarily, from tearing out my throat, I wasn't about to argue.

Straining to keep hold of the sword with one hand, I placed my free hand on the flat edge of the blade and tried to force it deeper into the wolf's mouth, using it as leverage to push it away. Snarling around the edges of the blade as it fought back against my efforts to push it away, I was surprised to find that the creature showed no sign of pain or discomfort from the sharp edges of the weapon, noticing that its jaw was, in fact, clenching downwards.

Is it trying to bite— I had barely begun to form the thought before Razor suddenly shattered right before my eyes, wicked metal shards flying in every direction as the wolf's jaw snapped shut.

"Shit!" I gasped as all resistance from the two now shattered halves of Razor in my hands vanished, Valefor lunging forward to take a large bite at my face before I could react, sinking its teeth into my cheek and jaw.

I felt flesh tear, and bone break as the wolf snapped its head to the side, causing mine to jerk in sympathy, the familiar cold sensation of my mana being drained returning with a vengeance. Dropping the broken shards of Razor, I reached up to grab at the spectral wolf at the same moment Amaranth leaped upon it.

<Lyrian!> Amaranth's mental roar seared my mind as I saw him sink his massive teeth into the back of Valefor's neck, his weight shoving the wolf down hard onto my chest, making it impossible for me to breathe. *<Hold on!>*

Trapped underneath the two creatures, I felt my body shake and jerk awkwardly as Amaranth attempted to dislodge the wolf from on top of me. Valefor, though, stubbornly refused to give up its iron hold on my head. Feeling the last bits of my mana begin to ebb away, I began to panic, reaching out towards the wolf on top of me, hoping to return the favor or at the very least nullify whatever it was draining from me. Pressing my hands deep into the shimmering essence that comprised it, I reached into the wolf expecting to feel the creature's mana, my mana flow back into me, hopefully giving Amaranth a chance to dislodge it.

But I felt nothing.

There was no mana in the creature at all, at least not anything that my ability could pull from. It was as if the spirit on top of me consumed the energy it was draining from me the moment that it left my body, leaving nothing inside of it for me to recover. My panic rose to new levels as I worked my hands up towards the wolf's face and reached for its eyes, hoping to find some vulnerable spot I could jab my finger into and force it to release its hold.

But before I could do anything, I felt an insatiable hunger rise up and consume me, banishing any sense of rational thought away from my mind as my vision involuntarily took on an azure hue. Four fleeting alerts appeared in the corner of my eye before vanishing as quickly as they appeared.

You have run out of Mana!
You are affected by [Ætherial Hunger]!
Your body consumes itself for 1 point of damage!
Your body consumes itself for 2 points of damage!

A horrific scream tore itself out of my throat as the hunger dwelling inside of me intensified, a distant part of my mind identifying it as being exactly the same as the one I had heard from the Ætherwarped ghouls several weeks earlier. My vision blurred as everything reduced itself to varying shades of azure, all other detail and color vanishing as the hunger within continued to grow with every second that passed.

I felt the weight on top of me shift in surprise, which was followed by a jerking motion that tore something free of my jaw. Yet whatever had happened, I felt no pain, my head automatically snapping back towards the now black silhouette on top of me. The hunger that now drove me regarded it carefully, gazing into the void of energy for several long heartbeats before a primal anger surged through me as it recognized what the shape was.

A rival predator.

With an unearthly snarl, my hands shot up of their own accord, fingers outstretched as they thrust themselves into the void that was perched on top of me, immediately eliciting a loud canine howl of pain. Writhing around my hands faster than I could react, the silhouette *shifted* into a strange inky blot and leaped off me, revealing yet another shape, this one a dark azure. Instinctively I reached out towards the shape, but before my body could even begin to move, it bounded away from me, chasing after whatever I had just wounded.

The hunger gnawing at me from within continued to intensify, my mind no longer able to focus past it, everything that I once was vanishing under its all-consuming presence. Drawn by a sense I couldn't identify, my body continued to move without active input from me as I rose to my feet, taking in all the various shades of azure that appeared around me. Some were bright and alluring, while others were dark and thus barely worth my notice.

It only took me an instant to take in all the bright azure shapes around me, something within me instinctively drawn to the brighter shapes, like a moth to the flame.

There! I was already in motion before the thought struck me, a bright azure shape, the *brightest* azure shape, looming before my eyes as I rapidly closed the distance towards it. A second, darker shape danced in front of it, its form shifting strangely in sync with the brighter one. I was far too gone to understand what the shapes were doing, all that mattered to me was getting towards the brightest azure shape in range.

The hunger demanded it.

Without even a second thought, I barreled past the dark shape as I closed the final distance between me and my target, one of my hands shoving it out of my way as I passed, sending it sprawling out of my vision. It was then, with nothing else before me that I thrust my hands towards my target, desperately attempting to reach into the bright azure shape where I knew the energy that my hunger craved was stored.

But to my frustration, the shape recoiled at my attempt to reach out to it, my hands hitting something hard that I couldn't quite see. My balance then shifted as a weight pressed itself into my shoulder, the hunger within me crying out for some reason I didn't understand. Redoubling my efforts, I launched myself forward again, this time sweeping my hands wide as I tried to step in closer to the shape, once again feeling a hand hit something hard and the other running ineffectively along something soft, but unyielding.

While I tried to make sense of what had just happened, another weight pressed into me, this time in the center of my chest, which for some reason caused my footing to falter, the hunger reaching new levels that I could have never dreamed possible. I began to feel strength leave my body, no longer able to keep up with the demand placed on it as a deep fatigue came over me. I stumbled forward, weakly sweeping a hand towards the shape once more, only to have it leap backwards away from me once again, escaping my reach.

The hunger demanded that I follow it, until it found what it needed to sate it, but my body was no longer capable. I felt my legs buckle as the final dregs of energy left my body, sending me falling to the ground. Craning my head upward as I fell, I caught one last glimpse of the bright shape that had evaded me, its presence somehow smaller than it was before.

Then I hit the ground, and everything went black.

Loading, please wait...

Chapter 27

Aldford – Town Hall

I hit the ground hard as I resurrected in Aldford, my mind flailing in momentary panic as it tried to pull myself together after yet another death, this one being perhaps the most traumatic that I had experienced to date. No sooner did I try to begin to process what had happened to me, did a powerful wave of nausea cause my stomach to clench as an all too familiar hunger welled up from within me.

Why didn't it go away?! I thought as I reflexively curled into a fetal position and retched. *I died and respawned, it should be over!*

The hunger shifted as I writhed on the ground, transitioning into a blinding spike of pain that radiated through my head as if there was something buried deep inside of it that desperately wanted to claw its way out. My vision blurred as the agony intensified, causing everything to go completely white as I felt something touch the edges of my mind, leaving me grinding my palms into my eyes, desperately paging to the menu that held the logout option.

But just before I was about to trigger the logout process, the pain vanished, my head suddenly snapping back to perfect clarity, leaving me gasping in a heavy sweat as my heart hammered in my ears and the familiar feeling of *Death Sickness* settled onto me.

What the hell was that? I took in a deep breath, and I tried to process what had just happened. In all my time playing Ascend Online, I had never felt anything close to what I had just experienced. Save for the time that I had fallen into the Ley Line. *Was it because I ran out of mana and died?*

"Lyrian!" Sierra's voice reached my ears, followed quickly behind by several rushing feet. "Lyrian, what happened to you?"

I felt a hand touch my shoulder as I pulled my hands away from my face, looking up at the concerned face of Sierra, who kneeled over me, with Constantine and Helix standing over her shoulder. Their eyes all widening as they looked down at me, their expressions shifting from concern to outright worry, if not fear.

"Marc," Constantine whispered as he joined Sierra in a kneeling position, who had inhaled sharply in shock as she looked at me. "Are you okay?"

"No," I replied as I reached up to rub my face and felt it strange to the touch. My hands still shook badly from what I had just experienced, the death sickness not helping any with my condition. I knew it was going to take me some time until I felt normal again, but until then I had to try and force my way through the apathy and moroseness that threatened to consume me if I let myself focus on it for too long.

"I ran out of mana," I explained.

Sierra and Constantine exchanged looks between one another, before looking back down at me. They all knew what that meant for me, though fortunately for them, they had also missed the spectacle that I had put on.

What the hell happened while I was out of mana? I asked myself, remembering my azure-tinted vision and how all-consuming the hunger had been. Even discounting my more recent episode, I had completely lost control after Carver's wolf had drained my mana, even going as far to hurt it somehow with my bare hands.

After it broke Razor, I remembered with a sudden pang of sorrow, one of my hands reaching down to where I expected my sword to be, only to find nothing.

"Lyrian," Constantine said after a few seconds, his concerned tone snapping me back to the present. "Your Ætherwarping...it looks like it got worse."

I froze, the hand searching for Razor freezing in place. "How bad?"

"Even gaunter," Sierra replied quietly her expression not wavering as she spoke. "And I can see slightly glowing veins in your face now, and down your neck. Similar to how it looked like when we were at the hub, just not as bright."

"Great," I let out a sigh, the pain that I had felt earlier now making a little more sense if my body had changed once again. I felt a wave of frustration, anger and depression surge through me as I realized that everyone would once again be flinching at me whenever they saw my face. Then I ruthlessly pushed the confusing array of emotions to the side. I didn't have time to worry about my appearance right now. Not while Carver was still out there, and the rest of the guild was in danger.

With a resigned shake of my head, I moved to get up to my feet, shifting the topic of conversation as I did so. "I'll figure that out later; we have a huge problem—"

"*Carver*, we know," Sierra stated darkly as she rose with me, both her, Constantine and Helix continuing to give me a worried look. "A few of the others who resurrected ahead of you already told us. Both about him and the bandits."

"I completely forgot about him," I said, silently cursing myself a second time for thinking that the man had moved onto somewhere else. "We just hadn't seen him for so long..."

"That he fell out of mind," Helix added softly. "It happened to all of ussss, Lyrian. Even with everything that he did."

"He isn't the worst of our worries though," Constantine cut in as we reshuffled ourselves into a standing circle,. The movement allowing me an opportunity to look around and see the rest of the respawned guild members standing a short distance away in their own cluster, which I was surprised to see included Lazarus and his group.

"Sierra and I ran into Orcs in the forest while we were scouting. We didn't even see them until they practically stepped out in front of us," Constantine continued. "They were *perfectly* camouflaged in the brush, likely with magic of some sort."

"Not just any Orcs either, Lyr, but NPC Orcs," Sierra clarified. "And Constantine is right; during our fight two of them started channeling fireballs, and we couldn't get to them both in time, though I'm pretty sure that Amaranth managed to jump one of them before he got his spell off."

"*Orcs?*" I replied in surprise as I remembered my familiar's panicked shouts during the battle and the rogue fireball that had impacted in the middle of Carver's group. "We didn't see any Orcs at all during our fight!"

"That's what Helix said too," Sierra told me with a nod. "For whatever reason, Carver held them back."

"That doesn't make sense," I replied as I forced my brain to work through the death sickness that hung over me and tried to work through Carver's motivations. "As it was, he had us dead to rights with just the people he brought with him. If the Orcs attacked too..."

"I'm guessing because he didn't want us to know he had them," Constantine said. "Though I'm pretty sure he'll figure out we know when he finds the handful we killed, plus hopefully the one Amaranth got."

"*Hopefully*," Helix agreed in a gravelly voice.

The four of us stood silently for a moment as we collected our thoughts, hearing the rest of the guild chatting nervously nearby. Many of them had known little of Carver's reputation and what he had done to the first group of Adventurers that had come to Aldford under Graves. Though judging from the general tone of some of the conversations I overheard, I was confident that they would all be brought up to speed very quickly.

"Fuck. As if this day wasn't bad enough already," I growled, turning my attention away from the guild members, feeling yet another thing land on top of my shoulders as I considered our next steps. It hadn't been enough to have the threat of the ruptured Ley Line and Eberian spies on my plate, but now I had to deal with potential Orcs living in the region.

Led by Carver of all people.

"No kidding," Constantine replied, sensing my thoughts with a grim nod. "When it rains, it pours."

"We need to get back to the others," I said, turning my head briefly as Lazarus walked into view, breaking away from the other group of guild members and approaching us. "The battle was too close to call when I died, but the others have to still be alive, no one else has respawned here after me."

"It'll take us a while to get there," Helix said cautiously, shifting to the side as Lazarus wordlessly fell into the group. "By the time we get there...what could we do?"

"We can take the horses," I countered shaking my head at the lizardman. "They may not all be bred for riding, but they'll be a hell of a lot faster than going on foot. I'm sure the new settlers will understand the need and let us borrow them."

"Hmm," Helix paused for a moment, considering what I had just said, then bobbed his head in agreement. "That would work. We could be there in a couple of hours, depending how fast the horses move."

"We'll be too late to affect the battle," I said, glancing at everyone in the circle. "But if we move fast, we might be able to save the wagon, or drive off Carver's forces if they're harassing the survivors."

"If nothing else it'll make us feel better than sitting here and waiting," Sierra added in a small voice. "And give us the chance to pick up our Soul Fragments where we died, at least before we lose too much more experience."

"Then that sounds like a plan," I finished, turning my head towards Lazarus and acknowledging the man, who wasted no time in speaking.

"We want to help," he stated simply. "What can we do?"

The half-giant's expression was completely serious as he waited for my answer, leaving me in no doubt that the offer was genuine. I motioned with my head in the direction of the pasture that we had set up on the outskirts of Aldford.

"You can saddle up with us."

———

Finally! I breathed with silent relief as we galloped across the plains over an hour later. The cloud of apathy and depression that was Death Sickness releasing its hold on me and allowing my mind to function clearly once more. I had experienced the effects of the death penalty a handful of times over the last month and was more than used to it.

At least as much as a person can be, I added dryly to myself. Dying was rarely a non-violent experience in Ascend Online after all.

The trick that I had found to avoid dwelling on the effects of the sickness was to keep moving and to prevent it from gaining hold on your psyche. The longer that one sat contemplating one's death, the more it tended to dig in and re-enforce itself, eventually leaving you with the desire to crawl into a corner and fall asleep, which often resulted in at least eight straight hours of sleep. Regardless of how rested you were before your death.

But now that the death sickness had let go of me, I was no longer in danger of spiraling into a depression, and I allowed myself to relax fractionally as I considered what was ahead of us. Thus far, even an hour after we had left Aldford on our horses, no one else had died from the battle with Carver. We had told everyone in the guild to keep careful track of their Party Sense as we travelled and to shout an alert if anyone happened to respawn in the direction of Aldford.

So far so good, I thought, checking on my own Party Sense once more and noting that Halcyon and Caius were still ahead of me, and from what I could tell, together, something that I considered to be a *very* good thing. The last I had seen of Halcyon was him riding on top of the wagon as both he and Thorne barreled through Carver's raiders and out onto the plains. If he and Caius had managed to regroup, then it meant that they were able to fight their way out of the forest and were already hopefully heading towards us.

Speaking of heading towards us, I thought with a start as I realized that I now sensed Amaranth with much clearer detail, and that he was rushing towards me with impressive speed. We weren't close enough just yet for our mental communication, but at the speeds that we were both travelling, that would change in minutes.

"Amaranth is closing in on us," I called out to the group, not wanting to startle anyone when an azure furred puma sprinted out of the tall grasses that covered the plains. The last thing we needed was a friendly fire incident with someone taking a shot at my familiar.

<Lyrian!> Amaranth's relieved voice filled my mind a few minutes later as he finally came into range, his words coming out in a rush. *<What happened? You somehow injured the creature…but your mind changed too, all I could hear was you screaming! Nothing I did could reach you!>*

I paused for a moment, taken back by Amaranth's concern and how quickly he had spoken. I had never heard such worry coming from my familiar before and I couldn't help but feel shaken at what he had told me. I held up a hand and signaled for everyone to stop as I mentally comprised my reply.

<I'm sorry, Amaranth,> I sent first and foremost to the cat. *<I don't know exactly what happened, save that the wolf drained all of my mana and I lost control. I don't remember all too well what happened afterwards.>*

<You fought like the warped creatures Carver set upon us ages ago,> Amaranth replied, the concern in his voice still present. *<Magic flowed off you completely, and you showed no reaction to any wounds. At least until you fell…>*

<What happened after that?> I asked, hoping to shift the topic of conversation. *<Did Carver retreat? Did we win?>*

<I don't know,> Amaranth told me with frustration. *<After you died…all I could think of was rejoining you. I left the battle the moment I sensed where you were.>*

<Oh,> I said suddenly remembering the compulsion that consumed Amaranth if I died and he still lived. It would have driven him to ignore everything that he was doing and rush to rejoin me as soon as physically possible, even if it meant leaving the battle behind.

<No one else resurrected in Aldford after me,> I told him, hoping that it would set him at ease. *<And everyone seems to still be alive and together.>*

Amaranth didn't reply for a few moments, causing me to worry that something had happened to him, but just as I was about to send another message his way. I noticed the grass part far ahead of me from on top of my horse, followed by glimpses of an azure colored streak heading towards us. Dismounting from my horse, my feet barely had hit the ground before Amaranth erupted from the grass, his fur covered in blood and panting heavily.

He wasted no time in crossing the distance between us, moving to lean his body heavily onto mine, relief shuddering through his body the moment that we made contact as the compulsion that had been driving him released its hold on his mind. I paused for a moment to run my hands through his fur, silently noting that all of his wounds had since regenerated from the battle, despite there still being missing patches that would take longer to regrow.

<That is better,> Amaranth said after a moment, his large head shaking from side to side. *<My mind feels…clearer once more.>*

"Good," I replied, hearing other horses approach behind me as the rest of the party closed around me.

"Any news?" Sierra asked as she pulled up on the other side of Amaranth, leaning down from her horse to offer the cat a hand to touch.

"Nothing, unfortunately," I answered, watching Amaranth reach up to rub his face on Sierra's outstretched hand in greeting. "He left to rejoin me the moment that I died. He didn't see the rest of the battle."

"Then we should keep moving," Constantine said from behind me, prompting a nod from me and a croak of acknowledgment from Amaranth, who had since managed to regain his breath.

"Yeah," I agreed as I climbed back onto my horse and looked back down at my familiar. "Are you okay to keep going?"

<Of course,> he answered with a snort, his mood having improved rapidly after reuniting with me. *<A short run across the plains would hardly wind me.>*

"Then let's get back at it," I said with a smile, spurring my horse to continue the journey back towards the rest of the guild.

The next hour and a half passed with almost blinding speed as we closed in on the surviving guild members, the wagon becoming visible on the darkening horizon long before we got close enough to see the individual people following beside it. It seemed that they had managed to get away from Carver and his group intact and based on what we could tell, weren't being actively pursued.

Though given that Carver knew exactly where Aldford was, I didn't consider that to be a clear sign that today's conflict was over or that it had been the last we'd seen of him. From what I could tell as we rode closer to the wagon, the first round ended in somewhat of a draw, the both of us having suffered a bloody enough nose that neither of us could claim any sort of victory.

"Hey!" Freya's voice was the first to greet us as we entered earshot, a waving hand signaling us from Thorne's side at the head of the wagon.

We all split up as we formally rejoined the party, the mounted members of the guild taking up position around the wagon. Party Sense had helped make it clear who we were as we approached and prevented any unpleasant accidents from occurring, but despite the fact that we were up to full strength, I could tell that everyone was on edge from the way they glanced around us, searching the plains for any sign of movement.

"We came as soon as we were able to get ourselves sorted," I said in greeting as I brought my horse alongside the front of the wagon to where Freya, Thorne, Halcyon, and Caius, were sitting. No sooner did I pull up close, did I see all of their eyes widen as they noticed the changes in my appearance.

"It's okay," I said, preempting their questions with a reassuring smile that I didn't quite feel and pushed onwards, hoping to keep the conversation off myself. "What happened with the rest of the battle after…I, uh, went down? Is Carver following you at all?"

"Doesn't seem like it," Freya replied after a moment, not quite believing my statement, the concern remaining on her face. "As for the battle…"

"It was a mess," Caius said, picking up as Freya trailed off. "They had the numbers, but we were better geared and trained as a whole. It was a stalemate for the longest time…at least until you did…whatever you did to Carver…"

"What *did* you do, Lyrian?" Freya asked, finding her voice as she continued to look at me with concern. "I never saw you fight *anything* like that before."

"During the fight, Carver's wolf managed to drain all of my mana," I said simply, before going on to explain what I remembered after I had lost control of my body, taking pains to downplay just how all-consuming the hunger had been. "…and then, I resurrected back in Aldford, badly shaken, and a little bit more warped."

"Damn," Halcyon commented, shaking his head from side to side. "That's brutal Lyr."

"It's not something I hope ever to repeat," I admitted, turning my attention to Freya. "If I remember right…I think I may have hit you during the fight, I'm sorry—"

"Shoved would be more accurate, and don't worry about it, really; I know it wasn't you," Freya replied with a shrug. "What you did to Carver though...how much of it do you remember?"

"Next to nothing to be honest," I said, feeling a sense of relief that she understood what had happened to me. "What happened exactly?"

"You broke his shield," Freya told me with a shake of her head. "Cracked it nearly in half."

"I did?" I looked at her with confusion. "I don't remember doing that at all."

"What about when you tore his arm apart?" Freya asked with a raised eyebrow. "Or brushed his spells off completely?"

I blinked at her and shook my head in negation, "None of that matches up to what I remember at all."

"It happened, Lyr," Caius said softly. "I didn't see the shield bit, but I definitely saw Carver run off with a mangled arm."

"Huh," I grunted before falling silent to reconsider what had happened during the fight from my perspective. Digging through my memories, I couldn't pinpoint a time where a spell might have landed on me, though I did vaguely remember my hand clawing something soft at one point. "What about Carver's retreat? What happened there?"

"Not much to say," Freya shrugged while letting out a deep breath. "After what you did, Carver was too wounded to continue fighting and was desperately trying to disengage when you...fell. He started calling for a general retreat afterward, and we just let him go. We were in no shape to pursue."

"After that, we gathered everyone still alive and pulled out of the forest," Freya continued nodding her head towards Thorne and Halcyon. "Eventually we linked up with these guys, and started making our way back to Aldford as fast as we could."

"God, what a shitty day," I said with resignation as I looked back at the large chunks of metal still on the bed of the wagon. "At least we didn't lose the metal."

"Small victories," Thorne commented. "Right?"

"*Right,*" I agreed with a heavy sigh. "But our day isn't done yet. A handful of us still need to go back and collect our Soul Fragments. There's no way we can afford to eat a twenty percent experience loss. Not knowing that Carver and his group are out here."

"Soul Fragments?" Caius asked, voicing the question on everyone's face as they turned sharply to look at me. "You don't lose a fragment of your soul if you die to players. You I can understand, but the others?"

"The fireballs that landed in the middle of us weren't cast by players," I told the group in a heavy tone. "Constantine and Sierra told me they were cast by Orcs, specifically ones that were working with Carver."

"*Orcs?*" Freya repeated with a surprised expression on her face. "Then that means..."

"Yeah," I confirmed with a nod, my eyes shifting between everyone.

"We're not as alone out here as we thought."

Chapter 28

Tuesday, March 19th, 2047 - 1:57 pm
The Northern Plains

"They're riding out to meet us!" Bax called back to me from the point of our formation as he motioned for us to slow our horses to a walk. "Er, well, walking out to meet us at any rate."

"That makes things easier," Natasha commented happily from Bax's side, the elven woman not having strayed far from it in the last few weeks. "We should probably slow down not to look threatening though."

"Good idea," I said distractedly, staring off into the distance where a trio of roughly made buildings stood in an area recently cleared of trees, barely able to focus my eyes on them. I was so tired that it was all I could do to keep myself steady on my horse, let alone fully be aware of my surroundings.

The days since the surprise attack had done much to contribute to my level of exhaustion. The revelation that Carver was still out in the region hadn't gone well once we had all managed to return to Aldford and word got out about his ambush. There were too many Adventurers that had a firsthand experience of Carver and wasted no time in painting the man as an unhinged sociopath, endlessly recounting their journey to Aldford as Graves' prisoners to anyone who would listen.

Which eventually escalated after several of them shared their own personal feed of Carver's antics.

As such, there was what could only be described as a knee-jerk reaction as the majority of the Adventurers practically demanded that we shift our focus from residential building to finishing the palisade surrounding Aldford. Carver on his own had been bad enough to unsettle everyone, but with the Bandit Adventurers under his command, and the potential alliance with at least one Orc Tribe, everyone was convinced that a defensive posture was a new priority.

Intellectually, I didn't disagree with them.

Practically, on the other hand, it meant that all of that new construction had to fall on my shoulders. Léandre still hadn't come back from his treatment, and at this point, we weren't sure if he ever would. Drace was consumed with the dig into the Nafarrian ruins, which was progressing at a slow if steady pace. Then lastly, Jenkins was far too busy catering to the new settlers, providing them with tools, equipment, and the countless other things that they would need to begin taming the land around Aldford. There was simply no one else to take over the construction efforts full time, or at least anyone else who had as much crafting experience as I did.

Needless to say, I hadn't been getting much sleep or downtime over the last few days.

"Lyr!" Constantine's sharp voice startled me and caused my eyes to snap open, making me wonder when I had even closed them.

Blinking furiously, I looked towards my friend and realized that he was holding my horse's reins in his hands and was in the process of getting my horse to stop, while Sierra on the other side of me had reached out to grab hold of my collar to keep me from falling straight out of my saddle.

"Ugh, sorry," I said with embarrassment, catching myself and then reaching for the length of leather in Constantine's hands, trying to replay the last few seconds and coming up blank.

"Damn it, Lyr. We've *all* told you that you've been working yourself too hard!" Constantine exclaimed in a soft tone, keeping his voice down but still trying to convey the message. "If you're that tired, you need to rest! The rest of us could have checked in here on our own!"

"I know," I replied quietly, bringing my horse to a stop as I rubbed my eyes with a free hand. "But I felt I needed to be here, to shake hands and greet them, if nothing else. We're not exactly bringing *good* news."

"You feel the need to be *everywhere*, Lyr," Sierra added from my other side, her tone matching Constantine's perfectly. "Which is fine if you're rested, but not when you're so tired that you nearly fall off your horse!"

I sighed in response to both of my friends' words, knowing all too well they were right. It hadn't been completely necessary for me to have made the trek all the way out here with Sierra, Constantine and the other two scouts, but I had been stubborn enough to insist on coming anyway, just to meet the *Hallowguarde* guild in person.

Great job, Marc, I berated myself as I made to dismount from my horse, realizing that during my almost imperceptible nap, we had drawn close enough to the advancing wave of people that there was no chance that they hadn't noticed my momentary slip-up. *Your first impression with them is going to forever be nearly falling off your horse because you were too tired to stay awake.*

With a huff of resignation, I pushed the thought out of my mind and moved to catch up with Bax and Natasha as they approached the group walking towards us, the pair clearly recognizing them as they approached. Slowing down, I forced my mind back into full awareness as our two groups closed in on one another, inspecting the three men before us carefully, having never had a chance to formally meet anyone from the guild before they had left Aldford.

The lead man, a tall and powerfully built Eberian in the center of the trio, caught my attention first, muscles rippling underneath his leather armor as he walked, hinting at him having chosen a melee oriented class, a suggestion somewhat confirmed by his completely clean-shaven head and the large axe hanging at his waist.

On the man's left, walked a grey-haired half-elf, dressed in a similar style of leather armor as his companion. Though instead of an axe, the man carried a large greatbow that stretched nearly as long as he was tall, a feat made all the more impressive given that he was at least a head taller than I was. From this distance, I could already see his eyes scanning each of us, attempting to determine if we were a threat.

Lastly, on the other side of the lead man, was another Eberian, bearing plain if almost forgettable features. In fact, the man was so decidedly average I found myself doing a double take just because of it, trying to pinpoint *something* about him that stood out, but ended up coming short. Dressed in a plain linen shirt with dark pants, the brown-haired man stared at us blankly, no emotion visible on his face as we approached. As far as I could tell, the man didn't even seem to have a weapon on him, something that I found to be rather peculiar given our proximity to the wild.

"Cassius!" Bax called, waving in greeting to the lead man in the group. "It looks like you're all doing pretty well out here!"

"Is that you, Bax?" The man's voice sounded both relieved and happy to see a friendly face, his posture immediately relaxing as his bright blue eyes swept over us. "Ah, Natasha! You came too! What do we owe the pleasure?"

"Just passing through," Bax replied as he motioned his head towards me. "We have some news that you should all know about."

"News?" Cassius asked with a raised eyebrow as he looked at me, his two other companions, doing the same. "What kind of news needs the Guildmaster of Virtus to deliver it?"

"Bad news, I'm afraid," I answered in a heavy voice, having long since gotten over the fact that people recognized me by sight. "We've had a bit of trouble in the area, and we were wondering if you had seen anything."

"What kind of trouble?" the half-elf asked, causing all our attention to shift to him.

"A few days ago, we were attacked by another group of Adventurers out in the wild," I said. "Some of them belonged to the *Grey Devils*, others...we knew from another incident—"

"Carver or Graves?" The brown-haired man asked, his head cocking to the side as he posed the question.

"Carver," I replied, taken aback by the man's question. "How did—"

"We watched your feed *very* carefully before we came out here," he explained not waiting for me to finish. "And as far as I know, that was the only other *incident* that happened out here. Plus, if it was anyone else...you wouldn't have come here in person."

There was a moment of silence as I stared at the brown-haired man blankly, my brain having skipped a beat at the man's eerily accurate insight.

"Damn it, Berwyn. Knock that shit off in front of guests!" Cassius growled in exasperation, casting a glance at the man. "Bad enough you interrupt me all the time!"

"Can't help that you're so slow," Berwyn replied with a dismissive shrug as Cassius took a step forward towards me, his hand outstretched in greeting.

"Nice to see that things are still in good spirits here," Bax commented with a smirk.

"Don't encourage him," Cassius chastened the scout as we shook hands, turning his head towards me as he did so. "By the way, if you didn't catch it, my name is Cassius Hart."

"Lyrian Rastler," I replied, my exhaustion making me momentarily forget that they likely all already knew my name. Panicking as I moved to cover my own faux pas, I gave the man a nod and pressed forward. "Nice to meet you formally this time around. I know we didn't get a chance before you guys set out on your own."

Smooth, I told myself sarcastically while simultaneously resolving to get through this meeting without a third slip up of some sort.

"Oh, don't worry about that. There's always too much to do when running your own settlement, though I'm sure you know that better than most," Cassius said understandingly before he inclined his head towards his companions and continued introductions. "You've already had the pleasure of meeting Berwyn here, so I'll just jump straight to the surly elf on the other side of me, Kilgore. The three of us make up the main council of the Hallowguarde guild and by extension our settlement here, Shadows Fall."

"You sure are building fast out here," I commented while Sierra and Constantine stepped forward to introduce themselves, taking the opportunity to look at the buildings in the distance a second time, realizing that I hadn't noticed that the settlement was on the edge of a rather large lake. The thick and wild tree line had partially blocked the body of water in the distance from my earlier vantage point, save for a small section that I could now see through.

Looking at the settlement, I could see several people moving about as they continued about their day, the majority of their attention being focused on a large ditch that was slowly being dug around the growing hamlet.

"Hope you don't mind us copying your idea for the ditch," Cassius said after the introductions were over, noticing where my attention had drifted to. "But as Berwyn said earlier, we watched your feeds and saw firsthand on how well that particular defense worked out for you guys."

"No problems here," I replied, feeling quite impressed on how prepared Cassius and his guild were. I couldn't help but wish once again that they had chosen to stay in Aldford, instead of settling out on their own. But I also understood their desire to be independent. "I was actually going to suggest the same if you hadn't already started."

One of Cassius's eyebrow rose at that statement, followed by inquiring looks from Berwyn and Kilgore.

"What's exactly going on, Lyrian?" Cassius asked. "You think Carver or someone is going to try attacking us out here?"

"I don't know…" I began with a sigh, before launching into my explanation of Carver's attack and our belief that he had allied himself with a tribe of Orcs, relying on more than one occasion for Sierra or Constantine to fill in any gaps that I missed. "We haven't seen or heard *anything* from him since our skirmish."

"Well, we haven't seen any orcs out here." Kilgore was the first to answer after my explanation. "Nor any Adventurers we couldn't account for either, though our hunting parties have largely ranged to the north and west."

"The land breaks up something bad about a day to the east from here too, becoming broken scree and nearly barren," Cassius added somewhat hesitantly. "We've been meaning to explore the area one day…but the creatures we've spotted out that way are in their mid-twenties level-wise, if not higher."

"The Orcs are more than likely not out that way then," I said, catching on to Cassius's reservation in revealing a high-level hunting spot, not that any of us would survive against a creature more than ten levels higher than us. "And don't worry, we won't come poking around your area without an invitation, as you can probably tell our hands are pretty full already."

"We'll definitely keep an eye out if we catch sight of any orcs or Adventurers," Cassius replied graciously while nodding in both understanding and appreciation. "Honestly, keeping you in the loop is the least we can do, and it costs nothing to send a message. On the other hand, Carver raiding each and every caravan that tries to make its way out here hurts all of us. The sooner we can put him and his group down for good, the better."

"No argument there," Sierra added. "Carver already had a lot to answer for, and it seems that his list keeps on growing."

Everyone chorused in agreement at the red-haired woman's statement, the three Hallowguarde members exchanging looks between one another and then focusing their attention back towards me.

"We're still in the middle of working for the day, but we can offer you guys a place to stay for the night if you're looking to wait until tomorrow to go back to Aldford," Cassius offered. "I know it had to be a long trek, even with horses."

"We appreciate the offer," I said with a shake of my head as I moved to take a heavy pack off my horse. "But we're going to have to keep moving; we just wanted to visit in person to let you know what was going on and to drop something off..."

I held out the pack in my hand towards Cassius, seeing Sierra and Constantine holding similar packages meant for Kilgore and Berwyn.

"It can be rough out here," I said as Cassius took the pack from me and looked inside, his eyes widening as he scanned through the contents of the bag. "And we want you to know that Aldford, and Virtus, are around to help if you need it."

"This is too much." Cassius shook his head as he glanced at the other bags that my friends were holding. "We're managing decently on our end here; we don't need anything."

"Think of it as a housewarming gift then. Plus, you might find yourself needing it later," Sierra countered from beside me. "There's no telling where any of this stuff with Carver might lead to. A bit of extra food and tools never goes wrong either."

"Especially when it makes us stronger to fight Carver or the orcs if we need to," Berwyn said pointedly, having already figured out one of the main reasons for our support.

"If it comes to that," Constantine acknowledged with a nod. "But also, because we know all too well how the wild can be here. It's the least we can do to help."

"Well, if that's the case, we certainly appreciate it," Cassius said, throwing the pack over his shoulder and sticking his hand out towards me a second time to shake my hand. "And we'll keep the sentiment in mind if we can ever repay the favor."

"Finding Carver or his base would be more than enough," Natasha chimed in, having been content to listen in for the majority of the meeting. "The sooner we can put him out of our minds, the better."

"Amen to that," Cassius echoed with a nod as our meeting drew to a close. "We'll be in touch if we find or hear of anything. Safe travels in the meantime."

"Safe travels," I repeated as we all turned away from the group, Sierra and Constantine having passed along their packages to Berwyn and Kilgore. Moving silently without another word, the five of us mounted our horses and turned away from Shadows Fall, ready to begin the trek back to Aldford.

But before we could make it further than a dozen feet, Sierra and Constantine cut their horses in front of me, their expressions a mixture of annoyance and concern.

"There, Lyr," Sierra began. "You made it to the meeting; there was no news of note. Like we expected there wouldn't be. It's time for you to take a break."

"We just barely left," I grunted in confusion. "It's going to take us hours to get back to Aldford."

"That's right; it's going to take *us* hours to get back to Aldford," Constantine said. "In the meantime, you're going to log off and get some rest. All of our play cycles are due for reset tonight anyway, so you can get a nice head start and maybe get more than three hours of sleep tonight."

"Come on, guys, I can hold out until we can get back," I protested, noticing that Bax and Natasha were completely ignoring the conversation, thanks to the filters the game world set in place to keep NPCs from reacting to out of character conversations.

Damn it, I cursed, my immersion breaking as I reminded myself that neither of the pair was truly *real*. For a split second, I had forgotten that all of this was a game, something that I found was happening more and more often the longer I played.

"No, you can't, Marc," Sierra countered waving a hand at me sharply. "You're working yourself so hard that even

Amaranth declined to come out with us today, and when the hell does *he* ever avoid going out for a run?"

"Uh," I stalled, vaguely recalling my familiar mentioning that all he had in mind for the day was sleeping in the sun and that he would bite me if I tried to wake him. "He was tired."

"He is tired because you're tired," Constantine shot back. "Amaranth is a lot more in sync with you than you think. If *he's* worn out, it's because you're worn out!"

"That's not how—" I began to say before sighing in defeat.

My friends were right. I was beyond tired, even more than I was willing to admit to myself. Ever since Carver had reappeared, I had been running at full speed, trying to do everything I possibly could to simultaneously prepare for our inevitable rematch and to make sure that Aldford was adequately protected.

At the cost of my own health and sanity.

"Everyone has their limits, Marc," Sierra said gently, sensing that my protests were coming to an end. "You are dangerously close to the end of yours. This game is fun and all, but you're taking it a bit too seriously. You need to rest or you're going to burn out."

"I never expected for us to end up in charge of everything," I admitted, feeling built up stress seep out of me as I said the words. "At least nothing as big as Aldford, or Virtus."

"Oh, please," Constantine snorted. "You're a workaholic, Marc. We all are in our own way. There was no question that we'd end up in charge of something, one way or another. But Misha is right. You really need to dial it back for a couple days and take a break. This next week is going to be busy enough, even if Carver doesn't throw a wrench into our plans. Especially once we get that ruin open. We're all going to need to be at the top of our game going forward."

"I know," I said rubbing my face as I remembered that we *still* had the Ley Line to deal with. "Okay, guys; you win. I'll knock off for the night. Are you sure you're going to be okay to get my body back?"

"Don't worry about that; we'll take care of it," Sierra stated. "You go get yourself some food and unwind a bit. Go to bed even."

"We'll be fine, Lyr," Constantine said confidently before he started shooing me away from him. "Go and take a break, we'll catch up later."

"Thanks, guys," I said as I mentally brought up the logout menu. "I'll catch you guys on the other side."

"Goodnight, Marc," Sierra added, giving me a wave.

I paused for a moment to look at my two friends, their faces watching me carefully as they waited for me to follow through on my promise. Without another word, I nodded to them before I triggered the logout process, watching the world gradually fade to black.

In what seemed like a blink of an eye later, I found myself back in Reality, the pod that I had been lying in opening as it slid out from the wall, a soft chime sounding once it was safe for me to climb out. Blinking repeatedly, I reached up to rub my face as my brain slowly readjusted itself back to the real world.

Logging out of Ascend Online had been a jarring process at first, the disconnect between the game world and reality often taking several minutes before one was ready to start moving around, but as with anything, it was something the body eventually got used to the more often it was experienced.

With a grunt of strong, yet largely unused muscles, I pushed myself out of the pod and into the deathly quiet apartment, my feet padding softly along the floor as I made a beeline to the bathroom. The first stop almost everyone had after any extended stay in virtual reality.

Pausing for a moment as I passed by the mirror, I couldn't help but notice once more that the last week and a half had served to further enhance the sharp lines on my face as I continued to lose weight, all thanks to the 'VR Diet' and its side-effects. I was fairly confident that this was the thinnest I had ever been in my life, a feeling that was made all the stranger considering that I also felt quite a bit stronger and fitter too.

I suppose it beats the alternative, I thought tiredly as I slowly stripped and stepped into the shower, turning the water to as hot as I could bear it, waiting patiently for the temperature to rise. *If I had to choose between losing a bit of weight to muscular atrophy...*

Any further thoughts I had dissolved into nothingness as I stepped into the spray of steaming water, the heat cleansing the exhaustion that clouded my mind. It wasn't until nearly an hour later that I was able to pull myself out of the bathroom, feeling much more rejuvenated and awake.

Glancing around the apartment, I found myself still completely alone knowing that it would still be hours until everyone else finished with their day and logged off for their rest cycle. After a few moments of consideration, I decided that I didn't want to spend the rest of the day waiting for everyone to log out, nor to be awoken once they did. It had been quite a long time since I had some peace and quiet to myself, which I felt was something that I really needed, given how busy I had been over the last few weeks.

So, with that in mind, I grabbed a warm change of clothes, scribbled a note telling everyone where I had gone, and left the apartment to go back to my condo, which had sat largely unused for the last month and a half.

Which means there's no food in it, I reminded myself as the elevator door opened on the ground floor of the building. With a resigned sigh, I realized that I would have to make a stop before heading home to pick up something to eat.

Moving with purpose, I left the building, briefly stepping out into the freezing winter air that refused to acknowledge that spring was here, before hailing a cab and practically leaping inside the moment that the car ground to a halt.

"Quiet Mode," I pre-empted the cab's question, then told it where to drop me off. As the car began to move, I reached to dig my phone out of my pocket, deciding to take the opportunity to catch up on what I knew would be a large number of messages and emails.

It had been quite an unwelcome shock the first time I had logged out of Ascend Online to realize that Reality had continued onwards without me, leaving me with hundreds of messages to sift through, and at first glance, this time was proving to be no exception either. Scanning through my phone, I found that I had several updates from Ætherworld Productions in my inbox and flagged them for later review, mentally cataloging them as earnings reports from our feeds.

Slowly as the car navigated its way through the automated traffic of the city, I paged through my inbox, eventually reaching the bottom of my list with the two most recent emails catching my full attention. Bringing the phone slightly closer to my face, I read the subject lines of both the emails, feeling my heart skip a beat in surprise.

Subject: 'Mom and I are going to be playing Ascend Online!' From: Dad. Sent: Today, 10:15am.

Subject: 'Hey, on my rest cycle too! Want to chat tonight? :)' From: Sonia. Sent: Today, 1:53pm.

I paused for a moment as I considered the two emails, a wide smile slowly spreading across my face. With barely a second thought, I clicked on an email and began to read, completely oblivious to the fact that I had already arrived at my destination.

Chapter 29

Thursday, March 21st, 2047 - 6:07 am
Aldford – The Crafting Hall

"Phew!" I exclaimed as the familiar kaleidoscope of colors faded away from my vision and I suddenly found myself in the heat of the Foundry, with a rhythmic hammering sound echoing around me. Taking a sharp breath, I felt a momentary wave of disorientation as images passed through my mind, the game world rapidly updating me on what had happened while I had been offline.

Pausing for a moment to sort through the new memories, I put my hand down on the stone table before me and shook my head, waiting for the information overload to pass. I saw Sierra and Constantine's journey back to Aldford as they escorted my digital avatar back to the town, which then blurred into crafting as my automated tasks took over. I saw glimpses of myself working away at mass producing items that would eventually be needed for the construction of the palisade or the guard towers that would be built into them. From everything that I could tell, there had been no issues over the last day, and everything was proceeding on schedule.

Almost everything at least. I felt my heart drop momentarily as I looked around the Foundry and saw Léandre's digital avatar working away at the smaller forge, a small tag notifying me that he was still offline.

[Léandre] – Offline – 121 Tasks Pending

The only reason why I could see his current status, was because before logging off, Léandre had given me permission to assign and modify his task list, a feature that we had all found to be very useful when it came to making the most of offline time. Unfortunately, on the other hand, since I could modify his task list, I could also see that he hadn't logged on in the last day while I was offline.

It was beginning to seem that Léandre's treatment hadn't worked out for him. None of the emails that I had sent had been returned, nor did anyone reply on his behalf. The only sliver of hope that I still had was that I hadn't found an obituary with Léandre's real name listed above it. With a shrug of resignation, I silently wished that I had thought to ask the elder man *where* he was getting his Age Regression done, so I could have called for an update, but I didn't think of it until after Léandre had logged off.

"Well, that's enough of that," I told myself with a shake of my head, trying to pull myself out of my funk. I had no way of finding out what had happened to my friend, and knowing Léandre, he would have insisted on me to keep working instead of spending my time pining. I just had to be patient and hope that he had pulled through.

Speaking of working, I looked down at the table I had been standing in front of and realized that it was the broken fragments of Razor I'd managed to collect when I recovered my Soul Fragment. Shattered almost beyond recognition, the bronze blade and core underneath had given up from all the strain that I had placed on it over the last month, and its final battle when that wolf spirit, Valefor, shattered it in its jaw. Despite my best efforts, I was forced to admit that the blade was beyond repair. At least in any state that would make it combat worthy once again and I couldn't quite bring myself to smelt it down to raw metal for use as nails or something equally mundane. Razor had been my first major find in Ascend Online, and I was reluctant to simply toss the weapon away or reuse it for parts.

No, I had decided that I would preserve the weapon by including a fragment of it in every weapon that I made going forward, so it would always be with me, one way or another. But while all of that was very sentimental, it didn't address what I had to do next, something that I had been both avoiding and looking forward to for several days now.

It was time to make myself a new weapon.

I was feeling much more confident with the Æthertouched Iron that we had recovered from the Tower to try my hand at making a weapon using the magical metal. In the few days since we'd brought it back, we'd managed to splinter enough fragments from the massive piece to give me enough to work with as I practiced smelting the iron. The experience had raised my blacksmithing all the way up to level seventeen while also teaching me how to work around its rapid cooling, at least when it came to smaller items. Larger pieces were still notably more difficult to shape due to the amount of work needed, and more often than not, simply fell apart when I tried to reheat them in the forge to make them more malleable.

But that had been several levels ago and I thought that it was time to put all my practice to use and try to craft a new weapon for myself, if not with the Æthertouched metal, then with something else that I had lying around the Crafting Hall.

"First thing first, let's light the forge and make something easy to begin with...like a hilt," I told myself as I mentally prepared myself to get to work. With a motion as I walked, I decided to call over Léandre's avatar to help me through the crafting process with the forge, having learned that two sets of hands with the forge made things much easier than just one.

Well used to the process, it took me only a moment to prepare the forge, the familiar azure-hued fire greeting my eyes as Léandre's avatar finished pouring the Æther. Signaling the man to stop, I pulled out several fragments of the Æthertouched Iron from my inventory and began the process of smelting them down into an ingot, remembering to toss in a fragment of Razor before the process was complete.

Pouring the metal into a cast, I waited for a while for the slag to cool, going on to smelt other, larger, shards in the meantime. After I had deemed the metal cool enough, I pulled it free and began crafting the hilt for what would become my new weapon.

Now that the metal had been refined, it only took a minute for the metal to heat, and barely three for me to hammer it into shape, the relatively small object strangely retaining the heat from the forge much longer than larger pieces I had worked with. Finishing the last strokes with the hammer just before it cooled, I carefully inspected the finished hilt for any defects or flaws, and to my pleasant surprise found none as the finished item description appeared in my vision.

Æthertouched Iron Hilt
Item Class: Magical
Item Quality: Mastercraft (+20%)
Durability: 120/120
Weight: 0.3 kg

"Well that turned out better than expected," I said with surprise. I had never managed to hit Mastercraft quality with the Æthertouched metal. The closest that I had ever come had been 'Good' quality on a simple drawing knife I made as an experiment. "Guess that little piece of Razor was lucky."

Heartened by my success, I put the hilt off to the side before I pulled out a larger ingot of metal and began to heat it in the hopes of making it into a blade, having long since decided that I would stick with a sword as my primary weapon. Given the amount of metal involved compared to the hilt, I had to wait patiently until it had heated enough before beginning to work it.

After a few minutes, I pulled the now gleaming azure ingot out of the forge and hefted my hammer high as I set to shaping the stubborn metal. Heavy hammer blows echoed through the air as I brought it down on the ingot, my hands dancing faster than they ever had before. At first, the metal easily gave way to my rapid strikes, gradually flattening as I worked it into a blade-like shape, but as the minutes passed, the metal hardened and refused to budge, forcing me to place it back into the forge and reheat it.

Hopefully, better timing will do the trick, I thought nervously as I mentally counted the seconds that the metal was back in the heat of the forge. So far, I had never been successful in crafting a piece that I was forced to reheat. Every time that I had done so, the metal reacted strangely afterward, either becoming badly misshapen at the first strike with the hammer or simply continued to melt itself down to slag, even after I had pulled it free from the heat.

"...eight, nine..." I counted aloud as I waited for the metal to heat, pulling the now faintly glowing ingot back out of the forge at the ten-second mark, this time aiming for the bare minimum of time.

Wasting no time, I set the metal back down and swung my hammer down at it, seeing it begin to shift under my rapid strikes once more. Feeling a sense of excitement surge through me as the metal continued to take shape, I redoubled my efforts, hoping to finish as much as I could of the piece before it hardened once more.

No sooner did the thought pass through my mind than a loud cracking sound filled the air just as I brought the hammer down. Wincing, I looked down at the half blade I had managed to create, seeing that I had somehow managed to crack it completely in half.

"Well, fuck; that's new," I grumbled in disappointment as I inspected the broken item, noticing that it had somehow turned brittle and even begun to flake. I set my tools down with resignation, then began to clean my workspace, tossing the scraps into a crucible for later use.

"Maybe there's something I'm missing?" I asked Léandre's avatar, not expecting a response. "I understand that it's a magical metal...but why can I forge a smaller piece in perfect quality, but larger pieces just don't come out at all? I tried once sticking it into the regular forge to heat it back up but ended up with the same problem we had before. It just doesn't do anything..."

Léandre's avatar stared at me blankly, before shrugging vaguely at my question but saying nothing.

"Well, if this was easy, I guess everyone would be doing it," I said with a sigh as I took another ingot that I had smelted and prepared to try again, this time planning on leaving the metal in a few seconds longer. "I guess this is going to be a bit of trial and error until we can find a process that works."

And for the next two hours, trial and error were all that I did, focusing specifically on the 'error' side of things. All my testing had reduced over two dozen blades to ragged scraps of metal in varying stages of completion before something inevitably happened and ruined the process. What frustrated me the most was that the failures I had were rarely consistent with regards to the variables I adjusted.

More often than not, the metal that I was working on destabilized, simply turning into a metallic mass of slag the moment I pulled it free from the forge, but it was the rare *other* incidents that had me wracking my brain wondering what exactly I was doing wrong.

On one occasion while working the ingot, the metal suddenly began to boil, large molten bubbles forming in the slag before popping violently in a spray of molten metal everywhere. On another, the hammer I was holding actually *caught fire* after I struck the ingot, the metal I had been trying to shape then freezing itself into a block of ice. But it was my latest experience that made me decide it was time to put my hammer down for the day and consider using something else to craft the blade for my sword.

On that particular attempt to forge a blade, I had been working the metal as fast as I could, faster than I knew was even remotely safe. At the speed that I was going, I knew that one slip up would likely cost me both tools I was working with, and likely several fingers too. Yet for all my haste, I didn't have a chance for an accident to occur, for the metal that I had been working on had simply decided to give up and explode in a blinding flash of colors, having vanished completely from the anvil that I had been working it on when my vision returned. Not so much as a fragment of it remained afterward that I could find.

"*Goddamnit!*" I swore in frustration as I blinked the afterimages from my eyes and threw my tools down. Whatever optimism I had started the day with, had long since vanished under the repeated failures. "What the hell am I supposed to do?"

I closed my eyes for a moment and rubbed my face, trying to cling to the only silver lining that I had been able to find during the morning. All of my repeated failures had given me enough blacksmithing experience to hit level 18 in the tradeskill, even if it hadn't made any appreciable difference for my current task.

"Okay," I said after a moment, exhaling deeply as I glared at the Ætherfire forge with resentment, then turned away from it and began to pace. "It looks like the Æthertouched metal is out, but what else can I use? Bronze won't be enough of an upgrade, nor will any of the spider claws that we have left. There's that ectoplasm from the Slave-King…but that's kinda useless in this case. Maybe I can carve myself a blade from the snake bone we found? Hmm…there's also that piece of Ætherwarped Oak…"

I stopped as the last item entered my mind, realizing that I hadn't given the crystalline wood a second thought after Jenkins had handed it to me.

"Would I even be able to get an edge on it though?" I whispered to myself as I pulled the length of wood out of my inventory and carefully inspected it. "And *keep* the edge on it?"

Glowing with a dull azure hue, the Ætherwarped branch appeared to be virtually unchanged over the last few days, the wood still cool and smooth to the touch. Staring at it closely, I could almost see a slight reflection of myself in it. Despite it having grown from a tree, it was obvious that it wasn't just wood anymore.

Given how hard it was for Jenkins to carve through it, this could be pretty durable, I thought while considering if it would be possible to carve the branch into a sword. I had made a few swords from regular wood in the past, and I did happen to have several Æthertouched Iron tools that I had made as practice.

"Why not give it a shot?" I decided with a shrug. "I don't have any better ideas at this point, and something tells me that carving wood is going to be much easier than snake bone…"

Excited that I had another option available to me, I cleaned up my area around the forge and left the Foundry, letting Léandre's avatar resume its tasks. Walking through the Crafting Hall, I set up shop in a largely unused workspace and spread out several of the Æthertouched carpentry tools that I had made. Taking a moment to come up with a plan for the carving, I began to carve the crystalline branch into a blade.

Initially, the work progressed rapidly as I cut off all the excess from the wood and exposed the inner core of the branch, which I found was much harder to carve as it took on an entirely crystalline appearance. Progress slowed to a crawl as I began to shape the core of the branch, the hours slowly passing by. The deeper into the core I carved, the more difficult it became to do so in a controlled manner, my knives no longer able to peel away the crystalline layers. After little progress for a time, I decided to resort to a hammer and chisel, gently splintering fragments off of the wood as I worked a single edge into my blade to be.

More time passed as I continued to work on the blade, my focus completely devoted to my crafting. The experience was nothing like my previous attempts at creating an item, where I had been mentally following a rote recipe in the back of my mind. This time I was completely in the moment, making it up as I went along. It reminded me of the time that I had made the pots and pans for Ragna a lifetime ago. I was making something completely new, that I had never done before.

I heard people walk past me as the Crafting Hall came to life around me, several of them stopping by to see what I was working on, some even trying to ask questions after seeing what was taking shape before me. But I was far too engrossed in what I was working on to reply. All I saw before me was what I had to do next, my hands moving with barely a conscious thought.

And then, after several hours of work, it was finished, the item description appearing in my vision, followed by a notification.

Ætherwarped Oak Blade

Item Class: Magical
Item Quality: Mastercraft (+20%)
Durability: 160/160
Weight: 1.3 kg

Your skill in Carpentry has increased to level 18!

"I did it," I breathed numbly as I straightened myself from my crouched over position and felt muscles in my back protest. It had taken much longer than I had thought it would, but I had managed to turn the Ætherwarped branch into an actual blade, the entirety of it having maintained its dull azure glow throughout the crafting process.

"Just one last thing to do," I whispered to myself as reached for the glowing blade with a shaky hand and pulled out the hilt that I had fashioned earlier with the Æthertouched Iron, carefully attaching the two pieces together. Fitting perfectly, the blade locked itself into place and then somehow *settled* into the hilt as I began to wrap a length of snakeskin around the hilt. The moment that I finished my work, I saw a prompt appear in the center of my vision, causing my heart to skip a beat.

You have successfully crafted a new item!
You have the opportunity to name this item!
Please enter a name:

There was no hesitation on my account as I entered a name, one that had popped into my mind the moment that I had begun working with the wood. I paused for the briefest of moments as I confirmed my choice and then accepted it, watching with wide eyes as my newly crafted sword's description appeared before me.

Splinter
  Slot: Main Hand
  Item Class: Magical
  Item Quality: Mastercraft (+20%)
  Damage: 35-50 (Slashing)
  Strength: +7 Agility: +7 Mana: +100
  Durability: 200/200
  Weight: 1.5 kg
  Class: Any Martial
  Level: 17
Special: Æthertouched – The potency of any magical spells or magic based traits channeled through this weapon are increased by 12%.

My already wide eyes grew even wider as I read through the item's description until they finally landed on the Æthertouched special ability. My mouth then fell open slightly as I considered the wording.

Magic based traits, I thought, reading and rereading the wording carefully as I looked down at the single edged weapon, its length slightly shorter than its predecessor but possessing a thicker and heavier blade. *Does the channeling part of that work both ways I wonder? Would this weapon allow me to mana drain a target every time that I hit them?*

I felt a surge of excitement course through my body as I considered the implications if it were possible. Grabbing hold or touching someone with a hand wasn't usually difficult prospect during a battle, but it also wasn't always the most feasible, especially against more melee oriented casters like Mozter or Carver. Having the ability to drain their mana just by hitting them would be a huge advantage.

Or in Carver's and his wolf's case, equalize the playing field.

"Ahem." A patient voice interrupted my thoughts from behind me. "Are you done crafting yet, Lyrian? Or perhaps I should come back a third time?"

I spun around, my heart leaping in my chest as I recognized the voice, seeing a familiar figure leaning against the doorway.

"Léandre!" I breathed in sudden relief, the man's face grinning as he met my eyes then dropped down to the sword in my hands.

"So," he began, nodding in appreciation at my work. "What did I miss?"

Chapter 30

"My risks were exceptionally high going into the treatment," Léandre told us as we all listened in rapt attention to the man's story. "And there were several complications during the process, more than were anticipated. I was forced to be put into a coma for several days while they tried to manage everything."

Everyone from both my group and Freya's - save Drace, who was still out digging at the ruin - had come running the moment that I had sent out a message that Léandre had returned. We had crowded around the man in the Crafting Hall before we decided to move our impromptu reunion to the Town Hall, taking over a pair of tables in the corner of the room, far away from where any of the other Adventurers or Townsfolk were sitting.

"I was told that it was a close thing, my surviving that is, and I am far from being out of the woods yet," Léandre continued in a small voice as he looked down towards his hands. "I won't bore you all with the medical details, but it was decided that my chances at survival would be better if they put me back into Ascend Online, rather than risk sedating me once more."

"Put you back?" Sierra asked in confusion. "Why would that matter? And why would they even think of doing that in the first place?"

"At my age, in my condition," Léandre replied. "I likely wouldn't come out of that kind of sedation a second time. But as for putting me back into the game...somehow CTI learned of my situation and took an interest in my treatment. Apparently, they believe that cases like mine are only going to become more common in the future and want to develop a treatment process that can be done 'in-pod', so to speak, over a longer treatment period."

"So right now, they're still...*uh,* working on you?" I asked hesitantly, unable to help but feel concerned about how such a treatment could affect Léandre's overall health.

"That's my understanding," Léandre replied with a nod. "And they will continue to do so, assuming I don't suddenly fall over dead that is."

Everyone gave Léandre a panicked stare, causing the feline man to raise his hands in a placating gesture.

"I will be fine," he soothed, before waving a hand dismissively through the air. "But please, enough of this. What will be, will be. I have long since accepted this and learned that one must make the best use of the time that they have in the moment. Tell me more about what I've missed, I have yet to fully sift through all my new memories, and it seems to me that it's been quite an eventful week, yes?"

There was a slight pause as everyone glanced between one another, then back to Léandre, still concerned about the ordeal that he had faced. Personally, I couldn't help but feel confused by CTI's interest in his treatment. To me, it seemed easier to let the already established businesses handle it, rather than attempt to integrate what had to already be a complicated process into their own technology.

They must think that they make money off it by targeting the older generations. Or maybe it will somehow help them manage our health better in the pods? I considered, before shrugging the question away. I didn't know the first thing about any of the technologies involved to create Ascend Online or the Age Regression process. If CTI thought that they could somehow improve the playing experience for us, I wasn't about to complain what they spent their research budget on. *Maybe they'll be able to get rid of the 'VR Diet' side effect that we currently have; I don't think I could stand to lose any more weight back in Reality.*

"—ambushed us few a days ago." Freya was in the middle of telling Léandre about Carver's attack when I tuned back into the conversation around me. "We fought a pitched battle against one another, but at best, it was a draw, and we were both forced to retreat."

"I see," Léandre said with a heavy sigh. "I remember Carver all too well from Graves' march. I had hoped that we had seen the last of him."

"I think we all did," Thorne grunted. "But it looks like he's put down roots to stay."

"And found Orcs to work with too," Constantine said bitterly before going on to recount Sierra and his portion of the encounter with Carver. "As of yet, we haven't had much luck in finding any sign of them, and we've scouted as far as two days north and northeast of Aldford on horseback."

"The best guess we have at this point is that they're based somewhere in the forests to the east," Sierra added. "But given the sheer size and density of that forest, exploring it quickly is impossible, even if we had several dozen people scouting at once."

"Getting more guilds out here is looking more attractive every day isn't it?" Halcyon asked in a whisper, elbowing me in the side as Constantine and Sierra continued updating Léandre. "We're drowning out here with all the space we need to cover and having more bodies would go a long way."

"No argument from me, Hal," I replied, having long since come to that conclusion myself. "Soon as we can get our house in order here, we can start reaching out, but until then…it might be premature."

"We can't wait too long," Halcyon warned. "Else all the shit going down in Coldscar is going to make the decision for us."

"I know, I know," I acknowledged, having heard this argument several times over the last few days. "Let's just see where we are in a couple days and go from there."

"Well, at least now the memories I have about the palisade make much more sense!" Léandre exclaimed, his yellow, feline eyes focusing on me as he spoke. "How has construction proceeded overall?"

"Good as a whole," I said, realizing that it was my turn to update Léandre. "We have enough housing now for everyone to have their own privacy, but nothing extra should anyone new arrive. Once everything with Carver became public, all of our building efforts shifted practically overnight to defenses."

"Understandable. And given what you've all said, likely a wise decision," Léandre agreed with a nod. "But did you manage to come up with a consensus for the design? The last time we spoke about the defenses, Drace and Jenkins were rather…*disagreeable*."

"Yeah, they definitely were," I said, remembering the arguments we'd had about what to do with Aldford's defenses and just how necessary they were. "But they're also far too busy to do the work themselves, so I made an executive decision. We've started on the heavy fortification design that you and I came up with, the one modeled after a Roman fort."

Léandre went completely still as he processed what I had just said. "A-are you sure about that, Lyrian? As I recall, that plan was…exceptionally ambitious, even for me. The amount of work and materials it would take…there is also the matter of, well…"

Léandre made a subtle downward pointing motion towards the ground.

"Right now, we *need* ambitious," I stated firmly, despite understanding Léandre's concern about the Ley Line below us. "Everyone is afraid of an attack by either Carver, his bandits, or the Orcs, and are willing to work *hard* in order to feel safe. This makes the best use of that energy and will set us up for the long term, assuming our other problem sorts itself out."

"Plus, it makes sure that people don't suspect that something is wrong," Sierra added in a faint whisper, Léandre's eyes shifting over to the red-haired elf. "If we stop building things and start preparing to abandon the town..."

"Then people will panic," Léandre finished with a shake of his head as his eyes glanced downward in memory. "I know. I have seen it first hand during my volunteering days."

There was a slight pause, as the man thought for a moment before he nodded to himself. "Very well. I can work with that for the time being. However, how is Drace proceeding on *that* particular front anyway? I would hate to see all of our hard work go to waste."

"Very well, last I heard," I replied, taking a moment to check on the man via Party Sense. I found myself surprised to realize that during the time we had been updating Léandre, Drace had managed to leave the Lakeside Ruins and was now walking through the town towards us. "He's actually on his way here right now. Hopefully, with good news."

"He did mention that he thought could break through today," Constantine said, turning his attention towards the open doors of the Town Hall. "Maybe he did."

"We'll find out in a moment," Halcyon added as we all turned to look towards the door, just at the same moment that Drace walked through it.

"Hey—oh," Drace started to greet us the moment that he entered the building and glanced in our direction, only to find us all already staring back at him expectantly. He floundered for a few seconds in surprise at our unexpected attention, before his eyes focused on a specific member of the group. "Léandre! You're back!"

"Hello, Drace," the man said with a smile, beckoning the half-giant over. "Lyrian sensed you coming and told us. How is everything going today?"

"Great!" Drace replied, matching Léandre's grin while crossing the distance between us. His stride paused for the briefest of seconds during his approach as his eyes briefly went out of focus, someone from the party no doubt updating him on what had happened with Léandre via private messaging and filling him in on what we were just talking about.

"We just broke through a small section of the collapse that opens up into a chamber of some sort," was the first thing he said in a low voice, everyone leaning forward to listen. "I decided to call a stop and block it off for the time being, but it should only take a few minutes more to break through the rest of it once we're ready to fully open it."

"What did it lead into?" I asked trying not to let the sudden anxiety that I felt seep into my voice. Despite the confidence I'd shown to Léandre, I was painfully aware that we had invested quite a bit of time and energy in digging out the collapsed route in the ruin. Now that we had broken through, I really hoped that our efforts paid off somehow and gave us a way to reach the Ley Line.

Because if it didn't, we'd be forced to start from scratch.

"A large room of some sort, in the same style as the ruin we dug from," Drace explained with a shrug, acknowledging how useless that explanation was. "I didn't want to risk shining too much light through the gap I made, just in case there was something in there."

"Probably a good idea," Halcyon agreed.

"I did find one interesting thing though," Drace added. "The air in the chamber smelled a bit *tangy*, but it was definitely breathable, and there was hardly a pressure difference when I broke through."

"That's...interesting," I said with surprise, noting that Léandre's face showed the same expression. "Can you describe the smell at all? Did it remind you of anything on the surface? I wonder if there's another route we missed."

"No, not really," Drace replied thoughtfully. "Best way I can describe it is that it smelled like mold, a little musky, a little damp, but nothing specific."

"Perhaps the Nafarr's magic extended to air purifiers?" Léandre queried. "It seems odd for a chamber so long buried to have not acquired its own particular stench, especially if bodies were present when it was sealed...as I assume, there must have been."

"Maybe. But it also seems odd that they'd be running this long too," I pointed out. "Shouldn't they have run out of magic?"

"With all the magic that we've seen through the Ætherscopes, they may not have," Caius countered. "We spotted dozens of sources the last time we took a scan; there's no telling what they could have been used for."

"That's a good point," I admitted, then shrugged my shoulders. "Beats me then."

"I guess we'll have to find out," Drace said as he cast a quick glance around the table then focused his attention on me. "Are we up for making preparations tonight and hitting it first thing in the morning?"

"The sooner, the better," I stated, seeing heads nod out of the corner of my eye in agreement. "We have no idea how much time we're working with here."

Everyone around the table nodded at my words and exchanged glances with one another, excitement visible on all their faces despite the seriousness of our situation. The chance to explore what could be an untouched underground ruin was one none of us wanted to miss, each of us having spent our fair share of time fantasizing to what we might find once we got down there.

Going into the ruin means putting looking for Carver on hold though, I thought, the memory of the half-orc still at the forefront of my mind. Even with all of the Adventurers in Aldford searching for the last week, we hadn't managed to find even a single clue to where he and his followers had escaped to, leaving me to think that he'd retreated at least a day or two's travel away from the town. *But given how much time we've already devoted searching for him with nothing to show for it, we need to move on. There's no telling how much time we have to find and seal the Ley Line before it erupts, we can't afford to sit here paralyzed until he shows up again.*

"We're still just taking our two groups, plus Lazarus's, right?" Freya asked, bringing everyone back to the moment. "Assuming we can all even fit down there..."

"For the time being, yeah," I replied, then remembered something I wanted to bring up with the group. "Though I actually wanted to add Alistair to our roster too. We're a little light on healing as it is, and he can help with that, as well as give us two full groups of eight."

"Extra healers are never a bad thing in my book," Constantine replied, earning a sympathetic grunt from Drace.

"It would certainly make my life easier," Theia commented from her side of the table, having been content to largely listen while everyone else talked. "Right now, I think Caius, Helix and myself are the only ones that can heal at all."

"And my healing isn't exactly the most reliable," Caius pointed out.

"Alissstair would be a great addition," Helix affirmed while nodding enthusiastically. "He has proven to be steady."

"Okay, seems like we're all on the same page then," Freya said with a smile, not seeing any arguments from the other guild members. "I'll send him a message and bring him into the loop once we're done here. We should also give Lazarus and his group a heads-up too."

"Yeah, I was going to send him a message when we're done here and let him know," I replied, looking around at all the faces at the table for questions. "Does anyone have anything else to bring up before we all split up?"

Everyone shook their heads in negation and glanced around the table for anyone else to speak up. After a few seconds pause, it became clear that no one had anything else to add for the moment.

"Alright," I said, standing up from my chair while mentally composing a private message to Lazarus and asking if he was available to meet with me. "In that case, let's start getting ready.

"Because tomorrow, we're going dungeon crawling."

Chapter 31

Friday, March 22th, 2047 - 7:01 am
The Lakeside Ruins

"I really hope that the whole ruin isn't this cramped," Alistair muttered aloud as the seventeen of us milled about in various groups, scattered throughout the main chamber of the Lakeside Ruins while we waited for Drace to excavate the last bits of the passage. "Otherwise, the only thing most of us are going to see is the back of the person in front of us."

"I hear you there," Constantine chimed in. "I'm not quite claustrophobic. But depending on how today works out...I just might be once we're done."

"I'm sure you'll be fine," I called to the rogue from my position leaning against the wall closest to the switchbacks. "But if you start feeling antsy, let us know, and we can let you take point once we get down there. Maybe then you can be useful and spring any traps before we can step onto them."

"I'm going to take a hard pass on that one, Lyr," Constantine replied without missing a beat. "I like my limbs firmly attached, and my flesh un-melted. Besides, Caius did a great job the last time with the trap springing; I don't see a reason to change things up now."

"How considerate," Caius grunted sarcastically. "You're a real team player."

"No problem, bud!" Constantine said with a grin. "I got your back."

"*To push it forward into danger you mean.*"

"I take it that you've all known one another for quite a long time," Lazarus asked me as the banter between Constantine and Caius continued, the pair clearly burning off nervous energy while they waited.

"Decades," I acknowledged, turning my head to see both Sawyer and Ransom standing beside the half-giant. "How about you guys?"

"Just a few weeks for me," Ransom replied. "Ever since…well, *you know*."

"I see," I said with a nod, before turning my head towards Sawyer.

"Almost since release day," Sawyer stated, giving Lazarus a grin as he spoke. "Though we didn't start off on the best terms."

"Oh?" I asked, raising an eyebrow as I looked towards Lazarus, who was shaking his head but shared the same smile that Sawyer did.

"Sawyer liked to make my life difficult in the beginning—" The half-giant started to say just before Sawyer interrupted.

"And I still do too!"

"—which hasn't changed." Lazarus paused to glare at the red-armored man. "*But* after beating the shit out of one another…five times, we decided that it was better to work together."

"That and because Eberia was *literally* on fire at the time," Sawyer added.

"That too," Lazarus agreed, his expression faltering slightly as he spoke. "As for the others—"

"Hey, we're through." Drace's low voice filtered out from the tunnel leading to the switchbacks a heartbeat before he appeared in the entranceway, causing my attention to shift towards him. "I had to make a bit of noise clearing the entrance, so we should get moving, in case something down there decides to investigate."

"Good idea," I replied, glancing back towards Lazarus and seeing that the emotion I had seen on his face had vanished, the moment having passed. "Let's get everyone moving then."

Turning around to face the rest of the guild, I cleared my throat loudly, the noise more than enough to cause all the conversations to stop as heads turned to look in my direction.

"It's showtime," I announced, seeing grins break out on several faces in the crowd as my words filled the air. "Everyone fall into their assigned formation and move as quietly as you can. The plan is to move carefully until we get a better picture of what's ahead of us. Keep your ears open and be sure to speak up if you see something interesting."

"Or if something interesting sees you," Constantine added dryly.

Murmurs of assent intermixed with laughter reached my ears as everyone moved into position, the sounds of weapons being drawn faintly echoing through the chambers. We had plenty of time to come up with a basic plan for exploring the ruin last night, and everyone was well aware of their roles and responsibilities.

The only thing left now was to dive on in and see what we found.

Nodding at Drace to take the lead, I followed him as he turned around back down the tunnel, waving at a somewhat sleepy Amaranth to follow close behind me.

<My kind is not supposed to be up this early in a new day,> the cat told me sullenly as he walked behind me. *<The sun wasn't even awake when we departed.>*

<We won't see the sun where we're going,> I replied to Amaranth with a smile on my face. *<Though if you're tired, you can stay behind and sleep a bit longer...while we go on without you.>*

<That will not be necessary,> he stated, his mental voice suddenly sounding much more alert.

The rest of the journey down the tunnel proceeded in silence, only the crunch of our feet on the broken stone sounding as we slowly stalked down the passage that Drace had spent the last week excavating. Taking care not to slip as I walked down the incline, I kept a firm eye on Drace's back as he led the way into the lower ruin, several motes of lights floating ahead of him and illuminating the way.

"Here we go," Drace whispered softly as we reached the bottom of the incline, which almost immediately opened up into a large, partially collapsed chamber, a maze of fallen stone preventing us from seeing deeper into the room.

I heard Drace take a deep breath before he stepped forward into the dark room before us, the large stone fragments protruding from the ceiling above us causing our lights to cast disturbing and eerie shadows as we moved. It only took me a handful of strides before my nose caught a whiff of the tangy, stench that Drace had mentioned earlier, which now that I smelled it, reminded me of moldy bread mixed with something extra that I couldn't quite identify.

Holding Splinter tightly in my hand as Drace and I picked our way through the fallen rubble, I couldn't help but notice that some of the larger fragments that we passed bore the same sort of architecture as the chamber above us.

It looks like a lot of whatever used to be here was affected or damaged by the explosion, I thought, my gaze landing on a massive piece of stone that had thrust itself through what I assumed was once a doorway, leading somewhere away from the chamber that we were in. *Just how big was this place when the Nafarr were still alive, and how much is still buried underground here?*

Questions about the ancient civilization continued to circulate through my mind as Drace, and I continued to navigate a path around the fallen chunks of stone, on one occasion needing to climb straight over a rather large shard when we couldn't find a way past. But eventually, after several minutes of slow progress, we finally worked our way past the worst of the collapse, entering into a relatively clear portion of the chamber where we decided to wait for the rest of the guild, and the motes of light, to catch up to us.

Looking into the gloom ahead of us, I decided to activate *True Sight*, my enhanced vision easily piercing through the darkness and illuminating the rest of the chamber. Blinking twice to get used to the sudden brightness, I was surprised that the first thing that I noticed were countless magical burns scarring nearly every portion of the chamber ahead of us.

Damn, it looks like a small war was fought down here, I observed, my eyes picking out large chunks of stone that had been blasted out from the floor and several splattered pockmarks that could have only been caused by acid. It was as if the damage that I'd seen in the chamber we'd come from above had repeated itself down here, except on a much larger scale. My gaze gradually continued to work its way further into the room as I followed the damage inward, eventually ending up at the far wall, roughly thirty feet away from us.

Cut into the wall, I saw two doorways roughly twenty feet apart from one another, both of them similar to the blocked one that Drace and I had passed earlier. One of the doors was wide open, the passage beyond it angling out of sight, while the other was sealed with what appeared to be a carved stone slab. There appeared to be some sort of design on the door, but I couldn't make out the detail from this distance.

An open doorway is a good sign, I told myself, happy to see that our dungeon crawl hadn't been stalled by the need to dig once more, or that a collapse had ended it before it had a chance to begin. My eyes dropped downwards from the two doorways to look at the rather large pile of rubble that littered the ground between the two entranceways. It only took me a second after focusing on the rubble to realize that it wasn't actually rubble at all. *Are those…*

I took a tentative step forward as I stared at the sight before me, my heart doing a flip once I figured out what I was looking at.

"Bodies," I whispered to myself. "They're all bodies."

"Lyr?" Drace whispered in concern as he stepped up to my side and regarded the darkness warily, unable to see through it like I could. "What do you see?"

"The remains of the people who were trapped in here, I think," I replied in a low voice as my eyes tried to make sense of what they were seeing.

Scattered everywhere on the ground between the two doorways ahead of us was what appeared to be well over a dozen withered and skeletal bodies. Many I could see were clad in armor of some sort, the finer details of which was obscured by the thick layer of dust that coated it. In several instances, I saw weapons protruding from the fallen bodies, which I couldn't help but notice were still clutched firmly in the hands of the other fallen. Whatever scene had once played out here long ago must have been one of complete chaos for the bodies to have ended up this way.

"It looks like there were two forces in here that fought one another," I said with a guess, taking my eyes off the fallen bodies ahead of me and turning around to face Drace and the others who had managed to navigate their way through the maze of fallen rubble. "The room is covered with battle damage further in, and the bodies are piled two or three deep in some places."

"The Irovians must have made it this far then," Drace commented, referring to the old dark elf empire that predated The Ascendancy. "It would make sense for them to try and secure the Ley Line from the Nafarr if they were attacking the city here. Assuming that all of this leads to the Ley Line in the first place."

"Maybe," I agreed. "But it doesn't look like it worked out that well for them."

"No, no it doesn't," Drace said wistfully before the two of us glanced over at the rest of the guild and saw that everyone had managed to catch up.

"Want to send a few lights forward so those of us without Darkvision can see?" Drace asked, motioning towards what I figured to be a near impenetrable darkness for his eyes.

"Sure," I replied, waving a hand to motion our casters over and repeating the request.

Seconds later, four motes of lights gently sailed through the air and illuminated the far end of the chamber, revealing the fallen bodies and twin doorways for everyone to see. There was a brief pause as the others took in the sight, the lights shifting ever so slightly to maximize their coverage of the area.

"Great, a bunch of bodies, lying suspiciously on the ground, weapons within reach," Constantine muttered softly as he moved to stand close to Drace and me. "Does the game think that we're stupid? Of course, the moment we get close to them, they're going to leap up at us."

"Probably," Drace agreed. "To the 'leaping up and attacking us' part at least, but do you really want the game making things *harder* for us? Compared to the last few days, I for one am happy with an underhanded toss once in a while."

"Eh, I guess," Constantine replied with a shrug. "I don't know; I was just expecting something with a little bit more...*flair,* to be honest. Maybe something like a—"

"Constantine, if you finish that sentence, I am going to hit you," Sierra said softly as she joined the conversation, drawing looks of concern from the rest of the guild members around us. "I don't need you jinxing us, or giving the game any ideas."

"*Fine*," the rogue groused, holding his hands up as he turned to look at the red-haired elf. "I just have our bottom line in mind, that's all. The more interesting our fights are, the better our feed ranks."

"*That* is the furthest thing from my mind right now," I growled, turning my head towards Sierra. "Can you peg one of the bodies with an arrow and see if it gets us a reaction? If it does, we'll light them up at range. If it doesn't, we can send Constantine forward for a more personal touch."

"You sure we can't start with that second option, Lyr?" Sierra asked hopefully, despite pulling an arrow from her quiver and nocking it on her bow.

"You guys are mean," Constantine muttered.

"*Quiet,*" I said to the rogue, then pitched my voice just high enough for everyone to hear. "Heads up! We're going to try and pull. Everyone line up!"

Within seconds of hearing my words, the sound of shuffling feet filled the room as everyone fell into their assigned ranks, their weapons held high as they focused their attention forward. Glancing over the line to make sure that everyone was ready, I nodded towards Sierra and signaled for her to proceed, taking up my assigned place at Drace's side.

Striding forward confidently a few steps ahead of us, I saw Sierra raise her bow to her shoulder and take aim at one of the skeletal bodies ahead of us. She paused for the briefest of moments as she steadied her aim, then let the arrow loose, the bolt leaving her bow with blinding speed and slamming into the side of a fallen body's head, piercing straight through it.

We watched the pile of bodies carefully, waiting for a reaction.

A handful of seconds passed with no visible reaction, then ten seconds, then twenty. When we reached the half minute mark with no sign of movement from the pile, I called out to Sierra in the softest voice I could manage.

"Try one more time."

With a nod, Sierra pulled another arrow free of her quiver and placed it on the string of her bow, taking careful aim at another target. The second arrow landed true to its mark, piercing through another skull with a loud crack, leaving us all waiting in suspense for a reaction.

Another half minute passed with not so much as a twitch from the pile of bodies, Sierra's head eventually turning back to look at me with a raised eyebrow.

"Alright, guess you're up, Con—" I began to say before two impossibly bright figures appeared from the wall before us, forcing me to shield my eyes out of reflex as they momentarily overwhelmed my *True Sight* with their presence.

"Oh shit!" I heard Constantine gasp, followed by similar exclamations from the rest of the guild around me.

Pulling my hand away from my face, I blinked the afterimages away from my vision and looked back towards the twin sources of magic that had blinded me, the images rapidly resolving from two bright blurs of magic into two ghostly women of a race I didn't recognize. The pair hovered at the far end of the room, their expressions twisted into one of rage as they regarded us, emerald strands of hair billowing out all around them. Two tags appeared in my vision as I stared dumbfounded at the sight before me, my focus shifting ever so slightly to read them.

[Ætherbound Specter] – Boss – Level 16

"Are you happy now, Constantine?" I heard Drace bark from beside me, a heartbeat before a screeching feminine voice assaulted my mind.

<**THE IROVIANS HAVE RETURNED!**> The words hit me with the force of the blow, causing me to wince in pain from the sheer volume and anger behind it. <**TO ARMS! TO ARMS! WE MUST NOT FAIL IN OUR DEFENSE!**>

No sooner did the words fade from my mind than a bright flash of magic filled the room as the two Specters thrust their ghostly hands towards the pile of bodies before them, an emerald wave of energy suffusing all of them and causing them to stir.

"Casters! Destroy the bodies!" I shouted while conjuring a *Flame Dagger* in my hand, instantly understanding what the Specters were doing. "Don't let them raise them all!"

My words were barely out of my mouth before I threw the burning knife that I had conjured, taking a step forward to impart extra momentum on the toss. But instead of targeting the bodies on the ground like I had ordered everyone else to, I had decided to try attacking one of the Specters, in the hope of distracting it from its efforts.

The dagger arced through the air, any hope of precision impossible at the distance between us and the Specters, but still accurate enough to pass through one of them, who let out a brief moan of pain, but otherwise did not react.

A wave of magic followed on the heels of my opening attack, several bolts of purple energy and a large fireball slamming into the skeletal bodies that littered the floor.

The impacts sent fragments of bone and shards of metal armor flying through the air, causing the two Specters to screech in response, their already rage-filled faces intensifying at the offense.

Immediately the pair shot forward, moving as one to put their ethereal forms before the fallen bodies that their magic was gradually animating. Glaring at us with incalculable hate, their mouths opened impossibly wide before letting out a primal scream that caused all of us to flinch in pain and drop down to our knees.

My head pounded in complete agony under the Specters' cry, my hands reflexively reaching up to my ears in an attempt to block the sound, but to no avail. It was all I could do to clench my eyes as tight as I could and wait for it to pass, the pain so intense I was barely able to focus on the two alerts that had appeared in my combat log.

An [Ætherbound Specter]'s [Psychic Scream] hits you for 128 points of damage!

An [Ætherbound Specter]'s [Psychic Scream] hits you for 114 points of damage!

Then, what seemed like hours later, the mental scream vanished as if it had never been, allowing me to reopen my eyes and gaze back in the direction of the Specters. The two spirits still hovered in the spot that I had last seen them, their mouths having returned to their normal shapes. Looking through them, I couldn't help but notice that during their attack's duration, several of the bodies had managed to rise to their feet, and were now steadily plodding forward toward us. Sensing what my eye was focused on, the game wasted no time in assigning a tag to one of the risen creatures, identifying it for me.

[Ætherbound Revenant] – Level 14

A Revenant? I thought numbly, still reeling from the aftereffects of the scream as I tried to make sense of what

I was seeing. The creature's flesh appeared to be completely dry and appeared as if it were stretched too tightly over its bones. I could see tears in the flesh and exposed bone underneath where it wasn't covered by the damaged armor that hung loosely from its body. In its hand, I saw that it clung to a tarnished sword, its gleaming emerald eyes staring mindlessly forward as it strode towards us.

A flare of magic from the Specters caused my attention to shift back towards them, as they both began to conjure large azure orbs of energy in their hands, the Revenants now steadily rising from the ground without any apparent effort on their part.

"They're casting spells!" I shouted in a panic, trying to warn everyone while simultaneously forcing myself to my feet. "Everyone get up!"

No sooner were the words out of my mouth than the Specters let their attacks fly, the two azure orbs speeding from their hands. Flinching from one that seemed to have been targeted directly at me, I braced myself for pain, only to have the orb prematurely explode, its energy washing away from me as a shimmering wave force filled the air before me.

"Shit that was close!" Halcyon gasped from behind me as other bursts of magic echoed through the chamber, followed by cries of pain. "I think I only got the one though..."

"Better than nothing!" I exclaimed with sudden relief as I realized that Halcyon had managed to put yet another timely *Force Shield* in front of me to save me and the others from an attack.

"We need to get in there, Lyr!" Drace grunted from beside me as he pushed himself to his feet. "More Revenants are rising by the second."

"Got a plan how to manage that?" Constantine's voice shouted from the other side of Drace.

"Attack the Specters to keep them focused on us and take out what Revenants you can," I said while casting *Lesser Shielding* on myself. "We need to make a path for the casters to the bodies that haven't risen yet, so they can thin them before they rise. If we don't do that we'll get swarmed!"

"We can do that!" Caius added from behind. "But we need to move! The other group took a beating from that spell!"

"Then let's go!" I barked, Halcyon taking my words as a cue to drop the Force Shield in front of us.

Rushing forward as a group, I focused my attention back onto the two Specters and saw that the pair had begun conjuring yet another round of azure orbs and by my best guess were moments away from unleashing another volley.

We won't be able to get to them before they finish their spells, I realized, seeing that nearly a dozen Revenants - about half of the bodies lying on the ground earlier - were now directly in our way. *They'll slow us down too much...unless I jump ahead.*

"Meet me in there! Going to try and disrupt their spells!" I called out to Drace in warning, a heartbeat before I triggered *Blink Step*, angling my teleport towards the far side of the room where I still had a clear line of sight, and nothing would block my spell.

In an all too familiar blur of colors, I reappeared barely an arm's length away from the sealed doorway on the far end of the room, which was thankfully an area free of any Revenants. Pivoting on my foot, I used the momentum I had teleported with to angle myself towards the twin Specters, having appeared nearly adjacent to them.

My unexpected movement attracted the attention of the Specter closest to me, causing her head to turn in my direction just as I closed in on her floating form. Moving on reflex, she twisted to throw the azure orb that she had conjured at me, but my charge had already carried me in far too close, and it sailed cleanly over my shoulder as I ducked under it, before it impacted on the far wall behind me with a thunderous crash.

Leading with Splinter, I thrust out with my newly crafted sword and drove it through her ethereal body, catching her just above where her hip would have been, had she'd been a physical entity. I felt only slightest tug on Splinter's edge as it passed clean through the spirit, leaving me wondering for the briefest of moments whether or not my attack had any effect.

The scream of pain that followed seconds afterward banished any doubts that I had.

Continuing my charge forward, I saw the second Specter flinch at its twin's cry, and it instinctively twisted its body in the direction of the noise, the slight movement giving me the perfect opportunity to sweep my blade straight through its chest. For a second time, I only felt the barest resistance as Splinter passed through the second Specter with hardly any effort on my part. A second, even louder scream greeted my ears as my momentum carried me past the two now screeching spirits, leaving no doubt in my mind that I had achieved what I had set out to do and successfully distracted the pair.

Unfortunately, I hadn't given a lot of thought to what I would do afterward.

What's your plan now, Marcus? I shouted mentally as I focused my attention forward and saw myself charging directly towards a quartet of Revenants that were heading towards the party.

I glanced around in a momentary wave of panic as I tried to find a way to avoid the impending collision with the Revenants, but no matter where I looked, the situation didn't look any better. There were far too many of the undead creatures on either side of me to have a clear line of sight to Blink Step out of the way, which meant that I had only the least worst option available to me.

Which was plowing straight into the four Revenants ahead of me and just plain hoping for the best.

This is going to suck! I shouted internally while tucking my head down into my shoulder and bracing Splinter on my hip as I readied to crash into the first Revenant.

The impact rattled my teeth as I blindsided the Revenant with the crunch of breaking bones, who up until this moment, had no idea that I existed. Stepping into the creature, I was surprised to find that it was much lighter than I had anticipated, the collision sending it sprawling to the ground, where it then crashed into a second Revenant and took out its legs from under it.

Seizing the unexpected opportunity, I ran past the two fallen Revenants and used the last bits of my momentum to chop Splinter into the side of yet another Revenant's head, caving half of it in and causing the undead creature to stagger to its knees from the blow. With my advantage spent, I spun to face the fourth Revenant that I had momentarily lost track of, immediately feeling the price of my failure as something sharp thrust itself into my hip, piercing deeply enough to grate against the bone.

Three for four isn't bad! I thought through clenched teeth as I twisted to face the Revenant and knocked a follow-up attack away, mindful of the two Specters that I knew were right behind me. I had only seconds to either find a clear line of sight to Blink Step somewhere safer or come up with a way to somehow prevent myself from getting turned into the magical equivalent of a pincushion. Swinging Splinter in a short chop, I caught the Revenant's blade and drove it backward, momentarily pinning it against its chest. The maneuver gave me an opportunity to cast a quick glance upwards towards the ceiling, checking to see just how much vertical room I had available above me, which to my disappointment, turned out to be very little. *Damn, the ceiling is too low! If I use my Jump spell in here, I'll just end up giving myself a concussion!*

Starting to feel panic rise from within at the prospect of being trapped, I released my hold on the Revenant's sword and exchanged a pair of blows as I worked to circle around the undead creature, hoping to put it between me and the two Specters behind me. Accepting a bruising chop on my elbow as part of the price for the shift in position, I managed to trade places with the Revenant and found myself with my back to the wall, spotting the two spirits hovering in the air where I had left them.

Only this time, their attention was focused entirely on me, and they were both holding bright azure orbs of magic.

Oh, this is going to hurt, I realized in a perfect moment of clarity as the two spirits prepared to cast their spells in my direction, only to have a hail of magic suddenly lash out from beyond the crowd of Revenants and splash across one of the Specters. Letting out a wail of pain as its spell came apart in its hand, the spirit instantly shifted its attention away from me and towards the source of the attack, a panicked voice cutting through the chaos of battle.

"Well we have its attention now! Now what?" I could just barely make out Ransom's shout as the Specter glided away from me, leaving me staring at the other spirit as it finished casting its spell and threw the orb it was holding in my direction.

Okay, on second thought, maybe this won't be so bad! I thought as I stared at the oncoming missile which appeared to move with glacial slowness in my heightened state of awareness. Acting on pure instinct, I reflexively tried to duck in front of the Revenant that I just traded places with, desperately hoping that its body would provide some cover from the coming attack.

I had barely begun to move before a bright azure light filled my vision, followed a heartbeat afterward by a thunderous crash of sound as the orb detonated and vented its magical fury on everything around me. I felt something hard crash into me and knock me backward, my back slamming into the wall. At the same instant, a brief, yet searing sensation of pain washed over me, causing the skin on my face to blister and burn. Passing as quickly as it appeared, the azure light vanished, my vision returning with several alerts flashing in the corner of my eye.

A [Ætherbound Revenant] hits you for 58 points of damage!

An [Ætherbound Specter]'s [Arcane Orb] hits you for 163 points of damage!

You are low on Health!

HP: 267/792

"Ugh," I let out a low moan as the weight that had slammed into me fell away from my body, leaving me staring down at the charred husk of the Revenant that I had taken shelter behind. It had taken the worse of the blast for me, but enough had still managed to get through to send my health down to critical levels.

A screeching wail along with a surge of adrenaline brought me back into the moment, causing my head to snap upwards and temporarily banish the pain coursing through my body. With a new orb growing in its hands, I saw the attacking Specter soar towards me with malice on her face, a clear, Revenant-free path now directly between us.

Something tells me that trick isn't going to work twice, I thought, desperately glancing for a way out. While the Specter's blast had inadvertently killed or knocked down the Revenants immediately around me, it did nothing to provide an avenue of escape, short of me somehow running straight through it. I was a sitting duck with nowhere to go and didn't have nearly enough health to survive—

Wait a second! My eyes widened as I replayed the last thought in my mind for a second time, it *should* be possible for me to pass through the spirit ahead of me! After all, it *was* a ghost, and I had done the same before to the Slave-King when I had fought him! Why would this occasion be any different? All I had to do was get close enough so it couldn't hit me with its spell...

With a snap decision I pushed myself forward off the wall, well aware of all the qualifiers I had attached to my desperate rationalization. Putting as much power as I could into my legs, I managed two large steps forward to build up some momentum, then triggered a short *Blink Step*, using the spell to teleport me directly point blank in front of the advancing Specter, my third step taking me directly inside the spirit.

Passing through the ghost felt as if I had plunged my entire body into an icy river of pure rage, an unearthly cold washing over me as I moved. I felt a maelstrom of alien emotions whip through my mind as I charged through the spirit, lasting until I erupted from the far side of the Specter, exhaling a deep breath of relief as I continued to put space between me and the spirit.

L-let's not do that again! The thought pounded through my mind as I shook off the unsettling cold that I had experienced and angled my sprint towards the relative safety of my friends. Distracting the Specters had turned into a hell of a lot more than I had anticipated, and I knew I was damned lucky to have survived, something I had to credit to Ransom and the other spellcasters timely intervention.

"Lyrian!" Helix was the first to spot me as I rushed towards their line of battle, his head towering over the Revenants between us. "This way! Make an opening! We'll cover you!"

Trusting that I would have somewhere safe to end up, I angled my sprint towards the lizardman shoving past a pair of a Revenants in my way and sending them staggering to the side. As I ran towards safety, I saw the familiar figures of Freya, Cadmus and Myr race past me, the three of them headed in the opposite direction as they continued to press the attack forward, passing by me in a blur.

Crossing the final distance to safety, I arrived just in time to see Helix obliterate a Revenant's head with his axe, then kick the now twice dead creature to the ground where it lay still for good. Beside him, I saw Abaddon and Thorne in the process of finishing off two other Revenants, their pair clearly eager to rush forward. I had barely come to a stop before Helix grabbed my arm roughly, his gravelly voice echoing through the air.

"You need healing," he said in a tone that wasn't a question as a wave of energy shot up my arm, causing the burns that I had suffered to fade in intensity. "That's the best I can do. *Theia*!"

Letting go of my arm without another word, he then rushed forward to follow Freya and the others, leaving me momentarily standing by myself until Theia came running from behind Abaddon and Thorne.

"Oh, Lyrian, what did you do?" she asked, her pale grey eyes widening as she saw me.

"Got lucky, to be honest," I replied as the lizardwoman raised a clawed hand to my face and began to channel healing magic into me. "I had to keep them from casting spells at the group, so I convinced them to cast them at me."

"That was you—" Theia started to ask before shaking her head in resignation. "Of course, it would be you."

"I had to do something," I protested, just before a deafening wail echoed through the chamber followed by another explosion of magic.

Spinning away from Theia reflexively, I twisted my body to look back towards the two Specters that I had run away from, a sudden panic gripping my heart. I had been so focused on trying to survive and get to safety that I hadn't even given them a second thought after I'd managed to escape.

But to my relief instead of the two Specters continuing their rampage, I saw that a handful of group members had finally managed to a clear a path through the Revenants and made it into melee range, their attacks causing the two spirits to howl in pain.

"Stop moving!" Theia shouted as she grabbed hold of me before I could run off and sent one large surge of healing energy into me. "There! Now you can go break yourself again!"

"Thanks, Theia!" I called out to the lizardwoman before charging back into the battle, this time not having to deal with any Revenants in the process. In the time that it had taken for me to be healed, Freya, Helix and the others had managed to advance, using their numbers to quickly cut through the handful of undead in their way.

As I ran to rejoin the fight, I focused my attention on the Specter closest to me, just in time to see Freya slash the edge of her spear through one of the spirits before her, the weapon causing a momentary stream of magic to bleed out from it before the temporary wound sealed itself. The Specter flinched from under the attack and lifted a clawed hand to strike at the blonde-haired warrior, only to howl in pain as Lazarus's translucent greatsword interrupted the motion and swept through the spirit's center mass.

Falling in line at Freya's side, I could visibly see that the Specter before me had weakened since I last saw it, appearing more and more translucent as the magic keeping it alive seeped out of it. Not waiting for an invitation to join the fight, I stabbed out with Splinter, simultaneously sending a *Shocking Touch* into the blade, the Ætherwarped Oak that I had crafted the weapon from easily conducting the magical energy.

Once again, there was barely any resistance as my weapon passed into the Specter, a flare of magic marking the spot where it pierced into the spirit. Dragging Splinter to the side, I widened the spectral wound that I had inflicted, this time activating my *Mana Leech* ability and instantly feeling a stream of cool energy travel up my arm as magic began to spill out from the Specter's body.

I was right! I can drain mana through Splinter! I thought with excitement, seeing the Specter recoil from the barrage of attacks and attempt to glide away from us, seeking safety closer to its twin, whom I noticed was being similarly pressed by Drace, Constantine and Sawyer.

"It's weakening!" Lazarus's voice shouted as he led the charge to follow the retreating spirit, his large blade sweeping out to carve another line through the Specter's form.

Rushing forward, we began to encircle the two spirits as they desperately fought back to back, abandoning their earlier magical attacks in favor of wicked swipes with their spectral claws that left searing internal wounds despite not breaking flesh. But for all their intensity, they gradually began to falter as spells eventually reached out to slam into them as the mages, and the rest of our melee fighters joined the fight, the Revenants that they had summoned now a shattered mass of bone and broken armor lying lifeless on the ground.

<*YOU WILL NOT SEIZE THIS PLACE INTACT!*> A mental cry rang out through my mind as a barrage of magic slammed into the two Specters, causing them both to flicker ominously, their ethereal bodies now steadily streaming magic with every second that passed. <*WE WILL DESTROY IT ALL BEFORE WE LET YOU HAVE IT! YOU WILL CLAIM NOTHING BUT ASHES AND DEATH!*>

With one last wail of agony, the bodies of the two spirits then vanished in a final puff of emerald light, the energy sustaining them no longer enough to keep them intact. Their cry, however, continued to echo through the chamber long after they disappeared, gradually diminishing until the only sound remaining was our panting breaths.

No one said anything as we glanced around the chamber, our victory taking a moment to sink in, which was expressed by rushed exhalations of relief as people began to lower their weapons.

"Well!" Constantine exclaimed, the first to break the silence that had fallen over us. "I sure as hell didn't expect that!"

Chapter 32

"So, what do you think about what the Specters said?" Lazarus asked me as the others around us explored the room. "Something to worry about?"

"I don't know," I replied with a sigh sharing Lazarus's concern, having mentally replayed the two spirit's last words several times over in my head. "The city that used to be here has long since been destroyed, and everything down here looks to have been abandoned for centuries. It's possible that we're seeing a ghostly memory of what happened before."

"Hmm, maybe," Lazarus allowed with a thoughtful nod and scratched his face. "They did call us Irovians before the fight began."

"Yeah, they did..." I replied hesitantly, having made a note of that particular fact too. "But, if they *weren't* living through a memory and were just reacting to us, then they would have had a good reason to think that we actually *were* Irovian attackers."

"Huh?" Lazarus looked at me in confusion. "Why?"

"Our armor," I said, motioning to the chainmail that I was wearing. "I crafted this armor from scraps of armor that we found in the Irovian Tower, and the majority of us are wearing it. From the two Specters' point of view, we would have looked like Irovian Soldiers."

Lazarus's eyes glanced down to my armor then back up to my face. "Ah, shit."

"Yeah," I said in complete agreement. "I noticed that some of the Revenants had similar armor to us too, no doubt being the Irovians that originally tried to invade the place."

"So, it's probably best that we assume that they *do* have a way of destroying the place," Lazarus stated.

"Given what we know about the Ley Line, that's probably a safe assumption," I acknowledged while glancing around the room. I spotted Halcyon, Caius and Constantine walking towards us with several items in their hands. I couldn't help but notice that whatever Constantine had in his hands, seemed to be emitting out a dull azure glow.

"Just finished sorting through the loot," Caius said, drawing my attention away from Constantine as he waved a piece of armor in one hand and a broken sword in the other. "Not much to help us out right now, unfortunately, though. Just a bunch of armor scraps and a handful of weapons that need to be re-forged."

Caius extended his arms to show me the items that he was holding, their descriptions appearing in my vision.

Blackened Chainmail Scrap
　　Quantity: 40
　　Item Class: Relic
　　Item Quality: Fine (+10%)
　　Durability: 0/0
　　Weight: 0.3 kg

Broken Irovian Longsword
　　Item Class: Relic
　　Item Quality: Fine (+10%)
　　Durability: 0/0
　　Weight: 0.5 kg

"I'm sure one of us can fix it up," I said after looking at the items. "Doesn't look like the sword was enchanted though."

"I don't think any of the weapons we've found were," Halcyon added, indicating a broken axe and shortsword he was holding. "We've found nearly a dozen different weapons, both of Irovian and Nafarrian make. I'm thinking we can offer them to the new recruits if they end up being any good when repaired."

"Not a bad idea," I agreed, knowing that many of them were still using the weapons that they had arrived at Aldford with. "We haven't really had the metal to create new weapons for them from scratch, but repairing these should be easy enough now that we have the Æthertouched Iron to work with."

"Plus, we can sell any extra for money," Constantine added, motioning towards me with what I now saw was a faintly glowing azure ball.

"We'll see," I commented, my attention having focused back on whatever was in Constantine's hand. "And what did you find?"

"Don't know," Constantine answered with a shrug as he moved to show me the emerald ball of light that he held, the item's description appearing in my vision. "Was hoping you'd be able to figure it out."

Essence of Suffering

   Item Class: Magical
   Item Quality: Good (+15%)
   Weight: N/A

"Huh," I grunted, disappointed at how vague the description was. "I have absolutely no idea."

"Weird right?" Constantine replied with a shrug. "But check this out, when I squeeze it…"

"Oh, please don't do that again!" Caius managed to say as both he and Halcyon preemptively winced.

Ignoring the warlock, Constantine squeezed his hand around the ball of light, which let out a faint, all too familiar wail, causing both Lazarus and I to flinch.

"What the hell?" Lazarus snapped, his hand having moved halfway to his sword before he caught himself.

"Kinda neat, isn't?" Constantine said with a grin, before squeezing it even harder and eliciting a louder response. "Like a spooky version of a whoopee cushion, but instead of gas, you get an unearthly wail of terror."

Lazarus and I were speechless as we stared at Constantine, who slowly released his hold on the Essence of Suffering and let the wailing cry fade away.

"I literally can't believe that these words are about to leave my mouth," I began, not breaking my eye contact with Constantine as I spoke. "But please stop tormenting that soul of the damned you're holding and give it to me."

"Oh, *come on, Lyr*!" Constantine exclaimed, pulling the Essence close to his chest. "Let me at least get Stanton with it!"

"Oh, I'd pay to see that," Lazarus said, suddenly sounding enthusiastic as he looked over towards me with a raised eyebrow. "Or Veronia?"

"Tempting, but no," I stated extending my hand towards Constantine. "Give."

"*Oh, fine,*" he grumbled, handing over the essence to me, which felt oddly spongey in my grasp.

"And the other one," I said, extending my other hand, still not breaking eye contact with the rogue.

Constantine stared back at me for a moment, completely unblinking as he froze in place. After a few seconds, he let out a sigh of defeat and pulled out a second Essence from his inventory and placed it in my hand. "*Man*, how'd you know there was a second one?"

"I didn't," I replied, smiling back at him as I accepted the second Essence.

"You mean…" Constantine started to say, then scowled. "Ugh, I walked right into that one!"

"That you did," Lazarus said as we all shared a laugh. "Oldest trick in the book too."

"Who walked into what?" Sierra's voice asked as she, Freya and Amaranth approached us having just walked out of the one open doorway in the chamber.

"Constantine," Caius answered without missing a beat. "Lyr didn't want him playing with the souls of the damned he found."

"Oh," Freya replied completely unfazed, glancing at what I was holding then back towards Constantine. "Is that all?"

"You guys never let me have any fun," he grumbled. "It was going to be for a good cause."

"We let you have fun once," Sierra said, her face completely deadpan. "Then you fed a bunch of mushrooms to our new guild members and got them all violently sick."

"Heh," Constantine let out a chuckle. "Yeah, that was pretty great."

"*Moving on*," Sierra said in a dismissive voice while jerking her thumb towards the doorway that the three of them had just exited from. "There's a short hallway through that door over there, and another door that looks similar to this one. From what we can tell, there's a crystal set in the side of the wall that *might* open it."

"Might?" I asked. "You didn't try it?"

"*Well*," Freya said, looking at me with a smile. "Sierra said that you're the resident expert at touching magical switches and things, so we figured we'd leave it to you to try."

"*Just in case*," Sierra stated, her grin matching Freya's.

"Just in case something goes wrong, so you can blame me for it you mean." I grunted as Amaranth padded over to me, his curiosity focused on the two Essences that I was holding.

"Isn't that what I just said?" Sierra asked, her smile not fading as she looked towards my familiar.

<This looks amusing,> the cat told me, his nose twitching briefly as he sniffed the Essences, then reached up as if to bat it with a paw.

"Hey!" I shouted, pulling the orbs I was holding away from his sweeping paw. "You can't play with these either!"

<But—> Amaranth began to protest, the emerald light from the Essences gleaming in his eyes as he moved to follow me.

"No buts!" I said firmly, turning away from the cat while simultaneously putting the two items away into my inventory.

"Let's go, Lyrian," Sierra said in mock impatience as Amaranth growled at me in frustration. "That switch isn't going to touch itself and as nice as this place is, I don't want to spend my entire day down here."

"Hrm," I grunted, not bothering to answer the woman as I stepped around my familiar and stepped out of the group, moving towards the open doorway. I could hear both Sierra and Freya laugh faintly behind me as I walked, followed moments after by everyone's footsteps.

<Nothing living has passed through here in ages,> Amaranth told me the moment that we passed through the doorway and into a long stone hallway. *<There is no scent at all through this place, save that thick musk that lingers.>*

<It looks like they fought here too,> I commented mentally to my familiar as I walked down the hallway, noticing that the damage hadn't been contained to just the main room. Magical burns covered nearly all the stone walls around us, leaving me wondering how the Irovians could have managed to fight their way through the hall.

Judging by the damage, the death toll must have been staggering, I thought briefly, before dismissing the thought with a mental shrug. *But then again, everyone down here died anyway when the entranceway collapsed.*

Reaching the end of the passage, I came to a door that appeared identical to the one that I had seen in the main chamber, save that this one had a small panel set in the wall beside it, with two crystals fixed directly inside it. The panel reminded me of the one that I had seen back at the Translocation Hub, and there was no doubt in my mind that they had been crafted by the same people.

Pausing for a moment to activate *True Sight*, I saw one of the crystals brighten with a faint glow of azure energy, the second one beside it appearing completely inert.

"See anything, Lyr?" Sierra asked, having caught sight of my glowing eyes.

"One of these looks to be active," I replied, motioning to the one that I saw glowing. "Best guess is that one opens the door, the other closes it."

"Makes sense," she agreed. "Want to try it and see what happens? I don't see a horde of time-locked spiders around this time for you to unfreeze."

"So, if I push this button and something horrible happens, I'm off the hook?" I pressed for a second time as I reached out towards the crystal.

"Oh, hell no," Sierra replied. "Where's the fun in that?"

"This sounds like a bad deal, Lyrian," Lazarus said from down the hall, despite the humor in his voice. "You're screwed either way."

"Tell me about it," I grumbled just as my hand came in contact with the crystal, instantly feeling something warm shoot through my hand and up my arm.

Nothing happened for a few seconds as I maintained contact with the crystal, then without warning a loud grinding sound filled the air. At first, I had thought that the door beside me had begun to move, but a loud shout from Constantine caused me to turn my attention back towards the doorway that we had just come from.

"Hey, hey! The door's closing over there!" He called out in surprise as he urgently stepped out of the doorway that he had been standing in. In the short time that I had been touching the crystal, a heavy stone slab had slid partially out from the side of the doorframe as if to close us into the hall.

Flinching at the unexpected event, I took my hand off the crystal, and the door stopped moving, having closed nearly half of the entranceway.

"Well, that didn't do quite what we expected," I said, feeling relieved that I hadn't managed to trap us.

"Not at all," Freya stated, just as several surprised voices rang out from the main chamber.

"What did you guys do?" Thorne's head poked through the partially closed doorway. "The other door started opening but stopped halfway."

"It did?" Sierra asked, casting a look back at me, then started moving to walk back towards the main chamber, all of us following behind eagerly.

Seconds later we all stood in front of the second doorway and found ourselves peering into a nearly identical hallway, the only difference being a different pattern of battle damage, and the fact that neither crystal in the far panel was active.

"So, any guesses on how to move forward?" Constantine asked after we had taken the time to explore the second hallway and confirm that neither of the two crystals there responded to touch. "Only the one crystal in the first hallway seems to still be active, and all that it seems to do is open the doors, the other crystals seem to be dead."

"Well, right now they do," Halcyon said, waving his hand at the two partially opened doorways. "The doors are only opened partially; the other crystals could activate when the first door is fully closed."

"Maybe, but that means we're going to have to risk locking someone in there to try that," Freya pointed out. "And we have no idea if we can get them out afterward."

"Getting out doesn't worry me as much as what's behind the two doors," I said, watching everyone's eyes focus on me. "Worse come to worse, and we get trapped, then we can...uh, *force* ourselves to respawn back at Aldford, then make our way back down here."

"Yeah, that's a morbid way of thinking," Constantine noted with a grumble. "But Lyr has a point. If we do manage to open the doors and there's something behind it...a single person is going to get overwhelmed."

"And eighteen people aren't going to fit into a hallway like that," Sierra finished with a sigh, casting a look around the group. "Are you guys thinking what I'm thinking for this place?"

"That it's a split dungeon?" Alistair offered.

"That's the feeling that I'm getting," Sierra replied with a nod. "Assuming we're right in thinking that the other crystals are going to activate once the door is closed, we're going to have to send a group into each one. One group to close the door behind them and see if the crystal activates, which if my guess is right will open the door for the trapped group..."

"Then the trapped group will have a way to open the door for the other group," I finished, considering the option before us. "I've seen similar things in other games before; it makes sense."

Everyone paused for a moment to think over the logic for a few seconds, and after a while, it was clear that no other ideas were going to be forthcoming.

"Well, it looks like we're going to be splitting up then," Freya said glancing over at Alistair then towards Lazarus and his group. "Stick with our usual parties and divide you four between us?"

"I think that's probably the best move," Lazarus replied with a nod. "Sawyer and Ransom can go with you. Alistair and I can tag along with Lyrian's group."

"That'll keep our melee ranksss balanced," Helix noted. "And grant us more magical support."

"Works for us," Sawyer added.

"Alright then," I replied, happy that we had managed to iron out who was going where without any issues. There was just one last thing I wanted to do before we put our theory to the test. "But before we get moving, let's take a quick look around with the Ætherscopes and see if we can figure out what's ahead of us."

"Good idea," Halcyon said, not wasting a second in pulling out a bone wand from his inventory.

Seeing Caius and the other spellcasters following suit, I drew my Ætherscope and stepped out of the loose circle that we had formed while talking to one another and turned my attention towards the wall, watching my vision gradually shift as distant sources of magic gradually became more visible. Gazing through the first hallway, the first thing that I noticed was the faint magical essence of the crystal that I had seen before, followed by several weaker and distant sources of magic. I vaguely recalled the shapes from the last time that I had looked through the Ætherscope and little had changed about them since. Unfortunately, though, despite the progress we had made, they were still simply too far and too weak for me to make out.

With a mental shrug, I shifted my gaze and slowly continued to scan the area before me, focusing my attention on the door at the end of the hallway. At first, there was nothing behind the door, but as I panned my vision downwards, three bright sources of magic bloomed in my vision, each of them set a fair distance apart, yet in a relatively straight line in relation to one another.

I wonder what they are, I thought idly as I continued to shift my vision towards the other hallway, spotting three more identical sources of energy that were also lined up the same way that the first three had been.

"That's interesting," Halcyon commented before I could say anything. "You guys see the six sources ahead of us?"

"I do," I answered, hearing similar words of affirmation from the other spellcasters. "They're both in line to each hallway, just deeper underground."

"But no moving sources of energy anymore," Caius pointed out. "Maybe those were the two Specters we killed?"

"Could have been," Zethus spoke up in an unsure voice. "But...how many were there when we last looked? Was there just two, or more?"

"There were several if I remember right," I said, recalling the first time that I had scanned the area and realizing that I couldn't see any sources of magic moving anywhere I looked.

Which for obvious reasons, didn't make me feel any better.

"They're missing," I told everyone, dismissing the enhanced vision that the Ætherscope gave me and putting the device back into my inventory. "I have no idea what they were, but something's changed now."

"We'll have to be ready for them then," Halcyon replied with a shrug. "Nothing we can do about it but move forward."

"I guess," I stated, before looking towards the non-magical members of the group and seeing the blank looks on all their faces.

"So," Drace was the first to speak. "You guys see anything interesting?"

"Or...*didn't* see something interesting?" Sawyer asked, his tone sounding unsure.

"The moving sources of magic we saw earlier are gone," I told the group, then went on to describe what I had seen while scanning the area.

"So, there could be other Specters or other magical...*things* waiting for us going forward," Freya said after I had finished my explanation.

"Probably safe to assume that there are," Halcyon replied. "And I think we were right in thinking that this is a split dungeon, with the three different magic sources down below on each side...this might only be the first checkpoint that we have to be working together."

"Shouldn't be a problem for us," Thorne chimed in. "We're more than used to that already!"

"That we are," I agreed, then cast one final look around the circle. "If no one else has any objections or ideas then, shall we get moving?"

"Just point me to where you need me," Lazarus grunted with a shake of his head as he moved to stand beside me.

"I think we're good to go," Freya said, meeting my eyes as everyone began to form up into their two respective groups. "We'll give our first plan a shot and see what happens."

"Sounds good to me," I replied, our two groups giving one another a brief wave before moving into our assigned hallways.

The relatively small passage made for a rather tight fit once we had all piled into it, Lazarus, Drace and Amaranth visibly appearing cramped as they squeezed in close to one another in an attempt to give the others space.

"Is everyone ready?" I asked, holding my hand just above the crystal that would send the stone door closing and hopefully activating the panel near the other group.

"Hurry it up," Drace grunted. "Something's jabbing me in the back and think I'm standing on someone's foot."

<He means my tail!> Amaranth growled to me mentally while simultaneously letting out an angry snarl. *<Do what must be done and quickly!>*

"Right!" I said, wincing at the volume of my familiar's distress and placed my hand on the crystal.

Once again, there were a few seconds of delay before the door began to move, the stone slab noisily grinding along the floor as it closed. Then with a loud boom, it finally closed, cutting us off from the main chamber.

Taking my hand off the crystal, I looked back towards the group and offered them a thin smile.

"Well, there's no going back now."

Chapter 33

"Finally!" Drace's voice boomed through the cramped hallway as the door beside me began to grind to one side, our hunch having clearly paid off.

It had been less than a minute since the door had closed behind me and closed the nine of us in the hallway, but the duration had been more than long enough for us to begin to worry and for claustrophobia to set in. Shoving his way forward, Drace didn't wait for the door to finish opening before shoving his bulk through it, bumping me hard in the process and eliciting yet another angry yowl from Amaranth as the half-giant stepped free of his tail. Following close on his heels, everyone in the group moved to follow the man, the gasps of relief and rushed footsteps echoing loud enough to drown out the sound of the grinding door.

"Phew!" Constantine exclaimed as he moved by, the last to push past me as I maintained my position in front of the panel. "I was starting to think that we were going to be stuck in here!"

"You and me both," Sierra muttered. "I like you guys, but I like my personal space a bit more. If you know what I mean."

"Keep on your toes, everyone!" I heard Lazarus call out from somewhere at the front of the group. "We don't know what's ahead of us, and that door opening wasn't exactly quiet."

Everyone's voice immediately died out at the half-giant's warning, and a quiet stillness filled the air as everyone turned their attention forward, listening to see if there was anything ahead of us. Caught at the back of the party, I couldn't make out where the passage ahead of us led, both because of everyone blocking my way and because my attention was still focused on the panel.

Is this other crystal going to light up? I thought while watching it carefully, waiting for any sign of magic in the crystal to appear.

With our earlier theory having been proven true, I could only assume that one of the crystals on Freya's side had activated itself once we had sealed ourselves into our hallway, and that one of our crystals would become active soon after the second door had opened. Which would then, in turn, allow me to return the favor and unlock the second door for the other group.

Was this intended as some sort of a security feature to keep people from getting deeper into the ruin? Or did something break when this place collapsed? The thought filtered through my mind as a spark of magic finally bloomed in the second crystal set into the panel. Without any hesitation, I reached out to touch it, feeling a similar sensation of warmth shoot up my hand as the crystal activated itself and a faint rumbling echoed through the wall behind me, coming directly from where I knew the other hallway to be.

"It worked," I whispered, looking back towards the rest of the party as the rumbling noise came to a stop, followed by a loud clicking sound, which then began to repeat itself, each interval between clicks gradually getting shorter and shorter.

"Lyr!" Sierra exclaimed, beckoning me forward as everyone's eyes widened at the audible timer that was echoing through the air. Years of gaming having taught us all too well what a sound like that meant.

"Coming!" I replied, letting go of the crystal and rushing the short distance past the doorway, easily passing through it as the party backed down the hall to give me space.

We had enough time to put several feet between us and the doorway as the noise continued to speed up, before it suddenly cut out at the exact second the heavy stone door slammed shut, moving faster than the eye could follow.

Trapping us inside the ruin.

"Well, I guess we're doubly committed," Constantine said in a low voice as I turned around to look at the party. "And so much for keeping things quiet, if they didn't hear the door opening, they sure heard it close."

"Probably," Halcyon agreed with resignation. "But given that the Specters likely set off some sort of alarm, it's safe to assume that anyway."

"True," I stated, motioning towards the wall. "It sounded like Freya, and the others managed to get past their door at least."

"Hopefully," Sierra said. "Nothing we can do about it now."

"Only to move forward," I acknowledged with a nod, before turning my attention towards the passage ahead of us. "Speaking of which, what do we have ahead of us?"

"Stairs going down from the looks of it," Lazarus answered from the front of the group. "My guess is another set of switchbacks."

"Man," Constantine grunted. "The Nafarr had all this technology on their hands, and they couldn't have figured out an elevator?"

"Would you trust an elevator that hadn't had any maintenance done to it in who knows how many centuries?" Drace asked pointedly before sharply motioning us to follow him down the stairs.

"Probably not," Constantine replied with a sigh, conceding the point. "But still…"

With nothing left to say, we all fell into a wary silence as we began to move down the stairs ahead of us, Lazarus's guess that the stairs ahead of us led to another set of switchbacks proving to be correct. Moving forward carefully with several orbs of magical light guiding our path, we descended down several flights of stairs, the walls all around us covered in more of the same battle damage we'd seen earlier.

Looks like the Nafarr made the Irovians pay for every inch they took, I considered, carefully scanning everything around me as we continued downward, our footsteps and shuffling armor the only sound reaching my ears. *But in the end, it doesn't look like it made much of a difference.*

After descending what I could only guess had been about eighty feet, we rounded the final switchback and found ourselves basked in a familiar azure light, which emanated from a hall at the bottom of the stairs.

"Guess we're about to find out whatever that source of magic was," Halcyon whispered practically in my ear as we all stopped for a moment before continuing forward.

"Looks like it," I agreed in hushed tones, before gently pushing myself through the group and making my way to the front, seeing that Lazarus had already partially descended down the stairway in an attempt to get a better view of what was ahead.

Creeping silently, I saw the lithe half-giant slowly step down the stairs in a half crouch, pausing once he had traveled far enough to see where the azure light ahead of us was coming from. He stayed still for a moment, before slowly turning his head back towards us, his eyes landing directly on mine. I saw something in them that I couldn't quite identify, meeting his gaze for several seconds before he motioned for me to join him.

Following his lead, I slowly moved forward and climbed down the stairs until I was directly by his side and pressed against the opposite wall, entering the azure light emanating from the hallway ahead of us. Squinting from the brightness, I was forced to wait a moment until my eyes adjusted, temporarily stricken blind by an intense source of magic ahead of me as it overwhelmed my magically enhanced sight. When my vision finally cleared, however, it was all I could do not to gasp in surprise.

The short hallway rapidly opened up into a larger chamber, stretching further than I could see from my limited angle, but not far enough that I was unable to miss the large glowing crystal that was suspended high in the air over a circular dais. Encircling the floating crystal were two gleaming metal disks, each of them rotating sedately as they gradually traveled from the crystal's base then back up to its tip, pausing for a second at each end before reversing its direction and repeating the motion. Thanks to my *True Sight* ability, I could see the waves of magic emanating from the crystal, filling the air around it in a thick azure haze of power.

Wow! I thought, completely speechless at the magic before me. I had accepted the possibility of us discovering still functioning Nafarrian technology in the ruin, but even in my wildest dreams, I hadn't expected anything like this. *This must be the source of magic that we saw through the Ætherscopes! I wonder—*

"I think there's at least nine of them." Lazarus's barely audible words were enough to bring me crashing back to the present as he whispered almost directly in my ear. "Some are on the other side of the crystal."

Flinching slightly from the unexpected sound, I glanced over towards Lazarus in surprise, caught completely off guard by whatever he was talking about. Watching an eyebrow rise in question as he waited for me to reply, I shook my head and temporarily deactivated *True Sight*.

"Hold on," I whispered back as my enhanced vision faded and the near blinding magical aura that was the crystal faded.

Don't get distracted, I admonished myself as I narrowed my eyes and looked back into the chamber, searching for whatever Lazarus had seen. To my dismay, it only took me a second to spot what he had been talking about, which prompted me to mentally kick myself. *Damn it, Marc! How the hell did you miss that?!*

Standing arrayed in a circle around the azure crystal, were the charred armored figures of several people, or what I assumed had once been people, before magic had twisted them into whatever they now were. Each of them was visibly burning with deep emerald flames from within their armor as if all of their flesh had become living fire. I saw the vague shadow of a skull visible from under the dancing flames, hovering just above each of their shoulders. A set of tags appeared in my vision, pointing to all the figures that I could see before me.

[Ætherbound Soldier] – Level 15

I missed them because they're made of magic! I realized, remembering the haze of magic that I had seen clustered around the crystal. I couldn't begin to guess what had happened to the soldiers before me, but at first glance, it seemed like they had been transformed to something akin to what the Slave King was when his spirit had interacted with the Ley Line, giving him a physical body to inhabit that was made completely out of Æther. The only difference that I could see in this situation was that each of the soldiers ahead of me had managed to retain their armor, which despite its blackened and almost charred looking appearance, I recognized as being of Irovian make, similar to armor that we all were wearing.

"So, the Irovians did at least make it this far," I whispered back to Lazarus, silently wondering what had happened to them to transform them so completely. It didn't appear as if they had been Ætherwarped, yet every single one of them appeared to be completely fixated on the large crystal in the center of the room, their bodies frozen in place as if drawn to the magic. *What else happened in here when this place was destroyed? This looks like something completely beyond Ætherwarping, but as if the Æther itself is animating it.*

"Looks like it," the half-giant replied softly, before motioning for us to ascend back up the stairs and return to the rest of the party.　　Allowing the man to go first, I took one last look towards the chamber then turned around to follow.

"What did you see?" Drace asked from the head of the party, having been in perfect position to see our reactions.

"There is a giant crystal in the room," I said, before going on to describe the undead-like creatures in the chamber ahead of us and how they had been warped by magic. "The Ætherbound Soldiers all look like Irovians based on their armor and, from what we could see, are all level fifteen."

"Hrm," Drace grunted, his face scowling slightly at the mention of the level, knowing that the majority of us were still level fourteen. A few levels weren't an insurmountable difference when it came to fighting as a group, but it was a clear indication that we would have to take the fight seriously. "Do we know how many for sure?

"I counted at least nine," Lazarus added, glancing over at me as he finished his sentence. "But that's just a guess based on their spacing around the crystal; there could be more in the room we couldn't see."

"We can't rule out the possibility of a boss ranked creature somewhere in there too," I pointed out, seeing both Drace and Lazarus nod at me in agreement. "This is a dungeon after all. It's not going to make it easy for us."

"That's probably a safe assumption," Drace said before motioning down the stairs with his chin. "What's our plan?"

"Keep moving forward," I replied without hesitation. "I'll scout just a bit further down the hall to make sure that there isn't anything else waiting for us in the room out of sight, but if there isn't, I think that if we rush the soldiers around the crystal, we can probably take a handful of them right off the bat if we focus our attacks. Plus, once we're out in the open, we can use our numbers to our advantage. This passageway would suck to fight in."

"Yeah, I definitely don't want to do that," Drace said, glancing upward at the ceiling which was barely three inches above his head.

"I'll second that," Lazarus added sympathetically, only being a few inches shorter than Drace.

"Alright," I said, shifting sideways on the stairs so I could see the rest of the party and pitching my voice so everyone could hear. "I'm going ahead to make sure there's nothing waiting to ambush us. If it's clear, I'll signal you all forward, and we'll charge the crystal together. If not, I'll figure something else out."

Pausing for a moment for my words to sink in, I waited to see if anyone had anything to add, but after seeing several nods from the group members, I figured that everyone was happy with my plan. Motioning for everyone to follow me to the bottom of the stairs, I slowly turned around from my position at the head of the group and led the way back down a second time, silently drawing Splinter from its sheath as I moved.

Taking the approach slowly, I stalked into the short hallway at the base of the stairs and approached the room beyond, the faint steps of our less stealthy party members causing me to wince as they moved behind me. Pausing at the entranceway into the chamber, I pressed myself into the leftmost wall and listened, hoping that my ears would be able to catch any noise coming from ahead of me.

After several seconds of silence, I decided it was safe enough for me to poke my head gingerly around the corner of the doorway, silently hoping that the movement wouldn't attract anyone's, or perhaps more appropriately, *anything's,* attention.

Moving with infinite care, I scanned the interior of the chamber, starting on the side closest to me, and immediately felt my heart leap in my chest once more. Lined in a row on the far-left side of the chamber were three small daises, similar to the one that was in the center of the room save for the fact that none of them bore any crystals upon them. Instead, there was a large collection of crystalline shards and fragments of metal littering the area, causing the smaller circular daises to glitter with countless azure reflections.

What the hell happened here? I couldn't help but ask myself as I continued to survey the room, mentally wincing at the damage. *Could this have anything to do with whatever destroyed the Nafarrian city?*

Pushing my surprise at the destruction to the side, my eyes continued their sweep, noting that the damage only appeared to be limited to the one area of the room. Turning my head towards the opposite side of the chamber, I passed over the still functioning crystal, and the Ætherbound Soldiers gathered around it, until my eyes landed on a single rectangular stone pillar set into the distant wall. The strange object barely reached shoulder height and appeared to have several crystals set into it, though from this distance I couldn't even begin to discern what its purpose was.

Something to worry about later, I thought, carefully completing my inspection of the chamber and not finding any other inhabitants inside, making me suspect that the cluster of magically twisted Irovians were going to be our only challenge for the room. *Assuming there isn't anything else hiding behind the crystal that I can't see.*

Making a decision to proceed with our assault, I waved a hand behind me and signaled to everyone that the way was clear, then stepped into the chamber and to the side so I wouldn't be in the party's way when they came charging through. With how fixated the Ætherbound Soldiers were on the magic crystal, we would have to be fools not to take advantage of their lapse in attention, a tactic that I also hoped would help mitigate the level disadvantage we had.

Rapid and heavy steps began to echo out of the hallway beside me, forcing me to push any doubt that I had to the side. Gripping Splinter tightly in my hand, I focused my attention on the Soldiers ahead of me, holding a single thought in my mind.

Here we go!

Chapter 34

Drace burst free of the hallway first, the long strides of the half-giant turning him into a blur as he rocketed past me and towards the oblivious Ætherbound Soldiers gathered around the crystal. Pushing off the wall, I then pumped my legs as hard as I could to fall into place behind Drace, my rapid steps allowing me to match his speed.

Completely mesmerized by the magical crystal, none of the Ætherbound Soldiers ahead of us reacted as we closed the distance with them. It wasn't until we were practically on top of them that their attention finally began to shift towards us, the emerald burning skulls that were set atop their shoulders eerily spinning around to look in our direction despite their bodies remaining fixed in place.

Moving with surprising reflexes, I then saw them all begin to turn their bodies towards us, each of their hands moving toward weapons hanging by their side.

All far too late to counter our charge.

With a bellowing shout, Drace was the first to make contact with the twisted undead-like creatures, simultaneously slamming into the still-turning form of one Soldier with his shoulder and bringing his sword down heavily onto the shoulder of another. I had just enough time to see the twin blows knock the pair of them off their feet, the first Soldier being thrown heavily into the dais below the floating crystal and the second being driven right down onto its knees.

Then it was my turn.

Having seen the two Soldiers that Drace had temporarily taken out of the fight, I focused my attention on the next one in the circle, timing my attack as it turned to meet our charge. Channeling all of my momentum into the blow, I lunged forward with my final step and swung Splinter into the heaviest attack I could manage, the gleaming blade crackling through the air before slamming viciously into the side of the Ætherbound Soldier's skull. I felt bone crack under the brutal impact as my attack completely obliterated the undead creature's jaw, sending fragments of it flying everywhere.

Reeling from the impact, the Soldier visibly staggered as it continued to turn, giving me a perfect opportunity to spend the final energy of my charge and slam my shoulder into it while fouling its balance with my foot. Completely overwhelmed by the brutal assault, it tumbled to the ground in a heap, falling directly on top of the first Soldier that Drace had knocked down.

Flailing in a tangle of limbs, the undead creature barely had time to complete its fall before Drace's sword came slashing down on the back of its already damaged skull, shattering it so completely that the emerald flames comprising its body winked out, whatever magic fueling it unable to keep up with the punishment that we had inflicted upon it.

That's one down! I thought with excitement as I took a step forward towards the other fallen Soldier that was trying to push the now empty armor of his companion off his body. Not giving the Ætherbound entity a chance to re-enter the fight, I slashed Splinter in a backhanded chop towards its exposed head, catching it right in the side of the temple and cleaving straight through bone.

Pulling Splinter free, I heard several loud shouts and crashes fill the air as the others joined the fight behind us. As I raised my blade for a second time to strike the undead Irovian, an azure blur appeared in the corner of my eye as Amaranth practically flew past me, pouncing on a pair of

Ætherbound Soldiers that had finally reacted to our presence.

Putting my familiar out of my mind for the moment, I brought my blade down a second time onto the trapped Soldier's skull, this time splitting the crown of the ancient bone in two, causing the emerald flames that animated it to dissipate in a burst of light.

There goes another one! I started to feel a surge of confidence shoot through me after seeing the second soldier go down, making me feel that we would be able to take care of the entire group without too much difficulty.

Of course, that was right when a bright flash of magic, followed by a thunderous burst of sound forced me to change my mind.

"Shit!" Constantine practically screamed from somewhere to my left. "There's a boss creature here—wait, no! There are *three* of them!"

In a heartbeat, I felt my blood go cold as I processed Constantine's words, my head spinning towards the sound of his voice. In a glance, I saw him, Alistair and Amaranth nearly surrounded by a quartet of the twisted Irovians, with two of them wearing notably different armor than the rest of the Ætherbound Soldiers.

One of the pair was clad in complete full plate, the heavy, black-charred armor clanking loudly with every step that it took towards the group. A thick helmet completely masked its features, save for the wisps of emerald fire that were visible through its eye sockets. In one of its hands, it held a massive shield, made from the same metal as its armor with the other carrying a wicked looking mace. Staring at it in momentary awe, an identifying tag appeared in my vision.

[Ætherbound Knight] – Boss – Level 15

Damn! I cursed, my mind immediately going into overdrive. We had known very well that there was a good chance that we would be up against a boss ranked enemy during this fight, but none of us had even dreamed that we would be facing three of them at once! Forcing myself to stay calm as I assessed the sudden change in battle, I shifted my eyes from the Irovian Knight and towards its partner walking in sync beside it.

The first thing that I noticed was that it was substantially lighter armored than the Knight, its armor namely being a metal cuirass protecting its chest, with a flexible layer of chainmail extending out to cover the rest of its body. Its head was encased in an open-faced helmet, the black silhouette of the skull within its emerald flames giving it a deeply sinister appearance. Armed with only a short, double-edged blade in its left hand, its remaining hand was empty and poised high at its side as if it were waiting for the right moment to cast a spell. Gazing at the creature as it advanced, another helpful tag appeared in my vision.

[Ætherbound Battlemage] – Boss – Level 15

"Drace! We need help on this side!" I shouted, turning my body to run towards the group, seeing that in addition to attracting the two boss creatures, Amaranth, in particular, had managed to catch the attention of the two Ætherbound Soldiers he had attacked earlier and was slowly being driven backward from their combined assault.

"One second!" Drace called back from behind me, just as a loud shout from Lazarus and another thunderclap of magic filled the chamber. "Okay, maybe two!"

Rushing forward, I approached the two Ætherbound Soldiers from behind, glancing around urgently for the third boss creature that Constantine had warned us about, but not seeing it anywhere nearby. Putting it out of my mind for the moment, I focused my attention on relieving the pressure on my familiar and thrust Splinter deep into one of the Soldier's back as I reentered combat, the charred armor giving way under the impact.

I felt the blade grate against metal before it pierced through into nothingness, the burning azure flames comprising the inner part of the undead creature's body providing no resistance to the sword's intrusion. But despite the creature no longer being one of flesh and blood, it recoiled in pain from the blow, a burst of magic seeping free from the rent in its armor.

<I think the armor and bones are helping contain the magic that's animating it!> I sent to Amaranth, as I pulled my blade free and delivered a second stab to the creature, this one higher up its body. *<Try to rend its armor or crush its skull!>*

<Easier said than done!> my familiar growled back at me as he swiped a massive paw at the other Soldier threatening him, succeeding only in knocking it off balance after striking it in the hip. *<Its armor resists my claws!>*

<Then bite this one!> I shouted back mentally as I pulled Splinter out of my target's back for a second time and then kicked it in the back of the knee, sending the wounded Soldier down to one knee.

Without a second's hesitation, Amaranth pounced forward, his jaws closing down on the Ætherbound Irovian's skull that was floating within its emerald flames. A loud crunch of bone then echoed through the air a heartbeat afterward, followed by the now empty armor falling to the ground with a thump.

<How hard was that?> I shot to Amaranth, just as Drace came rushing past us, not even bothering to stop to attack the one still standing Ætherbound Soldier. Instead choosing to simply trample it, using his massive bulk to simply bull it

out of his way and knock it down as he charged directly towards where I had last seen the Knight.

"Move!" I heard Drace shout ahead of him as he ran, followed shortly after by the ring of metal on metal. "Get him back and heal him! Lyr! I could use your help up here!"

"Coming!" I yelled back at the warrior, Amaranth and I already moving to attack the Soldier that had fallen to the ground before it managed to regain its feet.

Moving with blinding speed, Amaranth leaped onto the fallen Soldier's back, his weight pinning it to the ground, giving me the opportunity to bring Splinter down on its skull, having long since deduced that destroying it was the most efficient way to put an end to the creature. Bringing my sword down on the skull twice, I sent large cracks spiraling through the bone, until Amaranth pounced forward and bit into it, his powerful jaw effortlessly crushing Soldier's head and causing the emerald flames to wink out.

These Ætherbound Soldiers are little more than trash mobs, I thought to myself as I rushed to Drace's aid, leaving Amaranth to deal with yet another of the Soldiers that had finally rounded the floating crystal and was heading towards us. The sole purpose of the weaker creatures seemed to only be a distraction, forcing us to spend time dealing with them instead of focusing our attacks on the more dangerous Knight and Battlemage.

As I ran, I was forced to detour around a burnt-looking Constantine who was sitting on the ground and clutching at a visibly broken knee while an also singed Alistair desperately tried to heal it.

"Watch the Knight, Lyr!" Constantine shouted as I ran past the pair. "He is fast and hits hard! The Battlemage has instant spells too!"

"*Great!*" I called back, seeing that Drace was not only squaring off with the Knight but had managed to catch the attention of the Battlemage as well.

Which I suppose is actually his job, being the party tank, I added mentally as I decided to focus my attention on the Battlemage, feeling that I was better equipped to fight a magic using enemy, rather than one covered in nothing but heavy armor.

"Coming up on the right!" I shouted, giving Drace a heads-up as to which side I was going to take, then I immediately slashed at the Battlemage with a *Shocking Touch*-charged Splinter as a way of greeting, the blade sparking along its armor as it discharged into the creature.

"Lazarus is managing both the other Knight and Soldiers right now!" Drace told me without any preamble. "So, we need to hurry the hell up with these two and give him support before it steamrolls him and the others!"

"*There are two of these Knights?*" I replied in shock, barely catching the Battlemage's sword on Splinter's edge as it shifted its attention towards me.

"Yep!" Drace bellowed as he absorbed a punishing blow on his shield from the Knight's mace, using the opportunity to stab the tip of his sword into the armor protecting its knee, drawing forth a small flare of magic from the wound. "So, if you have any ideas on how to kill these things *fast*, I'm all ears!"

"Destroy their heads!" I said without hesitation, exchanging another set of blows with the Battlemage, which resulted in the both of us scoring minor wounds on one another.

"How the hell do you suggest we do that?" Drace barked in frustration, punctuating his point by slamming his sword into the side of the Knight's head with no visible reaction. "Have you even seen this guy's helmet?!"

"Figure something out!" I spat back hurriedly, seeing a bright crimson ball of fire begin to form in the Battlemage's free hand.

Reacting at the speed of thought, I instinctively reached out with my free hand towards the spell that the Battlemage was conjuring, only able to execute the reckless maneuver because it held its sword in its left hand. Had I been facing a right-handed opponent, reaching across my body to try what I had just done, would have likely resulted in me getting injured, or more even more likely, the loss of my entire hand.

In this case, however, the move caught the creature completely off guard, my hand thrusting through the partially formed spell and grabbing hold of the Battlemage's hand. No sooner did I tighten my grip on the hand did a wave of mana travel up my arm as I interrupted the creature's magic, causing the tiny ball of fire it was holding to fizzle and fade out of existence.

Instantly, I felt a wave of panic surge through the Battlemage as it realized what I had done, and it desperately began to thrash in my grip with surprising strength. Refusing to let go, I yanked on the creature's hand in an attempt to send it off balance, using the opportunity to thrust yet another *Shocking Touch*-charged Splinter into its shoulder, piercing through the thinner layer of chainmail where it joined with the cuirass. My efforts were rewarded by a bright spurt of azure energy as the power that was animating the Battlemage bled out from the armor containing it.

Almost immediately, the creature's sense of panic turned into a complete frenzy as I continued to drain mana from it, its sword swinging wildly through the air as it tried to force me to let go, cutting out viciously towards my face and eyes. Pulling Splinter free of its shoulder, I instinctively moved to intercept the sweeping blade and ducked my head away from the coming attack. Only to have the Battlemage suddenly redirect its arm and send the point of the weapon straight into my forearm, burying its short blade nearly to hilt.

"Aaah!" I couldn't help but cry out in pain as the Battlemage then twisted the weapon into my flesh, feeling the edges of the blade grind against the bones in my arm.

Sheer animal instinct demanded that I try to pull my arm away from the source that was causing me pain, but it was now my turn to find my hand being held in place, the Battlemage having decided that losing some mana was an acceptable price to pay in exchange for crippling one of my arms.

Snarling from the pain, I repeatedly hammered Splinter into the side of the Battlemage's head in a panic, not bothering to conserve any mana in the process, sparks of electricity shot into the air as my blade slammed into the creature's helmet. Showing no reaction from my assault, the Battlemage stoically maintained its tight grip on my arm and tugged sharply on the blade, causing a spray of blood to pour free from the widening wound.

Feeling my arm go numb from the pain, I readied myself to shout at Drace for help, when Amaranth's head shot into my vision, his jaw clamping down on the Battlemage's arm. Teeth sinking in deep into the chainmail sleeve, the big cat then snapped its head backward, the motion causing the Battlemage's weapon to pull itself free of my flesh. Gasping at the sudden relief, I reflexively brought my wounded arm close to my chest, while delivering a vengeful chop into the undead Irovian's shoulder, directly on top of the wound I had inflicted earlier and widening it in the process.

<Thanks!> I called out to Amaranth mentally as my familiar bit down even harder on the Battlemage's arm and

held it in place, effectively rendering the creature's weapon useless. Taking advantage of the gap in the Battlemage's defenses, I thrust out with Splinter directly towards its face, hoping that I could land a heavy enough blow to put an end to it.

Unfortunately, however, the Battlemage had other ideas.

Shifting its head upwards, it accepted my stab directly across its jawline, Splinter's edge obliterating nearly an entire row of teeth as it deflected off bone and sank ineffectually into its mouth, instead of the eye socket that I had originally aimed it at. Without any visible reaction of pain, the Battlemage then unleashed a sudden burst of flame from its free hand, bathing Amaranth's head in fire and forcing the cat to release his hold on the arm in its mouth.

<Rah!> Amaranth's snarl echoed through both my mind and ears as he pulled away from the Battlemage's flames and rubbed his face with a paw, seeking to put out the burning bits of fur that had caught fire from the Battlemage's attack.

"Whoa!" I let out a yelp and barely deflected an unexpectedly fast slash from the Battlemage's shortsword as it regained control of its arm.

Forced to take a step backward from the Battlemage as it renewed its attack, I exchanged another pair of blows with the creature before it suddenly decided to disengage from Amaranth and me, reversing its advance and leaping away from us. Pausing for a heartbeat, I reflexively scanned the area around me for an incoming threat that would have caused the undead Irovian to retreat, but found nothing, the closest thing being Constantine and Alistair having fallen beside Drace and had their attention focused on fighting the Knight.

What is it doing? I asked myself, the thought barely having enough time to form in my mind before the Battlemage suddenly vanished in a brief flare of magic, leaving Amaranth and I standing by ourselves.

"Shit!" I cursed in frustration as I spun around and scanned the room urgently, recognizing the spell that the creature had used as being something akin to *Blink Step*. The Battlemage having decided to go look for an easier set of targets, rather than allow Amaranth and I to continue double-teaming it.

I had barely begun to move before a pained scream filled the air, echoing out from somewhere behind me, which was followed by a surprised shout and the clang of metal on metal.

"Halcyon is down!" Caius's voice called out in a panic. "We need help over here *now*!"

Completing my turn, I looked in the direction of Caius's voice and spotted the Battlemage standing right in between Sierra and Caius; the pair caught completely off guard by its unexpected appearance. In the split second that it had teleported away from me, the Battlemage had managed to cross the length of the room and stab Halcyon in the back, the mage now writhing on the floor and clutching at a bloody wound at its feet.

<Help Drace and the others kill the Knight!> I told Amaranth, forcing my body to move towards the other half of the group. <I'm going to help the others in the meantime!>

Grunting in acknowledgment, Amaranth didn't bother with a mental reply, choosing instead to rush past me as the two of us began to move in opposite directions. Taking only a single step forward to give myself some momentum, I picked a spot near the Battlemage in the distance and triggered *Blink Step*.

A mix of azure light filled my vision as I crossed the room in an instant, appearing right on the creature's left flank, just as it raised its sword to strike at Sierra, who had just dropped her bow and was in the process of drawing her sword. Hoping to buy her the time that she needed to finish the motion, I brought Splinter heavily onto the Battlemage's already wounded shoulder, splitting the gaping rent in its armor even wider and spoiling its attack. As I drove the blade into the wound, I began to absorb the Battlemage's mana through Splinter, feeling the familiar cool wave of energy course into me.

"Lyr!" Sierra shouted in surprise at my timely intervention, just as the sound of her sword leaving its scabbard reached my ear.

"Try and hack its arm off!" I called out to the woman without any preamble, seeing that my latest blow had managed to seriously damage the chainmail connecting the sleeve of the Battlemage's armor to the rest of its body and that the emerald energy stored within had begun to flare out in spurts. "I think the armor is containing whatever is animating it! If we damage it enough, it'll die!"

"Works for me!" Sierra shouted back as the two of us fell into a practiced pattern, effectively pinning the Battlemage between us, the undead creature having spun to keep the both of us in its vision, its burning visage somehow managing to display annoyance at the tactic. "Caius! Get Hal out of the way! He's going to get stepped on here!"

"I'm on it!" the warlock replied a heartbeat later. "But he's going to need healing, which means you're going to have to distract that thing for me to lifetap afterward!"

"Just warn us when you're ready!" I yelled as the Battlemage finally managed to twist its way out from between Sierra and me, our blades carving a pair of gashes in its armor as it did so.

Falling in before us with its sword held high, the Battlemage now streamed an almost constant flow of magic from its body where its armor had been damaged, the largest of the rents still being the one on its left shoulder. Appearing less solid than it had earlier in the battle, I could tell that the wounds had taken a toll on the Battlemage, the emerald energy that was animating it having greatly dimmed in intensity.

It hasn't cast any spells in a while, I thought, noticing how much weaker the fire encasing the Battlemage's head had become and that its skull hovering within was slowly becoming more distinct than it had been earlier in the fight. *I think it's running out of energy and a few more solid hits should do it!*

Eager to put an end to at least one of the boss creatures, I lunged forward recklessly with Splinter, putting complete faith that Sierra would cover any openings in my guard if things didn't go according to plan. Feinting high with the blade, I purposefully moved slowly enough to draw the Battlemage's sword upwards as if I were going to bring it down on his head, only to at the last second, pull it away and bury the *Flaming Dagger* that I had conjured in my free hand straight into the Battlemage's stomach.

Feeling my injured arm scream in pain at the movement, I forced myself to hold onto the molten blade until the spell ended and it dissipated back into nothingness. No sooner did the blade vanish than yet another burst of magic erupted from the now gaping wound in the Battlemage's stomach, causing it to stagger as it belatedly swept its sword down in an attempt to slash at my now retreating hand.

Not one to pass up an opportunity, Sierra's blade came crashing down on the Battlemage's shoulder, the blow catching the already weakened section of armor and tearing it completely free from the cuirass. Almost instantly the Ætherbound creature's arm vanished as the energy animating it was cut off, the ruined sleeve of armor now hanging limply by its side.

"I'm ready!" Caius's voice called out, sounding weak despite the urgency behind his words. "Just—"

A loud grunt of pain followed by a crash of metal interrupted the rest of the warlock's words as Lazarus's body visibly tumbled into my vision over the Battlemage's wounded shoulder. Taking in his appearance at a glance, I saw that the half-giant's body had been almost completely pulverized, his armor battered and dented, with several gashes in the metal streaming a steady flow of blood.

"Lazarus is down, and the Knight is loose!" I shouted, remembering what Drace had said earlier and that Lazarus had been single-handedly keeping the other boss creature at bay. The key words in that statement being 'had been', his ragged and broken appearance clearly indicating that the Knight had finally managed to get the better of him.

Which meant that it was likely coming this way.

"Sierra, take care of this guy for Caius!" I ordered, making a snap decision as I threw myself forward into the now literally disarmed Battlemage, slamming my shoulder into his chest and hooking a foot around its ankle. With a shove, I pushed past the weakened Irovian and tripped it for Sierra and Caius to finish off, knowing that I had to find the other Knight before it caught up to Lazarus and finished him off.

Where is it? I thought in a frenzied panic, glancing briefly at Lazarus once more and seeing that he hadn't moved since he had fallen to the ground. Tearing my eyes off the injured half-giant, I scanned the chamber, in the direction I had seen him come tumbling from, logically assuming he had been thrown backward.

My hunch immediately paid off as I turned my head towards the floating crystal that centered the room, which was now partially blocked as the large and heavily armored Knight came into view, slowly plodding forward with its attention fixed directly on Lazarus. Appearing identical to the other Knight that Drace had been fighting, this particular Knight visibly displayed several large scars and gashes in its armor that streamed a steady flow of magic as it moved, the wounds a testament to how hard Lazarus must have fought against the creature.

Without a second's hesitation, my feet angled themselves towards the Ætherbound Knight, quickly building momentum with every step that I took. Analyzing the magically fueled entity with a practiced eye, I glanced over the wounds that Lazarus had inflicted upon it, trying to find a weakness that I could exploit.

Two large gashes across the torso. I noted to myself, time slowing down all around me as I sprinted forward. *Probably too hard for me to cut through though.*

I took another step towards the Knight.

Knee could be a weak spot, I continued, my gaze dropping downwards to see a puncture wound in the side of the being's left leg, just above the joint. *Destroying that could slow it down.*

The Knight's head began to shift in my direction as my foot hit the ground once more.

Armor on its shield arm looks— my train of thought instantly stopped as the creature completed its turn, its helmeted head revealing a long rent that burned with a bright azure fire. Fixing my attention on the tear in the armor, I could see a faint glimpse into the burning flames within, catching sight of the undead Irovian's skull.

There! I exclaimed within my mind, feeling my heart race with excitement as I focused my attention on the gap in the

Knight's armor, a plan of attack falling into place. Casting a glance upwards towards the ceiling, I checked to see if I would have enough room to pull off what I was hoping to do, and was happy to see that the chamber had plenty of space to work with. Gritting my teeth as I took yet another step towards the Knight, I mentally rehearsed what I was about to attempt, pushing aside the distant voice that told me just how reckless it was.

I think the situation calls for reckless at this point, I told myself dryly, carefully timing my upcoming maneuver while simultaneously trying to ignore the wicked axe that the Knight was holding in its hand. *Here goes nothing!*

Flicking the fingers on my still injured arm, I cast *Jump* on myself, instantly feeling my body become lighter as I ran. Taking two more bounding steps as I closed the distance between the Knight and me, I made sure to build up enough momentum for what I was about to attempt. Then, on my third step, I leaped high into the air, twisting my body into a corkscrewing flip that would have caused an Olympic gymnast to go green with envy.

Sailing directly over the stunned Knight as I spun through the air, I swung Splinter downwards with all the strength that I had in my arm, aiming the Æthertouched blade directly at the open scar in its helmet. Completely surprised by the maneuver, there was little the Knight could do to avoid the blow, my sword finding the gap in the helmet and biting deep into the skull housed within. Feeling the impact travel up my arm, I continued in the arc that my momentum had committed me to, my vision twisting wildly as I completed my flip and landed back on my feet behind the knight.

I can't believe that worked! I thought in amazement, moving from the spot that I had landed and glancing at the message that had appeared in my combat log.

You [Power Attack II] a [Ætherbound Knight] for 126 points of damage!

Happy to have confirmed that I had indeed managed to hurt the Knight, I dismissed my combat log and focused on putting some distance between me and the creature, knowing all too well what it was going to do next. Moving as if my very life depended on it, which in hindsight I knew it did, I planted my left foot on the ground hard then pushed off on it, sending me leaping to the side and towards the dais that the large crystal was set on.

Just in time to avoid the Knight's axe as it came down on the spot that I had just been standing.

The crunch of metal on stone echoed through the chamber as my leap carried me away from the Knight, who had recovered even faster than I had anticipated, spinning around with a vicious attack that would have crippled me, had it connected. Pushing back a sense of creeping doubt as I realized that my margin for error was now even slimmer than I had originally thought, I felt my right foot touch down on the side of the dais, the attached leg bending briefly as it absorbed the energy from my leap, then sprang forth, sending me flying back towards the Knight.

Aided by the *Jump* spell, I angled myself to slide across the ground, my trajectory carrying me past the now turned around Knight for a second time. Timing the attack carefully as I reentered melee range, I slashed across my body with Splinter, targeting the blade directly for the armored Irovian's wounded knee. Aided by momentum and the already damaged armor around the joint, my sword easily bit through the metal, widening the tear that Lazarus had inflicted earlier until it stretched completely around the back of the Knight's knee. As I continued my slide, now moving past the Knight, I caught a brief glimpse of magic out of the corner of my eye, followed by the sound of something heavy falling to the ground.

Coming to a stop just outside the Knight's range, I forced myself back up onto my feet and twisted to look back towards the undead Irovian, seeing the heavily armored creature now kneeling on the ground.

That should hopefully buy us some time to regroup, I thought, letting a small breath of relief escape my lips, only to have it cut it off as the knight pushed itself back up onto its feet. *On second thought, maybe not.*

Watching the Knight rise, I noticed a constant stream of magic pour free from the wound that I had inflicted on its knee, the injury visibly affecting it as it tried to maintain its balance, but not managing to cripple it as I had hoped. Not wanting to wait until the Knight finished climbing back up to its feet, I instinctively rushed back towards it, intent on inflicting as much damage as I could before the opportunity was lost.

Sparks flew from Splinter's edge as I channeled a *Shocking Touch* in the blade and leaped forward with the weapon outstretched. Caught half-risen from his kneeling position, I had a near perfect shot to drive the blade through the damaged portion of the Knight's helmet and into the skull housed within. Unfortunately for me, however, that opportunity vanished as the Knight unexpectedly turned its head, taking Splinter's edge off an undamaged section of the helmet and leaving my arm throbbing from the force of the blunted blow.

Oh shit, I thought, my eyes widening with the realization that I had been suckered in. Instinctively, I tried to retreat, to put any distance I could between the Knight and me before whatever counter attack he had in store for me landed.

I never had a chance.

A heavy metal shield slammed into my chest with the force of a sledgehammer, cracking and breaking countless ribs as it drove the air from my lungs and sent me staggering back, all of my forward momentum lost in a single blow. I managed a single agonizing cough as I struggled to keep balance, a watery sensation suddenly filling my chest. Numb from the sudden turn of events, it was all I could do to stare at the single log entry that had appeared in my combat log.

An [Ætherbound Knight] critically hits you with [Shield Slam III] for 274 points of damage!

The next thing I knew, my entire body was screaming at me in pain, and I was somehow lying on my back a short distance from where I had been standing, desperately struggling to catch my breath. As my mind slowly cleared and adrenaline caused the pain to fade away, I gradually became aware of loud clanging footsteps, vaguely sensing that there was something large and blurry approaching me. Blinking rapidly to get rid of the tears that had formed in my eyes, I cleared them just in time to see the Ætherbound Knight standing over me; its axe raised high in the air.

I'm screwed, I realized with sudden clarity as the stunning effects of the Knight's Shield Slam finally began to wear off, leaving my mind too scrambled to cast a spell and my body reacting far too slowly to roll out of the way of its coming attack.

"Hold on, Lyr!" Halcyon's voice cut through the fog that clouded my mind, just as two large balls of magic slammed into the side of the Knight, visibly rocking it from side to side. "We're coming!"

No sooner did the words fade from the air than a thunderclap of magic took their place as a wave of azure energy erupted out of nothingness directly in front of the Knight, forcing it to take an unsteady step backward to check its balance. Wincing from the proximity of the spell, I felt the searing heat from the spell wash over me, happy to endure a little bit of friendly fire from Halcyon's *Pyroclap* instead of experiencing the likely life ending impact of the Knight's axe as it sank into my chest.

The Knight bobbed unsteadily as its damaged leg struggled to keep itself upright under the onslaught of magic, the axe in its hand waving wildly in the air in an attempt to restore its balance. Taking advantage of my temporary stay of execution, I rolled my body to the side and put some distance between me and the heavily armored creature, feeling my lungs protest from the exertion. Once I felt I was at a safe distance, I rolled one more time onto my stomach, and let out a wet sounding cough that sent a spray of blood misting through the air, coating the floor beneath me.

Staring at the blood numbly as I struggled to take in a deep breath, a near deafening shout of rage, followed by the sound of tearing metal and even more shouting voices forced me to keep moving. Pushing myself up off the ground with a shaking hand, I turned as fast as I could manage back towards the Knight, all while coughing up another spray of blood from my damaged lungs.

"Hit the leg!" Drace's voice boomed over the cacophony of combat that had erupted in the few seconds it had taken me to regain my feet. "Take it down then finish it!"

Completing my turn towards the noise, I saw that both Lazarus and Drace had managed to join the fight, or perhaps more aptly in Lazarus's case, rejoin the fight, his body having clearly been healed since the last time that I had seen him. The pair of half-giants had flanked the now singed looking Knight, keeping the creature contained as Constantine, Alistair and Amaranth rushed around the floating crystal.

Of the three, my familiar was the first to arrive, the powerfully muscled cat lunging forward at Drace's instructions and sinking his thick teeth into the Knight's damaged knee. With a shake, I saw him tear the last shreds of metal that held the armor together apart, causing a brief flare of magic to erupt from the wound before the leg finally gave way, sending the Knight falling to the ground.

No sooner did the creature land than the rest of the party leaped upon it, their weapons flashing remorselessly through the air as they chopped or thrust deep into undead Irovian's armor, wisps of magic escaping its body with every new tear and puncture. Sensing that the battle was coming to a close, I moved to aid my friends, unwilling to stand idly by and watch while I was still able to contribute, especially when they all had just saved me from had looked like certain death.

It only took me seconds to reach the fallen Knight, during which time the party continued to fill the creature's armor with countless holes and scars. Yet for all the damage that they had done, the Knight did not want to die peacefully, one of its arms being held in place by Amaranth's teeth, biting down hard on its wrist, the other with Lazarus's sword thrust straight through it, pinning it into the ground. The pair visibly strained as they attempted to keep the creature contained as it thrashed desperately to free itself from their holds.

"Destroy its skull!" I shouted a heartbeat before I rejoined the party, sidestepping around Drace who had taken it upon himself to restrain the Knight's one remaining leg.

"*What do you think we're trying to do, Lyr?*" Constantine growled, both him and Alistair coming into view, standing above the flailing Knight. "He's making it a bit difficult, as you can imagine!"

Ignoring Constantine's words, I rushed in even closer to help the pair, instantly realizing the extent of their difficulties as the Knight constantly shifted its helmeted head to blunt or deflect the weapons that came towards its face, preventing them from taking advantage of the open wound in the metal. However, with its attention fixed solely at keeping the two of them at bay, it left itself completely open for my attack.

Lunging forward at the Knight, I threw everything I had into my attack, planting my knee directly into its chest as I thrust Splinter downwards through the broken gap in its helmet. I felt a jolt travel up my arm and into my shoulder as the sword tip bit into the Knight's skull, the bone standing up to the impact for a split second before all resistance suddenly gave way. With the sound of shattering bone, Splinter sank even deeper into the Knight's head, all movement from the creature freezing as it absorbed what had just happened.

Then without any warning at all, the emerald fire that burned within it winked out, and the armor deflated, leaving me kneeling atop an empty shell of metal. With the creature no longer thrashing, silence fell over the chamber, save for our rapid breathing. Breathing a sigh of relief, I gently pulled Splinter free of the now empty helmet before me, pausing to read the two messages that had appeared in the corner of my vision.

You have slain an [Ætherbound Knight]!
You have gained Experience!

Chapter 35

"Kill stealer!" Constantine accused as I pushed myself up off the disintegrating form of the Ætherbound Knight, the body fading away into nothingness and leaving a familiar loot bag in its place. "I had him!"

"You were taking too long," I told Constantine, letting out a ragged cough as I parroted the exact words that I had heard him use what seemed like a lifetime earlier. "I wanted to kill him before the sun set today."

"Very funny," Constantine grunted while rolling his eyes at my statement, clearly not having missed the reference.

"Is everyone okay?" Drace asked, clearly hoping to put an end to Constantine's and my bickering before it could really take off. "I don't think we lost anyone in that."

"We got pretty close," Halcyon replied amid a chorus of voices as we all accounted for one another and gathered in a large circle. "Thanks for the save there, Lyr. A few seconds later…"

"And it could have all gone differently," I acknowledged, nodding at Alistair as he went about his post-battle healing duties, laying a glowing hand on my shoulder. "Thanks for the save on your end too. I thought I was a goner."

"No problem, Lyr," the mage answered with a shrug. "That's what teamwork is for."

"Definitely," I replied with a smile as Halcyon's statement triggered something in my mind. "Hey, speaking of teamwork, did you all notice how…uncoordinated all the Irovians were during the battle? I don't think any of them moved to support one another even once."

"Huh," Drace grunted thoughtfully. "Now that you mention it…yeah. They pretty much all fought like individuals, hell, if I didn't know better, I'd say they actually fought more like robots, completely without emotion at all. All that was left to them was their fighting ability and basic self-preservation."

"Well, they were *kinda* undead-like, right?" Caius asked. "Maybe not quite the traditional necromancer version of undead, but an *Ætherwarped* version of undead?"

"Maybe that's what the *Ætherbound* prefix of their name means?" Lazarus offered with a shrug.

"Could be," I agreed, once again reminded about just how little we knew about Æther, even after all of our experiences with it. "I'd be really interested to know what caused them to transform into...*whatever* they were."

"Maybe we'll find out," Halcyon said, pointing towards the large crystal that still hovered a top of the dais beside us, showing no reaction to the battle that had been fought around it. "Some of the technology here looks to be intact; there's no telling what we might—"

"*Erm,*" Constantine loudly cleared his throat while giving both Halcyon and me a pointed look. "I know you guys are big on this whole magic and lore thing, which is great, don't get me wrong, but do you guys mind if we start sorting out the loot? I mean, that bag is just sitting there, begging to be opened and the rest of us are all just standing around..."

There was a moment of silence as everyone's attention focused on Constantine, then shifted back towards both Halcyon and me, faint echoes of agreement filtering through the air.

"We did just fight *three* dungeon bosses," Alistair said, speaking up in a small voice.

"So there has to be something nifty inside it," Drace added, trying and failing to hide a bored tone in his voice.

"Ugh, you guys have no patience." I grunted, waving a hand dismissively at the loot bag and inviting Constantine to sort through it.

"This coming from the guy who looted the Moss Snakes while we were all still dealing with the wounded?" Sierra asked with a grin on her face as both she and Constantine stepped towards the bag.

"You guys had it under control," I replied dismissively. "I was just being efficient."

"Well, you and Halcyon have the magic and lore conversation under control right now," Constantine shot back as he untied the bag that had been sitting on the ground and began sorting through it. "Now the rest of us are going to be efficient and see what loot dropped."

Without wasting another second, Constantine then began to pull several items out from the bag, pausing only to hand them over to Sierra or one of the other party members as we all gathered around him to watch, the item descriptions appearing in our vision.

Blackened Iron War Mace
  Slot: Main Hand
  Item Class: Magical
  Item Quality: Good (+15%)
  Damage: 30-45 (Crushing)
  Strength: +5 Constitution: +5
  Durability: 160/160
  Weight: 2.5 kg
  Class: Any Martial
  Level: 15

Blackened Iron War Axe
  Slot: Main Hand
  Item Class: Magical
  Item Quality: Good (+15%)
  Damage: 30-45 (Crushing)

Strength: +5 Constitution: +5
Durability: 160/160
Weight: 1.5 kg
Class: Any Martial
Level: 15

Blackened Iron Assault Shield

Quantity: 2
Slot: Off Hand
Item Class: Magical
Item Quality: Good (+15%)
Armor: 175
Strength: +3 Constitution: +3
Durability: 180/180
Weight: 3 kg
Class: Any Martial
Level: 15

Blackened Iron War Knife

Slot: Main Hand or Offhand
Item Class: Magical
Item Quality: Good (+15%)
Damage: 25-40 (Slashing or Piercing)
Strength: +4 Agility: +4
Durability: 120/120
Weight: 0.5 kg
Class: Any Martial
Level: 15

"That's actually a pretty great haul!" I exclaimed with surprise as Constantine finally pulled the last item out of the bag. "The first time we didn't get any crafting components either."

"Considering how brittle and charred the armor that all of the Irovians were wearing was, I consider that a good thing," Drace replied having exchanged both his old weapon and shield for the War Mace and Assault Shield. "I don't think even you would have been able to salvage that stuff into something I'd trust my life with. Whatever happened that transformed their bodies, it sure did a number on it."

"I guess that's true," I said, looking around the group and seeing that Alistair had laid claim to the other Assault shield as well as the War Axe, none of the other party members having a use for the melee oriented weapons. "Nice to see that these weapons are enchanted though, unlike the ones we found upstairs."

"The Knights and Battlemage were probably the leaders of the attacking force," Constantine commented, holding the Battlemage's weapon in his hand. "Makes sense that they would get the best gear."

"Yeah," I agreed, watching the loot bag on the ground disintegrate now that it was empty, its sole purpose for existence having been fulfilled.

With the loot out of the way, our attention then shifted back to the chamber that we found ourselves in, all of us splitting up into smaller groups as we wandered off in our own directions. Given each of our magical specializations, it was only natural that Caius, Halcyon and I grouped up together as we explored the room, choosing to start our exploration on the far side of the chamber where I had originally seen the pile of shattered crystal.

"Whatever was here looks like it exploded from within," Halcyon said to both Caius and me as the three of us scanned through the crystalline debris. "Look at the wall; you can see bits and pieces of crystal embedded in the stone."

"Good eye," I replied, inspecting the pockmarked wall in more detail and seeing that it also appeared cracked and burnt as if it were exposed to intense heat. "Maybe it was another set of crystals?"

"That would then explain these metal fragments here," Caius noted, bending down to pick up a flat, inch thick, fragment of metal that had several runes inscribed on it and showed it to the both of us. "Looks kind of similar to the rings on the still intact crystal over there."

"Hmm," I said thoughtfully as Caius turned the broken piece of metal over in his hand. "I wonder what they're for."

"Your guess is as good as mine," Halcyon replied as he bent down and picked up two metal fragments from the ground. "Maybe it has something to do with regulating the Æther stored in the crystal? Or somehow shifting Æther from its liquid state that we see in the Ley Line into whatever state it is in the crystal?"

"Either is a good theory," I stated, glancing at the two shards of metal that Halcyon was holding and seeing that both of them bore similar runes to the piece that Caius had picked up. "Though I wish we could read whatever runes were inscribed on them."

"Donovan might be able to if we bring him back enough pieces," Halcyon pointed out. "Or one of the other mages...assuming we trust them enough to show them."

"*Trust* being the keyword in that statement," I replied doubtfully, scanning the ground and finding another metal disk fragment lying amid the crystalline rubble. "But I think you're onto something. If we can recover enough pieces of these shattered disks and reassemble an intact one..."

"...then we can try building our own *Æther Crystal* using the crystals that we recovered from the Tower!" Caius exclaimed excitedly. "I...don't really know what we'd use them for yet, but we could figure that out afterwards!"

"Æther Crystal," Halcyon repeated as if testing the word. "I like that."

"Worse come to the worst, we can also try copying the runes on the disks around the still floating crystal," I said enjoying the pair's excitement as I stooped down to pick up the metal shard that I had seen earlier. "But that'd require us to draw it out on paper...or figure out a way to disassemble the thing. If we can find enough pieces to rebuild a disk back in Aldford, I can then use them to make a mold and cast it as one piece, rather than handcrafting from a sketch."

"Sounds like a plan to me!" Caius said enthusiastically, the three of us then beginning to sift through the piles of broken crystal in search of the metal disk fragments.

With the three of us working in tandem, it only took us a few minutes to scour the area, recovering over three dozen different fragments of the inch-thick metal, the largest concentrations of the pieces appearing to center around each individual dais that the crystals had once sat upon. Taking pains to keep each collection of fragments separate depending on which dais it was found at, we split the shards between ourselves, ensuring that we didn't accidentally mix pieces together that were found in a different location.

It was going to be a tough enough puzzle reassembling the fragments of the disks, and we didn't want to make it any harder on ourselves than it was already going to be.

"Hey, are you guys done digging through all that?" Sierra's voice called out from across the chamber. "Because we're blocked in here by another door, and none of us want to poke any of the crystals on this box without one of you checking it for magic."

"You mean taking the blame if something goes wrong!" I called back, straightening from my bent over position and looking in the direction of Sierra's voice, which was coming from the other side of the crystal.

"You already used that one today Lyr," Sierra said, sounding disappointed in my reply. "You need to work on some new material."

"Doesn't make it any less true!" I exclaimed while turning to look both at Caius and Halcyon with a raised eyebrow.

"I think we've found all the fragments that we're going to find," Caius replied, sensing my silent question. "If there are any pieces left, they're too small to find or buried in this wall somewhere."

"But we won't know for sure until we try reassembling the disks," Halcyon added as the three of us left the damaged portion of the chamber and began walking towards the other side, passing by a coiled Amaranth, who had decided to take up residence directly under the large Æther-infused crystal and was basking in its light as he would the sun.

<Don't fall asleep,> I sent to the cat, seeing an azure-colored eye open to look in my direction. *<We're going to be moving soon.>*

<Hrmpt,> Amaranth grunted unintelligibly in response before closing his eye again and lying his chin down on his paws. *<Wake me then; it is nice and warm here.>*

Shaking my head at the cat, I turned my attention back towards the other side of the room, seeing that the entire party had gathered around the strange rectangular pillar I had spotted earlier.

"This is the only thing that looks like anything resembling a switch," Sierra told us as we arrived. "Aside from a few stone workbenches over there, there really doesn't seem to be that much in this room, even before whatever happened to this place, happened."

"I see," I replied, scanning the other half of the chamber, seeing both the workbenches that Sierra had just mentioned as well as a door, identical to the one we had seen upstairs, set into the far wall.

"Best guess I have is that either this place didn't get a lot of traffic," Lazarus said. "Or, more likely, that they got far enough warning of the attack that they cleared out as much stuff as they could."

"And locked the door behind them," I added, looking back towards Sierra, then at the crystal filled pillar.

"Looks like it," the red-haired elf replied.

"Well, let's see what we can do about that," I said while activating *True Sight* and seeing several of the crystals set into the pillar begin to glow. "Hrm, well, whatever this thing is, it's definitely active."

"I'll say," Caius muttered as both he and Halcyon moved up to stand beside me, the rest of the party backing away a step to give us room.

"So," Halcyon began, waving a hand at the alien array of crystals set into the pillar. "Any idea where to start? Poke one of them and see what happens?"

"I guess," I replied with a shrug, counting seven active crystals on the pillar, with another nine crystals lying dormant. It seemed that whatever method that the Nafarr had used to label their switches, or crystals, in this case, had died with them, leaving no visible indication to what any of them did. "I don't have any better ideas, to be honest."

"You know we can hear you guys, right?" Constantine called out from behind us, his voice sounding nervous. "You aren't exactly filling us with a lot of confidence right now."

"Relax," I said soothingly, waving a hand in a reassuring manner over my shoulder where everyone could see while picking an active crystal at random on the pillar and reaching out to touch it with the other, feeling a familiar warmth travel up my arm. "I'm a professional at this sort of stuff; don't worry."

There was a short pause as my hand rested on the crystal, then without any warning at all the room went completely dark as the azure light emanating from the crystal suddenly vanished, plunging us all into complete darkness.

"Yep, this is about what I expected," Sierra was the first to comment.

"Are you *sure* you know what you're doing there?" Lazarus's voice followed a second afterward.

<What happened?> Amaranth asked sleepily in my mind. *<Where did the warmth and light go?>*

"Uh, just hang on a second," I replied loudly, seeing that all the crystals on the pillar had gone dark. Terrified that I had broken the device, I took my hand off the crystal and reached out to touch one of the others, hoping that I could undo whatever I had done earlier.

"Shit, did the whole thing die?" Halcyon whispered from beside me, reaching out to also touch one of the crystals on the pillar we had grouped around.

"Looks like it," Caius whispered back, going as far as to poke several of the crystals with his fingers. "It almost looks like it turned itself off."

"Who the hell puts an off-switch right in the middle of...whatever this thing is?" I said under my breath as the three of us went through each of the crystals on the pillar, testing to see if any of them elicited any sort of reaction.

Minutes passed as we continued to poke and prod the crystals in an attempt to reactivate the pillar and undo whatever it was that I had managed to do, but no matter what we tried, there was no visible reaction to our efforts. With every second that passed, it became more and more difficult for the three of us to hide our frustration at the lack of results, until I finally threw up my hands in the air, ready to admit defeat.

"Okay, this—" The words were barely out of my mouth before once again without any visible signal, the room suddenly illuminated itself as if some distant switch had been flipped, the familiar azure light from the large crystal set in the center of the chamber resuming its bright glow and banishing the darkness.

"—should work," I finished, trying to hide my surprise while turning my head to look around the chamber as several white lights set high in the ceiling above us also activated, shifting the room from the deep azure tint that had been there just seconds earlier to a near daytime brightness.

"Well, that's better I guess," Constantine commented as I turned to look in the party's direction, all of them visibly squinting from the change in light.

"Must have needed a chance to reboot?" Halcyon muttered quietly, sounding slightly unsure as he spoke. "Looks like the crystals are slowly reactivating one by one too."

"I honestly have no idea, Hal," I replied, turning around to look at the pillar and seeing that nearly all of them were now steadily flashing with a magical glow. "But seeing what happened last time, I'm a little hesitant to poke it again."

"I know what you mean, Lyr, but we're going to need—"

<Error in display system detected!> A distorted mental voice rang through my head without warning, causing me to flinch and look at the pillar in surprise. *<Switching to mental communication mode.>*

"Did that thing just talk to us?" Caius asked, the rest of the party behind us immediately falling silent, surprised at the voice that had just appeared in our heads.

"Whatever it was I heard it too," Sierra said, her footsteps echoing across the floor as she moved closer to us.

"Same here," Drace added, a shuffling sound indicating that he too was following Sierra. "What did you guys do?"

"No clue," Halcyon replied with a shrug, just as the voice echoed through our heads once more. "I think it's some sort of leftover technology..."

<Alert! Emergency Lockdown Procedures are in effect! Catastrophic failure of Ley Line Tap detected! Security systems are currently active!> the voice announced with urgency. *<Time since event: five hundred and fifty years, ten months, three weeks, one day, seven hours, fifty-four minutes, thirty-four seconds. Warning: Based on elapsed time, Æther ignition is believed to be imminent! Please evacuate the facility immediately unless assigned to a Containment Team!>*

"Huh," I grunted as the mental voice temporarily faded from my mind, then glanced around at the party that had grouped up behind me, seeing all their surprised expressions. It seemed that the large floating Æther Crystal wasn't the only piece of technology that had survived the destruction of the ruin.

Maybe it's a security system of some sort? I thought to myself, making the best guess I could, based on what it had just said. No sooner did the thought cross my mind that I remembered the security system back at the Transport Hub and how we had been forced to destroy it after it went haywire and tried to kill us, if somewhat indirectly. *Hopefully, this one isn't hostile.*

"Well, I guess we know when this place was destroyed now," Halcyon said, breaking the silence as we all processed what the voice had just told us. "Hard to believe that this place was just...buried under here for so long without anyone finding it, and bits and pieces of it are still active."

"I think that's only because there was no one *left* to find it," Sierra answered with a sad note in her voice.

"Or more likely because the Irovians either didn't have time to, or didn't want to dig into an active installation to repair the Ley Line right in the middle of a war," I offered. "And instead, they used whatever they built at the Tower and the Annulment Sphere to keep the Ley Line in check."

"*Great*," Constantine stated. "That worked for them, but now what do *we* do? Because we can't exactly get out of here now, short of dying that is, and I think pretty much all of us want to avoid that."

"Yeah, that'd be nice," Caius agreed. "I'm pretty close to level fifteen now, and I'd really rather not have to deal with an experience debt from a Death Penalty. Not to mention the skill loss..."

"I think we're all on board for that," Lazarus added dryly.

"Well, we're open to any ideas on how to get this thing talking," Halcyon said while waving a hand at the pillar.

"Hmm, hang on a second," I replied thoughtfully, an idea popping into my head. "It said mental communication mode before, and the way it spoke to us wasn't that much different than the way that Amaranth and I speak to one another. I can maybe try reaching out to it, and see where that gets us."

"So...you want to think at that stone pillar full of crystals and hope it replies to you?" Constantine asked me dubiously.

"No, I want to think at the stone pillar full of crystals and sweet talk it into opening the door for us," I replied while rolling my eyes at the rogue.

"Oh, well, that makes much more sense then," Constantine said in a sarcastic tone. "Try *'open sesame'*. Maybe that'll do it."

"If you prefer, I can try touching one of the crystals again," I offered, reaching out blindly towards the pillar behind me.

"Try that mental thing first," Sierra cut in quickly. "If that doesn't work, then you can try playing with the lights again."

"Works for me," I said turning away from the group and looking towards what I was beginning to suspect was the Nafarrian equivalent of a computer. Pausing for a second to consider how I would even begin communicating with it, I decided not to over think it, and simply willed my thoughts in its direction, the same way I separated my internal thoughts to myself, versus those I wanted Amaranth to hear.

<Hello?> I sent cautiously towards what I now mentally thought of as a machine, not knowing any better way of introducing myself.

<Mind Print is not recognized.> The very same distorted voice I had heard before filtered directly into my head, causing me to flinch at its mental volume. *<Resorting to secondary identification mechanism. State your name and purpose.>*

"It worked," I told the group, glancing back towards them with a smile on my face, before turning to the face the pillar once more, hoping that my idea would play out and that the machine wouldn't question it too much.

<Lyrian Rastler,> I sent, crossing my fingers as I spoke. *<I'm part of the Containment Team.>*

There was a long pause as the Nafarrian device considered my answer, leaving me staring at the crystals and waiting nervously for a response.

<There is no record of your name listed on a Containment Team,> the distorted voice replied. *<Identity cannot be verified.>*

<Of course, I wouldn't be on a local list,> I told the machine without missing a beat. *<It's been over five hundred and fifty years since we were forced to abandon this place! Everyone on record has died from old age!>*

<Checking statement,> it replied to me once more, before going dormant for several seconds. *<Report: Situation has been deemed plausible. Last contact with previous Containment Team was five hundred and fifty years, ten months, three weeks, three hours, thirty-six minutes, eighteen seconds ago. All attempts to reach the team has failed. It is logical to assume that they are now deceased.>*

They only survived little more than a day after the Ley Line ruptured, I noted, doing a quick mental calculation based on the Nafarrian computer's report. *They must have known they wouldn't be able to get out of here.*

<The door in this chamber is locked,> I told the machine, deciding to see if I could entice it into helping us out. *<We need to have access to the rest of the facility if we're going to be able to assess the damage and try to repair the Ley Line.>*

<Unable to comply.> The voice barked almost instantaneously. *<As per procedure, the facility is in lockdown mode until all Ætherial Anomalies have been eradicated.>*

<That's what we're here to do!> I replied enthusiastically, sensing a track that I could take. If I could convince the machine that we were here to help, then maybe we could find a way forward and out of this room. *<We've already cleared all the, uh…Ætherial Anomalies from this room, but*

unless you can open the door for us we can't go any further.>

<Checking statement,> the machine's rote reply had my stomach suddenly twisting in knots as I considered what we would do if I wasn't able to get it to open the door going forward. *<Report: All previously detected Ætherial Anomalies in this chamber have been eradicated. Updating. Warning: Two new Ætherial Anomalies have now been detected in this chamber. Lockdown cannot be lifted until all Ætherial Anomalies are contained or eradicated.>*

"Oh shit," I cursed as I glared at the crystal, not having even paused to consider that the device would detect Amaranth and me as being Ætherwarped.

"What's wrong?" Sierra asked, her voice sounding worried.

"It can sense that Amaranth and I are Ætherwarped and won't open the door yet," I replied while trying to think of a way around the machine's statement. "Hang on a second."

<The two new Ætherial Anomalies you're detecting are part of the Containment Team,> I sent to the device. *<They are not a threat and we have them under control.>*

<Checking statement,> the Nafarrian security intoned once more. *<Unable to verify. Clearance from someone ranked Supervisor or higher, including any members listed on a Containment Team must be obtained before proceeding.>*

<There is no one else alive in this facility to grant clearance and I am the Containment Team Leader,> I said to the machine, wondering if it would allow me to approve my own access. *<I will accept the risk.>*

<Checking statement,> it replied once again before falling silent for a few seconds. *<Query: Is there another Containment Team here with you?>*

<There is,> I replied suddenly hopeful, realizing that it must be referring to Freya and her group. *<We split up to ensure that we cleared the facility as quickly as possible.>*

<Understood.> The device stated, falling silent for a moment. *<Report: Ad-hoc provisional access deemed appropriate given the emergency situation. Lockdown will be lifted sequentially as you and your Containment Teams progress through the facility. Ensure that any Ætherial Anomalies encountered are eradicated or contained. Report progress at the console near the next Æther Matrix on your route.>*

Without another word, the door at the end of the chamber began to grind open, causing all of us to spin and glance in its direction as it gradually revealed a pitch-black passageway that visibly descended further downwards. As the door slowly opened, I felt a wave of relief shoot through me, along with seeing a skill notification followed by a quest update appear out of the corner of my eye.

Your skill in Wordplay has increased to Level 13!

Quest Update! The Ruptured Ley Line!

After excavating the collapsed passage, you and your party have confirmed your earlier suspicions and have discovered another level to the Nafarrian Ruins, leading even deeper underground, possibly towards the Ley Line. Since entering the ruins, you have encountered twisted remains belonging to both the Irovians and Nafarr who had been trapped within, each of whom appears to have been warped by magic.

During your exploration of the ruin, you have managed to make contact with a still functioning Nafarrian device, successfully convincing it that you are part of a Containment Team sent to clear the ruins of 'Ætherial Anomalies' and repair the Ley Line. As such, the device has agreed to unlock the route to the next Æther Matrix.

Attempt to excavate the collapsed passage and see where it leads: 1/1
Gain access to the Nafarrian Ruin: 1/1
Secure the next Æther Matrix: 0/1
Ley Line Sealed: 0/1

I must have missed an earlier update, I thought to myself, noting that there was a completed stage in the quest that I hadn't seen earlier. *Though considering how this day is shaping up, that's not surprising.*

With a mental shrug, I dismissed both the notification and quest update from my vision and took a step towards the door, flashing a smile back towards the rest of the party that looked towards me with surprise, none of them clearly having expected that my idea of 'thinking at the crystal pillar' would have worked.

"Well," I prompted, motioning for everyone to follow me. "Shall we see what else this dungeon has in store for us?"

Chapter 36

"Aaah!" I let out a brief shout of surprise and pain as I felt my feet leave the ground, a blast of intense energy sending me cartwheeling through the air. I barely had the chance to process what had happened before my body, and very shortly afterward, my head, collided with smooth, unforgiving stone, leaving me lying on the floor rattled and staring upwards at a new combat log entry.

An [Unstable Ætherbound Shade] hits you with [Æther Bomb] for 81 points of damage!

Damn, I cursed internally, reflexively sitting up despite how badly my head was spinning. *Where did that one come from?*

"Lyr!" Drace shouted over the incessant voices that echoed through our minds, the near deafening cacophony not having changed in volume or content since the encounter had begun. "We need you guys back here, *now!*"

"Us guys?" I asked dumbly, feeling my brain slowly start to function again as it recovered from its most recent impact on the ground. Glancing around me, my blurry vision sharpened, revealing both Constantine and Lazarus lying on the floor a short distance away from me, appearing just as dazed and confused as I felt.

Movement from ahead of me caused my eyes to shift from the pair and focus on several ghostlike shapes that were running towards us, my mind gradually rebooting as the last few seconds of battle came rushing back.

The three of us had been trying to break through a group of Shades, I recalled as I forced myself back up onto my feet while yelling something unintelligible at both Lazarus and Constantine in hopes of getting them moving. Standing up,

I reflexively scanned through the advancing attackers, carefully reading the four tags that appeared in my vision and remembering that we were supposed to look out for one type of Shade in particular.

[Ætherbound Shade] – Level 12

No Unstable Shades in this batch, I breathed with relief as I leaped forward to meet the oncoming group, sending a *Shocking Touch* into Splinter's edge and swiping it through the lead Shade's outstretched arm, feeling no resistance as the blade passed through the ghostly limb and severed it from the apparition's body. *That last one came out of nowhere; I never even saw it coming.*

Sidestepping a lunging slash from another Shade and repaying the favor in kind, I shook off the last of the cobwebs that still clung to my mind and returned to near full awareness, unable to stop myself from replaying just how we had gotten ourselves into this situation.

After the Nafarrian security system had finished opening the door for us, we had continued in our exploration of the ruin, delving even deeper and descending several more stories downward as we reached another set of switchbacks. But unlike the still intact portion of the ruin that we passed through earlier, we had begun to see signs of damage and destruction from whatever cataclysm had befallen the region.

As we descended, we passed by several collapsed or completely blocked passageways, some of them appearing as if the entire bedrock had shifted just enough to send entire hallways off their original course and blocking them from access, while simultaneously cracking others below them wide open. Navigating through the ruined passages carefully, we slowly pressed onwards, until we had eventually reached a nearly identical copy of the chamber that we had just left upstairs, complete with a floating

Æther Crystal set in the center of it. Completely identical except for the one tiny difference, that instead of glowing with a pale azure light, like the crystal before it, this one instead emitted a sickly green one and had a palpable haze hanging over it. Curious to what may have caused the difference, we had all waltzed into the otherwise empty room, thinking that because we couldn't see any creatures standing around, that there weren't any to find.

Unfortunately, that line of thinking only lasted for a few moments, just long enough for us all to approach the emerald colored crystal and to be in prime position when a horde of angry Nafarrian ghosts began pouring out from inside it, their angry mental howls filling our minds. The pitch of the voices changed with every word spoken, interchanging seamlessly between one another, with the rare word distorted almost beyond recognition.

<Invaders! Kill the invaders! They did this to us! Kill them! Kill them! KILL THEM!> A discordant shift in the chorus of voices caused me to slam back into the present, my train of thought interrupted by the mental noise. Redoubling my efforts to ignore the ghost's never-ending mental chant, I focused on stabbing Splinter into the sickly green aura that compromised an attacking Shade's form, the magical blade putting an end to the spirit's undeath as it faded from existence, hopefully heading towards a more peaceful afterlife.

"There's no end to them!" Constantine called out to me as he finally climbed back up to his feet and fell in beside me, both of his short swords slashing out at one of the three remaining Shades. "How the hell do we beat them all?"

"I have no idea!" I replied, using Constantine's arrival as a brief reprieve to cast a glance behind me, noticing that Lazarus was slowly rising to his feet with his translucent sword in hand. "But we need to get back to the rest of the group!"

I turned away from the still rising half-giant and returned my attention back to the Shades before me, seeing that we had managed to attract two newly spawned Shades that had just emerged from the tainted Æther Crystal. "Lazarus! We need to go! Can you move?"

"Nyah," the man grunted what I hoped was an affirmative response because no sooner did I hear his reply than I lunged forward at the two Shades loosely arrayed before me, accepting a grazing slash from each of their spectral claws in exchange for cleaving Splinter through both of their stomachs.

Reacting as if they were still creatures of flesh and blood, the two Shades howled in pain and reflexively clutched at their abdomens, which now trailed a stream of ectoplasm as the energy that bound them together gushed from the open wound. With both of their clawed hands no longer threatening me, it only took me a heartbeat to reverse Splinter's momentum, slicing the blade through their now unprotected heads and putting an end to the two undead creatures.

Not waiting to see if Constantine had dealt with his own Shade, I immediately took off at a run, angling myself in a sprint across the chamber, looking to circle around the tainted Æther Crystal and rejoin the rest of the party. As I ran, six more Shades emerged from the Crystal, their ghostly bodies falling to the ground soundlessly before slowly scrambling to their feet.

Individually, or even in small groups, the lower leveled Shades were nearly effortless to kill, as evidenced by how easily I had managed to kill three of them, suffering only a small wound for my efforts. It wasn't until their numbers grew, however, that they became dangerous, their ghostly bodies allowing them to stack on top of one another in a way that no physical creature could ever hope to mimic, forcing you to defend against a dozen ethereal claws all coming from the same direction at once.

"There's an Unstable one in that pack!" Lazarus's voice boomed from just behind my shoulder, causing my heart to leap in my chest as I glanced back towards the Crystal, my eyes landing on an all too familiar shifting form. "We won't make it far unless—"

"I'll take care of it!" I shouted back to the man, angling my desperate sprint across the room directly towards the tainted Æther Crystal. "You guys keep running! I'll catch up with you on the other side!"

"Lyr—" I heard Constantine begin to call from behind me as I shifted directions and immediately cut him off.

"Go, Constantine!" I barked, putting any further replies out of my mind as I rushed towards the six still-rising Shades, my attention focused solely on the one Shade that was roiling with azure light, the magical energy dancing across the emerald ectoplasm that was its body. We had learned early in the battle that any of these multicolored Shades with an 'Unstable' prefix attached to their name were substantially more dangerous than their more common variant.

Namely by having the ability to explode with extreme force after rushing into near point-blank range and sending everything around them flying through the air and crashing to the ground, allowing the rest of the Shades to quickly swarm any prone victims.

Which hopefully I can keep from happening…again, I thought while gritting my teeth and speeding up into a sprint. It was because of the Unstable Shades that Constantine, Lazarus and I had managed to get ourselves separated from the rest of the party in the first place. The three of us having been caught on the wrong side of the crystal when the encounter had first begun, and then forced to keep moving in order to avoid the seemingly never-ending stream of Shades emerging from the strangely-colored Æther Crystal. *If I can try and trigger the Unstable Shade early, and try to get out of its way before it can explode…*

I put on one last burst of speed as the distance between me and the Shades vanished, throwing myself forward directly into the middle of them as I entered melee range, sweeping Splinter in the wildest arc that I could manage. The Æthertouched blade sang through the air harmlessly as the three Shades centering the line before me reflexively leaped away from my attack, some spark of self-preservation having stuck with the creatures despite their now undead state.

Just how I had hoped they would.

Maintaining my sprint, I sped past the cluster of Shades, taking advantage of the opening and passed through the gap between their ranks; my eyes focused on the Unstable Shade standing just behind the trio. I had just enough time to see the multicolored Shade begin to raise its claw to strike me before I drove Splinter's point directly into its chest, discharging the *Shocking Touch* that I had stored in the weapon into the spirit's body.

There was a slight pause as the ghost shuddered from the after effects of my spell, giving me the chance to pull my blade free and take a step past it, before its allies all spun around and attacked me from behind. Recovering slowly from my attack, the Shade spun to follow me, swinging a claw wildly in my direction and earning a savage cut along its forearm for its efforts as I brought Splinter up just in time to block it. Snarling from the combined attacks, the

Unstable Shade's body immediately began to glow with bright azure light.

I think that's my cue, I thought as I dodged a second swipe from the Shade's other claw and slashed a shallow cut into its shoulder, the wound causing the light emanating from it to intensify. *Time to get out of here!*

Disengaging from the fight before the now brightly glowing Shade could work itself up into a frenzy, I spun on my heel and rushed around the raised dais of the Æther Crystal looming over us, before triggering *Blink Step*. My vision blurred into a familiar kaleidoscope of colors as I teleported across the room, rematerializing midstride just as a blinding flash of azure light filled the air behind me, followed closely by a thunderclap of magic.

"Lyr!" Constantine's voice rang out from much closer than I had expected, causing me to flinch in surprise as I turned my head towards its source, spotting both the rogue and Lazarus angling towards me, the pair having made great time circling around the Æther Crystal. "You made it!"

"Barely!" I exclaimed, feeling the sting of a wound I never remembered taking flare up on my back.

"We're not through yet!" Lazarus grunted, breathing hard as the three us of fell into line with one another. "The others are getting swarmed! Look!"

Taking my eyes off the pair, I snapped my head in the direction that I assumed the rest of the party to be, immediately seeing what Lazarus was referring to. In the time that the three of us had been separated from the group, they had been forced back into a corner of the room as a veritable horde of Shades had descended upon them, stacking atop themselves in a sea of emerald light, their ethereal forms allowing several of them to occupy the same space at once. Standing at the front of the group, I saw the bloodied and exhausted forms of both Amaranth and Drace doing their best to keep the enraged spirits at bay as a never-ending avalanche of claws continuously swept out from the mass before them.

"Shit!" I spat as we all adjusted our approach to hit the Shades from behind. "Anyone have a plan how to handle this?"

"We don't need a plan!" Lazarus barked harshly, anger boiling in his voice as he shouted, "Just follow me!"

Putting on an extra burst of speed, the enraged half-giant pulled away from both Constantine and me, his long legs pumping wildly as he charged the distracted Shades from behind. With a mighty cleave of his greatsword, Lazarus carved through a pile of the Nafarrian spirits clustered before Drace, turning the Shades near overpowering strength in numbers into a fatal weakness as the blade passed through several of them that had all been caught occupying the same spot at once.

With Lazarus's one attack, the pace of the battle shifted as a gap opened up in the Shades ranks, many of them shifting around in surprise to see what had attacked them from behind.

Just in time for Constantine and me to arrive.

Taking up position on either side of Lazarus, the two of us set about attacking the small army of Shades, scything through the mass as they all scrambled to meet our attack, only to have the rest of our party slam into them from the other side.

"Take the shield down!" Drace shouted, a thundering clap of magic filling the air a heartbeat afterward as a burst of Ætherfire from Halcyon's *Pyroclap* rolled over a cluster of Shades followed by a constant stream of fire from Caius's skull-tipped staff. "Hit them with everything we have before more spawn!"

Caught between the two forces, the Shades melted under our combined onslaught as we all surged forward, capitalizing on the ghost's tightly packed ranks, each one of our attacks hitting several of them at once. But yet, for all of our success, the sheer quantity of Shades meant that wounds were inevitable.

Ugh! I cursed mentally, unable to move my arm in time to prevent a spectral claw from running itself across my arm, the ethereal nails passing through my armor as if it were nonexistent and slicing through the flesh underneath. In retaliation, I reflexively thrust Splinter into the body that the claw was attached to as well as at least two others that happened to occupy the same space at the moment. Feeling no resistance to my attack, save for the cool flow of mana up my arm as I trigged my *Mana Leech* ability, I then twisted the blade sideways before sweeping it out of the several Shades' bodies, watching a spray of ectoplasm fill the air.

Over the next few minutes, the battle gradually shifted until the bulk of the Shades that had once threatened the party had been cleared out, allowing Constantine, Lazarus and I to finally fall into our proper places, forming a solid line of battle and giving the ranged members of the party the space and time they needed to pick off any Unstable Shades at a distance.

"If anyone has any bright ideas for putting an end to this fight, feel free to speak up!" Alistair shouted in an uncharacteristic display of anger and frustration. "Because I'm almost out of mana and I'm not going to be able to heal you guys anymore!"

"Same here!" Halcyon shouted. "I'm running on fumes!"

"Try to destroy the Crystal from range!" Lazarus offered through the chaos of battle.

"We tried that already!" Sierra replied immediately. "It just absorbed any spells directed at it, and my arrows just bounce off it harmlessly."

"Then we'll have to break up close!" Lazarus shot back.

"Hang on! Breaking it could cause the Crystal to explode!" Caius stated urgently. "All the Æther stored inside it is going to have to go somewhere!"

"All I'm hearing are problems!" Drace snarled. "Does anyone have a solution?!"

"What about that fancy box with the crystals over there?" Constantine called out. "It looks exactly like the one we saw upstairs!"

"Right! The security system thing!" I exclaimed, my eyes shifting to the wall closest to us and seeing a familiar looking rectangular pillar set into the side of it a short distance away from us. Eyes widening, I tried to make mental contact with the device but didn't get any reply. "I see the box, but I don't think I'm close enough to activate it!"

"Then we need to move before we get swarmed again!" Drace stated, the big man swinging his heavy mace through a cluster of Shades before him and taking a large step forward. "Everyone on my tail, now!"

Not waiting for a reply from any of us, Drace then went on to blaze a path through the gradually thickening wall of Shades that had steadily continued to pour from the Æther Crystal, these newly spawned spirits quickly replacing the batch that we had killed just moments earlier. Unless we found a way to stop the Crystal from spawning any more of them, it was only a matter of time before Alistair ran out of mana and exhaustion took its toll on us, allowing the Shades to slowly wear us down, or for a handful of the Unstable Shades to get close enough to disrupt our ranks.

Hopefully, this ancient Nafarrian...computer thing, or whatever it is, can help us before that happens! I thought desperately as I worked to keep pace with Drace and the other melee fighters, slashing and stabbing at every Shade that came into range. Moving with purpose through the thinned ranks of Shades, it didn't take us long to cut our way through them until we reached the pillar and formed a protective circle around it.

"You're up, Lyr!" Drace shouted as we all stopped moving. "I don't care what you have to do, but get that thing to turn this Crystal off!"

"I'm on it!" I answered, having switched places with Lazarus in our traditional line of battle and placed myself directly along the wall that the device was on, reducing my defensive responsibilities in case I needed to divide my attention. Crossing my fingers, I mentally reached out to the pillar once again, silently hoping that it would reply to me now that we had gotten closer.

<Hey, we need help!> I sent, far too caught up in the rush of battle not to be blunt with the machine. *<We are getting swarmed here!>*

There was no answer from the device for several seconds, the delay lasting long enough for me to begin to think that a reply wouldn't be forthcoming, but just as I was about to turn to inspect the crystals protruding from the pillar, a distorted voice filled my mind.

<Mind Print recognized. Welcome, Lyrian Rastler.> It intoned calmly at first, oblivious to the battle that was raging around it, before. *<Warning: Multiple Ætherial Anomalies detected nearby. Request status update on containment process.>*

<Failing!> I mentally shouted at the machine as several Shades wandered into my defensive sphere, forcing me to slash out at them with Splinter. *<The Æther Crystal in this*

chamber is different...its contaminated somehow! Spirits of the dead are emerging from it and trying to kill us!>

<Checking statement,> the Nafarrian intelligence replied as it paused for several seconds, giving me a chance to look in the direction of the Crystal and see another pack of Shades emerge free from it. *<Error: Display matrix is non-functional. Cannot verify statement. Engaging troubleshooting mode. Please describe the nature of the contamination.>*

Is this thing serious right now?! I thought to myself, unable to believe what I was hearing. *I need to deal with the Nafarrian equivalent of tech support right in the middle of a battle?*

<The Æther Crystal is glowing with a pale green light and hordes of deceased Nafarrian spirits are emerging from it believing that we are attempting to invade the place!> I practically shouted at the machine, hoping that my mental volume conveyed just how serious the situation was. *<We have killed scores of them, but they keep coming!>*

<Processing statement,> the Nafarrian device answered, completely unperturbed by the anger in my tone. *<Query: Are the Æther Transmogrification Rings of the Æther Matrix enveloped within a spectral or flesh-based protuberance?>*

<I have no idea what that even means!> I mentally screamed back at the device as the realization that we were all going to die began to sink in.

<Clarification: Have the metallic rings encircling the Æther Matrix grown arms?> it asked, still retaining a calm and collected voice.

<That can fucking happen?> I exclaimed just as a blast from an Unstable Shade that had managed to get too close to the line knocked me off balance and forced me to catch myself against the wall. Pushing myself back upright, I glanced towards the tainted Æther Crystal and didn't see

anything surrounding the metallic rings that gently spun around it. *<No! It doesn't have any arms at all!>*

<Noted. There are no further queries at this time. Please hold while diagnostics are performed,> The voice said before falling silent.

"How is it coming, Lyrian?" Drace shouted from the front of the line. "This is starting to get too much to handle!"

"It put me on goddamned hold is how it's going!" I snapped back at the warrior. "We need to wait until it's done!"

"Are you serious?" the half-giant roared, disbelief in his voice.

"Why the hell would I lie about something like that?" I retorted, the stress of the situation finally getting to me.

"Whatever! But it better not be too long!" Alistair added with a desperate note to his voice. "Because I'm officially out of mana now! Everyone's on their own!"

"Rah!" Drace growled in response, which was shortly followed by a loud clap of magic as a distant Unstable Shade detonated.

Turning my attention back to the battle at hand, I couldn't help but notice that the sheer quantity of Shades pouring free from the Æther Crystal had steadily managed to increase, with more and more of the undead spirits filling the chamber. Fighting side by side with Amaranth, my world shrank as the two of us worked to keep our portion of the defense pocket intact, countless minor wounds piling up from the sheer quantity of Shades that surrounded us.

<Diagnostic complete.> The device finally announced after what seemed like a lifetime, but in reality, had been less than half a minute. *<Situation is deemed to be a Class Five Spectral Infestation, centering on the chamber's Æther*

Matrix. Recommendation: Activate purge mechanism to drain Æther from infected Æther Matrix.>

<Great!> I replied, feeling as if a single ray of hope had appeared. *<How do I activate the purge mechanism?>*

<A purge can be activated by the express command of those ranked Supervisor or higher, including any members listed on a Containment Team,> the mental voice explained patiently.

<I'm the Containment Team Leader!> I told the Nafarrian machine, feeling a wave of frustration surge through me that I had to repeat myself. *<Purge the Æther Matrix in this chamber immediately!>*

<Command Received,> the device replied. *<Checking authorization: Success. Executing Command. Standby.>*

"Something is happening!" Drace announced, just as the light emanating from the Æther Crystal started to dim. "The energy around the Crystal is fading!"

"I activated some sort of purge mechanism!" I replied, noticing that the Nafarrian spirits before me seemed to be growing more and more indistinct with every second that passed. "It looks like it's affecting the Shades too!"

"About time!" Lazarus exclaimed from somewhere behind me, his voice sounding completely exhausted beyond measure. "I don't know how much I have left in me."

"Just a little bit longer!" I affirmed, slicing Splinter through the rapidly fading form of a Shade as the chamber steadily grew darker, the mental voices from the spirits also beginning to diminish in volume.

In the seconds that followed, both the chamber and the Shades continued to darken before they both finally winked out as if snuffed by an invisible hand, sending the chamber into pitch black darkness and silence. Several more seconds passed before a few orbs of light flared into existence, conjured with the final dregs of Halcyon's and Caius's mana.

Letting Splinter's edge drop down, I looked in the direction of the now dark Æther Crystal and saw that the tainted energy that once surrounded it had completely faded. Breathing a sigh of relief, I let my body relax, hearing the Nafarrian device voice filter into my head.

<Report: Æther purge complete. Spectral Infestation deemed neutralized.>

Chapter 37

"So, does anyone else think it's weird that all of the Nafarrian ghosts and spirits we've come across think that we're invading the place, but this...security system thing which Lyr is talking to wants us to kill them all anyway?" Constantine asked out loud as we all recovered from the fight and waited for our spellcasters to finish regenerating their mana - after they had each graciously allowed me to *Mana Drain* them to top my own reserves. "I mean, that just sounds kinda wrong to me. Shouldn't the security system be on their side?"

"If they were still alive, it probably would be," I replied with a shrug and continued scratching Amaranth's head, the big cat having practically sat on my feet in demand for attention. "But based on what I've noticed so far from the security system, and from what happened when we unfroze all the spiders back at the other ruin, it seems that the Nafarr made sure to have protocols in place when an 'Ætherial Anomaly' occurs."

"Clearly for a good reason," Sierra stated. "Look at what happened when a handful of spiders managed to get to the Ley Line, if we weren't here to stop the infestation before it got worse, this entire region would have been overrun."

<It would have at least been enjoyable to hunt the Many-Legs,> Amaranth told me mentally, clearly paying attention to the conversation. *<These...spirits...that we have faced recently give no satisfaction to the kill. They merely fade away into nothing.>*

<Hopefully we won't come across any other spirits,> I told my familiar, somewhat understanding where he was coming from. From his point of view, the ghosts that we

had been fighting were completely outside his realm of experience and nothing like the typical prey that he hunted. *<But I honestly don't know what else to expect down here.>*

"I guess," Constantine said, his face shifting to a thoughtful expression then looking towards me. "Has it given you any more problems about your Ætherwarping since the first room Lyr?"

"No, nothing." I replied, shaking my head at the rogue. "I have no idea how the Nafarr set up this system or if it has been damaged along with the ruin, but during an emergency the Containment Teams seem to be able to do or access anything. Even self-approve their own access, which seems like bad security design."

"I'm not so sure about that Lyr." Sierra stated. "Given how fast all this Æther stuff can get out of hand, I think reaction speed over security is more important."

"That is a good point," I agreed.

"It's also likely that they didn't just put *anyone* on a Containment Team," Halcyon offered, joining the conversation. "I mean, what did you say this whole thing was, Lyr? A Spectral Infestation? They wouldn't just send regular people after that. It'd likely be a specialized team of some sort."

"That's true too," I replied with a nod, unable to help myself from looking at the now dormant Æther Crystal, or how the security system referred to it as, the Æther Matrix. "The system said it was a 'Class Five Spectral Infestation'."

"Which leads me to believe that there are at least four other classifications to how badly this could have gone for us," Lazarus said pessimistically.

"The system *did* ask me if the Crystal had grown arms," I noted, agreeing with the half-giant's statement.

"Wait, I thought you were joking when you said that," Caius's head whipped around to look at me with concern. "Please tell me you're joking."

"Does this look like my joking face?" I asked the warlock while pointing to the serious expression I was wearing. "It asked if the arms were made out of flesh, or were spiritual in nature."

There was a moment of silence as everyone absorbed that mental picture, several heads turning towards the crystal.

"Well, just when you think you've run out of nightmare fuel, the game just finds a way to top you up again!" Halcyon exclaimed, his voice projecting a false, shaky confidence. "If that ever happens to us, I'm giving you all fair warning now, I'm just going to log off."

"Not if you want any loot, you won't," Sierra said, looking pointedly at the mage.

"Bah, what loot?" Halcyon grunted, waving his hands dramatically around the empty chamber. "These Shades didn't drop anything for us at all! To be honest, I feel a bit cheated."

"Eh, we've already gotten a pretty big haul from this dungeon already," I said, motioning towards the new gear that Constantine, Drace and Alistair had managed to get from the last fight. "Plus, if you look at it this way, we've also secured a completely intact *and* unpowered Æther Crystal."

"Hrm," Halcyon snorted dismissively. "With my luck, it'll still be full of ghosts the moment that we power it up."

"Maybe. But that also sounds like a problem for the future," I replied, using what had to be my favorite phrase. "Anyway, how are you guys doing on mana? Should I tell the security system thing to open the next set of doors for us?"

"I'm ready," Alistair announced, followed a heartbeat later by Caius saying the same.

"Yeah, I'm good," Halcyon said with a sigh, waving a hand at the crystal-filled pillar. "Do your thing."

Nodding at the group, Amaranth and I both turned to walk over towards the console with me mentally reaching out towards it the moment that I came into range.

<We're ready to keep moving,> I told the security system. *<Can you unlock the next door?>*

<Affirmative.> It stated, a grinding noise filling the air as the door at the far end of the chamber began to slide open. *<Warning: Detection apparatus beyond this chamber is non-operational. Cannot confirm presence of Ætherial Anomalies. Report: Based on last verifiable data, a Sentinel-class security unit was activated to safeguard the local Æther Matrixes. Contact with the security unit was lost: five hundred and fifty years, five months, two weeks, nine hours, eight minutes, twenty-two seconds ago. Recommendation: Proceed with caution.>*

A security unit? I thought to myself in surprise, once again doing the mental math and calculating that it had managed to survive for over five months down here before it too had lost contact. *But did it lose contact because it broke? Or because something managed to overwhelm it?*

<What can you tell me about the security unit?> I decided to ask the device, hoping it had a bit more information for me.

<Report: The unit was a standard Sentinel class model, designed for in close defense and assault. Its primary function was to protect any nearby Æther Matrixes, or serve as a backup to local Containment Teams.> The security system replied without any hesitation.

<Do you know what happened to cause the unit to lose contact?> I asked, starting to wonder just how often these

'Ætherial Anomalies' occurred if the Nafarr had security units on hand to deal with them.

<Unknown.> The system answered. *<The last recorded contact with the unit was when it was pursuing a high threat class Ætherial Anomaly, as per its last standing orders. Contact with the unit was suddenly lost during the engagement that followed. It is theorized that the unit was either destroyed or suffered enough damage to no longer be able to communicate.>*

<Hold on,> I told the system, my eyes widening as I considered the implications of what it had just said. *<If the Sentinel unit is still active, will it perceive us as a threat?>*

<Negative.> The voice replied. *<The security unit has full mental imprints of all Facility and Containment Team members to avoid friendly fire incidents.>*

<Even us, who were just added to the list?> I prompted the device, wondering if it would come to the same conclusion I had.

<Processing statement,> the mental voice intoned before falling silent for several seconds as it considered my question. *<Warning: If Sentinel unit is still active, newly updated Containment Teams will have not been uploaded into its memory core. Probability of unit regarding you as hostile is to be considered one-hundred percent. Recommendation: Disable and dismantle Sentinel unit until memory core can be updated.>*

"You better believe we're going to *dismantle* it," I muttered as I moved away from the crystal-filled pillar and turned to face the group, several of them already staring in my direction, clearly curious as to why I had been talking to the security system for so long.

"Everything okay, Lyr?" Sierra asked having raised an eyebrow after hearing my words. "What are we dismantling now?"

"Possibly a security unit. Whatever that exactly is," I said with a sigh. "Assuming it's still active...which I'll bet any money that is it."

"Uh, you've lost me here, Lyr," the red-haired elf replied, her expression shifting to confusion. "What security unit? Is it the system that you're talking to?"

"No, not that one," I said with another, even deeper, sigh as I ran a hand through my hair, then began to repeat what I had learned from the security system. "So, based on all that. I'm thinking that we either have a damaged security unit of some sort ahead of us..."

"Or something that was strong enough to destroy it," Lazarus finished, nodding along with my explanation. "*Or* maybe even both of those things...depending on how things shook out five-hundred years ago."

"Damn, I didn't think of that," I said, definitely not wanting to fight *two* powerful creatures at once.

"Is anyone else finding it hard to think on that sort of timescale?" Constantine asked. "I mean it's been so long, maybe this Sentinel thing managed to kill whatever it was chasing and just broke down afterward. It's been over five centuries since this all happened after all."

"I think that's wishful thinking, Constantine. We haven't found a single thing that's broken down here," Caius replied to the rogue while indicating the Æther Crystal. "The Nafarr built things to last."

"I'm trying hard to be optimistic here, Caius," Constantine said, putting both his hands behind the back of his head and taking a deep breath. "But you're making that really difficult right now."

"There's a time for optimism and a time for realism, Constantine," Sierra stated. "Right now, based on what we know, we need to prepare for the worst."

"I'm sure we'll be able to manage," I said, meeting everyone's gaze as I spoke. "It hasn't been exactly easy, but we've made it this far. I'm sure we can take it the rest of the way."

"We'll see," Drace replied wistfully, before motioning towards the crystal pillar with his chin. "I don't suppose that box can tell you how Freya and the others are doing? I'd feel a hell of a lot more confident if we could join up with them again."

"It should be able to," I said, sending a thought towards the security system. *<Where is the other Containment Team right now?>*

<Report: The other Containment Team was last detected leaving the Æther Matrix opposite to this one approximately: Six minutes and twenty-two seconds ago. Detection apparatus beyond that point is non-operational.> The mental voice answered promptly.

"According to the system, they're about six minutes ahead of us," I replied to the warrior while mentally picturing a map of the magical energy sources we had seen through the Ætherscope. Based on our exploration so far, it seemed that each and every major source of energy that we had detected, corresponded with the rough location of an Æther Crystal, which meant that there was only one more set of Æther Crystals ahead of us.

Plus, whatever else that was lying in wait.

"Then we better get moving," the half-giant stated, turning away from the group and waving for everyone to follow him as he headed towards the now open door at the far side of the chamber. "No telling what the damage is going to be like, and I'd rather not leave the other group hanging if they end up needing our help somehow."

With those words, we all left the darkened chamber behind us and filed through the doorway, Drace setting a demanding pace in the hope of catching up with the other group. Much like the previous route we had taken between the two Æther Matrixes, there was plenty of damage evident in the passageway, with large cracks running through the walls, and countless fragments broken off from the ceiling above, now littering the ground. The further that we walked, the more confident I became that the entire hallway itself seemed to be somehow off-center as if it had not only sunken downwards from its original path, but had also twisted slightly, causing our balance to be shifted almost imperceptibly to one side.

<The musk is growing thicker here,> Amaranth told me as we continued down the passageway. *<The air is heavier as well.>*

<Is it?> I asked my familiar, taking a deep breath and noticing that the vague moldy scent that filled the air had indeed grown more noticeable while also increasing in humidity. *<You're right; I can smell it now too. I wonder what it's coming from.>*

<I am not certain,> Amaranth replied, his ear flicking as he spoke. *<Perhaps there is stale water trapped down here?>*

<Maybe,> I acknowledged, a little surprised at my familiar's insight. There was much about the world that he simply didn't have a frame of reference for, yet it was becoming clear to me that the cat was much smarter than I had originally given him credit for.

Something to consider going forward, I guess, I thought, making a mental note not to hold anything back from Amaranth. I didn't want to inadvertently stunt the development of his personality by treating him as if he were less intelligent than he truly was.

"Hold up," Drace suddenly announced, pulling me out of my thoughts as he came to an abrupt stop, squinting at something further along the passageway. "Something doesn't look right up ahead."

"Trouble?" I asked, reflexively gripping Splinter's hilt tightly in my hand as I waited for an answer.

"I...don't think so," the half-giant replied, edging forward with careful steps, the orb of light that hovered around him gradually illuminating the pitch-black hallway as he advanced. "The passageway looks like it just...*ends* ahead of us here."

"What do you mean ends?" Constantine's voice filtered up from behind me. "It's collapsed?"

"No," Drace called back, turning back towards us and beckoning us forward, his voice having shifted to amazement. "Not collapsed, but opening up into...whatever this place is...*was*."

Curious to what he had found, I moved to catch up to Drace, seeing what had caught his attention in the first place. As I moved forward, the floor of the passageway gradually became blackened rubble, cracked and loose beneath my feet, with the wall on my right side giving way into complete darkness.

"Whoa," I gasped as I looked out into the pitch black that now surrounded me, then back towards Drace, seeing that the man had continued forward, stepping out onto what had to be a truly massive pile of stone as it continued downwards and out of sight.

"Whoa indeed," Drace agreed, motioning me forward towards him as the rest of the party caught up and stared out into the abyss around us.

"It's a...tunnel," Caius was the first to announce, his Dark Elven ancestry allowing him to see as clearly as if it were day. "A really, *really* big tunnel."

"But for what?" Constantine asked.

No one had an answer for the rogue as Caius and Halcyon wordlessly conjured several more orbs of light and began sending them out to illuminate the area, bits and pieces of the tunnel slowly becoming more and more visible. While the two mages ensured that those without enhanced vision could see, I decided to activate *True Sight*, the darkness around us vanishing as the magical enchantment took over.

Looking around the chamber, the first thing that my mind processed was the sheer size of the tunnel, which at my best guess measured at least fifty feet in each direction. I couldn't even begin to imagine the amount of work that would have gone into excavating the space and once again was in awe of the technology the Nafarr must have possessed.

This place must have been ancient even before it was destroyed, I theorized as I scanned my surroundings, seeing that there was a large collapse in the tunnel leading backward the way that we came. *This would have taken ages to plan and build.*

"This place looks wrecked," Halcyon said as he and Caius finished their conjuring, his voice vanishing out into the tunnel around us. "This tunnel almost looks exactly like what we saw in the room with the first Æther Crystal, the walls here are all burnt and shattered...just on a much larger scale."

"I'll say," I agreed, finishing my initial observation of the area, making a note of the damage that Halcyon had pointed out. It seemed like every spare inch of the walls around us had either been vitrified, and taken on a glassy sheen, or it had shattered and broken off completely, now a part of one of the many piles of stone that littered the area. "I think either something happened further down the tunnel and the blast carried up this far, or the Nafarr somehow moved Æther through this tunnel, and it erupted. That would explain all the damage we've seen."

"Honestly, it's anyone's guess at this point," Halcyon replied. "I wouldn't even know where to begin to piece together how this all happened."

"And I don't think we ever will." I nodded with a sigh, looking out at the collapse that had blocked the tunnel behind us, silently wondering how far it traced back to the path that we had already travelled. Turning around to face Drace, I noticed that he had kept himself busy while the rest of us had been caught glancing around the chamber, the man having taken several steps out on the rubble that was piled against our side of the tunnel wall. "See anything interesting out that way, Drace?"

"Eh," the half-giant grunted. "The remnants of the passageway we were just walking in from the looks of it. Looks like the whole chunk of stone it was carved out of shifted into the tunnel, then cracked and splintered off."

"Damn," I replied, looking around the area for a way forward and seeing that our only other option was to slide straight down the rubble before us and then to try climbing up another pile. "Can we keep going that way at all?"

"Don't hold it against me if I'm wrong," Drace answered a little hesitantly. "But yeah, I think so. If we hug the wall, we should be at least able to get to the next major pile of rubble I can see from here…"

"And where do we go from there?" Sierra asked, clearly not enthused with the man's lack of confidence.

"Forward?" Drace proposed, his shoulders moving in a large shrug. "I don't see any better options available to us. It's not like we passed another route behind us."

"He's right, Sierra," I said, waving a hand down at what I knew would be pitch-black darkness to her. "The only option I see is trying to slide down into all the rubble that's fallen down here, and try to pick our way through it."

"Hard pass on that," she replied, exhaling sharply as she did so.

"Then let's keep moving," I said, waving for everyone to follow me as I moved to catch up to Drace and resume our journey through the ruins.

Keeping close to the wall, we fell back into our usual formation, carefully following the broken remains of the passageway before crossing over onto the large pile of shattered stone that Drace had mentioned earlier and continuing onwards through the partially collapsed tunnel. Travelling across the rubble in search of a route forward, we followed it nearly the entire width of the tunnel before coming across a large fragment of the far wall that had broken off and formed a makeshift bridge connecting to yet another mountain of rubble ahead of us.

Making sure to test that the precariously balanced stone slab would be able to bear our weight before crossing, we cautiously continued forward, the sound of our crunching boots the only noise filling the chamber. Glancing around with my enhanced vision as we moved, I noticed that the further that we traveled, the thicker and denser the debris that filled the tunnel became.

The damage looks worse this way, I thought as I looked around the chamber with my enhanced vision, now leading the party across the sea of broken stone, having offered to take over for Drace since I could see near perfectly in the dark. Pausing for a moment to pick a better route, I noticed the fragmented remains of several passageways had been exposed and torn free when the walls had collapsed, silently wondering if we could find one intact enough to climb into and leave the tunnel behind. *It's almost as if something huge exploded in here and shattered a good portion of it, exposing all the passages and rooms that were built alongside.*

"This place is endless," Constantine grumbled as I led the party across a massive chunk of stone that had fallen from the ceiling above, somehow managing to remain in one piece when it landed.

"We've travelled less distance than you think," Lazarus said to the rogue. "We're crossing from one side of the tunnel to the other more often than not; I'd be surprised if we've moved more than a hundred feet forward."

"Ugh," the rogue grunted dramatically. "If there's a dead end at the end of this, I'm just going to throw myself into the abyss, rather than backtrack the way we just came."

"If you did that, then you'd have to come back down here and get your Soul Fragment anyway," Lazarus pointed out.

"Oh, right," Constantine replied dejectedly. "I'll get Drace to carry me then."

"To the edge of the ledge before tossing you off?" the warrior asked, clearly enthused by the idea. "I'm on board for that. In fact, I can do that right now if you'd like. I'm sure I can get you some great airtime before you fall onto all the sharp and pointy rocks down there…"

"Hey, Lyr, need some help up the front there?" Constantine's mood suddenly changed as several rushed footsteps echoed out from behind me.

"I think I'm doing okay, actually," I said with a smile, looking back towards the group and seeing Constantine rushing forward to catch up with me.

"Okay, no problem," Constantine replied, glancing behind him nervously, the motion causing a laugh from both Drace and Lazarus to filter forward. "I'm going to be right here though if you need anything."

"Sure," I said with a chuckle as I turned my attention back towards the path ahead of me, seeing that the large stone piece that we were currently walking on took us very close to the wall which had what appeared to be a large chunk missing from it. Angling our approach to investigate the damage, I hoped that I would find another stable platform of some sort that we could drop down onto and keep moving forward.

What I found, however, was something immeasurably better.

"There's a fissure in the wall that looks like it leads down," I told the group, having taken one glance at the sight below then turned around to fill everyone in. "We have about a ten-foot drop downwards onto what I assume used to be a hallway, which we can use to get closer to the hole. I can't quite make out what's inside it from this angle, but it definitely looks like it goes somewhere."

"Well, I'm ready to get out of this tunnel," Constantine said enthusiastically. "Let's go."

"Hang on," Sierra stated, motioning towards the rest of the area. "Do we have any other options before we throw ourselves into a hole? Climbing back up is always a pain, or may simply not be possible."

"Pretty much all our options are to go down at this point," I replied, stepping sideways to look out into the tunnel and motioning towards a very large collapse that had blocked the entire left side of the chamber ahead of us, realizing halfway through the gesture that Caius and Lazarus were the only party members that had the ability to the see in the dark.

"The entire left side of the tunnel is completely caved in," I explained, recovering from my mistake. "We'd have to drop down to the hallway below us anyway, then find a way to drop down even further before circling around all the fallen debris assuming we could at all."

"So basically, our choice boils down to jump down blindly into a hole that could be a dead end, or jump down blindly into a sharp pile of rocks," Drace summarized.

"Pretty much," I agreed. "Though to be fair, whatever is on the other end of the hole could also be filled with sharp rocks."

"A risk I'm willing to let you take for me," Sierra replied, letting a smile creep across her face as she looked around to the group. "All in favor of Lyrian jumping into the hole first?"

"Aye," the party echoed without missing a beat, including Amaranth's belated mental voice. *<Aye.>*

"Everyone else, I get. But why you?" I looked at the cat, puzzled at how quickly this had turned from me finding a route out of the tunnel, to everyone deciding I should be the first one down it.

<In order to bond fully with the pack, I must be seen as siding with them on occasion,> Amaranth replied. *<That, and even a blind kitten knows not to leap where they cannot see the ground.>*

"Traitors, all of you," I announced with a grimace, hearing everyone laugh as I turned away from the group and began to move towards the edge.

"Let's get this over with."

Chapter 38

"Ugh, Lyr!" Sierra exclaimed as she limped across the room angrily, her eyes staring daggers into mine. "You said that it was 'just a short drop with nothing to worry about'! I nearly broke both my ankles landing!"

"Actually, I think Lyrian added 'if you're careful' to the end of that sentence," Constantine chimed in with a chuckle. "Besides, Amaranth and I landed fine."

"Only because Amaranth is a giant fucking cat," Halcyon seethed through his teeth as he sat on the ground, clutching at one of his shins. "And you have a skill that specifically reduces falling damage."

"Psh, even without *Acrobatics* I would have been fine with that landing. Right, Lyr?" Constantine asked, looking over towards me with a wide smile. "It wasn't so bad."

"N-not at all," I replied to the rogue stoically as I leaned heavily against the wall with a bored expression on my face, doing my best to hide the fact that I too had badly sprained one of my ankles after I had lowered myself down through the hole and landed badly on the giant pile of rubble directly under it. "Piece of cake."

"*Sure, it was,*" Sierra commented grumpily as she took a seat on a large stone, breathing out in relief as the weight left her feet. "If that's true, why don't you put that left leg of yours on the ground and stand up straight?"

"Because if I stand like this," I replied, indicating my current pose and then waved the entire party ahead of me. "I can enjoy all of your misery at once without having to turn my head."

"Very funny, Lyr," she commented just as Alistair tapped her on the shoulder with a healing touch, causing her face to shift in relief. "Thanks, Alistair."

"No problem," Alistair said nonchalantly as he continued to work his way around the party, pausing briefly to lend a healing touch to those who needed it. "I'll send you all my bill at the end of the day. Healthcare isn't free you know."

"Shhh," Constantine waved a hand in Alistair's direction. "Healbots just worry about healing, not things like talking or getting paid."

"Or healing rogues," the priest replied, completely deadpan while giving Constantine a meaningful stare as a chorus of laughs echoed from the party.

"Everyone ready to get moving again?" I asked, finally able to put weight back on my injured foot as the last bits of pain faded away. "This passageway here looks like it follows the tunnel we just left and is completely straight from what I can see. No more debris hopping for us."

"Thank god for that," Lazarus stated, taking an eager step forward as several people echoed the man's sentiments.

"That and it also happens to be our only way out of...whatever this room once was," Caius added, glancing around at what must have once been a substantially large chamber, but had been badly damaged, leaving it almost filled with rubble.

"Well, yeah, that too," I agreed before turning around and motioning everyone to follow me as I set off down the passageway.

Leaving the ruined chamber, I set a brisk pace as I led the group forward, mindful of the fact that Freya and her group were still ahead of us. Bounding up to my side before anyone else could, Amaranth joined me at the front of the group; his attention focused sharply forward.

<This is a much better path to travel,> Amaranth told me barely a minute after we had resumed our journey, during which we made more forward progress than we had during the entire trek through the tunnel. *<It is much easier on the paws.>*

<No kidding,> I replied to the cat as I stepped over a large chunk of stone that had been forced through the floor of the passageway. *<Hopefully—>*

<Wait.> Amaranth suddenly interrupted me, his body pausing midstride, forcing me and everyone else behind us to stop. *<I hear something.>*

"What's—" Drace began to ask before I silenced him with a gesture, holding a hand to my lips and pointed at Amaranth.

<What do you hear?> I queried my familiar, the cat having crouched down low to the ground and was now slowly stalking forward.

<Shouting…it is Freya's voice!> Amaranth replied, taking several more steps down the passageway, his ears visibly twitching. *<Along with what sounds like the thunder of magic! It is distant from us, but the noise carries well in here.>*

"Shit!" I cursed and glanced back towards the rest of the party, filling them in on what my familiar had just told me. "We have trouble ahead; Amaranth can hear Freya shouting, along with magic too."

"Damn," Drace replied, his expression tightening. "Think they ran into that security unit?"

"Either that or something else!" I answered as I spun to race down the chamber ahead. "We can't waste time; let's go!"

Breaking into a sprint, we all rushed down the passageway, the sounds of our feet and rustling armor echoing loudly in the enclosed space. But as we drew closer to the conflict ahead, the noise that we were making was occasionally drowned out by the sound of crunching stone and several more loud shouts that I identified as belonging to Helix, Abaddon and Thorne.

I hope we're not too late, I thought desperately as the passageway that we were running down abruptly shifted to the left before immediately correcting itself, forcing us to shed some of our precious speed in order to keep our balance. Rounding the bend, I leaped over a pile of debris that littered the ground and pushed off the wall with my free hand, using it to both steady myself and regain some of my lost momentum. Continuing my sprint onwards, a bright flash of crimson light suddenly filled the far end of the passageway, which I now saw opened up into a vast chamber ahead.   Heart in my throat, I put on a burst of speed, the passageway blurring past me as I ran, practically exploding into the room beyond.

And entering into chaos.

My first reaction after stepping out of the passageway was to boggle at the size of the chamber that we had just run into, my brain skipping a beat until I realized that we had just managed to rejoin the massive tunnel that we had been following earlier. But instead of being filled with debris, this portion of the tunnel appeared as if it had been turned into magma and then allowed to cool, leaving the ground and walls covered in a layer of porous rock. Taking several steps forward into the cavernous room, another flash of crimson light filled my vision a second before a deafening explosion thundered through the air, followed by a pained shout.

That's Freya's voice! I thought in a panic, recognizing the voice and immediately turning my head in its direction, only to have my eyes land on two brightly glowing shapes that belonged to a pair of Æther Crystals hovering in the air.

Spinning awkwardly and off balance, both of the Crystals appeared visibly damaged with large burns crossing their otherwise translucent faces. But just as I was about to look away from the almost overpowering aura of magic in search of the noise that I had heard, a large shadow stepped in front of one of the crystals. *Wait. What the hell is that?*

Slowing down in shock, I gaped at the towering creature, realizing in an instant that it was easily twice my height despite the distance between us. Blinking to make sure that I wasn't imagining the sight before me, everything around me fell away as I took in its appearance.

Made entirely out of a tarnished dark metal I couldn't identify, the creature bore a bipedal shape, complete with two arms and two legs. In one of its arms, I could see the shadow of an incredibly long greatsword that had clearly been designed for a being of its stature. Its other hand was pointed straight ahead of itself, focused on something that I couldn't see, a wicked array of claws flashing in the azure light emanating from the Æther Crystals as it opened its palm and shifted its arm ever so slightly.

Then it unleashed an intense blast of crimson energy.

"Holy shit!" I gasped in surprise as the cavern flared brightly with a crimson light once more, the subsequent explosive blast causing me to first flinch mid-step, then stagger as my foot caught a protruding piece of rock.

<What is that?> Amaranth's mental voice roared in my head, having effortlessly kept pace with me during our sprint.

<A golem!> I shouted back at the cat as I worked to keep my balance, refusing to take my eyes off what I had mentally pegged as being metallic construct, its tag appearing in my vision.

[Nafarrian Sentinel] – Elite Boss – Level 16

It survived after all, I grimaced, feeling my stomach twist as I finished recovering from my stumble, glancing briefly at the ground to check for more obstacles, then back towards the Sentinel, only to see it begin to gradually turn in my direction, having sensed either my curse or our mad dash into the chamber. *How the hell do we even—*

"Lyrian!" Freya's voice interrupted my thoughts as she suddenly came into view, crouched down as low as she could possibly manage from behind a fused pile of igneous rock. "*Get down! All of you, get down!*"

Not questioning the blonde warrior's words, I dropped down into my knees and angled my slide towards Freya, seeing Amaranth vanish out of the corner of my eye as he leaped in the opposite direction away from me. The second that I came to a stop, another flash of crimson light filled the cavernous chamber, only this time, it was much, *much*, closer than it had ever been before.

Stone shards slammed into me as the rock pile that I had slid behind exploded from under the Sentinel's attack, forcing me to shield my face from the flying projectiles. With barely enough time to process what had just happened, I felt Freya's iron grip grab onto my wrist and yank me forward.

"*Move!*" she shouted, using her superior strength to practically drag me behind her as she abandoned her old hiding spot and desperately searched for another. "The moment that…*thing* sees anything, it tries to blast it with its hand cannon, then comes to finish the job with its sword. Believe me; you don't want to get hit by it!"

"No kidding!" I called back to Freya, struggling to regain my balance with her pulling on me as she led the two of us behind another pile of volcanic rock then turned around to face me.

"What the hell took you guys so long to get here?" Freya demanded, staring at me with a wide-eyed expression, rivulets of both blood and water visibly dripping from her hairline. "We've been here for *ages* playing hide-and-seek!"

"We came as quickly as we could!" I replied defensively, despite knowing that anything I said would fall flat. Seeing the annoyed expression on her face, I attempted to shift the conversation, asking the first thing that came to mind, "Why are you soaking wet?"

"Because I fell into a fucking pool of water!" Freya snapped, shaking her head dismissively and causing a spray of droplets to fill the air. "That's not important right now! Right now, we need to figure out what the hell that thing is, and how we're going to kill it!"

"It's a Nafarrian security unit," I told Freya, wincing as yet another flare of crimson light flashed in the distance, followed by the familiar sound of exploding stone. Based on the sounds of moving feet, it seemed that the Sentinel was moving away from our hiding spot, giving Freya and me a chance to quickly exchange notes. "I made contact with some sort of Nafarrian security system in charge of this place, and it said that it was damaged and non-responsive."

"Does shooting exploding death beams look non-responsive?!" Freya shouted back before shaking her head and dismissing the question. "Did the security system have any suggestions of how to deal with the stupid thing at least?"

"Nothing helpful," I answered, drawing Splinter from its sheath. "So, it looks like we're back to the old tried, tested and true tactic that works when all else fails..."

"...keep hitting it until it stops moving," Freya finished, her face turning into a grimace. "I don't know, Lyr, in order to do that we're going to have to get in *close*."

"I don't see another option here, Freya," I said impatiently. "Either we risk getting chopped to pieces or turned to ash. Either way, the end result is going to be the same!"

"You're right," Freya replied with a sigh, visibly deflating. "With all of you here now we might just stand a chance."

"Here's to hoping," I said dryly, taking a moment to cast *Lesser Shielding* on myself, hoping that if I did get hit, either by the Sentinel's beam or its sword, that the slight boost to my armor and spell resistance would make a difference. "Is there anything in here that could help us maybe? I made contact with the security system upstairs…maybe I can do the same here?"

"I don't think so, Lyr," Freya shook her head to the negative as she readied her spear, having been holding it in her free hand all this time. "The only thing I've seen in here so far were the same two mana crystals you just saw."

"They look a little worse for wear," I said, remembering their burnt and scarred appearance.

"Do you think we can use them for something?" Freya queried while twisting in place and peering over the mound of rock that we had taken cover behind.

"In general, yeah, probably," I answered, hearing the loud crunching steps of the Sentinel slowly grow louder as it made its way around the room. "But for this fight? No clue. Let's just try and see if we can damage the thing first."

"Okay," Freya said, letting out a short breath as she ducked back into cover. "It's coming this way anyway. Any plan of approach?"

"Give me a few seconds head start," I told the woman, gripping Splinter's hilt as I prepared myself to charge the Nafarrian golem. "I'll hopefully catch his attention and try to dodge one of its blasts while you and any others get in close."

"Sounds good," she stated with a nod, meeting my eyes with a grim expression. "See you out there."

Giving Freya what I hoped was a reassuring grin as I left, I forced myself up onto my feet before I could reconsider the action and rushed around the pile of fused stone that we had been hiding behind, sending a quick mental message to Amaranth.

<Going to try charging the Sentinel!> I warned my familiar, hoping that he had managed to escape the blast that I had heard earlier as I worked myself up into a sprint, already seeing the construct in the process of turning around to face me.

<Is that wise?> Amaranth's voice came back, sounding unsurprised at my statement.

<Probably not,> I admitted to the cat, *<but it's the least worst option we have right now!>*

Shifting my attention away from Amaranth's mental sigh, I focused my attention back to the Sentinel, seeing it complete its turn, my eyes being drawn towards a glowing light on its chest.

Shaped like a massive breastplate, the first thing that I noticed was that the golem's midsection was covered in a thick layer of grey, crud-like filth, mixed with visible spots of rust and battle damage. Set into the center of its chest, was a large crystalline sphere that glowed with a faint azure light, pulsing ever so slightly in sync with the Sentinel's movements, almost as if it were some sort of magical heart.

Drawing my gaze upwards to the construct's head, I found myself staring into an unrecognizable and partially melted visage, whatever little details that remained obscured by more of the crud-like substance that covered its chest. All that was visible on the Sentinel's head was a single bright azure-hued eye that glowed brightly on the right side of its misshapen face.

An eye that I couldn't help but notice was focused solely on me.

Watch the arm carefully, Marc, I told myself as the Sentinel extended the limb forward towards me, letting the tip of the large sword in its other hand drag along the ground. *You might only get one shot at this, and you don't want to catch a face full of whatever exploding magic it's throwing.*

Time slowed down as I continued to rush towards the ancient construct, carefully watching its left hand open, revealing another crystalline sphere set in its palm, this one glowing with a bright crimson energy. With *True Sight* still active, I saw the energy stored within the crystal rapidly accumulate as the Sentinel readied its attack. Holding my breath as the light intensified, I carefully waited for the moment that signaled that the beam was on its way.

Then I *Blink Stepped*.

Having decided to pick a spot diagonally away from where I had been standing, I reappeared on the Sentinel's flank, just outside of its range, planting my foot hard on the ground as I adjusted my approach towards it, the sound of exploding stone barely registering in my ears as I ran. Even with my sudden change in position, I saw the golem's damaged head already beginning to shift towards me, with the rest of its body following suit a heartbeat behind.

Shit, this thing is fast! I cursed, surprised at the Sentinel's quick reaction time as the edge of its glowing heart came into view, my eyes fixating on it once more. *Wait, maybe I can use this!*

Going with the idea that had just fallen into my mind, I snapped my hand out and cast *Jump*, leaping into the air the moment that I felt my body weight fade with Splinter's tip thrust out before me. Timing the Sentinel's turn, I aimed the point of the sword directly at the crystalline sphere centered in its chest.

Landing almost dead center on the crystal, I felt my sword skip along its faceted face, carving a thin line across it and causing several small fragments to break free from the impact. Reacting instinctively as I began to fall back to the ground, I grabbed hold of the depression that the crystal heart was seated in with my free hand, feeling the crud covering the construct's body squish wetly underneath my fingers. Tightening my grip in an attempt to hold on, I glanced at an entry that had just appeared in my combat log, eager to see just how effective my attack had been.

You hit a [Nafarrian Sentinel] for 23 points of damage!

Well shit! That sucked! I thought bitterly after seeing such a low number despite the direct hit that I had managed to score. *But then again, maybe I shouldn't try and cut a crystal with a sword!*

Deciding to try something different while I still had the chance, I pulled myself upwards, hoping to slam the end of Splinter's hilt into the crystal as hard as I could, with the thought that the heavier and blunter end of the sword would be more effective against the hard crystal. Unfortunately, however, the Sentinel picked that exact moment to violently twist its body, causing my grip to slip free of the crud-covered handhold that I was holding onto and sending me falling to the ground.

Still aided by my *Jump* spell, I landed effortlessly, silently cursing my missed opportunity while forcing my thoughts to shift into survival mode, knowing deep in my gut that an attack by the Sentinel was only seconds behind. Making a split-second decision, I rushed in even closer to the Nafarrian machine, figuring that the risk of being kicked or stepped on was a much more manageable one to take, especially considering that every other option before me included dodging a massive sword or a magical beam, if not both at the same time. No sooner did I start moving than a metallic crash echoed from behind me as something heavy slammed the ground, no doubt being the very sword I was trying to avoid.

<We are coming!> Amaranth's voice entered my mind as I ran past the Sentinel's leg, uselessly slashing Splinter against it to no visible effect. *<Distract it for a moment longer!>*

<That's easy for you to say!> I called back to my familiar, just as the construct kicked out towards me with a crud-encrusted leg, forcing me to throw my body blindly to the side in a desperate attempt to evade the attack. *<You're not—>*

A brutal impact from behind cut off the rest of my thought, followed by an explosion of pain as I felt my feet leave the ground. Gasping for air, I saw everything around me blur as I sailed past one of the Æther Crystals, then landed on the ground in a heap a short distance away from it, a flashing alert in my combat log screaming for my attention.

A [Nafarrian Sentinel] hits you with [Haymaker] for 312 points of damage!

"*Ugh,*" I groaned, lying on the ground in agony as I tried to twist an arm around to clench at my back where the blow had landed, dimly aware of the fact that I couldn't move my other arm. "*That hurt...*"

Lying on the ground wheezing from the blow, I slowly collected myself, forcing myself back into reality as the sound of rushing footsteps caused me to pull my eyes off the ground and look in the direction of the noise. Running towards me at full speed, were both Theia and Zethus with a familiar shambling shadow following the latter lizardman close behind.

"Lyrian!" Theia shouted as she saw me glance up at her. "Are you okay?"

"Got blindsided," I replied, wincing in pain as I twisted to get a better look at whatever was following Zethus, my eyes widening when I recognized it to be a near identical Revenant to the ones that we had fought at the ruin's entrance. "Hey, behind you!"

"It's fine, Lyrian," Zethus said quickly, seeing where my attention was focused. "I'm controlling it as one of my minions."

"Oh," I stated, exhaling sharply as Theia sent a wave of healing energy into my shoulder. "I've never seen you do that before."

"It's the first time," Zethus said with a shrug. "I haven't been able to find any creatures worth raising until now."

"We can talk about that later!" Theia exclaimed as she continued to mend the muscle and bone that had been damaged in the Sentinel's attack. "Right now, the others need our help in dealing with the Sentinel!"

"How are they doing?" I asked, unable to see what was happening behind me while lying on my stomach.

"Looks to be touch and go," Zethus answered nervously. "But at least it's no longer shooting those beams."

"It probably won't, unless there's no one in melee range," I theorized as Theia finally finished her work and the last of the pain faded. Pushing myself up off the ground, I stood and turned to look back towards the battle, seeing that it had shifted away from the two Æther Crystals.

In the short time that I had been knocked away from the fight, both parties had managed to emerge out of hiding and were in the process of surrounding the Nafarrian Sentinel, the ranged members of the group immediately letting their spells and arrows fly as the more melee-oriented members rushed to close with the construct.

This looks like some of the raids I've run in other games, I thought as I briefly took in the sight, unable to help but notice just how much larger the Sentinel was than the rest of us. *But then again, so were the snakes we fought last week.*

"Alright," I stated, bending down to pick up Splinter from where I had dropped it. "Let's get back to it."

"We'll link up with some of the ranged," Theia told me as we all began to move. "Try not to get hit again!"

"I'll *try*," I told the lizardwoman just before we all split up to go our separate ways, save for Zethus's minion who remained by my side as I ran to rejoin the fight. "But no promises there!"

Now, how the hell can we bring this thing down? I thought as I turned away from the pair and ran towards the Sentinel, watching a wave of magical fire from one of the spellcasters splash against the golem's body and bathe it in intense heat. The flames raged for several seconds on the construct's side, but when they finally vanished I saw that it had only managed to burn off a layer of the filth that had covered the spot earlier, revealing a section of pitted and rusted metal. *Damn! What is all that crap it's covered in?*

Grimacing at the sight before me, I came to a stop just outside of melee range a short distance away from the two Æther Crystals as the Sentinel swung its massive sword through the air just in front of me, causing both Freya and Thorne to leap backward towards me in an attempt to move out of the blade's path.

"Lyrian!" Thorne exclaimed, casting one quick glance in my direction before focusing his attention back onto the Sentinel as it continued to sweep its sword in a circle around its body, forcing everyone clustered around it to either retreat, or take their risks by rushing inside its guard. "We saw you get hit!"

"Theia healed me," I replied, watching Zethus's minion recklessly charge towards the golem with single-minded determination, only to get sliced completely in half as it practically ran straight into the Sentinel's sword, which had come by for a second pass. "How are we doing?"

"*Poorly*," Freya grunted, her eyes glancing at Zethus's dead minion before darting back to the Sentinel as it completed its turn and immediately swung its sword out towards Drace, who was nearly knocked off his feet as he caught the weapon on his new shield and deflected it away from his body. "Right now, we're going to try and take it down at the knees. I have no idea what that grey stuff that's growing on it is, but it looks like it's slowly eating its way through the metal—"

"Heads up!" Thorne barked at Freya and me, urgently motioning towards Lazarus who had leaped inside the Sentinel's guard and landed a punishing blow to the side of its knee, visibly deforming the filth covered armor surrounding the joint. "Get ready to rush it! Focus on the same spot he just hit!"

As soon as the words were out of Thorne's mouth, the Sentinel twisted its attention away from Drace and took a large step sideways, bringing its sword down to bear in one smooth motion on the spot Lazarus had just been occupying. I had just enough time to see the half-giant's head appear as he completed his roll, now behind the turning golem, before Freya and Thorne charged forward.

"Lyr, let's go!" Freya shouted, pausing just long enough for Thorne to take the lead before rushing to follow him. "Hit it hard then pass through the other side!"

"Wha-?" The question was half out of my mouth before I shoved it aside and charged after the pair, trusting that they had a better sense of the Sentinel's tactics than I did at the moment.

Turning its back towards us, the Nafarrian golem twisted as it searched for Lazarus, who continued moving from where I had seen him and was now running back out of melee range on its opposite side. Focused on searching for the elusive half-giant, the Sentinel was caught completely by surprise as Thorne slammed his heavy mace into its knee, targeting the exact same spot that Lazarus had just hit a few seconds earlier.

The loud ring of metal on metal filled the air as the golem's already weakened armor crumpled and rent apart, revealing a finger-sized hole in the filth-covered metal that protected its knee. With his attack spent, Thorne continued past the construct, slowing only to rush around its leg as he made for the edge of its reach and out of harm's way.

Less than a second afterward, it was Freya's turn, her long spear arriving long before her body did, its point driving deep into the wound and widening it as she put her entire weight behind the attack. Once again, metal groaned in protest as her spear touched something delicate housed within the Sentinel's knee, causing a strange grinding noise to briefly hiss out before she was forced to pull her weapon free and continue onwards on Thorne's heels.

Then, trailing several steps behind Freya, I finally arrived.

With the hard work already done for me, I didn't hesitate in thrusting Splinter into the now large gash on the side of the Sentinel's knee, the blade crackling with a stored *Shocking Touch*. Passing through the shorn metal with ease, I put all my momentum into the attack, feeling the Æthertouched sword bite into something hard within the construct's joint. Immediately, the sword jerked in my hand as the same grinding noise that I had heard earlier returned, only this time much louder and vicious. Gripping the now vibrating hilt of my weapon tightly, I discharged the electricity stored within, causing the Sentinel to shudder mid-step as the entire leg seized and its balance shifted precariously.

Well, that finally did something! I exclaimed mentally, feeling the vibrations suddenly intensify as Splinter began to violently shake in my grip. In a heartbeat, my triumph for damaging the construct was replaced with the desperate need to pull my weapon free of whatever it was caught in, lest I end up with a broken sword. Unfortunately, before I could do anything to pull Splinter free, the Sentinel's balance finally failed, and it stumbled forward, the movement causing the blade to wrench free of my hand.

"Shit!" I cursed, half in panic at losing my sword and half at the prospect of being crushed, unable to help; only able to instinctively flinch as the golem's body nearly came crashing down on top of me before it awkwardly caught itself by falling to one knee and planting both of its hands on the ground in front of it.

That was too close! I thought as I stared at the now semi-prone golem before me, its wounded leg stretched straight out behind it with Splinter's hilt protruding from the side of its knee. Reacting instinctively, I rushed forward to grab my weapon again, intent on pulling it free before it could break. Grabbing hold of the hilt, I looked back up at the prone construct, my brain finally catching up to the moment and sending a spark of a realization through my mind.

We can all finally reach it now! My eyes widened, seeing that the bulk of its body was now easily within melee range, giving everyone a chance to attack the Sentinel without needing to worry about its sword or taking turns striking at its legs.

"Hit it while it's down!" I shouted out to the group, as I added my free hand onto Splinter's hilt in an attempt to hold it steady, the grinding noise from the limb increasing in pitch with every second that passed. Hoping to take advantage of the golem's prone position, I attempted to drain mana from it, but found that there was nothing at all to absorb, likely because I wasn't in direct contact with the crystal powering it. "Try hitting the crystal in its chest with something heavy!"

Even before the words were fully out of my mouth, I noticed that some of the guild members were already moving to take advantage of the Sentinel's vulnerability as I caught sight of Myr and Cadmus rushing in behind me, the pair's attention focused on the golem's opposite flank. Just as they vanished out of the corner of my eye, a flash of azure fur appeared in front of me as Amaranth suddenly rushed into view on the opposite side of the Sentinel's leg, his mental voice greeting me a heartbeat afterward.

<You have crippled the metal creature!> he announced, jumping onto the back of the Sentinel's leg, his weight causing it to strain.

<Temporarily!> I told the cat while trying to twist Splinter free yet finding it impossible to budge. Given our advantage at the moment, I didn't want to completely pull the blade free of the joint and give the Sentinel the ability to regain its feet, but if I couldn't at least loosen it a little bit while I still had the chance, I knew I wouldn't be able to for the rest of the fight, if at all. *<But my sword is stuck in it! I can't get it out!>*

<Then we will tear it out!> Amaranth replied, a savage snarl echoing out from his maw as he bit down into the armor that covered the construct's knee, his large teeth flashing inches away from my face as they pierced through the filth covered metal. *<It may not be as soft as flesh, but my teeth work on it just the same!>*

Feeling a surge of surprise shoot through me as I watched my familiar snap his head to the side, twisting the already weakened metal, until I had a near perfect look at the inner workings of the Sentinel's knee, noticing that whatever the substance was that covered the outside of the construct, also covered everything inside of it.

That's why I can't pull Splinter out! I realized, temporarily dismissing the presence of the grey crud after seeing that I had managed to jam my sword through the center of the Sentinel's mechanical knee, which had closed from its original open position, trapping the blade in between.

<I need you to jump up and down on the knee!> I told Amaranth, just as a burst of magic flared out from the front of the Sentinel, followed by several loud shouts. I had no idea what was going on from my vantage point, but I knew that it was past time that I rejoined the fight. <I should be able to get my blade free if you can get it to bend!>

Not bothering to question my thinking, Amaranth did exactly what I asked of him, the azure-furred cat leaping high into the air off the Sentinel's leg, before coming down directly on top of the knee, causing it to sag, and by extension forcing the joint to open ever so slightly. With a sharp yank, I managed to pull Splinter out a few inches as the joint opened and before it caught a second time.

<*Again!*> I called to my familiar, the endless sound of metal on metal and the thunder of magic intensifying with each second that passed. <*We're almost there!*>

Once more, Amaranth leaped into the air and came down heavily onto the Sentinel's leg, causing it to bend even further than it had before, allowing me to pull Splinter free of its prison.

"Yes!" I exclaimed in relief as the blade came free and I took a staggering step away from the Sentinel, unable to keep myself from checking the sword for any sign of damage. Seeing only the faintest of markings on the

Æthertouched weapon, I turned my attention back towards Amaranth, whose voice rang out in my head.

<It is beginning to rise!> my familiar shouted urgently as the Sentinel began to regain its senses and shift its weight backward onto its undamaged knee in preparation to stand up again, the movement also allowing it to free its hands.

"Damn!" I swore, taking in the sight at a glance and then lunging forward, thrusting Splinter back into the wound that Amaranth had managed to rend open, this time aiming the edge of my weapon at a spot where a metal piston joined to the side of the Sentinel's knee.

Guiding the Æthertouched blade towards a crud-covered bolt that anchored the piston in place, I felt it bite deep into the weakened metal, prompting me to thrust down at it for a second time with all the force that I could put behind it. Unable to stand up to the assault, the rusted bolt split in two, immediately causing the attached piston to hang loosely.

"I think that's the best we're going to do!" I said, seeing Amaranth leap off the leg as the Sentinel pulled it forward as it prepared itself to stand. Motioning at the cat to follow me, I backed away from the moving leg, intent on seeing how the rest of the party was faring, when without warning, a bright surge of azure light erupted from the front of the Sentinel.

"*Shit! Look out!*" I heard Freya's voice boom through the air as I shielded my eyes from the sudden brightness, several other panicked shouts echoing out in sympathy. "Constantine, move!"

"Oh, fu—" the rogue started to shout in response, before being cut off with a sudden finality as a thunderclap of magic erupted in front of the golem and Constantine's presence vanished from Party Sense.

Ending as abruptly as it began, the bright azure light faded, allowing me to pull my hand away from my face just in time to see a scorched and singed Freya tumble out from in between the Sentinel's legs before landing on the ground directly before me, her armor smoking from whatever attack the construct had just unleashed.

"What the hell just happened?!" I demanded, grabbing Freya by the collar of her armor and yanking her backward as the Sentinel pushed itself up off the ground, its foot coming down right in the spot that she had just been lying in.

"It shot a beam from its chest!" she replied, grabbing onto my arm and pulling herself back onto her feet, immediately motioning for us to get away from the construct. "I don't know what the hell that crystal is, but it sure as shit isn't a weak point!"

"Damn," I grunted as the three of us rushed out of the Sentinel's range, casting a single glance over my shoulder to see that it had regained its feet, but was visibly favoring its left leg. "I think I managed to break something in its leg at least!"

"I'll take whatever small victories we can get at this point," Freya said with a sigh as we reached what we hoped was the edge of the Sentinel's reach and turned to face the construct warily, forced to squint our eyes due to the brightness of the two Æther Crystals now almost directly across from us.

Standing at an angle to take the weight off its bad leg, I could see that the Sentinel had taken a fair amount of damage in the brief time it had been within reach. Several new gashes now adorned the metal across its chest and body, including countless more burns and scars marking the spots where spells had landed. But, despite all our efforts, it didn't seem like anything critical had been hit, leaving me wondering if we would be forced to reduce the Sentinel to scrap in order to kill it.

I guess a certain amount of resilience would be important when designing a security unit, I allowed grimly, watching the Sentinel swing its sword at Cadmus as the lizardman belatedly leaped off the construct and threw himself forward into a desperate roll to avoid the sweeping blade.

"So, any ideas how to handle this now?" I asked Freya, watching the Sentinel plant its foot unsteadily on the ground as its attack just barely missed Cadmus, the leg that I had damaged hindering its movement.

"Hit the other leg?" Freya suggested as the spellcasters finally resumed their onslaught on the golem, their spells flying through the air and splashing across its tarnished metal shell, causing the construct to shift its head in their direction. "Maybe we should try and target the—"

A flash of crimson light caused Freya's words to die in her throat as the golem's arm snapped out in one smooth motion, pointing itself in the direction of the ranged attackers and unleashing a searing beam of magic. Almost instantly, the waves of magic pouring out from the ranged attackers stopped as a thunderous explosion echoed through the chamber, causing all of us to flinch in surprise at the Sentinel's unexpected change in tactics.

"Shit, it's shooting beams again!" Freya exclaimed, grabbing me by the arm as the Sentinel shifted its arm towards the rest of us scattered around it and unleashed another blast of energy. "We need to get behind cover!"

Spinning on our heels, the three of us turned and sprinted away from the Sentinel as several more explosions erupted around us, filling the large and cavernous room with a deafening echo and causing the ground to shake beneath our feet. Diving behind a large pile of stone, the three of us barely managed to avoid being struck directly by the beam, instead only suffering a punishing hail of stone as countless fragments slammed into us, some even managing to pierce through our armor.

"Ugh!" I growled in pain, grabbing a particularly large shard of stone that had managed to embed itself into my side and yanking it free. "If this thing doesn't kill us outright, it definitely will when it brings this whole place crashing down on us!"

"No kidding," Freya replied wearily while holding her hand against the side of her face, blood dripping down from under it.

<The metallic creature is moving,> Amaranth told me from his crouched position in front of me, his ears twitching as they shifted through the reverberating noise still echoing through the chamber. *<...but away from us.>*

"Huh?" I grunted at the cat's statement, my mind shifting off the countless aches and bruises that the flying rocks had inflicted on my body. <Why would it do that?>

<I know not,> Amaranth replied, slowly crawling forward to peer around the stone that we had taken cover behind. *<It is approaching the glowing crystals.>*

"The Æther Crystals?" I repeated, twisting from my seated position to peer over the stone myself. "What does it want with them?"

Spotting the construct, I saw that the Sentinel had indeed broken away from us after unleashing its barrage of attacks and had taken several long strides towards the two Æther Crystals, having gone as far as to turn its back completely towards us as it moved. Frowning at the sight, I felt a sense of worry bloom in my chest as I considered our options. Given our experiences so far, anything interacting with the Æther Crystals was a cause for concern.

And I was confident that this time would be no exception.

"We need to stop it," I said, glancing over at Freya as she twisted around to join me, the two of us watching the Sentinel step right in between the two Æther Crystals and drop its sword to the ground before raising its hands to grab each crystal, stopping them both from their spin. "I don't know what it's doing, but it can't be any good for us!"

Pushing myself back up to my feet, I ran out of our hiding spot, keeping my attention focused solely on the Sentinel as the already thick aura of magic that hung around both of the Æther Crystals intensified and became almost painful for me to look at with my *True Sight* ability active. With every second that passed, I could see the magic before me gradually become more and more substantial as the Sentinel began to somehow draw on the energy stored in two Æther Crystals that it was touching.

"I have a bad feeling about this, Lyr!" Freya exclaimed as the three of us ran forward, seeing an orb of shimmering magic form around the Sentinel and the Æther Crystals. "That looks like a Force Shield!"

"It is!" I confirmed for her, seeing the dome of magic before us solidify in my enhanced vision, making the Sentinel appear to me as a ghostly silhouette within an orb of azure light. "But why does it need—"

A large ball of azure energy burst free from the well of magic that the Sentinel had fashioned around itself, causing my words to die in my throat as Freya, Amaranth and I ground to a halt, surprised by the floating orb.

"What is that?!" Freya exclaimed as a second identical ball of magic emerged from the dome that the Sentinel had cast around itself, followed closely behind by a third, then a fourth. "Uh, *Lyrian...*"

"I have no idea," I replied, staring at the four beachball-sized orbs of magic as they all came to a stop for a brief moment, then slowly began to glide towards us, gradually picking up speed as they moved. "But I'm going to guess not good for us!"

Taking a step backward from the advancing orbs, I couldn't help but notice that another two had emerged from the Sentinel's dome, making me wonder just what exactly we were supposed to do at this stage in the encounter. This had been by far the most difficult boss fight that we had experienced in Ascend Online, and I couldn't help but begin to feel overwhelmed at how the fight was playing out.

The kid gloves are clearly off now, Marc, a pessimistic voice in my head said to me as the three of us continued to backpedal away from the orbs of magic, each of them appearing to have fixated themselves on one of us, with me being the odd one out and having attracted the attention of two of the four. *This is the part where the game finally tests you to see if you've been paying attention the whole time.*

"I think we need to split up," I said quickly, forcing the voice in my head to be quiet while I tried to come up with a plan. "It looks like each of those orbs is going to slowly get faster and faster until they finally catch up to us."

"I think you're right," Freya agreed, before jabbing her spear in the direction of the Sentinel. "But what are we supposed to do now? Just endlessly outrun them? The way that thing is spawning orbs, we're going to get overrun in no time!"

"I haven't thought that far ahead, to be honest!" I replied, watching the four newest orbs begin to glide forward, having fixated on one of the other members of the guild elsewhere in the chamber. "My guess is that either we need to survive until the Sentinel drains those crystals dry and runs out of power, or we need to try and attack that shield and bring it down somehow!"

"That's going to be next to impossible with the way it keeps creating those orbs!" Freya stated while casting a glance at me. "Can't you do your mana absorbing thing and bypass the shield like you did during that fight with Mozter and his group? Then maybe you can force the Sentinel to stop casting more of them!"

"Shit; that's a good idea!" I replied, kicking myself for not having thought of the tactic myself, having been more focused on figuring out a way through the mechanics of the encounter, rather than ignoring them completely. "I'll give it a shot!"

"Good luck! I'm going to warn the others!" Freya shouted as both she and Amaranth split up, going off in their own direction away from me, the azure orbs that had targeted them gradually adjusting their course to follow.

It looks like the orbs are slow to change course, I observed, noticing that there was a slight delay from when Freya and Amaranth began moving and their two azure orbs shifting to follow them. *That might make it easier to dodge them if they get too close.*

Keeping that bit of information in mind, I stopped backpedaling away from the Sentinel's dome and began to circle around it, breaking into a slow jog as I considered my options. At the moment, there were already a dozen orbs of magic gliding through the air, yet from what I could tell, only two of them had fixated their attention on me.

Which shouldn't be too hard to avoid, especially since I can Blink Step out of the way if they get too close, I thought, watching them slowly angle themselves to follow me, while all of the other orbs continued onwards to the rest of the party. *But if I rush to approach the dome, I need to make sure that I don't accidentally run into another orb, or get too close to one that just spawned. With my luck, these*

*things might just decide to explode the moment they sense
something close to them, even if it isn't their target.*

Checking to see how closely the two orbs were following
me, I increased my pace and cut in closer towards the
dome, looking to shorten the distance between me and the
magical barrier once I finally cleared the path that all the
other orbs were following. My plan right now was to see if
I could get in close enough to the dome to touch it and see
if I could force my way through it while saving Blink Step in
case I needed to make a quick escape.

"Here goes nothing!" I exclaimed, taking in a deep breath
as I passed by the final cluster of orbs and angled myself
directly towards the barrier.

Switching my steady jog into an all-out sprint, I closed the
distance between me and the force dome, seeing several
more orbs emerge from within as I ran. Fortunately for me,
however, all of the new orbs of magic were far enough
away from me that I didn't have to adjust my angle of
approach. With my free arm outstretched, I thrust it into
the shimmering dome of force the moment that I came
close enough to do so, feeling a torrent of energy shoot up
my arm. But instead of passing through the dome of force
as I had expected to, I felt the shield under my hand bend
and deform as a veritable torrent of mana surged into my
body, making me feel as if I had tried to take a drink from a
firehose.

"Whoa!" I couldn't help but gasp under the sheer
quantity of energy surging before me as the Sentinel's force
dome absorbed all of my momentum and left me standing
in place with my hand slowly being pushed out of the slight
depression that I had managed to make.

I can't absorb enough of it fast enough! I thought, for the
first time realizing just how much power was surging
through the magical barrier before me. All I had managed

to do was slightly weaken a small portion of it, but it hadn't been anywhere close enough to allow me to break through it. Remembering that the two orbs were still hot on my tail, I glanced over my shoulder and spotted the pair speeding towards me at high speed. *Shit! I have to move!*

Reacting at the speed of thought, I picked a spot directly behind the two orbs and triggered *Blink Step*, my vision blurring out of focus as I teleported. Reappearing at the very edge of the range that I could manage, I heard a loud thunderclap of magic echo through the chamber, prompting me to immediately spin around and look back at where I had just been standing. Gone was any sign of the two orbs that had been chasing me, replaced with a large cloud of rapidly fading magic.

Those pack an even bigger punch than I was expecting, I thought, seeing the force dome ripple from the blast, the energy swirling through it appearing to grow slightly dimmer in my augmented vision, making my eyes widen in surprise. *Wait! That blast affected the barrier!*

Focusing my attention on the magic forming the dome, I watched it gradually regain its former intensity, the whole purpose of the encounter suddenly crystallizing in my mind. *We need to lead the orbs it spawns back into the barrier! If we can get enough of them to hit it at the same time, then maybe we can bring it down or weaken it enough so I can break through!*

"The only trick now is getting enough orbs following you and surviving long enough to lead them back to the barrier," I said to myself grimly, glancing around to see if there were any party members nearby, my eyes landing on three sprinting figures that happened to have seven orbs trailing closely behind them. Breaking into a run, I waved wildly at the trio, recognizing them as Lazarus, Halcyon and Drace as I got closer.

"Hey!" I shouted in between steps, seeing each of their heads swivel in my direction. "I need you guys to lead your orbs to the dome!"

"You need us to do what, Lyr?" Halcyon answered first, panting heavily as he ran.

"I need you to lead your orbs to the dome and cause them to crash into it!" I explained, falling in line with the trio. "It should either destroy the barrier or weaken it enough so I can get through it!"

"Are you sure that's going to work?" Lazarus asked, barely sounding winded from the run. "Getting close is one thing, but getting out..."

"It'll work!" I affirmed. "I just tested it with two orbs, but it wasn't nearly enough. I'm hoping the ones following you three will work."

"Lyr," Halcyon gasped. "I have *four* of these things gaining on me, and I'm already running as fast as I can! There's no way I'm going to make it all that way, let alone out!"

"Hal—" I began, in an attempt to reassure the mage but found myself interrupted by Drace.

"Don't worry, man; you'll make it." He grunted while glancing over at Lazarus with a meaningful look, who nodded and then shifted his positioning until he was a few steps behind Halcyon. "One way or another at least."

"Huh?" the mage grunted, his hand clutching at a stitch in his chest as he tried to look over his shoulder. "What is that supposed to mean?!"

The words were barely out of the man's mouth before Lazarus came rushing up from behind Halcyon at a full sprint, a palpable red aura hanging around him in my vision. Without breaking stride, he effortlessly scooped up the running mage in his arms with one smooth motion and threw him over his shoulder.

"*Heeeey! What are you doing?*" Halcyon yelled, sheer terror tinging his voice. "Stop! Put me down!"

"I'm sorry, Hal. I'm afraid we can't do that right now," Drace replied, a note of humor evident in his voice. "Just enjoy the ride, and maybe cast a Force Shield if it looks like we'll need it."

"Uh, wait, you're not going to—" Halcyon began to protest just as Lazarus's words cut him off.

"Quiet!" The half-giant barked with barely restrained rage, the aura around him flaring brightly. "We're going! Follow me!"

Without another word, Lazarus took off like a gunshot, pulling ahead of both Drace and I as he sprinted directly towards the dome.

"I hope this shit works, Lyr!" Drace shouted a heartbeat afterward as he too put on a burst of speed to keep up with the enraged half-giant.

"It will!" I told the warrior, simultaneously crossing my fingers where he couldn't see. "Just be ready for whatever happens afterward!"

"Yeah!" I heard Drace call back as I split away from him, mindful of the fact that I needed to arrive *after* the orbs trailing him impacted the dome, or be caught right in the middle of the blast that I was trying to cause.

Taking several steps away from the line that Drace and the others had been following, I slowed just enough for the seven rapidly accelerating orbs to fly past me, using the opportunity to check and see if any newer orbs had managed to lock onto me in the meantime. Thankful to see that nothing had targeted me, I turned my attention back towards the dome, just in time to see the first of the orbs slam into it.

Immediately, everything in front of me vanished in a bright azure light as orb after orb collided with the dome and subsequently vented their fury onto the magical barrier that the Sentinel had created, filling the air with a palpable haze of mana. Rushing in half-blind on the heels of the blast, I threw any semblance of caution to the wind and charged forward with my free hand outstretched once again, ready to try and break through the barrier for a second time.

Plunging my hand into the swirling maelstrom of energy, I once again felt a cool wave of energy shoot up my arm as I began to absorb the mana powering the dome. This time, instead of it resisting my attempts to push through it, it dissipated under my touch, the multitudes of impacts from the orbs having weakened it past the point of resistance, allowing me to pass straight through it as if I were parting a curtain.

It worked! I exclaimed mentally, feeling a surge of elation course through my body as I rapidly brought myself to a halt, gazing up at the Sentinel's back as it maintained its grip on the two Æther Crystals, completely oblivious to my presence. Casting a glance behind me out of reflex, I saw that the barrier behind me had already sealed and was rapidly regenerating in strength with every second that passed, effectively trapping me inside the dome with the Sentinel. Glancing around, and then up at the construct, I suddenly felt a surge of doubt shoot through me as I considered what to do next. *Well, I wanted badly to get in here, but what the hell am I supposed to do now?*

Staring at the Sentinel for several seconds as I considered the options before me, I weighed the prospects of trying to climb it, then stab it, in what I hoped would be a vulnerable location, such as the one remaining eye it had, or coming up with an alternative solution. Shifting my gaze off the construct and onto the Æther Crystal, I carefully inspected the object, noting once again that it was perfectly identical to the crystals that we had seen earlier in the ruins, right down to the rings encircling it.

The rings, I noted with excitement, recalling the metal fragments that we had recovered in the first chamber. *The rings are somehow important to the Æther Crystals. Maybe if I broke them…*

Decision made, I sprang into action, grabbing hold of Splinter with both hands as I crossed the short distance between the closest Æther Crystal and me. Timing my attack for when the two rings descended to the lowest point of the crystal, I lashed out with Splinter, chopping the Æthertouched blade into the ancient metal with all the strength I could manage.

Which in hindsight, I later recalled, had been completely unnecessary on my part.

Both of the rings shattered violently under the impact of my blade, exploding into countless metal shards as if they had been wrapped around a stick of dynamite. Pain flared as several of the ring's fragments sliced exposed skin, forcing me to take a step backward in reflex and belatedly shield my face. Before I could even begin to voice a curse at what had just happened, a loud cracking sound filled the air before me. Pulling my hand away from my eyes, I glanced up at the Æther Crystal that I had just tried to sabotage, my mouth falling open as millions of tiny cracks began to snake through it. Reacting quickly, the Sentinel took its hand off the Æther Crystal and twisted its head down to look towards me, the energy powering the dome fading drastically.

"Shit! Time to go!" I said to myself, tearing my gaze away from the Sentinel as it reached out towards me with its now free hand, prompting me to turn away from the rapidly destabilizing crystal and trigger *Blink Step*, reappearing right beside the other Æther Crystal with Splinter raised high in the air.

Without a second's hesitation, I slashed out with my sword once more, catching the two rings on the second Æther Crystal as it came into range. This time ready for the blast, I made sure to turn my face away as I connected with the rings, feeling them practically explode from the impact, several of the shards finding their way into my flesh. But despite the pain shooting through me, I couldn't help but smile as another loud crack filled the air, echoing in sympathy with its twin.

Almost instantly, the dome of magic surrounding me vanished, leaving me staring out into the cavernous chamber and at several orbs still floating through the air as they chased their respective targets. Twisting back to look over my shoulder as I forced myself to run away from the two now damaged Æther Crystals, I saw that each of them had violently begun to shatter, the energy stored within them roiling as it refused to be contained. Shifting my glance ever so slightly, I caught sight of the Sentinel still standing directly between the two Æther Crystals as it slowly turned on its bad leg in an attempt to see where I had gone.

Taking my eyes off the Sentinel, I put on a burst of speed as I tried to put as much space between me and the crystals as possible, having a strong suspicion about what was going to happen next. Sprinting as if my life depended on it, I put every iota of strength that I had into my legs, watching the cavern blur by.

Then without any warning at all, everything suddenly went white, followed by a massive wave of force that swept me off my feet. I felt myself soar through the air for a distance spinning wildly without control, before I crashed back into the ground heavily, sliding until I struck something hard. Stunned from the impact, I lay completely insensate for a time, until my brain finally finished rebooting itself, leaving me staring upwards into a now pitch-black chamber, seeing a single azure orb sail through the corner of my vision.

<Are you okay?> Amaranth's mental voice thundered into my mind, a moment before his face appeared above me.

<I'm a little rattled,> I replied, despite feeling my body screaming at me in pain as I sat up. *<But I think I'll be okay.>*

<Good!> Amaranth replied, gently grabbing my arm in his mouth and trying to pull me up onto my feet. *<You are still needed! The fight isn't over yet!>*

<What do you mean it's not over?> I asked the cat numbly, wincing as his teeth dug into my arm.

<The rest of the group is still battling the metallic creature!> Amaranth explained. *<We require a distraction!>*

<Wait. What?> I exclaimed, accepting Amaranth's help in standing up and scanning the chamber, my eyes landing on the incredibly damaged form of the Sentinel as it took a lumbering swing at Drace with its only remaining arm. *<I can't believe it's still alive!>*

<It is certainly resilient,> Amaranth agreed as the two of us ran forward one last time towards the Nafarrian construct, spotting Drace, Freya, Thorne, Cadmus, and Lazarus having formed a loose circle around it.

"Lyr! You're up!" Drace greeted wearily as the Sentinel drunkenly twisted to take a swing at Freya. "Great, we might just have a chance now."

"Is this all of us that are left?" I asked, checking Party Sense and suddenly realizing that Caius was no longer nearby and had respawned with Constantine back in Aldford.

"Pretty much," the warrior grunted. "Sierra, Myr, Abaddon and Halcyon are all down and seriously injured with Theia tending to them. All the others are dead."

"Shit," I replied, letting out a deep sigh before realizing that there was a name missing. "What about Alistair?"

"Bringing the last orb in for a final pass," Drace told me. "We're hoping to use it to take down the Sentinel, but we missed the last time. This is our last chance with it."

"Okay," I acknowledged, turning my head until I spotted Alistair's sprinting figure in the distance. "Just one more time."

Nodding in wordless reply, Drace, Amaranth and I took several steps forward towards the Sentinel joining the rest of the group in keeping it distracted. One by one we then took turns stepping in close to the Sentinel, getting in close enough for it to attempt a swing at us, only to back away from the damaged construct, and forcing it to shift its attention to the next person in line. Watching carefully out of the corner of my eye, I saw Alistair close the distance between us, the azure orb glowing brightly just over his shoulder as he approached.

We had purposefully timed our turning of the Sentinel so that its back would be facing Alistair when he arrived, random chance allowing it to be my turn to distract the construct when he finally made contact, giving me the perfect view as he ran straight in between its legs and dove to the side, a heartbeat before the closely following orb slammed into the back of the golem's leg. Detonating, the orb consumed itself in a magical conflagration of energy, going as far to blow the Sentinel's leg clean off its body and sending the mechanical goliath crashing down onto the ground.

Sensing a chance to finally put an end to the battle, we all surged forward with a primal roar and charged the fallen

Sentinel. The scream of metal drowning out our cry as we all began to chop, thrust, or smash our weapons into the construct, rending apart the armor that hid the delicate machinery within. With every attack that landed, the Sentinel's movements gradually began to slow, smoke and sparks billowing out from within.

But for all the damage that we had caused, it wasn't until Alistair, recovered from his desperate sprint, brought his axe down on the golem's melted head, splitting it nearly in two, that the Sentinel finally stopped moving, all signs of life fading away, prompting a set of rapid messages to appear in my vision.

Alistair has slain a [Nafarrian Sentinel]!
You gain Party Experience!
Congratulations! You have reached Level 15!
You have been awarded one Class Skill Point!

Chapter 39

"Well, I don't think I'm going to forget that fight anytime soon!" Thorne's voice echoed out through the cavern as we all struggled to catch our breath from the battle, watching the Sentinel's body dissipate into nothingness to be replaced by a large loot bag. "An old Nafarrian robot was the last thing I would have expected to find down here."

"Didn't the security system warn you?" I asked while exhaling in a controlled manner, hoping that by slowing my breathing I would be able to calm my still rapidly beating heart. Hitting level fifteen had done wonders in healing all the wounds that I had suffered during the battle, but now that the fighting was over, I had to find my own way of calming down.

"Not that I know of," Thorne replied with a shrug. "Ransom and Zethus were the only ones that made contact with it, and they didn't mention anything."

"Hrm," I grunted, matching the dwarf's shrug with one of my own before turning my head towards the sound of approaching footsteps.

"Please tell me the Sentinel is dead," Sierra called hopefully as she and the others who had been seriously wounded towards the end of the fight rejoined us.

"It's dead," Drace affirmed turning around to face the approaching group. "And from the looks of it, I think most of us just leveled up."

"About time too!" Halcyon agreed with excitement on his face, nearly everyone between the two parties nodding enthusiastically, save for Alistair and Lazarus.

"Still have another quarter to go," Lazarus commented wistfully.

"And I am literally twenty experience short of level fourteen," Alistair added with frustration. "So close…"

"Oh shit. We got a class skill point this level!" Thorne said suddenly, his demeanor shifting to one of all-out joy as his eyes glazed over while he focused on a menu in his vision. "I completely forgot about that!"

"That's right!" I said enthusiastically, seeing all the other surviving guild members do the same as the dwarf as they looked to see what they could spend their new skill point on.

Casting an understanding look at both Alistair and Lazarus, the pair shrugged at me in response before turning to walk towards the Sentinel's loot bag, content to busy themselves with looking through the spoils while the rest of us adjusted our character sheets. Not wanting to seem rude, but also eager to see what new abilities I had available to me, I waited until the pair began searching through the bag, then brought up my ability list, immediately seeing a prompt fill my vision.

You currently have 1 unspent Class Skill Point.

Please select an ability from the following list to learn:

Traits:

Improved Familiar Bond

Type: Trait, Class

Duration: Permanent

Trait Requirement: A bonded familiar with Relationship rank 'Loyal' or higher.

Description: As your relationship with your familiar improves, the connection that the two of you share deepens, giving you the ability to channel self-targeted spells across your bond and gaining enhanced insight to one another's senses when in close proximity.

Effect: When you and your familiar are within fifteen

feet of one another any spell that could previously only be cast on yourself, can now also be cast on your familiar. Furthermore, when within range you each subconsciously share in one another's senses, giving insight into what the other is experiencing.

Mana Devourer

Type: Trait, Special
Duration: Permanent
Trait Requirement: Die from the effects of Mana Void.
Description: You have experienced the depths of your body's hunger for mana firsthand as it consumed your flesh and blood, feeling something stir deep within you. Even now, recovered from your ordeal you can't quite shake the feeling that there is something just past your perception within you, something more that you could tap into...or allow to tap into you.
Effect: Unknown.

Spells:

Cone of Cold

Type: Spell, Class Skill
Duration: Instant
Arcane Tree: Evocation
Spell Mastery: Evocation - Level 9
Mana Cost: 140
Description: You unleash a blast of arctic wind before you, freezing and slowing any who are caught in its blast.
Effect: You instantly cast a wave of freezing energy centering from either your hand or mouth, dealing 80-120 cold damage to everything in front of you.

Shocking Touch II

Type: Spell, Class Skill
Duration: Instant
Arcane Tree: Evocation

Spell Mastery: Evocation - Level 19
Mana Cost: 170
Description: You charge your hand with electricity, discharging it through the first thing you touch.
Effect: You shock the next thing you touch for 55-95 points of Electricity Damage. This attack can be conducted through metallic weapons, items, and water.

Martial Arts:

Rend

Type: Martial Art, General Skill
Skill Requirement: Swords Level 14
Stamina Cost: 60
Description: Twisting your sword through the target's flesh, you leave behind a wicked gash that bleeds for a short period.
Effect: You inflict a bleeding wound on your target, dealing 25 damage every 2 seconds, for the next 8 seconds or until healed. This effect scales with your weapon.

Ambush

Type: Martial Art, General Skill
Skill Requirement: Stealth Level 9
Stamina Cost: 60
Description: Taking your target by surprise, you strike them in a vulnerable location before combat has begun.
Effect: You ambush an unaware target, dealing weapon damage+125. This ability can only be used against enemies who are not aware of you, nor are in combat.

Oh damn! I thought, unable to keep my eyes from widening as I read through the list of traits, spells, and abilities that I had available to me. *This is like level ten all over again!*

Shaking my head, I re-read the list a second time, trying to figure out what abilities I could live without for the time being, and what others I could maybe attempt to learn the old-fashioned way, through endless practice and training.

Assuming I could ever find enough time to devote to doing that, I couldn't help but think, letting out a low sigh as I began to eliminate choices from the selection. *I think I can eliminate Cone of Cold, Rend and Ambush out of hand. Cone of Cold just costs too much mana for the amount of damage it deals...and I don't have that multi-cast ability that Mozter had to augment it. As for Rend, it'd be really useful to have...but I don't think it stands out enough from the other options available.*

I guess the same thing goes for Ambush too. I continued, looking over the ability and realizing that I tended to favor direct melee combat over stealth. *Being able to one-shot an enemy out of hiding would be awesome, but it'll be useless once the fight begins, and more often than not, I find myself right in the thick of things...*

Which I guess leaves the last three options available to me, I scrolled the list in my vision until I was looking at the upgraded version of *Shocking Touch*. It was easily the most popular spell in my Spellbook and one that was responsible for a substantial portion of the damage I inflicted, something that would greatly increase with this newest rank. Yet I couldn't help but feel hesitant in taking it as an option, noticing that the spell mastery put it five levels above what my current Evocation skill was. *Which means that I'd fail at fifty percent of my casts until I manage to level Evocation high enough, and that would be a bit of a pain considering that I can't regenerate mana.*

Running a hand through my hair, I temporarily took my eyes off the skill list in front of me to look at the rest of the party, seeing the intense expressions on their faces as they too wrestled with their skill options.

Nothing puts the pressure on like spending a skill point, especially considering how rarely we get them, I thought grimly, turning my attention back towards the list hanging in my vision and to the two remaining traits that were available. *Now, I guess that just leaves Improved Familiar Bond and…Mana Devourer…which sounds worrying if nothing else.*

Pausing for a moment to read over the latter trait's description for the third time, I couldn't help but feel unsettled as I recalled my experience resurrecting in Aldford after the battle with Carver. I remembered feeling like there was something trapped inside of me that was actively trying to claw its way out, before it finally went dormant. It wasn't an experience that I ever wanted to relive again.

But the fact that a specific trait had appeared in response to what I had experienced couldn't help but make me curious. Was this an option for me to progress deeper into my Ætherwarped condition? Or was this something related to my contact with the Annulment Sphere? Or even a combination of the two? The lack of information made it difficult for me to gauge the risk of taking the trait, especially considering the fact that I wasn't quite enthusiastic about how it had already affected me.

What if it turns me into one of those ghouls full time? I thought, staring at the trait intently. *Even if I retained my sanity this time…how would that make me look? How would it change my playstyle? Would I regret the choice?*

But no matter how many times I asked those questions in my mind, an answer never appeared, causing my eyes to drift off the Mana Devourer trait and onto the last, or more aptly, first trait in the list: Improved Familiar Bond.

Amaranth and I are barely ever apart, I noted, glancing over the trait description once again while looking down at the azure-furred puma at my feet, who was busily grooming himself as he patiently waited for us to get moving again. *And if I'm reading this trait right, we'll be able to coordinate better between one another, and I'll be able to share my Lesser Shielding spell with him, which should help keep him safe in combat. I wish though that I had a few other spells that were more useful, if only I could give him the ability to Blink Step...*

I felt my heart skip a beat as I replayed my last thought a second time in my mind, causing me to stare numbly at the trait. *Wait a second...Blink Step is a self-targeted spell! That should actually work! Sure, I'd burn through my mana in no time flat if the two of us are Blink Stepping around, but it would give us both a huge amount of mobility and give Amaranth an escape option if he needed it!*

Feeling that I was close to making a decision, I looked once more at the Mana Devourer trait, unable to completely let go of the curiosity that I felt. *I guess it's possible that I'll have another chance to take the trait when I get my next skill point at level twenty and there's also that Class Challenge thing at level nineteen before it, whatever that entails...*

Satisfied that the best choice for me, at the moment, was to take Improved Familiar Bond, I mentally selected the trait and confirmed my choice, feeling my awareness of Amaranth and by extension, my surroundings grow even sharper. I could suddenly hear faint sounds of rustling that hadn't been audible just a few seconds earlier, along with the potent stench of the moldy smelling musk that we had smelled ever since we had entered the chamber.

Whoa, I thought, raising a hand to clench my head as I tried to sort out what I was experiencing, realizing that I wasn't in fact hearing or smelling everything around me, but that Amaranth was. *Is…is this what Amaranth is hearing and smelling down here? Is this what the trait meant by sharing our senses?*

<Something is…different,> the cat stated, interrupting my thoughts as he paused from his grooming efforts and turning his head to look at me, his azure eyes wide with surprise. <I can sense…more, somehow.>

<I can too,> I replied to Amaranth, unsure of how to explain what had just changed. <I think our bond between one another is growing stronger.>

<I agree,> he answered after a moment. <Before…the link we shared felt more distant, but now it feels closer somehow. I can sense what you hear, what you smell…almost as if it came from my own ears and nose.>

<That's the same for me,> I acknowledged, happy that Amaranth was taking the deepening of our bond in stride. <But I don't think that's all that we can do, I think I may even be able to share some of my magic with you now.>

<You can?> Amaranth asked curiously, standing up from his half-seated position. <What kind of magic?>

<My shield spell,> I replied. <And maybe my Blink Step too, but I'm not sure.>

<You think you could give me the ability to flit from place to place?> Amaranth's mental voice was suddenly filled with excitement as he took a step closer towards me. <What must I do to accept this magic?>

<Uh,> I hedged, taking a step back from the overeager cat, having expected for him to be a bit more hesitant for some reason. <Well, I'm not sure. We may have to experiment a bit.>

<Right now?> the Puma asked impatiently.

<Sure, we can try,> I said while preparing myself to cast *Blink Step* and hoping that I hadn't set Amaranth up for disappointment. He hadn't ever shown any interest in being able to 'flit from place to place' as he called it, but given how enthusiastic he was right now, I would hate to have to let him down. <Tell me if you feel anything.>

Preparing himself, Amaranth visibly tensed as I went through the mental steps involved in casting Blink Step but stopping just shy of actually triggering the spell, holding it fixed in my mind.

<Do you sense anything?> I asked, seeing the cat cock his head to the side.

<I do...> he replied, his mental voice sounding unsure. <Like there is something being held slightly out of reach...>

<How about now?> I asked, mentally trying to push the spell in his direction the same way that I did with my thoughts. <Can you—>

Before I could finish my words, Amaranth vanished from in front of me, followed seconds later by several very loud and surprised shouts.

"Whoa! Amaranth! Where did you come from?" I heard Freya exclaim.

"Shit! He just appeared out of nowhere!" Halcyon added with a yelp.

"Wait, was that just a Blink Step?!" Sierra asked, cluing in the fastest out of the three.

<It worked!> Amaranth's voice sounded overjoyed as I turned my head to see him now standing right in front of Freya, Halcyon, and Sierra a short distance away from me. Turning away from the surprised trio, the cat quickly padded his way back over to me, clearly excited as he moved. <The magic came close enough to grasp, and in an instant, I felt like I could go anywhere!>

<That's great, Amaranth!> I replied, flashing a grin towards the three party members as they all gave me a surprised look. *<You were able to choose where you wanted to step to without any problems?>*

<Once I held the magic, yes,> Amaranth said. *<Though it was a bit unsettling as I...changed places.>*

<It always is,> I sent to my familiar. *<But practice will help get past that.>*

"Sooo, Lyr," Halcyon said loudly as he, Freya and Sierra began to walk over to me, their eyes flitting from Amaranth then back to me. "Learn anything new with your level fifteen skill point?"

"Eh, nothing too exciting," I replied with a shrug. "Just a bit of a boost to the bond that Amaranth and I share."

"A boost that lets him Blink Step?" Freya asked, a smile evident in her voice.

"Well, that's one thing," I said. "But I can share pretty much any self-targeted spell with him now."

"Oh, wow!" Halcyon exclaimed. "That's pretty badass! So, things like Blink Step and Lesser Shielding then?"

"Those and *Jump* are the only self-targeted ones I have so far," I replied. "And I'm pretty sure that Shocking Touch doesn't fall under the 'self-targeted' category, as useful as that may be."

"I think a giant blink-stepping puma is going to be terrifying enough for people to handle," Sierra stated. "Having it also be electrified may be just a little too much to ask..."

"Considering that spiritual wolf that Carver had, maybe not," I said, recalling our last battle with the man. "That thing had a mana draining ability on top of being able to do something like Blink Step."

"I remember that," Freya commented, her eyes taking on a faraway look for a second before focusing back onto me.

"Maybe you'll have an option to develop more abilities later? I'm not sure what you all had as part of your skill choices, but mine were damn near overwhelming."

"Tell me about it," Halcyon grumbled. "I still haven't made up my mind..."

"Yeah, they definitely were." I nodded at Freya. "And you're right. There's no way of knowing what else we might have available to us when we get our next skill point."

"Or that class challenge thing at level nineteen," Sierra mentioned, voicing the same thought that I had a few minutes earlier. "We—"

"Hey, everyone!" Lazarus's voice called out, causing all of us to turn and look in his and Alistair's direction. "I know you're all having a great time enjoying spending your skill points without us. But Alistair and I would *really* like to get moving so we can hit the next level too. You mind if we sort out the loot?"

"Uh, sure," Halcyon replied as we all turned to face the pair standing over the Sentinel's loot bag. "But get moving to where? Aren't we...done?"

"Don't think so," Lazarus replied, motioning towards the far end of the chamber that vanished into the darkness. "The tunnel keeps going onwards, and we still haven't found the Ley Line. You know, the reason why we came down here in the first place."

"Should we keep going without the others though?" Drace asked, joining in on the conversation as we all walked towards Lazarus and Alistair. "We're down a third of the group, and I don't know about you, but I could use a bit of a break."

"I hear you," I replied. "But the others are going to have to make their way back down here anyway to pick up their Soul Fragments. We might as well push a bit further until they can get back down here - if only to make sure that the area is clear."

"Fair enough," Drace acknowledged before motioning at the bag that Lazarus was holding open. "What dropped?"

"A hell of a lot," he said, reaching into the bag and beginning to pull items out, their descriptions appearing in my vision as he handed them out. "Some of it immediately useful; some of it...not so much."

Nafarrian Sentinel's Æther Core

Item Class: Relic
Item Quality: Mastercraft (+20%)
Strength: +3 Agility: +3 Constitution: +3 Intelligence: +3
Willpower +3
Weight: 0.1 kg
Level: 16

Nafarrian Sentinel's Focus Crystal

Slot: Main Hand
Item Class: Relic
Item Quality: Mastercraft (+20%)
Damage: 25-55 (Arcane)
Intelligence: +7 Willpower +7
Durability: 120/120
Weight: 0.2 kg
Class: Any Arcane
Level: 16

Nafarrian Sentinel's Iron Gauntlets

Slot: Main Hand and Off Hand
Item Class: Relic
Item Quality: Mastercraft (+20%)
Damage: 25-45 (Crushing)
Strength: +7 Agility +7
Durability: 160/160
Weight: 1 kg
Class: Any Martial

Level: 16
Filth-covered Iron Scrap
  Quantity: 200
  Item Class: Relic
  Item Quality: Mastercraft (+20%)
  Weight: 1 kg

"Damn, this is a ton of metal!" Drace exclaimed after the last item had been pulled free of the bag. "It won't be enough by a long shot to fill what we need for Aldford, but it'll help tide us over a bit longer and keep us from needing to use that Æthertouched Iron."

"Yeah, Léandre is going to love this stuff," I replied, wiping my finger through the filth coating the iron. "We're going to have to give it a really good clean though. I don't know what this crap all over it is, but it's everywhere."

"Looks like a mold to me," Drace said, inspecting a fragment in his hand. "Kinda smells faintly like that musk hanging in the air. Based on the pitting on the metal, I think it might have been slowly eating it."

"Think that'll post a problem with our gear?" I asked, checking to see if I had managed to get any of the pasty substance onto my chainmail.

"Dunno," Drace answered with a shrug, sounding unconcerned. "The Sentinel was completely covered in it and look at the punishment that it stood up to. It probably took centuries for the mold to make the progress that it did."

"Maybe," I said, not completely convinced. "We should quarantine it just in case, then burn all this stuff off it before letting it loose in Aldford."

"Yeah, that's probably a good idea," the big man agreed, putting the piece of scrap he was holding in his pocket, then turning back towards the group. "Anyone have any claims yet?"

"I do," Cadmus replied, holding the pair of heavy gauntlets in his hand. "These are a huge upgrade for me, at least twice as good as my current gloves."

"Then they're yours," I said, nodding towards the Lizardman, who immediately stripped off his existing gloves and put on the oversized gauntlets. "Anyone else?"

"Since all the other casters are dead, I'll take the Focus Crystal for now," Halcyon answered, holding the crystal that had been embedded into the Sentinel's palm for everyone to see. "I may need some help in attaching it to something, but this would make a great wand. The four of us can sort out who gets it after we get back."

"I think Drace or I could help you out with that," I told the mage with a nod, appreciating the fact that he hadn't forgotten about the other casters.

"Well, that was easy enough," Freya said, holding up the Sentinel's Æther Core in her hand. "All that's left is this thing now. From the looks of it, I guess it's used in crafting."

"Yeah, I think so too," I replied, looking at the fist-sized crystal that was glowing with a faint azure light. "Maybe I can set it into a weapon or maybe some armor...plus three to all stats across the board is a pretty serious bonus."

"It definitely is," Lazarus chimed in. "Perks of being the first to clear a dungeon, I guess."

"No kidding," I agreed while motioning for Freya to hang onto the crystal for the time being. "We can figure out what to do with that thing once we get back to town. It might be worth hanging onto it until we craft our next round of armor...whenever that'll be."

"Considering that it's a 'Mastercraft' item, that's probably for the best," Freya said, putting the Æther Core in her pocket. "It'd suck to waste it on something that would be replaced right away."

"We'll have to see what Léandre, Drace and I can come up with over the next few days, or weeks," I said, indicating for everyone to take a share of the Iron Scraps we had recovered, intending to split the load between the groups. "Maybe we'll be able to figure out how to forge larger pieces of the Æthertouched Iron and make something out of that."

"Hopefully," Drace stated as we all collected the scraps and prepared ourselves to resume exploring the ruin. "We sure have a lot of the stuff lying around now."

With the loot sorted and no pressing reason to stay in place, we set off down the tunnel that Lazarus had pointed out earlier, a handful of the group members still muttering to themselves as they considered what to spend their skill point on. As we walked, I remembered that I had yet to spend my attribute points and took a moment to consider where my points would be best placed for this level.

Strength and Agility are doing pretty well, but I can never get enough of those anyway, I thought as I scanned through my character sheet and tried to gauge what I needed most at the moment. *Compared to everything else though, my Constitution is falling behind. It's my second worse attribute after Willpower...and the one directly responsible for keeping me alive.*

Realizing what I needed to do, I mentally added my five attribute points to Constitution and confirmed my choice, feeling the still eerie sensation of my health and stamina improving. With the choice made, I briefly glanced over the top portion of my character sheet, familiarizing myself with the changes a new level always brought.

Lyrian Rastler – Level 15 Spellsword
   Human Male (Eberian)
Statistics:
   HP: 891/891

Stamina: 810/810
Mana: 940/940
Experience to next level: 534/31700
Attributes:
Strength: 55 (74)
Agility: 50 (71)
Constitution: 50 (51)
Intelligence: 54
Willpower: 20

Looking pretty good, I couldn't help but think as I saw my new hitpoint total, feeling more confident in my ability to endure whatever the game decided to throw my way. I knew that no matter how good I was at dodging or avoiding attacks, my luck would run out at some point, like it had with the Sentinel, and I wanted to be sure that I'd be able to stay standing for when it happened again.

Deciding that I would read through the full character sheet later, I dismissed the rest of it from my vision and turned my attention back towards the tunnel around us. Much like the larger cavern that we had just left, it too had been subjected to intense heat until it had partially melted, causing the entire passageway to shrink and deform as the molten stone dripped down from the ceiling above, forcing us to pick our way through, and in several cases over, piles of solidified lava.

"Whatever happened to this place, happened really close to here," Halcyon said, breaking the temporary silence that had filled the air as we moved. "This looks nothing like the tunnel that we passed through before. It must have all been melted."

"Seems like it," I replied to the mage, noting that the walls and ceiling around us had narrowed drastically, barely stretching more than twenty feet wide in some places, which was a far cry from the fifty feet that it had been before.

Falling back into a companionable silence, we all continued to follow the snaking path through the melted tunnel, eager to see if we would finally reach the Ley Line or another intact portion of the Nafarrian ruin. Moving at the head of the party with Amaranth by my side, I couldn't help but notice that in the short distance that we had traveled, the ever-persistent musk had grown practically impossible to ignore. Growing from a faint, yet potent, stench in the air, to an aroma so heavy that I felt as if it were sitting on my own tongue.

<We have to be coming close to whatever is causing that musk,> I told my familiar, letting out a sharp cough in hopes of driving the smell out of my nose. *<It is becoming nearly unbearable.>*

<This?> Amaranth queried, turning his head to look at me curiously. *<It is...unpleasant, yet pales in comparison to a skunk.>*

<Anything pales in comparison to a skunk!> I replied to the puma, letting out another cough.

My mental reply back to Amaranth was cut short as the two of us rounded a bend in the twisting tunnel, and a bright source of magic unexpectedly filled the entirety of my vision, forcing me to shield my eyes reflexively from the intensity. Never before had I seen any source of magic as bright as what I had just experienced, causing me to immediately deactivate *True Sight* just as Amaranth's stunned mental voice filtered into my head.

<Oh,> he stated, a sense of excitement and wonder coming across the bond that we shared. *<I would never have imagined finding anything like this underground.>*

"Finding what?" I asked, blinking furiously to get the afterimages out of my eyes, and pulling my hand away from my face, my jaw dropping as I took in the sight before me.

Opening up just past the bend that Amaranth and I had just passed, the tunnel expanded drastically before us, widening until it joined a vast, almost impossibly large cavern that practically blazed with azure light. I felt my leg tremble as I rushed across the remainder of the tunnel, hearing voices call out from behind me as I moved. Coming to a stop at the tunnel's mouth, I found myself staring out into a sight beyond my wildest dreams, barely able to process what was before me.

Just past a large ridge of stone, was a veritable forest filled with what could only be described as mushroom-like trees, each of them glowing with a faint azure light. Slowly turning my head away from the glowing forest, I noticed that the side of the cavern had been covered in patches of glowing moss, the combined light from the two almost perfectly illuminating the chamber in a dull azure haze.

Has this place been under Aldford all this time? I asked myself as I continued my scan of the cavern, gradually following the walls upward, until I had worked my way towards the ceiling, where I spotted countless brightly glowing crystals protruding from it, along with several larger ones on the far side of the cavern.

Hang on a second, I thought, squinting my eyes at the larger crystals in the distance, noticing that they didn't look quite right to my eye. *Those aren't crystals at all! Those are the Ætherwarped Oak's roots!* Feeling my heart thundering in my chest as I stared up at the cavern's ceiling, a twinkling light in the distance caught my eye, causing me to drop my gaze downwards. Squinting over the canopy of the mushroom forest, I could just barely make out a glowing waterfall at the far end of the cave as it dropped off a distant cliff face and out of sight.

That's not a waterfall! The thought caused my heart to beat even faster as I tore my eyes from the sight before me and spun backward towards the rest of the guild, seeing them all slowly approaching me, awe written all across each of their faces.

"We found it," I said to the group, watching as every single pair of eyes shifted onto me.

"We found the Ley Line."

Chapter 40

"Wow," Halcyon said gazing at the cavern before us, shaking his head from side to side. "Just...*wow*. I can't even describe what I'm feeling..."

"I don't think any of us can right now, Hal," Sierra stated, standing beside the mage. "This is beyond anything that I was expecting...this is..."

"A completely new zone," I said, turning my head to look at the pair and seeing them nod in agreement without taking their eyes off the cavern.

"This must have been ground zero for whatever destroyed the ruin and ruptured the Ley Line," Halcyon commented, his head slowly moving as he scanned the area. "Look at how some parts of the walls are all smooth, while others are porous and cracked..."

"Just like the tunnel," Freya noted. "Something in the ruin must have exploded in here and hollowed out a good chunk of the place. Then earthquakes must have then done the rest."

"Probably the Æther they had stored here," I suggested, remembering the size of the blast from the two depleted Æther Crystals during the battle with the Sentinel.

"That's what I'm thinking too," Halcyon agreed, taking his eye off the cavern just long enough to nod at Freya and me before glancing back. "It must have been a hell of a lot to create a cavern like this though. Earthquakes notwithstanding, this place has to be miles across."

"And yet, it's next to nothing compared to whatever made Crater Lake," I pointed out, trying to imagine the scope of the devastation that would have been left behind after erasing an entire city from existence. Shaking my head at the depressing thought, I focused my attention back to the massive cavern, unable to help but feel intimidated by its sheer size.

And here I thought the hard part was over after making it through that dungeon, I thought, feeling a mixed wave of both resignation and excitement shoot through my body. On the one hand, we had a brand-new area to explore, and the Ley Line was finally within reach. But on the other, I had a sinking suspicion in my gut that going forward wouldn't be easy.

As it was, we had already been hard-pressed to fight our way through the Nafarrian ruins, the level gap between the dungeon inhabitants and ourselves widening the further that we progressed. Even with the new level under our belts, I expected that this new area would continue the trend, if not increase it drastically.

We'll figure out a way to manage. We always have so far, I thought, pushing my reservations to the side as I brought up my quest log, deciding to check on the status of our quest. Lately, I had begun to ignore the almost constant updates that had appeared in the corner of my vision as we explored the ruin, the majority of them being either a summary of recent events or just an incremental notification that had reached a new area.

Which I guess this one isn't really any different, I noted as I skimmed through the newest update.

Quest Update! The Ruptured Ley Line!

Following the path that the Nafarrian device had opened for you, you and your party delved deeper into the ruins, encountering tremendous damage and destruction on your route to the next Æther Matrix, which proved to be infested with the spirits of the dead. With the aid of the device, you were able to overcome the spirits and continued onwards until you rejoined with the rest of your guild members, caught in the middle of a battle with an ancient Nafarrian construct. Rushing to their aid, your combined efforts proved enough to destroy the machine, despite incurring heavy losses.

After taking a moment to recover from the ordeal, you and the rest of your party resumed your exploration of the ruin, travelling through a large burnt out tunnel until you found yourselves overlooking a massive underground cavern filled with strange glowing plants.

From your vantage point, you can see a bright, azure-hued, waterfall glowing in the distance. Could this be the Ley Line that you came here looking for?

Explore the Cavern: 0/1

Ley Line Sealed: 0/1

"So, who feels up to exploring the place?" I asked, dismissing the quest update from my vision and checking Party Sense to see where Caius and Constantine were, finding them to be somewhere above and in front of us. "It doesn't seem like the others have left Aldford yet for some reason, so we have plenty of time to kill before they get back."

"Hrm," Drace grunted, his head glancing up towards the cavern's ceiling. "You're right; they haven't left yet. I wonder what's going on."

"Now that you mention it," Theia spoke up. "Our group hasn't left yet either. Maybe they're waiting for their death sickness to wear off?"

"Maybe," Freya acknowledged. "But it's also only been what? Ten or fifteen minutes since we finished off the Sentinel? They could be waiting to see if anyone else pops in before leaving, they're all going to have to go through those double doors again at the ruin's entrance."

"Oh right," I replied, having completely forgotten about the two doors that controlled access to the ruin. "I'll have to see if I can get the security system to disable that."

"We can do it on the way out," Halcyon said eagerly, motioning towards a small ramp of dried lava that led off our vantage point and downwards into darkness. "Let's go and take a look around first!"

"I'm down for that," Drace stated, casting a glance at the rest of the party and me before taking the first step down the ramp. "If the others are going to be a while in getting back down here, I'd rather be moving around in the meantime, rather than just standing and waiting."

"Sounds good to me," I replied, moving to follow the half-giant and casting a *Light* spell to brighten the path as he led the way down, Freya and Amaranth taking up places beside me as we walked.

"I bet there are a bunch of interesting creatures down here!" Alistair announced from the middle of the party. "This place reminds me of zones I've seen in other games years ago…they've always ended up being my favorite places to explore."

"And to hit level fourteen in?" Lazarus prompted, with a note of humor in his voice.

"Hopefully!" Alistair replied. "Though I haven't been able to see any creatures here yet."

"Me either," Sierra chimed in as we continued to move. "Maybe they're just good at hiding? The spiders in the Webwood were pretty hard to find at first."

"Oh please, don't use that 'S' word down here," Halcyon groaned theatrically. "I've had my fill of those for several lifetimes. It can be literally anything other than spiders, and I'll be cool with it."

"Like scorpions?" Drace prompted from the head of the group, flashing me a smile over his shoulder as he spoke.

"Okay, spiders and scorpions," Halcyon corrected. "Everything else should be cool."

"What about a giant praying mantis?" Thorne suggested.

"Or giant mosquitos?" Abaddon added with a throaty chuckle.

"Guys, do you want me just to come out and say it?" Halcyon stated uneasily. "I'm terrified of giant bugs in general."

"Is that really a fear though?" Lazarus asked, barely stifling a laugh. "I thought that was just called common sense."

<Why should Halcyon fear the Many Legs?> Amaranth sent to me. *<They are an excellent source of meat, and taste fairly good when eaten fresh.>*

"Hey, Hal," I called, twisting to look at the mage behind me. "Amaranth wants you to know that spiders taste pretty great and that you shouldn't worry about them."

"Oh god, I hate you all," the mage grumbled, causing a chorus of laughter to erupt from the group.

With all of us eager to see what the new area held in store for us, we descended the ancient lava flow and headed towards the cavern floor, the azure-tinted jungle in the distance vanishing from sight as we descended below it. Chancing a quick glance with *True Sight* before the brightness of the cavern overwhelmed me, I managed to see that we would have to descend downwards into a small valley that separated the cavern wall and the ridge that the alien forest was set on, then find a way to climb upwards and get back up to the higher elevation.

"This place is a hell of a lot rockier and jagged up close," Halcyon commented while conjuring several orbs of light, allowing us a chance to glance around the valley that we had found ourselves and finding it free of any vegetation, glowing or otherwise. "Hey, speaking about that, shouldn't we name this area? Since we're the first people here, we can do that, right?"

"Yeah, we can actually!" I replied enthusiastically, remembering how I had named the Webwood a few weeks earlier. "Anyone have any suggestions?"

"The Glowing Abyss?" Lazarus suggested before shrugging his large shoulders. "I'm terrible at naming things, so don't expect anything better than that from me."

"The Mushroom Forest?" Halcyon chimed in, his face turning into a scowl. "No, on second thought, not that. That's awful."

"How about the Æther Gardens?" I said, looking around the group for reactions.

"Not bad," Freya commented thoughtfully. "But I think it's missing something."

"What about Fungal Grove or maybe Twilight Cavern?" Sierra paused for a moment, clearly not happy with her choices, before suddenly snapping her fingers. "The Twilight Grove!"

"Oh, I like that one!" I said right away, looking up towards the azure-hued ceiling and testing the word. "The Twilight Grove."

"It has my vote!" Freya exclaimed. "I think it fits perfectly!"

"Works for me!" Halcyon agreed, the rest of the group chiming in a second behind. "Do we need to do anything specific now?"

"I don't think so," I answered, recalling that all it had taken was me coming up with a name and writing it down on my map for the area to be named. "I'll make sure to include it on the map that I'm making, but the game should take care of it automatically."

"Oh, I remember you scratching away at that thing," Drace commented. "How's that coming along anyway?"

"Glacially slow," I grunted, not able to remember the last time that I had taken it out to sketch out any updates. "I honestly haven't had the time to get to it, Maybe when things calm down…one day."

"Well, Lyrian's crazy schedule aside," Halcyon began. "We should see if the name stuck if we can find a creature here somewhere, right?"

"That's how it's worked out so far," I replied, nodding at the mage.

"Well, then, let's go find a creature and see!" he exclaimed, motioning for us to continue onwards, his orbs of light leading the way.

"And then kill it for experience, right?" Alistair queried as we all turned to start moving again, prompting another laugh from the group.

Resuming our journey through the newly named Twilight Grove, we gradually made our way through the valley in search of a route up the ridge, the sound of the crunching rock underneath our feet filling the air. Despite the presence of the strange forest in the distance, it seemed that this particular valley was still in the middle of establishing its own ecosystem, appearing completely barren of any plant life or creatures.

Was this place growing here all this time? Or did this all sprout into existence soon after the Ley Line started leaking again? Questions filtered through my mind as I glanced between the walls high above us, staring at the strange mold that I had seen earlier. It had only taken a few weeks for the Ætherwarped Oak in Aldford to grow to massive proportions. With the energy from the nearby Ley Line, I didn't consider it a far stretch that everything here could have sprouted and grown to size in just a handful of days. *I guess it's impossible to know for sure.*

"Looks like we can probably climb up the ridge over there," Drace said, pulling me out of my reverie as he pointed at a section of stone that had broken away from the ridge, creating a rough path that we could use to climb upwards. "We just need to pull ourselves up onto that rock there; then we should be able to scramble up the rest of the way."

"Ugh, more climbing," Halcyon grunted. "You know, the best thing about Ascend Online has to be that even if I'm a mage, I still have better upper body strength in the game than I do in Reality."

"That's because coffee and junk food aren't real food groups, Hal," Sierra said as we all grouped around the rock that Drace had indicated seconds earlier, the large warrior having already pulled himself up.

"What is this?" the mage replied defensively. "Pick on Halcyon day?"

"Well, Constantine isn't here right now..." I said, flashing the man a grin as I moved to follow Lazarus, who had climbed up behind Drace.

Putting Halcyon's grumbling behind me, I easily pulled myself upwards onto the boulder and then carefully made my way up the rough path of stones. Reaching the ridgetop without any difficultly, I quickly spotted both Drace and Lazarus, The pair had moved away from the edge and were gazing in the direction of the dimly lit jungle, which had come back into view.

"Well, this place is going to be interesting to navigate," Drace said, glancing over his shoulder as I approached, waving his arm out towards the jungle before us. "Looks like we're going to have to blaze a path through all of that before we can get to the Ley Line."

"Yeah," I replied with a sigh, my eyes scanning through the countless strangely shaped plants that made up the forest. "I guess it would be too much for us to ask to be able to just have a clear straight shot at it."

"Of course not," Lazarus agreed, matching my tone. "We'll have to suffer first, and earn our way towards it. Like everything else in this game."

"Hopefully we'll have enough time to do that," Drace said, his eyes remaining fixated on the forest. "I still don't see any creatures ahead of us, but if you listen closely, you can hear a sort of...*chittering* sound in the distance."

"I hear it too," I replied, the sound suddenly intensifying as Amaranth finished his climb and came into range of our now augmented bond. "Seems like there is a hell of a lot of whatever it is making that noise."

"Good," Lazarus commented. "And hopefully it's easy to catch too. I have a hell of a lot of catching up to do with you guys."

Giving the half-giant an understanding nod, I turned to glance back at the rest of the party who had finally made the climb up the ramp, their eyes focused on the jungle ahead. "Last chance, everyone. Ready to see what this place has in store for us?"

"Just about," Theia said, amid a chorus of affirmative replies. "I have a spell I want to try out on us before we go. I picked up a buff with my level fifteen skill point!"

"Oh, awesome!" Freya exclaimed as all of us huddled close to the lizardwoman at her prompting. "What does it do?"

"It gives a slight boost to hit points, armor and health regeneration," Theia said as she began to emit an aura of violet energy from her body that reached out to encircle us. "It's not much, but every bit helps in the long run!"

A surge of energy coursed through me as Theia completed her spell, the aura surrounding us gradually flowing into our bodies. When the last traces of it finally vanished, I could feel myself become slightly healthier as the magic took hold, seeing a pair of notifications appear in my vision.

Theia casts [Inner Fire] on you!

You gain +50 hit points, +30 to armor, and +2 to Health Regeneration for 3 hours!

"Hey, this is pretty great!" Thorne announced. "Though I hope we're not in a situation where fifty hit points are all that keeps me from dying..."

"I am for any situation that we live through," Abaddon grunted in response. "Thank you, Theia."

"Happy to help," she replied graciously and then turned her attention back towards me. "Alright. Now I'm ready to go."

"Great!" I replied, giving her a thankful nod and turning back towards the jungle. "Let's see what this place has in store for us."

With the chatter amongst the group dying down, we set off, our eyes cautiously scanning our surroundings. None of us had the vaguest idea of what to expect going forward into this place and we were all seasoned enough to know that pointless noise was a sure way to attract attention that you didn't necessarily want to have at that moment.

Once we get a better feel for this place we can think about relaxing, I thought as I stepped past the tree line and entered into near darkness, the chittering noise that we had heard earlier intensifying until it seemingly came from everywhere at once.

<The noise nearly drowns out all other sound,> Amaranth commented, a note of frustration filtering over our bond. *<And this musk is potent enough to mask all other scents. This will not be an easy place to hunt in.>*

<No kidding.> I replied to the cat, finding that the already potent odor was even more intense inside the jungle. *<Do*

you see anything yet? Whatever creatures are making this noise can't be far.>

<No creatures,> Amaranth stated before inclining his head towards a vine-like growth that hung loosely from a large mushroom tree, swaying gently in the air. *<Yet it seems that we've interrupted something that was just eating.>*

"Hmm," I grunted thoughtfully while motioning towards the vine for the others to see, pointing out the several large bites missing from it.

<I didn't even see anything move,> I told the cat, scanning the area around the plant and not seeing anything of note on the soft, grey-tinted dirt below. *<There are no tracks surrounding it either.>*

<None that we see from the ground,> Amaranth corrected, his eyes glancing upwards. *<Yet given the thickness of the canopy above...>*

<There might be creatures above us,> I sent back to Amaranth while turning around to face the group, filling them in on our train of thought. "...based on the lack of tracks, whatever was eating it may not use the ground to travel at all, or at least not all the time."

"I was starting to think the same thing," Sierra replied, staring up at where the savaged vine had attached itself to the tree. "I could swear I keep seeing shadows or something moving up above us, but it keeps moving too fast to get a good look at it."

"You think we're moving in too large a group?" Thorne asked. "I mean anything with half a brain isn't going to stick around with a dozen of us tromping through the area."

"That's a good point," Drace pointed out. "Some of us might be half blind in here, but the creatures probably aren't."

"I think you're right," I replied, staring at the half-eaten vine before me and silently reconsidered my approach. With us entering into an unknown area with poor lighting, potentially filled with creatures of an unknown level, I had wanted to keep us all close together until we could get a better idea of what we were up against. My reasoning being that if we came across something drastically higher leveled than us, we could simply swarm it with raw numbers and then regroup from there.

Unfortunately, it seemed that tactic wasn't about to work.

"Looks like it's up to our scouts," I whispered to Sierra, seeing her turn her head to look at me and give me a nod.

"About time," Sierra replied, flashing me a grin as she signaled for Lazarus to follow her into the surrounding brush. "The two of us will take a quick look around and see if we can find something interesting to bring back. You guys just sit tight here for a bit and keep an eye out for any creatures."

"But if you hear any loud noises or screaming while we're gone, please assume it's something trying to eat us," Lazarus said softly as he moved to follow the red-haired elf. "And come running."

"Can do," Drace replied with a soft chuckle. All of us watched the two stealthy members of our group fade away into the forest.

"Wish Caius would have made it," Halcyon commented sadly. "His 'Bloodsense' ability would have helped here. He could tell us if there was anything close by."

"Yeah," I agreed as I pulled Splinter from its sheath, getting myself ready for when one of the scouts hopefully brought back a group of creatures for us. "Though something tells me *close by* isn't a problem."

Waiting patiently, I felt the minutes pass by slowly as I waited for the scouts to return, passing the time tracking them via Party Sense. At first, they moved quickly away from us as they spread out away from one another, then slowed as they gradually fanned outward. During this time, those of us left waiting kept a careful eye on our surroundings, making sure that nothing tried to sneak up on us while the others were away.

<Sierra and Lazarus have gone pretty far,> I told Amaranth as I stared out in the direction that I sensed them in. *<I can't believe that they haven't found anything yet.>*

<A good predator must have patience,> the cat replied dryly, fixing me with a glare. *<Else he will find himself hungry more often than not.>*

Grunting, I accepted Amaranth's rebuke and resumed patiently waiting, paying careful attention to Sierra and Lazarus's presence as they continued to move through the jungle.

If the creatures here don't want to have anything to do with us, then maybe we'll actually have a clear shot at the Ley Line, I thought while trying to temper my expectations. In all our experiences so far, between the Webwood and the Greenwood that we had taken the new guild recruits to the other week, forests had always been packed full of hostile creatures, often to the point where it was difficult to take a step without disturbing something lying in wait. To make it this far into a virtually untouched area to be actively ignored by the creatures seemed extremely unusual.

"Hmm," Drace let out a sudden moue of interest as he turned his head in the direction of Sierra and Lazarus, his expression shifting to one of curiosity and a heartbeat later I realized why.

Lazarus is coming back towards us! I thought excitedly, sensing him rapidly getting closer. *And Sierra stopped moving.*

Waiting on pins and needles, we all eagerly waited for Lazarus's return to the group, gripping our weapons tightly in case he arrived with a horde of creatures in tow. Emerging from the foliage at a quick pace, Lazarus's hands immediately shot up in front of him as he spotted us, and shook his head side to side.

"Nothing following me," the half-giant stated, watching all our faces fall at the news. "But Sierra and I found something else interesting that you all need to see. Follow me."

Intrigued by the man's cryptic statement, we fell into line behind him and retracted the path that Lazarus had just blazed, trampling over the already damaged foliage with ease. Moving at a demanding pace, it didn't take long before we finally arrived at where Sierra was waiting, spotting the woman standing directly in front of a large jagged piece of stone that protruded from a barren patch of ground, her attention fixed intently upon it.

"Hey—" My greeting barely had the chance to leave my throat, before the rock Sierra was staring at suddenly flared with countless emerald colored runes, each of them appearing to crawl across the stone's face before fading into nothingness.

Speechless, we all ground to a halt as we stared at the stone before us, watching the strange symbols continue to play across it before everything gradually faded away, leaving the face blank once more. Taking her gaze away from the stone, Sierra turned around to face us, her eyes wide with wonder.

"Hey," she greeted, her voice sounding slightly stunned. "So, I know it wasn't a creature, but we found something else interesting."

"I'll say!" I replied, shaking off my astonishment and approaching the stone, everyone else following closely behind me.

"It flares up every few minutes or so," Sierra told me, stepping to the side as I placed my hand on the stone's surface, feeling it perfectly smooth to the touch. "Then lasts roughly about as long as you saw before fading away again."

"We didn't see anything like this in our half of the ruin," Freya commented, taking up position beside me and looking up at the stone. "Did you guys?"

"Nothing even remotely close," I replied. "Just the Æther Crystals."

"Damn," Halcyon breathed in a low voice as he too approached the stone. "I figured that everything from the ruin here would have been destroyed."

"I think we all did," I said to the mage, my eyes following the edges of the stone then down towards its base. "Look at the edges to this though. It almost seems like it broke away from something even larger…and landed here."

"But what is it?" Freya asked.

"I don't even have the faintest idea," I answered with a shrug. "Though the runes that appeared earlier almost seemed like spell notations, similar to how a scribed spell would look like in a Spellbook."

"I noticed that too," Halcyon commented before suddenly shielding his eyes. "Ugh! Damn, that's bright! Don't look at it with Arcane Sight, Lyr. It's definitely magical, even if it's not showing anything right now. More so than anything I've ever seen before too."

"Interesting," I replied, wondering just how much longer it would be before the runes appeared again.

"So, you think that whatever's on the rune might be a spell?" Sierra asked, taking a step away from the rock and rejoining the bulk of the group.

"I don't know," I said, turning around to look at everyone. "Scribed spells don't normally move around like that one did, but maybe we'll be able to..."

My words trailed off as the incessant chittering that filled the air abruptly stopped, the jungle around us falling deathly silent. Standing beside me, Amaranth let out a low growl as we all looked out into the brush with confused, yet wary expressions.

<Something happened in the jungle.> Amaranth hissed, his fur standing on edge as he glanced around rapidly and crouched low on his haunches. *<Perhaps a predator is somewhere nearby?>*

<Maybe,> I sent back to the cat, staring out into the jungle nervously, but not seeing any sign of movement through the dark gloom.

"Everything just stopped making noise," Alistair announced from within the group. "I can't hear anything at all now. Just us."

"Me either," I replied, surprised to find that even with me sharing Amaranth's senses, I couldn't pick up any noise from the forest surrounding us, everything seemingly having agreed to fall silent at the same time.

<Can you see anything?> I asked the cat, not wanting to blind myself by activating True Sight again.

<No...> he replied a heartbeat afterward. *<The jungle is too thick to see through. If something is out there, it is a masterful hider.>*

"You think the creatures finally clued in that we're here?" Thorne asked somewhat rhetorically, gripping his mace tightly as he searched the canopy above us.

"I don't know what else it could be," Freya said from beside me, holding her spear high. "But I still can't see anything."

"What's our plan?" Lazarus asked, taking up position alongside Drace and Abaddon, the trio shifting until they were each back to back.

"Let's pull—" I started to say when a flash of movement appeared in the corner of my eye, causing my head to snap to the side and land on a set of yellow eyes staring back at me from within the jungle.

That's not just one pair of eyes, I thought, feeling my words catch in my throat as I realized that there were dozens more eyes peering out at me from the depths of the jungle, causing a single thought to slam into my mind. *We're surrounded.*

Feeling adrenaline surge through me at the revelation, I felt everything stop for the briefest of moments as if the world itself was taking a deep breath in preparation for what was about to come.

And when it finally did, the jungle *screamed.*

"Holy shi—" I could barely make out Lazarus's curse through the deafening noise that filled the air, yet as I glanced up at the jungle canopy, there was no doubt in my mind to what he had just seen.

Leaping out from seemingly everywhere at once, was a veritable swarm of claws and teeth, each of them belonging to a small gremlin-like creature, bearing the very same yellow eyes I had just seen a heartbeat earlier. Gazing at the incoming avalanche of creatures descending upon me, I had just enough time to read the tag that appeared in my vision.

[Twilight Grove Gremlin] – Level 17

No sooner were the words burned into my mind than I was driven to my knees from the weight of two of the creatures landing on top of me, their sharp, needle-like teeth and claws passing through my armor as if it wasn't even there. Thrashing wildly from the pain, I instinctively reached up to tear one of the Gremlins off me, feeling flesh tear as its talons came free. Slamming it against the ground and pinning it in place, the impact stunned the beast long enough for me to look over it, getting a better sense of what we were up against.

Measuring just over two feet tall, the Gremlin was vaguely bipedal in shape, its body covered in a thick, grey-colored hide. Baring a set of three razor-sharp talons on both of its arms, and a pair of thicker claws on its more powerful legs, there was little doubt in my mind that the creature was a predator in whatever passed for an ecosystem in this grove. A fact that was only re-enforced by the presence of countless jagged teeth in its maw as it shook its head and snarled viciously at me, fighting angrily to escape my grip.

Feeling the bite from the other Gremlin still on top of me, I instinctively thrust Splinter's tip into the beast's open maw, driving it straight through the roof of its mouth and into its brain, causing it to fall limp in my grip. With no time to enjoy my success, I began to reach towards the other that had landed on top of me, the Gremlin having since sunk its teeth into my shoulder. But before my free hand could even travel halfway across my body, two more of the creatures rushed into view, one of them leaping to bite the arm that held Splinter, with the other launching itself directly at my face.

"*Shit!*" I shouted to myself in panic, desperately moving my free arm to intercept the airborne Gremlin.

Catching the vicious creature on my forearm, I managed to shove it away from me, earning a bleeding cut across my cheek in the process as a flailing talon lashed out to scratch me. No sooner did I knock the Gremlin away than Amaranth suddenly came bounding beside me, biting down onto the creature that affixed itself to my arm, crushing its body easily in his powerful jaws.

<We must flee!> my familiar called to me in a panic as he swept a massive paw at the Gremlin on my shoulder, batting it clean off me in a single blow. *<Something large approaches!>*

<What do you mean?> I shouted back, staggering slightly from Amaranth's assistance, but managing to force myself back up to my feet. *<We need to regroup—>*

"Lyrian!" Freya's panicked shout interrupted my thought, causing both Amaranth and me to spin in its direction, catching sight of the blonde-haired warrior several steps away from us as she stared at something looming behind the now glowing stone beside me.

It's not behind the stone, I corrected myself as I followed Freya's gaze, craning my head practically straight up until they landed on two massive yellow orbs that seemingly hung high in the air above me. *It's standing over the stone.*

Appearing out from behind the stone, I saw a gargantuan paw reach out from the dim shadows, gripping the side of the jagged rock, causing me to reflexively take a step back in shock as I numbly counted five massive talons protruding from the claw, each of them at least a foot in length. Drawing my gaze back upward towards the eyes that I had seen earlier, I saw a beastly face lower itself down into the light, its maw already open and dripping with saliva.

"Oh…" The word escaped from me involuntarily as I stared up at the colossal creature, watching its eyes fixate right upon me. Taking a step backward, I felt a primal terror take hold of my heart as it slowly opened its mouth, revealing rows and rows of jagged teeth.

And then it *roared*.

Staggering from the noise as if it were a physical blow, I found myself completely paralyzed, unable to move, unable to think, unable to do anything other than gaze into certain doom. Closing its mouth after what seemed like eternity, the massive creature began to pull itself forward, revealing its near pitch-black body as it rounded the stone, causing a new, golden tag that I had never seen before to point towards it.

[The Beast] – Raid Boss – Level 19

That's not fair, I thought numbly as The Beast suddenly launched itself at me, moving faster than any creature of its size should ever have been capable of moving. *That's just not fair at all.*

Teeth filled my vision for the briefest of moments, before everything plunged into darkness, followed by an intense wave of pain.

And then there was nothing.

Loading, please wait…

Chapter 41

Passing through the veil of death yet again, I felt my consciousness slowly return as the darkness surrounding me faded away, leaving me looking out at the familiar surroundings of Aldford. Blinking numbly as I processed my rather traumatic death, I felt myself sway on my feet unsteadily, images of gnashing teeth and blinding pain still fresh in my mind.

Damn, I cursed mentally, bringing up a hand to rub my face, feeling the weight of Death Sickness land on top of me. *That death isn't going to be easy to—*

"You guys have no right to hide shit like this from us!" A nearby harsh voice cut through the air, interrupting my train of thought.

"Huh?" I croaked, more confused by the angry voice than anything else. Taking my hand off my face, I blearily looked in the direction of the noise and found myself staring at a handful of Adventurers that I didn't recognize, facing off with the missing members of our guild. Standing directly between the two groups was Dyre, along with a visibly angry Constantine and another Adventurer that wore a rather familiar set of armor.

That's the armor that I made a few days ago, I noted distantly, my brain still not having fully caught up with my resurrection, let alone beginning to process whatever was going on here.

Having heard the sound of my voice, I saw Constantine's head snap in my direction, the near rage on his face shifting into dismay. "Lyr!"

Turning away from the small crowd, Constantine made to move towards me but froze before he could take more than a single step as several faint flashes of light began filling the air around me, all conversation around us immediately coming to a halt.

The rest of our group, I realized with a hard swallow, turning my head to see Freya appear an arm's length away from me, along with Drace a short distance away from her, the rest of the group gradually appearing as the seconds passed. Gritting my teeth, I waited for the heart-rending twist of pain that would herald Amaranth's death, realizing that my familiar was unfortunately out of range of our mental link.

Yet as the seconds passed, the pain never came, and I could tell that Amaranth's presence was gradually getting further away from me, kindling the faint hope that the cat had somehow managed to survive.

If any of us could escape that Beast, he would have the best chance, I thought optimistically as I tried to shake off the mental image of the creature's teeth once again. All that I remember in the split second that I had seen it was a brief flash of dark, leathery skin.

"Lyrian," Constantine finally repeated, having crossed the distance between me and the group of Adventurers, his arm landing on my shoulder drawing me out of my spiraling thoughts before they could firmly take hold. "What happened? Did the…"

"Something else got us," I replied, not so far gone that I didn't sense the implied question behind his words. Pausing for a moment to look into his eyes, I couldn't help but notice the anger that still burned in them, causing me to shift my gaze past him and onto the Adventurer wearing the armor that I had made.

"What's going on?" I asked, keeping my voice low. "Who are those people and why is Dyre here?"

"That…*vulture*…" Constantine began to hiss angrily, "was snooping around the ruin this morning and found the dungeon entrance. It was just dumb luck that I overheard him talking about assembling a party after I respawned here."

"We…haven't exactly made it a secret we were working on something in there," Freya replied wearily, as she joined the conversation. "But, it's *Virtus's* ruin in the end. He can't go into it without our say so."

"That is part of his problem," the rogue replied. "He doesn't think that it's fair we've claimed so much."

"Not this shit again!" I spat, feeling a spike of anger shoot through me at the familiar topic. It had been annoying enough to deal with Stanton's mock attempt to seize the ruins, and the last thing we needed right now was to replay that experience with a group of Adventurers. "We don't have time for this! We need to get back down there, not just us, but the whole guild. *We found it,* Constantine. We found what we were looking for."

I saw my friend's eyes widen at my statement, excitement briefly replacing the anger in his eyes, lasting just long enough until a familiar voice barked out a second time.

"I'm still waiting for an answer, Constantine!" the voice called. "Or maybe now that Virtus has bitten off more than it can chew, I should talk to the Guildmaster directly! Seeing how he's the one who is *really* in charge here!"

"He's been trying to bait me into hitting him ever since Dyre arrived," Constantine warned through gritted teeth. "Can't say I'm not tempted."

"Let's keep that option on the table for the moment," I growled as I motioned for Constantine to lead the way back to the man, my already foul mood at being jumped by a *Raid Boss* of all things, growing worse by the second. Having my emotions cluttered by the wild swings that

Death Sickness always brought wasn't helping either. "Who is this guy? Is he part of another guild?"

"Dunno," Constantine replied quietly. "But his name is Ignis."

"Must be someone from the new group of settlers," Freya whispered to me as the three of us approached the man and the waiting Adventurers. "I don't recognize the name at all, nor the others with him."

"Hrm," I grunted, fixating my attention on the man's familiar armor, pegging it specifically as one of the Serpentine Striker armor sets that I had crafted. Despite whatever problems he claimed to have with Virtus, they clearly didn't extend to buying my armor.

Nor bitching at the person who crafted it in the first place, I thought grimly as the three of us came to a stop in front of Ignis, the Adventurers milling behind him having taken several steps back at my arrival. *Hmm, maybe everyone isn't on the same page here.*

Saying nothing as we came to a stop, I glared at the man, my eyes taking in the sharp features on his face and the thin line of white hair that protruded from the edges of his helmet. *Looks like a half-elf, or maybe an elf.*

"So," Ignis began, looking me up and down, his eyes noticeably lingering on the damaged portions of my armor. "I know you guys are hiding a dungeon from all of us."

"I'm afraid I have no idea what you're talking about," I replied, keeping my expression neutral as I spoke, knowing that it would aggravate the man.

"Bullshit, you don't know!" the elf exclaimed, his face turning into a scowl. "I saw the ruin entrance myself!"

"You did?" I asked, shifting my eyes over to the Justicar. "So, you admit to trespassing. Did you hear that, Justicar?"

"I most certainly did," Dyre replied, turning his faceless gaze onto Ignis. "Did you have express permission to be on Virtus's property?"

"*Permission?*" The man snarled. "I don't need permission to explore a ruin!"

"An unclaimed ruin, perhaps," Dyre stated. "Yet this one has been legally claimed by Virtus."

"*That's because everything here has been claimed by Virtus!*" Ignis hissed. "This town, the nearby ruins, that's all any of us ever hear! Virtus owns this! Virtus owns that!"

We earned all of those claims," Freya answered. "Through blood and sweat. You want something of your own? *Go and find it.*"

"You earned them by being *first*," Ignis countered. "Now you're cockblocking the rest of us from catching up!"

"Now who's spouting bullshit, Ignis?" I asked, motioning towards the armor that he was wearing. "You're clearly not suffering."

"I'm wearing something I actually earned!" Ignis answered, slapping a hand on his chest.

"That's funny," Freya said. "Because I seem to recall that I was the one to kill that snake."

"You—" Ignis began to sputter.

"You have no idea what's at stake here, Ignis," I stated, cutting the man off and seeing his eyes widen in anger. "And I don't have the time, nor the obligation to explain it to you. Suffice to say when you *and* the other Adventurers have a reason to know, you will know."

"You mean *after* you've all had a chance to earn your glory and post it to your feed," the elf countered angrily. "I know—"

"You don't know shit, Ignis," I interrupted the man in a cold voice, letting my frustration leak into my tone. "And you'll just have to take me at my word that this is more important than anything we have in our feed. Now if you'll excuse me, we're done here."

"Like hell, we're done!" Ignis called to me as I stepped past him and his posse and began walking towards the Town Hall, the guild moving to follow behind me. "I'm far from the only one who is tired of Virtus running this town like its own personal kingdom!"

"What was that all about, Lyrian?" Lazarus asked in a tired voice as we entered the building, temporarily taking Constantine's place as he caught up beside me.

"Just an impatient idiot who knows we found a dungeon," I replied, angling our approach to the far end of the room and the stairs to the upper level. "Have you seen him before? He was part of your group that came up here."

"No, I don't know him," Lazarus said. "Though I'll ask Ransom and Sawyer too. Stanton kept us under a pretty watchful eye while we were travelling."

"What are we doing now?" Constantine asked from over my shoulder as we all thundered across the room, causing the handful of Adventurers sitting at tables to look in our direction.

"We need to let Aldwin know what we found," I said, then lowered my voice to a whisper. "And Stanton too, I suppose."

"Then after that, we need to get every single guild member still in town and get ready to head back," I continued. "Amaranth is still alive down there, and I don't want to leave him any longer than I have to."

"Oh, damn, Lyr; I didn't know Amaranth survived!" Freya commented, casting a wide-eyed glance at me. "I'll start sending out private messages to anyone still around town. Hopefully, we'll still have a good core around."

"Thanks, Freya," I replied, pausing to look back at the rest of the guild that had followed us into the Town Hall, the majority of them taking a seat at our usual two tables and whispering between one another, the survivors of the battle with the Sentinel eagerly updating those who hadn't made it through the fight. "We'll need everyone we can get."

"And more," Lazarus grunted as I turned around to climb the stairs. "The last thing I expected was to have a damned *Raid Boss* jump us. I didn't even know this game *had* Raid Bosses at our level."

"Fun for us to find out the hard way," I groused, glancing behind me as I led the way to Aldwin's study, hoping that the Knight would be around.

Knocking on the door twice, I heard the Bann call out without a moment's hesitation, "Come in!"

Pushing the door open, I spotted Aldwin sitting behind his desk with several sheets of paper strewn across it, the man clearly in the middle of something. Looking up from his work, his eyes widened in surprise as he saw the four of us standing in the doorway.

"Lyrian!" he exclaimed. "You're back already? D-did something happen?"

"You could say that," I replied, giving the man a nod with a half-smile on my face. "I have good news and bad news, but we should also tell Stanton too. Time isn't exactly on our side right now."

"He's in the meeting room with Veronia," Aldwin said, sensing the urgency in my words and standing up from his desk.

Taking a few seconds to reorient ourselves as the Bann eagerly left his paperwork behind, we shifted back down the hallway and knocked on the meeting room door, not waiting for any reply before entering.

"We found it," I announced without any preamble, seeing Stanton and Veronia sitting across the table from one another, with a pile of paper and what looked to be a random assortment of knickknacks spread out around them.

"The Ley Line?" Veronia asked eagerly, showing no sign of anger or annoyance at our interruption.

"The Ley Line," Freya confirmed as we all moved to take seats around the table. "But that's not the only thing; we found something else."

"More like something else found *us*," Lazarus said with a note of bitter humor in his voice.

"What do you mean?" Aldwin asked. "Something...killed you all?"

"Perhaps starting at the beginning would be more efficient," Stanton stated, appearing completely calm as he clasped his hands together. "What did you find?"

"That a good portion of the ruin is still intact," I said before beginning to recount everything that we had experienced in the Nafarrian ruin, leaving nothing out during my explanation. "...and a massive beast appeared out of the darkness. We didn't stand a chance against it."

"*Gods*," Aldwin whispered incredulously, leaning forward in his seat as he glanced down at the table. "All of this was *under* us this whole time?"

"It seems like it," I soothed, more than understanding what Aldwin was feeling. From his perspective, the founding of Aldford had led from one crisis to another, each one seeming to somehow be more threatening than the one before it. "Though given how fast Æther can make things grow...we could be wrong."

"Five-hundred and fifty years is a long enough time for anything to happen," Stanton said, his voice sounding awed by what we had just told him. "You realize that this is the first time that we have a true understanding of the timeline of when the Nafarrian civilization fell? Nothing we've ever uncovered has even hinted at how long they may have been extinct for."

"A dying race usually doesn't really have time to leave notes behind," Lazarus said dryly. "And I imagine The Ascendancy wouldn't have been forthcoming with those answers."

"*Hardly*," Veronia agreed.

"We've also managed to recover a handful of artifacts and relics from the ruin," I said, glancing between Aldwin and Stanton. "I think I'll be able to salvage or re-create some of it, but the Ley Line has to be our priority for the time being."

"I absolutely agree," Stanton said with a nod. "But in the meantime, would it be possible to have your permission to send Samuel and Quincy into the ruin? The information that we could uncover…is beyond priceless, it could redefine all study of the Nafarr."

At least he knows how to ask politely, I thought as I shifted my gaze towards Aldwin, seeing him give me a nearly imperceptible shrug in return. I wasn't anywhere close to trusting Stanton at this point, yet given the seriousness of the situation, I couldn't see what there was to gain from denying him access to the ruin. The more we discovered about the Nafarr and their technology, the better prepared we would be when it came to deal with the Ley Line. *But still, it pays to be cautious…*

"You can," I stated after a moment of thought. "But I want a copy of all your research, and Halcyon, Caius, and Donovan will be in charge. Anything they say goes."

"That is more than fair," Stanton said in a surprisingly gracious manner. "I will be sure to impress upon Samuel and Quincy that we are guests."

"And how are you exactly going to tell them that?" Lazarus asked. "Everyone knows about the last time you and Lyrian met in public. Aren't you concerned your cover is going to slip?"

"Given the nature of our discovery, I believe it would be best that Lyrian and 'Stanton' bury the hatchet publicly," the agent replied, first to Lazarus, then glancing over to me as he spoke. "If what you've said about the cavern below is true, we don't have time for division in the ranks."

"We don't," I agreed. "As it is, we're going to need all of Virtus working on this, and even then, I think we're going to be hard-pressed. That giant beast aside, we were *all* outclassed by even the common creatures that inhabited the Grove. It's going to be a long learning curve for all of us down there."

"Are we sure we just want to limit this to the guild, Lyr?" Freya asked. "That cavern is *huge*, and even with all of us exploring it, I'm not sure if we have enough people to make a dent in all the creatures down there. At least not quickly."

"I was thinking the same thing," I replied hesitantly. "But if we tell people about the Twilight Grove, then we're going to have to tell them about the Ley Line too. That has a very real risk of blowing up in our faces. *Badly.*"

"As opposed to the ground literally exploding in their faces if we fail?" Constantine chimed in. "I can appreciate your hesitation, Lyr. But by the time evening falls, everyone is going to know that we were up to something today. A full wipe by Virtus's elite isn't something that is going to keep quiet for long."

"*Especially* if people see us heading to the ruin on a regular basis, let alone if we wipe again," Freya added, giving me a worried look. "And don't forget about Ignis, he found the ruin not even two hours after we'd uncovered it. It's only a matter of time until he starts telling everyone and they try to enter the ruins themselves. We may have a claim to the place, but unless we're willing to sit and guard it full time, they're going to get in regardless. But if we can be the ones to tell them…we can at least be in control of how the news comes out, maybe set some ground rules. Short term hurt feelings aside, it'll be better for us in the long run."

"I don't mean to seem like I am piling on," Aldwin began hesitantly, his attention focused on me. "But I believe that your friends are right in this matter, Lyrian. Keeping news of the Ley Line was a necessary tactic at the time. All it would have done was incite panic, and weaken Aldford before we knew what we were up against."

"But now," the Bann continued. "We have a clear vision of the task before us, and secrecy at this point will only put the town in more jeopardy. If what you have said is true about the creatures in the Grove below us, we need all of Aldford's Adventurers working together on this - if only to provide you all with some assistance, so Virtus isn't shouldering this alone."

"Doing this is going to disrupt everything in Aldford," I said, feeling the weight of my friends' advice land on my shoulders. "We need to be ready to handle that."

"You'll have my full support in whatever you need, Lyrian," Aldwin replied. "If anyone asks, I will stand behind our decision to keep the information privileged."

"And so will we," Stanton added, Veronia nodding her head in agreement. "Though I expect our words not to carry as far as Fredric's will."

"It will at least provide a united front," Freya said. "Which—"

A knock on the door caused everyone to turn around as Sierra poked her head into the room.

"*Hey*…" she said in an uneasy voice. "There are a bunch of Adventurers that have been showing up downstairs over the last few minutes, and they're all talking about the ruin. Some of them are even making plans to check it out..."

"How did they even—" I started to say before the realization hit me. "*Ignis.* Damn that man is fast."

"I saw him downstairs," Sierra confirmed. "Right now, everyone seems to be excited by the news that there's something so close to explore, but that can turn quickly."

"He must have gone to spread the word right away," Constantine commented angrily. "He's probably expecting us to either quash it and look like assholes, or give in and let everyone in the dungeon."

"Including himself by extension," Lazarus stated acidly. "Underhanded, but damned if it doesn't put you guys in a hard spot."

"You've mentioned this man twice now. He's an Adventurer?" Veronia asked, looking at us for confirmation.

"He is," I stated, reaching up to rub my forehead at this newest development. It wasn't enough for us to have a nearly impossible task in fighting our way through the Grove and repairing the Ley Line, but that we also had to do it while dealing with greedy players too. "He's angry about how much influence Virtus has around here and doesn't trust us."

"He must be a new arrival then," Aldwin stated, an angry expression crossing his face. "Else he would know that influence was justly earned."

"That doesn't matter right now," Freya said bitterly as she pushed herself up and out of her seat. "Ignis has forced our hand on this, and we need to make a statement about the ruins before anyone leaves."

"Yeah, the genie is definitely out of the bottle now," I grumbled, following Freya's lead and standing up from the table, hearing everyone else rise behind me. "I really hoped we'd have more time to get ready for this..."

"'Ask me for anything but time'," Lazarus quoted as we all got up and started to move, leaving the meeting room and following Sierra back down into the common area, the excited voices of the Adventurers below filtering up the stairs.

Damn, Sierra wasn't kidding, I thought as I looked out towards all the people that had answered Ignis's call. Seeing that several dozen Adventurers had managed to pack themselves into the Town Hall, and were all in the process of forming their groups and preparing themselves to head out for the day.

"Damn, that's a lot of them," Constantine whispered from behind me. "This has to be most of the Adventurers in town."

"It's barely after nine," I commented, glancing over all the excited faces in the room and wondering what exactly I was going to say to them. "Only the early risers have left for the day already. Most of the other Adventurers are just getting up."

"Saves us the trouble of having to tell them more than once then," Freya said, her eyes scanning the crowd, likely for Ignis and the other Adventurers that we saw with him. "How do you want to approach this, Lyr?"

"Directly and with the facts is probably our best bet. There's no sense in hiding any more than we have to," I replied, feeling my heart flutter as my nerves warred with the weight of the Death Sickness still afflicting me. "I was thinking to address them from right under the Webwood Queen's skull, with you and Aldwin standing beside me."

"A potent statement," Stanton said with approval in his voice. "It will remind them of what Virtus is capable of."

"And show them that you have my full support," Aldwin added.

"Hopefully that will be enough," I said, exhaling slowly in an attempt to control my wildly beating heart. "Let's get this over with."

Crossing the room, Freya, Aldwin and I made our way through the crowd of Adventurers until we reached the large fireplace that dominated the center wall of the hall, with the Webwood Queen's skull hanging over it. Sparing only a brief glance up at the trophy, I mustered my courage and then climbed on top of a nearby long table, where I was able to get a perfect view of the Adventurers in the hall.

And where the Adventurers were able to get a perfect view of me.

This is just marginally less stressful than seeing that Raid Boss come out of the woods, I thought nervously as I realized that this would be the largest crowd I had ever spoken to. Sure, I had made speeches before, but this was by far going to be the largest, and I didn't exactly have good news to share. *Just take it one step at a time, Marc, and let them know what the score is. You've done this before; there's nothing to worry about.*

Taking in a deep breath, I tried to hold onto my mental pep talk as I raised my hand high into the air and conjured a bright orb of light. Almost immediately everyone's eyes glanced over in my direction, curious to see what was going on, the voices gradually dying out as they recognized who I was. Holding my other hand high in the air, I signaled for silence, waiting patiently until I was confident I had everyone's attention.

"Good morning," I called out, unable to think of any other better way to start my speech off. "I understand that there have been rumors of a discovery floating around Aldford today and I wanted to take this opportunity to address them."

I paused for a moment, hearing several excited whispers echo up from the crowd in anticipation of what I was going to say.

"The first thing that I wanted to announce is that those rumors are true," I stated in a clear and loud tone. "An intact Nafarrian ruin has indeed been discovered a short distance away from Aldford, and—"

A cheer from the crowd interrupted me as several of the Adventurers shouted in celebration, causing me to hold out my hands once more and signal for silence.

"*And*," I repeated, once the noise had died down enough for me to continue, "as you may have also heard, Virtus *did* run into something that wiped out two of our parties."

All lingering traces of chatter died in the room at my statement, with a range of emotions crossing the faces of the Adventurers before me. Gazing out into the crowd as my words sank in, I saw expressions of concern, excitement, and in a handful of cases, fear, looking back at me, everyone eager to hear what more I had to say.

"But it isn't what killed us that I am here to warn you about," I stated, choosing my next words carefully. "I'm here to warn you about an even greater threat that has been lurking beneath Aldford, one that has the potential to erase all that we have worked so hard to build, and one that Virtus is no longer capable of managing on its own."

I felt the atmosphere in the room grow heavy with my last statement, all excitement of the new ruin suddenly vanishing as if it had never been.

Here goes nothing, I thought, chancing a sidelong glance at Freya who had climbed the table with me and was standing on my right. Sensing my stare, I saw her give me a reassuring nod out of the corner of my eye, giving me the confidence to voice my next words.

"Approximately two weeks ago, Virtus detected something strange in the Ley Line that runs under Aldford," I announced, hearing murmurs fill the hall the second that I mentioned the river of magic. "After taking a closer look at it, and bringing in the expertise of the Eberian Mages Guild members, we discovered that a portion of the Ley Line had ruptured and that Æther was leaking from it, pooling somewhere far beneath us."

"It was determined that unless this rupture were somehow repaired, the Æther leaking from the Ley Line would eventually reach a critical mass and detonate itself, catastrophically destroying everything in this region, Aldford included."

I waited for a moment to let my words sink in, watching shock and surprise play across the Adventurers' faces.

"Based on the severity of this situation and the panic that it could bring, we collectively decided that it would be best to keep this news to ourselves until—"

"Until you had no other choice!" Ignis's familiar voice shouted out. "The only reason why you're telling us this now is because—"

"Until we had more information," I countered loudly, seeing several Adventurers all shifting away from a spot, revealing where Ignis had hidden himself in the crowd, the elf glaring straight up at me with an angry expression. "Given the lack of information that we were working with, we did not want to cause a panic in the town if we could avoid it."

"A measure that I highly endorsed," Aldwin added from his place on my left. "Aldford has seen its share of trials of late, and more than anything, I wanted to preserve a sense of normalcy while we investigated this threat to the town."

"Don't give us that shit!" Ignis retorted hotly, several voices from the crowd shouting out in sympathy. "You would have kept this a secret forever if it wasn't for me finding the damn ruin myself!"

"Oy, shut up, ya twit!" a loud voice barked out from amid the Adventurers, which immediately prompted more shuffling as everyone took a step away from the new speaker, revealing an armored dwarf I'd never seen before walking towards Ignis. "Lyrian and his group have done far too much for us for you to be talking smack about his choices of how to run this town. If it weren't for them, saving our asses from them bandits, a good lot of us would be starting fresh back from Eberia! But not only that, they've been working like fiends to ensure that we are housed and fed!"

A loud chorus of agreement rang up at the dwarf's statement, causing Ignis to shrink backward a step as the man closed in on him.

"You know damn well that cowardly folk like you would have bailed the moment that trouble reared its ugly head!" the dwarf continued, taking several more threatening steps towards Ignis who finally managed to muster up his courage.

"How *dare* you call me a coward!" he spat at the dwarf. "I'm the one who brought *all* of this to light! You would have never even known about this if it weren't for me!"

"All you're doing, *boy*, is stirring an overboiling pot that Virtus is desperately trying to cool!" the dwarf answered, taking another step towards Ignis, this time with his hands raised before him. "And if you keep spewing your filth, I swear I'm gonna pop you in the gob hard enough that you'll be picking your teeth out from your pod!"

"There will be no violence here!" Dyre's voice rang out as he suddenly appeared between the dwarf and Ignis, having effortlessly made his way through the crowd. "If you must settle anything, it will be through a sanctioned duel, *outside* the Town Hall!"

"Something that I would do gladly, Justicar!" the dwarf shouted in response, to the cheers of several Adventurers in the crowd.

"Looks like we have more support than we thought," Freya commented quietly as the cheers devolved into shouting and Adventures began to form up behind either Ignis or the dwarf.

"Damn! This is exactly what I was afraid of happening!" I replied, gritting my teeth as the dwarf and Ignis continued to shout at one another. Pitching my voice over the crowd, I called out as loud as I could manage. "*Enough!*"

With my shout cutting through the din and Dyre's imposing presence, the voices in the hall gradually quieted, everyone's attention shifting away from the two Adventurers and back onto me.

"As I was saying," I said after the volume had died down to a manageable level. "We were waiting until we had more information before making a public statement about the Ley Line and as of a few moments ago we finally have something to share."

I paused once again for a moment, waiting for the lingering voices to completely die down.

"During our exploration of the Nafarrian ruins, we found a route that led deep underground, going as far to reach a massive cavern, set directly under Aldford," I announced, in as clear a voice as I could manage. "And in that cavern, we discovered an underground grove like none seen before. One filled to the brim with hordes of savage creatures along with magical plants and countless untouched resources.

"And, of course, the Ley Line rupture."

With my last words, excited murmurs broke out from the Adventurers, the argument just seconds earlier completely overshadowed by the promise of a rich and untouched area to explore.

"But this place, The Twilight Grove, is not for the faint of heart," I warned, hoping to temper everyone's expectations. "It is a place of extreme danger that only the strongest Adventurers and Guilds in Aldford are going to be able to survive in, and only if they all work together.

"As such, I am issuing a Call to Arms to all the Adventurers here before me," I announced, looking out into the crowd and meeting as many eyes as I could manage. "It will not be an easy task by any means, but we need your help in taming this new region and in finding a way to repair the Ley Line before it can destroy what we've worked so hard to build."

Wrapping up my speech, I spread my hands wide and hoped that my words would be enough to inspire everyone and keep the cracks that had just shown themselves under control.

"So now I ask, who among you is ready to stand up and help save Aldford?"

Chapter 42

With a sharp grunt of exertion, I thrust Splinter's point into the beast's armpit, forcing it through the tough muscle until the hilt came to a stop against flesh. Within a heartbeat of the blow landing, a pained roar filled the air around me, prompting me to duck under a razor-sharp set of claws, temporarily letting go of my sword. Feeling the breeze of the arm sail over my head, I used the opportunity to conjure a burning dagger in my hand and in one smooth motion, plunged it into the creature's far knee, the thick grey skin easily parting under the knife's searing edge.

The smell of burning flesh filled my nose as I continued to move. The dagger, its job done, turned to ash in my grasp. A step took me past the now falling beast, its large, muscular form twisting awkwardly as the momentum from its earlier attack, combined with its now-crippled knee, sent it to the ground in a heap.

Right into Amaranth's waiting jaws.

The gorilla-like creature barely had time to complete its fall to the ground before the azure-furred puma managed to sink his teeth into its throat and tear out a large chunk of flesh, turning its whining cry into a pitiful gurgle.

Time to end this, I thought, reaching out towards Splinter's hilt protruding from the beast's side and grasping it tightly. With a sharp yank, I pulled the blade free of the grey-skinned creature's thrashing body and unceremoniously thrust it into the back of its head, immediately seeing a pair of notifications appear in my combat log.

You have slain a [Twilight Grove Troglodyte]!

You have gained Party Experience!

<Give me your magic!> Amaranth's voice brought me back into the moment, the cat already leaping away from the body of the fallen Troglodyte, towards where more of its comrades were fighting. *<There are more beasts still standing!>*

With barely a second thought, I mentally channeled *Blink Step* in Amaranth's direction, the cat vanishing from sight the moment that I made the spell available to him and reappearing mid-leap just inches behind another Troglodyte. Moving to follow my familiar, I leaped over the rapidly dissipating body of the creature that we had just killed and triggered my own *Blink Step,* my world splintering into a blur of colors as I shifted places.

Reappearing just as Amaranth hamstrung a new Troglodyte, I saw the large creature fall to one knee with a roar, its sudden movement giving me a perfect view of both Sawyer and Sierra over its shoulder as the pair fought back-to-back against two more of the beasts that had managed to circle them.

"Nice of you to finally join the party, Lyr!" Sierra called out, catching sight of me out of the corner of her eye as she dodged under one pair of Troglodyte's claws while catching the second on one of the twin swords in her hands, leaving the other free for her to send a short stab into the beast's chest.

"I decided to take the scenic route!" I answered, moving forward to aid Amaranth, seeing him leap backward from a swipe of the Troglodyte's claw as it spun around, then dart forward to deliver a slash of his own along its side.

Leading with Splinter as I rushed towards the creature's flank, I took advantage of its awkward positioning and carved a line into its shoulder, prompting a pained howl from the unexpected attack. Dragging my blade across the Troglodyte's back, I felt a cool wave of energy travel through Splinter and up my arm as I absorbed the few dregs of mana its kind usually had, the sensation lasting barely longer than a couple seconds before fading. Quivering under my draining touch, I heard a confused roar escape from the beast's throat as it tried to shrink away from my blade, giving Amaranth the opportunity to land another swipe, this one landing with enough force for bones to audibly crack and send it falling towards the ground.

Which, much like its companion a few seconds earlier, heralded the end for the poor creature as Splinter's edge connected with the Troglodyte's neck and continued straight through it until it buried itself in the soft dirt underneath.

We've come a long way since the first day here, I couldn't help but think as I watched the creature's head fall away from its body, rolling limply along the ground as a dark grey ichor began to pour forth from its severed neck. Looking up from the fallen beast, I returned my attention to both Sawyer and Sierra, the pair gradually wearing down their two Troglodytes now that they didn't have to worry about the third one. *These things used to take three of us to take one down; now we can manage by ourselves, or nearly effortlessly in pairs.*

<Help Sawyer. I'll help Sierra,> I told Amaranth as I flicked the dark blood from Splinter's edge and rushed towards the Troglodyte's flank, charging the blade with a *Shocking Touch*.

"Coming in high!" I called out to Sierra as I approached the wounded Troglodyte from the side, seeing her slash one of her blades across the creature's stomach and then pivot to one side, causing it to reflexively shift its head to follow.

Giving me the perfect shot at the beast's head.

Swinging a crackling Splinter through the air, I chopped the blade into the side of the Troglodyte's skull and felt a shuddering crunch as the sword bit deep into the skull, imbedding itself in the bone. Discharging itself on contact, I then felt the electricity stored in my blade leap forward as it coursed through the creature's head, scrambling all thought stored within.

Assuming these Trogs are even capable of thought, I added dryly as I yanked on Splinter's hilt, pulling the now spasming creature's head backward in the process and exposing its throat towards Sierra, who promptly buried one of her swords into it. A sharp kick to the back of leg a second later then brought the gurgling Troglodyte down to its knees, where Sierra's other blade quickly found its eye and sent it along to join the rest of its companions.

Placing my foot on the back of the dead Troglodyte's back, I pushed against the body, needing the leverage to dislodge my blade which was still firmly imbedded into its skull. While pulling the blade free, I cast a quick look around the battlefield, catching sight of both Amaranth and Sawyer putting an end to their Troglodyte. I then continued onwards to check the rest of the group, having lost track of them in the melee.

Seems like everyone made it without too many problems, I noted to myself several seconds later, seeing Drace and Freya step out from the thick jungle nearby, and sensing that Constantine, Halcyon and Caius were gradually approaching us.

"Everyone doing okay?" Drace asked as he caught sight of us all, his voice breaking the relative silence that had fallen over our patch of the jungle now that the Troglodytes were dead.

"No problems here," Sawyer announced from behind me. "I think we're finally getting the hang of this. A hell of a lot better than our first day down here..."

"God, don't remind me about that," Sierra added in a pained tone as she exhaled sharply. "Just thinking about that day gives me Death Sickness."

"We had a lot to learn," Freya replied dryly, her eyes losing focus as she looked at something in her vision. "How's everyone doing? Just a couple thousand experience points shy of level eighteen."

"Roughly the same here," Sawyer answered with both Drace and Sierra also echoing similar values.

"I still have a fair bit to go," I replied, bringing up my character sheet and glancing over all the changes that had taken place over the last few days.

Lyrian Rastler – Level 17 Spellsword
Human Male (Eberian)
Statistics:
HP: 979/979
Stamina: 890/890
Mana: 1040/1040
Experience to next level: 15734/36400
Attributes:
Strength: 57 (77)
Agility: 57 (78)
Constitution: 54 (55)
Intelligence: 60
Willpower: 22

"Still leveling your Leadership skills?" Freya asked, prompting me to shift my focus away from the sheet. "You've been at that for a while now."

"I just need one more point," I said, giving the woman a nod before returning my attention back to the sheet and scrolling down towards the Leadership section, checking to see what my progress was. "I've managed to boost the other skills high enough to unlock the next Leadership tier, which costs three points and I—oh wait! I gained a point during that battle! Hang on a second."

Feeling a surge of excitement surge through me, I spent my newly gained Leadership Skill Point, having spent the last few days in this cavern with sixty percent of my experience gain allocated into the Leadership tree. Originally, my plan had been to continue to develop the three regeneration skills that I had already had focused on, and help decrease our downtime between fights. But when I had spent my thirtieth Leadership Skill Point, a new skill became available to me, which given our experience with The Beast, practically begged me to invest the time in earning it.

Now let's see what else I've unlocked! I thought eagerly as I confirmed my choice and felt an unexpected wave of confidence surge through me as a list of notifications appeared in my vision, along with a newly updated Leadership Skill Tree.

You have unlocked a new Leadership Skill – Form Raid Group!

You now have access to Tier 2 Leadership Skills!
Leadership Skills:
> *Increased Health Regeneration – Increase amount of Health Regenerated by 8. (8/10)*
> *Increased Mana Regeneration – Increase amount of Mana Regenerated by 8. (8/10)*
> *Increased Stamina Regeneration – Increase amount of Stamina Regenerated by 8. (8/10)*

Increased Movement – Increase mounted and unmounted speed by 6%. (6/10)

Improved Leadership I – Grants the ability to form a raid group and unlocks further leadership development. (1/1)

Improved Health – Increase total Health by 1%. (0/5)

Improved Mana – Increase total Mana by 1%. (0/5)

Improved Stamina – Increase total Stamina by 1%. (0/5)

"Oh damn!" I exclaimed excitedly as I finished reading over my new skill list, unable to keep myself from grinning as I read over it. "This was definitely worth it!"

"What was worth it?" Constantine asked as he and the other two casters finally emerged from the forest and rejoined us, their eyes scanning the area cautiously. "You guys find some loot?"

"No," I replied, my eyes still focused on the text hanging in my vision. "I finally earned that last Leadership point I needed to unlock the next skill tier."

"Oh," the rogue replied, his voice sounding slightly disappointed that my excitement didn't correspond to material wealth. "That's just as great, I guess..."

"What skills did you get?" Freya asked curiously, ignoring Constantine's lack of excitement. She had also unlocked the Leadership Skill Tree but hadn't chosen to progress as far down it as I had just yet. "Anything good?"

"Well, I can form Raid Groups now for one thing, so that'll be useful for later," I announced, watching everyone's face shift as they were reminded of my initial motivation to unlock the skill. "But I also unlocked these three other skills that'll scale pretty well with time..."

I then read out the new leadership skills to the party, watching their faces light up at the news. "...each of them takes three skill points per level right now, and I'm sure that'll only increase, but that's a pretty potent buff for just forming a party!"

"I'll say," Freya replied with envy in her voice. "Especially once you've got them all capped out, no one will begrudge an extra bit of health or mana; it could end up making all the difference."

"Damn right. I'll never turn down more hit points," Drace agreed. "Because when it turns out you need more hit points, you *really need more hit points*."

"I hear you there," I said, all the close calls and fights over the last few days floating through my mind. "But given that a Leadership Skill Point is costing me thirty-five hundred experience points now, I think I'm going to switch back to full leveling for a bit. Earning just a one percent boost to a stat compared against reaching level eighteen or higher just doesn't seem worth it yet. Being able to form a raid group was the thing I wanted the most at the moment."

"Makes sense—" Freya began to agree before Halcyon's somewhat shrill voice cut her off.

"I'm sorry, Lyrian, I think you're going to have to repeat all of that for us," he said glancing nervously around the party. "Because I know that I can't be the only one whose brain started going *'EEEEEEEEeeee!'* the moment that you suggested we'd be forming a raid group. You still seriously want to go after *The Beast*?"

"I don't see any other option, Hal," I replied firmly, despite sharing his reservations. "That thing has been effortlessly wiping out two or three parties a day. As soon as we get a decent enough core of higher levels…we're going to have to take a shot at it."

"That and the fact that it's a *Raid Boss*, Hal," Constantine added in a passionate voice. "It's our duty as Adventurers to put our immortal lives on the line, to find and slay this magnificent beast before it can wreak havoc amongst the NPCs in the region."

"First of all, that *thing* is too big to fit through the tunnel entrance." Halcyon breathed. "So, it's not threatening any NPCs at all. If we leave it in here, it'll never escape. Second—"

"Geez work with me here?" the rogue interrupted, reassuming his normal tone and glaring at the mage. "We want to kill the thing because it probably drops awesome loot and if we don't do it, another group might pull it off. Not to mention, a fight with that raid boss is probably worth half a mil' to us in feed value alone, maybe more if we're the ones to take it down."

Shit. I didn't even consider that! I thought as the revelation hit both the rest of the group and me with equal intensity, everyone glancing at one another with wide eyes.

"Holy shit," Sawyer whispered, the first to break the shocked silence. "You guys are *that* popular? I mean I had an idea but..."

"We're in the top thousand," I admitted to Sawyer, still a bit stunned by Constantine's logic.

"Damn," the red-armored man whispered with awe, his eyes brightening as he looked over at me. "Virtus need any more warriors by chance? Lazarus may be a good buddy, but he sure as hell doesn't pay in the six-figure range...or the one figure range, now that I think about it..."

"I'll keep you in mind," I replied, flashing a smile at the man before Halcyon called out again.

"*Lyr*," he stated in a serious voice. "After some serious consideration, I've changed my mind; we need to turn that creature into sausage as soon and in as awesome a manner possible."

"I thought that would bring you around to my line of thinking," Constantine said with a wide smile breaking out on his face.

"Oh, I'm thinking alright," the mage replied. "Mostly on how I'm going to stay the hell away from the thing, while you all kill it. Being eaten by that thing once in my life is more than enough for me."

"I think we're all—" I started to reply to the mage, only to have a massive roar echo out from somewhere distant in the jungle, filling all of us with a deep existential dread as the very creature we were talking about made itself known.

"Another one bites the dust…" Sierra said nervously, her eyes focused towards the shadow-filled canopy. "What's that? The sixth today?"

"At least," I replied with a sigh, the levity of our earlier conversation having vanished. The Beast's roar had become an almost staple noise in the Twilight Grove over the last few days, ringing out whenever the creature managed to claim a new victim, or more likely, a group of victims.

A noise that had been growing only more frequent with each day that passed.

"That sounded far enough away," I said, motioning for everyone to resume the trail that we had been following through the jungle. "But we should probably get moving just in case. If we can't find that stone soon, we'll have to turn back for the night."

"Based on what that other group told us, we should be getting close," Sierra assured me as she, Amaranth and I took point, resuming our trek. "Assuming we haven't accidentally intersected another group's path, but I doubt that's the case, it's impossible to get through this place without leaving a trail exactly where you've gone, and I haven't noticed any other trails."

"Me either," I replied, glancing out at the ragged path of broken plants and torn vines that signaled that a group of Adventurers had recently passed through here. The jungle was simply too thick for anyone except for the most patient to pass through without leaving some sort of evidence of where they had gone.

Pushing onwards, I kept my eyes scanning the foliage carefully as we moved, watching for any sign of creatures lurking in wait, while silently wondering if the group had actually found a second Runestone - which is what we had begun calling the large glowing rock that we had discovered during our first day in the Grove.

Which already seems like a lifetime ago, I thought, feeling the familiar weight of mental fatigue and exhaustion return as the excitement of battle faded. Ever since I had issued the Call to Arms and led Aldford's Adventurers down into the Twilight Grove, the days had blurred themselves into a veritable storm of blood and death as we all worked to tame the underground jungle.

The first day with all of Aldford's Adventurers entering the Grove had been sheer chaos. Despite all our warnings not to take the creatures lightly, the majority of the groups going into the cavern had done just that, treating the Grove as if it were just another area filled with monsters.

And consequently, they paid the price for it.

Nearly three-quarters of all the Adventurers that came down with us on that first day were torn to shreds by the jungle creatures, with a substantial number of them practically begging us or other well-organized guilds to physically escort them to their numerous Soul Fragments by the time the evening fell. Many of them then choose not to return to the Grove, in favor of spending more time leveling in the safer areas above ground before making a second attempt at the jungle.

But those who learned from their early mistakes, or had been smart enough to heed our warning in the first place, found themselves in a place where they could hone their skills against a virtually endless horde of creatures.

Or as gamers would more aptly describe it, *grind*.

Given the rather substantial level difference between the average Aldford Adventurer and the majority of the creatures in the Grove, gaining levels was by far the most important thing that anyone could do in the jungle, and Virtus was no exception. We had recalled every single member of the guild and outfitted them with the best armor and weapons that we had available, then set out en mass into the cavern, starting the process in bridging the level gap between us and the creatures that inhabited the Twilight Grove.

There were of course missteps and deaths at first as we were forced to develop tactics that worked against the creatures and which people fought best together. But as the days progressed, we slowly made headway against the seemingly endless array of monsters that crawled amongst the strange, alien plants that made up the jungle; we were now able to carve our way through the weaker hordes that would have once stopped us cold.

All part of the cycle, I thought dryly as I pushed a large fern-like plant out of my face and continued to follow the trail. *Find a new area full of tough monsters, kill them until you out level them, then go searching for newer and tougher monsters. Though in our case, finding tougher creatures means working our way closer to the Ley Line.*

After a few days of leveling in the Twilight Grove, we had all noticed that the creatures in the place progressively increased in level the further that one delved into it. Lower levels, for the area at least, seemed to be found around the edges of the massive jungle, their levels ranging from level fifteen to seventeen, and gradually increasing to eighteen and nineteen as one pushed into the heart of the Grove. Anything past that point, however, was still a mystery, with no Adventurer or group having managed to make it any deeper without being fatally swarmed by the local fauna, or attracting the attention of The Beast.

It's only a matter of time, I thought optimistically as I considered just how far we'd come in the last few days. *Just a few more days leveling, then we should have enough people leveled high enough to go hunting for that damn creature. Once it's out of the way, we can see about pushing our way towards the Ley Line.*

<Is that the stone we were looking for?> Amaranth's mental voice broke through my introspective thoughts, causing me to focus on our surroundings once more.

"Uh," I stalled, seeing the outlines of a large shadow loom distantly along the trail. "Let me see."

Bracing myself for the shock, I quickly toggled my *True Sight* while staring in the direction of the shadow, the darkness at the edges of our light vanishing into a blinding spray of azure energy before vanishing, leaving me clutching at my eyes as faint afterimages swam across my vision.

"*Yep!*" I announced, recalling the pillar of light that was exactly where the shadow had stood. "That's definitely another Runestone."

"Great!" Sierra commented excitedly from beside me. "...so, what does that mean?"

"I haven't the faintest idea," I replied as the stone came into view in the orbs of light that were illuminating our path. Taking a moment to inspect the area, I noticed that like the first Runestone we'd found several days earlier, this one was also deeply imbedded in the ground with much of the vegetation around it having been trampled, likely from the other party that had found it first. "We haven't even made sense of the first one we found, let alone this one."

"Donovan and the others haven't had any insight?" Sierra asked as the rest of the group joined us and we all walked around to the smooth side of the Runestone.

"Nothing useful," Halcyon supplied for me, having been working with the four mages with whatever little spare time he had. "After watching the runes play through a few cycles on the stone, Lyr and I decided to take some sketches to show them, and so far, we all agree that it's some sort of spell notation…but we haven't been able to figure out anything more than that."

"Probably because we don't have enough context of the overall spell," I said, motioning towards the stone. "We thought that the Runestone might have been part of something bigger before, and this is proof of it."

"Could be," Caius agreed. "But that only leaves to question how many Runestones there are…or if they're all even intact."

"We can ask around and see if anyone else has found any, now that we know for sure there is more than one," Sierra said thoughtfully. "Or make a formal announcement to all the Adventurers that we're looking for them. Pretty much everyone's found the first stone already, so it's not a secret by any stretch."

"My bet is if there are any others that they're even further into the jungle," Constantine said. "This one here is about as deep into the Grove as any of us have travelled so far. Any further than this and we're likely to start running into those level nineteen Praying Mantis looking things that Lazarus said wiped out his group last night."

"I think you're right," I told the rogue, while simultaneously shuddering at the memory of the half-giant's description of the creatures.

"So, what's the plan now, Lyr?" Drace asked after we all shared a sympathetic wince. "We found the stone, but I'm not keen on hanging around here any longer than we have to."

"We wait until it lights up," I said, sheathing Splinter and then reaching into my inventory to pull out a stick of charcoal, parchment, and a flat sheet of metal, seeing Halcyon do the same out of the corner of my eye. "And then we sketch it too, it's not like we can take it with us."

Drace paused to look up at the stone, before nodding in agreement. "No, definitely not through a jungle like this."

"Do you really think you guys will be able to figure something out with this?" Constantine asked as I found myself a place to sit in front of the Runestone, both Amaranth and Halcyon moving to take a seat on each side of me. "I mean the quest we have for the Ley Line didn't even react to us finding the stones."

"I really don't know, Constantine," I admitted with a shrug as I readied myself. "But these stones have to be important somehow. Otherwise, they wouldn't have survived the blast that formed this place."

As if it had been listening to my words, the Runestone chose that moment into flare to life, familiar runes and magical script appearing on its smooth face and beginning to crawl across its surface. Sitting up straight, I flattened the parchment onto the metal sheet before me, while watching the shifting lines flow across the rock, attempting to commit each and every piece of it to memory. I stared at the Runestone without moving, letting the entire sequence play out on its surface until it finally faded away.

It was only then that I looked down at the parchment before me and lifted the charcoal stick in my hand, placing it on the page carefully.

And began to draw.

Chapter 43

"*Finally!*" Constantine exclaimed as we passed through the long tunnel separating the Twilight Grove and the massive chamber that we had fought the Sentinel in, the sound of friendly voices and even laughter greeting our ears. "Home, albeit *temporary* home, at last!"

"What a long day," Drace agreed, the half-giant's tone carrying a heavy note of exhaustion. "I can't wait to sleep...hell, I might just log off and crash in my real bed tonight."

"That's not a bad idea," I told the man, looking out at the sprawling camp that had practically willed itself into existence the moment that Adventurers realized that after a long day of hunting in the Grove that they *still* had to make the trek back up through the ruin and then to Aldford.

I had no clue who first decided to throw their bedroll down on the ground in the chamber and simply fall asleep, but most of the Adventurers afterward had considered it to be a fantastic idea and joined in until nearly everyone exploring the Grove was spending their nights in the relatively safe area. After that, it wasn't long until a handful of them decided to clean up the rather battle-scarred chamber, and even shorter after that before several other enterprising Adventurers realized that there was coin to be made by providing services to those willing to brave the Grove.

And so, Camp Sentinel was born.

In the span of three days, the chamber that we had been caught fighting for our lives in against the Nafarrian golem, had been transformed into a sort of home away from home, filled with clusters of roughly made chairs and tables where weary Adventurers could rest in between their expeditions into the Twilight Grove. Yet the addition of new furniture wasn't what made the place feel homey; it was everything else that followed it.

With the Adventurers choosing to spend their downtime in a single spot, it was only a matter of time before the chefs among their ranks began to ply their trade and began turning the creatures and plants of the Grove into strange and exotic dishes, removing the one major need any of them had to return to the surface. Shortly after the chefs appeared, so did the merchants, each of them eager to lighten overburdened Adventurers of their spoils gained from hunting in exchange for piles of coin. Then eventually, following the merchants, came Shelia and Jenkins, the pair seizing on the opportunity to both cater to those who needed healing and those who found their equipment in dire need of repair, if not replacement.

"Every time I look at this place it seems that there is something new sprouting up," I commented to Freya, motioning towards a group of Adventurers that were setting up a large burlap tent in one corner of the chamber in an attempt to carve out some privacy for themselves.

"Never underestimate the power of an inconvenienced Adventurer," she replied tiredly, following my hand towards the group's efforts. "They'll move heaven and earth until they can be lazy again."

"That sounds about right," I said with a chuckle while glancing back at the group and seeing that they had all dispersed, some heading towards the tables where other members of Virtus sat, others heading straight towards their bedrolls before collapsing into them. "Are you going to bed or staying up a bit longer?"

"Bed, definitely," Freya replied, covering a yawn as she shook her head. "I don't know how you manage on four hours of sleep a night, but I can't do it, at least not after a day like today."

"I know what you mean," I said, despite feeling the exhaustion that only an entire day of fighting could bring. "But I shouldn't be too long; I just want to check on the camp, then take the new Runestone sketches to the mages and see if we can make sense of them. I'll sleep better knowing that everything here is going okay."

"I'll save you a bedroll then," Freya told me with a wave, her eyes already partially glazed over as she turned to walk towards the section of the chamber that Virtus had staked out, leaning heavily on her spear as she moved. "Good night, Lyr. Good night, Amaranth."

"Good night, Freya," I called back, my familiar also croaking in acknowledgment as the blonde warrior departed.

<Perhaps we can find some food too?> Amaranth asked a heartbeat afterward, his hopeful eyes shifting up to look at me. *<The meat from those beasts...the Troglodytes...tasted far too foul to be eaten and I find myself starving.>*

"Ah, I'm sorry, Amaranth!" I replied to the cat, suddenly realizing that aside from a single unlucky Gremlin in the morning, I hadn't seen him eat or drink anything at all today. Given my rather unique condition of no longer needing to eat, I wasn't in the habit of carrying any food with me, leaving me with nothing to offer the cat. "I didn't even think! Let's find you something right now!"

Moving deeper into the camp, the two of us made a beeline towards a collection of tables that served as a makeshift kitchen catering to the hordes of the Adventurers, while also making a brisk business buying meat and herbs recovered from the creatures of the Grove.

Angling our approach towards a tall, dark-furred Tul'Shar that was busily butchering various meats, I flagged the man down and pointed towards a table with a pile of uncut meat.

"Hey, is any of this meat for sale?" I asked, seeing his eyes widen in recognition as he turned to look towards me, still holding his bloody knife in his hand.

"Hmm?" He grunted in confusion before following my hand towards the table. "Uh, well, not until it's cooked. If you want a meal you can—*OH!*"

Halfway through his sentence, Amaranth decided to make his presence known and placed both of his paws on the heavily laden table as he lifted himself up off the ground, his nose twitching as he began to sniff at the meat.

"It's not for me," I told the understandably shocked butcher as the table groaned ominously under Amaranth's weight. "I'm just looking for something for my familiar."

"I-I can see that," he said, managing to recover from the surprise. "W-what does he want?"

<This piece,> Amaranth replied, licking a massive flank that must have once belonged to a truly large Grove creature, not waiting for me to pass the question along to him. *<Possibly more if I'm still hungry.>*

"We'll start with that slab that he just licked," I told the man, seeing him wince as Amaranth then bit into the meat that he had marked and lifted it off the table without disturbing any of the other cuts piled around it. "How much for that piece and let's say another cut roughly its size too?"

"Um," the Tul'Shar stalled as the sounds of Amaranth tearing into his meal reached our ears. "Three silvers should cover it. Maybe just have him come back when he's ready for seconds?"

"Works for me," I replied, taking out my pouch to pay the man, who accepted my coin with a numb expression, his attention focused in the direction of Amaranth's eating.

<You can take one more thing off the table when you're done that piece,> I told the cat as I turned away from the tables. *<I'm going to check on Shelia and the others to see how their day went.>*

Receiving a mental grunt in response from my familiar as he continued to messily feast on his meal, I left him behind to eat in peace while crossing the length of the camp towards where Shelia and her apprentices had set up shop. After the disaster that was the first day exploring the Grove, we realized that we needed to have a medical area to help treat the wounded who managed to make it out of the Grove under their own power.

I hadn't yet been unfortunate enough to come across any, but there were apparently a number of creatures in the jungle that were capable of inflicting lasting injuries on their victims, be it through some sort of wasting disease, burrowing spines, or a particularly long-lasting venom. None of which faded with the regular regeneration that we Adventurers enjoyed.

Instead, anyone so afflicted needed to be treated either magically or cured by alchemical means, which many of the Adventurers simply didn't have access to. It seemed as with many of the games before it, Ascend Online was no exception to the rule that Healers were often few and far between, with many players not gravitating to the support role.

Fortunately for us, however, we had Shelia and several other Adventurers that she had taken under her wing, who were all more than willing to aid those suffering in exchange for a chance to practice their skills.

"Thank you so much for your help," I heard an unfamiliar Adventurer say graciously as she stepped out from behind a set of several blinds that marked the healer's area of the camp, designed to give their patients some privacy. "I don't know what I would have done without you."

"It's what we're here for," Shelia replied a moment later, following the woman out from behind the enclosed area. "Do try and take care of yourself, will you? Perhaps *avoiding* the stinger of whatever beast you came across in the jungle would be a good start?"

"Believe me," the woman breathed, letting out a small chuckle before departing, "I'll *try*. I definitely don't want to go through that again."

"Hey, Shelia," I called out as I approached the priestess, seeing her eyes shift off of the Adventurer and onto me.

"Ah, Lyrian!" she greeted, her eyes dropping down to look over my body as if expecting to see an injury. "Are you just stopping by for a visit, or...?"

"Just a visit," I said quickly, not wanting to worry the woman. "We just got back from the Grove a few minutes ago, and I just wanted to check in."

"That I am glad to hear," Shelia replied with relief in her voice before motioning me towards a set of chairs that faced the camp.

"Was it a busy day today?" I asked once the both of us were seated. "Any problems?"

"Not particularly," Shelia replied, after cocking her head in thought for a moment. "The camp is in good spirits overall. Though I did have a few unfortunate souls earlier in the day that I hope have learned to be much warier about what plants they decide to eat...*oh*, and another handful that will hopefully take much more care when fighting those Quillbears that I have heard about. I must have removed enough of those jagged quills to fashion myself a cloak from them all."

"You know that may not actually be a bad idea," I replied, having only heard stories about the bear-sized porcupines that inhabited a section of the jungle. "It would certainly deter anyone from attacking the wearer from behind."

"Likely it would just fill the wearer's backside full of the quills once he attempted to sit down with the cloak on," Shelia said with a chuckle. "But how about your day, Lyrian? Was it a productive day hunting?"

"It was," I stated, shaking my head at the mental picture the priestess had just painted. "We spent the day thinning out the Troglodytes on the eastern side of the Grove and eventually got word that a group discovered yet another Runestone, so we went to verify that."

"And?" Shelia prompted, well aware of the strange Nafarrian artifact by reputation if not by sight.

"There was indeed a second Runestone," I said, then followed it with a shrug a moment afterward. "I still have no idea what to make of it, but we took a few more sketches of the thing, and I was going to deliver them to the mages in the upper ruins before turning in for the night. I just wanted to check in on you and Jenkins before I left the camp again."

"Well, unfortunately, you've just missed him," Shelia replied with a shake of her head. "He, Ritt and a pair of Adventurers just left for Aldford less than an hour ago. He briefly mentioned something about a group finding a large vein of ore in the Grove and needing more tools before taking off."

"Someone found metal?" I exclaimed in sudden excitement at the news. "That's amazing! Did he say what kind it was?"

"Unfortunately, no," Shelia answered, not surprised in the slightest at my enthusiasm. Having spent the last few weeks living with Jenkins, she was well aware of the shortages that Aldford faced when it came to the precious substance. "Given our needs...he was understandably excited."

"No kidding," I said, nodding along with her assessment while simultaneously feeling a sense of relief wash over me. A large vein of any type of metal would go a long way to meeting the demands that the rapid construction had placed on Aldford and perhaps allow us to use some of it for something other than building. Especially if we didn't need to use the difficult-to-forge Æthertouched Iron that we had recovered. "That could change everything."

"I think those were the exact words that came out of his mouth too," Shelia commented with a laugh before her face turned serious. "We'll have to see if the news bears fruit though; the metal has yet to actually be recovered."

"Definitely," I agreed, noticing a staggering Adventurer turn around a distant tent and begin to make his way towards us. "Oh, looks like you might have another customer coming."

"Hmm," Shelia replied, leaning forward in her seat to look past me, then stood up from her seat sighing softly. "More quills from the looks of it."

Standing up to follow Shelia, I turned to look towards the Adventurer, the man having approached close enough for me to identify him as a half-elf, likely either a rogue or warrior based on what I could see of his armor - where it wasn't completely covered in razor-sharp quills, protruding from nearly every part of his body.

"Hey," the half-elf greeted us with a noticeable quiver in his voice. "So...I kinda fucked up."

"I think we can see that," Shelia replied, indicating for the man to step behind one of the blinds. "But don't worry, I'll have you fixed up in no time."

"That would be great," the elf replied, managing half a nod before his face contorted in a wince. "Shit, ow."

"Did you win?" I asked the man as he gingerly turned himself to walk behind the blind that Shelia had pointed to.

Turning his head slowly to look towards me, the man flashed a happy smile. "Hell yeah. It was a rare creature too!"

"Right on, man," I congratulated, prompting an exasperated sigh from Shelia.

"I'll never understand you Adventurers," she growled. "Anyway, I guess I'll see you later, Lyrian."

"Good luck," I replied, waving farewell at the priestess as she and the quill-filled Adventurer stepped out of sight behind the blind.

I guess I'll need to catch Ritt and Jenkins later then, I thought as I left the medial area behind, hearing a loud yelp of pain echo out from behind me as Shelia began to de-quill her latest patient. With my plans now changed, I retraced my earlier steps across the camp as I made a line towards the passage that would take me to the upper ruins, the same one that Freya and her party had explored when we had first delved into the dungeon.

<I'm heading up to see the mages now,> I sent to Amaranth as I walked, wondering if the cat had managed to finish his meal. *<Are you coming with me?>*

<Must I?> Amaranth replied, his mental voice sounding tired and disoriented. *<I am rather tired...and full.>*

<Not at all,> I told my familiar, receiving the mental equivalent of a snore as the cat's presence faded away from my mind.

I don't blame him for being tired, I thought with a smile. *We were out in the jungle for the entire day today as well as the day before that…and even the day before that too…*

And likely for the foreseeable future, I added dryly, feeling my earlier grin fade away as I considered just how much of the cavern was still left for us to explore.

Letting my thoughts wander as I walked through the chamber and into the passage that led to the surface, I barely spared a glance at the damaged Nafarrian ruins around me, their novelty having somewhat worn off after several trips to the surface and back. Thankfully I had been able to convince the Nafarrian security system to permanently unlock one of the paths into the ruin, giving everyone an easy way in and out of the place. It also ensured that a portion of the ruin was completely blocked off from the regular Adventurers, ensuring that at least some of the Nafarrian technology wouldn't be damaged or tampered with.

Eventually, my feet carried me to the upper portion of the ruins, and I found myself entering a room bathed in a cool azure light, the familiar sight of an Æther Crystal hanging in the center of the chamber. Blinking as my eyes adjusted, I spotted both Donovan and Stanton standing on either side of the crystal with their outstretched hands pointed towards it. But despite their focus, the both of them spotted my presence and lowered their arms, turning their heads towards me.

"Donovan, Stanton," I greeted the pair as I crossed the room and walked towards them.

"Good evening, Lyrian," Donovan greeted, stretching his arms and shoulders as if he had been holding his pose for a substantial length of time. "How did the hunt go today?"

"Pretty well actually," I replied, before waving at the Æther Crystal. "What were you guys just up to?"

"We're trying to measure just how much Æther this crystal contains," Stanton said, taking a step around the crystal to better see me.

"And?" I asked, suddenly curious.

"We don't know," Donovan answered with a frustrated sigh. "We simply have no comparison to form a rational measurement. The power stored in here beggars anything we've ever seen before, by several orders of magnitude."

"That much?" I asked, looking over at the Crystal then back towards the two mages.

"Imagine one only ever having seen water in puddles all their lives," Stanton said. "And assuming that is a normal quantity found everywhere in the world."

"And then one day, stumbling unexpectedly on the ocean," Donovan added, waving at the Æther Crystal.

"Hrm," I grunted, somewhat better understanding the mental struggle that the two mages were experiencing. "What would the Ley Line itself be in that case?"

"The Sun," Donovan replied with a shake of his head. "Even if that disrupts the water analogy somewhat."

"It is apt regardless," Stanton agreed, nodding at the mage before returning his attention to me. "Was there something that you needed from us, Lyrian? Or were you just passing through?"

"Actually, I had some news to share," I said, pausing for a moment as I pulled both Halcyon's and mine's sketches out from my inventory, offering the both of them to the mages. "We found another Runestone in the Grove today."

"*You did?*" Donovan shouted as he lunged forward to grab the sketch out of my hand, Stanton only barely managing to restrain himself from doing the same as he too took the proffered sheet of paper and inspected it.

Silence fell over the chamber as the two mages excitedly examined the sketches that I had handed to them, before almost simultaneously rushing over towards a stone table at one end of the room. Moving to follow the pair, I saw that there were several other papers scattered across its surface, one of them namely being the sketch of the first Runestone.

"This is part of the same spell as the first one," Stanton stated, as he placed my newest sketch beside the one belonging to the first Runestone, unable to completely hide the sense of wonder in his voice. "Yet, looking at this...I still cannot fathom what it is actually supposed to *do*. It doesn't quite make sense."

"Me either," Donovan added, his voice mixed with both frustration and excitement as the pair shifted to make room for me at the table. "However, this *proves* we are not seeing the whole spell notation, there must still be more out in the Grove to be found."

"That's what Halcyon and I are now thinking," I replied taking a look at the two sketches before me, slowly working my way through the notation, having only had memory to compare against while sketching the second stone. After a few minutes, I noticed that a portion of the notation repeated itself, namely the trailing edge of one sketch, mirroring the leading edge of the next and said as much to the two mages.

"I had noticed that too," Donovan admitted. "Though I am not certain what to make of it."

"I think I do," I said while tapping my finger on the sketch thoughtfully. "Halcyon and I copied the script exactly how it appears when they activate, as well as how it moves across the surface."

"How do you mean?" Stanton asked, looking at me curiously. "I remember you mentioning that the script moves across the Runestone's face, but I admit I cannot picture that in my mind."

"It is hard to explain without seeing it yourself," I said, struggling to find an example that the two mages would understand. "But I'm starting to think that the script on this sketch..."

I paused to indicate the newer sketches that I had just shown the mages.

"...travels over onto the Runestone that bore the first sketch," I continued, pointing to the second piece of paper. "And repeats itself there."

"Which means we can disregard the repetition in the notation," Stanton said slowly, putting his hand on the sketch to cover a portion of it.

"That would certainly lend more context," Donovan said, nodding slowly at our logic.

"Let me redraw it," I stated, feeling a spark of excitement kindle within me as I grabbed a blank piece of paper and a stick of charcoal, then began to combine the two sketches together, removing the duplicate portion of the notation.

Paying special care to detail, it took me several minutes to combine the drawings as the two mages watched wordlessly over my shoulder. When I was finally done, I set the now shorter piece of charcoal down and took in the newly made sketch.

"It's...a containment spell?" I asked aloud after staring at the script for a few moments and trying to piece together the incomplete script.

"I believe so," Donovan replied, turning his head to the side as he stared at the paper. "But to contain what?"

"The Ley Line," I suggested, my heart suddenly pounding in my chest. If this spell was capable of affecting the Ley Line, then we might actually have a way to seal it when we finally managed to cut a path towards it. "What else would there be to contain?"

"Well, yes," Donovan agreed, but then pointed towards a section of the script located directly in the center of it. "But there's something else too…I can't make sense of it."

The three of us paused as we inspected the area that the mage had indicated.

"It is certainly particular," Stanton mused. "It seems to somehow allow the spell to…*adjust* itself without a caster's input, but how, I cannot say."

"If this were somehow used to contain or interact with the Ley Line, then it would make sense that it should be able to react automatically," I reasoned, glancing between the two mages. "We have no idea how complicated managing a tapped Ley Line could have been, I can't imagine that it was easy."

"Or safe," I added as an afterthought.

"You think this spell may have been a control mechanism of some sort then?" Donovan asked me.

"Maybe," I replied with a shrug. "If the Nafarr were using the Ley Line for power, then having a way to control it would have been critical."

"I am inclined to agree," Stanton said. "All that we have uncovered about the Nafarr over the decades has pointed to them being thorough in their designs. They would not have left something like containing the Ley Line to chance."

"Then I guess we're going to have to go back into the Grove and find the rest of the Runestones," I stated, looking down at my newly updated sketch. "This is the first lead we have in actually *fixing* the Ley Line; now we just need to actually find a way to get to it."

"I thought you said things were going well on that front?" Donovan asked, sounding slightly concerned.

"They are going well enough, but slowly," I sighed. "We haven't even managed to make it halfway through the jungle yet, and that still leaves a substantial portion of it for us to cover, the creatures inhabiting it notwithstanding."

"I don't envy you and your guild in their task, Lyrian," Stanton said in a grave tone. "I've noticed that many of the Adventures that pass through these chambers on route to the Grove always seem to have curses directed at *The Beast* at the edge of their lips."

"For good reason," I acknowledged. "That thing is the largest reason for our slow process so far. Sooner or later, we're all going to have to try and hunt it down."

"Do you really think you'll be able to kill it?" Donovan asked. "From the tales we've heard..."

"I don't know," I admitted as I stepped away from the table, memories of the creature floating to the forefront of my mind. "But we need to try...because one way or another..."

I paused for a moment as I looked both mages in the eye.

"Aldford's and maybe even Eberia's fate depends on it."

Chapter 44

Thursday, March 28th, 2047 - 5:58 pm
The Twilight Grove

A deafening shriek filled the air as a grey-colored blur slammed into me faster than I could react, the impact knocking me off my feet and sending me falling backward. Landing heavily, I felt the air rush out of my chest followed closely behind by a sharp stabbing pain in my hip as the grey shape leaped on top of me.

"Ah!" I barked in a mix of pain and defiance at the screaming creature now straddling me, the horror that was a Twilight Gloomstalker.

Resembling something akin to a Praying Mantis, the nearly six-foot-tall Gloomstalker towered over its diminutive cousin, its greater size lending it an infinitely more menacing appearance, which was only further enhanced by the presence of two wickedly serrated blades attached to its arms. But despite its massive increase in size, whatever passed for Mother Nature in the Twilight Grove hadn't yet finished with the creature, deciding to cover the bipedal creature in an array of sharp and cruel looking barbs, making being in proximity to it an exercise in pain.

It was those very barbs that happened to limit the extent of my options at the moment, giving me the choice of accepting my fate and letting the Gloomstalker bury its sharp claws in my chest before feasting on my remains. Or to try and stop its claws, by grasping hold of its barb covered forearms before the blades began plunging into my chest, likely delaying the inevitable by a few seconds at most, at the cost of great personal pain.

Needless to say, I took the second option.

"Arrrgh! Fuck!" The curse practically flew out of my mouth as I grabbed hold of what passed for the Gloomstalker's arms, willingly impaling my hands onto the sharp spines that protruded from them.

This is what I get for losing Splinter! I berated myself mentally, trying to focus past my newest set of injuries as I caught the descending limbs and pushed against them, just barely managing to stop the Gloomstalker's claws inches away from my chest. Exhausted from what had already been a fatiguing battle, it was all I could do to keep the claws at bay, my muscles straining under the creature's superior positioning.

Hissing angrily at my desperate attempt to preserve my life, the Gloomstalker threw its weight against me, forcing the barbs even deeper into my palms and causing its claws to sink just a bit closer to my chest. Reeling from the pain, but unwilling to surrender, I clenched my hands as tightly as I could around the creature's arms, feeling blood begin to ooze into my gloves. Feeling the strength drain away from my arms, I knew that I wouldn't be able to keep the creature at bay forever, a point driven home as one of the two blades sank low enough to pierce flesh.

I guess this is going to hurt even more than it already does! I thought grimly while gritting my teeth in preparation for what I was about to do, a desperate idea having come to mind. Taking a heartbeat to brace myself, I channeled *Shocking Touch* into my hands and let it flow into the Gloomstalker before I could have second thoughts.

Instantly, the massive insect began to thrash in my grip as its body seized, the motion from its movement causing the already intense pain in my hands to intensify. Yet despite the agony, I did my best to hold onto the creature, using the opportunity to shift my legs out from under it and brace both of my feet against its chest. Not letting up in the only avenue of attack I had, I sent another *Shocking Touch* into the Gloomstalker, causing it to hiss and thrash wildly for a second time as I began to push it away with my legs.

Enraged by my attempt to get away, the oversized bug threw itself against me even harder, its instinct driven mind unable to fully comprehend the extent of my strategy. As I extended my legs, I maintained my steady grip on the two arms that I had grabbed hold of, no longer needing to push against them to keep the creature at bay. Instead, I began to force the creature away from me with my legs, the movement causing its arms to stretch until they were fully extended. It was only when the sound of cracking chitin sounded from the two limbs that the Gloomstalker finally understood what I was doing, its angry attempts to close with me suddenly turning to a panicked thrash.

With a burst of energy, I savagely yanked on the creature's two arms while thrusting my legs against its chest with every ounce of strength I possessed. Holding for the briefest of moments, I felt the Gloomstalker's arms resist my pull, before suddenly giving way with a sickening crack as the limbs that I was holding tore free of its body. With all resistance vanishing, the Gloomstalker fell away from me in a spray of black ichor, a wailing cry of pain echoing up a heartbeat after.

"*Gah!*" I yelped in pain as I lay gasping on the ground, the Gloomstalker temporarily forgotten while I looked at the bloody mess that was my hands. The barbed spines of the creature's arms had rent my palms wickedly, causing a steady flow of blood to pour from them.

Better my hands looking like this, rather than my face or chest, I thought acidly as I forced my hands to unclench before gingerly pulling them free of the barbed limbs, hissing softly in the process. Once my hands were free, I forced myself back up onto my feet and turned my attention towards the now writhing Gloomstalker a short distance away from me, seeing a dark well of ichor that had pooled around its body. Staggering over to the dying creature, I didn't hesitate in delivering a savage stomp to the creature's head to put it out of its misery, all while I fished to open my belt pocket, finding it difficult to open with my torn hand.

Finally managing to get the clasp undone, I reached inside and pulled out a single glass vial filled with a familiar red liquid that every Adventurer ever born recognized. Thumbing off the stopper, I brought the vial up to my mouth, watching a small description appear in my vision as I tipped it back.

Minor Healing Potion

Item Class: Magical
Item Quality: Average (+0%)
Weight: 0.1 kg
Use: Regenerate 250 hit points over the next 10 seconds.

Downing the potion with barely a second thought, I immediately felt the strange liquid begin to do its work on my torn hands and the rest of my body, the bruised and broken flesh rapidly knitting itself together. Breathing an intense sigh of relief, I allowed myself a momentary pause, which was promptly interrupted by Lazarus's voice.

"Are you okay, Lyrian?" he shouted, pitching his voice over a shrieking cry similar to the one that I had heard just seconds earlier. "Because if you are, we could sure as hell use your help over here again! *Ah! Shit!* Ransom—"

Whirling at the half-giant's voice just as a loud burst of magic drowned out everything around me, I caught the tail end of a flaming blast that filled the jungle with smoke and the smell of burning vegetation. But before I could even begin to think about moving, a shape that I recognized all too well staggered backward out of the acrid mist, its body charred from the recent blast of magic as well as several more wounds that I didn't recall seeing from earlier in the battle.

Damn, that thing is still standing! I thought incredulously as a tag appeared in my vision, pointing towards the still smoking creature as it forced itself back fully onto its feet, where it then towered nearly half a body length over me.

[Twilight Grove Deathstalker] – Rare Boss – Level 19

Making the Gloomstalker that I had just killed appear like an innocent kitten in comparison, the Deathstalker was a paragon of its kind, improving on everything that defined its already vicious siblings and turning it into a veritable whirlwind of carnage.

Carnage being exactly what it had wrought since its arrival.

Pushing aside the chaotic memories of earlier in the fight, for the time being, I instead forced myself to focus my attention on the ferocious creature as my eyes searched for the one thing I needed to get back into the fight.

Splinter.

Good! It's still there! I breathed with a sigh of relief as I spotted the hilt of my blade protruding from the side of the Deathstalker's shoulder, exactly where I had thrust it into before being unceremoniously slapped away by a flailing claw and sent tumbling across the ground. *Now...to get it back without somehow killing myself.*

Conjuring and discarding half a dozen ideas, I quickly came up with a plan that I was reasonably confident wouldn't result in my untimely end. I forced myself to sprint towards the creature, watching its movements carefully as

I closed. With it still reeling from whatever magic Ransom had unleashed, I only had precious seconds to recover my weapon before it resumed its rampage.

Reaching the point of no return a short distance away from the Deathstalker, I leaped high into the air and triggered *Blink Step*, my vision blurring into colors before suddenly snapping back into focus an arm's length away from the creature's back. With momentum still carrying me forward, I barely had enough time to process my change in scenery before I slammed into the giant insect, causing it to stagger forward from the impact.

Pushing aside the sharp stab of countless barbs that covered the creature's carapace, I threw one of my arms around the Deathstalker's neck to keep me from falling, while my other reached out to grasp Splinter's cool hilt. Just as my hand wrapped itself around the sword's base, I heard a shrieking hiss erupt from the Deathstalker as it twisted violently in pain.

"Not quite what I was expecting you to do, Lyrian!" I heard Lazarus shout from somewhere in front of me. "But hell, if it works!"

"Yeah, well, I didn't have much of a choice!" I replied, struggling to hold onto the creature as it began to thrash in an attempt to dislodge me. "I had to get my damn sword back!"

"Well now that you have it, put it to use!" Lazarus called back, the ichor covered tip of his sword appearing briefly in my vision as he swung it towards the Deathstalker. "Ransom and your cat are dealing with another two of the smaller bugs!"

"Shit," I cursed softly, realizing that I hadn't heard anything from Amaranth since the battle had started, before having been jumped by a Gloomstalker the moment that I had recovered from my landing. Yanking Splinter free of the Deathstalker's shoulder with a spray of ichor, I mentally reached out towards my familiar.

<Amaranth! How is your side of the fight going?> I asked the cat as I stabbed Splinter back into the Deathstalker's body, sensing through our bond that my familiar had been injured several times.

<Poorly!> he replied in an angry tone. *<It is all I can do to keep these predators off Ransom! If we do not get some assistance soon…>*

<Damn, okay! Just hold out for a bit longer,> I told Amaranth, the urgency in his voice prompting me to channel a *Shocking Touch* into my blade before I pulled it free a second time. *<Lazarus and I just need to kill the Deathstalker!>*

Receiving a mental growl in acknowledgment, I was forced to turn the entirety of my attention back towards the writhing creature that I was currently hanging off as it worked itself up into a frenzy. Clinging on for dear life, I felt the flesh on my chest and the arm that I had wrapped around the Deathstalker's neck tear painfully as it desperately attempted to shake me loose, the creature's cruel barbs digging into me. Maintaining my grip on the Splinter's hilt, I sent yet another surge of electricity into the nightmare-sized creature, feeling it jerk wildly as its muscles spasmed.

Taking advantage of my distraction, I felt a heavy blow from Lazarus slam into the Deathstalker, the impact causing the creature to suddenly buckle and drop down to a knee. Hissing at the unexpected movement and the pain that it caused, I found myself staring almost directly into Lazarus's face over the creature's shoulder, a bleeding cut across his brow having covered it almost completely in blood. Then as quickly as he had appeared, he vanished, forced to duck under the Deathstalker's sweeping claw as it struggled to buy some time to regain its balance.

Time that I wasn't about to give it.

Tearing my sword free once more from the Deathstalker's back, I tightened my grip on the blade's hilt and then yanked myself upwards with the arm I'd slung around the creature's neck in one explosive burst of energy. Letting out a ragged gasp as the spines continued to dig into my body, I thrust Splinter into the base of the Deathstalker's head, using both my strength and momentum to drive it upwards through the hard chitin until I felt the blade exit through the other side. At once, I felt the creature go limp from the blow, the flailing movements of its body losing all sense of coordination as it pitched forward, just barely catching itself on its claws before it hit the ground.

Gritting my teeth at the Deathstalker's stubbornness, I twisted Splinter savagely and delivered a final S*hocking Touch*, all resistance fading away from the creature as the electricity traveled the length of my blade and coursed into its skull. Landing on the ground with a heavy thud, I felt the creature deflate under me as a pair of timely prompts appeared in my combat log.

You have slain a [Twilight Grove Deathstalker]!
You have gained Experience!

"Finally!" Lazarus rasped from nearby, causing my head to spin in the direction of the voice and spotting the man leaning heavily on his glass-steel sword while holding a badly bleeding arm to his chest. The Deathstalker had clearly managed to land its fair share of blows on the half-giant during the fight. "I was starting to think I'd never see that fucker dead!"

"It was a close thing," I agreed in an exhausted tone, hearing a vicious growl from Amaranth echo out from the jungle, reminding me that the fight wasn't quite over yet.

Pulling both myself and Splinter free from the dead creature, I couldn't help but wince from the newest round of wounds that covered my body. "You going to be able to keep up with that arm?"

"*Just watch me*," Lazarus growled, pulling his large weapon free of the ground. "Let's go!"

Rushing towards the sounds of the battle, it only took us a heartbeat to find both Amaranth and Ransom fighting back to back against the two remaining Gloomstalkers, and even less time for us to enter the fray. With my vision blurring into a spray of colors as I triggered *Blink Step*, I arrived behind the Gloomstalker threatening my familiar with Splinter already in motion, the blade's razor-sharp edge slicing through the creature's elbow as if it were paper.

<Finally!> Amaranth's voice echoed through my head as the insect-like creature recoiled in pain from my attack, giving the cat the opportunity to pounce on the creature and take it to the ground.

Landing heavily on top of it, I heard the familiar crack of chitin as Amaranth drove his weight down onto the Gloomstalker, seconds before his powerful jaws found its neck, easily piercing through the hard shell that protected it. With another crack, the cat snapped his head viciously, putting an end to the wounded Mantis, the single moment of opportunity being all that he needed to turn the tables on the creature.

Glancing up from the sudden and brutal end, I managed to look up just in time to see Lazarus's sweeping blade catch the other Gloomstalker directly in the side of the head. The impact took the surprised creature off its feet and sprawling onto the ground, where a bright blast of fire from Ransom and a stab from Lazarus put it out of its misery.

Just like that, the fight was over.

"Damn," Ransom heaved with exhaustion, his posture slightly bent over with both hands on his knees as he tried to catch a breath. "That was *close*. Too close! Shit!"

"You're telling me," I said with an equally exhausted sigh as I considered our losses. Out of the group of eight Adventurers that we had started the day with, only the three of us were left standing, in addition to Amaranth, of course. "Anyone see what happened during the ambush? I didn't even see the others go down."

"The big one dropped down on us from above," Ransom replied, shaking his head at the memory. "It landed with both claws in Cadmus, then sliced Myr apart a second after. They really didn't have a chance. After that…"

The half-orc warlock shook his head and motioned to the burnt and trampled vegetation surrounding us as if that explained everything.

"I saw Edanea go down," Lazarus added in a quiet voice. "We got caught in a no-win situation after the second pack of Gloomstalkers rushed out of the jungle. She managed to buy Connor, Thorne and I enough time to take the first pack down while you and Amaranth kept the Deathstalker busy."

"There was a second pack of those things?" I asked, completely dumbfounded that I missed them in the chaos. "I didn't even see them…"

"At least six of them according to my combat log," Ransom confirmed, his breathing having finally evened out. "After Edanea went down, it all became a scramble, and something got Connor soon after. I never saw what happened to Thorne though."

<He stepped in front of a blow meant for me,> Amaranth told me, his mental voice sounding low. *<It would have certainly been my end.>*

And mine most likely too, I added as an afterthought, realizing Thorn's train of thought. Amaranth's death would have likely weakened me past the point of being able to keep up with the Deathstalker, assuming the shock of his death hadn't caused me to freeze at an inopportune time in the first place.

"Well," Lazarus stated after a moment of silence. "We managed to kill the Deathstalker in the end…which means there's one less rare boss wandering this jungle."

"Small victories, right?" I said, trying to project a sense of optimism in my voice that I didn't quite feel. "Doesn't seem like it's our day for a Runestone though."

"Not today," Ransom added in a disappointed tone. "We should probably grab any drops from the creatures while we still can, then make our way back to the camp. After the beating we just took…going any further today is just asking for something else to jump us, if not *The Beast*."

"No complaints from me," I told the warlock while checking the arm that I had used to hold onto the Deathstalker and realizing that my antics had seriously damaged the armor. "Looks like I'm due for some repairs too. This jungle isn't easy on the gear at all."

"No," Lazarus agreed as he waved at the loot bag that now marked where the Deathstalker's corpse had just been a few moments earlier. "About the only thing this place is good for is the experience bar…and loot of course."

"That sounds about right," I said with a dry laugh as I walked over to the bag and took a look inside, watching the items appear in my vision.

Deathstalker Claw
Quantity: 2
Item Class: Magical
Item Quality: Mastercraft (+20%)
Durability: 0/0

Weight: 2 kg
Deathstalker Fangs
　Quantity: 20
　Item Class: Magical
　Item Quality: Mastercraft (+20%)
　Durability: 0/0
　Weight: 4 kg
Deathstalker Chitin
　Quantity: 10
　Item Class: Magical
　Item Quality: Mastercraft (+20%)
　Durability: 0/0
　Weight: 20 kg

"And we have even more crafting materials," I announced in an unsurprised voice, having grown used to the pattern that the game followed. Choosing to lean on the realistic side of things, wild creatures in Ascend Online were never considerate enough to drop fully forged weapons and armor when they were killed. Instead, choosing to consistently drop the raw materials needed to create something useful, relying on a crafter to give it shape.

Must be a sign of just how tired I am and how long this week has been if I'm complaining about having Mastercraft quality materials to craft with, I thought while rubbing my face, hearing both Ransom and Lazarus echo similar sentiments as they collected the loot belonging to the Gloomstalkers that had also been killed during the fight. *But that's what barely four hours of sleep a night will get me.*

Much like the few days that had preceded it, the last two days had passed at a breakneck pace since the discovery of the second Runestone. The promise of actually having a way to repair the Ley Line once we reached it having prompted us to dive back into the Twilight Grove with renewed excitement, intent on pushing faster and farther into the jungle than we ever had in the days before.

Yet for all our exuberance, we found our efforts neatly curtailed by the second wave of creatures that inhabited the deeper, yet unexplored section of the Grove, their numbers and ferocity increasing the farther we travelled. While we had all expected that there would be challenges in pressing on ahead, any hope I had about being able to at least progress as quickly through the deeper portion of the jungle as we had its border region were dashed after the third Gloomstalker ambush hit us, just barely thirty feet away from where the first one had ended.

Instead, I had been forced to resign myself to a slow grinding approach as we forced our way deeper into the jungle, whittling away at the seemingly endless horde of creatures that inhabited the place, buying every inch closer to the Ley Line with blood and sweat.

Which really wouldn't be a problem for me if it wasn't for our damn deadline, I thought, feeling a slight scowl cross my face as I looked in the direction that I knew the Ley Line to be in. *We don't know how long we have until the Ley Line is in danger of exploding, and our rest cycle is coming up fast! If we can't get this all sorted out by Monday morning...we're going to lose a day, and that'll only put us even further—*

"You coming, Lyrian?" Lazarus's voice interrupted my mental spiral, causing me to turn back in his direction and seeing that both he and Ransom were ready to leave.

"Yeah," I replied, breathing out a deep sigh as I moved to follow the pair, Amaranth moving silently beside me. "Just a little frustrated at the slow progress."

"You call clawing your way up to level eighteen in six days *slow?*" Ransom replied. "If we have another day like today, tomorrow, then I think we can all hit nineteen. If not, then the day after for sure."

"I meant more progress through the jungle," I clarified, despite nodding in agreement with the half-orc.

"Believe me, Lyrian," Lazarus stated, inclining his head to Ransom. "Neither of us are exactly *thrilled* to be here. You know full well that we'd rather be back in Eberia. But with that being said, levels *are* progress here. It's only a matter of time until we're cutting through these Gloomstalkers like we do with the Gremlin and Trogs."

"*Time* being the key word there," I pointed out.

"I'll give you that," Lazarus allowed with a nod in my direction. "But we're not exactly sitting on our asses here, and you forget that the rest of your guild too has been poking around the jungle. It's entirely possible that they've had more luck than us."

"You mean finding, *and surviving*, a rare creature in the deep jungle isn't luck?" Ransom interjected with a note of humor in his voice. "Two days ago, that Deathstalker would have killed us."

"Two days ago, that Deathstalker *did* kill me!" Lazarus spat. "There are going to be more than a few people back at the camp happy to hear that it's dead. Hey, by the way, I don't suppose you'd be able to throw a few of those chitin pieces my way? Believe it or not, I'm still wearing level thirteen gear…and it's not exactly holding together anymore."

"I know what you mean," I replied, glancing over at the half-giant's armor with a critical eye, spotting countless tears and scars on it. Staring at it for several seconds, I slowly considered what the man had just said before shaking my head and snorting. "Damn, I didn't really think about that."

"Think about what?" Lazarus queried as he glanced downward. "My armor?"

"That we've essentially out leveled everything that we're wearing," I said, bringing up my own character sheet to verify. "Everything I'm wearing, with the exception of my sword is still level thirteen."

"I wouldn't say no to upgrading a few pieces," Lazarus said. "We did get a fair bit of scraps from the early part of the ruins."

"And we've been collecting a hell of a lot of hide, leather and other stuff from these Grove creatures," Ransom stated, an optimistic note sounding in his voice. "Do you think you'd be able to craft something useful for us from all that, Lyrian? Better gear could go a long way…"

"Hmm," I mused thoughtfully, feeling a smile creep across my face as I mentally inventoried everything that we had found over the last few days, my mental frustration fading away under the impending excitement of crafting. "You know what…I think I just might be able to come up with something."

Chapter 45

Our journey back to Camp Sentinel was largely uneventful, in as much as a trio of Troglodytes, a quartet of Gremlins, and one *very* large Quillbear could be called such. Yet compared to the Gloomstalkers that we had faced deeper in the jungle, they were all barely noticeable speedbumps on our return route back to the camp, once again reinforcing just how much progress we had made to be able to deal with them so effortlessly.

Lazarus does have a point, I guess, I thought as I paused to look back at the sprawling jungle that filled the Twilight Grove from the high vantage point at the Camp's entrance. *It's not nearly as bad travelling through the border parts of the jungle. At worse, anyone will only have to deal with a handful of creatures at a time now, instead of the huge swarms that roamed around during the first few days in the Grove, when all the creatures were trying to viciously defend their territory.*

Staring out at the azure-tinted cavern for a few more seconds, I then turned away from the sight and began walking towards the tunnel, seeing both Lazarus and Ransom waiting for me.

"Are you planning on heading back up to Aldford to craft?" the half-giant prompted me as I rejoined the pair.

"No. I think I have enough materials down here already," I replied, thinking over everything that I had in my pack. "The crafting area that Jenkins set up down here is fairly comprehensive and should suit my needs for the time being. He even managed to get a small forge down here too."

"He did?" Ransom asked, giving me a surprised glance. "Wouldn't that foul the air in here?"

"Normally I'd say yes," I answered giving the man a shrug. "But it doesn't seem to be causing any problems. I guess the air flowing upwards through the open route and whatever magic the Nafarr enchanted the ruins with seem to be enough in keeping the air breathable. At least that's the only thing that I can think of. With how sprawling and sealed off this whole installation is, they must have taken that into account somehow."

"Makes sense," Lazarus agreed. "If not, then there's that whole jungle of plants and stuff that's probably producing air for everything to breathe."

"Assuming that magically fueled plants even produce oxygen," I said while shaking my head. "I don't even know."

"And here I thought you were the local Ætherbiology expert, Lyrian," Lazarus said with a chuckle.

"Falling into a Ley Line hardly makes you an expert," I replied, snorting at the newly coined name. "If anything, that should be a clear warning sign that I don't know what I'm doing. Besides, I'm pretty sure I flunked biology."

"So, mitochondria *isn't* the mana-source of the cell then?" Ransom asked in a sarcastic tone, flashing a wide smile at me.

"Ha!" I couldn't help but laugh, shaking my head at the warlock. "I didn't flunk *that* badly."

The next few minutes passed in a blur as we continued through the tunnel and entered the camp, the stress of the day gradually unwinding with each step. Filled with a fairly sized crowd, we were far from the first party to return back for the day, but nowhere near to being the last. Scanning the camp activity with a practiced eye, I gauged that easily half, if not closer to two thirds, of the regular Adventurers that normally filled the camp were still out exploring the

Grove, many of which would start trickling back in as the evening wore on.

"Well, Ransom and I are going to keep heading towards the surface and back to Aldford for a bit," Lazarus said as we all came to a stop just outside the camp entrance. "I don't know about you, but I'm long overdue to catch at least a glimpse of the sun before it sets and some fresh air before coming back down."

"I don't blame you," I replied giving the pair an understanding nod. While I wasn't quite missing the daylight myself, I knew what sort of psychological effect the sun had in perking someone's mood and couldn't begrudge him the break. "Just come find me in the crafting area when you come back so I can take some measurements for your armor. It's going to take me a while to get myself sorted out anyway, so no rush."

"Great!" Ransom exclaimed excitedly. "Thanks."

"No problem," I said, seeing Lazarus nod in sympathy to the half-orc's sentiments. "I'll see you guys later."

<Perhaps now would be a good time to mention that I am hungry again?> Amaranth told me as Lazarus and Ransom departed, cutting through the camp and towards the route that led to the surface. *<The Gloomstalkers were…adequate prey, yet hardly satisfying to one's stomach.>*

"Sure," I replied taking a single step in the direction of the camp butchers when Amaranth's voice caused me to stop.

<Actually,> he said, his voice taking on a hesitant tone. *<I am interested in purchasing the meal myself.>*

"Wait, what?" I said, Amaranth's reply taking me so far off guard that I had to process it a second time. "You want to buy your own food?"

<I believe that there is value in learning this version of…hunting…> my familiar replied, his eyes darting up to

look at mine. *<I have noticed the shiny metals you Adventurers trade amongst yourselves in exchange for trinkets and food, and I am curious to attempt the same for myself.>*

"Well, sure," I replied to the cat, wrapping my head around the idea and not seeing any logical reason to refuse. "I mean I don't see why you couldn't, though you not being able to talk may be a bit of a barrier."

<I have considered this,> Amaranth replied in a confident voice. *<And I have come to the conclusion that hunger transcends language.>*

"I suppose it does," I said, unable to completely disagree with the cat's logic. "How were you going to go about buying the food you want?"

<My plan was to present some of the shiny metals to the…merchant, I believe they are called,> Amaranth informed me. *<Then I was going to indicate which cut of meat I wished to devour. From there I believe that my intentions would be quite clear.>*

Maybe, I thought, thinking of several ways that Amaranth's plan could go wrong. Yet if he truly wanted to learn how to…*shop*, of all things, I wasn't about to stand in his way.

"I think that should work," I told the cat. "Or at least communicate enough for you to be able to improvise."

<Good,> Amaranth replied, bobbing his head in a feline approximation of a nod. *<Now…in order for me to execute this plan, I require some of those shiny metals that you Adventurers carry…they are called…coins, correct?>*

"That's right," I said to the cat as I caught the implied meaning in his mental voice and pulled out my coin pouch, counting out a handful of silver. Taking a moment to transfer the coins into a smaller bag, I offered it to my familiar, who gently took it from my hand with his mouth.

"This should be enough to buy two pieces, assuming you want that much."

<Perhaps,> Amaranth said, cocking his head to the side with the coin pouch in his mouth. *<We will see if I am successful first.>*

"Well, if you need any help, I'll be over in the crafting area," I told my familiar and received an acknowledging flick of the ear in return as he turned away from me, his tail hanging high in the air with confidence.

I guess if I don't hear any screaming or panic, I'll just assume things are going well, I thought, slowly trying to accustom myself to my familiar's sudden display of independence. It hadn't escaped me that Amaranth's personality was becoming more developed and nuanced as the weeks wore on, but having him expressing the desire to...*buy something* was the last thing that I had expected to hear.

But not a bad thing either, I added a heartbeat later followed by a mental shrug as I began to walk through the camp and towards the crafting area that Jenkins had set up.

I was hoping that I'd be able to catch the man at some point today, having barely had a chance to exchange more than a dozen words with him over the last two days. Ever since he found out that there were veins of metal readily available in the cave, both he and Ritt had dropped almost everything in favor of supporting the group of Adventurers that had claimed it and ensured that Aldford got the majority of the ore for its construction efforts.

That last move hadn't exactly won them any favors with the rest of Aldford's Adventurers, who also wanted all the metal that they could get their hands on. But since Ritt was willing to buy ore at above market rates and was bankrolled by Aldford's rather deep coffers, there was little that they could do about it, short of going out and prospecting themselves. Unfortunately, however, my hopes were dashed when I arrived at the makeshift crafting area and found it to be completely empty with neither Ritt nor Jenkins anywhere in sight.

"With how much work I have ahead of me I'm sure I'll run into them if I stay put," I said wistfully as I dropped my pack on the ground and began to unfasten my armor, unable to conceal the grimace that crossed my face as I ran my fingers over the seemingly countless broken rings that comprised the chainmail. "I think at this point, it'll probably be easier for me to dismantle the majority of this for scrap than it will be to fix it."

With practiced ease, I peeled the layers of the now well-worn armor off me and laid it out on an empty table, carefully inspecting the damage that six days of practically non-stop adventuring had wrought.

"This leather is going to have to go," I told myself as I appraised the now bloodstained hide that comprised the shoulder portions of the armor, my fingers tracing a deep scar in the leather that marked one particularly close call the day before. "I'll have to relink some of this chain, but I think I should be able to salvage a good portion of it..."

Whispering softly to myself as I continued my inspection, I felt the wheels in my head begin to turn as I assessed what sections of armor were worth salvaging and just how I could reuse them going forward. Once I had a better idea of what I was working with, I then turned to my pack and began to inventory the crafting material that I had on hand, watching all the items that I had accumulated in the Nafarrian ruins and the Twilight Grove appear in my vision one by one.

[Blackened Chainmail Scrap] x 5
[Gremlin Leather] x 23
[Gremlin Teeth] x 76

[Troglodyte Hide] x 46
[Troglodyte Claw] x 31
[Large Razor Quill] x 12
[Small Barbed Quill] x 34
[Gloomstalker Chitin] x 25
[Deathstalker Chitin] x 10
[Deathstalker Claw] x 2
[Deathstalker Fangs] x 20
[Iron Ingot] x 20
[Nafarrian Sentinel's Æther Core] x 1

"Huh," I grunted as I fished through the pack. "I forgot I still have a few chainmail scraps that we found in the dungeon; I guess that will make repairs easier. I can also use the Trog hide to replace the leather in the armor easily enough, assuming that Jenkins hasn't used up all that alcohol that Marlin sent down the other day…"

I felt my hand land on something that I wasn't expecting and pulled it out of the pack, revealing a glowing crystal, "…ah! I forgot Freya gave the Æther Core back to me…"

Turning the object over in my hand, I inspected the crystal carefully as I considered the best way to put it to use. It wasn't exactly doing anything useful sitting in the bottom of my bag, and I was all too familiar with the idea of 'saving' a rare item indefinitely while waiting for the perfect chance to use it.

You're making a new set of armor for yourself anyway, Marc, the pragmatic portion of my subconscious told me as I considered the item and the rather substantial bonus that it gave to all attributes. *Given how brutal the Grove has been so far…you're going to need every single edge you can get going forward. Plus, it's not like you're getting any closer to figuring out how to forge larger pieces with that Æthertouched Iron back in Aldford either.*

"Isn't that the truth," I grunted to myself as memories of the uncooperative metal came to mind. Ever since crafting Splinter, I hadn't had the time, or to be completely honest with myself, the inclination, to try experimenting with the Æthertouched metal. Having had a few days to think about it, I was confident that there was a fundamental step in the forging process that I was missing, and as satisfying as it would be to solve it, doing so simply wasn't currently the best use of my time.

Right now, everything depended on us getting to the Ley Line and somehow finding out a way to seal the rupture before it reached critical mass. Only then, and once we were all confident that the danger of the town and surrounding region exploding in a cataclysmic storm of raw magic had passed, was I going to try working with the strange metal again.

Which meant that at the moment, I was limited to the items I had on hand.

"Which *also* means that I'd be a fool not to use this," I said to myself, still staring at the Æther Core in my hand as I completed my rationalization process for using the item.

Confident in my decision, I then set the Æther Core in the center of a clear table and began to pull the other items I would need out of my pack, placing several pieces of Troglodyte Hide, a handful of Iron Ingots, all the spare chainmail scraps, and two large pieces of Deathstalker Chitin around the crystal.

"Alright," I announced to the air around me as I rubbed my hands together in anticipation before reaching out to grab a pair of heavy pliers I would need to disassemble my old set of armor. "Let's get started."

Diving into my work with fervor, the next two hours passed by in a blur as I began to craft myself a new set of armor, marked only by Amaranth's report that he had been victorious in his 'hunting' attempt, which was then soon followed by a mental snore as he began to digest his meal. Slowly but surely as the hours passed, my new armor began to take shape as I fashioned each piece in sequence, disassembling the old armor's piece, then immediately using what I had salvaged on its replacement and adding in the new materials that I had set aside, where appropriate.

It was towards the end of those two hours when I finally found myself finishing the final and largest section of my new armor set, namely being the chest piece. It was a roughly hammered cuirass with two large plates that would protect both my chest and back, linked together by a double layer of chainmail and chitin that gave some flexibility to the piece, allowing me to make the most of my speed and mobility. Set directly in the center of the cuirass was the glowing Æther Core, the otherwise clear crystal giving off a cool azure light from within.

Checking its setting one last time, I made sure that the crystal wouldn't fall out of the socket that I had fashioned for it, pushing and pulling on it as hard as I could. The last thing that I wanted to worry about was to have the item come loose in the middle of a fight and losing its bonuses, or heaven forbid, the Æther core itself. Satisfied that it would stay in place, I took a step away from the armor and the table that it was sitting on, seeing its stats appear before me.

Twilight Avenger Armor Set
Slots: Arm, Chest, Feet, Hands, Legs, Head, Shoulders
Item Class: Magical
Item Quality: Good (+15%)
Armor: 385
Set Bonus: (7/7)
Strength: +12 Agility: +12
Armor Type: Light

Weight: 12 kg
Augment: Nafarrian Sentinel's Æther Core. +3 to all Attributes.
Favored Class: Any Martial
Level: 19

"Well, that turned out pretty great!" I exclaimed, despite noticing that I didn't hit 'Mastercraft' quality on the armor set, likely since I had reused so much of my old gear. Yet I could hardly be disappointed in the result before me, and I couldn't help feel a shiver of anticipation for putting it on and seeing the boost that it gave to my attributes.

Which is exactly what I promptly did.

Practically teleporting myself into the waiting suit of armor, I dressed in what had to be a near record time, and before I knew it, I had tightened the final strap that kept the gear in place, feeling it hanging almost weightlessly off my body. Moving my limbs around to test the motion of the joints, I gradually became aware of the Æther Core's presence in the center of my chest, as if it constantly radiated a reassuring wave of energy through my body.

Hard to tell if that's just what the crystal is supposed to do, or if that has something to do with me being Ætherwarped, I thought as I touched the crystal with a gloved hand, feeling the energy then flow through my arm. *Maybe it's a little bit of both.*

Putting that particular consideration aside for the future, I stopped my delaying tactics and brought up the majority of my character sheet, looking over all the changes that the last few days had brought.

Lyrian Rastler – Level 18 Spellsword

Human Male (Eberian)

Statistics:

HP: 1056/1056
Stamina: 960/960

Mana: 1277/1277
Experience to next level: 11238/38900
Attributes:
Strength: 58 (84)
Agility: 58 (85)
Constitution: 56 (60)
Intelligence: 68 (71)
Willpower: 23 (26)
Skills:
Magic:
Evocation – Level 18 – 85%
Alteration – Level 18 – 17%
Conjuration – Level 17 – 13%
Abjuration – Level 17 – 1%
Weapons:
Unarmed Combat – Level 18 – 78%
Swords – Level 19 – 82%
Axes – Level 11 – 35%
Daggers – Level 16 – 73%
Other:
Stealth – Level 18 – 28%
Wordplay – Level 15 – 16%
Perception – Level 18 – 67%
Tradeskills:
Blacksmithing – Level 19 – 22%
Carpentry – Level 18 – 31%
Cartography – Level 2 – 3%
Tailoring – Level 14 – 69%
Cooking – Level 5 – 54%
Herbalism – Level 11 – 4%
Leatherworking – Level 19 – 17%
Mining – Level 15 – 1%

"Looks like I've let my other weapon skills and Tailoring slip a bit," I commented to myself as I looked over the character sheet. "Though hopefully once we get all of this sorted out I can spend some time bringing them up to speed...the same for my magic skills, assuming I can get some the mages to agree to be my mana batteries while I practice—"

"Talking to yourself already, Lyrian?" Jenkins's loud and jovial voice interrupted my thoughts, causing me to flinch and spin in the direction of the sound, spotting the smith and Ritt entering the crafting area with broad smiles on their faces. "That doesn't seem to be the sign of a healthy mind to me. Perhaps the jungle here is finally starting to get to you!"

"Talking to yourself is perfectly *fine*," I replied, matching the man's smile. "Just as long as you're not surprised by any of the replies that your mind comes back with."

"Heh, I suppose that *would* be troubling," Jenkins agreed with a chuckle as he eyed my new armor and began nodding appreciatively. "So, I see you've been making good use of my space while I was gone...though I really hope you didn't use up all my fuel..."

"There's plenty left," I reassured the man as he stepped forward to take a closer look at my new armor. "It wasn't exactly my best effort...since I decided to reuse pieces of the chainmail that I had before, but I think it's decent enough to help me push deeper into the jungle. Once we get everything sorted out down here, I was thinking to try and replicate it with the Æthertouched Iron that we have...after I figure out how to forge it properly."

"'*Wasn't his best effort*', he says as he produces a near flawless work," Jenkins muttered with a shake of his head as he continued to inspect my work. "I daresay there are many that would love to have this armor in your stead!"

"One of them being me right here!" Ritt exclaimed as he stepped forward to admire my work. "Please tell me you can make *more* of this kind of armor, Lyrian! That Serpentine armor you made last week barely lasted a full day at auction...if I could get a dozen more of these suits...*gods* the Adventurers would go into a frenzy! I would need Dyre to oversee the exchange just so I wouldn't get mugged!"

"Uh, I could," I said, tapping on the metal breastplate. "But this armor set is pretty metal intensive. As it was I used nearly my entire share out of the metal we recovered from the golem, plus a bunch of the scraps that I already had from the other set of armor to put this together. So, unless you're willing to share some of that metal that you guys are buying up...I *might* just have enough to get the core guild members armored up, and they take priority over selling to the rest of the Adventurers."

"I understand, Lyrian," Ritt replied, his eyes never leaving my armor as he spoke. "And I'm sure, well, pretty sure that we can get some of the iron we're buying your way, for a share of the profits, of course, Jenkins should be able to talk Le—"

"Oh, hell no, Ritt!" Jenkins barked, interrupting the man. "I'm not talking Léandre into *anything* involving diverting or taking away the metal he needs to finish his work."

"But—" Ritt started to say before Jenkins cut him off.

"But *nothing!* You saw that man when we handed him the first cart of ore! He nearly *cried* with joy!" The smith continued, turning away from me as he rounded on the merchant. "Which was nearly the same thing that *I* did when I first saw what those Adventurers pulled out of that damn jungle! We need that metal going to construction a hell of a lot more than we need more suits of armor right now!"

"I don't disagree, Jenkins. But pretty soon we're going to need ways of *paying* for all the ore that we're buying!" Ritt countered, his tone telling me that this wasn't the first time that he and Jenkins had this conversation. "Right now, we're buying up everything that's coming in, which is great, because we *need* the metal. But with every day that we do that, it's driving up the market rate that the other Adventurers are willing to pay to get metal of their own. All while our total supply of coin dwindles."

"*I know that*, Ritt," Jenkins growled. "I've dealt with Eberian Quartermasters every day during my service. Supply and demand isn't exactly a new mystery for me. Besides, you said you had a solution for that."

"I said I *might* have a solution, and that it's likely going to take metal anyway, along with Lyrian's help," the merchant said, casting a glance in my direction.

"I was waiting for my name to come up in all of that," I replied dryly, prompting a snort from Jenkins. "What do you need from me exactly?"

"The short version?" Ritt said. "I need you to verify and then buy a potential silver vein from an Adventurer that discovered it."

"And what's the longer version?" I asked, feeling my eyebrow raise at Ritt's news.

"Mostly the same," he answered with a shrug. "Yesterday someone came to me saying that he had found, and I quote, '*A giant fucking motherlode of silver*' somewhere in the depths of the jungle and expressed interest that he was willing to sell the location of it if the price was right. He said he has no interest, or skill in mining it himself."

"And you believe him?" I queried while trying to keep my excitement in check.

"He swore that it existed in front of the Justicar," Ritt told me with a pointed glance. "If he were lying, Dyre would have called him out on it."

"Huh," I grunted, taking a moment to process that bit of information. "How much does he want for it then?"

"He opened at six-hundred-and-fifty gold pieces," Ritt stated.

"Yeah, well, he's not going to get that," I grunted, shaking my head at the price. "I don't know how Aldford's finances are, but Virtus doesn't have that much coin on hand even if I bankrupted it."

"The town isn't any different, especially since we're buying up as much metal as we can," Ritt explained. "But, I think there is room to negotiate him down to a more reasonable amount."

"Which you want Virtus to foot the bill for, after we presumably verify its existence, and relative worth," I said, starting to catch onto Ritt's plans. "Then afterward you want us to haul it back to Aldford where my guess is that you're going to want to start minting that silver into coins."

"See, *I told you* Lyrian would understand!" Ritt exclaimed, casting a harsh glance at Jenkins before looking back towards me. "But actually, we'd want Virtus minting those coins; it should help expand your power base within the—"

"W-wait, you want *us* to start minting our own coins?" I felt my brain stop for a moment as I considered what Ritt had just said. "*Can* we even do that?"

"Why wouldn't you be able to?" Jenkins retorted. "Assuming it's the standard size and purity, the silver's value will be the same regardless of who's stamp is on it, and besides, Aldford is independent of Eberia. It's up to us to manage our own currency."

"Not to mention that the amount of hard coinage in the town is fixed," Ritt pointed out. "Unless we start minting more ourselves...or somehow bridge the distance between Eberia and us to get more through trade, our economy will eventually start to suffer."

"I understand that much," I said, nodding slowly at the two men. "But creating coins is usually the *government's* responsibility. Not an Adventurer's guild."

"And Virtus isn't part of Aldford's government?" Ritt asked, giving me a resigned look. "If you haven't noticed Lyrian, Virtus and Aldford are so closely knit that they might as well be one. Not that either of us are complaining of that."

"No," Jenkins added, meeting my eye as he spoke. "You and yours have done right by us, Lyrian, and Virtus is the only one who we feel we could trust managing something like this. Else it'd just fall to the two of us to manage, which, of course, as you know, would just end up with me doing all the work once Ritt got bored."

"Hey!" Ritt exclaimed in an offended tone.

"That seems about right," I agreed.

"Hey!" Ritt repeated in an even louder tone. "I *help!*"

"Help create trouble maybe," Jenkins grunted, waving a dismissive hand at the young merchant. "Anyway, wasn't there a second part to what you wanted to ask Lyrian?"

"Uh? Oh! Right!" Ritt said, shaking off the momentary wave of confusion that crossed his face. "Back to that Adventurer that I want you to buy that silver lode from. Once you buy it off of him, I need you also to sell him enough of your fancy arms and armor to earn back as much of the coin that you gave him."

"Uh, why?" I asked, cocking my head at the rather now convoluted request that Ritt was laying before me. "If he needs equipment, we can just barter."

"I don't think he'll go for that, at least not right away," Ritt replied. "But the reason why is because I think he's considering leaving Aldford..."

"Thus, taking a substantial portion of our gold coin supply out of the local economy," I finished, catching onto Ritt's concerns. "Okay, I think I see your point now."

"Do you think you could manage something like that?" Ritt asked. "I know you have enough worrying about this Ley Line business...but at the same time...we need to start thinking about what will happen if the region *doesn't* go up in a magical conflagration of death and destruction."

"I'll see what I can do," I told the man despite feeling more of the familiar pressure fall onto my shoulders at this newest development. It was one thing to have to worry about a tangible, existential threat to the town, but something very different when faced with an economic one. I simply didn't have a frame of reference for dealing with anything like this. "But I'll be honest though, for this type of negotiation Constantine would be the better person to handle it."

"Whatever works, Lyrian," Ritt said with a shrug. "You're just the first one I've managed to catch, though the Adventurer did tell me he wanted an answer by the end of tomorrow...else he'd announce it to the other Adventurers."

"That should give us more than enough time to work with," I stated, motioning towards the rest of the camp. "Let's go see if we can find him or the rest of the guild near the kitchens, I'm sure that most of the groups have to be back by now."

"Alright," Ritt said, turning around as the two of us moved to leave the crafting area. "Coming, Jenkins?"

"Nah," the smith grunted. "If Lyrian's going to babysit and keep you out of trouble for a bit, I'm going to use the time to get some work done."

"Har, har," Ritt retorted good-naturedly as we departed the area. "I'll see you—*oof!*"

No sooner did Ritt and I step out from the behind the large blind that concealed the crafting area, did a running blur slam into us, the impact sending all three of us tumbling to the ground in a confused tangle of limbs and shouts.

"Ugh, *what the hell?*" Ritt wheezed in pain, winded from the impact.

"Geez, man, what's the hurry?" I grunted as I pushed a pair of legs off me and twisted my body in the direction of whomever had just crashed into us.

Only to find myself staring into the panicked and pale face of Ignis.

"Ah, oh," Ignis gasped as he struggled to take a deep enough breath, a wave of fear briefly flashing through his eyes as he recognized me. "...rain coming, I didn't do it...but..."

"Rain?" I repeated, not able to make sense of what the man was trying to say, nor why he appeared so frightened. "It's going to rain outside?"

"N-no," Ignis said letting out a ragged cough as he inhaled a lungful of air. "*T-there's a train coming!*"

"*Wait, what?*" I exclaimed, a surge of adrenaline shooting through my body as I forced myself up. "What do you mean?"

"I-I-we were just in the jungle a-and," Ignis stammered, still trying to catch his breath from his recent exertions. "They just...came out of nowhere! Everywhere!"

"What came out of nowhere, Ignis?" I demanded, feeling the bottom of my stomach fall out from under me. "What did you lead back to the camp?"

"I-I don't know," he said. "We just, just *ran* and—*oh no*, there is it again!"

"There is *what*—" I started to shout at the man for a second time, when a mental voice I had heard before filled my mind, causing my blood to go cold.

<Invaders! Kill the invaders! They did this to us! Kill them! Kill them! KILL THEM!>

Chapter 46

We barely had the time to process the screaming chant that pierced through our minds before a pair of head-sized emerald blurs shot down from above us, prompting a surprised scream from Ignis as he dove out of the way.

"Shit! Lookout!" he wailed as he hit the ground hard and attempted to roll away from whatever that was attacking him.

"What the hell did you do, Ignis?" I demanded, the words flying out of my mouth as I drew Splinter and instinctively charged towards the spirits, scanning the two identical tags that appeared in my vision.

[Ætherbound Phantasm] – Level 17

"I-I—" the half-elf stammered incoherently in response as I swept Splinter's edge through the center of the closest spirit, which then immediately exploded in a blast of searing energy, prompting pained screams from both Ritt and Ignis. "No! Don't hit them! T-they explode!"

"Too late for that warning, Ignis!" I barked angrily, having taken the somewhat painful blast at point-blank range; I began to rapidly back away from the second spirit as it twisted in the air to face me.

Fixing my attention on the angry spirit as it glared at me with an angry wail, I was immediately reminded of the Ætherbound Shades that we had fought in the dungeon above us earlier in the week. But where a Shade had been a full-bodied spirit, the Phantasm was only a floating head surrounded by a mane of dull emerald energy, its facial features grossly deformed from whatever it once represented in life. Yet despite its lack of a spiritual body, I realized that it did little to hinder its movements as the

Phantasm shot forward through the air, crossing the little distance I had been able to put between it and myself in the blink of an eye.

This is the absolute last thing that we need to deal with right now! The angry thought couldn't help but cross my mind as I threw myself into a desperate roll to evade the oncoming spirit.

Completing my dodge as the Phantasm soared over me, I wasted no time in launching myself back up onto my feet, conjuring and throwing a *Flaming Dagger* at the spirit in one motion, which promptly exploded in a harmlessly spray of energy as soon as the hurled knife touched it.

"Shit, Lyrian!" Jenkins's voice shouted from the entrance of the crafting area as the blast from the Phantasm filled the air, temporarily basking all of us in an emerald light. "What the hell is going on?"

"We're under attack by spirits from the jungle!" I replied as I moved to check on Ritt, seeing that he had only been lightly singed by the first Phantasm's blast. "*Ignis* here dragged them back to the camp!"

"He did *what*?" Jenkins snarled, his voice suddenly laced with a cold rage that I had never heard from the man before.

"I didn't realize they were still following me!" Ignis protested as he scrambled up from his prone position on the ground. "I—"

"Save it!" I barked savagely as I pulled Ritt up to his feet while glaring at the man. "You've done enough already!"

<We're under attack!> I sent to Amaranth, taking advantage of the first free moment I had to collect my thoughts. *<There are spirits invading the camp!>*

<We are aware!> my familiar replied less than a heartbeat later from his place on the opposite side of the

camp. *<Their chant awoke us all, and we are rousing ourselves now!>*

<Good!> I sent back to the cat. *<So far it doesn't look so bad, maybe we—>*

As if drawn by the timing of my words, several loud screams suddenly echoed throughout the camp, interrupting my train of thought, which was followed closely behind by the rapid thunder of magic as other Adventurers discovered the attacking spirits.

"Damn!" I cursed, my head snapping in the direction of the noise. I had no idea just how much Ignis had managed to pull back through the jungle with him, but judging by the growing cacophony around us, it was far more than the two Phantasms that had just attacked us.

<Just fight your way towards us when you can!> I sent back to Amaranth as quickly as I could, watching an errant streak of magic fly high up into the cavern before fizzling out in a spray of sparks.

"What's the plan, Lyrian?" Jenkins asked as he drew a heavy sword from his belt, his eyes darting over towards Ignis, who had finally managed to regain his feet.

"What do you mean what's the plan?" Ignis replied, his voice tinged with panic. "We need to keep running and get the hell out of here!"

"Running is what got you into this damn mess!" I hissed at the man angrily. "No, we need to rally as many of the Adventurers as we can before we lose the camp or even the entire ruin!"

"You're—*oh, shit*!" the half-elf's reply was cut short as a massive shape chose that moment to crash through a pile of crates that had been stacked opposite of the crafting area, its landing reducing them to splinters.

"'Oh, shit' doesn't even begin to describe our problems right now, Ignis!" I shouted as Ritt, Jenkins and I reflexively scrambled to put some distance between us and the horrific, patchwork creature that had just crashed through the crates, followed closely by a blast of magic that washed over its grotesque body.

With negligible effect from what I could tell.

What the hell is this thing? I thought as I glanced at the abomination before us, feeling my heart skip a beat the as an identifying tag appeared in my vision.

[Ætherbound Monstrosity] – Level 19

Seemingly made from a patchwork of flesh, hide, and chitin, the Monstrosity was a nightmare to behold, appearing as if a mad god had decided to tear a handful of the Grove creatures to shreds before combining them together without regard to any of their original forms. At a glance, I could see the dark leather hide that once belonged to a Troglodyte covering one portion of the body, with the dull grey chitin of a Gloomstalker covering its back and chest, leaving the familiar quills, and the flesh they were attached to, of a Quillbear to cover even more. But for all that it had stolen from the Grove creatures, it wasn't enough to fully clothe the spirit, glimpses of its ghostly form shining through the torn patches flesh that it had covered itself in.

"*Gods,*" Jenkins gasped in a strangled voice as the Monstrosity slammed a massive spectral arm, bereft of any flesh, into the ground and forced itself back up onto a pair of mismatched limbs, one bearing the graceful leg of a Gloomstalker, with the other being the short and squat leg of a Troglodyte. "What—"

"Don't let it get up!" a loud familiar voice interrupted the smith as a second wave of magic slammed into the creature, followed by a group of charging Adventurers with their weapons outstretched before them. "Hit it with everything you have!"

"That's Alistair's voice!" I exclaimed, spotting the man a heartbeat afterward as he led a pair of guild members I recognized, and a few other Adventurers I didn't, to attack the still rising Monstrosity. Not waiting for a written invitation to join the fight, I sprang forward to assist, charging Splinter with a *Shocking Touch* as I ran. "Let's go!"

Expecting everyone to follow on my heels, I put the group out of my mind as I rushed towards the Monstrosity, it only taking me three long strides to close the distance and enter the fray. Announcing my presence with a loud shout, I swept Splinter through the large spectral arm that the Monstrosity had planted on the ground, feeling the blade pass effortlessly through the limb, discharging the energy stored inside it as it did. At that same instant, Alistair and the other Adventurers arrived, swarming around the creature and landing their own punishing blows.

Staggering from the barrage of attacks, the Ætherbound spirit faltered in its attempt to right itself, several bright sprays of energy erupting from its spectral body, causing it to let loose an unearthly wail. But despite its apparent pain, the Monstrosity was far from being finished, reflexively swinging its other arm, which appeared to be covered in a layer of Troglodyte hide in a wild arc before it. Moving faster than either of them could react, the sweeping limb caught a pair of the attacking Adventurers high in the chest, and sent them both sailing off their feet and out of sight, a distant tear of cloth and crunch of wood marking their landing.

"Lyrian!" Alistair called out a second afterward, not having missed my arrival. "What the hell is going on? Where are more of these things coming from?"

"Ignis found them!" I replied, stepping around the now flailing Monstrosity until I was directly behind it, slashing out with Splinter as I moved and drained what mana I could from the creature. "He pulled all of them back to the camp from the Grove!"

"*Are you*—" Alistair's reply was abruptly cut off with a loud grunt as the creature's thrashing reached a new level of intensity, forcing me to take a large step backward as a massive arm swept through the spot I was just standing in.

With my reflexes having been honed to a razor's edge after an entire week's worth of fighting in the Grove, I waited just long enough for the creature's attack to pass, before launching myself back into the fray. Burning through my mana with reckless abandon, I thrust another *Shocking Touch*-charged Splinter into the Monstrosity's body as I re-entered melee range, then immediately slashed a burning dagger through the flesh covering its side.

Howling under my blows, the spirit's movements became lethargic as the energy animating it fled its body in large spurts from the multitude of wounds now covering it. The creature's flagging efforts allowing all the other Adventurers, along with Jenkins and Ritt, to close with it, their weapons tearing into its spectral form. With a shout of triumph rising all around us as it lost its shape, the Ætherbound Monstrosity's body dissolved into a spray of energy, the flesh and hide covering it falling to the ground lifelessly once more.

"Ritt, Jenkins, are you two okay?" I called out the moment that the fight ended, my eyes worriedly darting over towards the pair, who I knew would have been grossly outclassed by the fight, yet hadn't hesitated for a heartbeat to jump in.

"I'm fine," Ritt said, breathing heavily from the short fight.

"Same here," Jenkins answered, a heartbeat behind the merchant. "Never in my life have I seen anything like that…*thing*!"

"Neither have we," Alistair stated, shaking his head as he stepped over the remains of the creature, casting a dirty glance at Ignis, who had taken up position a few steps away from us. "*Until today.*"

"There'll be time for blame once all of this is over," I said, seeing several other eyes turn in the direction of the elf. As much as I wanted to figure out *exactly* what Ignis had done to drag a horde of spirits and ghost back to the camp, we had more pressing matters to worry about right now. "But right now, we need to *move* and start rallying as many people as we can.

"*And then fight to save the camp*," I added pointedly, turning my head to glare at Ignis, who at least had the decency to not look me in the eye.

"As much as it pains me to say, Lyrian, I don't know how much we'll be able to help to fight these spirits," Jenkins stated in a steady voice. "But we're with you, whatever you need."

"I understand, Jenkins," I said with a nod, thankful that the man had recognized his limits on his own and wasn't afraid to admit them. "I'll take this group and head to the sounds of the heaviest fighting and try to hold the spirits back, if you and Ritt could comb the rear of the camp for any Adventurers and send them forward that would help us greatly. The same goes for evacuating any townsfolk down here to the surface."

"We can handle that," Ritt said, relief evident on his face that he wouldn't be heading straight to the frontline. "Right, Jenkins?"

"We can," he said with a nod, though his expression was one more of frustrated resignation of his inability to compete with the attacking spirits than relief. "We'll stop first at the healing ward with Shelia, and warn her to expect casualties. If she has any spare healers on hand, I'll be sure to send them forward too."

"The more help I can get on that front the better," Alistair agreed enthusiastically. "I won't be able to keep up forever."

"Alright!" I said as a new rush of magical thunderclaps sounded through the air. "That's a good enough plan for now! *We need to move!*"

With that, we split up from the two NPCs, both Ritt and Jenkins turning to run towards the rear of the camp, while the rest of us charged in the opposite direction, heading towards the sounds of combat in the distance. Positioning myself at the rear of the party as we ran, I made a point to keep a sharp eye on Ignis, not putting it above the half-elf to attempt to slip away during the chaos.

I might be actually doing him a favor if I let him run, assuming he runs as far as he possibly can away from Aldford, I thought, teeth clenched. *If the other Adventurers ever find out that he's responsible for dragging a train into the camp...*

I shook my head at the thought, unable to bring myself to care what sort of vigilante punishments the rest of the Adventurers would inflict if that happened. Maybe if they were severe enough, it would serve as a good enough deterrent for any other Adventurers thinking to do the same thing the next time they found themselves in over their heads.

Assuming we have a next time, I couldn't help but add, thinking of the disaster it would be if we were forced out of the camp and had to fight through the ruins a second time. With a sharp shake of my head, I forced myself away from that train of thought and decided to focus on what I could control, mentally reaching out towards Amaranth.

<*I've regrouped with Alistair and a bunch of other Adventurers,*> I told my familiar, sensing that he had made progress in moving through the camp since that last time that I had spoken with him. <*We're moving through the camp for survivors.*>

<*So are we,*> Amaranth replied. <*Drace, Constantine, Thorne and a few of the other guild members are with me, but we haven't seen any of the others yet.*>

<*They have to be around here somewhere,*> I said confidently, hoping that they had managed to survive the spirit's surprise attack.

Turning my attention back towards our rush through the camp, I followed Alistair's lead as the priest guided us towards the sounds of combat. Rounding a sharp corner, the source of the noise quickly became evident as we spotted a large group of Ætherbound Shades that had managed to completely encircle a handful of Adventurers. Judging from the twin piles of Grove creature flesh lying on the ground a short distance away from the circle, they had already managed to take care of two of the large Monstrosities, but the sheer number of attacking Shades had been too much for them to handle.

At least until we showed up.

"Rush them!" Alistair shouted from the head of the group, making the same decision that I would have in his place, prompting everyone to break into a sprint.

"That means you too, Ignis!" I yelled, noticing that the half-elf was hesitating in following Alistair's lead and delivering a rough shove to get him moving. "Go!"

"Damn it, Lyrian! I'm going!" he shouted, stumbling for half a step from my rather forceful encouragement, but regaining his balance and charging forward without any further complaint.

Following close on Ignis's heels to ensure that he didn't have a change of heart, I found myself slamming into the spirits ranks with him by my side before losing sight of him in the melee. Focusing on driving through the line of the Shades before me, I found myself reliving the desperate fight that we had the previous week at the infected Æther Crystal.

Countless Shades had packed themselves on top of one another, their incorporeal forms allowing several of them to occupy the same space at the same time, making it nearly impossible to defend against them without constantly giving ground. A feat that was next to impossible for the encircled Adventurers to manage indefinitely. Yet, that same fight had also taught me how to use their packed numbers against them.

Slashing Splinter in a wide cleave, I swept the Æthertouched blade through the ranks of Shades before me, feeling a trickle of mana course up my arm with each and every spirit that it passed through. Putting that energy to use immediately, I channeled it back into a *Shocking Touch* and slashed my sword through the wall of spirits a second time, seeing several of them fade away into nothingness as the magic binding them failed. Within seconds of our arrival, the tone of the battle shifted as the Shades registered our presence, and a ragged cry rose up from the trapped Adventurers.

"Help is here everyone!" Sierra's tired voice rang out from inside the circle of spirits. "Now's the time to hit them hard! Push!"

"Sierra!" I exclaimed in relief at having found one of my friends as the trapped Adventurers answered the woman's words with a shout and charged forward into the line of Shades separating us with renewed energy.

"Lyrian, is that you?" Sawyer's voice called out from inside the circle. "Damn, I thought we were done for!"

"Not by a long shot!" I yelled as I sliced through a confused cluster of Shades, all of whom seemed to have a different idea of who or what direction they should be facing.

Pinned between us, the Shades separating our two groups rapidly began to disintegrate as we carved through them, their ranks falling into complete disarray before finally vanishing in a spray of emerald energy. Continuing forward, we charged to support the once trapped Adventurers and slammed into the second line of Shades that had encircled them, our two groups managing to easily overwhelm the remaining spirits.

"Great timing, Alistair, Lyr," Sierra said breathlessly after the last Shade had fallen and our area was reasonably safe for the moment. "Things were looking pretty bad there for a second. Do you have *any* idea what's going on? Where the hell did all of these things come from?"

"The Grove and I'll tell you later," I stated, shaking my head before jerking it in Ignis's direction. "There's no time to get into it now; we need to keep moving. We have no idea just how many spirits are attacking us."

"*A lot*. Assuming that what we just faced is any indication," Sawyer growled, but nodded in agreement with my statement. "Let's go; we can catch our breaths along the way."

Taking a brief moment to consolidate our two groups, we resumed our search through the camp, the shouts and screams that had been echoing through the air earlier having faded as the surprise of the attack wore off, and Adventurers began to fight back. Using the sounds of fighting as a beacon, we rushed towards them, looking to rescue and relieve those who found themselves under attack. As the minutes passed, we gradually found ourselves working towards the front of the camp as we moved, coming across several groups of both Adventurers and spirits, adding the former to our ranks while ruthlessly dispatching the latter.

"Rah!" I grunted as I slashed a crackling Splinter across my body and into the slow-moving leg of an Ætherbound Monstrosity, feeling the tip of the blade shred the layer of Gremlinhide that armored it and discharge itself into the spirit underneath.

No sooner did my attack land than I yanked my blade back towards me, using its edge to intercept the outstretched claw belonging to a Shade that had chosen that very moment to press forward. Just barely slicing through the wrist that the claw was attached to in time, I was then forced to twist my body awkwardly to avoid a vengeful fist belonging to the Monstrosity that I had just injured a heartbeat earlier, the movement putting me square in the path of yet another Shade's claw that I hadn't seen until it was too late to avoid it.

Hissing as the spectral claws bypassed my armor and raked my chest, I forced the injury away from my conscious mind and returned the favor to the offending Shade, slashing Splinter through its head and seeing it vanish in a dull flash of energy. Bringing Splinter before me, I turned my attention back towards the Monstrosity, just in time to see Sawyer's axe sweep through its ghostly head, the attack causing it to vanish in a spray of energy and for its body to lose its shape a second afterward.

"It's down! Everyone forward!" I called out the moment that I saw the massive spirit disintegrate, all the melee Adventurers in the ragged line on either side of me rushing against the Shades that had clustered around it. Weapons flashed, and magic thundered through the air as we rushed the now unsupported Shades, their numbers far too few to pose any threat without the Monstrosity hindering our movements.

"I think that has to be it for the stragglers," Sawyer said to me after the last the Shades had been killed, the two of us watching Alistair and a few other healers rush forward to heal the newest group of Adventurers that we had rescued. "Anyone else has either linked up with another group and moved on, or didn't make it."

"Looks like it," I agreed, glancing around the disrupted camp all around us, hearing the constant thunder of magic and shouting echoing from the further areas of the camp. "Let's get—"

A near deafening boom of magic echoed through the cavern, cutting my words off as it reverberated through the chamber. Glancing at Sawyer in a momentary surge of panic, I felt Amaranth's voice shout through my mind.

<Where are you?> my familiar demanded, a wave of exhaustion seeping through our link. *<We need help! Urgently!>*

<We're around the middle of the camp!> I replied to Amaranth, instinctively glancing in the direction that I sensed him in, finding him near the camp's entrance. *<What's happening?>*

<A horde of the Deathless are erupting from the tunnel!> he answered almost instantly. *<Our numbers are too few to hold them back for long!>*

<Shit! Okay, we're coming as fast as we can!> I sent back, my feet already in motion as I signaled for everyone to follow me. "We need to move! More spirits are coming through the tunnel!"

Fueled by a sense of urgency that I'd never felt before, I sprinted through the heart of the camp towards where I sensed Amaranth to be, all the other Adventurers rushing to follow behind me. With the camp passing by me in a blur, it wasn't long before I saw what my familiar had warned me about, my heart skipping a beat as I took in the battle ahead of me.

Glowing with a bright emerald light, a massive horde of Shades and Monstrosities filled my vision, with several dozen of their Phantasm cousins soaring through the air high above. Before them, I could see a large group of Adventurers that were clearly trying to keep them from overrunning what remained of the camp, but were gradually being forced backward, lest they end up enveloped by the attacking spirits.

"Oh damn!" I heard Sierra's voice exclaim from behind me as we ran, followed by countless other, far more colorful curses from the Adventurers following us.

"You could say that again!" I called back, catching sight of Freya's spear as it briefly appeared over the thickly packed horde of spirits as a large number of them suddenly swarmed forward and over the group's flank closest to us. "Shit! They're getting overwhelmed!"

Pouring on every ounce of speed that I could muster, I charged forward towards the advancing spirits, watching them curl around the group's edge, quickly beginning to surround them. But before the spirits could completely send the Adventurers into disarray, we arrived, slamming into their extended line unexpectedly and scything straight through it. Within seconds, we cut down dozens of the attacking Shades and had them back on their heels, erasing all of their forward progress they had managed to make as well as giving the beleaguered Adventurers the time they desperately needed to reform their ranks.

"You guys made it just in time!" Freya greeted us with a relieved shout as both she and Amaranth fell in on either side of me as the ranks organized themselves, my familiar rushing to reunite with me the first moment that he could. "We barely had enough time to form lines before they hit us!"

"I know the feeling!" I replied with a grimace as I slashed Splinter through the horde of Shades in front of me. "It's been like this the entire trek through the camp!"

Before either of us could say anything more, the spirits surged forward to meet our reinforced ranks, a new level of ferocity appearing in their attacks. Forced to focus solely on staying alive under their onslaught, all rational thought fled from my conscious mind as instinct took over, guiding both my blade and body to wherever they needed to be at that instant. Flashes of combat intermixed with fleeting moments of pain were all that I could remember from the next few minutes that passed, the battle descending into sheer chaos as the living desperately tried to outfight the dead. It wasn't until I found myself taking a step forward that conscious thought began to return to me, several more steps passing until I finally realized what was happening.

"We're pushing them back!" I shouted as I took yet another step forward, seeing that the endless wall of spirits before us had thinned and was no longer as thick as it was before. I could even see the tunnel looming in the distance ahead of us, the once flood of ghosts erupting from the passage now only a trickle.

"This is our chance!" I roared, thrusting Splinter in front of me as I felt a second wind surge through my exhausted body. *"Everyone, charge! Send them back to the hell they came from!"*

A roar rose up at my words, and all the surviving Adventurers leaped forward with renewed energy as we cut through the scattered ranks of Shades and Monstrosities. A staccato of magic momentarily drowned out our cry as the few still-standing mages spent their last dregs of mana and rained down a hail of missiles on the spirits before us, their efforts adding to our momentum.

Charging at the head of the group with Freya and Amaranth on either side of me, we blazed a path forward and before long found ourselves rushing through the tunnel. Slowing ever so slightly as the terrain shifted under us, we relentlessly pressed onwards and eventually found ourselves on the very edge of the Twilight Grove. Resisting us with their last dregs of strength, the spirits put up a desperate effort as they tried to stop our progress, but they didn't have anywhere near the numbers that they had at the beginning of the battle and the result was a foregone conclusion.

A crackling slash of Splinter, combined with a powerful spear thrust marked the end of the last Monstrosity blocking the tunnel to the Grove, causing a ragged cheer to rise from the Adventurers in the front ranks as it died. Yet, even as the spirit faded, I noticed that a pale emerald light remained in the tunnel, shining through the nearby entrance. Exchanging a worried glance with Freya, the two of us rushed forward into the Twilight Grove, Amaranth and all the other Adventurers following closely.

"Oh," I breathed as I looked out over the distant jungle, standing in the very same spot that I had been when I'd first laid eyes on the place. "Oh, no."

"*What happened?*" Freya whispered from beside me. "This...this..."

Her words trailed off as we all focused on the distant Ley Line, the once azure light emanating from it was now a sickly emerald hue, bathing the entire cavern in its eerie light. We all stared onwards wordlessly for several seconds, the only sounds filling the air being the scuff of feet and everyone's labored breaths. Then without warning, a sudden tremor shook the entire cavern around us, causing everyone to shout in surprise. Reaching out reflexively, I grabbed hold of Freya as the two of us staggered from the unexpected earthquake, but managed to stay steady on our feet.

Ending as quickly as it began, the shaking stopped, and the distant Ley Line pulsed before growing ever so slightly brighter. At that same instant, a soft chime that I had never heard before sounded in my ear, followed by a bright text that filled my vision.

A *World Event has begun!*

Deep within a forgotten place, a legacy of a bygone age has been awoken, bringing forth a vengeful host denied passage to their eternal slumber. Driven by vengeance against an ancient enemy, they will reach for a river of unimaginable power, corrupting it with their foul touch. Unless their efforts are checked, they will bring about a cataclysm the likes of which the world has never seen, bringing ruin to the region and beyond.

My blood ran cold as I read the alert and I felt Freya's grip tighten on my arm. Tearing my eyes off the Ley Line, I turned my head slowly to look at her. Staring back at me with a numb expression, I saw her shake her head in disbelief, her mouth opening and then closing, unable to find any words to say.

"Lyrian..." she finally managed to get out on her second attempt, turning to look back towards the Ley Line as she spoke. "What are we going to do?"

"I don't know, Freya," I replied, feeling a heavy lump form in my throat as I too looked back at the Ley Line, watching its emerald light play off the cavern walls.

"I just don't know."

Chapter 47

The aftermath of the battle took us a few hours to sort out.

At first, we all found ourselves sitting on pins and needles overlooking the now tainted Grove as we nervously waited for a follow-up attack from the spirits or some further sign regarding the world event that had just started. But after a calm and eventless first hour, we all decided that there wasn't a second attack coming and turned our attention towards the damaged camp, making sure to leave a handful of vigilant guards to watch for any sign of movement from the distant jungle.

For the next two hours that followed that, we picked through the damaged, and in some cases, still burning, remains of Camp Sentinel. After getting the fires under control, it didn't take us long to determine that the Grove facing side of the camp was a complete write-off. All the furniture, tents and supplies that had been unlucky to find itself there had been destroyed or scattered during the chaos, making it easier for us to simply clear it all away and start over again.

Thankfully, however, the rear of the camp escaped with only superficial damage, isolated to the few sections where the spirits had managed to rush ahead before being pushed back by Adventurers. On top of that, the more critical camp features such as the kitchens, the crafting area, and the healing ward had escaped without so much of a scratch, allowing everyone to focus their attention on putting the place back together again. I was confident that given a day or two, the camp would be back on its feet and back to normal.

The problem I had with that thought though, was that I wasn't sure if we had a day or two to spare.

In the few hurried conversations that I'd been able to have with the group, everyone seemed to be thinking that the world event that we'd seen after successfully defending the camp marked the start of the countdown before the Ley Line erupted. The only problem was, is that none of us could venture a guess of just how long that countdown was.

Which was why the six of us were looking for Ignis and the rest of his group in hopes of getting whatever answers we could from them.

"Finished getting your stories straight?" The harsh words left my mouth the moment that I spotted Ignis and four of his newly resurrected groupmates huddled together, all of them whispering to one another in angry tones. Yet the moment that they heard my voice, they all stopped, spinning to face me and the others with looks of both anger and guilt written across their faces.

"Lyrian," Ignis greeted me in a tight voice, his eyes widening, then shifting off me once he realized that I wasn't alone. "Y-you said you wanted to see us?"

"Oh, we want a *hell* of a lot more than that," Lazarus hissed from my left as everyone fanned out to surround the five Adventurers, setting the tone for how we expected the conversation to go.

Holding my question for a moment, I waited until Freya, Constantine, and Sierra finished moving, breaking eye contact with Ignis to look down at Amaranth beside me who had begun to growl angrily.

<It is not too late for me to demonstrate my rage upon them,> he told me in a seething tone. *<Allow me to maim or kill one, it will ensure that they answer our questions honestly.>*

<Oh, I think they know all too well already how much their situation depends on an honest answer,> I replied to Amaranth, despite sharing in his thoughts. After the battle was over, it had taken every single ounce of restraint in me not to publicly call Ignis out about dragging the spirits to the camp in earshot of the other Adventurers, knowing that they would be quick to express their displeasure on the man.

No. As much as a dick move it was, I instead decided to hold that particular threat over Ignis's head until I found out what happened in the Grove and where the spirits had come from. If I didn't like his answers, then I would be more than happy to let word slip where more Adventurers could hear and let nature take its course from there.

A course that I expected to be incredibly painful for Ignis and his group, and would likely result in them being forced to leave Aldford entirely, something that I knew he was all too aware of, given his rather subdued and anxious demeanor.

"So," I finally began, making eye contact with the man as I spoke. "What the *hell* happened?"

I knew it was a simple question to start with, but I wanted to see just how much Ignis and his group chose to reveal on their own accord before we started asking more pointed questions.

"We fucked up," Ignis said simply, his shoulders drooping downward at the admission.

"While that's not exactly a surprise, I think we were expecting something with a bit more substance," Constantine replied dryly from his spot in the circle. "Specifically, *how* did you fuck up?"

"We were exploring the Grove and trying to find a way closer to the Ley Line…" Ignis elaborated, pausing to glance at the rogue contritely. "But instead of going through the heart of the jungle, we decided to cling to the cavern walls, you know, to see if we could bypass it entirely like you usually could in other games without anything jumping us."

"Sure," I replied, watching the half-elf's head turn back in my direction at my comment. Hugging the border of a region or zone had been a tried and true tactic for gamers of all stripes over the decades, allowing them to use it as a relatively safe path and bypass higher-leveled creatures that would otherwise kill them.

"Well, it kinda worked," Ignis said. "It took us a bit of time to figure out—"

"And several broken ankles and legs," one of Ignis's groupmates, a male elf, added.

"But today we finally managed to climb past the majority of the jungle and towards the far side of the cavern," Ignis finished, nodding at his companion's interruption as if pain and suffering would somehow gain our sympathy.

"Fantastic. You can climb a wall," Lazarus grunted, unimpressed by what he had heard so far. "Fast forward to the part where you nearly doomed all of us and kicked this event off, if you don't mind."

"I-uh, well, in that case," Ignis stammered, a brief wave of annoyance crossing over his face at the half-giant's comments before vanishing. "It all started when we found where the Æther leaking out of the Ley Line ends up."

That bit of information was enough to get everyone's attention.

"It feeds into a large...lake, for lack of a better word," he continued, sensing our sudden interest. "It's nothing like Crater Lake, but there's a large chasm that the Ley Line is slowly filling on the far side of the cavern, similar to the one that we have on this side, separating us from the jungle. I have no clue how deep it is, but it stretches almost the entire length of the far wall and curls back towards us. We were forced to get off the wall because of it, actually."

"Why?" I asked while trying to picture just how much Æther must have leaked from the Ley Line in order fill that volume.

"Æther Sickness," Ignis stated. "We wanted to keep climbing towards the Ley Line, but the moment we were over the lake…"

"You started taking damage," Constantine finished. "Probably the game world's way of keeping you from climbing all the way to the Ley Line and bypassing the jungle."

"Uh, I didn't think of it that way, but that actually makes sense," Ignis acknowledged with a nod before resuming his explanation. "Either way, we realized that there was no way we could continue towards the Ley Line, so we decided to climb down and take a closer look at the Æther, since it didn't quite look right, based on what we saw from both your feed and what we saw leaking from the Ley Line."

"What do you mean it didn't look right?" I asked, my voice taking on a dangerous tone as I mentally prepared myself for what he was about to say.

"*Well*," Ignis replied, this time hesitantly as he sensed the undercurrent to my voice. "It was…tinted slightly green…"

"*Of course, it was!*" I barked, seeing Ignis and all his group members cringe at the reluctant admission. "And what about the warning that we gave *everyone* when we led you into this ruin? Specifically, the part that sounded something along the lines of, 'if you see any Æther Crystals that happen to be glowing *green*, stay the hell away from it and *tell us*, because the last one we saw contained an endless horde of angry ghosts that nearly killed us!'"

"I-I remember," Ignis answered in a small voice. "B-but it wasn't a crystal, so we didn't think—"

"Oh, goddamn right you didn't think!" Lazarus hissed from beside me. "Why the hell would there be a difference?!"

"I don't know!" the half-elf exclaimed raising his hands in front of him. "W-we didn't think that you were being honest! You already have control of all the other Æther in the area! We just figured that the green type was just more valuable or something!"

"Are you *serious* right now, Ignis?" Freya barked angrily. "You thought we were warning you out of *greed?*"

"I...we..." Ignis countered weakly, his arms falling to his sides before he shrugged. "Like I said, *we fucked up.*"

"And you all decided to *keep fucking up!*" Sierra exclaimed. "Because when you did get close enough to the tainted Æther, and all the spirits started coming out of everywhere, you decided to run!"

"Actually, most of us just died on the spot as soon as the spirits started to appear," the same elf that had spoken earlier stated. "We didn't get a chance to do anything!"

"Which means that you were one of the ones dumb enough to actually get *close* to the Æther in the first place!" Sierra snapped.

"Fine, I'll admit to that!" the elf replied while pointing a finger at Ignis. "But *he's* the one who dragged the spirits back here. None of us were stupid enough to do that!"

"*Thanks, Hido,*" Ignis hissed turning to glare at the man who had just thrown him under the bus. "Do you want to say that a bit louder? I don't think the *entire camp* heard you the first time!"

"Screw you—" the elf started to reply.

"*Enough!*" I spat, cutting off the argument before it could gain any more steam. It was obvious that Ignis's group was in the process of fracturing, but I also didn't consider that to be my problem to fix. If they wanted to fight among themselves, they could very well go ahead and do it.

Just as long as they did it *after* I was done with them.

I glared at the group until I was sure that none of them would interrupt me, then shifted my attention to Ignis.

"So, you ran," I prompted the half-elf, watching his expression carefully as he replied.

"You know I did," he admitted petulantly. "The moment that I saw the spirits start pulling themselves out of the lake, I took off. I figured that if I moved fast enough that they'd lose interest in me like the Grove creatures usually do if you run far enough..."

"But they clearly didn't," Lazarus observed with a growl.

"No," Ignis replied with a sigh. "I made it most of the way through the jungle before I realized that they were chasing...and then I really started to panic."

"Have you ever heard of Hanlon's Razor, Ignis?" I asked, bringing up my hands to rub my temples as I considered what he had just told me. I knew that there was likely more to the story that he wasn't telling me, or had decided to leave out, like how he'd even managed to get through the jungle alive, but after hearing his explanation so far, I found myself hard pressed to want to hear it.

"Uh, it doesn't ring a bell," he said uneasily. "What is it?"

"An aphorism," I explained taking my hands away from my face as I gave him a resigned look, feeling the anger in me fizzle and morph into a dull exhaustion that began to radiate through my body. "Loosely translated, it means 'never attribute to malice that which is adequately explained by stupidity', which is the only way that I could even begin to rationalize everything you just told me. If you somehow actually set out to maliciously destroy this camp, I don't know how you could have possibly done a better job, short of literally not running into me when you did."

Reddening at my explanation, I saw a look of anger, frustration, and embarrassment, come across Ignis's face as he glared back me, immediately replying back in a sarcastic tone, "I guess I'll have to try harder next time."

"Don't make shit worse for us with your damn attitude!" Hido spat as he suddenly shoved Ignis from behind, causing him to stumble forward. "Bad enough we stood by you when you opened your fat mouth last week and got us blackballed by half the Adventurers here!"

"Oh f—" the beginning of a curse flew out of Ignis's mouth as he caught himself and spun towards Hido, only to have the elf's fist slam into the side of the man's face, sending him falling straight to the ground.

Almost immediately, the rest of Ignis's group rushed forward to attack him, all of them managing to land several blows before any of us had the presence of mind to intervene and separate them.

"Stop!" I found myself shouting as I grabbed hold of the elf that had started the impromptu brawl and pulled him off of Ignis, who lay groaning on the ground before us. "That's enough!"

"I think we've gotten all we're going to, Lyrian," Freya told me as she held the twisted arm of a thin half-orc in a tight grip. "They're ready to kill one another at this point."

"Looks like it," I agreed, looking down at Ignis, who was slowly pulling himself together with a dazed expression on his face.

"Then that's it?" Hido asked, breathing hard from the brief exertion, all the other Adventurers falling behind him as the group released them. "We can go? You're not going to punish us?"

"For what? Being stupid?" I replied half-heartedly as I motioned for the group to step back while Ignis picked himself up off the ground, his hand covering a broken and bleeding nose. "There's no point in doing that. Besides, I think having your Soul Fragments trapped in the middle of the jungle is more punishment than anything I could inflict at the moment."

"Ugh," Hido grunted as he and everyone else behind him visibly deflated at that reminder. "I forgot about that…"

"Good luck recovering it," I replied, doing my best to project an honest tone in my voice. "But with that being said, if you guys want to keep fighting between yourselves, go do it in the Grove or on the surface. Anywhere but the camp."

"Noted," Hido said, giving Ignis one last glare before promptly turning around and leaving with the other three Adventurers into the camp without another word.

Staring at their departure for a moment, Ignis gave us all a dirty glance before turning around and heading in the opposite direction by himself, leaving us all standing by ourselves as we watched the two groups depart.

"Well, that turned out to be a little bit more entertaining than I was expecting," Lazarus said, exhaling sharply. "We should have let them beat on one another a bit longer though."

"Talking to them was a waste of time," Sierra said in a frustrated tone. "I'm not sure I completely buy anything Ignis told us, or how he had the dumb luck to run through half the jungle without getting jumped by a creature, but *damned* if his group mates were pissed. That part was *definitely* honest."

"Well they should be pissed," Constantine stated. "You hear what they said about being blackballed? I have a feeling that sort of resentment has been brewing for a while."

"Does anyone know anything about that?" I asked curiously, scanning everyone's faces. "Has everyone who originally stood with Ignis the other week been getting the cold shoulder from the rest of the Adventurers?"

"I don't know," Freya replied with a shrug. "You'd have to ask Dunedin, if anyone's instigating against Ignis and his group, it'd be him. He took it a bit personally when Ignis pulled his stunt the other week."

"Huh," I grunted, recognizing the name as belonging to the dwarf that had stood up in favor of Virtus when we had first announced the discovery of the Nafarrian ruin and the Ley Line. I'd made it a point to thank him once everything had settled that day, but I couldn't really recall seeing him since then. "Has anyone seen him lately? I sure haven't."

"I have," Constantine said. "He's been working with Jenkins and Ritt quite a fair bit. Something about having found a huge vein of metal in the Grove."

"Wait, that was *him*?" I asked, remembering what the pair had told me just a few hours earlier. "Shit, I didn't know."

"If you had the time to keep up on camp gossip and everyone's whereabouts on top of everything that you were doing already, Lyrian, I'd be shocked," Lazarus grumbled. "As it is, I have no idea when you even find the time to sleep."

"I've learned to get by on the little I get while blinking," I replied dryly, prompting a chuckle from the half-giant. "But given what happened today, I think it would be good to check what the general attitude among the Adventurers is like. The last thing we can afford is fighting amongst ourselves when we have this world event to worry about now."

"I'll see if I can track him down once we're done here," Constantine promised.

"The rest of us can keep our ears open too," Freya added. "I'm sure we can ask the rest of the guild members if they're hearing anything too."

"Hopefully it's just Ignis and his group," I said optimistically, running my hand through Amaranth's fur as I spoke. "And not a bigger issue for us to worry about."

"Speaking of bigger issues," Constantine said, changing the topic. "What are we going to do about this...oh, what did that gizmo call it?"

"Spectral Infestation." Sierra supplied, prompting Constantine to nod in thanks.

"Right!" he acknowledged. "This *massive* new Spectral Infestation that Ignis and his team of idiots kicked off. I don't think we can turn the Ley Line off as easily as we did that infected crystal back upstairs."

"Well, we can seal it," I said. "Assuming we can find the remaining Runestones...and decipher the spell inscribed on them."

"That may keep the problem from getting worse," Constantine admitted. "But that weird green Æther is still going to be there, right? Won't we have to figure out a way of getting rid of that too?"

"I honestly don't know," I replied, shrugging my shoulders with resignation. "I feel like we've been tossed in the deep end regarding all this Æther stuff. First, it mutates every living thing it touches, and now apparently it can sort-of bring the dead back to life."

"Or the dead can use *it* to come back to life," Freya added, offering a different perspective. "Don't forget about what the Slave-King did. He used the Æther at that Irovian Tower to come back to life too."

"Yeah, but he wasn't like the other spirits; he actually had his shit together when he came back," I said. "These spirits are mindless, just driven by emotion, vengeance in their case, they aren't—"

"I'm gonna stop you right there, Lyr," Constantine stated, cutting me off before I could finish my thought. "Before your complaints start giving the game world *ideas*. Do you really want to be fighting all these spirits if they were actually *smart* and had a better sense of tactics?"

"Uh, no," I agreed, realizing that I might have very well been jinxing myself. "Dumb and swarming is perfect. Forget I said anything at all."

"As much as I agree with the both of you, that doesn't get us any closer to answers," Sierra said with a sigh. "Assuming there are any answers to this!"

"Well, I'm not exactly an expert on this Nafarrian stuff," Lazarus interjected. "But there was one thing in that world event alert that stood out for me."

"There was?" I asked as we all turned to look at the big half-giant curiously.

"Sure," he said, his eyes temporarily losing focus as he brought the notice up in his vision. "Specifically, the part that said, '*Bringing forth a vengeful host denied passage to their eternal slumber.*' The spirits are clearly the vengeful host, but it's that second part that's interesting. It mentions that they weren't able to pass on. Now I don't know about you guys, but based on that it's not a far mental stretch to assume that something is holding them here against their will."

"Like what though?" Freya queried as we all processed Lazarus's train of thought. "I have no idea how the afterlife or any of that sort of stuff is handled in Ascend Online, at least from the NPCs perspective. The Adventurer version of it is pretty clear-cut."

"Me either," Lazarus replied with a shrug. "But look at what we've faced so far here, both in the dungeon above and now in the Grove. The dead clearly aren't moving onto whatever type of afterlife they should be."

"That's a really good point," I said, feeling Lazarus's insight had a great deal of merit to it. "Well, I guess we should find out what happens when someone dies."

"How do you plan on doing that Lyr?" Constantine asked me. "That's...not something that we can exactly test."

"Easy," I told the rogue as I motioned for everyone to follow me. "We do what most people have been doing for thousands of years when faced with questions about death."

"And what's that?" Constantine asked as he fell in beside me, one eyebrow raised curiously.

"We ask a Priest," I replied, flashing a smile in his direction. "Or in our case, a Priestess."

Chapter 48

Moving with purpose, it didn't take long for us to make it to the healing ward at the rear of the camp to where I hoped to find Shelia and get a better understanding of how the general theology of the world worked. Or at least what people generally believed happened. I didn't know if any of the information would be useful, or even pertain to our particular situation with the Spectral Infestation that was currently afflicting the Twilight Grove, but Lazarus's words had resonated with me pretty strongly, leaving me with one recurring thought that I couldn't quite wrap my head around.

Why have none of the Nafarr in this ruin moved on to their afterlife?

Was it because they all died in anger? I asked myself, as I slowly filtered through the common tropes about ghosts that I'd seen or read over my lifetime, trying to pick one that would fit our current situation. *Or is it because they're trapped here somehow? Or maybe they're some sort of echo of sentience caught by the Æther and not really ghosts at all?*

Halting my train of thought as we entered the healing ward, I was happy to find the place quiet and completely devoid of patients, any wounded from the attack having long since been mended and sent on their way. After entering the area, it didn't take long for the sounds of our feet to draw Shelia's attention, her head poking free from one of the far blinds moments before the rest of her body followed.

"We're not injured," I said by way of greeting, after seeing her eyes drop down to inspect our bodies, searching for wounds or broken limbs.

"I figured as much," Shelia replied in a tired tone as her eyes darted up to meet mine. "It seems to be a new habit that I've picked up after my time down here. But what can I do for all of you? I'm surprised to see you all still up after that battle and all the cleanup…"

"I'm sure we'll turn in soon enough," I replied, despite knowing full well that sleep was a distant hope for me. "We're actually here because we have a few questions that we were hoping to get your perspective on as a Priestess."

"Oh?" Shelia asked, her curiosity suddenly piqued. "What about?"

"What happens to someone's soul when they die?" I queried, seeing her eyes widen in surprise.

"Now *that*," she replied, exhaling a deep breath as she spoke, "is quite the question, Lyrian!"

"Which is why we all came to you," Freya said as she joined the conversation. "As Adventurers, we're well aware of what happens to *our* souls if we die, but we also know that we're an exception to the rule. We wanted to get a better understanding of what a regular person's soul may face when they pass."

"This is because of the attack by the Nafarrian spirits?" Shelia asked, her eyes scanning all of ours.

"That's right," I replied, giving the red-haired priestess a nod, not surprised with how quickly she had come to that conclusion. "If we're to find a way to defeat them, or at least manage them somehow, we're hoping to understand *why* they're still here and haven't moved on to whatever afterlife that they believed in."

"And to do that, you want an idea of what a soul would normally do after its death," Shelia said, nodding at our logic. "Very well. I think I understand your question a little bit better now, but before I answer it, perhaps we should sit down first. This is not a conversation to have standing or one to rush."

Without another word, Shelia motioned for us to follow her and led us behind the blind that we had seen her appear from just a few moments earlier, revealing an area with several chairs and a pair of tables with pitchers of water and food on top of them. With a wave, she motioned for us to take our seats, taking one for herself, and waited patiently until we had all finished moving.

"I admit, I find myself at a bit of a loss at where to start," Shelia admitted as she looked out towards us. "When trying to answer what comes after death…all the scriptures and rituals of my faith come to mind, along with their meaning and symbolism. But I don't believe that is what you are all looking for. So, with that, I will try and explain what I can…and hope that helps, somehow."

Shelia looked down for a moment as she collected her thoughts, then glanced back up towards us.

"When a soul's vessel, their body, dies," she began, "there are several things that may happen, depending on their soul's temperament and the life that it led before its death."

"Should it have been a Faithful soul, one that actively worshiped and devoted itself to a god, then it will find itself called to join that god's host and pass out of this plane of existence, where it will be judged, and then find whatever paradise that their particular faith exalts if they are found to be worthy," Shelia explained, slowly making eye contact with each of us as she spoke. "Out of all the paths a soul may take, this is the most common."

"Yet in the cases where a soul was Faithless or did not profess any strong belief in a single deity, or…" Shelia paused for a moment as her lips tightened. "…died in the grip of strong emotional upheaval, then things… tend to get a bit more *complicated*."

It looks like I wasn't too far off with one of my earlier guesses, after all, I thought as I listened to Shelia speak.

"When a Faithless or Divided soul passes, they are judged by the gods on the virtues that they possessed in life, such as valor, altruism, kindness, or any of the countless others that can define a person's existence," the priestess continued. "And depending on the conviction behind those virtues, the soul may find itself called by a particular deity who personifies that virtue the strongest, even if they weren't adherents to the faith it represents."

"And those that aren't called?" Sierra asked.

"Then they are Lost," Shelia answered with a sad note in her voice. "They remain forever trapped in a state between life and death until their soul fades away into oblivion. However, as we all saw today, there are some souls that somehow manage to keep their essences from fading, often returning as a mockery of life in the form of undead. This is also where we most commonly find the last kind of soul that I mentioned."

"The ones who died with strong emotions," Freya stated.

"Indeed," Shelia acknowledged. "Those who die in such a state often have their souls consumed with whatever emotion they passed with, often making it difficult for them to hear the call of their god, or in some cases deafening them from it entirely. In every case, they return as an undead creature in some way, shape, or form, seeking some sort of revenge against the living or those they believe that have wronged them."

"And from the looks of it," Lazarus said. "We have an entire cavern of that exact kind to deal with."

"It certainly seems that way," Shelia agreed in a small voice. "I heard their mental chant as they attacked the camp. Even after all this time, they are incredibly angry. *Defiant* even."

"They think that they are still at war," I said, recalling their voices all too well.

"And they think that we are the invading Irovians," Freya added, turning to look towards me as she spoke. "The Specters we fought at the ruin's entrance said as much before they attacked."

"I'm sure it didn't help that we were wearing Irovian armor at the time," I noted, looking down at my new set of armor, then back towards the others, who all still wore the blackened chainmail sets that I had repaired from the scraps found in the fallen Irovian Tower.

"Maybe not," Shelia agreed. "But such a traumatized spirit may not have been able to make that distinction; they would have likely treated anyone as invaders."

"I suppose," I said, offering the priestess a small shrug as I thought back to our encounter at the ruin entrance. "I'm reminded about what the Specters said when they died...they threatened to destroy this place if their defense failed."

"I remember that too," Lazarus commented thoughtfully. "Do you think that's what actually happened here centuries ago? That the Nafarr destroyed their own city to keep the Irovians from capturing it?"

"I don't know..." I replied, shaking my head at the thought. "To sacrifice an entire city just because you're losing...that seems a bit extreme."

"Not when the option is death anyway," Lazarus said. "We have no idea of what the war being fought was like, and given that none of the Nafarr that lived in Eberia survived the city's fall..."

Lazarus let his words hang in the air, everyone understanding what was left unsaid. If the war between the Irovians and the Nafarr was so brutal that they'd willingly destroy their own city, with themselves still in it, then they must have felt like they had no other option.

"They could have wanted to go out on their own terms," Sierra offered, breaking the silence. "If they knew they were going to die no matter what."

"It is a good theory," Shelia said. "That would certainly explain the spirits anger and desire for vengeance. Such a vicious and genocidal conflict would make our war with the orcs look like a schoolyard fight between children…"

"That's for sure," I agreed as I reached up to scratch the side of my head, working through everything that Shelia had just told us. I now had a vague sense of how the spirits *might* have ended up here, though I couldn't be completely sure. We were working with precious little in terms of real information, and our guesses, were just that, *guesses*, based on what we thought made sense in the moment.

"I suppose that answers my question, Shelia," I said with a frustrated sigh as I leaned back in my chair. "Though I am afraid it only brings up several more."

"Good questions often have a tendency to do that," the priestess replied with a faint smile. "Are perhaps any of those questions ones that I can help answer?"

"I don't know," I said, putting both of my hands behind my head and lacing my fingers together as I collected my thoughts. "The last time that we fought the spirits, in the ruins above, they had managed to corrupt a single Æther Crystal and were constantly pouring from it to attack us. We only survived because we were able to use the Nafarrian security system to purge the Æther stored in the crystal, thereby starving the spirits and causing them to vanish."

"But you can't do that so easily to the spirits that are in the Grove," Shelia observed, nodding at me in understanding. "There is simply too much Æther."

"Yeah," I said. "At best, we can seal the Ley Line to keep more from coming in. But that won't do anything to what has already leaked from the rupture."

"So then, if I don't miss my guess, you want to know if there is any other way that you can get these spirits to move on of their own accord," Shelia stated.

"That's right," I answered with a nod, not at all surprised by Shelia's insight.

"Then I'm afraid to tell you that there is no easy answer to that question either, Lyrian," Shelia said in a consoling manner. "Vengeful souls can anchor themselves to anything. From the most innocuous of objects to buildings, to huge swaths of land, to even insubstantial ideals. I recall an incident I read about, set during the early days of *The War* where an Eberian battalion was killed to a man defending *The Bulwark* from a particularly determined orc assault that sought to breach the walls. Despite their desperate defense succeeding in driving the orcs back, their spirits clung to their fallen bodies, and they all rose up the following morning as Revenants, not unlike the ones I heard you face in the ruins, attacking anything and everything that came near them."

"It took the better part of a regiment to regain control of that section of the wall," Shelia continued. "Not by destroying all of the risen undead, but by reclaiming the battalion's standard, which despite all the battles that had raged around it, still stood where it had been planted. It is said that the moment that it was touched, whatever was holding those souls in place vanished, and the remaining undead all fell in unison."

"So, there could be something like that holding the Nafarrian spirits here?" Freya asked with a hopeful sound in her voice. "Something we could just do, or find, and they'll all just fade away?"

"*Possibly*," Shelia replied, stressing the word very carefully. "Spirits can fixate on anything that resonates with them, and it is almost impossible to determine what that is until after it was discovered. They may very well be anchored to the very *concept* of defending this place from any interloper, and there is nothing that we can do, short of starving them of Æther, to defeat them."

"Well if that's the case," Constantine said, reaching out from his seat to clap me on the shoulder. "Thankfully we have Lyrian here. We can just toss him into all of the Æther that the spirits are coming from and have him absorb it all."

"Yeah, and then have me end up even more Ætherwarped," I grunted, reaching up to bat his arm off my shoulder. "*Or*, god forbid, end up possessed by an angry Nafarrian ghost like Graves was."

"There is that," Constantine admitted. "But do you think that'd work? You just absorbing all the Æther?"

"Not in any reasonable timeframe," I replied, shaking my head. "I have a limit of how fast I can absorb mana in general, and I've been hesitant to try draining Æther. I don't want to accidentally warp myself any more than I am already."

"Bah," Constantine grunted. "I'm sure you'd be fine..."

"I'm sorry that I don't have more specific answers to give you all," Shelia said, causing us all to focus our attention back towards her. "But you are all going to go back into the Grove, right? Maybe you'll be able to observe what the spirits are doing, and perhaps something will stand out."

"Hopefully," I replied with a sigh, appreciating Shelia's optimism, even if it did ring a bit hollow to me. We'd managed to get a few bits of information with regards to the world's lore that we didn't know before, but nothing concrete. It would be up to us to find a solution on our own, rather than have it spelled out for us.

Which I guess is why this quest is considered 'Legendary' in difficulty, I mused, recalling the Ley Line's quest details, which I had been annoyed to note *hadn't* updated with the latest world event.

"Thanks for answering our questions, Shelia," I said, unlacing my hands and leaning forward in my chair. "You've definitely given us a better understanding than we had before."

"I am always happy to help," the priestess replied as she stood up, sensing that our impromptu meeting was coming to a close. "Hopefully we will be able to find a way to put these spirits to rest and seal the Ley Line. It may seem a bit unusual to say, but I'm starting to look back on the days where we only had goblins and giant spiders to worry about with fondness."

"Everything did seem simpler back then, didn't it?" Constantine asked as everyone chuckled.

"Maybe just a little bit," I said, sharing a smile with everyone as we stood up and moved to exit the healing ward. "We'll just need to see if we can make it through this latest trial."

"I have faith that we will, Lyrian," Shelia stated confidently. "The gods are not so cruel to have us endure so much with no possibility for victory. It's just up to us to find it."

"I hope so," I affirmed as we came to the entrance of the healing ward and turned to bid farewell to the priestess, everyone replying in kind after me. "Have a good night, Shelia; thanks again."

"So, is there anything else on our agenda?" Constantine asked as we turned back towards the heart of the camp. "Because if there isn't, I'm going to go crash. I want to get a group out in the jungle first thing in the morning to see what the spirits have done to the place, and I'd rather not be dead tired while out there."

"That sounds like a good plan, and count me in for the group," Lazarus said to the rogue. "I'm sure Ransom and Sawyer will be up for it too."

"I'll second that," Sierra said in a tired voice. "Especially the sleep part. I don't even know what time it is anymore. I was already out when the spirits attacked."

"It's late enough to be considered early," Freya answered, before looking over towards me. "And I don't think we have anything else that needs to be done? Right, Lyr?"

"Nothing for you all," I replied. "Though I was planning on staying up and crafting a bit. If you all don't mind dropping your armor off at the crafting area, along with any of the golem metal, hide, or leather you have, I should be able to get a new set made up by the time you wake up."

"Sleep *and* new gear when I wake up?" Constantine exclaimed, reaching up to undo a strap of his armor as we walked. "Sign me right up!"

"And when exactly were you planning on resting yourself, Lyrian?" Freya asked me pointedly. "We don't need you burning out."

"Soon as I'm done," I promised, having learned my lesson in how far I could push myself the other week. "And I think I'm going to have to pass on going to the Grove at all with you until later. I need to head back up to Aldford and devote a day to upgrading everyone's, including the guild's gear. Lazarus and I really noticed it when we were out in the Grove this evening, with most of us having hit level eighteen and approaching nineteen, we've really started to out-level our gear."

"Fair enough," Freya replied, her eyes drifting down towards my armor. "Though I'll admit that having some new armor *would* be nice..."

"Just armor?" I teased as we all shifted our direction to walk towards the crafting area. "What about a weapon?"

"You think you can make me a new spear too?" Freya asked excitedly, her earlier reservations suddenly vanishing.

"Oooh, that's smooth, Lyr," Constantine quipped, prompting a laugh from everyone in the group.

"Maybe you should spend some time learning to craft your way into a girl's heart, Constantine," Freya replied as she reached out to grab my arm. "So, Lyr, tell me more about this new spear of mine."

"Well," I began, breaking into a wide smile. "Earlier today Lazarus and I fought a rare boss called a *Deathstalker*..."

Chapter 49

Friday, March 29th, 2047 - 8:01 pm
Aldford – The Crafting Hall

"Shit!" *Léandre* shouted in a sudden panic as the ground beneath our feet began to rumble, the intensity of the earthquake climbing sharply until it was strong enough to knock the two of us off our feet. "This is a bad one!"

"Sure feels like it!" I called back as I rolled myself onto all fours and then attempted to pull myself under the crafting table that I had just been standing in front of.

Barely managing to avoid a falling set of tools as they shook themselves off the table, I managed to scramble under the sturdy object and instinctively grabbed hold of one of its legs, having had far too much practice in earthquake survival in the last day.

This makes for number four, I thought as I waited for the shaking to stop, my eyes scanning the room as the building shook around us to see that both *Léandre and Amaranth had managed to take cover under a pair of tables in the room. In the seconds before this latest earthquake had started, Amaranth had managed to growl out a warning, giving Léandre and me just enough time to set our tools down before it hit. Which might have been the only thing that saved me from accidentally stabbing myself with the knife I'd been holding.*

Maintaining my death grip on the table as the vicious shaking persisted, I saw several more tools and equipment fall off the nearby tables and clatter onto the floor, skittering around wildly. A large crate filled with finished armor then decided that it couldn't hold itself together any longer and gave up, one of its sides coming free and spilling its contents everywhere. Mentally wincing at the growing mess, I looked down at the floor below me, and closed my eyes, waiting for the event to pass. Eventually, after nearly a half a minute of constant movement, the shaking began to diminish, lasting for several more seconds until it finally came to a stop.

"Everyone okay?" I asked from my position under the table as I opened my eyes and looked out at the chaos, deciding to stay put for a moment in case there was a follow-up quake.

"Battered," Léandre replied in a shaky voice. "But still whole."

<I am uninjured,> Amaranth answered angrily, letting out a low growl as he did so. The earthquakes had been a brand-new experience for him, in that he had never even comprehended that the ground could shake, let alone as often as it had done over the last day, and it had left him incredibly anxious and on edge.

"That was the worse quake yet," Léandre commented, as we both spared a glance over at my familiar, who had coiled himself up under a table with his ears flat and teeth bared as if to warn away an invisible enemy that was shaking the earth. "Yet, thankfully, I didn't hear any buildings coming down, so it must have not been too bad.*"*

"Small victories," I agreed, feeling my heart still hammering in my chest from the excitement. "But that still means we're one step closer to running out of time."

"I know, Lyrian, but we are almost ready," Léandre said, straining to inject some of his usual optimism into the conversation as he poked his head free from under his table and began to survey the room. "Looks like that's all we're going to get from this quake, might as well start cleaning up and see where this has left us."

"Yeah..." I replied, struggling to push down the newest wave of anxiety that was dangerously close to overwhelming me as I looked at the mess before me.

The last twenty hours since the attack had been nothing but a blur to my mind and I couldn't help but feel as if it had taken place days ago. The memory of me talking to Freya and hurriedly crafting a set of armor for my friends while they slept was broken up with disjointed images of me logging out into Reality and staggering into a bed in our suite just as the sun began to rise. I vaguely recalled getting some sleep at that point, if only for a few hours, which was then followed by the memory of me practically inhaling an entire pot of coffee and reentering the game world.

Then, as my new memories filtered into my psyche once I had logged in, I learned that I had just missed the second earthquake as it shook both the Grove and Aldford above it, lasting only a handful of seconds before stopping. Yet once the rumbling ended, I was told that the intensity of the Ley Line had increased yet again and that the distant glint of flowing Æther had now become a constant flow as the rupture widened, just how the very first one had when the world event started.

It's just like a giant doomsday clock counting down towards the apocalypse, I thought as I crawled out from under the table and tried to figure out where to start my cleanup efforts. Each quake brings us one step closer to running out of time, except that none of us can see just how much time is left on the clock.

Well, maybe on second thought, that's not entirely true, I mentally corrected myself as I grabbed the knife that I had been holding just a few seconds earlier, the item having landed on the floor in front of me, and forced myself back up onto my feet. I know how much time we specifically have, which is only until Sunday morning. Then we're going to be forced to take our rest cycle and watch from the sidelines, hoping that everything doesn't go to hell while we're gone. After that…assuming everything's still here when we come back, we're going to be seriously understrength as everyone else is forced to take their rest cycles, unless we risk everyone taking them at the same time Sunday…

Breathing out a deep sigh as the familiar train of thought wormed its way through my mind, I tried to focus my attention on my current task and began to pick up all the tools that I could find, while tossing the scattered armor that had spilled out of the broken crate into a pile. I'd eventually need to find a new crate to stash all the gear in again before we took it down to the camp and handed it out to the guild.

Léandre and I had been working nonstop since I arrived back in Aldford to upgrade all the arms and armor that the Virtus members had in preparation for tonight's assault into the Grove. With so much on the line, we wanted everyone to be outfitted with the absolute best we could provide, knowing that it could very well make the difference between success or failure.

"Don't borrow any more trouble than you have to, Lyrian," Léandre told me from across the room after hearing my sigh, knowing all too well what was causing it. "We have a plan that we are working towards. We must see it through, even though the troubles that we are facing now are so distracting."

"I know, Léandre," I replied as I continued to sort through the mess. "It just feels different to be up here on the sidelines while everyone else is fighting and scouting down in the Grove to get ready for tonight. I know crafting all of this is the best place for me to be right now…but still…"

"You will have your chance soon, Lyrian," Léandre said soothingly. "We have what? Another two hours before the raid starts? Even with this setback, I'm confident that we will be finished within the next half-hour, perhaps slightly longer to get it all packed up again."

"That would be great," I agreed, appreciating the elder man's efforts to steady my nerves. "Thanks, Léandre."

"Think nothing of it, my friend," the Tul'Shar replied, waving a dismissive paw in my direction. "Besides, it will be good for you to lead the assault with a fresh mind, not one already fatigued from a day of combat...or god forbid, death sickness. It seems that there has been an unusually large amount of poor souls today that have run afoul of something in the Grove, if the curses that I occasionally hear from outside are any indication."

"I can't even imagine what the place is like now," I replied with a shake of my head, having managed to catch a brief report earlier in the day of the chaos that was unfolding below us.

Apparently, the Nafarrian spirits were attacking every living thing that they saw in the Twilight Grove, including the regular creatures that inhabited the place, which weren't exactly known for their sociable nature either. The result had been essentially an all-out war in the Grove between the two forces with us Adventurers caught in the middle.

At least until the Grove creatures lost, like we all knew they eventually would. The spirits' ranks seemed to be endless as they emerged from the tainted lake of Æther in the cavern, where, on the other hand, the creatures' ranks weren't. Attrition would eventually swing things in favor of the undead spirits, assuming of course whatever they were doing to the Ley Line didn't destroy the place first.

With nothing left to say for the moment, the two, well, three of us, once Amaranth felt confident enough to come out from under his table, focused our efforts on tiding up the aftereffects of the earthquake, and before long I found myself sorting through the armor that had broken free of its crate.

Had I known this crate was going to break, I would have sorted these two sets of armor separately like I did the other one, I thought as I glanced over at an intact crate full of armor, filled with the same Twilight Avenger set I'd made for myself yesterday. It wasn't exactly difficult to sort the scattered armor pieces based on their appearance, yet given the sheer number of pieces involved there was a small chance to accidentally mix them up if I didn't pay attention. After managing to finally collect two of the sets together, I made sure to check their descriptions to ensure that I hadn't missed a piece, carefully reading them over as they appeared in my vision.

Twilight Savant Armor Set
Slots: Arm, Chest, Feet, Hands, Legs, Head, Shoulders
Item Class: Magical
Item Quality: Mastercraft (+20%)
Armor: 355
Set Bonus: (7/7)
Intelligence: +12 Willpower: +12
Armor Type: Light
Weight: 6 kg
Favored Class: Any Arcane or Divine
Level: 19

Twilight Protector Armor Set
Slots: Arm, Chest, Feet, Hands, Legs, Head, Shoulders
Item Class: Magical
Item Quality: Mastercraft (+20%)
Armor: 455

Set Bonus: (7/7)
Strength: +12 Constitution: +12
Armor Type: Light
Weight: 18 kg
Favored Class: Any Martial
Level: 19

"I wished we'd been able to figure out a way to add a third attribute to these new sets of armor and weapons," I said aloud to Léandre as I bundled the two sets of armor before me together and set them to the side. "We seem to be stuck in a pattern where we can only include two main stats into a crafted item."

"Perhaps that is something that will come with time?" Léandre suggested in an amused voice. "Despite all of our achievements thus far Lyrian, I must remind you that we are still ranked as Apprentice craftsman in our tradeskills, and will be until we can reach level thirty in them."

"I know," I replied, mentally wincing at still how far I had to go until I hit that milestone. Despite all the crafting that I had done over the last day, I'd managed to only get Leatherworking and Blacksmithing up to level twenty-one before everything that we'd been working on turned trivial to create. "Just wishful thinking on my part, I guess. Being able to add just a few points of Constitution on these items would be perfect…"

"That it would be," Léandre agreed before we resumed cleaning up the room, gradually restoring order to the place and bringing it back to the state that it was before the quake.

<I found this under a table,> Amaranth told me a few minutes later as I finished reassembling the last set of armor I could find, prompting me to turn around and find him holding a long metal object in his mouth.

"Ah! That's Freya's new spear!" I exclaimed, setting the armor aside and reaching out to take the item from my familiar. "I forgot I had this leaning against the wall. Thanks, Amaranth."

Purring contently, the cat flicked an ear in acknowledgment as I took the item and looked it over, making it sure that it hadn't been damaged somehow.

Not that I expect it to be, I thought as I hefted the spear in both hands. *This thing is pretty much a solid iron bar.*

Convincing Léandre to allow me to use some of the iron that Ritt and Jenkins had sourced from the Grove, I had done my best to make good on my promise to Freya and crafted her a weapon that I was confident she would love. It was heavy enough for her to pierce through armor, yet also balanced to ensure that it wouldn't slow her down. Plus, it gave me the perfect opportunity to use one of the large Deathstalker's claws that Lazarus and I had looted from the creature, turning it into a rather vicious looking spearhead with only a minimal amount of modification. Finishing my inspection of the weapon, I was satisfied that the fall hadn't damaged it and brought up its description for one last look before I packed it away, this time properly.

Deathstalker's Revenge
Slot: Main Hand and Offhand
Item Class: Magical
Item Quality: Mastercraft (+20%)
Damage: 60-90 (Piercing & Slashing)
Strength: +9 Agility: +9
Durability: 200/200
Weight: 3 kg
Class: Any Martial
Level: 19

Probably the highest damage weapon I've made yet, I thought with a smile as I dismissed the item's description *from my vision and moved to pack the item for our trip back to the camp. However, no sooner did I manage to get the item stored, did I hear Aldwin's voice ring out from the hallway outside our room.*

"Lyrian! Léandre!" he called out. "Are either of you in here somewhere?"

"We're in here!" I answered as I stood up from the new crate that I'd begun to organize and turned towards the door, managing to make it nearly halfway to the door before it was pushed open and Aldwin's face appeared.

"Figures you'd be in the last room I checked," he greeted us with a sigh. "Everything in order here after that latest quake?"

"Just about," Léandre answered, waving at the mess we'd yet to finish cleaning up. "It was enough to throw the room into chaos, even with our regular precautions."

"Was there any damage to the town?" I asked, despite having a feeling that if there had been, Aldwin, or more likely someone else, would have come running with much more urgency.

"Nothing serious," he replied with a shake of his head. "The Town Hall is still standing without any apparent damage, but the southern watchtower has definitely shifted even more. I don't think it's enough to be a danger, not yet at least, but we all would appreciate your eyes on it when you get the chance, Léandre."

"I'll make it a priority once we're finished here," the Tul'Shar said, letting out a frustrated growl at the news. "Though if it has shifted again, we will likely have to dismantle it and rebuild the foundation anyway, which I expect to be a pain since the river has made the ground so soft in that area."

Aldwin nodded in silent understanding, obviously not truly worried about the damage a falling watchtower could cause given our current situation. He paused for a moment, eyes shifting between the three of us as he looked for a way to ask the question that I knew weighed heavily on his mind, the one he'd really come here to ask.

"And..." he finally managed to get out, his eyes landing on me as he spoke. "How goes our preparations?"

"We're ahead of schedule," I replied, seeing the Bann's stance relax at the news. I could appreciate how hard it had been for him not to hover around or request constant updates as the day wore on, but with the latest earthquake shaking the town and our time running out, he had a near perfect excuse to come and check on us. "We should be ready to head back to the camp within the hour...and then we'll be setting out into the Grove an hour after that."

"Good," Aldwin said, relief clear in his voice. "Then we will hopefully be able to put this nightmare behind us."

"We will," I affirmed with all the confidence I could muster. "We have practically every Adventurer in Aldford coming with us tonight. If we fail...it won't be from a lack of trying."

"That...is actually something that I wanted to mention to you as well, Lyrian," Aldwin said, his face taking on a stone-like quality to it as he looked at me. "I have decided that I will be coming with you all tonight, and I believe Veronia will be as well. I can't stay on the sidelines any longer, not when an extra pair of arms or two could make the difference between success or failure."

"Fredric," I replied, feeling my eyes widen in panic at the thought of having Aldwin and Veronia with us. "You both could die."

"And that is supposed to keep me from helping?" he replied, instant anger on his face. "I will have you know, I risked dying every day I fought for Eberia, why would I not want to do the same for my home now?"

"Because you have us to take those risks for you now!" I countered, knowing that the words were hollow the moment they left my mouth. "It may take multiple attempts for us to clear the Grove tonight and tomorrow; we can all afford to die as many times as we need to! You can't!"

"And does that somehow make my life more special…or somehow cheaper, than yours?" the Bann asked in a quieter voice, but still retaining the earlier anger. "Because I only have one to give?"

"No, it's because if I—we, screw up, you'll be gone!" I exclaimed while glancing at Léandre for support, only to see him raise both of his hands to ward me off, clearly smart enough not to get involved in the conversation.

"If my death is the price that it takes to keep Aldford, and by extension, Eberia, safe. Then that is a price that I am more than willing to pay," Aldwin said to me. "For this entire month, I've sat within Aldford while you've all taken unimaginable risks on the town's behalf and I find myself unable to stomach it any longer, Lyrian. Especially with everything we have at stake. Not if I want to be able to look at myself in the mirror again."

I stared at Aldwin silently for a moment as I tried to come up with a suitable reply, but found myself unable to disagree with anything that he'd said. Ever since the new settlers arrived, the administration of the town had taken almost the entirety of Aldwin's time, forcing him to watch from afar as we Adventurers hunted for food, found resources, and dealt with threats. I couldn't blame him if he wanted to take an active role in protecting everything that we'd built together, knowing that if our position were exchanged, I'd feel the exact same way.

"Okay, Aldwin," I said, breaking the silence that had hung between us. "I understand."

"I knew you would…eventually," he replied with a nod, the anger on his face fading. "And I have the utmost confidence that we will all succeed today. For if we didn't, the gods would have to go find someone else to torment, and I doubt they would ever find anyone worthy of replacing us."

"I think Shelia said something similar this morning," I replied with a smile, the momentary tension that had been in the air vanishing. "Though maybe not as…"

"Apt?" Léandre offered.

"Sure, let's go with that," I said with a chuckle.

"Anyway, that was all that I wanted," Aldwin said to us after the moment had passed, taking a step backward towards the door. "I will leave you two to finish your work. Veronia and I will be ready to depart shortly."

With a nod of his head, Aldwin turned and left the room, leaving both Léandre and me alone together once more.

"I never even doubted that he would be joining your expedition tonight," Léandre said after we heard the Bann walk down the hallway and out of earshot. "I thought you knew."

<I agree,> Amaranth added, letting out a raspy croak as he walked up beside me. <When there are predators outside your den…or beneath it, one does not sit inside it waiting for them to consume you. You either attack or flee. It was obvious he would choose to attack.>

"I guess I'm a little slow on the uptake today," I said, reaching up to run a hand through my hair as I turned back towards my half-packed crate. "But you're right; I should have expected it…it's not like he'd be in any less danger up here. If we fail…all of this here will be destroyed."

"A factor that he likely took into consideration," Léandre pointed out. "At least he will feel that he is doing

something, rather than waiting endlessly for the world to end...or for you all to return victorious."

"I suppose," I admitted. "As much as I hate to use Aldwin that way, his presence should hopefully help motivate everyone to just be a little bit more on their game tonight."

"There is that," Léandre said, picking up a large unstrung bow stave from the table before him and using it to motion over towards my crate. "Now, before we let the time get away from us, finish packing that box. I will need your help in a moment to string this new contraption for Sierra."

With that, the two of us went back to work, getting our newly crafted equipment sorted and putting the finishing touches on the pieces that we had yet to finish, eventually taking all the crates outside to where a horse-drawn wagon was waiting. We'd be able to use the animal in getting all the supplies to the mouth of the shortcut, but it would be up to us to haul it into the ruins afterward, the sheer quantity of items that we were taking just too much to fit into our inventories. Fortunately for us on that front, we had planned ahead, and had enlisted the services of Cadmus, Abaddon, and Helix, to both escort us to the ruins safely, and for the added muscle to carry everything down.

"Well, I guess that's everything," I found myself saying to Léandre less than an hour later as the two of us looked over the now loaded wagon one last time.

"Looks like it," the Tul'Shar agreed, the two of us then stepping away from the vehicle and glancing around at the deathly silent streets of Aldford. The repeated earthquakes today had done much to unnerve all the townsfolk, and many of them had resorted to hunkering down in their homes or the Town Hall for the evening, leaving Aldford to almost feel as if it had been abandoned, save for the lights that peered through the odd window.

"Alright, we're ready to go," I announced, taking my eyes off the dark town around me and focusing on Aldwin, who was standing nearby with the three Lizardmen.

More like using the Lizardmen as a buffer to keep away from Veronia, I mentally corrected, shifting my glance to see the woman standing by herself a few steps away from the group, her face completely expressionless as she gazed off into the distance, waiting patiently for us to get moving. *After walking in on her and Aldwin arguing the other week, I'd barely seen her around Aldford. Save, of course, for the meetings she'd shared with Stanton. I'd since come to suspect that she was actively avoiding me whenever possible. Which will be hard for her to do tonight.*

"Then let get moving," Aldwin said with obvious relief as he took a step forward towards the wagon, his voice drawing my attention back to the present and out of my thoughts.

"I'll drive the wagon there and back," Léandre told us as he stepped up into the driver's seat of the wagon and then motioned for the rest of us to climb on back, there still being plenty of room on it despite everything we were taking with us.

And then we were off.

Looking out at the town as we began to move, I couldn't help but notice once more just how quickly things had changed in the last month. The place had gone from a rustic frontier village to a booming town in almost the blink of an eye, the changes only made more apparent by the fact that I'd spent the last week in the Grove. I could make out several new plots that I hadn't seen before, their lines staked out near our path as we wound our way through the streets. Past them, I could also see the half-finished skeleton of yet another longhouse that I didn't even know

Léandre had started, leaving me to imagine what other countless details I had missed out on due to my absence.

Even with the majority of us gone, it doesn't seem like the construction has slowed down at all, I thought with a shake of my head as we drew closer to the town's edge and I saw the sprawling framework of the palisade come into view, noticing that the foundations for the northernmost section of the wall had already been prepared. *I just hope that it all wasn't for nothing.*

Continuing out into the countryside, we left Aldford behind and made our way to the shortcut's entrance, the journey passing by quickly and quietly, everyone in the group lost in their own thoughts. Before long, we were all watching the rear of Léandre's wagon heading away from us as it faded into the growing night on its way back to town, the last rays of the summer sun vanishing over the horizon. With a final look at Aldford in the distance, we then each grabbed the supplies that we had unloaded and set off towards the camp below.

Having passed through them more times than I could count by this point, the ruins blurred past me without notice, my mind already mulling over what the night had in store for us.

Not your typical Friday night raid this time, is it, Marc? I asked myself as I walked. *This one actually could have consequences if you fail. Far more than just a few digital coins to repair your gear and try again.*

I couldn't help but give Aldwin a sidelong glance at that thought, my mind then shifting as another realization bubbled to the surface.

If we fail…and Aldford ends up getting destroyed, we'll all respawn back in Coldscar or Eberia, I thought, feeling a wave of sadness roll over me. *Would we even bother to come out this way again, knowing that there would be nothing waiting for us? Or would we go somewhere else? Maybe try to find a place where we could restart without any guilt, and let someone else worry about the spirits here.*

Similar thoughts continued to swirl through my mind as we descended deeper into the ruin, until excited voices and shouting from up ahead brought me back into the moment.

"Looks like everyone is already excited for the raid," I mused, breaking the silence that had fallen over us as we approached the final turn towards the camp, the voices growing louder with every step.

"Ssseems like it," Helix agreed, with a curious voice. "Yet...it was nothing like this when we left."

"Perhapsss the spirits have surrendered?" Cadmus asked, barking a dry laugh afterward at the idea.

"As if thingsss would be so easy for us," Abaddon answered with an amused scoff.

Driven forward by curiosity, we all quickened our pace and entered the cavern, hearing the dull roar of excited voices echoing out from almost everywhere at once as Adventurers rushed about the camp, grabbing weapons and donning armor as if they were preparing to head out at a moment's notice.

"I thought we were early?" Aldwin asked me as we all took in the flurry of activity before us. "It seems like they're all rushing to leave..."

"That's what I thought too," I replied, suddenly catching sight of both Constantine and, strangely enough, Ignis, rushing to the front of the camp together. Without a second's hesitation, I called out to my friend before he could run past us "Hey! Constantine! What's all the rush?"

"Lyr! You're early!" Constantine shouted back, his head snapping in my direction at the sound of my voice and angling his run towards us. "That's great! Perfect actually!

We don't have a lot of time; a huge opportunity just fell into our lap, and we have to jump on it fast!"

"We do?" I asked, surprised to see a wide smile come across both my friend's and Ignis's faces as they looked at me. "What's going on?"

"We found another Runestone, Lyr," Constantine replied with excitement. "Well, really Ignis did, but that's not the only thing."

"You did?" I exclaimed, feeling my heart skip a beat at the news. "Where is it?"

"Well, that's the other thing," Constantine told me, both his and Ignis's smile growing even wider. "It's right outside The Beast's lair."

Chapter 50

"Everything looks to be going well so far, and we're on track to be ready shortly," Freya announced as she rejoined our ongoing meeting, her new spear clutched tightly in her hand. "All that new gear you and *Léandre* made is a hit with the guild. You wouldn't believe the dirty looks that all of the other Adventurers are giving us."

"I'll find a way to live with it," I replied, giving the woman a smile as she moved to stand beside me in the loose circle that we'd formed.

It'd been a whirlwind of activity since Constantine and Ignis dropped their bombshell on us and we'd all rushed to get the newly crafted equipment distributed to the guild, knowing that it would take time for everyone to sort themselves out. Thankfully, the three Thunder Lizards along with Veronia and Aldwin had volunteered to take charge on that front, giving me a chance to regroup with both Sierra and Freya who had taken on the task of preparing for the coming raid.

"It's great to hear that we're on time so far," I said, turning my attention back towards the rest of the group. "What else do we have outstanding right now?"

"Not too much actually," Sierra answered, glancing down at a list that she'd written for herself. "We've already told everyone to start forming themselves into parties, and that we'll extend raid invites to the group leaders shortly. Healing potions have already been distributed, and everyone should have at least one on them, though we told them to only use them in a real emergency since we've pretty much blown through our entire stock handing them out. I have both Drace and Huxley out and checking on everyone, but at this point, we're just giving the stragglers a bit more time to finish repairing their gear and get ready."

"Good," I said with a nod as I checked over my Raid Leader interface and made a few adjustments, choosing to designate both Sierra and Freya as Co-Leaders. "I just added some raid permissions to both you and Freya to help me manage this upcoming mess."

"Gee, *thanks*; here I thought you'd take over now that you're back," Sierra replied in a sarcastic tone, but I could see her eyes lose focus as she read something that appeared in her vision. "Actually, on second thought, this doesn't look too complicated to manage."

"It really doesn't," Freya agreed as she too scanned through the interface. "We can extend raid invites to group leaders, and it'll auto-add their entire party without us having to micromanage each and every person. Then we can filter our own Raid Sense, to get an idea of where all the group leaders are, and focus down onto their parties if we need to."

"We'll see how it works in practice, but that piece alone should make things easier," I said, happy that the game had a way to prevent me from automatically sensing where each and every single raid member was. With us expecting to have easily a hundred Adventurers joining us tonight, that sort of information overload would be impossible to ignore.

"Alright, that settles our preparations for leaving, now we just need to figure where it is exactly that we're going," I continued, dismissing the raid interface from my vision and turning to look back towards everyone else who had been patiently waiting through the interruption, my attention landing specifically on Ignis. "Now where did you exactly find The Beast's Lair, Ignis?"

"It's on the western side of the jungle, about two-thirds of the way into the Grove," the half-elf replied eagerly, his eyes darting over to look at me as he spoke. "There's a pretty large cave there, likely an old lava tube, or something similar."

"And you *found* The Beast in there?" I asked curiously, not having had a chance to hear the full story yet.

"Uh, no, we followed it there actually," Ignis replied with a shake of his head. "My group and I were trying to scout a path through the jungle again, looking to see if we could find anything useful for tonight's raid when we heard The Beast roar from practically right on top of us."

"At first, we thought it'd found us and that we were dead," the half-elf continued. "But we were wrong; it actually ran into a bunch of spirits that were roaming through the jungle just ahead of us."

"I can't imagine that they managed to do much to it," I commented, trying to picture The Beast attacking the Nafarrian spirits.

"I don't doubt it," Ignis replied with a shrug. "Though none of us saw the fight directly, just heard it, along with the spirit's chant...at least until it stopped. But once it was over, we did manage to catch sight of The Beast as it left the area. It was then we decided to follow it. We all felt so bad about the...*thing* yesterday...and wanted to try and find a way to make it up to you all..."

"Hang on," Freya said with a frown, jumping into the conversation. "You got back together with your old group?"

"Huh?" Ignis looked confused for several seconds before he gave us all an embarrassed nod. "Oh, yeah...*that*. Uh, well, we sorted out our issues, and things are...*okay*, for now."

"That was...*fast*," Freya said slowly.

"Well, realizing that no one else in the town would group with any of us had a lot to do with that," Ignis replied in a bitter voice, before managing to get it under control. "*Anyway*, we were hoping that being 'useful' somehow would convince everyone to give us a second shot...then we could all go our separate ways after."

"Fair enough," Freya said, conceding the point before steering the conversation back on track. "So, you followed it?"

"We did," Ignis confirmed. "*Carefully,* and from as far away as we could manage, but we thankfully didn't have far to go until we reached its lair just as it went inside."

"And what about the Runestone?" I asked, not wanting to forget about what was arguably the most important thing in the Grove at the moment, even more so than The Beast. Everything hinged on us finding the spell fragments written on the Runestones in the Grove in order to even have a chance at sealing the Ley Line. "Where did you see that?"

"It was right by the mouth of the cave," Ignis said almost apologetically. "We all saw it light up while trying to figure out what to do, but none of us wanted to get any closer, just in case."

"Probably a good idea," I agreed. "And unless I miss my guess, the rest of your group is watching over the place still?"

"Yep," Ignis confirmed. "They haven't moved much since I left, and with Party Sense leading the way I should be able to take you all there easily. Though Hido is the party leader now...so you'll have to invite us when we get there."

"That's fine," I replied, pausing for a second as I thought over the half-elf's description of The Beast's lair, while silently cursing the AI that ran the game. Placing the Runestone so close to the cave was a perfect way to force us to confront the creature if we wanted to get the spell fragment it contained, but that in itself presented risks that I wasn't sure I wanted to take.

On the one hand, this gives us a perfect opportunity to kill The Beast, and ensure it can't bother us anymore...while also getting a small measure of revenge for all the trouble it's given us over the last week, I said to myself as I considered our options. *But on the other, it means that we're going to be fighting a cornered animal...*

"What's on your mind, Lyr?" Freya asked, noticing that I'd fallen silent.

"Just wondering how we can tackle all this in the smartest way," I answered. "Can we really afford to get into a fight with The Beast right now? Even if everything goes right...we're bound to lose people."

"I think the better question is can we afford *not* to?" Constantine countered, speaking up for the first time in a while. "Runestone aside, this is the first chance we've managed to get The Beast in one spot. The last thing we need is for the stupid thing to sneak up on all of us in the middle of the jungle, or jump us when we're fighting another horde of spirits."

"Constantine has a point, Lyr," Freya said. "If we miss this chance...we might not get another one. Besides, even if we take casualties killing it, it'll still be gone for good. All we'd be out is an hour for everyone to get back down here from Aldford and push through their Death Sickness."

"Yeah..." I acknowledged with a sigh, then reached up to scratch the side of my head, a nervous tick that I felt myself exhibiting more and more often lately. "You're both right, if we have a chance to take The Beast out, we'd be idiots not to take it, especially with the whole night, and day tomorrow, to work with."

"That's the spirit, Lyr!" Constantine said excitedly at my response. "Don't forget about the loot either! That thing is bound to drop something awesome!"

"Let's worry about killing it first," I chided, despite feeling a bit more confident about our plan going forward. "Or better yet, *getting* there."

"Well, if there's nothing else we need to talk about, let's get a start on that second thing right now," Sierra said, taking a step out of our circle and turning towards the front of the camp where all the Adventurers were gathering. "It's about time we started the raid invites anyway."

"Sounds good to me," I replied as we all turned to follow Sierra.

It didn't take long for us to walk through the partially rebuilt camp until we reached the waiting crowd of Adventurers, many of them having formed into their own clusters, based on their guilds or their chosen party for the raid tonight. Looking around us as we made our way towards the front, I couldn't help but notice the sheer quantity of people around us, and how almost everyone glanced in my direction as I passed.

"This is the first time that I've seen all of Aldford's Adventurers in one place," I whispered to Freya beside me as we walked. "Even in the Town Hall we never saw so many at once."

"Well, I can't think of many better motivators for showing up than being among the first to kill a raid boss," she replied. "That or respawning days away if things really end up going south."

"Good point," I grunted, noticing that the crowd around us had started to look familiar and that we were finally amongst our Virtus guildmates, all of them dressed in the equipment that Léandre and I had brought down. A wave of cheers and words of thanks called out as I walked through the ranks, and I couldn't help but smile and wave back at everyone, despite doing my best to hide my inner thoughts.

Sure, they're happy about getting new gear now, I thought as we moved through the waiting guild members and towards the front, where I could see Drace, Aldwin, Ritt, Jenkins and Shelia standing in a circle while chatting amongst themselves. *But when they find out that I'm planning on using them as the tip of the spear because they're now the best-geared Adventurers in Aldford, I'm sure they'll be less happy.*

"Ah, there are you all are," Drace greeted us with a wave after we'd finally made it through the crowd. "You ready to get this show on the road?"

"Yeah, we might as well," I replied, turning around to take in the milling crowd of Adventurers. "I have a feeling this will be like herding cats at first."

I paused for a moment to glance down at my familiar as I considered my statement. "No offense, Amaranth."

<For what?> he asked, flicking his ear at me dismissively. *<There is a reason my kind is solitary after all.>*

"I actually don't think it'll be that bad," Drace said, motioning towards a group of Adventurers that were all standing separate from the larger crowd. "I had all of the group leaders stand in one spot so that we can sort out invites quickly, plus we should be able to give them marching orders and rely on them to get their troops moving."

"Oh, that'll be a huge help!" Sierra exclaimed with relief, then looked over towards me. "Lyr, if you give Drace the same invite rights Freya and I have, the three of us should be able to have this sorted out quickly."

"Sure," I replied, opening my Raid Interface and granting Drace the Co-Leader role. "There, it should be set now."

"Great," Sierra replied, before beckoning the others to follow her. "Alright, let's go start the invites, and while we do that, Constantine and Ignis, you two can give everyone a rundown about where we're going. I don't want this to end up as one of those raids where we spend two hours getting ready, and then another hour getting to where we need to be."

"God, I've had my fill of those," Constantine grumbled, hearing similar responses from both Freya and Drace as everyone turned to followed Sierra, leaving Amaranth and me with Aldwin and the others.

"You've surrounded yourself with very capable friends, Lyrian," Aldwin said as we watched my friends, plus Ignis, walk towards the waiting Adventurers. "Getting so many Adventurers moving in such a short amount of time is nothing short of a miracle. I've known some military units that would struggle to move so efficiently."

"Thanks, Fredric," I replied, acknowledging the compliment with a smile as I looked back to the man. "We've been lucky that Aldford has attracted a higher caliber of Adventurer. That and everyone is *extremely* motivated to see things succeed today."

"*Our impending doom being a good reason*," Jenkins grunted, his tone prompting an elbow jab from Shelia. "Erm, I mean, good luck, Lyrian. I really hope things go as smoothly as they can go out there."

"Smooth *and* successful," Ritt added, jumping into the conversation.

"I appreciate that, Jenkins," I said, giving both the men a smile in reply. "And here's to hoping, Ritt. Though no matter what, we'll try our best."

"We don't doubt that for a second," Shelia stated, matching my smile with one of her own. "And we'll make sure to keep the fires warm here for when you return. If anyone has injuries…or anything at all before then, just send them back, and we'll sort them out as best as we can."

"We'll do that, Shelia," I promised. "Hopefully we can keep a good pace moving for the night, though it'll depend on how our battle with The Beast turns out."

"I can't say that I envy you all going after that thing," Jenkins replied, shaking his head. "Based on the stories I've heard over the last week…"

"Bah, we'll be fine," I said, putting up my best attempt at bravado. "I think that your biggest concern should be figuring out how you're going to mount that head in the Town Hall when we bring it back."

"Ha!" Jenkins laughed. "Bring it back to me, and I'll have it up within a day! Even if I have to chain it to the ceiling!"

"Won't that be a sight for me to witness every morning when I have my breakfast," Shelia commented dryly. "I'm not so sure turning our Town Hall into some sort of…*hunting lodge*…with a beast's skull hanging from the ceiling strikes the proper cord for Aldford and its development, don't you think, Aldwin?"

"Hmm," Aldwin replied, running a hand through his beard as he considered the question. "I believe that you are quite right, Shelia; hanging such a display would send the wrong message."

"I thought so," she said, casting a glance at Jenkins and then over to me, a single eyebrow cocked in victory.

"No…no," Aldwin continued. "Such a ferocious creature deserves to be preserved in all of its original glory and taxidermized. Then all who visit Aldford will be able to witness it as we did, not simply gaze upon a barren skull and wonder at what was."

"W-wait, what?" The satisfied expression on Shelia's face vanished as she processed Aldwin's statement. "You want to do *what?*"

"I think that's a great idea, Aldwin!" I exclaimed as everyone in the group, save for Shelia, broke into a laugh.

"Where are the other women when I need them?" the priestess muttered as she glanced around for support. "We don't need such a...*ghastly* reminder..."

"I'm sure we can figure something out when the time comes," I said to Shelia soothingly, still chuckling from the exchange. But before any of us could continue, Halcyon and Caius chose that moment to arrive, with Stanton, Veronia, and Donovan, following closely on their heels.

"Hey, everyone," Halcyon greeted as we all readjusted our circle to include the new arrivals. "We're all set to go on our end of things. We wanted to make sure we had enough copies of the spell fragment to go around, in case one of us goes down during the battle. I also asked around a bit, and I've found a few people with steady hands who can draw if you and I aren't able to."

"That's great," I replied, happy for my friend's foresight. "I didn't even think of doing that."

"Thanks, and no worries," Halcyon said with a shrug. "Just want to make sure all the bases are covered. The last thing we need to slow our night down is running out of something as simple as paper. We have Samuel and Quincy taking care of that now."

"That would be something," I agreed, shaking my head at the thought and looking over towards Stanton and Donovan, realizing that I'd barely seen either of them in the last few days, nor the other two Eberian mages, for even longer. The entire last week seemed to have flown by in the blink of an eye, and I felt that it was all I could do to keep up in the moment.

"We hope that your expedition tonight proves fruitful," Stanton said to me by way of greeting, leaning heavily on his walking stick as he spoke. "I'd never thought that my journey here would lead to such a...*precipitous* event and leave us all standing on the brink of ruin."

"I don't think any of us could have," I replied, recalling my first meeting with the elder noble. "But we will persevere. This isn't the first occasion where we've been staring certain death and destruction in the eye."

"You could say that," Caius agreed with a snort. "Depends how we're counting, this is what...the fourth time maybe?"

"Fifth from my point of view if you count the first attack by the goblins," I said, seeing Aldwin and the other Townsfolk nod in agreement. "With so many crises one after the other, you'd almost start to think that this place is cursed."

"Perhaps by an endless horde of Nafarrian spirits?" Donovan offered, prompting another round of dry, fatalistic chuckles, the joke going as far to crack even Veronia's stony expression, her face softening ever so slightly before resuming its original shape.

"Nothing like the threat of unleashing a horrific blight of undead on the region to lighten the mood," Halcyon quipped, then glanced to the side as movement caught his eye. "Anyway, looks like Sierra and the others have managed to get everyone sorted out. They're on their way back."

"In that case, we should finish our farewells for now and get out of the way," Shelia said, giving both Aldwin and me one last look. "Good luck to all of you tonight."

With that, everyone who wasn't coming tonight offered us one last goodbye before returning to the camp, their departure signaling an increase of volume from the front ranks of the waiting Adventures as they realized that it was finally time to leave.

"Well," I announced after Sierra and the others had rejoined our party, and confirmed that there weren't any other details to be taken care of before we left. "Since I don't think anyone will actually *hear* a speech over all this noise, and because we really don't have time for one, we might as well get moving."

"Sounds good to me," Sierra said as she unslung her new bow from over her shoulder in preparation to leave. "Just lead the way, Lyr."

Nodding, I took one last look at the camp behind me and all the gathered Adventurers, hoping that there wasn't anything that we'd forgotten to prepare for. Taking in the sight for a few seconds, I then turned away and focused my attention on the tunnel ahead of me. With a deep breath, I took a step forward and quickly followed it with another. By the time I'd taken my third step, a roar of excitement had begun to fill the cavern, and by the time I'd taken my fifth step, it was all that I could hear.

The raid into Twilight Grove had begun.

Chapter 51

"Looks like there's another one," Constantine mused as a distant creature's dying scream rang out through the otherwise silent jungle around us. "You'd think they'd know we're coming through by now."

"*You'd think*," I agreed as I looked out at the thick foliage, unable to help but shake my head in sympathy at the poor Grove creature that had thought to attack, or had been caught by, one of the many groups following behind us. "But the creatures down in here tend to be all teeth and no brains, so I'm not that surprised they're attacking every so often."

"Heh, that's a pretty good way of describing them," Constantine said with a chuckle before cocking his head at me. "But what does that say about us then? Seeing how we're after the creature with the *biggest* teeth that this place has to offer."

"That we think we have even bigger teeth?" I replied, giving the rogue a shrug before turning my attention back towards Ignis who was leading the way. So far, we'd made excellent time since leaving the camp, managing to make it deep into the jungle without losing anyone or forgetting something important - a small miracle that anyone who's ever led raid could appreciate.

Especially when the particular raid in question is a loose collection of groups and guilds that have never worked with one another before, I thought, then glanced over to both Sierra and Freya who were walking beside one another and whispering softly. *Though all the credit, in this case, goes to those two. Without them managing all the details, we would have never left on time. If at all.*

"We're just about there," Ignis announced in a quiet voice, interrupting my thoughts as he looked over his shoulder and back towards me. "The jungle is starting to thin out, and the rest of my group is just up ahead."

"Good," I acknowledged, feeling my heart start to beat faster in anticipation of finally confronting the raid boss that had terrorized the Twilight Grove for the last week. "Let's slow down a bit in that case and let the rest of the raid catch up. We're stretched pretty far apart right now, and I want to make sure that we don't make any more noise approaching the lair than we need to."

"Good idea," Ignis replied as we all slowed our pace to a crawl and drew closer.

"So, any plan how we're going to approach this, Lyrian?" Freya asked in a hushed voice as we walked, our eyes watching the jungle ahead of us carefully. "None of us really know what to expect from The Beast or what it can really do."

"I know," I replied, the thought having crossed my mind while we were walking. Despite the countless people that had fallen prey to the creature over the last week the total sum of our knowledge of The Beast could be summed up as: it was strong, it was *very* fast, and that it was a near perfect ambush predator. That was it. Even after all the repeated attacks amongst the Adventurers, no one could completely agree how it looked. "But as for a plan...it's going to depend a lot on the terrain we have to work with. To be honest, I'll be happy just *not* to be surprised by the creature."

"I could live with that too," Freya agreed, using her spear to push a thick cluster of vines hanging from above out of our way, revealing the edge of the jungle as the foliage rapidly began to die off, and allowing the faint emerald gloom that now illuminated the Grove to shine through. "And it looks like we're going to get that answer shortly."

Stalking forward carefully, we picked our way through the final stretch of the jungle until all the plants gave way and gazed out at the now not so distant cavern wall, a chorus of sharp breaths filling the air as we witnessed what was ahead. Looming almost directly before us, was a large jagged cave, its yawning mouth standing out from the otherwise rough cavern wall.

"Well," Freya whispered as we all looked into the pitch black entrance that led into The Beast's lair. "Here we are."

"Looks like it," I replied, keeping my voice low as we all came to a stop at the jungle's edge and surveyed our new surroundings.

Completely barren, the approach towards the cave was devoid of any plant life as if the jungle had simply decided to stop growing after a point, leaving nothing but a field of rough, volcanic rock between it and the cavern wall. As I turned my head to scan the area, a reflection caught my eye, and I reflexively shifted my attention towards it, finding myself staring into a not insubstantial pool of water just a short distance to our right.

"Well, cave notwithstanding, I guess that makes sense why it picked this spot for its lair," I whispered to everyone in earshot, motioning in the direction of the pool. "Look over there."

"*Water*," Sierra said, following my hand as I pointed. "That's not easy to find down here, and if anything is strong enough to claim an entire pool for itself…it sure as hell would be."

"Yeah," I agreed, slowly taking a few steps away from the jungle and towards the pool, hearing everyone shift to follow me. While water wasn't exactly a scarce resource within the Grove, it wasn't a plentiful one by any means either, and a large pool such as this would be hotly contested by the jungle creatures had it been anywhere else.

Though maybe even that didn't stop other creatures from trying their luck, I thought to myself as we approached the pool, unable to help but notice a fairly large quantity of bones scattered around it, many of them having been crushed to splinters.

"Looks like it needs to enforce that claim every so often," I said as we all came to a stop a short distance away from the water.

"No kidding," Constantine stated as he bent down to pick up a shard of bone from the ground and then inspected it.

<It has been here recently,> Amaranth's voice said in my mind as he sniffed the air. *<It has a very weak scent, and one that dissipates rapidly, yet I recognize it from before.>*

<Well that's good to know,> I replied to the cat, before glancing back towards the jungle as I heard the leading edge of the raid begin to draw closer.

"Alright," I stated in a quiet voice, my brain shifting into action as I began to plan out the coming battle. "The rest of the Adventurers are going to start showing up pretty soon, so let's spread the word for them to keep as quiet as possible when they arrive. I have no idea how good The Beast's hearing is, but let's not take a chance."

"No argument there," Constantine agreed, everyone else murmuring in agreement.

"Good," I continued, giving the group a nod. "I'll leave that for all of you to sort out, but let's also get all the group leaders organized and up front. I'm going to go up ahead and look over the approach into the cave to see what we have to work with. Then we can iron out a plan of attack and have the group leaders pass it on to their respective people."

"Sounds good to me," Sierra agreed, then winced as several voices filtered out from the jungle nearby. "*Shit*! Okay, we need to get on top of all that noise *now* if we're going to keep things quiet. Let's go."

Moving with a sense of urgency, everyone save for Ignis, Amaranth and myself took off away from us as they rushed to quiet the arriving raid. Some of them headed straight into the jungle to head off nearby groups, while others made a beeline to those that had already emerged from the overgrowth.

"Hido is just up ahead, closer to the cave," Ignis said to me, pointing to indicate his direction. "The rest look like they've circled back to join the raid already."

"Then closer to the cave is where we need to go," I replied, as we began to move, picking our way through the barren and uneven landscape until we eventually found the aforementioned elf, who had taken shelter behind a large mound of volcanic stone that offered a near perfect view of the cave ahead.

"You certainly brought the cavalry quickly," Hido said by way of greeting, having sensed Ignis's gradual approach through the Grove.

"We had good motivation to come," I replied, motioning my head towards the cave. "Is it still in there?"

"Well, we're all still alive, aren't we?" Hido asked with a touch of sarcasm, before shaking his head at my question. "But really, we haven't heard a peep since we all got here, I think it's gone to sleep for the night…assuming that it sleeps in the first place."

"Your guess is as good as mine on that front," I said with a shrug as I moved to peer over the mound to get a better look at the cave, hoping that the closer view would give me some sort of inspiration of how to plan the coming battle.

Do we all try to rush into the cave and try to fight it inside? Or do we try to pull it out here and fight it in the open? I considered as I inspected the terrain, finding the approach to the cave rocky yet still relatively flat. *Fighting out here would let us all use our numbers more efficiently...but it would also let The Beast run around, and it'd be hard to keep it under control. Fighting it in the cave though...we'd be able to fight it head on and reduce its mobility, but we would be sacrificing the same—*

"There it goes again," Hido's whispered voice interrupted my thoughts as a flash of green suddenly appeared near the right side of the cave's mouth, illuminating a familiar shape.

"*The Runestone,*" I said as my eyes fixated on the distant light, watching it shift indecipherably for a time before fading. "Damn, I can't make out anything from this far away."

"Could try to get closer if you want to..." Hido suggested hesitantly. "It flashes often enough."

"No," I replied shaking my head, already having dismissed that option. "It's not worth the risk. We need to deal with The Beast first."

"And any ideas how exactly we're going to do that?" the elf asked.

"Several," I replied as I pulled my gaze off where I'd seen the Runestone and scanned the terrain a second time, hoping that I'd find something to make my decision easier. "But none that I'm really happy with."

"So, now what then?" Ignis asked.

"Now, we go back and come up with a plan," I stated, turning away from the cave and looking back towards the jungle, having noticed that Sierra and the others were moving towards us via Party Sense. It hadn't taken her and the others long to organize the arriving raid behind us, and

I could see that a smaller cluster of just over a dozen people had broken off from the main group and were slowly making their way towards us.

Deciding that it would be best to greet the oncoming group further away from the cave than where we currently were, I waved for the two to follow me, and moved to meet them halfway. As I walked, I could see a handful of familiar faces in the group aside from my friends, marking them all as the group leaders from our raid.

"So, Lyrian," Aldwin was the first to ask once we'd managed to form up into a tight circle, his voice barely above a whisper. "What exactly are our options?"

"A narrow cave or the wide-open area outside it," I replied, seeing everyone lean in to listen. "It's hard to make out from this far away, but I doubt we'd be able to get more than a dozen people in a line if we fought in the cave, less if the terrain inside doesn't cooperate."

"A dozen people would likely fold under The Beast's attacks like paper," a female Tul'Shar, whose name I didn't know, stated. "We'd have no room to maneuver, or use our numbers."

"I thought pretty much the same thing," I agreed, nodding at the dark-furred woman. "Which is why I think it'd be best for us to draw *The Beast* out of the cave and fight it out here in the open. If we were fighting people, or even smaller creatures, fighting in the tunnel would be a better tactic. But in this case…we'd simply be feeding the front ranks into its mouth piecemeal."

Everyone visibly grimaced at that mental thought but didn't disagree with my assessment.

"I'm a fan of anything that doesn't end up with me being dog food," Lazarus announced with several of the more melee-oriented group leaders echoing in sympathy. "Fighting outside sounds like a safer bet."

"Only if we can contain the creature," Aldwin said, the experienced warrior having arrived at the same concern that I had earlier. "We can attempt to box the beast in using our numbers while fighting in the open. But our success will largely depend on everyone standing their ground when it turns its attention towards you. If a group breaks…"

"Then it can run circles around us," Freya finished. "We—"

A shrill whistle suddenly interrupted Freya and caused all of us to flinch at the sound of the earsplitting shriek.

"What the hell is that?!" I exclaimed, feeling my heart begin racing in my chest at the unexpected noise. "Where is it coming from?!"

"I don't know; I can't tell!" Constantine replied as everyone in the circle glanced around in a panic trying to find the source of the sound, only to have a thunderclap of magic echo out from the direction of the raid.

Twisting at the newest noise, we all instinctively looked back towards the waiting raid of Adventurers, only to see several more flashes of magic erupt amid their ranks and for everyone to begin to scatter, confused voices and shouts filling the air.

"Shit!" Sierra cursed as we all watched the disaster unfold before us. "Are we under attack?"

"I have no idea!" Drace barked, taking a step towards the rapidly disintegrating raid with the majority of the group leaders moving to follow him. "But we need to get this under control *now* before it wakes the damn boss up!"

"All of you go sort out the raid!" I ordered while tearing my eyes off the Adventurers in the distance and glancing around us trying to find the source of the whistling sound that had preempted the chaos. "I'm going to find out what's making that damn noise!"

<*I hear it coming from behind us,*> Amaranth told me as the rest of the group rushed off towards the raid, prompting the both of us to turn around.

<*From the cave?*> I asked, my eyes darting towards the jagged entrance. Nothing seemed to have changed in the short time that we'd had our backs turned towards the place, at least nothing—

A flash of movement suddenly caught my eye, and I felt my heart lurch as I saw a figure jogging towards the cave, a figure that I couldn't help but recognize.

"*Ignis!*" I spat the name like a curse as a wave of both anger and confusion shot through me. "What is he—"

<*BEHIND YOU!*> Amaranth's mental voice suddenly roared through my mind as he let out the beginnings of a savage growl.

Flinching from the sudden volume of my familiar's warning, I reflexively twisted and fell into a fighting stance, managing to complete my turn just as a dagger sliced a line across my jaw, inches away from my throat.

"Shit!" I heard a voice curse as the now bloody dagger reversed itself and came in for another attack, forcing me to take a step backward to avoid it. "They weren't kidding when they said that you were *fast!*"

"Ugh!" I grunted, my hand reaching up to clench my face as a wave of pain and shock shot through me, my brain caught completely off guard by the unexpected attack. Forcing myself past my surprise, I followed the hand holding the now bloody dagger until I found myself staring directly at Hido, his teeth bared angrily as he rapidly backed away from Amaranth who had placed himself before me.

<*He attacked you!*> Amaranth shouted angrily through our link as he swiped his claw towards the elf, managing to connect with the forearm holding the dagger and drawing a line of blood across it.

"What the fuck, Hido?!" I shouted, recovering from my surprise as I reflexively reached down to draw Splinter from its sheath. "What the hell are you doing?"

"Isn't it obvious?" Hido replied with a laugh as he drew a shortsword from his waist, oblivious to the wound that Amaranth had just inflicted on his arm. "We're trying to wipe the raid!"

"*Why?*" I demanded, seeing another flash of magic erupt from the now disorganized cluster of Adventurers in the distance.

"Because *fuck you*, that's why!" he spat angrily before rushing forward with both of his weapons held high, uncaring of the fact that both Amaranth and I were ready to meet him.

"Damn it, tell me *why!*" I shouted as I stepped up beside my familiar, catching Hido's slashing sword on Splinter and trapping it while Amaranth simply dodged under the elf's dagger and sank his powerful jaws into the wrist holding it. "You have to know you can't beat the two of us! You missed your chance with your cheap shot!"

"Oh, I'm *aware*!" Hido croaked through clenched teeth as my free hand then grabbed him by the throat and pulled him closer. "But this was never about beating you…that would have just been a bonus if I'd managed to do it myself. This was just about keeping you busy for as long as I could."

"*God damn it*," I hissed angrily, having momentarily forgotten about Ignis after Hido's unexpected betrayal.

Glaring at the man's unexpectedly hate-filled eyes, I realized that I wasn't going to get anything more from him, and that every second I wasted here, was another second that I played into whatever plan that he and Ignis had concocted. Making a split-second decision, I released my hold on Hido and shoved him backward, watching him twist and fall awkwardly as my familiar stubbornly held onto his arm.

"Take care of him for me, Amaranth," I said, feeling a cold wave come over me as I turned back towards the cave where I'd last seen Ignis, my feet already moving towards it. "And make it *hurt*."

A vicious snarl, followed by a pained scream rang out behind me as I dug my heels in and began to sprint towards The Beast's Lair. Triggering *Blink Step* as I ran, I used the spell to give myself a head start towards the cave, eventually spotting Ignis, who was now standing completely still, directly in front of the cave's entrance.

They trained the camp yesterday on purpose! I thought to myself, the realization causing me to curse myself for my stupidity. None of us even paused to consider the fact that he and his friends would have tried to do it intentionally. Especially not after the majority of them had died. *But why? Why would they want to do that? This doesn't seem like simple griefing, and trying to screw us over for fun. Hido actually seemed angry about something...but what?*

Continuing my mad dash towards Ignis, I was eventually forced to put my questions to the side as I finally reached the cave's mouth, seeing him turn around to face me, still holding a whistle to his mouth. With a dying shriek, he pulled the object away from his face and broke into a smile as I approached.

"Lyrian! You made it!" He said with obvious joy. "I didn't think for a second that Hido had a chance in taking you down, but he really wanted *so badly* to try. I just *had* to let him. Though it looks like a close shave was all that he could manage."

"*What the hell, Ignis?*" I barked at the half-elf, his calm and collected tone causing my anger to soar to new heights. "Why are you doing this?"

"Well, I said I'd try harder next time, didn't I?" Ignis replied, his grin growing even wider. "You know, everything was going so well until I *literally* ran into you yesterday. Like what kind of fucking cosmic joke is that? Here I am trying to fuck everything up, and *boom*, there you were, just in time to save the day. God, I was so angry. Still am a little, to be honest."

"Why the hell would you want to do that, Ignis?" I asked, trying to keep my anger from boiling over as I took a step closer to the man, only to see him take a step backward towards the cave in response. "This entire region is going to be destroyed if we don't fix the Ley Line in time and get those spirits under control. I can't see you gaining anything from any of this!"

"It was never about us *gaining* something from doing all of this," Ignis replied with a shake of his head. "It was about sending a message. One that would be impossible to ignore."

"A message to who, Ignis?" I demanded, getting tired of the roundabout conversation. "And for what?"

The smile on Ignis's face grew wider at my question as if he'd been leading the conversation just to get to this point.

"Did you ever wonder how the *Grey Devils* kept finding all of the caravans that came out this way?" Ignis asked me, cocking his head to the side as he spoke to me.

"Huh?" I replied, confused by the unexpected shift in the conversation. "What does that have to do with this?"

"It has *everything* to do with this!" Ignis exclaimed, the smile on his face finally fading away and shifting into anger. "You and your damned guild ruined a good thing for us, Lyrian, and then when you had a chance to make amends...you spat in our faces and made life even *more* difficult for us."

"You're a damn *spy* for Carver," I said as I finally began to piece together everything that Ignis had told me.

"Ah! I knew you'd figure it out *eventually*, Lyrian," the half-elf replied, the half-smile on his face returning. "Which brings us back to where we are right now. Carver's decided that an *example* is in order, and given that we have this convenient world event to work with, he decided that it would be in all of our best interest if things just went...*kaboom* here. In fact, he and the others should be on their way to make sure that happens now."

"Carver is coming *here*?" I couldn't help but blurt out, feeling the bottom of my stomach fall out at the revelation.

"Actually," Ignis said, mockingly looking at his wrist as if inspecting a watch. "He should be here already, and on his way to the Ley Line if the timing is right, not that I really expect you to be able to do anything about it.

"Because in the next few seconds," the half-elf continued as heavy footsteps began to echo out from the cave behind him. "I think you're going to have a *hell* of a lot more pressing things to worry about."

No sooner did Ignis finish his sentence than a massive, familiar looking head emerge from the shadows of the cave, its bright yellow eyes glowing fiercely as it first gazed at me and then shifted over towards the half-elf standing closer to it. With a growl of agitation, I saw the pupils in the twin orbs narrow in anger, the noise coming from its throat increasing in volume as the rest of its body stepped out of the shadows, towering over both Ignis and me.

"Goodbye, Lyrian," Ignis said in a steady voice while slowly spreading his arms open in acceptance for what was about to happen. "It's a shame I won't see how this works out...but then again I really don't have any doubts what the final result will—"

Before the final word could leave Ignis's mouth, a massive maw shot down from above and swallowed him whole, the sounds of ripping flesh and cracking bones filling the air as it began to chew through his body. Making short work of its impromptu meal, I then saw the yellow eyes shift towards me, the maw opening wide as it took another step out of its cave.

"Oh fuck," I whispered to myself as I gazed up at the creature and took a step backward, everything in my mind going blank, save for a single thought repeating itself endlessly.

The Beast was awake.

Chapter 52

Time slowed as The Beast sailed through the air towards me, giving me a perfect view of my impending death.

I saw its long and wicked claws stretch out before its body, their razor-sharp tips angling themselves directly towards my chest. The creature's maw was open, a distant howl managing to pierce through my stunned mind as rows of jagged teeth grew larger and larger with each passing instant. As it grew closer, I could even see the bloody spittle that sprayed out from the side of its jaws, along with the bits of flesh that once belonged to Ignis.

That bastard. I felt a wave of rage surge up inside of me at the thought of the man, the emotion piercing through the terror of The Beast's presence and causing my mind to snap back into focus. *He expects all of us just to lay down and die, to let Aldford die! I can't let him get away with this! Not without trying!*

Feeling the paralyzing fear release its hold on me, time resumed its normal speed as I looked up at The Beast, and saw that the distance between us had almost vanished. In an instant, I realized that unless I did something *fast*, I'd soon be sharing the same fate as Ignis, something that he no doubt had hoped for when he'd lured me so close to the cave.

Fortunately for me, however, *fast*, was only a matter of thought.

Triggering *Blink Step,* I watched The Beast's open mouth and blur away into a spray of dull colors as I teleported out of its path, reappearing at the very edge of my range just in time for it to complete its pounce, the impact causing the ground to shake.

<The Beast is awake!> I shouted to Amaranth via our mental link as I watched the creature react with confusion after it had landed and didn't find me in its claws, buying me the precious seconds I needed to get my feet moving. *<What is happening with the rest of the raid?! We need them up here fast!>*

<They are still in disarray!> My familiar replied a second afterward. *<But the magic being thrown about has ceased.>*

<That's better than nothing I guess!> I replied as The Beast's head snapped in my direction, hearing the ground crunch underneath my feet as I put on a burst of speed. *<I'm going to need your help distracting it in the meantime!>*

<I'm already on my way!> Amaranth told me just as The Beast let out an angry snarl that prompted me to turn my full attention back towards it, and for the first time, found myself able to take in its full appearance without near crippling terror affecting me.

It must have some sort of fear aura, I thought as The Beast launched itself towards me, its thick and powerful muscles visibly rippling under what I now saw to be scales that covered its entire body. Gaining speed, the creature moved with a smooth serpentine grace despite its massive size, which with my newfound clarity, I was able to estimate was at least fifteen feet tall and nearly twice that in length. Catching sight of a reptilian tail whipping back and forth behind the creature as it moved, I felt an odd wave of familiarity come over me, feeling as if I *almost* recognized it from something I'd seen before.

It looks sort of like a wingless dragon, I said to myself, angling my sprint away from The Beast and back in the direction of the raid, hoping that Sierra and the others would be able to rally the raid before long and come to my rescue. *But it doesn't quite look like a dragon; it's more lizard-like and without the long neck...wait! I know what it is! It's a Land Drake!*

Glancing over my shoulder as if to confirm my guess, I saw that The Beast was rapidly gaining on me and decided that I had several much more pressing matters to worry about, rather than trying to identify exactly what species it was.

Chief among those concerns being to somehow find a way to survive the next thirty seconds.

Thinking desperately, I briefly considered switching my sprint into a zigzag pattern, but then just as quickly dismissed it, realizing that The Beast was likely better suited to twisting and turning than I was. The best chance for survival that I could think of would be for me to use my magic to confuse the creature and try to stay one step ahead of it for as long as possible.

<*I'm almost there!*> Amaranth called to me as I heard The Beast draw closer behind me. <*What do you need me to do?!*>

<*Run past it when I Blink Step!*> I shouted to the cat as I glanced over to my left, checking my flank for a safe spot to teleport to. <*We need to force it to stop and keep it in place until the raid is ready! Outrunning it isn't an option!*>

Not waiting for a reply from my familiar, I slowed my sprint for as much as I dared, allowing The Beast to catch up with me ever so slightly, then a moment before a set of teeth snapped through the spot that I was standing in, I triggered *Blink Step* once again. Feeling my world shift, I reappeared at the edge of my range laterally and away from The Beast, turning my head just in time to see it rush past me, the momentum of its charge carrying it forward.

Immediately, I heard a frustrated howl fill the Grove as The Beast planted all four of its clawed feet into the ground, its head whipping around wildly in an attempt to find me. But before it could twist far enough to see me, an azure streak blurred past it on the opposite side that I'd found myself on, causing its attention to instantly shift in that direction.

<*It's seen me!*> Amaranth called with a note of nervousness in his mental voice as the colossal creature twisted its body to pursue him. <*What now?*>

<*Turn it towards me and run past me as close as possible!*> I told the cat as I began sprinting directly towards the Beast, watching its dark scales gleam in the emerald light. <*Once it sees me, it should stop!*>

<*Should?*> Amaranth shouted at me angrily. <*What if—*>

<*Then just keep running!*> I yelled at the cat, not able to fault him for his concern, but also unable to do anything about it.

Maintaining my pace towards The Beast as Amaranth cut his sprint to the inside, I tightly gripped Splinter's hilt and hoped that my next move worked, or at the very least, didn't end up getting the both of us killed. Adjusting my timing as Amaranth rapidly approached, I glanced up towards The Beast's head, watching its eyes shift as it tracked my familiar, its body visibly coiling to strike.

Then, just before The Beast could pounce, Amaranth rushed past me, barely a stride's length separating us as our paths intersected, causing the creature's eyes to pass right over me and for its entire body to suddenly hesitate. Having been so focused on following my familiar, The Beast had temporarily forgotten about me, at least until I reappeared in the center of its vision and was rushing directly toward it, a tactic that immediately provoked an instinctive response. Fearing that it was under attack, The Beast instantly shifted its attention off Amaranth and onto me, its coiled body shooting forward with its maw opened wide.

Just as I'd hoped it would.

In the split second that The Beast had spotted me, it had hesitated for the briefest of moments between deciding to change targets and finally executing its attack, giving me just enough time to put on one last burst of speed and to drop down into a roll, just barely managing to dive under its snapping jaws. Springing up from my somersault, I forced myself to move as I found myself now directly under The Beast and rushed down the length of its body.

This is probably the best-worst idea that I could have come up with! I thought as I charged Splinter with a *Shocking Touch* and thrust it upwards into creature's belly above me, feeling the sharp tip of the blade pierce through the thinner under scales and sink into the flesh within. *But if this doesn't piss it off and keep its attention focused on us, I don't know what will!*

Discharging my blade into the wound, I felt The Beast's entire body convulse from the unexpected attack, an enraged howl following it less than a second afterward. Pulling Splinter free as The Beast began to twist in an attempt to get to me, I then rushed towards the creature's flank, looking to make a quick exit while I still had the chance. But before I could take more than a handful of steps, The Beast howled in pain for a second time and then immediately began to shake its body.

<*What's going on out there?*> I asked Amaranth as I ran, taking the opportunity to deliver another slash along The Beast's underside and managing to open a shallow wound.

<*I am upon it!*> Amaranth shouted back. <*Its scales are rather difficult to pierce!*>

<Wait, what?> I demanded, feeling my stride slow ever so slightly as I processed what Amaranth had just said. *<You're on top of it?>*

<That's what I said!> my familiar replied angrily as The Beast's thrashing intensified. *<We are to provide a distraction, are we not?>*

<I…uh, right! Carry on then!> I said back to Amaranth, this time making the most of his distraction to deliver a powerful two-handed thrust into The Beast's underside and attempting to drain whatever mana I could from the creature. Almost instantly, I felt a wave of cool energy travel up my arm before The Beast suddenly launched itself forward and pulled itself free from my sword. *<Amaranth, it's starting to—>*

Without warning, The Beast's heavy leg slammed into me, the impact taking me completely off my feet and causing me to fly through the air a short distance before landing heavily on the ground, eventually rolling to a stop. Gasping in pain from the unexpected blow, I instinctively looked back in the direction of the leg, only to see The Beast's clawed foot descending down right on top of the spot that I was lying in.

"Shit!" I cursed in sudden panic and forced myself past the pain coursing through my back and rolled out of the way of the descending limb, managing to just barely avoid being crushed as the massive paw briefly touched down before springing up again. Glancing upward as The Beast continued to move forward, I saw the rest of its body pass over me just as Amaranth's voice filled my head.

<I was forced to abandon my perch!> he warned me, sounding indignant and angry as he spoke. *<The Beast reached up with its hind leg and shed me like I was a common flea!>*

<It's okay,> I told Amaranth, as I slowly forced myself back onto my feet, feeling the pain in my back begin to fade into a dull throb. *<We did a pretty good job for our first try.>*

<And what will we do for our next?> my familiar asked me with sudden urgency as he reappeared at my side. *<Because it is about to return!>*

Glancing up at Amaranth's words, I saw that The Beast had managed to twist around after putting some space between us, its angry yellow eyes now tiny slits as it snarled with barely contained rage. Up until this very moment, we'd simply been prey to the gargantuan apex predator, barely worthy of notice, save for the effort that it took to catch and devour us. But now that we'd managed to injure it, to *dare* make it feel pain, we'd been shifted into another category entirely, one that forced it to take us much more seriously.

<We keep its attention split as best we can,> I told my familiar as we watched The Beast slowly advance forward, keeping its body low to the ground while its eyes fixated on Amaranth and me. A low growl echoed out from its throat as it coiled its muscles in preparation to strike. *<Just follow my lead, and be ready to grab my spell when the moment comes.>*

Taking a deep breath as the three of us readied ourselves to resume our dance, I briefly checked my Raid Sense, hoping to get an idea of just how much longer Amaranth and I had to survive. As the information flowed into me, my heart fell as I learned that a handful of the raid members had somehow died and were now back in Aldford, prompting me to mentally curse Ignis and his group once more. Yet pushing past that discovery, I sensed that several of the groups behind me were starting to make their way towards us.

"Help is on the way," I said to Amaranth as I took a step forward, sensing him do the same. "We just need to hold out a little bit longer."

Receiving a raspy croak from my familiar in response, the two of us then charged forward directly towards The Beast, our sudden movement causing it to spring forward to meet us. With the distance separating us rapidly vanishing, I made sure to ready *Blink Step*, holding the spell in my mind for Amaranth to use when the moment came. Waiting until the last possible moment, I let the gap between us shrink to almost nothing.

<Now!> I shouted at my familiar, feeling him grab hold of the waiting spell and vanish, allowing me to trigger a second casting a heartbeat later.

In an instant, the two of us vanished from sight and reappeared on either side of The Beast, who to my dismay, was already twisting its body in my direction, having grown wise to my teleporting tactic. Not even having the time to let out a curse, I found myself forced to dodge under a slashing claw and then leap over a sweeping tail as it threatened to take out my feet from under me.

Pressing its advantage without any hesitation, it was all I could do to keep ahead of The Beast as it unleashed its fury on me, its attacks now carrying a level of ferocity that I hadn't seen earlier. All conscious thought fled from my mind as I desperately tried to stay ahead of The Beast's reach, finding myself relying more and more on using Blink Step, just to buy a few seconds of relative safety before the creature was upon me again.

The deadly dance seemed to continue for ages as both Amaranth and I scrambled to stay alive, the Beast alternating its attention between the two of us almost seamlessly now that it had realized we weren't merely prey. Before long, I was panting heavily as my endurance began to falter and I felt myself hard pressed to keep up, just barely managing to dodge a sweeping claw and then immediately being forced to use Blink Step to evade a snapping bite that I hadn't even seen coming.

<Look out!> Amaranth's voice rang out in my mind less than a second after I'd reappeared from my panicked Blink Step, causing me to flinch in numb surprise as I saw The Beast's other claw rushing directly towards me.

Without being able to even form a thought, let alone react in time, the massive paw slammed into me with bone shattering force and slapped me straight off my feet, causing me to bounce and then tumble across the ground a fair distance, two red tinted alerts flashing in the center of my vision.

[The Beast] critically hits you for 548 points of damage! You are low on health!

Groaning as I came to a stop, it was all that I could do take a breath, the entire left side of my body feeling like it'd been run over by a truck, or more aptly in my case, slapped away like an annoying insect. Managing just the smallest of gasps, I felt a disturbing watery sensation in my chest, which then quickly became a ragged, bloody cough.

I think I have a punctured lung, I thought distantly as I reflexively tried to sit myself up, only to have an incredible wave of agony from my wounded side dissuade me from doing so. *Along with a broken everything else.*

<Are you okay?> Amaranth's voice shouted in my head, a sense of anxiety seeping through our bond.

<Not really,> I replied, unable to feel anything but pain combined with a sense of wetness from my left arm or shoulder. Curious about what that sensation could be, I reached to touch my side with my still working arm, while checking to see just how much health I had left. *<But I'm not quite dead yet...>*

Statistics:
  HP: 232/1056
  Stamina: 132/960
  Mana: 235/1277

Just one solid hit nearly did me in, I noted through gritted teeth as I brought back the hand that I'd used to check my side, seeing that it was completely covered in blood, specifically, *my blood.* Staring at the hand with a numb expression for several heartbeats, I slowly realized that The Beast's paw had also included a particularly sharp set of talons. Talons that I clearly hadn't been fortunate enough to evade when it had hit me. As I continued to stare at the blood now dripping down my glove, I heard a desperate voice shout out my name, causing me shift back into the moment.

"We're coming, Lyrian!" a male voice yelled amid the sound of running feet. "Hold on a bit longer!"

Is that Aldwin? I thought, recognizing the voice and trying to push myself up, feeling a wave of lightheadedness come over me as I moved.

Clenching my jaw through the pain as I pushed myself awkwardly up on one side with my good arm, I glanced around the battlefield, seeing that The Beast was now barely a dozen feet away, its hateful glare focused directly on me as it rapidly approached. But before it could close the distance between us, a hail of magic and arrows slammed into it, causing it to shriek loudly in pain and recoil from the sudden assault. As if encouraged by the pained cry, a chorus of triumphant shouting rang out through the air, moments before a horde of Adventurers charged into view, their massed ranks slamming directly into The Beast and forcing it to stagger backward from the sheer weight behind it.

It had taken time, but at long last, the raid had finally arrived.

In an instant, the thunder of magic and shouting voices took over the Twilight Grove, filling the air with a near deafening cacophony that was intermixed with the occasional howling cry from The Beast. Caught staring at the sight before me, I missed the sound of rapidly approaching footsteps, only recalling them in hindsight after Veronia's face came into view before me.

"V-Veronia?" I wheezed in surprise at the woman's unexpected arrival as she dropped down beside me, her eyes going to the wound in my side. "What are you doing here?"

"Saving your life, it seems," she replied tersely as she set down her shield and then shifted to get a better look at the damage The Beast's claws had managed to inflict. "We find ourselves rather short of capable healers, and I happen to have some ability to assist in that area."

"I d-didn't know that you could heal," I said, wincing in pain as she put both of her hands directly on top of my wounded side.

"There is *a lot* you don't know about me," Veronia stated in a harsh tone, glaring at me for several seconds before her expression softened. "Just keep still while I take care of this."

As soon as she finished speaking, a wave of heat surged into my wounds from Veronia's hands, causing the pain coursing through me to gradually diminish until it finally vanished, all while a string of identical messages appeared in my combat log.

Veronia heals you with [Lay on Hands] for 81 points of damage!

"There," the woman announced a few seconds later, taking her now blood-covered hands away from my side. "Good as new, I suppose."

"Thanks," I replied, breathing a sigh of relief now that the pain was gone and turning my head towards Veronia. "That spell you used...you're a Disciple, aren't you?"

"I am," she replied curtly as she grabbed her shield and stood up, then paused to offer her hand to help me up. "But this really isn't the time, nor the place to discuss that."

"You're right," I said accepting her hand and allowing her to pull me back up to my feet as the two of us then launched into a sprint to rejoin the fight.

Scanning the battlefield as I ran, I was happy to see that in the short span that I'd been out of the fight, the newly arriving Adventurers had managed to force The Beast back onto its heels as they continued to swarm it. But despite their success in changing the flow of the battle, The Beast had managed to make them pay for their efforts, and I could see several wounded or dead Adventurers lying on the ground as we ran.

"Of course, he would be right in front, *the fool*," Veronia's hiss reached my ears as we ran, prompting me to glance briefly at her, then back in the direction of The Beast where she was looking.

Only to find Aldwin standing right between Drace and Abaddon, directly in front of The Beast.

"And where else would he be?" I asked, just as I saw Drace catch one of The Beast's claws on his shield and hold it in place just long enough for Aldwin to deliver a powerful blow with his axe to the limb, all while Abaddon simultaneously stepped up to block the creature's maw from taking a bite out of the Bann's vulnerable side.

"*Somewhere safe!*" Veronia barked with sudden anger as she glared over at me, then immediately shifted her sprint and split away from me.

What the hell was that about just now? I thought with a wide-eyed expression as I saw the woman leave me behind, her reaction completely out of character based on everything I knew about her. *Maybe she doesn't completely hate Aldwin after all?*

Shaking my head at the thought, I pushed it to the back of my mind and focused back on the battle before me, catching sight of both Freya and Lazarus on The Beast's flank and angling my sprint towards them. Charging forward, I inserted myself into a newly formed gap between them, the Adventurer that had been standing there just a moment earlier being flicked away by The Beast's now flailing tail.

"Lyr! You're alive!" Freya greeted me with a shout as I stepped in beside her and delivered a two-handed slash into The Beast's side, adding a new wound to the countless others that now adorned its blood-covered side. "We thought we were too late!"

"It was a close call!" I exclaimed as we were all forced to leap backward in order to evade another swipe from The Beast's tail as it came for a second pass. "But I'm sure glad that you're all here now!"

"It was Ignis's group that caused all the chaos!" Lazarus shouted out as the three of us stepped back into our old positions, the tail having moved on to threaten the Adventurers on the other side of the creature. "They started targeting the healers in the raid and managed to take out a handful before we could get things under control!"

"Damn!" I cursed angrily, Veronia's earlier words suddenly making more sense to me. "Hido tried to take a cheap shot at me as soon as you all left, and Ignis was the one who pulled The Beast early!"

"Why would they do that?" Freya demanded angrily as she viciously thrust her spear into the raid boss's side, the heavy tip easily piercing through the tough scales and provoking an angry roar from the creature.

"Because they're working with Carver," I said, feeling a surge of anger shoot through me as the words left my mouth.

"Carver is involved in all this?" Freya snarled, her head snapping over to look at me. *"You have to be fucking kidding me!"*

"I wish I was!" I replied bitterly. "But that's not all. Apparently Carver is on his way down here too! He wants to make sure we don't seal the Ley Line before it blows!"

"So, all of this was just a damn trap to get us out of the way!" Lazarus exclaimed from my right as he carved open a large wound on The Beast's side.

"Looks like it!" I agreed, once more delivering a powerful thrust with Splinter. "That's why we need to put an end to this fight as soon as we can!"

"That might be easier said than done! Heads up!" Freya shouted at the same moment The Beast suddenly twisted away from Aldwin and the other warriors keeping it in place.

Turning its attention directly towards us.

"Shit! Aggro!" I exclaimed, scrambling backward as The Beast's snapping jaws filled the spot that we'd all been standing in, just narrowly missing us.

As we continued to rapidly back away from the turning creature, I saw its bright eyes fixate on me, the orbs widening in recognition. Letting loose a primal roar of rage, the creature swiped out with a claw directly at me, forcing all of us to dive in different directions to avoid it.

"Damn! It must really hate you, Lyr!" Lazarus shouted as we all desperately tried to regain our feet before The Beast could press its attack any further.

"No kidding!" I agreed as I pushed myself up off the ground and reflexively looked for another attack, only to see that the Beast had stopped in its tracks, the muscles on the sides of its throat undulating in a way that I'd never seen before.

"What is it doing?!" Freya asked as she climbed to her feet a short distance away from me, having noticed the same thing I had. "Is it trying to throw up?"

"I don't know," I replied, seeing a thin spurt of liquid leave The Beast's mouth as the contractions continued and land on the stone floor, where it then began to sizzle. Confused by what I was seeing, I stared at the dripping substance for several seconds, until the pieces finally snapped together in my mind. "It's acid!"

"Acid?" Freya repeated, a momentarily confused expression crossing her face before being replaced by panicked understanding. "*It's acid!*"

"Everybody *move*!" I shouted, my feet already in motion as I saw The Beast's mouth open wide, the muscles on its throat contracting sharply and releasing a thick green column from its maw that shot through the air. "It can breathe acid!"

Seeing Lazarus dive away in the opposite direction that I'd chosen to run, I felt my skin begin to burn as acid splashed up from the spot where I'd just been standing, seeing an alert appear in my combat log in the process.

[The Beast] hits you with [Acid Spray] for 87 points of damage!

Like we needed this thing to have a special ability on top of being a raid boss! I thought as I ran to get out of range of the spray, seeing Freya already several steps ahead of me. A chorus of panicked voices rose all around me as everyone reacted to The Beast's new ability, the tide of the battle suddenly shifting as everyone scrambled to get out of its path. Yet as I moved, I noticed that the torrent of acid shifted to follow me as The Beast tracked my attempt to escape, trying to catch me with the full force of the attack. *Damn! It won't leave me alone!*

"Lyr! Over here!" I heard Halcyon shout through the chaos, my eyes shifting to spot him and several other mages that had lined up together and were all channeling several *Force Shields*, providing a safe pocket for nearby Adventurers to take cover in.

"Coming!" I shouted, risking a glance behind me and realizing that it was only seconds until The Beast adjusted to my speed. Faced with no other choice, I dipped once more into the now pitiful pool of mana I had left and triggered *Blink Step*, fixing my destination just past the edge of the closest *Force Shield*.

Vision blurring as I crossed the intervening space, I reappeared at the spot that I had chosen just in time to see Freya rush past me, having been forced to cross the distance bereft of the aid of magic. Glancing around me, I noticed that the majority of the people around me were all Virtus members and I breathed a sigh of relief to be back among friends.

"Lyr!" I heard Constantine's tired voice call out from amongst the crowd, prompting me to spin in its direction to see both him and Amaranth rush towards me, both of them covered in blood and looking the worse for wear. "Please tell me I heard wrong and this thing isn't really—"

"Incoming!" Halcyon's shouting voice interrupted from beside us. "Get right up against the shield if you can!"

Not waiting for a second warning, the three of us reflexively rushed to obey the mage's warning and piled in close behind him, just in time to see The Beast's acid spray splash across the *Force Shield* he'd conjured, before shifting to continue towards the other mages.

"Does that answer your question?" I asked, glancing back towards Constantine, who had gone noticeably pale at the sight.

"Unfortunately," Constantine grunted as he lifted an arm to protect his face from the stinging mist that began to filter down from above.

"If anyone has any bright solutions on how to get out of this I'm all ears!" the mage called out, visibly flinching as the spray of acid slammed into the barrier again, causing the shimmering field to waver. "Because we're not going to be able to keep this up much longer!"

"We won't have to!" Freya's voice called out excitedly from beside us. "Look! Help is on the way!"

As one, we all moved to look through the distorted lens of Halcyon's *Force Shield* just in time to see the other half of the raid rush out from behind The Beast, having found itself temporarily forgotten in the chaos. Without a second's hesitation, they swarmed forward as one, intent on making The Beast pay for its lapse in vigilance. Seeing several familiar faces in the distant crowd, my eyes were drawn to the row of people leading the raid's charge, managing to catch sight of Drace, Aldwin, Veronia, and Lazarus a heartbeat before they all slammed into The Beast's flank.

"Here's our chance!" I shouted, the stream of acid spewing forth from The Beast's mouth abruptly stopping as it staggered from the impact of the raid's brutal charge and howled in pain. "Take the shields down! Everyone, *forward!*"

Sensing that the end was finally at hand, a deafening roar tore itself out of our throats as the *Force Shields* fell before us and we all charged forward towards The Beast, a veritable storm of magic crackling out over us to herald our arrival. Flinching from the now combined onslaught, I saw The Beast look uncertain for the first time in the fight as it turned its head back towards us and took a halting step backward as if contemplating retreat.

But before it could do anything, we too slammed into the creature and began to swarm around it, our weapons slashing and chopping through flesh. Bellowing in agony, The Beast wasted no time in responding to our attacks, its claws and teeth lashing out through our ranks and claiming their fair share in casualties. Yet as the battle began to wear on, the mighty creature finally began to falter, its once glorious hide nothing but a patchwork of carnage and gore, its attacks growing slower and less accurate.

Staggering drunkenly from the loss of blood as the epic battle came to an end, The Beast opened its mouth one last time in a desperate attempt to send another spray of acid through our ranks, only to invite an avalanche of magic and arrows straight into its maw and down its throat. Coughing violently, that final onslaught proved to be last that the creature could withstand and it collapsed to the ground in a heap, a river of blood and acid pouring free from its ravaged maw as it lay completely still.

Silence fell over the battlefield, save for our ragged breaths as we all stared at The Beast's body in complete exhaustion, none of us daring to believe that it had truly fallen. That after all that had happened that we'd all somehow managed to end up victorious. Then without any visible cue, a short and victorious fanfare followed by a familiar chime echoed through my ears as several lines of golden text appeared in my vision.

Congratulations! Your raid has successfully defeated [The Beast]!

As a reward for your legendary accomplishment everyone in your raid has been awarded:

   1 Class Skill Point

   500 Renown

You gain Raid Experience!

Congratulations! You have reached Level 19!

You have unlocked a Class Challenge opportunity!

Chapter 53

"…and that was the last thing he said before The Beast ate him," I finished, spreading my arms out wide in a shrug as I looked out towards the group, hearing several curses fill the air in response.

"*The camp,*" Caius said in a sad voice. "If Carver and his group came down here, they had to go through the camp, which means…"

"I know, Caius," I replied. "Depending on what they did…Shelia, Jenkins, all the others."

"Are we going to go back?" Freya asked in a quiet voice.

"We can't," I said, shaking my head as much it pained me to say so. "What's done there…is done. We won't be able to change anything at this point. It's more important that we try and find Carver before he can find a way to screw with the world event here and destroy everything."

"You think he'd actually do that?" Lazarus asked, sounding a bit hesitant. "He and all of his followers then would have to eat the Death Penalty from dying. There'd be no way they'd be able to get their Soul Fragments back from this place afterward."

"In a heartbeat," Drace said bitterly. "We're not exactly his favorite people. Even less so if what Ignis told Lyrian is true."

"Damn that man," I spat angrily. "I still can't even begin to imagine just how much he would have fed back to Carver. No wonder we never ended up finding him after the battle at the Tower."

"Or why he pushed us so hard to get into the Dungeon," Halcyon added. "He wanted to know exactly what we were up to…"

"I bet he and his group are probably long gone from Aldford by now," Constantine said. "Assuming they didn't change their bind points beforehand. Hell, if they already knew they were going to destroy the place…they likely would have. Else their death could have them resurrecting back in Coldscar or Eberia if Aldford was…*gone*."

"They tried to cover all their bases," Sierra noted. "Well, almost all of them. They couldn't have counted on us actually *killing* The Beast, after Ignis's stunt."

"Which means that we have a very short window to get things back under control," I said, glancing towards the scattered groups of Adventurers that had survived the battle with The Beast, and seeing them all in various stages of recovery as the few healers we had still standing did their rounds and soothed injuries. "We need to get everyone ready to move as soon as Halcyon and I can get a sketch made of the Runestone. Hopefully, we can get it down in just one cycle."

"We will, Lyr," Halcyon said to me in a confident voice.

"You two go sort that out then," Sierra told us, then went on to indicate Drace and Freya with a wave. "The three of us will sort out the raid and reorganize the groups."

"And I guess Lazarus and I will get the loot sorted then," Constantine said. "I think given the urgency right now, no one will complain if we hand it all out later…"

"That all sounds good to me," I stated as I glanced in the direction of the Runestone then back towards the group. "Halcyon and I will regroup with you all once we have our sketches done."

With tasks assigned, we all then splintered into our assigned groups and headed off in separate directions, the need to get moving putting a spring in all our steps. Falling in beside Halcyon, the two of us made a beeline towards the Runestone at the mouth of The Beast's Lair, which we expected to illuminate any minute.

"Hey, Lyr," Halcyon said to me as we made our way to the cave's entrance. "By any chance did you hit level nineteen and see our Class Challenge thing?"

"Uh, not yet," I replied, noticing one of the several alerts still needing my attention in the corner of my vision. "I mean, I hit level nineteen, but I haven't checked anything yet."

"You should," Halcyon told me. "It's...*interesting*..."

"Hmm," I said thoughtfully as I called up the notification and saw a large block of text appear in my vision. "*Whoa,* that's a lot...give me a second."

Congratulations! You have unlocked your first Class Challenge opportunity!

In order to cater to as wide of a variety of playstyles as possible, Class Challenges are designed as a way to further develop your character attributes and abilities beyond what normal level progression and equipment are able to grant.

For your first Class Challenge, you will be able to gain a substantial boost to an attribute of your choice by performing an exceptional act of prowess that best embodies that trait. Please note, you will only be able to gain a boost to a single attribute. Good luck!

Perform an Act of Strength: 0/1
  Reward: +10 to Strength
Perform an Act of Agility: 0/1
  Reward: +10 to Agility
Perform an Act of Endurance: 0/1
  Reward: +10 to Constitution
Perform an Act of Magic: 0/1
  Reward: +10 to Intelligence
Perform an Act of Faith: 0/1

Reward: +10 to Willpower

"Huh," I said after I finished reading the update and dismissed it from my vision. "That's pretty cool."

"Yeah, that's what I thought too," Halcyon replied. "Though...I'm not sure what exactly would qualify for some of them. I mean, like what does it exactly mean to perform an act of magic or faith? The other ones are pretty easy to explain."

"I'm not sure," I said as I considered the question. "We're among the first to hit this level, so we're breaking new ground here. Maybe the idea behind the Class Challenge is to try and push us to our limits, and then reward us afterward?"

"That's as good as an explanation as any, I guess," Halcyon said with a shrug as we arrived at the still blank Runestone. "It'll be something fun to work towards to when we have the time, an extra plus ten to an attribute is worth a bit of effort to figure out."

"Definitely," I agreed as the two of us sat down in front of the Runestone and readied ourselves to copy the spell fragment when it appeared. Sitting in silence with charcoal in hand as we waited, I found it difficult to keep my hands steady, the aftereffects of the battle and Ignis's betrayal still weighing heavily on my mind.

I should have expected something like this, I thought as I clenched my hands tightly. *Why did I think Carver would leave us alone for so long? I let myself get too roped up in the dungeon and then everything here in the Twilight Grove...meanwhile he was just biding his time, all the while knowing what we were up to.*

"Did I screw up, Hal?" I asked with a sigh, forcing my hands open. "I mean, I didn't see anything coming...about Carver or Ignis...and he literally *ran into me* as he was dragging a train through the camp."

"You're too hard on yourself, Lyr," Halcyon replied. "*None* of us saw the bit with Ignis coming, and once we found the Grove, after nearly a *week* of looking for Carver with nothing to show for it, it'd make sense he'd fall off our radar."

"Still feels like I could have done more," I said. "Maybe if I'd taken that espionage training that Stanton offered us all…"

"And what would you have exactly dropped in favor of doing that, Lyr?" Halcyon asked me while shaking his head. "I'll admit, maybe we were all a bit naïve thinking that someone wouldn't betray us from the inside, but we also had no reason to believe that someone *would*."

"Until it bit us in the ass," I grunted.

"That's usually how these things work out," Halcyon admitted. "Sure, it sucks right now, and if we make it through all of this, we're going to have to be more careful going forward, but you can't be stressing yourself out over something we didn't, *couldn't*, have anticipated."

Before I could say anything in reply to Halcyon, the Runestone chose that moment to activate, prompting the two of us to abandon our conversation as we fervently rushed to copy the spell fragment. Drawing faster than I ever had to before, I didn't dare take my eyes off the display as my hand moved across the paper before me, only shifting my eyes downward after the display had faded and I was forced to rely on memory. Scrambling to get every piece of detail down before we forgot, we sat in silence for nearly a minute as we worked, well aware that we were trying to accomplish a task in a single pass that would have normally taken us three if not more cycles to verify.

"I think I got it," I announced, taking my hand away from the paper and looking over the detail.

"Same," Halcyon replied, shifting over towards me so we could begin to compare our sketches, realizing that they were completely identical. "Well, that's good news. Though this one didn't seem as large or complicated as the other two."

"I noticed that," I said in agreement as we then compared the latest spell fragment against the two that we had already found, finding that it fit seamlessly with one of the pieces and effectively completed that half of the spell. "Looks like there's just one last piece left then if this is any indication."

"Here's to hoping," Halcyon replied as he carefully read the combined spellwork and then looked back up towards me. "This looks right to me, Lyr. At least, in that, I can't see anything *wrong* with it. Though I guess we won't know for sure until we find the other fragment and actually try to cast the spell."

"We'll cross that bridge if, or when, we come to it," I said with a shrug, knowing that this was currently the best we could do. "Right now, we have to try and track Carver down. Once we have that taken care of..."

I let my words drift off as Halcyon began to nod in understanding, "I hear you, Lyr. We'll figure it out. But speaking of Carver, where'd you think to start looking for him? The Ley Line?"

"Yeah," I agreed as I turned my head towards the bright emerald light that shone over the jungle. "The only way I can see Carver somehow forcing this world event to kick off, is if he screws with the Ley Line, specifically, the ruptured part of it."

"I was thinking the same thing," Halcyon said as he followed my gaze. "Though you know...Carver won't be the only thing to deal with if we head that way. There'll be spirits too."

"I'm counting on that actually," I told the mage as I turned back to face him. "We're likely going to be outnumbered when we manage to catch up to Carver and his group, but if we can somehow use the spirits against them..."

"Then maybe we can give them a taste of their own medicine," Halcyon said with a smile. "Seems fair after all they put us through."

"I certainly think so," I replied, briefly returning the man's smile before resuming my serious expression and looking towards the raid, which was still in the process of getting itself together. "Well, we might as well get back to the others and help get things ready; we got what we came here for. We'll have to come back another time to explore this cave. If there is another time."

"There will be, Lyr," Halcyon said optimistically as the two of us began our trek back towards the raid. "There will be."

Falling into a companionable silence as we walked, I decided to take the time to focus my attention on one of the two notifications still flashing in the corner of my vision, the first being my newly gained attribute points. Giving the matter a few seconds of thought, I decided to invest the five new points into Strength, realizing that it'd been a few levels since I'd improved the attribute. With that out of the way, I then turned to the second notification, seeing that it pertained to the Class Skill Point that we had all gained from killing The Beast.

Well, I guess we're back to this choice again, I said to myself as I brought up the skills and abilities available for me to spend my skill point on, noticing that it was the same list as when I had turned level fifteen. Staring at the list blankly for a second, I found my eyes ignoring all the other options and shifting towards the trait that I had begrudgingly passed up before, reading over it again to refresh my memory.

Mana Devourer

Type: Trait, Special
Duration: Permanent
Trait Requirement: Die from the effects of Mana Void.
Description: You have experienced the depths of your body's hunger for mana firsthand as it consumed your flesh and blood, feeling something stir deep within you. Even now, recovered from your ordeal you can't quite shake the feeling that there is something just past your perception, something more that you could tap into...or allow to tap into you.
Effect: Unknown

I still don't feel any more confident about this Trait looking at it a second time around, I thought, trying to tease any sort of hint or insight about what the trait might bring if I chose it. *Breaking it down based on the requirements, it seems like it has more to do with Mana Void Trait rather than my Ætherwarped one. But does that mean if I take the trait that it'll only improve my mana draining abilities and nothing else? Or will it have something to do with that ghoul form that I transformed into when I ran out of mana? Or maybe a combination of both?*

Shaking my head at all the questions that had popped into my mind, I realized that I wasn't going to find a logical solution to my problem, to somehow discover what the game was purposefully hiding from me. The Trait was designed to be a leap of faith, to give me an option to explore the strange circumstances that had given me my mana draining ability and see what lay beyond it.

The question simply was, did I want to?

"Fuck it," I whispered to myself as I made a snap decision and quickly assigned the skill point, going as far to confirm the choice before I spent any more time endlessly overanalyzing it.

"Hmm?" Halcyon asked, turning his head to look at me. "Did you say something, Lyr?"

"Only to my—" I started to say before I felt *something* stir inside of me, causing my stomach to twist with nausea as a powerful, all-consuming wave of hunger came over me. Gasping from the sudden sensation, I stopped walking and gripped my stomach, unable to help but feel a sense of panic shoot straight through me. But before I could do or say anything else, a spike of pain shot through my head, forcing me down onto my knees in agony, feeling as if razor sharp claws were dragging themselves along the insides of my skull.

This almost feels like what happened after I respawned from the fight with Carver, just…worse! I thought, the painful memory flashing through my mind. So complete and consuming was the pain, that I barely felt Halcyon grab me by the shoulders, only vaguely recalling it after the fact. As the seconds passed, the pain began to mercifully fade, leaving only the faint sensation of hunger behind as if I had recently missed a meal.

"Lyr! Are you okay?!" I heard Halcyon's shout as a cool flowing sensation came over me. "What's going—hey! What are you doing? Hold up! *Stop!*"

I felt a sharp tug pull me forward, causing me to lose my balance and catch myself with one hand against the ground, the other holding onto something that continued to try and yank itself backward. Not understanding what was happening, I looked up and saw that my hand had wrapped itself around Halcyon's forearm and was squeezing tightly, an expression of pain written across my friend's face.

"Shit!" I cursed in surprise as I saw what was happening and forced my hand to let go, the cool flowing sensation that had been coursing through my body vanishing the moment I broke contact, leaving me feeling satiated and no longer hungry. "W-what's going on?"

"I think that's supposed to be my question!" Halcyon replied, stumbling backwards half a step from my sudden release before he managed to recover. "What the hell was that about? You don't just go start stealing mana without at least a courtesy warning!"

"I-I didn't even realize I was doing it," I replied, holding up a hand for the mage to wait as I sorted out what I was feeling and waited for my heartrate to return to normal. "I spent my skill point on a new trait just now, and then everything went a bit *off*..."

"I'll say," Halcyon grunted as he rubbed his forearm in pain. "For a second there I thought you were going to break my arm. What Trait did you take?"

"It was the one I mentioned before. The one I wasn't sure about," I told the mage, taking deep breaths as I slowly regained control and tried to make sense of what I was feeling, eventually pushing myself back up onto my feet and noticing a flashing notification in my vision that was demanding my attention.

"Hang on a second," I said as I mentally called up the prompt and saw my vision fill with text. "An alert just popped up."

You have experienced the full depths of your body's demand for Arcane Energy, going as far as to have it consume your very life, which has now awoken a primal hunger from within that now permanently lurks at the edges of your mind. As a result of this development, your potency of your abilities have intensified, as well as their drawbacks.

The Trait: **Mana Void** *has been upgraded to* **Mana Devourer**!

Mana Devourer *– For as long as you have mana, you do not require to eat or drink, however as your mana reserves diminish, your hunger will increase correspondingly until it becomes impossible to ignore. Should you completely deplete your mana reserves, your body will immediately enter a feral state as it begins to consume itself at a rate of five hit points for each second in a mana deprivation state, the rate increasing by another five hit points every second afterward until at least 50% of your total mana is restored or you are consumed. All mana regeneration is permanently reduced by 100%.*

The Ability: **Mana Leech** *has been augmented!*

Mana Leech *– Its power enhanced by the effects of the [Mana Devourer] trait, you are now able to momentarily enhance your mana leech ability by expending your life force, allowing it to disrupt a single nearby spell. At the cost of 8% of your total health, you are now able to disrupt the formation of any spell within 30 feet, absorbing 50% of mana used to cast it, and prevent your target from casting spells for the next two seconds. Due to its strain on your body, this ability can only be used once every five minutes.*

You have learned the new Ability: **Mana Torrent**

Mana Torrent *– By fueling the ever-present hunger that now lurks within your body with your life force, you are able to momentarily draw in all nearby sources of mana directly towards you and absorb it. At the cost of 20% of your total health, this ability will instantly drain all mana sources within a 15-foot radius of you for 200% of your [Mana Leech] rate, and temporarily disrupt the formation of any* *spells for the next three seconds. Due to the strain on your body, this ability can only be used once an hour.*

"Huh," I grunted as I finished reading the update and dismissed it from my vision.

"Good news?" Halcyon asked, his voice sounding a mix between curious and concerned.

"It's…not bad actually," I replied with a note of surprise as I gave the mage an outline of everything that I'd just read. "The only downside I can see is that I actually feel hungry again, but for mana instead of food. It feels similar to what I felt when I'd lost control during the first battle with Carver, but nowhere as intense."

"And you think that will change depending on how much mana you have left?" Halcyon asked, homing in on one of the things that I'd mentioned in my explanation.

"That's what it sounds like," I said with a nod, unsure of how I felt about that particular development. At the moment, the newly awakened hunger was barely noticeable in the back of my mind, yet I couldn't help but wonder how that would change as I used up my mana pool. "Though we'll have to see how that works in practice."

"Well, we have a few seconds right now," Halcyon said, waving at the still assembling raid in the distance. "Cast a spell now and see what it's like so it doesn't surprise you later. I can top you up afterward."

"Good idea," I replied, pausing for a moment as I considered what spell to use, eventually settling on *Lesser Shielding* due to its larger mana cost. Casting the spell, I felt the protective shield fall over me, followed a heartbeat behind by the hunger intensifying as I went from being satiated to feeling like I should find something to eat soon.

"It's noticeable," I told Halcyon, who offered me an arm to replenish my mana. "But it's not too bad at the start; it'll likely get more and more intense the less mana that I have."

"That makes sense," he agreed, wincing slightly as I briefly absorbed enough mana from him to replace what I'd used to cast the spell, the spike in hunger that I'd felt fading away. "Though that *Torrent* ability that you said you got should really help keep your mana levels up."

"Yeah," I said while nodding in thanks to the mage as I released his arm. "It has a pretty steep cost in health...but I have a few ideas of how to put it to good use, I've seen similar abilities in other games before."

"I remember too," Halcyon commented. "*And* with that in mind, I'm happy you're on our side. You're shaping up to be a regular mage slayer, Lyr."

"I guess I am, aren't I?" I replied, realizing that my friend's assessment was true. With my mobility and speed, combined with my mana draining and now spell interrupts, I was a living nightmare for a caster to face. I could get into melee range fast, and then negate anything that they did long enough to inflict serious harm if they didn't have any support nearby. "Though that's probably the role that Spellswords would have normally fit into anyway. I just have a few extra tricks that make me stand out."

"Maybe," Halcyon agreed as he motioned for us resume our journey back towards the raid. "Though I think everyone is going to start coming into their class roles in the next few levels. I remember overhearing people talking about their new class skills back at level fifteen, and a little bit more now with this point we just got. Options for spell interrupts, buffs, and crowd control abilities or spells are starting to become available."

"And that doesn't even include whatever we'll find at level twenty," I said, nodding in sync with the man's train of thought. "And then past that...it's only nine levels away until we hit our Advanced Class."

"Definitely looking forward to that," Halcyon said excitedly. "Though that is probably ages away. It took us *two months* to get this far after all."

"That's true," I acknowledged. "Though what I wouldn't give for two months of *peace,* just to catch up."

"I hear you, Lyr," Halcyon said. "But something tells me that's just not in the cards for the next little while."

"Probably not," I agreed with a heavy sigh, Carver and his gang appearing at the forefront of my mind. Even if we managed to stop them here today, we'd have to start looking for their base again right away. They'd proved today that they were simply too dangerous to leave unattended.

Walking the final distance back to the raid in silence, we eventually spotted Constantine, Lazarus and Amaranth standing together in a half circle, with a smattering of the other Adventurers from the raid milling around. Everyone seemed to be interested in coming by to peek into the bag that the two were holding, before moving off to excitedly chat with their respective groups. Curious to what was going on, I motioned for Halcyon to follow me as we approached.

"Want to see the loot, Lyr?" Constantine asked as we approached. "Sierra and the others are just consolidating the last few groups that are missing their leaders or have taken too many losses. We figured we could show everyone else what The Beast dropped while we waited. It was a pretty good haul, though before you get too excited, it's more crafting stuff and its skull...plus...something else that we're really not sure of."

"What exactly aren't you sure of?" I queried, only to see both Lazarus and Constantine shrug in response.

"Take a look," Lazarus said to me, shaking the loot bag he was holding. "You'll see."

"Uh, okay," I replied, taking a step forward to peer inside the pack and seeing a list of items appear in my vision.

Pristine Drake Scale
> *Quantity: 180*
> *Item Class: Magical*
> *Item Quality: Mythical (+30%)*
> *Weight: 60 kg*

Pristine Drake Fang
> *Quantity: 32*
> *Item Class: Magical*
> *Item Quality: Mythical (+30%)*
> *Weight: 10 kg*

Pristine Drake Talon
> *Quantity: 20*
> *Item Class: Magical*
> *Item Quality: Mythical (+30%)*
> *Weight: 10 kg*

Pristine Drake Bone
> *Quantity: 120*
> *Item Class: Magical*
> *Item Quality: Mythical (+30%)*
> *Weight: 60 kg*

The Beast's Skull
> *Item Class: Trophy*
> *Weight: 10 kg*

Greater Essence of Ferocity
> *Quantity: 4*
> *Item Class: Magical*
> *Item Quality: Mythical (+30%)*
> *Weight: N/A*

"*Essence of Ferocity?*" I asked, looking at the two who then shrugged back at me. "That's similar to the essence that we found from the Specters in the ruins."

"Seems like it, Lyr," Constantine said. "But...what is it *for*? And why did The Beast drop it? Wasn't that like...an undead spirit thing?"

"Guess not if we're seeing it here," I replied, it being my turn to give the pair a shrug. "I have no idea."

"Best guess is that it has something to do with crafting that we haven't figured out yet," Halcyon suggested as he finished looking through the loot bag. "Maybe for one of the Advanced Tradeskills, like Enchanting or Runecrafting?"

"Huh, I forgot about those," Constantine said, glancing over to one side as he caught movement out of the corner of his eye. "Well, at any rate, it looks like that's going to go on the back burner for now. Because unless I'm mistaken, we're ready to move."

Turning my head to follow his gaze, I saw that Sierra and the others had just emerged from the raid with a handful of the group leaders following closely behind them. Spotting the five of us right away, it didn't take long for all of them to make their way to us.

"We've managed to get everyone who's still standing sorted out and are ready to go," Sierra said by way of greeting. "You guys have everything you need from that Runestone?"

"Yep," I replied, without a moment's hesitation.

"We're all set," Halcyon confirmed a moment afterward.

"Great," she stated, giving the both of us a nod, then shifted her attention over towards Lazarus and Constantine. "All the loot is accounted for?"

"It is," Lazarus replied.

"Perfect. Unless anyone else has something they need doing...?" Sierra let the question hang as she looked around the group, giving time for anyone to speak up if they had any concerns. A few seconds of silence passed as everyone around us shook their heads and stayed silent.

"Alright then," the red-haired elf said, breaking the silence as she gave us all one last look.

"Let's go find Carver."

Chapter 54

<It is as we thought,> Amaranth announced in my mind as I pushed my way through the thick foliage before me, the smell of burning vegetation growing stronger with each step I took. *<Someone has been through here.>*

<Good!> I replied, feeling my heart begin to beat faster at the news, which in turn then prompted me to move faster through the thick brush. *<Hold on a moment; we're coming to you now.>*

It had only been a handful of minutes since we'd left The Beast's lair. Minutes that had the jungle blurring past us as we recklessly blazed a path through it, sacrificing any pretense of stealth in favor of raw speed. The few spirits or creatures finding themselves unlucky enough to be in our path barely had time to process their mistake before a veritable avalanche of Adventurers trampled them.

Yet despite the progress that we were making, it was the most recent turn of events that had me holding my breath in anticipation of what I would find next. Up until just a few moments earlier, our sprint through the jungle had largely included us cutting our own trail through the heavy overgrowth as we headed in the direction of the Ley Line, at least until Amaranth had announced he had caught the scent of several unfamiliar beings, mixed in along with the smell of smoke. With the entire raid following behind me and this being the deepest that any of us had ever ventured into the Grove, that bit of news could have only meant one thing.

We'd caught wind of Carver's trail.

Shifting to follow the scent, I ordered for Amaranth to scout ahead and to report back on what he'd found as I followed with the rest of the raid.

And here we are, I thought as I cautiously stepped out of the overgrowth with Splinter held high and into a newly trampled clearing, my eyes scanning the area around me and seeing signs of recent battle. Almost all the vegetation nearby was either in tatters, trampled flat, or singed from a blast of magic. *It looks like a portion of Carver's group was jumped by a bunch of the Grove creatures or spirits and were forced to fight.*

<The battle here was brief, yet vicious,> Amaranth told me, trotting into view with his tail held low to the ground. *<I smell the blood of several beings nearby, some belonging to the Grove creatures, others not. Yet there is no doubt that the invaders persevered, for there is a path leading onwards.>*

<It's only fair that Carver's group get a taste of what we had to face in here,> I replied to the cat before glancing behind me as the rest of the raid began to arrive.

"What's the news, Lyr?" Drace asked, the first to appear from the jungle behind me with Constantine and Sierra close behind.

"Looks like we've found his trail," I replied, motioning that it was safe to come out as even more of the raid began to appear behind them. "He and his group fought *something* here then continued onwards.

"A lot of somethings from what I can tell," Sierra stated as she stepped around the half-giant and glanced around the battle-torn area. "But that's a big help for us; we'll be able to move faster if we're not blazing our own path through the jungle."

"True," I agreed as I gave the area another look, trying to picture just how many people had passed through the area.

"Seems like he has a pretty big group with him, likely much more than we saw him with at the Tower."

"We kinda expected that though, Lyr," Constantine said while indicating the jungle around us. "Besides, quantity didn't exactly work out in his favor the last time we fought him."

"That it didn't," I acknowledged, trying to project a sense of confidence in my voice despite how I truly felt. I knew firsthand just how much could change over the course of a few weeks, especially when it came to training and practice. The only reason why we were able to beat out Carver and his group the last time was because we had all drilled together as a team and had better gear in comparison, if he'd found a way to make up for that difference *with* their larger numbers since we'd last fought them, there'd be little we could do to stand up against it.

Focus on worrying about things you have control over, Marc, I thought, stopping that train of thought before my thoughts could begin to spiral. *First things first, we need to find Carver, and that means keeping everyone moving. You can worry about how you're going to fight him once you know where he is.*

"Alright," I stated, taking my eyes off the jungle and turning my attention back towards the raid, which had just about finished arriving. "Since Carver's been so nice as to give us a path we can follow, let's get everyone organized nice and close, that way we can all travel quickly together, instead of being spread out and arriving piecemeal when we find him."

"Works for me," Drace grunted as both Constantine and Sierra nodded in agreement, the four of us then moving to pass on our updated plan to Freya and the others.

Within a minute we were all moving again, this time following the trail that Carver and the rest of his group had left through the jungle. The simple difference of not needing to cut a path through the thick foliage allowing us to speed through the jungle at a near sprint. As we ran through the far reaches of the Twilight Grove, I gradually noticed a familiar feeling come over me, a sense of soothing warmth as the air somehow grew heavier.

We must be getting close to the Ley Line, I thought as the sensation continued to increase, prompting me to temporarily pull my glove off to check the veins in my hand, seeing that they'd begun to glow with a soft azure energy. *Very close.*

"We're almost there," I announced, turning my head slightly towards Sierra who had taken up position on my left.

"How can you ev—oh, you're glowing again," Sierra replied, her eyes widening in momentary surprise as they shot up to look at my face. "I forgot you double as a handy Geiger counter when it comes to Æther."

"That's one way of putting it I guess," I replied with a snort as I raised a hand upward to signal the raid to slow down. With us getting this close to the Ley Line, and presumably Carver, the last thing I wanted to do was to have us all burst free of the jungle en masse and ruin any element of surprise we might have. Continuing forward at a more sedate pace down the trail, I was eventually able to make out a distant glow of emerald light ahead of us as the jungle came to an end.

"There it is—" Sierra started to say as we approached the jungle's edge when a discordant mental voice suddenly slammed into our minds, causing our hands to reflexively shoot up to cover our ears.

<Invaders! Kill the invaders! They did this to us! Kill them! Kill them! KILL THEM!> The spirits familiar chant tore

through my head with an intensity that I'd never heard before, making me feel as if I'd been physically struck.

"Ugh, that is *loud!*" Sierra gasped, her hands moving away from her ears to clutch at her head as she closed her eyes in pain.

"Angrier too," I stated, gritting my teeth as I tried to push the mental noise out of my mind while forcing my feet to continue moving forward, the urgency of our situation refusing to let me stop, hearing a wave of groans echo out from behind me as the rest of the raid was affected by the mental assault. "Just a little bit farther."

Pushing through the psychic assault, we rapidly approached the jungle's edge and the glowing emerald light beyond it. With every step we took, I felt the mental pressure of the screaming voices in my head increase, until it was practically the only thing I could hear, drowning out the sounds of the raid behind me. Feeling a hand grip my arm, I turned to see that Sierra was trying to get my attention, her mouth saying something that was immediately lost amid the voices swirling through my mind.

"What did you say?" I shouted, leaning in closer towards in the hope of being able to understand what she was saying.

"Combat!" She yelled back at me, almost directly into my ear. "I hear combat ahead!"

Eyes widening in surprise, I looked back at my friend then back towards the jungle's edge, a brief moment of clarity coming over me as I heard a thunderclap of magic echo in the distance, followed closely by shouting voices. Rushing forward without a second's hesitation, I charged towards the edge of the jungle, now just barely ahead of us, pushing the foliage out of my way as I moved. Squinting from the intense emerald light as I stepped out of the undergrowth,

I forced myself to look through the brightness, feeling my heart skip a beat at the scene before me.

Stretching as far as I could see, was a massive canyon almost completely filled with the emerald-colored Æther, its sickly light drowning out the azure-hued cascade that fell from a large tear in the cavern wall above. Feeling my mouth drop open at the sight, my attention was drawn to the massive body of tainted Æther, its surface roiling with countless ghostly shapes, some of which broke free and soared high up into the air. Shifting my eyes to follow one of the spirits as it left the body of Æther behind and flew upwards, I saw it join a huge swarm of similar looking shapes that were all swirling intently around the mouth of the ruptured Ley Line and the Æther pouring from it.

"Lyr!" Sierra's voice caused me to tear my eyes off of the torrent of spirits high above as her hand came into view, pointing at something much closer. "Look!"

Following her outstretched finger, I dropped my gaze downwards and found myself staring at a large outcropping that stretched over the canyon, stopping just shy of the Ætherfall pouring from the ruptured Ley Line. Yet it wasn't the outcropping itself that had commanded Sierra's attention, but the fierce and vicious battle being waged on top of it. Blinking to make sure that I wasn't imagining the sight before me, I saw a large host of unfamiliar Adventurers flanking either side of the outcropping as they clashed with a seemingly endless horde of Nafarrian spirits that were climbing out of the Æther-filled canyon and scaling the rock upward.

We found them, I realized as I looked out towards the chaotic battle, seeing that the Adventurers were just barely managing to keep the onrushing spirits at bay due to their superior positioning on either side of the outcropping. Glancing inward from the two forces, I saw a small reserve of Adventurers standing by a large jagged rock, enjoying a pocket of relative safety as they tended to the wounded or moved to shore up flagging sections of the line. *But I don't see Carver or his pet anywhere in that mess…unless he's on the other side of that stone—*

"Shit! That's the other Runestone!" I practically shouted, the revelation interrupting my thoughts with the force of a sledgehammer. "*Of course, it'd be here!*"

"Is it?" Constantine demanded from my other side, having appeared seemingly from nowhere while I'd been staring at the battle, along with several others as everyone in the raid eagerly pushed their way forward out of the jungle. "Are you sure?"

"It looks the same as the others," I replied, feeling my heart begin to thunder in my chest as a surge of adrenaline shot through me. "And *where* else would the game put it? Just like sticking it in The Beast's Lair, putting it here *forces* us to confront the spirits. To do *exactly* what Carver and his group are doing right now!"

"We need—*wait, what's that?*" Sierra yelled as a bright flash of magic appeared at the edge of the outcropping in the distance, prompting all of our heads to snap in its direction where we now saw a figure standing inside a bright orange aura.

"*It's Carver!*" I snarled angrily, recognizing the one antlered helmet that the figure in the distance wore, the magic flaring around him as it began to take shape. "And he's casting some sort of spell!"

"Then that means we're almost out of time!" Sierra exclaimed as she unslung her bow from her shoulder. "We need to get in there!"

"Here is our chance!" I shouted, making a snap decision as I took a step forward and looked back towards the raid, knowing that there wasn't enough time to lay out a battleplan or give a speech. Not if we wanted to have any hope of stopping Carver in time. So instead, I kept my message as short and as simple as possible. "This is where we decide if Aldford lives or dies today! So, hit them as hard as you can! Everyone, with me!"

With my words still hanging in the air, I turned back towards the distant battle and launched myself into a sprint, hearing a loud wordless roar split the air behind me as the raid rushed to follow, the thunder of their feet echoing briefly before it was lost amongst the spirits' endless wail. Running as fast as I could over the rough terrain, I saw both Constantine and Amaranth appear either side of me, the three of us spearheading the raid's charge.   As the distance between us and the rapidly approaching battle diminished, I felt a tingle of energy play across my skin, followed by an alert in my vision.

You have entered an area permeated with Æther!

All mana regeneration rates are increased by 100 mana per second!

All magical effects are increased by 25%!

The Æther is affecting this place just like it did at the Hub! I exclaimed mentally as I scanned the notification, feeling my eyes widen at bonuses that this area provided. *No wonder everyone is throwing magic around nonstop! It regenerates almost faster than you can spend it!*

My mind racing at the unexpected development, I dismissed the alert from my vision and focused my attention back towards Carver's forces, trying to decide where our arrival would do the most harm.

The right side looks the weakest between the two, I noted as we approached, seeing that the majority of the Adventurers clustered by the Runestone had their attention focused in that direction, with several of their members moving to relieve overwhelmed sections of the line. *If we can hit them hard enough, we can force them straight off the edge and into the Æther, then continue rolling forward until we reach Carver. If the other half moves to attack us, then they'll end up sandwiched between us and the spirits.*

"They've seen us!" Constantine warned with a shout, prompting me to swing my attention back towards the center pocket where the reserve had been standing, seeing several of the Adventurers pointing in our direction while trying to raise the alarm.

"Far too late!" I shouted back, feeling a surge of vengeful glee shoot through me as I saw the wave of panic sweep through all of the Adventurers ahead of us, their heads snapping towards us in disbelief.

In their eyes, we'd already been a defeated force, fallen prey to Ignis's plan to have The Beast kill us and put us out of the fight. Seeing us suddenly appear in near point-blank range with the majority of our numbers intact, was something that none of them expected, causing many of them to freeze in surprise.

Giving us the extra few seconds we needed to slam into their ranks.

Shouting at the top of my lungs as we rudely interrupted the battle in progress, I fixated my attention on a stunned Adventurer before me, the mace in his hand coming up far too slowly to prevent a crackling Splinter from slicing a line across his throat. Feeling the blade grate across bone as I completed my opening swing, I shouldered the man out of my way and continued onwards, seeking to use my momentum to drive as deep as I could into the invader's ranks before I was forced to stop.

Shoving my way forward, I didn't hesitate to make full use of the area's regenerative effect on my mana pool, channeling *Shocking Touch* with every swing I took while simultaneously conjuring *Flame Daggers* in my offhand and putting them to deadly use. Melting from under our brutal onslaught, we carved a swath through the invaders, managing to make it almost halfway across the outcropping and towards Carver, before we met the first signs of resistance.

"*YOU!*" The hate-filled word brought me back into the moment as Splinter's edge slammed down on a metal shield's edge, leaving me staring into a dwarven face that I instantly recognized from what felt like a lifetime ago. "*You're not supposed to be here!*"

"That's funny," I replied in a savage tone as I sent a surge of electricity through the shield and into the dwarf holding it. "I happen to feel the same way!"

"You should have known this was coming!" Phillion barked, barely twitching from my magic as he retaliated with his own attack. "We were never going to lie down after what you did to our guild!"

"Maybe you damn well should have!" I retorted as I caught his sword on Splinter's edge and trapped it, channeling yet another *Shocking Touch* through the metallic item. Visibly wincing from the attack this time, the dwarf tried to take a step backward in an attempt to disengage his weapon from mine, only to have Amaranth dart in from beside me and sink his teeth into his leg.

"Aaah!" Phillion yelped in pain a second before he lost his balance and fell awkwardly to the ground, giving me the opening I needed to thrust Splinter deep into his stomach and then step past him, trusting that my familiar would finish the job.

Hearing a pained scream ring out from behind me as I moved, I thrust Splinter into the side of an Adventurer facing away from me, his attention still focused on the spirits climbing up the outcropping's side. Feeling his body go stiff from the pain, I wasted no time pulling my weapon free, then kicked his legs out from under him, sending him tumbling off the edge and into the tainted Æther below.

Finished with the dwarf that I had left behind, I saw Amaranth bound into view as he leaped past me, followed closely behind by Aldwin, Constantine and Freya.

"We have to keep moving!" the Bann shouted as he caught an Adventurer's attack on his shield, then retaliated with a chop of his axe into their shoulder that sent them crashing to the ground. "They're starting to rally their forces! We need to force them back on their heels while we still can!"

"I'm with you!" I shouted back at the knight as I rushed forward to join the group, finding myself a spot on the far right in our line of battle, right against the edge of the outcropping.   Pushing forward with deadly purpose, the five of us scythed through a wave of scrambling Adventurers along with several spirits that had managed to finish the climb up the outcropping's side, giving us a new threat to worry about.

I guess that was inevitable at some point, I thought as I swept Splinter through a Shade before me, its body vanishing in a burst of energy. *But all that matters right now is stopping Carver and whatever he's trying to do. Once he's out of the way, we can deal with the spirits afterward.*

Our attack so far had devastated nearly the entirety of the invaders right flank, allowing the spirits that they'd been keeping at bay to finish their climb up the rock face and join the battle. A quick glance towards the other flank showed me a similar scene in the making as our mages and ranged attackers took advantage of the invaders positioning, focusing their attacks to hit the opposite line of Adventurers from behind without fear of reprisal, lest they turn their attention away from the spirits. In what seemed like an instant, the balance that Carver's force had achieved in keeping the spirits at bay had been lost, and panic was beginning to spread amongst them as fractures in their lines started to appear.

Continuing to press forward with the others, I thrust Splinter through an Adventurer's guard and stabbed the tip deep into his shoulder, discharging a *Shocking Touch* through his body and then followed up with a burning dagger thrust sharply upwards and under his ribs. Shoving the falling body to the side, I made to keep pressing onwards, only to hear a startled shout from Freya.

"Shit! Reinforcements from the left!" Her voice rang out from down the line, prompting my head to instinctively snap in its direction as our line suddenly shifted to adjust.

Only to see a brightly glowing sword heading straight towards my face.

Shouting in surprise at the attack, I reflexively swept Splinter upward before me, feeling the Æthertouched blade knock the attack out of the way, which was then immediately followed by a surge of electricity shooting down my arm and into my body. Grimacing from the unexpected pain, I finished twisting in the direction of the attacker and felt my heart skip a beat as I found myself staring into a face that I'd never expected to see again, let alone *here* of all places.

"*Lyrian!*" The man's voice sliced effortlessly through the combined crash of battle and spirits' chant as he sliced out with another attack, taking advantage of my momentary surprise and carving a line across my arm. "I'm so happy you were able to make it here in time! After Carver told me what he had planned for you...I had my doubts you'd even show up at all!"

"Mozter!" I snarled with sudden rage as I pushed past the unexpected revelation and retaliated with my own attack. "What the hell are you doing here?!"

"Isn't it obvious, Lyrian?!" the dark elf shouted in reply, displaying a savage grin on his face as he caught Splinter on his sword and knocked it out of the way. "I'm here for round two! You didn't think that just because you managed to get me and my group exiled, that I wouldn't try and take a second shot at you if I had the chance?"

"What I'd *hoped* is that you came to your damn senses after I handed your ass to you, and that you got a fresh start somewhere else!" I retorted, slapping a thrust from Mozter to the side and delivering a searing cut across his thigh with a hastily conjured *Flame Dagger*, a part of my mind finally noticing that he was wearing the same roughly cut leather armor that I'd seen Carver wearing the other week.

"Oh, but that's exactly what we did, Lyrian!" Mozter replied, showing no sign that my attack had hurt him. "It turns out Carver and his group are big fans of our winner-take-all approach to things...*well,* at least the winners are! But then again, *that's the point!*"

Launching himself forward with a laugh, the two of us exchanged a rapid flurry of blows that made me realize that whatever level advantage that I'd previously enjoyed against Mozter was now gone. Moving with a speed and strength that he hadn't possessed earlier, the dark elf set me back on my heels as I rapidly tried to adjust to his new skill level, finding it to be a near perfect match for my own. Chancing a glance towards the rest of my party in the hope of support, I saw that the entirety of Mozter's old group had joined him in his attack, stopping our assault cold, and keeping all of them far too busy to help.

Damn it! I don't have time for a duel right now and especially not here! I thought as I traded electrified blows with the dark elf, the two of us burning through our mana pools as if they were bottomless, which given the area's special effect, they effectively were. *Plus, with how fast we're regenerating mana here, draining it is pointless!*

Backpedaling as Mozter pressed his attack, I couldn't help but keep his multi-cast ability at the forefront of my mind and forced myself to fight cautiously, not wanting to be caught by surprise by a blast of magic that I knew I'd have no chance to recover from.

Assuming I survived it in the first place.

"What's wrong, Lyrian?" Mozter taunted as my conservative style gradually forced me backward to the edge of the outcropping overlooking the tainted Æther below. "Are you feeling hard-pressed to keep up? I expected better than this from you!"

Ignoring the man's jab, I replied by parrying a sweeping attack from his sword, immediately riposting in return, scoring a wound on the dark elf's bicep. Seeing him wince from the attack, I quickly followed it up with a yet another *Flame Dagger*, throwing the burning knife directly at his face and forcing him to leap backward to evade it. Pressing forward, I fought to give myself some space from the edge, hoping that a spirit didn't pick that moment to climb up behind me.

I can't keep wasting my time here, I thought as it became Mozter's turn to fight cautiously, the dark elf now focusing on pure evasion, not wanting to risk contact with my sword, lest it carry a current of electricity. *I need to put an end to this and get to Carver before it's too late!*

Continuing to fight in our own pocket amid the greater conflict around us, the exchange between the two of us grew in both speed and intensity. Minor injuries piled up as the battle progressed, each and every one gradually slowing our movements, it being only a matter of time before one of us made a fatal mistake, allowing the other to put an end to the contest. Forming a desperate plan in my head as I felt myself being forced backward again, I decided to give Mozter that very mistake that he was looking for, while silently hoping that I'd be able to turn it around on him in time.

"Ha!" Mozter exclaimed in triumph as I feinted a slip off of the edge of the outcropping, the man taking advantage of the opening to thrust his sword directly into my abdomen just above my left hip, while simultaneously extending his free hand towards me, a glowing ball of azure light forming in his palm. "Looks like I win this time, Lyrian!"

"I wouldn't be so sure of that, Mozter!" I hissed through clenched teeth, adrenaline the only thing keeping the pain at bay as I reached out to grab the dark elf by the collar of his armor while triggering my newly improved Mana Leech ability. In a heartbeat, the growing spell in Mozter's hand came apart as an overwhelming surge of hunger came over me, the spell's mana flowing across the short distance between us and into my body. Eyes widening at his interrupted spell, I managed to see a fleeting look of terror cross Mozter's face as I then threw my weight backward.

Pulling us both off of the ledge.

"Lyrian you fu—" I heard Mozter scream in a panic as the two of us began to fall, his words abruptly cutting themselves off the moment that I triggered *Blink Step*.

With my vision blurring in a wild array of colors, I felt myself land heavily back on the outcropping's edge that I'd just thrown both Mozter and myself off of, a wave of sheer agony passing through my side from the impact. Somewhere in my desperate maneuver, Mozter's sword had managed to tear itself free of my body, leaving a steady stream of blood pouring from it.

"Goodbye, Mozter," I whispered to myself as I placed a hand over the wound and glanced down the outcropping's edge, only seeing the tainted Æther below with no sign of either the dark elf or any climbing spirits. "And good riddance."

Breathing a sigh of relief, I reached into my belt pocket and pulled out a healing potion, downing its contents quickly before scanning the battlefield, having been too focused on my duel with Mozter to keep track of everything going on. Taking in everything at a glance, I saw that in the time that I'd been fighting Mozter, the rest of the raid had continued to press against Carver's forces, ravaging their ranks until only a small fraction of their original numbers remained standing.

Hang on, I thought as I finished taking in the scene, noticing that while there were a substantial number of spirits on the outcropping now, there was nowhere near the amount that I'd expected now that Carver's forces weren't able to keep them at bay anymore. *Why aren't there more of them up here? We should be getting swarmed by now!*

As if sensing my thoughts, it was at that very moment that a vicious tremor shook the cavern all around us, causing everyone to momentarily lose their balance. Within seconds of the event occurring, I felt the spirits' chant suddenly die off, temporarily bathing all of us in an eerie silence. Looking up at the unexpected event, I glanced in the direction of several of the spirits' seeing them visibly wincing as if they were in pain, their bodies rapidly losing shape with every second that passed.

"What the hell?" I managed to gasp from my kneeling position as the spirits before me dissolved into an insubstantial ball of energy and hovered in the air. Glancing around towards the other spirits that I'd seen just seconds

earlier, I saw the same event repeat itself endlessly, each of the ghosts transforming into a hazy mote of emerald light.

<What is happening!> Amaranth asked a moment before he bounded into view, his voice filtering through our mental link as I forced myself back up onto my feet. *<The spirits have…shifted somehow!>*

<I see it too,> I replied to the cat, just in time to see all the motes begin to move towards us. *<Wait, something's happen—>*

<No! Stop!> an ethereal voice suddenly demanded, its mental volume causing me to wince in pain. *<Don't do this! You have no idea what you'll unle—Ah!>*

Cutting off with a scream, the voice vanished from my mind just as quickly as it had appeared. But before I could even begin to make sense of what exactly it was that I'd heard, I was forced to scramble out of the way as several of the shimmering motes shot past me, their speed increasing the further that they traveled. Feeling a spike of dread shoot through me as I twisted my body to follow the wave of disembodied spirits as they sailed through the air, seeing them rush to join a growing maelstrom of energy right at the edge of the outcropping overlooking the Ley Line Rupture.

Right where I'd last seen Carver.

Oh, fuck! I swore silently as I looked up at the well of power, seeing that the torrent of spirits that had been swirling around the Ley Line Rupture earlier in the battle had since been consumed by whatever spell that Carver had managed to conjure and was growing in size with every second that passed.

<Where are the others?> I asked Amaranth as I tore my eyes off the spell and looked behind me, only to see that the battle between the raid and Carver's followers had

begun anew, now that they weren't forced to keep the spirits at bay any longer.

<They're still fighting with the invaders!> my familiar replied. *<I just barely managed to escape before being drawn in again!>*

*"*Shit!" I cursed aloud, realizing that time was rapidly running out. Making a decision, I signaled for Amaranth to follow me and turned my body towards the far edge of the outcropping where all the spirits were being drawn to. *<We can't wait for the others! We need to stop whatever Carver is doing before it's too late!>*

Launching myself into a sprint, Amaranth and I left the growing battle behind as the two of us charged towards Carver, watching more and more of the emerald motes fly past us. Using *Blink Step* to help the both of us cross the distance even faster, I didn't even feel my mana deplete as I carried the both of us forward, all of my attention focused on reaching the distant half-orc before it was too late.

Sensing our approach as we rapidly closed the distance, I saw a familiar crimson shape by Carver's side shift around to look in my direction, its hackles rising the instant that it spotted us. Letting out a savage bark it leaped to put itself between us and its master, who spun around in our direction.

"*Carver!*" I shouted as I cast *Blink Step* once again, causing Amaranth and me to appear at near point-blank range in front of the pair. With my familiar leading the way half a step ahead of me, I had just enough time to see him slam into the crimson spirit wolf and knock it out of my path, giving me a perfect opportunity to swing Splinter at Carver's head.

"Lyrian! Well isn't this a surprise?! You actually made it!" The half-orc exclaimed as he caught my sword on an upraised spear tip and blunted the blow by taking a step backwards, the storm of magic crackling with energy above us. "I guess I'm going to have a few failures to punish once this is all over!"

"You mean Ignis and his group?!" I growled at the man angrily, chopping Splinter viciously into Carver's spear, noticing that he no longer carried a shield in his off-hand and instead was clinging onto a brightly glowing totem. "Feel free to send them back to us! I'll *happily* sort them out for you! In fact, why don't you tell me where I can pick them up?"

"Heh, I bet you would love to do just that," Carver replied, a wide grin crossing his face as he retaliated with a combination of spear thrusts that forced me to dance backwards out of reach, both Amaranth and Carver's spirit wolf also taking the opportunity to break free of their respective battle to fall in by our sides. "But I'm afraid I prefer to handle all my discipline matters internally. Better for morale that way. Besides, I don't expect you and your little town to be around much longer anyway."

"Like hell we won't be!" I retorted, conjuring a *Flame Dagger* in my hand, hearing Amaranth growl fiercely as I prepared to renew my attack against Carver. "My raid is finishing off the rest of your followers right now, and the moment that I put you into the ground, I'm going to unravel *whatever* the hell you're trying to do here!"

"Haha!" Carver barked a sudden and slightly maniacal laugh at my statement while shaking his head viciously to the side, the totem in his hand suddenly pulsing with a wave of emerald light. "God, I've always wanted to say this…but you're too late, Lyrian! You can't stop any of this now!"

Glancing down at the totem as Carver began to thrust it upwards, I reflexively threw the *Flame Dagger* in my hand towards it, while lunging forward with Amaranth beside me. But before either the knife or the two of us could reach Carver, a blinding burst of emerald light erupted from the totem, followed closely behind by a wave of force that slammed into us, sending us both stumbling backward.

"In the end, I suppose it's only fitting that you have a front row seat to this, Lyrian!" I heard Carver's voice call out as the raging storm of energy above us shifted. "I just hope that this will teach you to keep your nose out of my business in the future!"

"What the hell did you just do, Carver?" I demanded, seeing all of the individual motes that had once been spirits suddenly shooting downwards towards the massive pool of Æther below us, causing what parts of it I could see to roil and churn.

"Oh, nothing too special," the half-orc replied in a smug voice as a faint tremor shook the cavern. "All I did was give these spirits a little inspiration and a little nudge in the direction they were going anyway. Just to help speed things along."

As if waiting until that very moment for its cue, a loud mental howl slammed into my mind, the sheer intensity behind it powerful enough to cause my thoughts to momentarily go blank. Gritting my teeth as I tried to focus past what sounded like a million angry voices screaming out at once, I felt the ground begin to shake underneath my feet, this time with more force than any that I'd ever experienced before. Unable to keep my balance, I dropped down to my knees just in time to see a column of tainted Æther erupt before me, shooting straight up into the air, several others joining it seconds later.

What the hell is—oh no! The fleeting thought crossed my mind before shifting into outright terror as I gazed upwards at the emerald-tinted Æther, seeing it suddenly begin to shift and distort as a familiar ghostly haze enveloped it.

Within seconds it then began to rapidly elongate itself, each of the Æther columns transforming themselves into an array of bizarre and twisted looking appendages. Staring on in horror as the strange limbs continued to take shape, I saw massive spectral claws come into being at the ends of a handful of them, while others shifted into twisted, gaping mouths that gnashed at the air.

We're too late, I couldn't help but think to myself as a massive shape then rose from the tainted Æther just past the edge of the outcropping in front of me, growing until it towered high above it. Staring up at the entity, I found it almost physically painful to look at, its ghostly, ooze-like form warping and undulating wildly as countless eyes, claws, and mouths played across its body, eventually vanishing from one spot, and reappearing somewhere else.

With the colossal spirit reaching its full height, the shaking in the cavern abruptly stopped, and the mental scream lost some of its intensity, making rational thought possible once more. Feeling like I could finally move again, I shakily pushed myself upwards, despair blooming in my heart as I focused on the massive entity and the tag that I had just seen appear in my vision.

[Ætherbound Shoggoth] – World Event Boss – Level 20

Chapter 55

"Well, Lyrian!" Carver's voice called out, causing my attention to shift downward towards the man, seeing a wide grin on his face as he put his now faintly glowing totem away and gripped his spear with both hands. "Now that we have *that* bit of ugly business out of the way, where were we?"

"You have no idea what you've just done, Carver!" I screamed, feeling the despair within me morph into white-hot rage as I stared at the half-orc. "You've doomed everyone! Us! Aldford! Even Eberia!"

"Do you think that I really didn't know that?" Carver replied with a savage laugh. "Why do you think I chose this way to do it? Just because it gave me an easy way to wipe out your little town? *Ha!* I'm playing a much bigger game here, Lyrian. One that goes so far beyond this region."

"God damn you, Carver," I hissed as I took a step towards the half-orc, gripping Splinter's hilt so tightly that I felt the bones in my hand crack. "No matter what happens here today, I am going to be coming for you, and I'm not going to stop until I put you in the darkest hole that I can find. Somewhere you'll never be able to escape from."

"Oh, I'll be ready, Lyrian!" Carver announced with another laugh as both he and his wolf fell into a fighting stance. "Now...why don't you come over here and see just how sorry you can make me? Something tells me we aren't going to have long until our *friend* over there decides to join the party."

"Good thing I won't need too much time!" I spat as I lunged forward with Amaranth by my side.

Crossing the distance between us in an instant, the two of us slammed into our respective counterparts and resumed the battle right where it had left off just seconds earlier. But this time, instead of being completely drawn into our own individual conflict, Amaranth and I stayed together, fighting almost on top of one another in perfect sync, effortlessly switching our focus between Carver or his spirit wolf as the situation demanded.

Deflecting a spear thrust from Carver, I pushed the pointed tip of his weapon out of the way, allowing Amaranth's claw to lash out and rend open a line of flesh on the half-orc's leg. Shifting my focus as my familiar attacked, I then swept my blade downward to intercept Carver's spirit wolf who had leaped forward to snap at Amaranth, and slashed through its spectral body, sending it flinching backward with a yelp of pain. Without missing a beat, I then conjured and released a *Flame Dagger* in my free hand, throwing it almost lazily in Carver's direction as I turned my head back towards him, watching the knife fly just past his face, leaving a wicked burn across his jaw.

"Having trouble keeping up, Carver?" I taunted the man as I seamlessly switched targets with Amaranth and slashed out with a crackling Splinter, purposefully driving the blow into Carver's spear. "I expected more from you after the last time!"

"*Hardly!*" The half-orc replied fiercely, oblivious to the fact that his voice lacked the same confidence that it had a few seconds earlier. "You haven't seen anything yet!"

Throwing themselves forward with a roar, both Carver and his spirit wolf renewed their attacks, compensating for their relative lack of teamwork with a vicious burst of ferocity that forced Amaranth and me to rapidly give ground. As the pair pressed forward recklessly, I saw an orb of sickly green light flash in Carver's hand a heartbeat before he threw it forward, the ball of magic moving too fast for me to get out of its way.

Splashing across my shoulder, I felt a wave of sickness come over me, slowing my movements just enough to allow Carver's spear to reach out and cut a shallow wound across my ribs. Hissing from the blow, I forced myself to embrace the pain in an attempt to shift my attention away from my roiling stomach and threw another burning dagger at the half-orc Shaman to buy myself some space.

"How do you like that, Lyrian?" Carver shouted as he effortlessly evaded my flaming missile by dancing backward away from me, his hand bursting into a pale yellow light. "You may be faster and stronger than me now! But my magic gives me a few tricks that yours doesn't!"

Opening his palm as he finished speaking, I saw the spell that he had conjured flow directly into his body, causing the wound that I had inflicted on his face to vanish and for the bleeding slash on his leg to instantly scab over.

Shit! He can heal himself! I cursed with sudden annoyance as I instinctively moved to launch myself back at the man, seeing yet another orb of yellow light appear in his hand, but before I could even begin to move, Amaranth's panicked voice thundered through my mind.

<Above us!> he shouted, a wave of sheer animalistic terror seeping through our bond. *<We need to flee! NOW!>*

Feeling my heart stop as I reflexively glanced upwards at my familiar's words, I saw that two of the thrashing tendrils had begun their descent downward towards us, one bearing a set of nightmarish claws on its end, while the other bore a gnashing maw. Leaping backward from Carver at the speed of thought, I quickly cast *Blink Step* for Amaranth and me, reappearing at the very edge that the spell could take us. No sooner did our feet land on the ground than a massive impact shake the entire outcropping beneath us as the two massive tentacles slammed into the spot where we had just been standing.

Spinning to look back at the impact, I saw that only Carver had managed to avoid the Shoggoth's opening attack, if only partially, his wolf nowhere in sight as he desperately scrambled across the ground, dragging one of his legs uselessly behind him. With all its tentacles and appendages flailing wildly through the air, the entity let out a loud mental roar as the countless eyes on its body all focused themselves downward towards us. Surging forward, huge splashes of tainted Æther sprayed upwards as the Shoggoth moved to envelope the section of the outcropping that we'd been standing on, a gargantuan maw full of teeth taking shape in the center of its spectral body.

Staring in stunned disbelief as the nightmarish being bit down, I felt the entire outcropping twist and shake underneath me as it tore free a portion of the rock in its maw, then began to chew on it as if it were flesh. Struggling to keep my balance as the ground threatened to shake itself to pieces, a flash of light caught my eye, causing me to shift my eyes off of the spirit and onto Carver, who was forcing himself back up onto his feet, his ruined leg now partially healed.

Feeling a renewed spike of rage shoot through me at the sight of the half-orc, I wasted no time in turning towards him, eager to get some measure of vengeance before the chance was taken away from me. Launching myself forward into a charge, Amaranth and I covered the distance to Carver in what felt like an instant, barely giving the half-orc the time to raise his spear to receive our attack.

"All the healing in the world isn't going to save you from me!" I shouted at the man as the two of us rapidly forced him backward, the spirit wolf no longer around to divide our attention. Within seconds, I landed several vicious cuts across Carver's body, followed by Amaranth delivering a staggering slap with his paw to the man's hip, the sound of cracking bone sending him stumbling badly onto his still wounded leg.

"Talk all you want if it makes you feel better, Lyrian," Carver replied to me through gritted teeth as our attacks continued to force him backward. "But we all know how this battle is going to end. I came here fully willing to die to make sure this place went off properly, whether it happens by your hand…or something else's, doesn't matter to me in the slightest."

"If that's the case," I snarled, seizing an opening in the half-orc's weakened guard to chop a crackling Splinter deep into his shoulder at the same time Amaranth lunged forward to bite down onto his spear and tore it from his grasp. "Let me send you off in a way that you'll never forget!"

Pulling my blade free of Carver's shoulder with a spray of blood, I then planted the heaviest kick I could muster straight into his wounded leg, hearing a snapping sound fill the air as he fell heavily to the ground.

"I'm sure I'll be seeing you soon, Carver," I said to the half-orc as I took a step backward away from the man, having seen the Shoggoth's tentacles unwind from the spot that they had slammed into and ready themselves for another strike. "But until then…I hope eating the loss of your *Soul Fragment* keeps you full of happy thoughts."

Seeing Carver's eyes widen as Amaranth and I rapidly backed away from him, I saw him glance upwards just in time for a wicked set of claws attached to one of the Shoggoth's tentacles take him directly in the chest and then lift his body straight up into the air and out of sight.

Feeling the rage within me turn to ash at Carver's death, I spun on my heel as I saw the other tentacle swing in our direction, Amaranth and I both rushing to get out of its reach. Working ourselves up into a full sprint, I felt the ground shake again as a loud crunch of stone echoed out from behind us.

Not wanting to risk a glance behind me at the noise, I cast *Blink Step* once more, taking advantage of my near limitless mana pool to get both Amaranth and myself firmly out of its reach. With the world blurring as we shifted places, the two of us reappeared further down the outcropping and practically crashed headlong into the fractured remains of the raid.

"Lyrian!" Sierra's voice shouted out in surprise from the head of the group, everyone coming to a stop as they saw both Amaranth and me appear. "We were just coming to help! What the hell happened up there?"

"Carver happened," I replied, breathing heavily as I looked over the raid, seeing all my friends rush forward to surround me. "I tried to stop him, but I was too late. He did...*something* to the spirits and turned them into *that*."

"Shit!" Constantine exclaimed before giving me an asking look. "Did you at least get him?"

"Yeah," I replied, hearing several grunts of approval from the raid. "For all the good it does us now."

"It's not over until it's over," Aldwin said in a tired voice. "There must be something that we—"

A loud crunch followed by a tremor suddenly interrupted the Knight, causing everyone to glance in the direction of the Shoggoth, just in time to see it take another chunk out of the outcropping.

"Gods!" Aldwin exclaimed as the chunk of stone vanished into the creature's maw. "Is that creature...trying to eat the place?"

"It sure looks like it!" I answered, shaking my head as half a dozen tentacles then erupted from the tainted Æther.

Two of the six immediately questing upwards towards the Ley Line while the other four began to rapidly grow massive bulges on their sides as they reached out to hover the outcropping. "Look! It's reaching for the—"

Before I could finish my statement, the bulges on the tentacles burst open with a spray of emerald-tinted Æther and several large globs fell from each of them, the majority of them landing wetly on the outcropping before us, with a handful falling back into the Æther below. Shifting rapidly, the shapes that had managed to land on the outcropping quickly sprouted their own array of tentacles, mouths and eyes, appearing as miniature versions of the larger Shoggoth.

"Shit! It's spawning minions!" Drace exclaimed, the big man's voice echoing over the raid's surprise as another wave of bulges burst from the tentacles, repeating the process a second time.

"Forget the minions! Look at what it's doing!" I shouted as I pointed directly at the Rupture, where the two other tentacles had transformed themselves into the gnashing maws that I had seen earlier and were beginning to devour the stone surrounding it. "It's trying to widen the Rupture!"

As one, everyone's eyes shot up to look at the Ley Line high above with the azure-tinted Æther still pouring steadily from it before vanishing out of sight behind the Shoggoth.

"Oh, fuck it is," Constantine whispered. "What the hell are we going to do? What *can* we do at this point?"

"What we came here to do," I said, turning my head to glance towards the middle of the outcropping to where the final Runestone was. "We need to try and seal the Ley Line."

"Do you really think that'll work, Lyr?" Freya asked, her head shifting to look at me.

"It's the best thing that I can think of right now," I replied, giving her what I hoped was a confident nod. "If we can get the final spell fragment from the Runestone and seal the rupture, then we just *might* keep things from getting worse."

"I have to agree with Lyr here," Halcyon said. "And that's not just because I don't want to get *anywhere* near that damn monster! It's really the best chance we have!"

"Uh, guys!" Drace called out, having kept his eyes down low while we had all focused on the Ley Line. "Speaking of *getting worse*, those minion things are starting to head this way!"

"Shit!" Freya cursed, shifting her gaze towards the onrushing horde of creatures. "Okay, Lyr! Your plan sounds like the best option we have right now! Take some people to watch over you in case some of these critters get past us and seal that damn Ley Line!"

"Got it!" I replied as Drace and Aldwin began shouting to get the raid organized, their two voices prompting everyone to move. "Halcyon! Constantine! Lazarus! Let's go!"

Splitting apart from the rest of the raid the five us, Amaranth included, rushed back down the outcropping, trusting that Freya and the others would keep the Shoggoth's spawn at bay. Crossing the distance quickly, thanks to the fact that we didn't need to fight Carver's forces along the way, it didn't take us long to reach the Runestone, Halcyon and I immediately reaching into our packs to pull out a clean sheet of paper and something to draw with.

"I have no idea what the timing on this one is, Lyr!" Halcyon said as the two us prepared ourselves. "Could be seconds, or minutes! I didn't see it flare at all during the battle earlier."

"Me either!" I replied, vaguely remembering myself running past it before encountering Mozter. "We'll need to wait...and hope that it doesn't take too long."

"Is there anything we can do to help?" Lazarus asked, his glass-steel sword in hand as he surveyed the area.

"Warn us if anything gets loose from the rest of the raid," I replied, seeing him nod as our eyes met. "But not while we're drawing. We can't afford any distractions."

"I understand," the half-giant acknowledged, before turning to look in the direction of the raid as several thunderclaps of magic announced the start of battle.

Sitting quietly as we waited for the Runestone to activate, I felt my heart hammer in my chest as I held the stick of charcoal over the paper, focusing on tuning out both the sounds of battle behind me and the Shoggoth's mindless screams until all I heard was my own breathing. Staring blankly at the Runestone for what seemed like ages, but could have also been seconds, I waited, my mind completely blank.

Then without any warning, the Runestone activated.

With my breath catching in my chest as I saw the spell fragment appear on the stone's face, I felt everything in the world fade away except for the symbols before me. Drawing even faster than I had when I had copied the Runestone at The Beast's lair, a distant understanding began to grow in my mind with every line that I drew on the page, eventually realizing that at some point I had taken my eyes off the glowing rock and was now staring at the completed spell fragment.

Taking a deep breath, all the noise that I had tuned out came crashing back onto me, this time sounding much closer than it had before. Glancing over at Halcyon to see how he was doing, I saw that the mage was also staring at a finished page before him, his expression one of bewilderment.

"All good, Hal?" I asked as I shifted my spell fragment towards him, ready to compare our sketches as quickly as possible.

"Y-yeah, Lyr," he replied, shaking his head as he showed me his page. "I feel like I *almost* understand the spell at this point."

"I know what you mean," I said as the two of us then reviewed our sketches, once again finding them to be completely identical to one another.

"Hey, I don't mean to rush you guys…" Constantine called out. "But could you maybe hurry it up just a little bit? Things are starting to look a bit hot!"

Turning at Constantine's words, I looked back towards the raid, seeing that several other tentacles had emerged from the Æther and were in the process of wreaking havoc among the raid's ranks. All while the Shoggoth continued to steadily chew through both the stone surrounding the Ley Line and the outcropping itself.

"Oh damn!" I heard Halcyon curse as he too twisted to look at the raid, taking the words right out of my mouth.

"We can try!" I shouted back at the rogue as the two of us turned back towards our papers and pulled out the other spell fragments from our pack, lining them up side by side with one another until they formed one cohesive spell.

Bending down to read the spell in its completed entirety, I found my eyes dancing across the combined pages as they followed the swirling symbols and inscriptions that we had so painstakingly collected from across the Grove. With every symbol that I read, I gradually felt that familiar understanding I'd just experienced return. But this time, instead of fading away into nothingness as I finished reading the spell, I felt a sudden rush of knowledge burst into my mind, followed closely behind by a large block of text appearing in my vision.

Congratulations! You have unlocked a new spell type: Ritual Magic!

You have learned the [Ritual of Ætherbinding]!

Ritual Magic encompasses a special class of spells that are more complicated and mana intensive than the typical spells used by Arcane and Divine casters. These spells are designed to have a lasting or large-scale impact on the world and require two or more Spellcasters working in concert over a longer period of time to successfully cast it.

In order to cast a Ritual Spell, all of the Spell Mastery requirements must be met at the time of casting. These requirements can be split amongst multiple participants in the ritual as long as their combined skill levels meet or exceed the spell's requirements. When casting a Ritual Spell, the Initial Mana Cost will be divided proportionally amongst all the participants, thus forming the base of the spell. In order to complete and fully cast the Ritual Spell, the Total Ritual Mana Cost must be channeled into the spell via all of the participants at whatever rate that they choose to contribute. Once the spell is completely charged, the participants may then choose to finish the Ritual and activate the spell.

Ritual of Ætherbinding
　　Type: Ritual, General
　　Duration: Permanent
　　Participants: 2 or more
　　Spell Mastery:
　　　　Abjuration – Level 15
　　　　Alteration – Level 15
　　　　Conjuration – Level 20
　　　　Evocation – Level 20

Initial Mana Cost: 2,500
Total Ritual Mana Cost: 57,500
Description: Constructing a massive magical matrix, you and the ritual participants create a network of spells and layer it onto a nearby Ley Line via an anchor point, creating a tap that can be used to contain, and control the energies that it possesses.

"We did it, Lyr!" Halcyon announced from beside me, his voice sounding full of both awe and relief. "We can use this to seal the Ley Line!"

"Are you sure?" I asked as I dismissed everything from my vision, unable to help but feel slightly overwhelmed by everything that I had just read. "My Evocation skill is high enough for this, but my Conjuration sure isn't!"

"Don't worry, mine is!" Halcyon replied enthusiastically as we both pushed ourselves off the ground, collecting the pages that contained the newly reassembled Ritual. "I actually meet all the requirements myself, thanks to that *Magical Aptitude* trait I took at character creation!"

"Damn lucky choice that was!" I exclaimed with a shake of my head, wondering what we would have done if we hadn't met the ritual's Spell Mastery requirements. "You think we can handle this spell together? By the time we run back to the raid to get another caster..."

"We should be able to manage it ourselves," the mage replied as he readied himself to begin the ritual. "With the mana regen bonus that this place is giving us...we should be able to cast it in just under five minutes."

"Hopefully we have that much time," I whispered as I glanced towards the battle and saw that the raid was being steadily forced back towards us.

"Fingers crossed," Halcyon said, a look of determination coming across his face as he motioned for me to stand across from him. Once I was in place, he then raised his hands before him in preparation to begin the spell, and I saw a glowing prompt appear in my vision.

Halcyon has invited you to participate in the [Ritual of Ætherbinding]!

Accepting the invitation without hesitation, I looked up towards Halcyon and gave him a nod, already feeling the beginnings of the spell take shape.

"Here goes nothing," I whispered as a tiny azure-colored orb of energy sprang into existence between us, which quickly began to grow as we poured more mana into it.

Feeling nearly the entirety of my mana vanish as the base of the spell came into being, an incredible wave of hunger suddenly shot through me, prompting me to stagger unexpectedly. Catching myself before I could fall, I forced the sudden feeling down, feeling the nearly overwhelming hunger diminish as my mana pool gradually replenished itself from the area's enhanced regeneration. Focusing all of my attention on the orb hovering between us in an attempt to distract myself, I watched it slowly float upward, where it then began to rapidly expand until it became a swirling sphere of arcane energy.

"Are you okay, Lyr?" Halcyon asked out as the first stage of the ritual completed itself and we began to pour mana into the spell.

"I'm fine," I replied, the hunger having faded to a manageable level. "It was just a little bit intense going that low on mana all at once."

"Shit, Lyr, I'm sorry!" Halcyon exclaimed. "I completely forgot about that!"

"Don't worry about it," I said, shaking my head as I increased the flow of mana into the ritual to match the regeneration rate that the Æther infused area was providing. "I'm okay—"

"Heads up, guys!" Lazarus suddenly called out. "Looks like we have one that got through!"

Spinning my head towards the sound of Lazarus's voice, I saw that one of the Shoggoth's spawn had managed to somehow find a way through the raid and was now bearing down towards us. Staring at the creature as it moved, I saw an identifying tag appear and point towards it.

[Ætherbound Shoggoth Broodling] – Level 19

"It doesn't look too tough," Constantine replied as he rushed over towards Lazarus's side. "Lazarus and I should be able to take it easily together. Amaranth, watch Lyr and Hal while we go sort this out."

Hearing Amaranth give him a raspy growl in acknowledgment the pair sprinted towards the oncoming Broodling, leaving Halcyon and me to watch from afar as we continued to fuel the ritual. Working in tandem, I saw Constantine and Lazarus rush the creature without any hesitation, their weapons flashing in the distance as they set about their deadly work, the details of battle lost in the distance between us. But no sooner did the Broodling fall, did I notice that another one had managed to make its way past the raid, prompting them to move once more to intercept it.

"We're half-way there, Lyr," Halcyon told me as the two of us waited in our relative pocket of safety, able to do nothing but stare helplessly onwards at the moment. "Just a little bit longer."

"Yeah," I acknowledged, feeling my jaw tighten as I saw a third Broodling break free of the distant raid. "Hopefully—"

<I hear scratching!> Amaranth suddenly announced, letting out a low growl as he sped past me and rushed towards the side of the outcropping, his body pressed against the ground. *<There is something climbing up the side of the cliff!>*

"Oh shit," I cursed, glancing at my familiar before looking back towards Lazarus and Constantine. "Amaranth says we have something coming up the side of the outcropping."

"'Oh shit' is right, Lyr!" Halcyon exclaimed, his eyes growing wide as I looked towards him. "I need to worry about keeping the Ritual up, and I can't cast any spells while doing that! What are we going to do?!"

"Whatever we have to!" I replied to the mage as I drew Splinter, only needing one freehand to continuing fueling the ritual. "If things get close enough, I can at least still use this!"

Waiting with our hearts in our mouths as we stared at the edge of the outcropping it didn't take long before three tentacles shot upwards and crashed down into the stone, their clawed tips biting deep for purchase. Feeling my breath catch in my throat as the tentacles then began to pull their bearers up, I saw Amaranth's body tense in preparation to pounce, launching himself forward the moment that the first Broodling's body appeared with his claws outstretched.

Slamming into the leading creature with over eight-hundred pounds of angry cat behind it, Amaranth's ambush took the lead Broodling completely by surprise and knocked it straight off the outcropping, its lone tentacle scraping across the ground before vanishing over the edge. Without pausing to celebrate his victory, my familiar then immediately leaped to bite down onto the next closest tentacle, his teeth and claws sinking deep into the ooze-like ectoplasm that it was made of. Thrashing once in surprise from the attack, it didn't take long for the appendage to come apart under the cat's savage mauling and for the second Broodling to lose its grip on the stone, falling away before it could even come into sight.

But despite Amaranth's heroic delaying efforts, the third Broodling managed to finish its climb, pulling its amorphous body over the outcropping's edge, whipping its tentacles through the air angrily.

"Lyr! We have one climbing up on the other side!" Halcyon exclaimed. "Its tentacle just hit the ground!

"Constantine! Lazarus!" I wasted no time in shouting for the other two group members, seeing my familiar throw himself directly at the Broodling before him, the big cat snarling and hissing wildly as he laid into the creature with his teeth and claws. "We need help back here! They're climbing up the sides!"

Turning my head away from the nearby conflict as I continued to shout, I looked towards where I'd last seen the pair, seeing that their situation didn't look any better than ours. In the short time that I'd looked away, the two had killed three more Broodlings that had managed to evade the raid and were currently in the process of dealing with another two.

Unfortunately, that doesn't matter right now, I thought as I repeated my shout a third time, finally seeing one of the two figures look back towards us, the fighting making it impossible to tell who it was. *If we can't get this spell off in time to seal the Ley Line, none of this is going to matter!*

"Heads up, Lyr!" Halcyon's shout brought me back into the moment and caused me to spin towards the Broodling that he had warned about earlier, the creature having completed its climb up the side of the outcropping and was now surging towards us.

"Oh, this is going to suck!" I shouted as the Broodling charged forward, one of its claw-tipped tentacles slashing through the air towards me and forcing me to catch the attack across Splinter's entire edge, lest I end up being sliced to ribbons.

Grunting from the impact, I felt my feet slide across the ground a short distance before the clawed tentacle pulled itself away from me and another lashed out to take its place. Shifting desperately to catch the claws of the second tentacle I just barely managed to get enough of Splinter into position to avoid a fatal hit, but still found myself gasping in pain as something sharp tore into my right hip and leg. Hissing from the blow, I slashed out at the offending appendage, slicing a deep gash through and prompting a spurt of emerald-colored liquid to spray across the ground.

Reeling back from the attack, the tentacle quickly vanished as the Broodling finally lumbered into range, leaving me staring at its nightmarish body, with countless eyes and mouths opening and closing across its body. Feeling a sense of hesitation come over me as I looked at the large creature, I felt myself at a complete loss of what to do next. I couldn't leave my place in the ritual circle, lest I disrupt the spell, but if I stayed where I was, it was only a matter of seconds until the creature overwhelmed me, causing the spell to fail anyway.

We're fucked, I thought, a sense of crushing defeat falling over me, the world suddenly going into slow motion, giving me a perfect view of the Broodling's massive maw as it lunged forward towards me. *We came this far…but it wasn't enough. Aldford is going—*

A bright red object suddenly flew past the corner of my eye and slammed heavily into the Broodling without warning, causing it to abort its attack and scream in pain, its body writhing as it recoiled away from me. Looking on in surprise I wondered at what could have possibly stopped the creature in its tracks, only to find my eyes widen as they saw a flaming greatsword imbedded in its side.

A Flaming *Glass-Steel* greatsword.

"I'm coming, Lyrian!" I heard Lazarus's voice shout, my head twisting to see the half-giant barely a dozen strides away, running at full sprint towards me. "Hold on!"

Crossing the distance remaining in the blink of an eye, the half-giant slammed into the Broodling at full speed, the impact sending the creature rolling backward with Lazarus on top of it, his hands already around the hilt of his burning greatsword.

"Finish the Ritual, Lyrian!" Lazarus shouted to me as he pulled the blade free and thrust it back into the Broodling, prompting another pained scream from the creature.

"Halcyon! How much time do we have left?" I shouted, turning to look back towards the mage as a spark of hope kindled in my chest.

"Less than a minute!" the mage answered. "Sooner if you can put more mana into it!"

"I'm on it!" I replied, choosing to drop Splinter to the ground as I thrust both hands towards the massive spell forming above us and sent every bit of mana that I could spare into it, feeling the hunger return with a vengeance. "What do we do when it's finished?!"

"We cast it onto an anchor point!" Halcyon told me. "I was thinking to use the *Tree*!"

"What?" I shouted back at the mage in confusion. "What do you mean a tree?!"

"Not a tree, Lyr!" Halcyon exclaimed as he thrust his head upwards. "*The Tree!*"

Eyes widening as I glanced upwards, I suddenly remembered that the roots belonging to the Ætherwarped Oak in Aldford were right above us. Right where we had first seen them a week ago, protruding through the cavern's ceiling when we had first entered the Grove.

Right where we needed it to be.

"*The Tree!*" I exclaimed as a wave of comprehension shot through me. "*That's brilliant, Hal!*"

"Thank me if it works!" Halcyon replied as the ritual neared its completion, the spell having absorbed all the mana that it needed to be cast. "Are you ready, Lyr?"

"Do it!" I shouted, seeing the crackling orb of power above us shift itself into a complicated and constantly changing spell matrix that my eye could barely follow.

"Here it goes!" Halcyon shouted as the two of us triggered the final step of the ritual and sent the swirling matrix speeding upwards into the air and towards the Ætherwarped Oak's roots high above.

Craning my head upwards, I looked up just in time to see the spell begin to rapidly unfold as it spread out to encompass the entirety of the exposed root system. At first, there was no sign of anything happening, the magic continuing to grow until the very air began to shimmer with a bright azure light. But then slowly, I began to see one of the larger root fragments begin to grow, its glowing body lengthening and twisting as it started to quest towards the exposed Ley Line, gradually gaining speed the closer that it approached.

Until it suddenly shot forward like an uncoiled snake and plunged itself directly into the Ruptured Ley Line.

"Whoa!" I exclaimed, both in surprise at the root's unexpected movement and the bright azure light that shot up its length. In an instant, all the other roots protruding from the Cavern's ceiling flared with a similar energy and began to push their way out of the rock, rapidly growing in size. "Look at that!"

"It's working!" Halcyon shouted as the root system began to splinter, some of them heading towards the Ley Line, while others continued straight down towards us. "It's sealing the rupture!"

Turning my eyes towards the Ley Line, I saw another root thrust itself into the breach, followed by another and another, their combined onrush crushing one of the Shoggoth's flailing tentacles as they filled the breach. Slowly as the tree continued to twist and grow, the Æther leaking free from the Ley Line began to diminish until it slowly came to a stop, the now bright azure roots basking the cavern in its cool glow.

"We did it, Hal!" I shouted as I saw the final drop of Æther spilling from the Ley Line fall out of sight, feeling a near overwhelming torrent of relief come over me, followed by a wave of sheer exhaustion. "We sealed it! We—wait! What is it doing now?!"

Instead of stopping now that the Ley Line was sealed, the other Ætherwarped roots continued to twist and spiral through the air, until they reached the canyon of tainted Æther surrounding us, plunging themselves into the roiling surface.

Where they then exploded with sheer uncontrolled growth.

Moving faster than our eyes could follow, countless more Ætherwarped roots shot downwards from the cavern's ceiling above as they hungrily dove into the Æther. Within seconds, all we could see was a thick glowing nest of intertwined roots as they began to absorb all of the Æther within the massive reservoir.

"Lyr, look!" Halcyon called out, grabbing my shoulder as he pointed straight down the outcropping. "The Shoggoth!"

Flinching at the urgency in his tone, I turned my head to follow his hand, just in time to see a pair of large roots shoot down from above and pierce straight through the colossal entity, causing it to scream in pain as it shook. Thrashing its tentacles uselessly through the air, the creature tried to slap away a second wave of roots that snaked out towards it, only to have the ooze-like appendage bounce harmlessly off the Ætherwarped wood before they all thrust themselves into its body.

Twisting and wailing wildly, the Shoggoth attempted to escape from the roots now binding it, but to no avail, its form beginning to rapidly shrink and lose substance. Staring onwards with my mouth open, I saw the creature fall forward onto the outcropping before it, its body and tentacles losing all shape and coming apart in a spray of Æther, the few Broodlings that were still standing following a heartbeat afterward. Then finally, with one last mournful cry passing through our minds, the Grove fell silent once more as all the emerald green light that was the tainted Æther and Nafarrian spirits faded away.

Staring onwards in numb shock, I looked up towards the now impenetrable network of glowing azure roots that covered the Ley Line before us, realizing all too well how close to defeat we'd managed to come.

"It's over," I whispered, breathing out a deep sigh, feeling my hands shake as I began to come down from what had been a truly epic battle. "We did it."

"We did," Halcyon replied, his voice sounding hoarse and tired. "But what is that light at the end of the outcropping there?"

"Hmm?" I asked, shifting my gaze I caught a faint gleam of emerald light at the very edge of the outcropping where the Shoggoth had fallen. "I don't know. Let's take a look."

Turning to see that both Amaranth and Lazarus had both survived our side of the battle, the four of us then began walking forward, at first turning our attention to the remnants of the raid. Numbering nearly a hundred Adventurers when we had left the camp, there were now barely two dozen of us left, the near constant fighting over the last few hours having reduced our ranks to a small shadow of what we'd started with.

But for all the casualties that we had suffered, I still found myself seeing a handful of familiar faces as we approached and felt a knot in my heart unwind as I spotted an exhausted-looking Aldwin standing next to an equally tired looking Veronia, the two having managed to survive the deadly battle. Continuing to walk through the raid, I saw several other faces belonging to both my friends and others from the guild, including Freya, who rushed towards me the moment that she saw me.

Enjoying a short reunion as we all exchanged notes from the battle, we all then pressed onwards in search of the strange light that Halcyon and I had seen earlier, curious to find out what it was, in case it was something that we had to be worried about. But as we approached the edge of the outcropping, I saw that the light was coming from a glowing emerald crystal lying on the stone, roughly the size and length of my forearm. Wondering what it could possibly be, I stepped forward to inspect the object, seeing a tag appear in my vision and point towards it.

Cocking my head curiously at the tag, I then reached out to pick it up, seeing the rest of its description appear in my vision. Reading it, I felt my eyes widen as I realized what I was holding, barely hearing the chime that signaled a new level, or all the other notifications that suddenly began clamoring for my attention as I turned around and looked back at the raid with awe.

We did it, I thought as I raised the crystal over my head, hearing the raid break out in cheers. Against all odds, we'd somehow managed to find a way to persevere. The Beast had been killed, Carver had been stopped, the Spirits had been put to rest, and most importantly, the Ley Line had been sealed.

We had won.

Chapter 56

Saturday, March 30th, 2047 - 10:12 am
Aldford

I awoke slowly as I felt the sunbeam crawl across my face, its warmth causing me to slowly drift out of a deep dreamless sleep until I found myself looking up at a wooden ceiling. Staring blankly for a moment, it took a minute for my brain to wake up, leaving me in a halfway state of total peace. Yet as full awareness began to dawn on me, broken and random memories started to surface, causing my heart to beat faster.

Did all of that really happen yesterday? I thought as the previous day's events came floating to the forefront of my mind, leaving me almost doubting that they had ever happened in the first place. *Is it all really over? Are we safe now?*

Closing my eyes for a moment, I exhaled a slow breath in an attempt to clear the rapid thoughts that had flooded into me, eventually feeling my body relax. Reopening my eyes, I stared back up at the ceiling again, this time noticing a trio of notifications that I hadn't bothered to fully read or dismiss before I'd gone to bed. Realizing that I was fully awake by this point, I decided to get a start on with my day, picking the first item in my list and watching it fill my vision.

Quest Complete! The Ruptured Ley Line!

> *Congratulations! After spending days exploring The Twilight Grove and unraveling the mystery of the Runestone, you and your companions have managed to successfully piece together a Nafarrian ritual spell and used it to seal the Ley Line beneath Aldford, thereby*

preventing a catastrophe that would have spelled doom for the region, and quite possibly the world beyond.

It is still too early to tell what the long-term consequences of your actions might be, but you have ensured that Aldford will at least live long enough to see it!

Ley Line Sealed: 1/1

Reward:

  Experience Points: 40,000

  Renown: 5000

I definitely didn't imagine that part of yesterday! I thought to myself with a smile as I finished reading the completed quest update, going on to remember that I had also hit level twenty, thanks to the quest's reward for completing it. *Oh, that's right! I also managed to finish that Class Challenge thing, though mostly out of luck than anything else!*

Dismissing the quest update, I then brought up the corresponding notification in my vision, vaguely remembering what it had said when I read it last night.

Congratulations! By successfully casting the [Ritual of Ætherbinding] you have performed an Act of Magic and have completed your first Class Challenge!

Perform an Act of Magic: 1/1

  Reward: +10 to Intelligence

"I might not have chosen that one if I had a chance to do it all again, but I guess I can't complain though," I said to myself as I once again cleared my vision and dismissed the notification, leaving only a single one remaining. *A big boost to Intelligence now means I can focus on my other attributes for the next few levels. Plus, I'm sure the extra mana won't hurt.*

Giving myself the mental equivalent of a shrug, I then brought up the last notification, remembering that on top of everything else that I'd gained, I'd also managed to get another Class Skill Point with a new batch of skills to choose from.

And they aren't any easier this time around either, I grumbled mentally to myself as I watched the somewhat familiar text appear in my vision, followed by a list of new skills available for purchase.

You currently have 1 unspent Class Skill Point.

Please select an ability from the following list to learn:

Spells:

Alacrity

Type: Spell, Class Skill

Duration: Maintained

Arcane Tree: Alteration

Spell Mastery: Alteration - Level 20

Mana Cost: 10 per second.

Description: By channeling a steady stream of magic into your body, your movement speed and reactions are greatly increased.

Effect: While active, this spell grants you a 10% boost to both movement speed and attack speed.

Concussive Blast

Type: Spell, Class Skill

Duration: Instant

Range: 20 feet

Arcane Tree: Evocation

Spell Mastery: Evocation - Level 20

Mana Cost: 160

Description: You unleash a targeted burst of magic at a nearby target, causing a wave of magical force to flare into existence.

Effect: When cast, this spell inflicts 30-60 points of Arcane Damage to your target and temporarily staggers them, possibly knocking them off their feet.

Frigid Grasp

Type: Spell, Class Skill
Duration: Instant
Arcane Tree: Evocation
Spell Mastery: Evocation - Level 20
Mana Cost: 170
Description: Summoning an intense magical frost in your hand, you send a freezing burst of cold through the first thing you touch.
Effect: You freeze the next thing you touch for 45-80 points of Cold Damage. Should this spell be used on a living creature, it will also temporarily slow its attack rate and movements for 5 seconds. This spell can also be used to freeze objects and liquids for a short period of time.

Martial Arts:

Sword Mastery I

Type: Martial Art, Passive
Skill Requirement: Swords Level 20
Description: Taking the first step along the path to mastering the blade, your attacks while wielding a sword have become all the much more deadly.
Effect: All damage inflicted with swords is increased by 5%.

Adrenaline Rush

Type: Martial Art, General Skill
Skill Requirement: Any Weapon Skill Level 20
Stamina Cost: 300
Description: With a massive burst of adrenaline surging through your system, you unleash a wild

flurry of blows putting extra strength and ferocity behind them.

Effect: For the next 10 seconds all attacks by you deal weapon damage+20%. Due to the toll that this ability takes on your body, it can only be used once every hour.

Cold Blooded

Type: Martial Art, General Skill
Skill Requirement: Stealth Level 20
Stamina Cost: 250
Description: Purging yourself of all remorse or hesitation, you prepare yourself to unleash a brutal and savage blow at a nearby target.

Effect: For the next 15 seconds any attack dealt to an unaware target as part of your opening attack out of stealth is increased by 50%. Due to the toll that this ability takes on your body, it can only be used once every hour.

I think I'm going to need to take a few days to think about this one, I thought as I read over all my skill options. If I had the chance, I'd take each and every single one of them, but unfortunately, that was outside the realm of possibility. *Maybe I can talk with the others and see what—*

"Mmm," a feminine voice suddenly groaned from beside me, followed by a gentle shuffling. "You awake?"

"I am," I replied with a smile crossing my face as I dismissed the Class Skill menu and looked down towards the body pressed up beside me, seeing myself looking into Freya's half-opened eyes. "Good morning."

"I'll say," the woman said with a matching smile as she drew herself even closer towards me. "This was the first night in a long time that I've been able to sleep without needing to worry about a disaster waking me up."

"I know how you feel," I agreed. "You know, when I first woke up, I almost didn't believe that yesterday happened. With everything that went on...and how fast it all happened..."

I let the words drift off and then shook my head.

"It ended up being really close at the end, didn't it?" Freya asked, placing her hand on my chest.

"More like every step along the way," I replied, reaching up to put my hand on top of Freya's. "I can count half a dozen times where if things had gone differently...we wouldn't be here right now."

"But we are," the blonde-haired woman replied. "And really, that's all that matters right now. We don't need to keep scrambling anymore, and we can finally take some time to breathe."

"Yeah," I said. "At least for a little while..."

"Until we go looking for Carver," Freya finished, her voice hardening. "This time he won't have someone feeding him information on the sly."

"No, he won't," I stated, feeling a momentary surge of anger shoot through me as I remembered Ignis and his group. As we'd suspected, the group had indeed changed their bind point before attempting to betray us yesterday, leaving us with no obvious trail to even begin looking for them. "Anyway, we can worry about that later. Right now, our rest cycle comes first. I think we all deserve at least a day to unplug."

"Hah, after everything we've been through?" Freya asked, raising an eyebrow as she looked up at me. "I think we deserve a whole rest *week!*"

"That would be something," I said with a chuckle. "But we'll have to take what we can get."

"I suppose," Freya replied, shifting her body into a stretch. "What's your plan for the day now? Are you going to head back down into the Grove?"

"I don't know yet," I said, giving Freya the best shrug I could manage while lying on my back. "I was thinking of visiting Léandre and arranging a crafting plan for my avatar while I'm offline, then I was going to check in on everyone and get a sense of what our next steps should be. Now that everyone knows that the ground won't explode right under our feet, maybe we can start building again."

"That would definitely help things get back to normal," Freya said as she gave my chest a squeeze and then pushed herself up into a sitting position. "Not to mention getting that palisade up and finished would go far for making everyone feel safe."

"That it would," I agreed, already envisioning the amount of work that would need to go into upgrading Aldford's defenses. Though fortunately for us, I knew that we had a more than ready and willing labor force to draw from. "What about you? What are your plans today?"

"Guild management stuff first," Freya replied as she pulled herself up and out of bed, running her hands through her air. "We have a few people who went above and beyond yesterday. I want to make sure that they know we appreciate it. But past that, I was actually thinking to make a trip back down to the Grove with whoever is willing to come. I feel a little hesitant to leave the place without giving it a thorough look. Not to mention we have a pretty large group of people that are going to need to find their Soul Fragments."

"That's a good idea," I said as I untangled myself from the blankets and forced myself out of bed. "Let me know when you're going…if I can swing it, I'll come too."

"Great!" Freya exclaimed, turning around to smile at me before she started to get dressed. "Oh hey, any more thoughts on what you're going to do with that crystal thing that you found yesterday? I know people are going to start asking me about it today, along with the rest of the loot from The Beast."

"Hmm, I was thinking to keep it," I replied as I bent down to pick up my pack lying on the floor nearby. Shifting through it quickly, I then pulled out the very crystal in question and held it before me, seeing its description fill my vision.

Legacy of the Nafarr
Item Class: Magical
Weight: 0.1 kg
Lore: Shimmering with a strange emerald glow from within, this crystal contains the fragmented memories of the Nafarr that once lived in this region from eons past.
Special: Skill Crystal – By activating this crystal and keeping it in close proximity for four consecutive weeks, you will gradually absorb the knowledge stored within. Upon completion of the process, you will be granted full understanding of the Nafarrian Language as well as a wide cross-section of knowledge regarding their culture. Should the crystal leave your possession before the process is complete, you will have to begin the process anew. Upon successful absorption of the knowledge, this crystal will dissolve.

"Given that we've managed to seal the Ley Line...and that we've claimed all three of the ruins in the area, I think its best this stays with us. The knowledge that it could give us is just too valuable to let anyone else have."

"That's fair enough," Freya said as she turned around to face me while pulling on a shirt. "But if that's the case, everyone's going to want to know how that's going to affect our share of The Beast's loot. We need to still be fair to the other Adventurers that aren't in Virtus."

"I know, and I'll see if I can figure that out while I'm talking with Léandre today," I replied, still hanging onto the emerald crystal. "If anyone asks you about the loot, just send them my way. I'll figure something out."

"That I can do," Freya stated as she tucked her shirt into her pants. "Now hurry up and get dressed! You may not need to eat while in game, but *I do*, and I'm starving!"

Chuckling, I put the crystal away back into my pack and threw on a set of clothes before leaving the room of the longhouse that Freya and I had spent the night in, the two of us having finally acknowledged the feelings for one another that had slowly grown over the last two months. It was still far too early to tell where our relationship was headed, or if there was going to be one at all, since the previous night had only happened in virtual reality and not back in the Real World.

But we do have a rest day coming up tomorrow, I thought as I gave Freya a kiss before the two of us parted ways, with her heading towards the Town Hall and me to the Crafting Hall. *Maybe we can make some sort of arrangement to meet in person, and see if the spark carries there.*

Making a mental note to bring it up with Freya later in the day, I set out across the town, unable to help but notice the stark change in demeanor for both the townsfolk and Adventurers. Where they had been nervous and highly-strung yesterday, they were relaxed and cheerful today, with the threat of the Ley Line exploding no longer hanging over their heads.

I can't imagine how it would have looked from everyone else's perspective in Aldford yesterday, I thought as I walked. *Adventurers would have respawned here in dribs and drabs, each of them during a different battle and giving everyone here something new to worry about. And then of course when the tree started to change…*

At that thought, I looked up towards the sky, seeing the now gargantuan Ætherwarped Oak towering above us, the tree having easily tripled, if not quadrupled, in size after it had made contact with the Ley Line. Now it dominated the horizon, stretching well over two-hundred feet into the air, its azure glow making it a beacon for everything in the region. But in addition to its size increase, there had been a particularly interesting development due to the tree's connection to the Ley Line, one universally loved by all of the spellcasters in the town.

Somehow after coming in contact with the Ley Line, the Ætherwarped Oak had begun to emanate a low-level aura of magic until it completely permeated the air around Aldford. The end result of that was an increased level of mana regeneration for all of the spellcasters within the town's limits, not unlike what we'd experienced during the battle at the Ley Line, if only on a lesser scale. I had no idea what would come of that particular benefit in the coming weeks, or if it would end up having side effects in the long run, but I was happy to take whatever benefit that I could.

Especially since there wasn't really a lot I could do about it anyway.

Continuing my walk through the town, I made my way to the Crafting Hall and entered through its main doors, the sound of industry greeting my ears. With how fierce the battle was yesterday, many of the Adventurers were taking the time to repair their gear today or craft entirely new replacements if the item was too damaged to be saved. Poking my head into a few of the rooms in search of Léandre, I made sure to wave at whatever Adventurers I interrupted, eventually finding myself walking into the

Foundry, hearing the rhythmic thunder of hammers on metal as I entered.

"There you are!" I exclaimed as I finally found the craftsman standing in front of the smelter as he waited for the ore within to melt.

"Lyrian, good morning," Léandre replied with a smile, one of his eyebrows raised. "Or perhaps I should say *good afternoon* with how late it is!"

"Hrm," I snorted as I crossed the room towards the Tul'Shar. "I think that after saving the town and sealing the Ley Line I'm entitled to sleep in for at least *one* morning."

"I *suppose*," Léandre said, drawing the word out as he shook his head. "So long as it doesn't become a habit. I am going to need your hands more than ever now, especially with the bounty of iron we've finally found ourselves with!"

"No disagreement here," I told the man as I watched him check the ore in the smelter, seeing that it wasn't quite ready yet. "That's why I'm here actually. I was hoping to coordinate my rest cycle and get all that set up before I log off later tonight."

"Ah! That's right!" Léandre exclaimed as he turned away from his work with a toothy smile. "That means I will have the full well of your talent to draw from for the next day! Perfect!"

Laughing at the man's undisguised glee to put me to work, the two of us then outlined our plans for the next few days, which largely focused on us exploiting the metals that we'd found in the Grove and getting them into workable shape. By the time I finished talking with Léandre, I'd resigned myself to the fact that the Foundry was likely going to be my second home for the foreseeable future as I either churned out ingots by the truckload, or worked them into the tools and construction materials we'd need to start building the palisade around the town.

"Speaking of crafting stuff by the way," I said after Léandre and I had finished organizing my crafting plan, and I'd given him the rights to assign me tasks once I logged off. "We need to talk about the loot that we managed to recover from The Beast, specifically how we're going to sort them out between the other Adventurers. Everything aside from the skull and a handful of bones at least, which Aldwin has claimed for Aldford."

"Mmm, I was about to ask you about that," the Tul'Shar replied, a sudden excitement appearing in his voice. "I've managed to take a look at what was recovered...and I am truly itching to get my hands on the scales in particular."

"Me too," I said, appreciating Léandre's sentiment all too well. "But we need to make sure that everyone gets an equal share for their efforts, at least all the Adventurers that aren't in Virtus. None of our members will complain if we hang onto our portion of the loot, since they know we'll just turn around and hand them new gear once we finish crafting it into something useful."

"I understand," Léandre stated with a nod. "Yet...giving away such high-quality crafting materials..."

The elder craftsman paused to shake his head, a look of distaste coming across his face.

"Between the two of us, I can't think of any others in Aldford who have the skill needed to craft them into something useful," he finished. "At least not yet."

"I get what you're saying, Léandre, but unfortunately that's out of our hands. If unskilled crafters want to try their hand at crafting something that's beyond them and ruin their materials, that's their choice," I said with a shrug. "But, I do have a couple of ideas on how to mitigate that."

"Oh?" The man replied curiously. "And what would they be?"

"First, we offer to pay the other Adventurers out of their share of the loot in cash or precious metals," I replied, watching Léandre's eyes widen at the suggestion. "There's a large vein of silver down in the Grove that I'm considering buying off of an Adventurer, which we can then use to mint our own coins or just trade wholesale. Combine that with the money we have in Virtus's coffers we can probably afford to buy a decent chunk of the scales, since that's probably what we'd be the most interested in. Given how tight the currency supply is out here, I think most of the Adventurers will jump at a chance to get their hands on a pile of coin. Especially once they hear we're churning out iron weapons and armor for everyone to buy."

"And they will then spend the money they sold the scales for!" Léandre exclaimed with an amused laugh. "Very crafty, Lyrian! I heartily approve! What's your other idea?"

"I knew you'd appreciate it!" I said with a smile. "As for the other idea I had in mind, I wanted to go back to what you said earlier, about some of the other crafters not being as skilled as we are. I think if we put out that we're accepting crafting commissions, we can get other Adventurers to *pay* us to craft new gear for them if they supply the materials."

"Thus paying ourselves, increasing our own skills, *and* ensuring that none of the material goes to waste!" Léandre finished, his enthusiasm increasing with every word that he spoke. "I think this will all work nicely, Lyrian! I am onboard for anything you need from me."

"Great!" I exclaimed, my smile growing even wider. "I'll let—"

A loud bang followed by the sound of several things falling to the ground interrupted me, the noise prompting both of Léandre's and my head to twist in its direction just as a string of expletives filled the air.

"Oh fucking, stupid hell!" Jenkins growled as he bent over to pick up a rack filled with tools that he'd knocked over.

"Oh shit, Jenkins!" I called out in concern as Léandre and I both rushed towards the man. "Are you okay?"

"I'm fine, I'm fine," Jenkins grunted as he lifted the rack off the ground and stood it up again. "I just need to get used to this stupid thing and completely forgot I'd moved this rack by the door the other day."

"Are you sure you don't want to take it easy for at least a day? None of us would begrudge you that." Léandre asked, prompting Jenkin's head to snap back to glare at us.

Giving me a perfect view of the large eyepatch that covered where his right eye had been.

"*I'm fine,*" Jenkins replied a bit testily, before shaking his head and waving a hand at Léandre in apology. "I have it easy compared to the others."

"Yeah..." I said sadly, suddenly feeling my heart drop like a stone as a wave of crushing memories that I'd been purposefully avoiding rushed to the forefront of my mind.

Despite our victory in managing to seal the Ley Line below Aldford, there had been one particularly sour note to take away from our victory, one that we all knew was coming but at the time hadn't wanted to face.

Namely being the aftermath of Carver's attack on the camp.

With ash in our hearts as we made our way back after sealing the Ley Line, we returned to the burnt out and largely destroyed remains of Camp Sentinel, the place having been razed nearly to the ground. Brought low from our triumphant victory as the consequences began to set in, it didn't take us long to find Quincy's body along with a handful of the townsfolk among the wreckage, burnt and sliced to pieces. Fearing the worse, we then all tore through the camp in search of the others, only to find that they had managed to escape down the other passageway that led into the camp and warding it tightly enough that Carver's group hadn't been able to follow.

But despite managing to evade being massacred by the invaders, there had still been several injuries among the survivors, with the two most serious ones falling onto both Samuel and Ritt. The mage having been caught in the wrong place at the wrong time and suffering the loss of both of his legs from a particularly deadly blast of magic that had sent a wave of acid splashing over them, leaving little for Shelia to save by the time she was able to assist. Ritt on the other hand, had earned his injuries through heroism, desperately holding the tunnel's entrance with Jenkins by his side as the invaders tried to overrun them before the ward could be put into place, the effort costing him his entire right hand and the better part of his forearm.

"Speaking of that," Léandre said breaking the morose silence that had fallen over us. "How are they doing today?"

"As well as they can be," Jenkins replied with a shrug, immediately knowing who Léandre was asking after. "Ritt is in…*decent* if somewhat low spirits, which is understandable given his loss. Samuel on the other hand…"

Jenkins paused to shake his head with a sad expression, "…may never be quite the same again, even if he eventually does receive the healing to replace his legs."

"He lost a friend," I said, feeling a wave of a guilt and anger surge through me at the loss. "One that he'd been through a lot with."

"Yeah," Jenkins said with a deep sigh. "A loss like that hits the heart deeply."

"I think I'll go and drop in on them both," I stated, feeling that I had to find a way to assuage my guilt of being drawn into Ignis and Carver's scheme which had resulted in us not being around to defend the camp. "Are they still both at the Town Hall?"

"They are," Jenkin confirmed. "Shelia's set aside a room for them where they can rest in peace."

"Good," I replied as I took a step towards the door before turning to look back at the smith. "And are you sure you're doing okay yourself?"

"I really am," the man said, this time without any venom or anger in his tone. "Like I said yesterday, I've lost an eye before during *The War,* and I eventually had it regrown by one of the army chaplains a few weeks later. Shelia thinks she'll be able to do the same thing…*eventually*, once her faith reaches a point to where she is able to wield such magic, but I'll also be the first to admit that I don't know what that means exactly."

It means that she needs more levels, I thought silently as I nodded at Jenkins, knowing that there was no way of simply telling him that.

"We'll figure it out one day," I said to the man before giving him and Léandre a wave as I turned to leave. "Alright, I'm off. I'll drop by again in a bit."

Hearing the pair bid me farewell as I left the Foundry, I made my way outside and started walking towards the Town Hall, the good cheer that I'd woken up with now slightly muted. Cutting through Aldford, it wasn't long until the building came into the sight, which I couldn't help but notice was completely dwarfed by the now massive trunk of the Ætherwarped Oak tree.

If that thing gets any bigger, we're going to have to tear the Town Hall down and rebuild it somewhere else! I thought, glancing up at the tree for the second time in the day. It was definitely going to take time until the tree no longer caught my eye every time I stepped outside.

Moving to walk past the tree as I approached the Town

Hall's entrance, I managed to get nearly halfway past it before I heard my name.

"Hey, Lyr! You're up!" Halcyon called out, the greeting causing me to look over my shoulder just in time to see him and Stanton come into view, the older man leaning heavily on his cane. "Have a minute?"

"Sure," I replied as I turned away from the Town Hall and towards the two mages. "What's up?"

"We're just doing our last checks on the tree," Halcyon explained, his gaze shifting over towards Stanton. "Everything looks to be good. *Very good* actually. That spell we cast somehow managed to anchor itself *in* the tree. It's working perfectly as far as we can tell."

"As much as *any* of us can tell what 'working perfectly' should look like in a Nafarrian spell such as this," Stanton said, his voice sounding cautious yet lighthearted. "Yet since the ground has not erupted into a fiery conflagration of doom I am tempted to agree that we are safe for the time being."

"And what about Eberia?" I asked, remembering that the completed quest hadn't mentioned anything about the Æther being restored to the city. "Do you think the Æther will flow back towards the city now?"

"I believe so?" Stanton replied, giving me what I thought looked like an honest shrug. "I have no idea how long it will take the Æther to reach the city, but barring any other complications, it should."

"Which means," Halcyon stated. "Eberia should at least now have a fighting chance to stand up to The Ascendancy."

"That is our hope," the spy said in an earnest tone. "But as you all know, the future is never certain."

"No," I agreed. "It really isn't."

"Anyway," I continued after a brief moment of silence. "I was just heading to check on both Ritt and Samuel. I haven't seen them yet today."

"I haven't either," Stanton said as grimace came over his face. "And I should as well."

"Same here," Halcyon added in a somber tone, the three of us then turning towards the Town Hall.

Just in time to see a flash of light fill the air as an Adventurer respawned, followed by another and another until there were well over a dozen people standing in front of the Town Hall.

"What the fuck just happened?!" Halcyon exclaimed as loud cursing and shouting erupted from newly respawned Adventurers. "I didn't think anyone went out today!"

"Those aren't our people, Hal," I replied, my blood going cold as I rushed forward towards the group.

The screaming and cursing continued to build as I approached, prompting a crowd of Adventurers to rush out of the Town Hall to investigate what was happening. By the time that I managed to get to the group, the building had nearly emptied itself, with dozens of Adventurers all pushing forward to see what the commotion was. Scanning the group of people that had just respawned, I found my eye land on a trio of familiar faces in the crowd, my heart stopping the moment that they met my eyes.

"*Cassius*," I breathed, seeing the man's angry expression fixate on me.

"*Lyrian*," the man replied with barely contained rage. "Shadow's Fall...is gone."

"What?" I exclaimed, taking a step forward towards the man. "*What happened?!*"

"*Carver happened!*" Cassius snarled loud enough for everyone to hear, which prompted angry shouts from the crowd around us. "He destroyed it! All of it! For no reason at all!"

"Tell me everything," I said, feeling all of the joy from last night's victory vanish at the mention of the man's name, replacing itself with a burning hot rage that began to roil within me.

Damn that man! I shouted internally, feeling my hands shake as I listened to Cassius explain what had happened, his voice barely audible with how loud my heart was pounding. Staring at him blankly as he spoke, I eventually felt the anger within me cool, until it formed an ice cold hate centered on my heart.

"I'm sorry you all got dragged into this, Cassius," I heard myself say in a calm voice the moment that the man finished speaking. "This is our fault. My fault."

"*Fault?*" Cassius repeated almost in disbelief. "I don't care about *fault!* I care about vengeance! About making Carver *pay* for what he did to us!"

A deafening chorus of angry voices shouted out in agreement at Cassius's statement, the mood instantly turning bloodthirsty. I could hear demands being shouted, along with angry threats and vengeful promises, the crowd rapidly whipping itself up into frenzy.

"Enough!" I shouted, thrusting my hands in the air before the emotions reached a boiling point. Repeating myself, I turned my body to look out towards the crowd while keeping my arms raised, waiting until the noise died down and everyone's eyes were on me.

"We all want vengeance for what Carver has done!" I declared pitching my voice loud enough for everyone to hear. "And why wouldn't we? He has done countless things to demand vengeance for! First, his followers spent weeks attacking and raiding our settlers! Then when we put an end to that, he ambushed us in the wild! Demanding that we *apologize* for defending our own people! Everyone here knows how we answered that!"

A vicious roar rose up from the crowd in response before dying back down to a dull roar.

"Then, when he realized he couldn't beat us with force, he turned to betrayal, using someone we had taken on in good faith to exploit our trust, and came dangerously close to succeeding," I continued, hearing a low hiss echo through the air, everyone knowing all too well who I was talking about. "And when we stopped that plan, he lashed out at our ally, one who had done *nothing* to deserve it, and burned Shadows Fall to the ground.

"Which in turn has brought us here to this very moment," I stated, spreading my hands to indicate everyone standing around me. "Carver has proven time and time again that he will stop at nothing to see us dead, to see this town, this region, completely razed of anyone who isn't under his direct control. Which means that we only have one recourse left to us if we want to hold onto our freedom, and everything that we've worked so hard to build.

"As such," I stated, slowly turning around to look at everyone around me, meeting as many eyes as I could. "I declare that as of this very moment...

"*We are at war.*"

Epilogue

Monday, April 1st, 2047 - 11:34 pm
Eberia – The Royal Palace
Graves

I climbed the stairs to the tower with a nervous energy coursing through me, prompting me to clench my hands tightly as I ascended up the stone passageway with nothing but my thoughts to keep me company. Something that I was all too used to by now.

Today's the day, I announced in my head for what had to be the hundredth time. *I've done everything that has been asked of me and more. It's time that I got something for my end of the bargain, instead of moldering away in this castle for another month.*

Steadying my resolve as I continued upwards, I eventually reached an ornate wooden door at the end of my journey.

Pausing to make sure that my robes were presentable, I then reached out and knocked on the door exactly three times then lowered my hand in preparation to wait. To my surprise the door opened almost immediately, swinging soundlessly on well-oiled hinges and revealing a warm and welcoming chamber beyond.

That was the fastest she's ever opened it for me, I thought, making sure to keep my face completely impassive as I entered the room, feeling the door drift shut behind me and close softly. *Is that a good sign? Or a bad one?*

Glancing around the room silently, I found her sitting in the open windowsill, legs drawn up close to her chest as she stared out at the two waxing moons in the night sky, the rest of Eberia visible below. Turning to face her, I took a few steps forward before stopping, preparing myself to wait once more. But once again, I found myself surprised as she didn't wait to speak out.

"I just found out that against all odds he actually succeeded," she said to me, her head unmoving from her gaze on the moons above. "Two days ago."

"Did he now?" I replied, feeling yet another surge of surprise shoot through me. There was no need to explain who *'he'* was. "That was…*unexpected*."

"It was," she agreed, falling silent as she stared out for window for a time. "Yet it presents us with options that we didn't have before. Ones that were otherwise closed to us."

"Is there something that you wish to change then?" I asked, dreading a positive reply. It would be impossible to change what we'd already set in motion here in Eberia, at least not without a drastic and bloody effort.

"No," the woman replied with a shrug. "It will play out how it is meant to play out."

"Then what are our next steps?" I asked, her mercurial moods having long since ceased to surprise me. At one moment she could be raging hotter than an active volcano, the next as cold as a blizzard, then as serene as a monk. Though whatever she was today was something I hadn't seen before.

"That depends," she replied, finally turning away from the window to look at me, her eyes boring into me with a knowing look. "Are you finally going to voice the request that has sat on your tongue for this long?"

"As I've said before, *numerous times,* if I recall correctly," I hissed feeling a sudden spike of anger shoot through me. "Stay. Out. Of. My. Head."

"Oh my, I've forgotten how your anger kindles at that." The woman let out a short giggle. "But rest assured, I didn't need to peek inside your mind to see that you are growing restless within this golden cage, Graves. You hide it better than most people in your place would."

"Then you understand I need to get out of this castle, this city even," I stated, the nerves that I'd felt earlier vanishing completely now that the ice had been broken. "I think it is time that I was rewarded for my service, or if not, at the very least the freedom to leave."

"You want to try for your revenge already?" I saw a look of surprise cross the woman's face. "Even after what I just told you?"

"What I want," I said slowly, choosing my words carefully. "Is a chance to rejoin the other Adventurers out in the world, and *perhaps*...move events along in a different direction than we had originally planned."

"Oh?" the woman replied, her eyes taking on a curious expression. "And what direction would that be?"

Here it goes, I thought as I began to lay out the basic plans of what I had spent the last month carefully researching and putting together, having spent all my free time watching whatever feeds I could get my hands on to help paint me a picture of what was happening out in the world.

"Interesting," she said after I had finished, raising a hand to stroke her long raven-colored hair. "Very interesting indeed...but how do you plan to actually accomplish it?"

"That depends," I answered, letting a smile cross my face. "Can you get me a Nemesis?"

The woman's motions stopped, and her eyes shot directly towards me, burning with an intensity I'd never seen before. Nearly a minute passed as she glared at me, making me think that I'd somehow overstepped and asked for too much, but eventually her voice echoed through the air.

"What would you do with it *if* I could?" she asked.

"Well," I began, my smile growing even wider as I told her, seeing laughter appear in her eyes by the time I was finished.

"Oh, Graves," she replied. "*That is perfect!*"

Lyrian's Character Sheet at the end of Legacy of the Fallen

Lyrian Rastler – Level 20 Spellsword
Human Male (Eberian)
Statistics:
HP: 1144/1144
Stamina: 1040/1040
Mana: 1370/1370
Experience to next level: 5426/44300
Renown: 7110
Attributes:
Strength: 65 (91)
Agility: 65 (92)
Constitution: 60 (64)
Intelligence: 84 (87)
Willpower: 25 (28)
Abilities:
Sneak Attack II (Passive) – Attacks made before the target is aware of you automatically deal weapon damage+35.

Power Attack II (Active: 50 Stamina) – You slash viciously at the target putting extra strength behind the blow. Deal weapon damage+25.

Kick (Active: 20) – You kick your enemy for 10-20 points of damage, and knock them back 1-2 yards. Depending on your Strength/Agility score, you may also knock down the target.

Shoulder Tackle (Active: 40 Stamina) – Stun enemy for 1-2 seconds with chance to knock enemy down based on Strength and/or Agility attribute.

Unarmed Mastery I (Passive) — All Unarmed attack damage is increased by 12.

Skills:

Magic:

Evocation — Level 20 — 1%

Alteration — Level 19 — 96%

Conjuration — Level 19 — 53%

Abjuration — Level 18 — 12%

Weapons:

Unarmed Combat — Level 19 — 18%

Swords — Level 20 — 45%

Axes — Level 11 — 35%

Daggers — Level 18 — 13%

Other:

Stealth — Level 20 — 3%

Wordplay — Level 15 — 16%

Perception - Level 20 - 25%

Tradeskills:

Blacksmithing — Level 19 — 22%

Carpentry — Level 18 — 31%

Cartography — Level 2 — 3%

Tailoring - Level 14 — 69%

Cooking — Level 5 — 54%

Herbalism — Level 11 — 4%

Leatherworking — Level 19 — 17%

Mining — Level 16 — 1%

Leadership Skills:

Increased Health Regeneration — Increase amount of Health Regenerated by 8.   (8/10)

Increased Mana Regeneration — Increase amount of Mana Regenerated by 8. (8/10)

Increased Stamina Regeneration — Increase amount of Stamina Regenerated by 8. (8/10)

Increased Movement – Increase mounted and unmounted speed by 6%. (6/10)

Improved Leadership I – Grants the ability to form a raid group and unlocks further leadership development. (1/1)

Spells:

Flare

Light

Blink Step

Shocking Touch

Lesser Shielding

Flame Dagger

Jump

Racial Ability:

Military Conditioning (Passive) *– All defenses are increased by 5% and total hit points are increased by 10%.*

Traits:

Open Minded *– Accepting of racial differences and radical ideas, you have learned to accept wisdom and the opportunity to learn no matter what form it takes, allowing you to make intuitive insights where others would give up in frustration. Grants a substantial increase in learning new skills, and the ability to learn all race locked traits, skills, crafting recipes, and abilities that are not otherwise restricted.*

Re-Forge *– You have learned the basics of how to recreate a broken relic and are able to bring back some of its former glory. This skill will function across any and all Tradeskills you acquire.*

Improvisation *– Your study of goblin craftsmanship has given you the insight to make adjustments to standard and learned recipes by replacing required materials with something else. E.g., Replacing metal with wood* *in an armor recipe will create a set of wooden armor instead of metal. The higher your level in a Tradeskill, the more changes can be made and the fewer materials they will require.*

Ætherwarped – *Due to high exposure of Raw Æther, your body has undergone unpredictable changes! You have gained the following Sub-Trait(s) and Abilities as part of your condition.*

True Sight – *Your eyes have been enhanced by exposure to Æther to the point where they are able to pierce through natural darkness and all facets of magic to see things as they truly are. This ability replaces Arcane Sight and can be suppressed at will. When this ability is active, the player's eyes will visibly glow a bright blue.*

Mana Devourer – *For as long as you have mana, you do not require to eat or drink, however as your mana reserves diminish, your hunger will increase correspondingly until it becomes impossible to ignore. Should you completely deplete your mana reserves, your body will immediately enter a feral state as it begins to consume itself at a rate of five hit points for each second in a mana deprivation state, the rate increasing by another five hit points every second afterward until at least 50% of your total mana is restored or you are consumed. All mana regeneration is permanently reduced by 100%.*

Mana Leech – *Its power enhanced by the effects of the [Mana Devourer] trait, you are now able to momentarily enhance your mana leech ability by expending your life force, allowing it to disrupt a single nearby spell. At the cost of 8% of your total health, you are now able to disrupt the formation of any spell within 30 feet, absorbing 50% of mana used* *to cast it, and prevent your target from casting spells for the next two seconds. Due to its strain on your body, this ability can only be used once every five minutes.*

Mana Torrent – *By fueling the ever-present hunger that now lurks within your body with your life force, you are able to momentarily draw in all nearby sources of mana directly towards you and absorb it. At the cost of 20% of your total health, this ability will instantly drain all mana sources within a 15-foot radius of you for 200% of your [Mana Leech] rate, and temporarily disrupt the formation of any spells for the next three seconds. Due to the strain on your body, this ability can only be used once an hour.*

Player versus Player:

  Ranked Duel Statistics:

   Current Title: Neophyte

   Regional Rank: 56

   Global Rank: 13,326,784

   Glory Points: 13

   Personal Rating: 1531

   Wins: 1

   Losses: 0

   Draws: 0

  Current PvP Skills Available for purchase:

    Increased Health – Increase total health by 0.5%. 0/5 (200 GP)

    Increased Stamina – Increase total Stamina by 0.5%. 0/5 (200 GP)

    Increased Mana – Increase total Mana by 0.5%. 0/5 (200 GP)

Familiar:

  Name: Amaranth

  Type: Ætherwarped Puma

Level: 20
Relationship: Fanatically Loyal
Familiar Abilities:

Mental Link – *The magical bond linking you and your familiar has created an intimate mental link between the two of you, allowing each of you to communicate mentally between one another for a distance of up to one mile, regardless of intervening objects. Magical wards, however, will block this form of mental communication.*

Soul Bound – *During the familiar bonding process, you have anchored the being's soul directly to your own. Should the familiar be slain in your service, you will immediately suffer a 10% penalty to all attributes and skills for the next 24 hours until the familiar is reborn. Should the familiar survive your death, it does not suffer any penalties, but will be compelled to travel to your place of rebirth as quickly as possible.*

Improved Familiar Bond – *As your relationship with your familiar improves, the connection that the two of you share deepens, giving you the ability to channel self-targeted spells across your bond while gaining enhanced insight to one another's senses when in close proximity.*

Afterword

Thank you so much for reading Legacy of the Fallen! I hope you enjoyed the book and Lyrian's latest adventure! Sharp eyes for this may notice that Lyrian never spent his skill point in his final chapter, and I happy to announce that I will be leaving Lyrian's next skill choice up to my Patrons to decide which one he is going to take! If you're interested in having a hand in Lyrian's development in the next book, consider joining my Patreon page and letting me know what you think! You can find my Patreon page at: www.patreon.com/LukeChmilenko

On my Patreon page, I am going to be posting exclusive sneak peek previews of Lyrian's next adventure, specifically the next one in the series titled: 'Glory to the Brave'! I will also be posting sketches of cover artwork and other projects that I'm working on too!

Please consider leaving a review of this book on Amazon! Reviews are critical to both help me improve as a writer and to help gain exposure! If there are things that you like or didn't like in this story, please let me know! I unfortunately don't have the ability to read minds (yet), but all of your feedback is greatly appreciated!

You can also get in touch with me directly at LyrianRastler@gmail.com, friend me on Facebook or join my Ascend Online Facebook Page! I welcome questions, comments, and suggestions! Also, if you happen to spot any errors, please let me know and I will fix them right away!

If you are interested in other books that fall into the "LitRPG" genre, you should also check out the RPG GameLit

Society Facebook group, it is an awesome community filled with authors, contests and LitRPG news!

If my book has you hooked and you're looking to get in on all the Ascend Online news, sign up for my mailing list on my website www.lukechmilenko.com